Alan Golbourn

# ✝ FAMULI CANI ✝

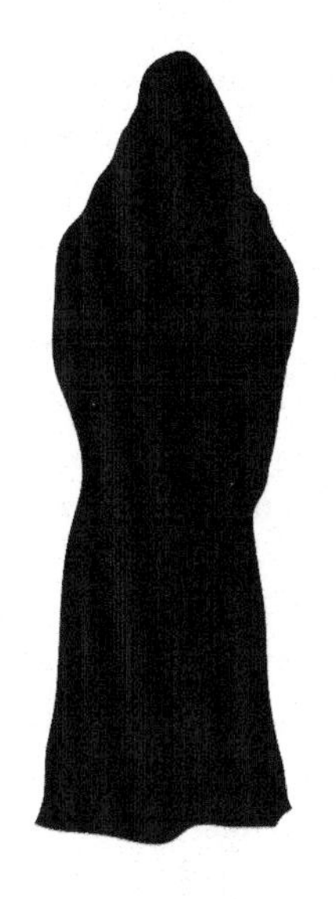

First published in Great Britain in 2021 by Gelbs Publishers Ltd
GelbsPublishersLtd@protonmail.com

ISBN (Paperback) 978-1-9993795-0-6
ISBN (eBook) 978-1-9993795-1-3



A CIP catalogue record for this book is available from the British Library.
Formatting by Polgarus Studios
Cover design by Creative Covers

*To Mum & Oscar – always and for ever*

She slowly turned her head and looked up with him. She stood in her bloodstained nightie, her face still emotionless but now painted with her deceased husband's blood. Murdered, by her hand. Her eyes were wide and as black as onyx.

# Chapter One

## 25th June, 2018

It was a summer's afternoon, a Monday …

"Anyway, I'm sure you know by now, why I've brought you in, David? I've just got to let you go. You aren't the only one, as you've no doubt heard. But we've got to have cutbacks and unfortunately, you're one of the select few who has to be made redundant. I really am sorry." The manager tried to sound as sincere and sympathetic as he could.

"I know, Paul. Don't worry about it. It's not exactly the 'End of the World.' I'll miss the money, though." David shrugged as he sat slumped in the black, faux leather chair, across the desk from his manager.

The room was fairly hot. The late afternoon sun was shining through Paul's office window directly onto David. The office having no air conditioning didn't help.

"Even though, David, I still feel bad about it. It's nothing personal. I've always thought of you as a good worker. It's just head office have told me it's 'last in, first out,' the usual protocol. Despite you being with us for three years. I really am sorry. It's just out of my hands."

David laughed. "Honestly, Paul. It doesn't matter. It's not like I won't find another job."

Paul smiled back. "I know. But if you need a reference, I'll always give you a good one, you know that."

"I know you will. Thanks. What about notice?"

"I've been told only two weeks, I'm afraid. I know it's very short notice, but it's the best I can do." Paul gestured with his hands. "We will sort out some redundancy for you; you won't leave empty-handed. Don't worry about that!"

"Yeah, that's cool. I'm probably going to take a few weeks off first anyway, before I look for work again. I've got a bit saved up and enough to pay for my flat. I might even take a holiday, seeing as it's summer. I'll see how it goes, I guess …" David tried his best to sound upbeat. He'd known the redundancy was coming. There was talk of it a few weeks back. It was expected. Not to mention others had also been given their notice earlier in the day. He wasn't overly fussed. Yet still, he was a little disappointed.

He had been at Wellman's Furniture Ltd for just over three years, assembling all sorts of furnishings. It was still a job at the end of the day. It was still money. Pretty good money at that. None of that cheap minimum wage crap. The company actually respected their workers. He'd had three significant pay rises since he started. Even though it was hard work, he actually quite enjoyed it. Along with the money, he'd also miss the banter with his work colleagues. Soon to be 'ex' work colleagues. Paul was a good boss to work for as well. He was easy-going and had a good sense of humour. All the workers liked him. They liked David too.

"Sounds good. Anywhere in particular?" Paul asked, trying to move away from having just made David redundant and feeling awkward.

"I don't know, really. I might go abroad. I could even see my uncle up north as he has a farm up there. I could help out. It would be good to see him again. I've not seen him for a while. He's a great guy. He's often said I'm more than welcome to go up there. It would be good exercise at least."

"Once again, I am sorry."

"Stop apologising." David smiled at Paul as he rose from the chair.

The slightly overweight Paul laughed as he got up and held out a warm and sweaty hand, which David welcomed and they shook hands. David then left the office, closing the door behind him.

It was not long after five, when David exited the building. The meeting had only lasted a few minutes. His backside was sweating from sitting on the chair in Paul's office where the sun had been beating in. "Fuck's sake," he muttered to himself, walking towards the car park.

"You too, eh? You *loser*!" came a shout from a parked car.

There was a guy smoking a joint, grinning. He was sitting on the hood of his car, a bead of sweat beaming on his forehead.

"Piss off." David smirked.

It was his best friend, John.

"Guess that makes two of us, then? Told you it was going to be us, didn't I?" John took a huge intake of weed, before exhaling profusely, almost coughing his lungs out.

"I thought you were going to pack that shit up?" David approached the car. "You can smell that from over there ... It was pretty obvious. We all knew the few of us who started last were most likely going to be the so-called 'casualties.' Who cares, anyway?" David tried to sound unbothered.

"You do!" John said abruptly, before grinning.

"Maybe a bit. I just can't be arsed right now to have the hassle of looking for another job. Plus, I'm going to miss that Jane in the office."

"Yeah, what happened about that? I'll bet you miss seeing those big jugs of hers, eh? Weren't you supposed to have gotten her number? You were always flirting. She definitely liked you."

"I didn't see the point really, seeing as she had a boyfriend. He's a big bastard, too."

"Whatever," John replied casually, leaping off the hood of his car with his rolled-up joint still in his mouth, making the car wobble slightly.

David Hammond and John Addams had been the best of friends since childhood and school. They were like brothers. John would joke and sometimes refer to David as *My brother from another mother.*

Both the only children of their families, they lived away from London and the noise and traffic that came with it. The countryside that surrounded them was pleasant and they welcomed it. Growing up was great. From video games, to bike rides, building dens in the fields and getting up to the odd 'mischief' here and there – although they were both relatively well-behaved kids – they did most things together. Both were now twenty-four years old, with only a week separating their birthdays.

David was the better looking out of the two, with his 'pretty boy' looks as John often teased; he had blue eyes and thick eyelashes, along with his short dark hair and stubble. David most definitely took after his parents' good looks. He had inherited good genes.

John, in contrast to David, had brushed back fair hair and also had blue eyes and was good-looking.

Like all friends, they had had their differences and falling-outs for sure. But they were always there for one another, especially David for John, when his mother died after a long battle with cancer. John had been just sixteen and it was a hard time for him; he went off the rails a little. It was a tough couple of years to say the least, with John drinking quite heavily at times and dabbling a fair bit in drugs, although, it was never anything hardcore. David did his part in helping him through it, along with his parents and John's own father. Despite the pain of his mother's death, John never lost his wicked sense of humour and was more the joker out of the two.

"So, where we going anyway, mate? Few drinks?" John asked as they both got into John's 2006, grey, Renault Clio.

David himself, didn't possess a driving licence.

"Maybe later. I need to pick up Benji from my mum and dad's first."

Benji was a sweet, three-year-old, chocolate Labrador, who was looked after most days by David's mum, Annette, at his parents' house. David didn't like leaving him alone by himself when he was at work. Annette didn't work herself, but his father, Jason, worked as a pretty big-time lawyer in the capital.

"Sounds good." John smiled back.

David shook his head smirking. John had had a crush on David's mother since childhood.

"What are we both going to do now?" John asked seriously, flicking the small remains of the joint out of the window.

"Who knows? I can't say I'm too bothered about the job 'per se.' I suppose it was a bit boring at times, but the money was good. And now there's the annoying task of having to find something else … It's a laugh as well working there. Those three odd years I was there have flown by."

"I know, mate. I was only there for a year and a half. That's gone well quick!" John drove out of the car park of Wellman's Furniture Ltd. "Let's go for a bit of a spin," he suggested.

*****

The hot afternoon was turning slightly milder by the time they reached David's parents. A soft breeze had kicked in, making the heat more bearable. The smell of freshly pruned roses struck them as they walked up the stone pathway to the open front door. Benji came charging out, his tail wagging excitedly.

"Hello, boy!" David said passionately as Benji jumped into his arms, furiously licking his beloved owner's face.

"He heard the car pull up," a voice came from the front door and David's mum appeared. Annette's straight, naturally, dirty-blonde hair blew slightly in the summer breeze. "I was just attending to the front garden. I thought you'd be back soon for Benji. You're a bit later than usual, aren't you?"

"Hi, Mrs Hammond." John raised a hand cheerfully.

"Call me, Annette. I keep telling you that; you're not children anymore. Come on in!" Annette laughed.

"Yeah, we went for a drive after work, Mum. I had a brief meeting at work as well."

"Oh?" Annette asked curiously.

John and David both entered the house followed by Benji. Annette shut the front door behind them.

"Well, you knew the chances of you two being included in the redundancies was highly likely, love. You'll just have to keep looking out for another job. You'll soon find something. You too, John."

"I know, Mum. I can't say I'm too bothered. It's just frustrating I suppose. There's not always a lot of jobs out there."

"We'll soon get another one, Mrs H. No big deal," John said cockily.

Annette laughed. "At least you both have your forklift driving licences. That can be an advantage workwise. Your father should be back soon. He'll understand. He was expecting this. Would you boys like to stay for tea?"

John clapped his hands and rubbed them enthusiastically. He loved Annette's home cooking. "Yes, please! What are we having?"

*****

David's father, Jason, arrived home to the scent of potato and bacon casserole hitting his nostrils. He tossed his keys onto the coffee table, making a clinking sound as they hit the glass top. He then threw his coat over the armchair. *I don't know why I took this today.*

Benji came from the kitchen to greet him, licking his hand.

Jason followed him back into the kitchen to see his son and his friend sitting at the table, tucking into the casserole. "Hey, honey, I'm home," he quipped, walking over to his wife and kissing her on the cheek.

"What have I told you about throwing your keys on that table?" Annette frowned at him.

"It's okay, babe. I'll just buy a new one if it breaks," Jason replied blasé. "You all right, Son?"

"Not bad, Dad," David answered with a mouthful of food.

Jason patted David on the back affectionately.

"Mr H." John nodded at his best friend's father.

"You all right, Johnny?" Jason took his place at the table and waited for his dinner to arrive. "I might have known you'd be here. Being joined at the hip and all." Jason gave the two lads a warm smile.

Annette and Jason were in their early fifties, having married when they were twenty-seven. Annette's attractive face and blue eyes defied her age. She could quite easily pass for a woman in her forties. They met by chance at a café, where Annette worked and which Jason often frequented whilst a budding lawyer. There had been an immediate spark of attraction between David's parents. Annette was attracted to Jason's sense of humour as well as his good looks, with his dark brown hair, brushed back to the side. He had worn the same hair style pretty much his whole life, although it was shorter now than when they met, and had acquired a 'salt and pepper' tint with age. He was still handsome. Friends often referred to him as a 'silver fox.'

Jason had certainly achieved what he wanted in life. His job always came second. Family came first. But with his job came a nice life, with a 'little luxury.' He had the son he always wanted. He and Annette would have liked more children, but it never happened. They weren't too concerned; they had David.

*****

After dinner, they all moved into the elegant living room with an ebony wood wall unit housing their huge TV. Crystal chandeliers hung from either end of the room. Jason had brought the wine and glasses in for Annette and him.

"You're okay for money, David, yeah?" Jason poured himself another glass.

"I don't need hand-outs, Dad," David said annoyed.

"I know, Son. But I'm happy to help, if need be."

David had too much self-respect to ask his parents for financial help. He had bought most of his things himself and was proud of that virtue; he was also a good negotiator. He had managed to negotiate the rent down on his flat from six hundred pounds a month to only four hundred and persuaded the landlord to let him keep his dog there too.

"Any ideas on what you're going to do?" Jason asked.

Benji had fallen asleep on David's lap.

"I thought about maybe taking a holiday. I've got some cash saved up."

"That's good, David. Let your hair down and then come back and start looking for a new job. Maybe something that's more of a career move? Take a break first, though."

"I was actually thinking of perhaps going up and seeing Uncle Bob on his farm, see if he needs any help. I've not seen him since Christmas."

"My brother Bob and Hamish Farm? That's not a bad idea, I suppose. He would probably appreciate any help."

"I know, Dad. It would be good. A change of scenery as well up in Scotland."

"I thought you'd be more interested in going abroad, somewhere with women and a beach." Jason laughed.

"Yeah. Why the bloody hell Scotland, and a farm at that?" John questioned.

"I just like the idea. I've always liked Uncle Bob and Aunt Betty. They've always said I would be welcome anytime. You too, John. I think Benji would love it as well. It's in that big forest up there."

"Yes, that's right; the forest is huge. Me and your father have been a few times, albeit a long time ago, mind," Annette recalled. "It's beautiful scenery up there. Mountains, too. I believe the last time we went there was around ten years ago, when you were away on a trip with school for a week or so. The other times before that, were when you were only very young ..."

"Maybe I could come, too? If you're serious? It could be good. There may be a lack of women, I'd imagine." John scratched his cheek.

*****

When David and John left, Annette kissed them both. The sun was setting into a vibrant orange and pink sky. It still felt early.

"You fancy a few drinks, pal?" John asked as they drove off.

"Nah, just take me home. Going to have a bath and probably an early night." David yawned.

"Okay then, you old-timer," John joked.

A few minutes later, they reached David's flat. The flat itself was small, yet adequate. David had been there for almost four years. Although he loved his parents and was very close to them, he liked having his own independence and privacy. But at the same time, he liked that his parents weren't too far away.

The two friends clasped hands as David got out of the car. He let Benji out of the back and waved John off. John beeped his horn as he raced down the street and turned the corner. As he entered the flat, David almost tripped over a pair of his boots in the hallway. Benji raced straight over to his personalised BENJI food bowl in the kitchen.

David kicked off his trainers as the light in the flat was diminishing. On the small sofa bed lay a pizza box with a few leftover crusts. A few empty beer bottles remained on the small, wooden table from two nights ago, when he had John over.

He fetched a bin bag from the cupboard under the kitchen sink. Benji was happily munching on biscuits in his bowl. David shook the bin bag open and scooped up the near empty pizza box and beer bottles. They made a clinking sound as they plopped into the bag, making Benji look up. Leaving the bin bag next to the table, David picked up the TV remote, brushed a few crumbs onto the floor and lay on the light blue sofa bed, with his legs outstretched. He switched on the TV.

"Come on, Benj."

Benji jumped up and snuggled onto David's stomach. David started flicking through the channels.

*****

After watching the last part of a film, David didn't find anything else worth viewing. He listened to the weather forecast, which predicted mostly hot weather for the next two weeks. "Nice," he said to himself, before switching off the television.

Benji was fast asleep by now. David smiled as he listened to his soft snoring, staying there in the dark for a few minutes with his hands behind his head, contemplating unemployment and the possibility of going to Scotland. He closed his eyes and he too, fell sound asleep.

# Chapter Two

## 9th July, 2018

On David's first day of freedom after working his notice period, he awoke to the sound of his mobile vibrating on the floor next to a pair of jeans. "Urgh," he groaned, rubbing the sleep from his eyes. He bent down to answer the call. It was 08:32 according to his phone. "Hello?" David yawned widely.

"All right, David?"

"Grant? Have you got a new number?"

Grant laughed. "Yep. I got a new phone yesterday. You okay? I hope I didn't wake you?"

"Well, yeah. You kind of did, mate. It's not like I have to be up early for work anymore, though," David half-joked. He looked over at Benji who had slunk off into the kitchen to drink from his water bowl.

"Welcome to The Unemployment Club," Grant quipped. He had mentioned recently that work for him was sparse of late.

Grant Smith was the most intelligent of the three friends, as well as the eldest at twenty-eight. He was also the shyest. He tried to keep up to date on global current affairs and was a regular blogger. Initially, he was more a friend of John's than of David's. They met a few years previously on a drunken night out. Grant knew that John and David were closer than he was to either of them, but he never resented it. He called them the *Three Amigos* and he meant it.

With his floppy black hair and glasses, Grant often came across as a bit of a 'nerd.' Especially, as he spent a lot of time on his computer and the internet. He loved computers and his gaming. Bits and pieces of computers with various gadgets were strewn all over his flat, presenting obstacles for his friends to trip over; "Jesus Christ, Grant. We're going to break our necks one of these days!" John had commented on his last visit.

His main income was from fixing and repairing computers for people. Sometimes 'off the record,' cash in hand. He would even build them for people. He deemed it more of a hobby than a job. Grant earnt enough to keep himself ticking over, and to pay for his own place and the bills that came with it. He was a prudent guy, spending sensibly, so he never struggled financially.

David laughed. "Yeah. The *Three Losers* now." He was glad to hear from Grant, particularly today.

"What are you up to this morning?"

"Not much. I haven't given it much thought to be honest. It's going to be another stinker today as well, really hot apparently."

"Fancy breakfast at Gino's?"

David's stomach rumbled at the thought. "Yeah, why not?"

Gino's was a regular haunt for the young men; a burger van not far from where David and John use to work. Gino sold fry-ups, various baguettes, and more recently with John's encouragement, chips. David liked to watch his figure somewhat, so sometimes opted for a healthier option, whereas the other two didn't really give it too much thought. John and David would go there before work or during their lunch break, either to get a bite to eat or just to chat to their friend, Gino. In winter, they would sit in the heated mobile unit next to the van.

Gino was a warm and generous soul, often offering to feed the boys for free. They only once accepted his generosity, when they didn't have enough money on them, and Gino refused to let them pay him back later. It had been a while since they last saw Gino; he'd been visiting a friend in Wales.

"Cool. John's happy to pick us up – say in around an hour?"

John was the only one of them who had a car, even though Grant could drive.

"Sounds good. It will give me time to sort myself out and shower and stuff." David yawned again.

They both hung up and David headed to the bathroom, rubbing Benji's head on the way. While showering, his mind was eagerly thinking about breakfast and how he would treat himself to a 'less healthy' option, rather than his usual ham salad baguette. 'Comfort food' for having lost his job.

*****

David dried himself off. Despite his 'milk bottle legs,' he threw on a pair of white shorts and a blue T-shirt. He briefly switched morning telly on until his friends arrived.

David heard a horn beep. He shielded his eyes from the sun and shouted to his friends from the living room window, "Be there in a minute, guys."

He hooked Benji's lead onto his collar and grabbed a pair of sunglasses from the shelf by the front door. Above it was a small mirror, where he gave his hair a final check before locking up. Outside, the air was already muggy and sticky. Potentially the hottest day of the year so far. The kind of day where you could see for miles. David was looking forward to spending the morning with his two closest friends, and to a good breakfast.

"You okay then, mate?" Grant moved his head forwards between the car headrests to speak to the guys in front.

"Better now I'm with you guys." David beamed.

"Sweet." Grant grinned.

They chatted briefly about John and David losing their jobs.

"You won't follow your dad and become a lawyer, then?" Grant mused.

"Nah, not for me. I've never been interested in law school or anything like that. As long as I earn a half decent wage doing something and enjoy myself in life, that's all that matters to me. And to eventually have a family, of course."

"You never thought about a career, then?" Grant continued.

"Sure. But it hasn't really interested me. People might say get a 'proper' job and stuff. But define proper? All jobs are the same overall. Unless you're a highly paid doctor, lawyer, or something like that." David sounded assertive.

"Your dad never tried pushing you into being a lawyer?" Grant asked, not for the first time.

"Not at all. He always encouraged me with whatever I wanted to do. He wanted me to try and make something of my life and to do my best, obviously. But he always respected my decisions. I've had numerous jobs. Some have been well paid; some I left off my own back and some I lost through no fault of my own. Probably the one I just had was the best. It was the best pay, definitely. Driving the forklift was a laugh as well. Although me and John were packing and assembling furniture most the time. Anyway, what's with the questions? I've told you this several times before!"

"I don't know." Grant made a face, raising his eyebrows.

David smiled and pushed Grant's face back affectionately.

John looked over his shoulder and grinned.

*****

With the windows open, turning into Gino's road, they could already smell his cooking. The smell of fresh bacon filled the car.

"Ahh … Heaven!" Grant inhaled, closing his eyes.

"It sure is, boyo," John agreed.

"Yep," David confirmed.

John pulled up just short of Gino's. Surprisingly, it was pretty quiet. *"Hey up, you Italian bastard!"* John shouted affectionately to Gino.

A couple of already-served customers turned their heads.

Gino was flipping bacon. *"Buongiorno!"* he called back. He came out of the side door wiping his hands. They all shook his hand. Gino was a big man with a sturdy handshake. He walked to the front of his van, reached over for a streak of bacon and handed it to Benji, rubbing both hands on the side of Benji's head. "Shouldn't you two be in work by now?" he asked in his thick Italian accent.

"We thought we'd come and spend the day with you instead, amigo. It's been a while," John joked. "How was Wales?"

"Ah … you're too kind, boys," Gino joked back sarcastically. "Wales was great!"

Gino Mossatelli was a lovable man. He was in his late fifties. With his olive skin and balding, yet greying hair, he had been working his food van for around eight years, having been in the country since his late thirties. He had met an English woman on holiday in Italy and eventually married her and moved to England. Although the marriage didn't work out, he decided to stay in the country, doing various jobs before finally opening his own food catering business. He didn't have family in England or many friends, so aside from his genuine like of the three lads, he was grateful for their friendship.

*****

The four of them sat around one of the small, plastic, fold-up tables by the van, talking about Gino's business and his trip to Wales. Gino asked what the two boys were going to do about getting another job, whilst they tucked into Gino's fry-up on white paper plates.

"This is great, Gino." John chewed away.

"You got another couple of sausages, please?" Grant asked.

Gino got up to offer seconds, checking whether David wanted some too.

"Go on then. Why not?"

John put an extra bit of ketchup on his plate.

"You know, I could maybe do with an extra hand or two. At least one of you boys. I'm not too sure yet. Business is good, but it might still be hard to employ someone else." Gino wiped his mouth with a napkin.

"Don't worry about it, Gino. We'll sort something out," David replied.

"Yeah. We don't need your pity." John grinned.

Gino playfully smacked him across the back of the head, just as his phone rang. He wandered back to the van deeply engrossed in an Italian conversation.

"John says you're thinking about going up to Scotland, to help out on your uncle's farm?" Grant suddenly said.

"Yep. Definitely considering it. Have to speak to him first though, to see if he's okay to have me."

*"Us!"* John said sharply.

"What, you're serious about wanting to come?"

"Why wouldn't I be?"

"I just thought you may find it a bit boring."

"Nah. It'll be cool. Besides, I can still check out some of those Scottish chicks, eh?"

"Erm, not sure about that. It's pretty remote up there." David finished the last of his bacon.

Grant took a gulp of his Coke and cleared his throat. "You got room maybe for one more?"

"What?" John and David both asked, taken aback.

"Well, I don't really want to be on my own for the summer, or however long you're planning on being up there … To be honest, I haven't got much work to do with my computers, and a few of my other friends have already gone away or are about to. It's going to be pretty boring without you two."

"Awww," John replied sarcastically, pinching and shaking Grant's left cheek.

"I really don't know if my uncle will have all of us, guys. He may not even need or want me. I just like the idea of seeing him and getting away. It would be something different I suppose." David shoved his sunglasses up on his head and looked at them both.

Gino had finished his call and was smoking a cigarette away from the van.

"He did say you'd be welcome up there any time … and me," John reminded David. "He obviously knows we're close. I'm sure he wouldn't mind Grant as well … I met your uncle, once. He seemed a nice guy. I think it would be good. You know, the three of us. And Benji, of course."

Benji was drinking water Gino had put out for him.

"He's right, David. It would be good," Grant urged.

David sighed. "I don't know, guys. Don't get me wrong, I genuinely like the idea, but just thought I'd be going on my own, and I don't want to take the piss with my Uncle Bob."

"No harm in asking though, right?" John pulled the back of his T-shirt away from his sweaty back.

"Yep," Grant added.

"Okay, let's do it. I'll ring him later. I need to get his number from my folks, first."

Gino dropped most of the cigarette to the ground, stamping it out. He returned to his van to attend to some hungry customers.

The young men sat and discussed Scotland and waited for Gino to finish serving. When Gino rejoined them, they told him their plans for going away and promised to catch up before leaving if they went. Gino shared that his call was from his mother back in Italy, asking him when he was coming home to visit. It had been almost a year.

"You ever consider moving back? You must miss it, and your family?" Grant asked politely.

"I don't know, sonny … I guess I just like the English way of life. Don't get me wrong, of course I miss my family and my mamma's cooking!" Gino laughed. "I probably should go back more often."

"Isn't your mum like ninety-six?" John asked amazed.

*"Ninety-eight!"* Gino fired back.

The guys looked astonished.

"Us Italians know how to look after ourselves."

"Yeah, right …" David joked, pointing at the burger van and the bacon and eggs sizzling on the grill.

Gino looked over and laughed.

*****

Eventually, the lads left.

"What do you guys fancy doing next? I might head off home. I'm starting to feel a bit headachy," John announced.

Grant and David had swapped seats, taking turns to sit in the back with Benji. Nearly midday, the temperature was uncomfortable. Benji hung his head out of the window, panting with his tongue out.

"I'm going to walk Benj, let him loose for a bit. Let him enjoy the weather," David suggested.

"You want me to drop you off at the playing fields?" John looked back.

"Yeah, please, mate."

"How about you, Granty? Where you want taking?"

"You can drop me of at my parents' … if it's okay? I've not seen them for a while. I can mention about Scotland, in case it comes off. I feel a bit tired too, after all that food."

"No, I don't mind. After I've dropped you two off, I might take a nap. I think I've got one of my migraines coming. Must be the heat." John's face was grimacing.

"Not good. Make sure you take something for it," David advised, his hand on Benji.

They exchanged a few more words before John dropped David off at the playing fields, then Grant at his parents' house. John headed back home where he lived with his father, although he was currently at work.

John and his father didn't always see eye to eye while John was growing up, but the death of his mother brought them closer together, strengthening the bond between father and son.

John walked in through his front door, headed straight to the kitchen and pulled out a couple of painkillers from one of the top cupboards. He washed them down with a glass of water and headed upstairs to sleep off his headache.

*****

Meanwhile, David was sitting under a tree in the shade, trying to take some cover from the glaring sun. The temperature continued to rise. He welcomed the occasional slight breeze as it stroked his face momentarily, cooling a few drops of sweat from his forehead. It was even hotter now. He was throwing a stick for Benji to fetch, making sure not to overdo it. He didn't want to tire Benji too much or give him a heat stroke. Suddenly, he felt something touch his right elbow. A football rolled next to him.

"Can we have our ball back please, Mister?" a young boy asked innocently.

David smiled. He pulled himself up and kicked the ball back to the boy and his playmates.

"Thank you," the boy called back as he turned to rejoin his friends.

"No worries," David shouted back, again smiling. *Cute kid.*

David slumped back down and heard a shriek. To his left, a young couple were mucking about. The guy had poured water down his girlfriend's back and he was chasing her. David laughed. He missed that. Not being with someone. He was a fantastically, good-looking young man, but he was fussy when it came to women. Yes, he had had a few past relationships and offers; he just never really felt 'that' connection. He loved his two friends, John and Grant very much, but he still yearned to fall in love again with someone.

His last relationship with Rachel had lasted a year and ended two years ago. It had reached a point when he didn't love her anymore. The first few months were great, but as time went on, he wasn't sure he felt the same way towards her. He'd always spent a lot of time with his two friends, particularly John. Rachel never liked that. David had thought her unreasonable, because he and Rachel still spent a lot of time together. He and John had always been tight knit. That would never change. No matter what happened or who they both met. Though, that wasn't the main reason David and Rachel broke up. It just wasn't the same as when they first met, so he decided it would be best to part ways. He had no regrets.

David lay in the shade for a few minutes more watching Benji who was a few yards away, chewing and biting on the stick that he was chasing back and forth with.

David heard the tune of an ice cream van. "Come on, boy," David called to Benji, putting him back on his lead to head for the ice cream van, where he ordered a 99. He enjoyed the rapidly melting ice cream in the summer heat. Because he tried to eat it quickly to avoid getting it all over his hands, he soon got brain freeze.

*****

It was still early afternoon by the time David got back to his flat. Some mail had arrived whilst he was out.

Holding the mail between his teeth, he unhooked Benji's collar, who then went for a drink. David sat down on the sofa bed, scanning through his mail with his legs up on the table. There were bills, a credit card application form, junk mail, and more junk mail. In one of the envelopes was a scratch card. He pulled his keys out of his pocket and scratched off the silver bits. He checked the symbols to see if any matched and he had won something. Nothing.

He placed the bills on the table in front of him and then dropped the unwanted mail into the kitchen bin. He decided to check his bank balance and emails, whilst seated on his only one soft armchair. He pulled his laptop open and turned it on. While he was checking through, his mobile rang with an unknown number. "Hello?" David answered seriously with a hint of curiosity.

"David?" It was a soft female voice.

"Err, yeah?" David scratched the back of his left ear.

"It's Aunt Betty, dear."

"Oh, hey!" David was surprised.

"I hope you don't mind me calling?"

"Don't be silly. Of course not. I'm just surprised. I didn't know who it was, as I didn't recognise the mobile number."

"Well, dear ... I spoke to your parents last night, to see how they were doing, and they told me about you losing your job. I'm sorry to hear that. Your mum said that you were perhaps interested in coming up here? They gave me and Bob your number. I'm actually ringing from one of the nearest towns, as we don't always get a decent signal on mobile phones where we are. Particularly of late, as there's been some strange interference at times."

"Yeah. I was considering it and I was going to call Uncle Bob once I'd got his number from Dad. I just wasn't sure if you two wanted to have me at all, or if you could, even?" David sat forward in the armchair. He scratched his cheek.

"We would love to have you here, dear. We would appreciate the help as well. It's just that ... maybe the timing isn't too great ..." Aunt Betty sounded hesitant.

"How do you mean?"

"Well ... it's just that the past couple of weeks or so ... some strange things have kind of, well, some things have been happening."

"Strange things? Like what? You sound worried, and I'm worried now."

"Oh, don't worry about me, David, love. I'm fine."

"Please, Aunt Betty. You can't leave me hanging. Please, tell me. I'm intrigued now; it would be unfair not to tell me."

"I'm sorry, my dear. It's best if Bobby tells you himself. I, I promise I will get him to call you sometime this evening. I thought I'd just ring you and give you a 'heads up,' if you will ... He was going to call you himself earlier, but ... it's best you speak to him."

David sensed something bad had happened, or rather, was happening. "Okay, Aunt Betty ... that's fine. Any idea what time he might call me? Not that it matters too much. I always have my mobile with me."

"I'm not sure, David. I'll make sure he calls you. It will most likely be on our landline if you wonder what the number is, when it shows up. Although, we've started to get bad interference on that too, lately. It should be okay. I just thought I'd give you a call whilst I was doing some shopping."

"Okay, Aunt Betty. I look forward to speaking to him."

"Okay, David. You take good care, okay?"

"I will. You too, okay?"

"I, I will, love. Bye, bye."

David wondered what the conversation had meant and immediately decided to speak with his mum. "Hey, Mum!" David said loudly.

"No need to shout, David. I'm not deaf. I might be now," Annette joked.

"Sorry, Mum. It's just that I got off the phone with Aunt Betty."

"Yes, she said she would call you. I don't think you should go up to Scotland ..." Annette was drying her hands on a towel after doing the washing up, with the phone cradled between her neck and shoulder.

"Why not? Did she tell you about what had happened? She was very reluctant to tell me, not to mention how worried she sounded." David heard a sigh from the other end.

"She seemed a little upset. Something about how some of the animals they had on the farm had been killed."

"What do you mean, killed?" David asked perplexed. "Like by another animal, or by someone?"

"She wouldn't go into details ... just something about how her and Bob and a couple of workers found some of their livestock missing. Some of them were found. Well ... what was left of them."

"Well, was it an animal or a person that did it?"

"I honestly don't know, David. One of their cats died, too. She wouldn't go into too much detail. I don't think you should go up there; it's not a good time and I don't think her and Bob would appreciate it. Maybe another time. You can go away somewhere else. I'm not sure why you'd be that concerned about going there anyway; it's not really ideal for someone of your age." Annette was trying to convince her son and to sound reasonable.

"Sorry for wanting to do something different. *Fine*, I won't bother!"

"Don't get annoyed at me. I'm just saying how I see it. Or rather how I hear it ..." Annette said calmly.

"Well, Betty said Uncle Bob was going to call tonight about it. So, we can see."

"Okay. Well, let me know what he says, won't you?"

"Will do. I'm sorry for getting annoyed at you, Mum."

"It's fine, love."

"What's the name of the place where they live?"

"I asked your aunt last night. I'd forgotten myself. It was a little hard to understand her though, as there was bad reception, like static over the phone. The farm itself is called Hamish Farm and it is pretty remote. The forest is called Rothiemurchus. It's a lovely place. Very scenic."

"Okay, thanks, Mum. Love you."

"Love you too, David."

David sat there for a while twiddling his thumbs and thinking. He would have to wait to hear more until his uncle rang. He did his daily search online for any jobs he could apply for. As usual, he didn't find anything appropriate. Most he'd seen advertised before needed experience or a driver's licence; they always had something he didn't have. There didn't even appear to be any temporary summer jobs. He wouldn't mind working outside with it being summer. He wasn't afraid of getting his hands dirty.

The only one suitable, he had already enquired about. It was a warehouse job, not too far from where he used to work. By the time he had rung up about it, the job had already been filled. The advert should have been removed. He was frustrated with himself for not looking for a job as soon as he had heard mention of redundancies.

# Chapter Three

## 9th July, 2018

Just after seven in the evening, David lay in the bath chatting to John on his mobile. Benji was on the floor next to him, dozing off on the white, memory foam bathroom mat.

"Didn't she say?"

"Nope. Only my mum gave some details about it. Even then, it wasn't really that clear." David swished the water over his hairy legs back and forth. He made sure he didn't drop the phone in the bath.

"What did she tell your mum?"

"Just how some of the farm animals had been killed. Their cat died, too."

"What, like by a wild animal? Or a madman? Did he have his way with the animals first, you reckon?" John tried to make light of the situation. He could hear his mate was worried.

"Jesus." David half-smiled. "I'm really worried, John. Intrigued, too. Something doesn't seem right up there. I've just got this hunch."

"Sorry, mate. I'm only messing. I know you're worried. You're quite close with all your family. You're a family-oriented guy. It's one thing I admire and love about you, boyo."

"It's just the way I am. Always have been. If nothing else, I'm bloody interested and curious."

A few drops of water splashed out of the bath onto Benji's side, making him jolt his head up. He then began to lick his slightly wet, chocolate brown fur.

"What time is your uncle calling you back? You think he will? I'm intrigued, now."

"Could be any time. I better not speak too long, in case he's trying to call."

David's fingers and toes were beginning to get wrinkled from being in the water too long.

"Well, don't waste time speaking to me, then!" John half-joked.

David promised to call John back with any news and placed his phone at the side of the bath. He stood up and dried himself off, almost knocking his phone into the receding water in the process. *That was close.*

Getting out the bath, he carefully clung onto the basin to step over Benji who was still asleep on the mat. He didn't want to wake him; he'd tired himself out playing fetch in the hot weather. As David was about to turn the bathroom light off, the light on the ceiling began to dim and flicker. *The bulb might be dying.* He couldn't remember when he'd last had to change it. He pulled on the cord to turn off the light.

The temperature was still high. As soon as David had dried himself off, his back and stomach were already growing wet again from his sweat. He needed air conditioning in his flat for days like this.

He pulled out a stand-up fan from the corner of the living room and switched it on. He found it hard to believe that it had been almost a year since he last used it. The time seemed to fly by since he got that little bit older. He plugged his phone charger into the other socket, balanced the charging phone on the sofa bed arm, and laid down with just his damp towel around him. The fan cooled him.

David was beginning to doze off when his phone rang, from a landline number. "Hello?" He sat up quickly.

"David? Is that you?" It was definitely his Uncle Bob. He recognised the gruff voice almost straight away. Smoking almost twenty cigarettes a day until eleven years ago hadn't helped Bob's voice.

"I'm doing good thanks, Uncle. What's been happening on your farm?" David got straight to the point.

"I'm sorry about you losing your job, David," Uncle Bob said calmly.

"Don't worry about that. Please, tell me what's been happening with you and Betty. She sounded really concerned." David's heart was beating a little bit faster from being woken up, and also at the intrigue.

The phone crackled a little bit and he remembered what his aunt had said about the interference they were experiencing. He really hoped they wouldn't get cut off.

Bob sighed. "Oh, David. It's *awful*. Horrible … Everything was fine. But less than two weeks ago, things started *happening*." Bob sounded downbeat.

"Like what?" David's eyes widened, his mouth open.

The phone crackled again. David thought he heard a hiss and something that sounded like a person exhaling abnormally. It sounded dark, ghostly. *It must just be a dodgy line.* He wanted to hear what his uncle had to say. He'd waited a few hours for this. His heartbeat increased.

"We woke up one morning last week and went to feed the animals like we usually do. We have a number of animals here, David. But this one morning, we noticed a couple of pigs weren't in their pen and some chickens were missing from their coop. Some blood was splattered on the side of the pen and chicken coop. We thought they caught themselves getting out. But it's impossible for them to get out by themselves. There's no gaps, nothing like that. There was no sign of any break in or damage at all.

"It also rained during the night. We didn't hear anything from the house, even though we'd slept with the window open. But what was even more odd, was not only was there no sign of breaking and entering, there weren't even any signs of footprints around the area at all. You'd think there would be, with some of the mud. Okay, maybe the rain washed them away, but it's so strange. And that's only part of it ..." Bob tried to catch his breath.

David listened intently.

"Anyway, a couple of our workers arrived not long after. We checked on the other animals and they seemed fine and were all there. We counted them and checked. We then had a look around the farm and outline of the forest but found nothing. The four of us decided to go back into the house and Betty cooked us all breakfast, although we weren't particularly hungry. I said we needed to eat and then go from there. I decided to go look near another part of the forest we live in. We're surrounded by rich forest here. It can get pretty dark here, early at times, too. As I got to the edge of one part of the forest, I wish I hadn't had any breakfast at all ...

"What I saw made me sick to the stomach, David. *Literally.* There, at a small opening, was one of our pigs, Mandy. There were flies and maggots everywhere. We name all our animals here and we become attached, as we don't have them sent away to a slaughterhouse. But she was there, mutilated, and ... her h-head was impaled on a pike in the ground. I didn't think it was her at first. I didn't want to believe it. On the ground was her collar we gave her, like we do with most of our animals here ..." Bob's voice began to break through with emotion.

David gulped, shocked and unsure what to say.

Bob paused a little bit before speaking again, trying to compose himself. "I went a little bit more into the forest and I saw all this blood and feathers. It was our chickens that had gone missing, killed. I then looked around and saw another trail of blood which led off a little. I followed it and-"

There was another loud crackle over the phone. This time it was louder, causing David to drop his phone. *"Shit!"* he said sharply, holding his ear. He picked up his phone. "Bob, Uncle Bob? Can you hear me?"

"What happened? I heard this horrible crackle."

"It's this interference. What happened next, after you saw the trail of blood?"

"I, I saw this pool of blood and inside it, entrails. And just behind a tree ..." Bob paused again, this time there was no crackle. "Our other pig, Shelley. Again, mutilated. Her collar bloodied on the ground. Only her head wasn't to be found." Bob's gruff voice choked up a little.

David could tell this was hard for his uncle. He understood why it was so difficult for his aunt to talk about it. "I don't know what to say, Uncle ... I am *so* sorry."

"Things have gotten even stranger though, David. And *worse* ... We've been hearing strange sounds ever since. Like this whispering coming from the forest, and this interference. Not all the time, but every now and then. In fact, the interference started around a week beforehand. The farm animals sometimes act strange as well and become frantic. And ... one of our cats, Daisy, she went missing eight days ago. Today ... early this morning ..." Bob yet again paused, "we, we, found her body, hanging on the clothesline by her collar. Completely skinned and gutted ... the p-poor thing ..." Bob started to sob.

David had his hand over his mouth. A chill ran straight through him. His eyes welled. He could hear Betty in the background crying. He wiped his tears away. "I am so, so, sorry, Uncle. I didn't know what to expect with what was happening. But I *never* thought this. Have you ... have you phoned the police?" David felt stupid. Surely his uncle would have done that. But it was the only thing he could think to ask.

Bob cleared his throat. "I did ... They came and looked around and helped us clean up the remains. Apart from that, they found nothing at all. They just wrote it off as some kind of sick joke."

David shook his head.

"There was something else, but I'm taking up your time, David. I don't want to worry you with our problems ..."

"Uncle, you're *family*. *Of course* I'm worried about your problems! What else happened? Tell me everything. Try not to leave anything out."

"Well ... when they removed the head ... I mean, Mandy, sorry ..." Bob started sobbing again. "There was a strange symbol carved into the back of her head."

"What?"

"From what I recall, it was a circle with like a star in it." Bob tried to control his voice.

"You mean like an inverted pentagram?" David got up and fetched a glass of water. His mouth was becoming dry.

"Yes, I think that's what it was … I think there was another symbol, too. I … I can't remember …"

David almost spat his water out; his throat cramped up from swallowing too hard and fast. He then heard an unnatural groan on the call. "What the? Bob, did you just hear that?"

"I didn't hear anything, David. Apart from this annoying interference over the phone. What was it?"

"I just thought I heard a groan … Must be the poor reception." David wasn't sure what he had just heard. "Listen, Uncle. I'm coming up," he said abruptly.

"No, my boy. You are not," Bob responded. A little calmer now, but firm. "We can cope. We just have to be more careful and watch out for the animals. I have my shotgun, too. Besides, whoever's doing this, we don't know what they're capable of. It could be dangerous. Though, I'm sure it isn't and it'll stop soon enough. If it hasn't already … We started paying overtime to our workers as well, to work during the night, to guard our animals. I'm sure we'll be fine, David. Plus, I don't think your parents would appreciate me letting you come up here, right now."

"Don't worry about them, Uncle Bob. It's my decision. You mentioned other strange things. What about this whispering?"

"It's probably just us. We're being paranoid. We're all feeling it. Our imaginations are running wild … It's just a weird sensation here. It feels like we are being watched."

"Explain the whispering?"

"It's inaudible, really. It isn't all the time. It just happens sometimes outside, whilst we're working. It's probably just the wind, like when it picks up."

"Anything else strange happening?" David was trying to get his head around all of this.

"Some of our farming equipment has been moved or has disappeared. Things like that. It's just someone's idea of a sick joke. A *bloody sick* joke, mind."

"I still want to come up, Bob. I'm worried about you two and the animals. Me and John have been talking about it. We can help out at night, too …

keeping guard. I insist. It would be good to see you again as well. It's been months."

"Ah … John. How's he doing? I remember him, I think. Fair hair? Nice guy? Always likes a laugh and a joke? You're best friends, aren't you?" Bob tried to change the subject.

"Yeah, we are … But listen. We're going to come. If you don't want us there after a day or two, I promise, we will leave."

Bob sighed. "Okay … We could do with the extra help and lookout, I suppose. Honestly, David, I'm not comfortable with it. Under normal circumstances, I wouldn't have a problem with it at all. It would be lovely to see you."

"Great," David answered, glad he had talked his uncle round. "It's okay if I bring John? Well, he'd be bringing me actually. He has the car."

Bob sighed a little more. "That's fine. We have room at our homestead. We can easily accommodate you both."

"Oh, there's one final thing …" David said a little awkwardly.

"Go on …"

"We erm, have another friend, Grant. He-"

"Let me guess … He'd like to come too, eh? You really have been talking about it, haven't you? It's fine, David. Any friend of yours is a friend of ours. I still feel uncomfortable about it all, being such an odd time … I have a feeling you'd come here anyway, even if I said no?"

"Okay, you got me there. I would, yes. But we won't be any problem, the three of us. I promise."

"I know you won't be. You'd be the *least* of our problems."

"I'll talk to John and Grant, fill them in on everything and get back to you, Uncle."

Bob finished the call asking David to send his love to Jason and Annette. After the call, David's ear was ringing from the weird static sounds.

Benji was still fast asleep as David went into the bathroom to relieve himself. He glanced over at the bathroom mirror casually and saw his own good-looking reflection staring back at him. His right ear caught his attention. It was red and inflamed with blisters. It was beginning to burn. He pulled himself closer to the mirror and stared at his glowing ear. He tried to soothe it with some cold water, but the relief was only temporary. He grabbed some cream from the bathroom shelf above the toilet, wincing as he proceeded to rub some in.

Although the alarm caused by his uncle's call had subdued somewhat, his heartbeat quickened again when he heard a light tapping sound from his front door. It sounded as though someone was tapping their fingernails on the wood. He stood there, still in his towel, frozen for a few seconds.

He walked quietly into his room and put on a pair of boxers and a T-shirt. He walked hesitantly towards the front door of his flat, treading softly. He looked through the spyhole … There was no one there. He carefully opened the door and peered out. No one. His pulse increased. It was quiet out, although he could smell a barbecue somewhere. He walked out a little into the street and took a look around, resting his hands on his hips. Not a soul in sight.

He went back inside closing the front door and walked towards his bedroom.

"BOO!" came a loud shout.

Two hands came up from behind David and grabbed his shoulders. David's heart skipped a beat. He spun round and without thinking, grabbed the person instinctively and threw them against the wall with a thud, shaking a signed photo in its frame of former Arsenal captain, Tony Adams, lifting the 2002 Premier League trophy. The noise awoke Benji, who raised his head and stared out from the bathroom.

"*Argh*, Jesus," Grant said, rubbing the back of his head. His glasses lay on the floor next to him. "What the hell did you do that for? It was a joke, dammit."

David stared at his friend in a crumpled heap. "What the *hell* did you think you were doing?"

"I just wanted to scare you … as a joke. I tapped on the door and then hid behind that bush, then snuck in when you went out onto the street," Grant answered defensively, looking up at David and noticing his red ear. "I hid in the living room."

"Shit, mate … You almost gave me a heart attack." David reached down and held out a hand to help Grant to his feet; he then picked up Grant's glasses from the floor and handed them to him.

"Good job these weren't broken." Grant wiped his glasses with his T-shirt and placed them back on the ridge of his nose.

"I wouldn't be paying for them if they were," David half-joked. He put a hand on Grant's shoulder and then went to sit back on his sofa bed.

"I tried ringing you first, but it went straight to voicemail."

"Really? I was on the phone to my uncle. I didn't get any incoming call notification."

"You spoke to your uncle? Great!" Grant was excited.

David just sat there not saying anything.

Grant was still rubbing his head and looked at David. He was concerned for his friend. "David, what is it? What's up with your ear, too? Have you been bitten?"

David told Grant everything about his uncle's call; the mutilations, strange sounds, how his ear was fine previously, and how this had all freaked him out when Grant had surprised him. The pair of them sat there momentarily, looking into space and trying to collect their thoughts. David's ear was still irritating him. He placed a bag of ice on it to sooth it.

"This is so freaky. You're still serious about going up there?"

David turned to look at Grant. He nodded slowly.

"Jesus. I was up for going. Now, I don't know. You think it's safe? What do you think is going on up there?"

"I have no idea, Grant. But I intend to find out. One way or another. These sick people need to be stopped. I'm an animal lover, so this upsets me even more. But I'm concerned for my aunt and uncle. They're family, you know? It's all very strange. It seems even more important that I go, now."

"I'm intrigued as well. I can't say I'm excited about it, but I'm with you, mate."

"You don't have to come, Granty. It was originally just going to be me."

"I know ... Do you, erm, think that something supernatural is going on?" Grant felt a little silly for suggesting it.

"Honestly? Maybe. I really don't know. I mean, this whispering my uncle and his workers have been hearing on the farm sounds weird. The strange noises down the phone. My *ear*. Doesn't seem natural, does it? Although, I can't exactly say I believe in things like that."

"So weird ... Scary thinking about it. Christ knows how your aunt and uncle are feeling up there. I guess we're going to find out."

David nodded. "That we are," he said, biting his fingernails.

"We should call John. Let him know about what's happening."

"Most definitely. I was just thinking the same thing. I'll do it now."

Grant gave a nod.

"John, what you up to?"

"Sod all, really. I was about to call you."

"You fancy popping round?"

"For sure. I'm going to jump in the shower first. I'll be around in say, half an hour or so. You all right? You sound a bit serious?"

"Not really, bud. I spoke to my uncle."

"What did he say?" John asked eagerly.

"Best if you come round. Grant's already here."

"Okay, I'll be as fast as I can. Want to freshen up a bit first. I kind of stink."

# Chapter Four

## 9th July, 2018

Forty minutes later, David and Grant heard John's car door slam and David jumped up to let him in.

The first thing John noticed, even in the low light, was David's right ear. It was still red and blistery, although it had started to fade a little. "Sorry, I'm a bit late. My dad was asking me about work and stuff. But it's okay, I'm 'ear' now." He grinned cheekily.

David forced a smile and sat down on the armchair. "You really don't miss anything, do you?"

"Nope."

"There's quite a bit to explain."

"Well, I'm all *ears.*" John tried to remain straight faced.

David recounted the whole story for the second time that night, and saw that John was unconvinced.

"Bollocks," John said half-laughing. "You're having me on … And you're telling me it's something supernatural involved?"

"Straight up," Grant replied.

John looked to Grant, then back to David.

"You know I wouldn't lie about something like this," David added.

John dropped his smile. "No, no you wouldn't."

David got up to feed Benji, topping up the biscuits in his bowl and then walked over to the window in the living room. It was growing darker now and the temperature was cooling. The fan was still spinning and oscillating in the room. "We're going to have a big storm soon, I reckon." David stared out of the window.

"What are we going to do? When are we going?" John asked.

"Soon as possible," David answered, still staring outside.

"Well, I don't mind driving us up there," John offered.

"Could always fly?" Grant suggested. "It would be easier and a hell of a lot quicker."

"Nah. That won't work. I have a fear of flying," John answered.

"You can drive; we'll fly. Right, David?" Grant responded only half-serious.

"No … We go together. It's best. Flying would be quicker and I don't want to waste time, but John doesn't want to fly. Besides, I don't think there's an airport nearby."

"Yeah, but going up in his old car, to Scotland? No offence, mate," Grant said, looking at John.

"At least I've got a car!" John shot back.

*"Touché!"* Grant laughed. "It'll probably break down within the first fifty miles."

John smiled and threw a small cushion that bounced off Grant onto the mesh cover of the fan.

David picked it up. "When's the earliest you guys can go?"

"Whenever, really."

"Yep. I'm fine with that." Grant nodded in agreement.

"How about tomorrow evening? It's going to take a long time to get there. We could arrive by morning."

"Erm, yeah, can do that."

"Granty?" David asked.

"Whatever you guys want to do, I'm in." Grant began to feel more nervous.

"I'm going to want to see my folks first though, tell them about it. I don't want them to worry, but I'd rather be honest with them. I know my mum will probably try and talk me out of it." David remembered his earlier call and Annette's reluctance for him to go.

"Where exactly is it?" asked John.

"Damn … I can't remember. Rothy, something. Rothymicus?"

The laptop was on the table.

"Well, there's only one way to find out." Grant reached for the laptop. "We can do some research. See what comes up on good old Google."

"Bloody updates; always take an age," John moaned. "Anyone else hungry?"

"I am, actually," David replied.

"Pizza?" John suggested.

"I'm game," Grant answered.

"Me, three," came the reply from David.

John pulled out his phone from his pocket and scrolled down to the number for their favourite pizzeria. They ordered a twelve-inch Meaty Feast pizza each. David insisted on paying for them all.

"We should get Gino to do pizzas," John joked as they waited for the updates to finish …

*****

"Finally!" Grant exclaimed as the updates finished. He then asked for the name of where David's aunt and uncle lived up in Scotland.

A sudden gust of wind blew the curtains out distracting them momentarily.

"Where did *that* come from?" Grant sat in the middle of the sofa bed with the other two either side of him.

David was leaning his elbows on his thighs with his hands cupping his chin. "It was something like Rothymicus, murcas?"

After a couple of failed attempts, Google suggested the place name.

*"Rothiemurchus,"* said Grant in a raised voice.

"That's it," David confirmed.

"What's it say?" John asked.

"A few things … This and that …" Grant said enthusiastically. He was in his element. Pushing his glasses up his nose, he moved his face closer to the screen. The screen reflected in the lenses. "It looks like there's a few activities we can do up there."

John and David leaned in, both looking at the screen.

"I'm not really interested in that. Not now. I think my uncle's farm is pretty much secluded, anyway. It's quite a bit from anywhere, where we're going."

"I know. I'm just saying," Grant said back.

They looked up some more and saw pictures of Rothiemurchus Forest which surrounded his uncle's farm.

"That's one big arse forest," John remarked.

Rothiemurchus Forest sat within the Cairngorms National Park.

"Where abouts is your uncle's place?" John queried.

"No idea," David answered. "I'll find out more when I let him know when we're coming up."

They scanned a few more pages, trying to gain more information and looking up the area in more detail. They discovered that 'Inverness-shire,' appeared to have been the county that Rothiemurchus was in, and that

'Inverdruie' was a small rural hamlet in the area. 'Aviemore' seemed to be one of the main towns with beautiful scenery.

"Try looking for 'hauntings' there, or in that region, will you, Granty?" David asked.

"Not sure if this is significant or not but check this out. There is something." Grant pointed at the screen. "Read this ..."

> *In a remote corner of Rothiemurchus Forest is the burial site of Seath Mór Sgorfhiaclach, a chief of the Clan Shaw, who was alive during the 14th century. Shaw had a reputation for being a formidable warrior, being well over six feet tall, with a twisted smile that struck terror into the hearts and souls of even his own followers. Over the centuries, people travelling through the forest have spoken of encounters with a gigantic figure challenging them to a battle. If they accepted his offer, then no harm would be done to them and the scary figure would disappear. But if anyone showed fear when they crossed paths with him, they would perish, never to be seen again.*

John acted scared, his eyes wide and pretending to bite his nails.

David and Grant smiled and shook their heads.

"Oh, come on," said John. "It's an urban myth. You don't believe this rubbish, do you? Okay, maybe something sinister is happening at your uncle's farm, but this is horseshit, guys. And it doesn't relate at *all* to what may or may not be happening to your Uncle Bob, Dave."

"No one's saying it's true," replied Grant.

"No, but from the look on your faces, you believe it. You're supposed to be the rational one out of the three of us, Granty."

There was a knock on the door.

*"Pizza!"* John slapped his thighs and got up from the sofa bed.

"Take some money out of my jacket pocket, hanging in the hallway. That should cover it," David called after him.

Stood at the door, was a cute looking girl with soft features; she looked like she was eighteen and smiled at John, showing a couple of small dimples on either side of her freckly cheeks.

John took the three pizzas from her delicate hands and placed them on the carpet in the hallway. He asked what the damage was and then handed her David's money. "Keep the change." He winked. He closed the door and picked up the pizzas; the boxes felt hot in his hands and the smell already filled the hallway.

"Any change?" David asked, still focusing on the laptop.

"I told her to keep it. It was only a couple of quid. She was cute, too."

"Two quid's, two quid," David replied only slightly annoyed.

"She was cute!" John repeated.

With their hunger accentuated by the aroma of melted cheese, they abandoned the laptop and tucked into their late dinner.

"Um-um," John said speaking with his mouth full. Long elastic, stringy cheese hung from his mouth as he pulled the slice of hot pizza away.

"This is great," said David.

"Best pizza I've ever had," Grant added.

"Anyone want a beer?" David asked.

"Sure," Grant replied.

"Here, here," John seconded.

David went to the kitchen and opened the fridge. A magnet slipped as he slammed it shut. It read *I Love New York!* It was a small memento from a holiday with his parents a few years ago in America. It had been a great holiday. A small hiss escaped the bottles as they were opened and a cool smoke emerged.

"Cheers," John said, raising his bottle.

"Here's to Scotland, and my aunt and uncle." David raised his bottle.

They clinked their three bottles together.

*****

Between researching the Rothiemurchus area on and off, John was doing something on his phone and Grant and David watched telly, digesting their full bellies. David's arm flopped down touching Benji's chocolate coloured head.

"Who you texting?" Grant asked intrigued.

"I do have other friends as well you know," John remarked jokingly, not looking up from his phone.

"How dare you!" Grant joked, smiling.

John smiled and raised his eyes.

"Well, I'm thinking of getting some shut-eye soon, guys." David yawned, stretching his arms above his head.

"Yeah, I think that's wise. We've got a long journey ahead of us tomorrow," Grant replied. "You okay to take me home, Johnny?"

"Huh?" John seemed oblivious as he looked up from his phone. "Oh. Yeah, that's fine, dude." He put his phone away.

"You going to see your parents tomorrow morning?" Grant asked David.

"I think I'm going to stay round there for most of the day, before we head off. Going to pack some stuff in the morning, take Benji for a walk, then of course speak to my uncle, just to make sure everything is okay and to confirm. I'll let him know we expect to be there Wednesday morning. Hopefully, we won't have any problems finding it."

"Remember to see Gino, too," John said.

"Definitely," David replied.

"Be good to see that old Italian bastardo before we head off," John joked warmly.

The other pair both agreed.

After a high-five and hugs, David collected the empty beer bottles and pizza boxes and shoved them into the kitchen bin, squashing down on the boxes. He tied a yellow knot in the top of the bin bag. He planned to take it outside in a short while.

*****

David walked outside and placed the rubbish next to his main bin which was already full, ready for the bin men in the morning. The air was now cool and a tad nippy.

Just as a breeze picked up, he heard what he thought was a slight whisper from behind him. He spun around sharply. *Grant again?* He felt the hairs on the back of his neck stand up. Goosebumps formed on his arms. He swallowed hard. Nothing was there. It must have been the wind. A stronger breeze hit him harder and rustled the bin bag noisily. No whisper this time. He was spooking himself now. He laughed. Shaking his head, he started to walk back inside.

A couple of metres away from his front door, out of the corner of his eye, he saw a shadowy flicker between the curtains of his living room window. A bark came from inside.

He stood, frozen. A chill shivered down his spine and his breathing felt heavy. *"Benji!"* David dashed into the flat and straight to the living room, leaving the front door open. *"Benji!"* David's heart was racing.

Benji was nowhere to be seen. The living room was empty.

David checked his bedroom, then the bathroom. He was panicking now. *"Benji?"* he shouted louder. *"Where are you, boy?"*

The flat now felt cold.

David suddenly had an idea. He darted back into his bedroom and checked under the bed, where he found Benji, cowering and whimpering. "There you are, boy," David said calmly, relieved he had found him. He slowly lifted the bed up onto its side so the pillows toppled onto the floor and gently pulled Benji out from underneath. Benji was limp. "Jesus." Benji was shaking and felt cold. "What was it, boy?"

Benji's big brown eyes looked up at him. David rubbed him firmly, trying to comfort him and give him some warmth. After a few minutes, Benji stopped shaking and his body temperature returned to normal. David hugged him on the floor and kissed him affectionately. Benji returned the love by licking his face.

"Better, Benj?" David smiled.

David left Benji in his room and went to close the front door. He then went back into his living room where he felt a strange sensation; static electricity. He hadn't felt it before. The hairs on his limbs were pulling away from his skin and he could feel his head hair rise. He crossed his arms and rubbed the tops of his arms and shoulders. The temperature seemed to be dropping dramatically. Dumfounded, he walked over to the window and stood there, searching for where he'd seen the shadowy flicker. It was clear that something had terrified Benji. David heard growling. As he turned round, he saw Benji sitting at the doorway of the living room staring towards him, still growling.

David knelt beside him and put his arm around him. "What is it, Benj?"

Benji started to bark aggressively and then growled harder. David could feel the vibration of it on his hand. Since owning him, he had never, ever heard him growl or bark like this. David's panic resurfaced, his mouth becoming dry. His heart was pounding in his ears. He licked his dry lips. Suddenly, a strange humming sound filled the room and the light above them flickered profusely. David thought that the bulb was going to explode. But it just stopped as suddenly as it had started. Everything went quiet and the light returned to normal, the static, now gone. Benji, too, had stopped growling and barking. He casually trotted to his food bowl in the kitchen as if nothing had happened.

David looked at him, perplexed. "What the hell is happening?" he said, looking around the room.

*****

David felt like a kid that night. Not since he was a child, had he slept with the lights on. But that night, he did. He had Benji on the bed with him. He was too terrified to sleep. He contemplated going to his parents' house and sleeping there. But if he was going to go up to Scotland, this might only be the beginning. He had to *man up*. Whatever was happening at his uncle's place was possibly affecting him too now. He didn't want his parents involved either. He wanted them to be safe. Everything had been fine this morning. What a difference a day made. He felt scared and confused, wondering what on earth had just happened.

He started to contemplate how events had unfolded. If he hadn't lost his job, he wouldn't have thought of going to Scotland. He should tell John and Grant; he didn't want them involved if it was going to be dangerous. Perhaps things were happening because someone or *something* was trying to scare him off from going. Perhaps it would stop if he stayed at home? Perhaps it was an isolated incident, or there was a rational explanation behind it all? *No.* He was worried for his aunt and uncle. He *had* to go.

# Chapter Five

## 10th July, 2018

"Just doing this one, Chris," a bin man shouted.

"You do number eleven, yeah?" another voice shouted back.

David slowly opened his eyes, woken by noises and voices outside his flat. He then felt a warm, wet sensation on his neck that spread to his left cheek. "Oh, morning, Benj," David said, still half-asleep as Benji continued to lick furiously.

David lay there for another minute, stretching and groaning as he did so. He moved Benji away from his face, roughing his fur up and sat up yawning. He rubbed his eyes and then remembered what had happened last night. Perhaps he dreamt it? But then, it hit him. *Hard.* It wasn't a dream. He wished it had been. He threw his legs out of bed and hung his head, with his eyes still half-shut. He had managed to sleep after all.

He had a fair bit to do today. He needed to tell John and Grant what had happened after they left, and how he didn't think it was a good idea for them to join him on the trip to Scotland. He didn't want to risk anything happening to his friends. He wanted to see Gino too, as he didn't know when he would be back from up north. That was *if* he came back. He was feeling very nervous about it all. He also needed to see his parents and talk to Uncle Bob. Plus, he must pack. He had to plan how he would get to Scotland, now he'd decided John wouldn't be driving him. A flight would be quickest. First, he would have breakfast.

He got out of bed and checked his ear in the bathroom mirror, holding his ear lobe up. It was fine. *Weird.* He drew the curtains back in his flat and looked out of the living room window. *No static.* It was overcast. It had rained in the night. The pavement was wet and the grass had a sheen to it.

David put some dog meat in Benji's food bowl and then added fresh water from the tap to his water bowl. He poured some cornflakes into a bowl for himself and walked over to the fridge for milk. The microwave clock read 09:24, which seemed early for the bin men.

As he opened the fridge door, he retched involuntarily; a putrid stench made his eyes water. *"Good, God,"* he said aloud, turning his head, covering his face with his right forearm. He keeled over, coughing and spluttering, nearly vomiting. Strangely, he'd smelt nothing until he opened the fridge.

All the food in the fridge had decayed. Fresh packaged bacon was somehow now open and looked dark brown, speckled with yellow pus. Maggots were writhing in and out of the rotted meat. Some of them wriggled and fell to the bottom of the fridge. David retched again, his arm still over his face. The milk was congealed and frothy and the mayonnaise was on its side dripping down, along with a bottle of ketchup. A small dollop dropped onto the wriggling, fallen maggots. The ham was streaked with green. Even the bottle of Coke which was standing upright inside the fridge door was congealed and tinted green.

David had lost his appetite. He pulled out some rubber gloves from under the kitchen sink and a new tea towel. He tied the tea towel around his face like a bandana, covering his nose and mouth to protect him from the smell. He pulled out a bin bag and scooped the rotten food into it along with the maggots. It was gross. Benji scampered into the bedroom away from the stench.

*****

After half an hour, David had finally returned the fridge to its normal fresh state. The freezer compartment was fine.

He put the bin bag into the now empty bin outside, including the gloves, wishing the bin men had come at their usual time today. *Typical.* After washing his hands, he opened the windows, trying to get some fresh air into his home. He sprayed the kitchen and the living room with an apple air freshener. Shortly after, he turned on his phone. He heard four beeps and saw four notifications where he had missed calls and voicemails. All, from John:

08:30 - *"David. Give me a call when you can. We need to speak. Something's happened."* John sounded anxious.

David then listened to the second voicemail from John. This one, seventeen minutes after the first ...

08:47 - *"Christ's sake, David. Turn your phone on!"* John sounded more anxious than before, but also annoyed.

09:18 - *"Fuck, mate. We need to talk!"*

The final voicemail, was left twelve minutes ago …

09:49 - *"Please, mate. Call me when you get these messages. It's my car. Someone's trashed it! I'm at the garage … "*

David could hear the clanging of metal tools on a concrete floor. After hearing the voicemails, he immediately phoned John.

"Finally! You've been asleep all this time?"

"Not quite," David replied. "There's a lot to talk about, John. Something has happened here as well."

"What?" John covered his other ear so he could hear David over the noises of the garage workshop. The garage was working on his car and others, making a racket.

"I'll explain later when we're together. What's with the car, what happened? I've only just turned my phone on and listened to your voicemails." David struggled to hear John.

"I tried calling you numerous times, but my signal kept dying. Some bastard slashed my tyres, took out the windows and dented the bodywork."

"What?"

"Yeah," John shouted back over the noise, "and what's even more odd, is I didn't even hear a single damn thing in the night! My car was parked right out front and I had my bedroom window open. I told my old man, who's at work. He heard nothing, too."

David heard his letterbox open in the hallway. "We really need to speak. Is your car going to be okay?"

"It's going to take a little while yet, bud. It's a good job I know these guys well. They're prioritising it for me. They've already changed the tyres. We should still be good to go later on this evening, for when we head off up north, mate."

David heard an air tool in the background. "Erm, yeah. We need to speak about that, too."

"Why, what's happened?"

"Let's talk later when your car is done, yeah? We'll get Grant, too."

"Oh, okay, sure – I'll phone you when the car's fixed."

David went to collect what he thought was the post. Instead, there was a small piece of paper on the mat. It looked blank. He bent down to pick it up. He felt an excruciating sharp pain in his head. He dropped to his knees crying out with the pain.

He dropped the paper to hold his head in his hands. It felt like someone was stabbing his head with a hot dagger, piercing right through his skull. It lasted only a minute, but it had been by far the worst pain he had ever felt in his life. When it stopped, still kneeling, he noticed a few drops of blood fall on the front door mat. His nose was bleeding. He got up and steadied himself, pushing against the wall. He stumbled, dizzily to the bathroom. Benji was sitting outside the bedroom, watching his faithful owner.

David wiped his nose, which stopped bleeding, and washed his face and hands. He returned to retrieve the paper from the floor. It was no longer blank. Not wanting to feel the pain again, he reluctantly picked up the note. His head was fine this time. The note read STAY AWAY! in bright red.

In the top right-hand corner was a symbol, a hexagram, also in red, in what looked like blood. David felt a chill run through his body. Whoever or whatever was doing this, they didn't want him to go up to Scotland. 'They,' were trying to scare him and his friends from going. At least, so it seemed.

# Chapter Six

## 10th July, 2018

Grant had slept in pretty late that morning and was woken by a slow, but constant banging coming from the front door of his flat.

Still weary and half-asleep, he pulled himself out of his bed, picked up his glasses from the bedside table and put on his slippers and an old green T-shirt that was screwed up on his bedroom floor. Stepping over the clutter of computer components and other technical stuff, he made his way to the front door. The banging grew louder as he edged closer to it. "H-hello?" he asked nervously.

The banging stopped. As he stood there, a note was pushed through his letter box. It floated to the floor. At first glance, there didn't appear to be anything written on it. He knelt down and picked it up.

He stood up staring at the piece of paper and then turned it over. The words STAY AWAY! shouted out at him in blood red. Unlike David's note, there was no symbol on it. Grant stood there, feeling confused and still half-asleep. He then saw something else come through the letter box. It was his mobile phone. "What the ..." He bent down and picked up his phone. The phone screen had a video on it. With the note in one hand, he pressed play with the other ...

The video was about thirty seconds long. It was a video of him sleeping. The camera focused fleetingly on his alarm clock on the bedside table; 03:00. Someone had been in his flat and used his *own* phone to film him in the night. Grant could hear laboured breathing as the film scoured his room.

As the video finished, Grant froze in shock as he felt an icy-cold breath on the back of his neck. He tensed, clenching his fist with the note in it. His eyes started to well up as he felt warm urine trickle down his right leg. He dropped his phone. Too scared to look round, he charged out of his flat and ran all the way to David's, forgetting to close his front door and forgetting he was still in his boxer shorts and slippers.

He charged down the street in tears. Passers-by stared at him, pointing and looking alarmed as he sprinted past them. Drivers beeped their horns and shouted profanities at him as he ran across roads. He banged and shouted on David's door in hysterics.

*****

Once John's car had been fixed, he had gone straight to David's. He had arrived a few minutes after Grant. Grant's eyes were still red behind his square glasses. John put a sympathetic hand on his shaking shoulder. Grant didn't respond. He was still in a state of shock. It had taken them some time to calm him down.

They noticed Grant had something in his left hand. They had to pry his hand open to see what it was. It was the crumpled-up note.

Standing in David's living room, they stared at the two STAY AWAY! notes.

"So, you both got them?" John was concerned for all of them.

"How do they know where I even live? How did they get in?" Grant sobbed again. "What have we gotten ourselves into?"

David then recounted his stories from the previous night and this morning. John shared with Grant what had happened to his car. At least Grant shouldn't feel that he was being singled out.

"This is getting serious, now," John said to David.

David nodded. "That's why I don't want you guys coming with me to Scotland."

"We're already involved, and I'm not letting you go up on your own, David," John said strongly. "It's my duty to watch your back; you two are my best friends. You've always been there for me."

They left Grant in the living room to speak alone, just the two of them, out in the black carpeted hallway.

"It's obviously all related," John said. "Whatever this presence was in your flat, was most likely the same as in Grant's place."

"Highly possible. Could it even be more than one thing or persons? Maybe we're fortunate to be alive? You don't hear of ghosts or spirits writing notes, though." David tried to remain calm.

"I don't think there's any doubt that there's some kind of entity or entities at work here. Something supernatural. Something *evil* ... They did a number on my car. Why wouldn't they write it off for good, though? It doesn't make sense."

"I think they are like warnings for us ... It's like a catch-twenty-two situation. Do we stay here, get on with our lives and forget about it, and all of this weird stuff just stops? Or, do we leave and go and see my uncle, and find out more, make sure they're okay, and in the process, possibly make matters worse?" David was thinking aloud and trying to sound rational.

"Will it stop, though?"

"I honestly don't know. I'm concerned for Uncle Bob and Aunt Betty, all alone up there on that farm. I'm thinking about their welfare. They don't even know what's happened to us. Not yet, anyway."

They stood there quiet for a few seconds.

"I'm not sure I even *believe* in ghosts and shit like that," John said.

"I know what you mean, mate. I'm the same. It's hard to believe. Maybe it's some kind of sick joke? But what the three of us have experienced so far, it's happened so hard and fast ... I'm going to risk it. It's kind of ironic. Whatever it is, is trying to scare us off. Yet, all it's doing is making me more determined to go up there. If you're in, or out, that's fine."

"I'm in, mate. All the way! But what about Grant?" John motioned his head towards the living room.

"I don't want him to come. Not now. If he's terrified now, what's he going to be like when we get to my uncle's farm, if things start to happen further? It's not fair on him. I don't think he's going to come now, anyway."

"Yeah, I hear you. But what's he going to do? I don't think he's going to go back to his flat. And he's right, too ... how on earth *do* they know where we live?"

"I guess that's the paranormal for you."

Overhearing them in the hallway, Grant called out to them, "You're right ... After what has happened, I can't go up with you. I'm s-sorry."

John and David walked back into the living room.

"It's fine, Granty," John said softly. "We can't expect you to go now. You're freaked out. We *all* are."

"I, I just feel like I'm letting you guys down."

David crouched down to Grant at eye level. "Look at me ..."

Grant looked up, his eyes still watering.

"You've got *nothing* to feel sorry for. You're scared. Who *wouldn't* be?"

"B-but you're still going to go. You and John ... I feel like such a wimp. A coward." Grant sniffed.

John handed him an unused tissue from his own back pocket.

"You're *not* a coward. I'm going up because it's my uncle. I'm worried for him. And my aunt. John's going to watch my back. And me, his ..." David placed his hands on Grant's shoulders.

Grant wiped his nose with the tissue and sniffed. "I, I can't go back to my flat … Not now. Not yet. My phone is there, too. I left my door open."

"We'll go and check the flat out. Together." David patted his friend's face gently with his hand.

"Yeah. You can wait in my car, bud."

Grant looked down and nodded, still sniffing.

*****

The sun tried to break through, but the sky was still heavy with clouds. The three of them drove back to Grant's flat. Despite John's car being repaired, there was still some visible damage on parts of the bodywork. Grant sat in the passenger seat, nervously biting his nails as they approached his home.

"You wait in the car with Benji, okay?" David said.

Grant looked down and nodded.

David got out of the car and shut the door. "Stay here, Benj …" he said through the window, rubbing his dog's head.

The front door was still open. A faint sound of thunder rumbled in the distance. It looked darker over to the south. David and John both looked across as a flash of lightning shot through.

"Nervous?" John asked.

"A bit."

They slowly walked through the doorway and paused to take a look around. They tried to ignore the damp yellow patch on the pale green carpet where Grant had urinated himself in fright.

"Jesus. The poor guy …" said John.

David picked Grant's phone up and they watched the video.

"Jesus," John said again, rubbing his smooth chin.

"You check the bathroom and living room, I'll check the bedroom …" David suggested.

David walked into the bedroom and checked under the bed and the wardrobe. It was clear. Everything was normal. The only odd thing he noticed was the alarm clock on Grant's bedside table. It had stopped; the red digits flashed 03:00. He adjusted it to 12:09 and placed it back down. There was a crash from one of the other rooms and John shouted out.

David dashed towards the noise and found John lying on the living room floor which was littered with computer parts. "John! You okay? What happened?"

John sighed. "I'm fine …" He picked himself up off the floor and brushed himself down. "I told Grant about leaving all this crap on the floor."

They cleaned the yellow patch in the hallway and doublechecked the flat as thunder continued to rumble outside.

"Well, everything seems to be okay in here at least," John said.

"It doesn't mean anything, though … I'm not sure Grant is going to be safe here. Not on his own … Are any of us?"

"I can't see him coming back in here. Not anytime soon."

"We'll have to talk to him. See what he says. I still need to go and see my folks, then ring my uncle back."

"You going to tell your mum and dad about all of this? Any of this?"

"I have no idea, mate. I want to … But one, I don't want to worry them. Two, I don't want them involved, and three, will they believe us anyway? They're unlikely to believe us if we tell them that we think there's a supernatural explanation."

"Yep. I see where you're coming from, completely. I'll go grab a pair of Granty's jeans and trainers for him."

It had begun to rain hard outside and the sky had grown darker. They took Grant's keys from the hallway hook and locked his front door. They ran as a huge flash of lightning ushered them into the car, reflecting on the wet ground and metallic of the car. A crack of thunder followed as they closed the car doors. All four were startled at the sound of the thunder.

David handed the phone and keys to Grant.

"We checked the flat, bud. It's all good," John said softly. "We cleaned the stain you made as well …" John smiled affectionately and leant his face towards Grant's. "I took some jeans and trainers for you."

Grant was still staring down, picking at his nails. He managed to force a slight smile. There was a long pause. "I still can't go in there. Not on my own …" Grant finally said, looking first at John, then turning to David behind him.

"It's completely understandable." David made eye contact with John in the rear-view mirror.

"Where are you going to stay?" John asked.

"I might stay with my parents. I've got nowhere else to go, really. My other friends have gone away. Well, most of them. The only place I might feel safe is with my folks."

"What are you going to tell them?" asked David.

"I, I don't know yet. They may not believe me. If they do, they'll probably call the police. I don't think that's going to help."

There was another flash of lightning. The three of them looked out of the window and up at the sky. It was still raining heavily.

"You want to go see your parents now, Dave?"

"Yeah, let's do it. I'll tell my mum about our plans. My dad will probably be at work." David put on his seat belt.

Another crack of thunder struck as John started the engine.

*****

By the time they arrived at David's parents' house, the rain had stopped and the sky was no longer as dark. The brief thunderstorm had moved on to the east. The sun was starting to beat down again. It looked like another hot afternoon ahead, with the rain already evaporating from the drenched pavements.

David rang the doorbell and then knocked ... Just as he was about to try for a second time, his mother came to the door.

Benji wagged his tail and jumped up at Annette.

"David, love! Sorry, I was just baking a cake." She sounded surprised and happy.

"You okay, Mum?" David gave his mum a hug and a kiss.

"I wasn't expecting to see you again so soon, after you coming for Sunday's roast." She hugged him back.

"Just keep keeping up appearances, Mum," he teased her.

She slapped her son affectionately across the face.

"It's okay if we come in?"

"Of course."

John gave Annette a hug too as he entered.

"You okay, Grant?" Annette was puzzled by their seriousness.

Grant tried not to make eye contact. He managed a slight smile as he walked in.

*What's up with him?* Annette mouthed.

John just screwed his face up and shook his head.

They all stood in the kitchen while Annette tended to her cake in the oven. David opened the back door to let Benji have a run around in the garden now the rain had stopped.

"You okay?" Annette asked, taking off her oven gloves and shutting the oven door. Her fruit cake wasn't quite ready.

"Not too bad." David didn't want to worry her and wasn't sure she'd believe their story if they told it. He hated keeping things from his parents, but he believed this was the right thing to do. At least for the time being.

"I'm glad you came by. I was going to tell you later. But seeing as you're here," Annette said. "Me and your dad are going to Spain for a couple of weeks ... we leave Friday. I know it's a bit sudden. After you left Sunday, my sister, your Aunt Sarah, called us. She asked us if we wanted to go over and see her. We decided this morning. Your father isn't too busy at the moment. What work he does have, he can take with him. She said you and John could come as well, if you liked? Seeing as you were thinking about going away."

"Oh, okay. Sounds good. Me and John are actually going away too, Mum."

"Really? You decided on somewhere, then?"

David hesitated. "Erm ... Yep. Uncle Bob's."

"Bob's? I told you, David. It isn't really a good idea going up there. It's not good timing at all."

"Well ... Bob's cool with it. At least I care about what's happening up there."

"What's that supposed to mean? What's happened on your uncle's farm is horrible, of course it is. But I don't see how you and John going up there is going to help anything. Believe me, if your uncle needed and wanted me and your father's help, we wouldn't hesitate in going up there. And besides, your father spoke with your uncle this morning as it happens. He said he was sorry about what had happened and that we were going away, but if there was anything he needed, to let us know."

"I'm sorry, Mum. It's just that, well, I think something's happening up there and it's affecting me as well," David said apologetically. He realised he was being harsh on his mother. She had no idea how severe the situation perhaps was. It was wrong of him to criticise her.

"Affecting you, how?" Annette asked, looking curious and straight at her son.

David tried to brush it off. "Just in general. Bob's family and those poor animals. You know?"

"I know ... It's horrible. I'm sure it's probably okay, now."

John and Grant looked at each other. If only she knew.

"I still think it's best if you stay away for a while. Give your aunt and uncle some space. But, if Bob said it's okay, then I guess it is. I can't stop you."

"I haven't told Bob when we're coming yet. I promised we won't get in the way." David looked out at the garden. Benji was springing and hopping about. It made him smile.

"When are you planning on going?"

John scratched his forehead. "Erm. This evening. Tonight."

"Tonight? How are you getting there?"

"John's going to drive us. He's happy to drive. It's going to take about nine or ten hours, we think. Give or take. We might drive a few hours then stop off maybe at a hotel. Get some sleep, then carry on. So maybe longer perhaps. A hotel may be difficult with Benji, though. We might have to sleep in John's car."

"And you don't mind driving, John?" Annette looked at John.

"Not at all, Mrs Hammond."

Annette sighed. "Well, as long as you two know what you're doing. It's a shame you don't drive as well, David. You really ought to retake your driving test. You could have shared the driving whilst the other got some sleep."

"I know, Mum."

"What about you, Grant? You're not going too, are you?"

Grant was still standing there quietly. He didn't say anything.

David jumped in. "Er, no. Three of us might be a bit too much for Bob … Grant's a bit busy with his computers and stuff, anyway. Isn't that right, Grant?"

"Yes," Grant answered.

"Well, if that's what you want to do. It's up to you."

"I'm going to pop round later before we head off. I'm going to pack some stuff. Have you got Uncle Bob's mobile number? It might come in handy as I only have Betty's and their landline one."

"Hold on. Let me see …" Annette walked into the living room and over to a small antique table with a phone and lamp on it. She pulled out an address book from one of the drawers. She licked her finger and flicked through her addresses. "I'll give you Aunt Sarah's numbers too, just in case you need to contact us while we're in Spain."

"Yeah, that makes sense." David was standing in the doorway of the kitchen that led into the living room.

"Okay, here they are …" Annette read them out while David entered them into his phone. She then popped to the loo.

"Shall we go and see Gino, soon?" John asked.

"Yep. We said we'd go and see him before we left," David replied.

"That okay with you, Granty?" John asked.

"Fine," Grant mumbled, still suffering.

*****

David had said goodbye to his mother, leaving Benji in his parents' garden until he returned that evening with John.

There were a few people queuing up outside Gino's van. They could smell the food cooking from the car. Gino didn't notice them at first as he was too busy attending to his customers, so they stood in line, behind the short queue.

"All right, Gino?" John called over.

Gino looked up from flipping one of his burgers on the hot grill. The burger made a sizzling sound as it flopped over onto its uncooked side. "Afternoon, gentlemen." Gino raised a smile.

David and John took their bacon rolls with dollops of ketchup, along with their coffees, to sit at one of the tables. Grant wasn't feeling hungry, but reluctantly drank a can of Coke to appear more sociable.

Gino joined them once he had a break from serving his punters. "You didn't waste any time in going away, chaps." Gino smiled. "You're not going too, Grant?"

Grant took a sip of his can. "No. I don't feel too good."

"You do look a bit pale. Perhaps you're coming down with one of those summer colds?" Gino suggested. "*Bah* ... I hate them."

They sat there for a little while and then told Gino that they had better get going. Gino wished them well and David promised they would come to see him after they got back. They didn't see the point in telling Gino what had happened. It didn't seem worth it. It would sound crazy.

John and David finished their coffees and placed the empty cups in the bin. Grant dropped his half drunken can on top of them.

"If you're going to your parents, Grant, we can come now and help you get a few things, if you'd like? Or do you need to let your folks know first that you're coming?" John asked.

"I'd appreciate it, guys. Thanks. And nah, it should be okay. My parents won't mind me turning up unannounced. They're fine."

John beeped his horn and Gino waved to them wiping some sweat off his face with a towel. They headed for Grant's.

*****

"I'll come in this time," Grant said quietly when they arrived.

"You sure?" John asked.

Grant nodded and he stepped out of the car.

John and David exchanged glances and followed him. Grant stood wearily in the open door, staring in. He started to feel more nervous.

"It's okay, mate," David said quietly in Grant's ear behind him.

Grant took a deep breath and entered, leading the way into his bedroom.

"Not so bad, eh?" John tried to encourage but felt as if he was patronising his friend.

"I guess I've got to come back here eventually." Grant looked around his room tentatively.

John stayed with Grant in his room whilst he packed. David had another check around the flat to see if anything had been disturbed or if he noticed anything out of the ordinary. Though with all the mess in the flat, it was hard to tell if anything had been moved.

Grant packed some clothes into a large rucksack. He hadn't a clue how long he would stay with his parents, nor what to tell them to explain his turning up out of the blue with his things.

David went back to join them.

After he was done with his clothes, he proceeded to the bathroom and collected some toiletries and plopped them into the rucksack too. "All done, guys." Grant looked at his two friends.

*****

It was mid-afternoon when they arrived outside Grant's family home. His parents' car wasn't parked outside. Grant assumed they had gone to do their weekly shopping. It wasn't a problem though, as Grant had a key to his old house.

"You okay then, buddy?" John asked.

"I, I think so ..."

"We'll be in contact, okay? Everything is going to be fine," David said.

"If you need anything, we're just a phone call away, remember." John placed a hand on Grant's shoulder.

Grant undid his seatbelt. "Thanks, guys. I really appreciate the support."

"It's what friends are for, Granty. Isn't that right, David?"

"Sure is."

"What are you two going to do up there, exactly?"

"Christ knows," David answered. "Initially, I was going to go up there to the farm to help out. Just to have a change of scenery and see my relatives. Take a break. Now, I'm hoping we can get to the bottom of all this weird shit and find out *exactly* what is going on."

"We'll just see what happens," John added.

"I, I really am sorry for chickening out." Grant looked sad again.

"Don't be silly. You're fine. If anything, you're being sensible for *not* going." David tried making Grant feel better about himself.

John laughed. "Yeah. We're fucking stupid for *going* up there!"

"We'll see you when we get back, mate. Count on it," David said reassuringly.

The three of them had a group hug in the car. Grant got out and trundled off to his parents' front porch through the hedge archway. He stopped momentarily to wave back to his two friends. He was genuinely worried for the pair of them, and not least, for himself. He wondered if he would ever see his two friends again.

"What do you think he's going to tell his parents?" John asked.

David climbed into the front passenger seat. "I have no idea. I'm not sure he'll actually tell them anything. I guess we'll find out when we next speak to him."

John pulled down the sun visor to shield his eyes from the sun. "You want me to drop you off at yours, then?"

"Please. I've got to ring my uncle and check everything is still okay and get the directions. Then obviously pack some stuff as well. I'm sure he won't mind us driving up tonight."

"Cool."

David was a little distracted. He was checking out a girl in a skimpy miniskirt. He bent his head forward and peered over his sunglasses, pulling them down to get a better view.

"You're not supposed to make it too obvious, right? That's the whole point of wearing sunglasses, so no one knows where you're looking!" John joked. It felt good to laugh.

*****

John had dropped David off and went home to pack and get a few hours' sleep before tonight's long trip. David stood outside for a minute, looking at the window where he had seen a shadow the previous night. The rubbish he had dropped into the bin this morning had attracted a haze of flies hovering over it. David shivered.

# Chapter Seven

## 10th July, 2018

There was no post. Once inside the living room, David looked at the window again, feeling a little nervous. He decided it was time to call his uncle and confirm that they were leaving tonight and expected to arrive first thing tomorrow morning.

"Hello?" said the hoarse, yet polite voice.

"Hey, Uncle Bob. It's me, David. You okay? I got your mobile number earlier from Mum."

"David … I'm a little tired, but not too bad, considering. I'm just at the store waiting for your aunt to come out. We're not at the farm at the moment. Though you can probably tell, as there's no interference."

"There's a *lot* I need to tell you, Uncle. Something has happened. Or rather, some things have happened," David said anxiously.

"Are you okay? Is it your parents?"

"No, they're fine. It's just … it's just that since I spoke to you last night, things have been happening, similar to the things you were telling me about …"

There were a few seconds of silence before Bob spoke again. "Tell me *everything*, David …"

So, David took his uncle through everything that had happened, speaking fast and trying to get everything out at once. "… and then we dropped Grant off at his parents' house because he was scared."

"Woah … Slow down, boy," Bob said calmly.

"I'm sorry, Uncle."

"It's okay … Did you tell your parents?"

"I wanted to. I really did. But I didn't want to worry them. Especially as they're off to Spain at the end of the week. I wasn't sure if they would believe it, either."

"I know. I understand. I'm not sure if they would have believed any of it. I wasn't sure if there was anything paranormal going on up here. I don't believe in any of that stuff. Neither does your Aunt Betty. I've always been a rational kind of man. But, after everything that has happened up here and now with you down there too, it's making me question it. Even more so after last night. Something else happened here, too …"

"Really, what?" David positioned himself forward, awaiting his uncle's response …

"We lost one of our workers this morning. He quit. He got freaked out by something. We have a couple of guys working now and keeping an eye on the animals whilst I'm at the shops with your auntie. To be safe. But last night … Eric, who had been with us for a good number of years, a really nice and honest man, was working the night shift we've arranged along with Gavin, another of our workers. They were taking it in turns whilst the other one slept.

"First up, was Gavin. Nothing too much had happened as such, no whispering this time, but he said that around midnight, not too long before Eric was due to take over, he heard some kind of weird chanting coming from deep inside the forest. He climbed a ladder onto one of the barns to see if he could get a better vantage point of where the chanting was coming from. In the distance, he could see some kind of glow rising up, which he could only assume was a fire. The chanting stopped and the glow vanished, just like that. A mist then fell …"

David swallowed hard.

"He thought it was strange. Despite what's been happening here, he didn't think too much of it; I suppose he was tired. Gavin is probably the most rational one out the group of us here. After a while, he went to wake Eric up for his shift. We've been sleeping in one of the barns as we feel it's better to be closer to the animals in case something happens. Gavin didn't want to worry Eric about what he had heard or seen. Eric took over and again, everything was pretty much okay. *But*, just before five in the morning as the sun was coming up, Eric saw something … *something* that scared the shit out of him.

"He was walking by the pens when he happened to glance up and saw some kind of cloaked figure, *float* into the forest and disappear! He then heard whispering and felt a cold breath on the back of his neck. When he looked behind him, there was nothing there …"

David swallowed harder. Grant had felt an icy-cold breath in his flat when he pissed himself with fright. "Oh, God," David muttered, his hand over his mouth.

"He raced to wake Gavin up, who tried telling him it was just his imagination and that it was due to a lack of sleep. Gavin blatantly refuses the idea of it being anything paranormal. Even though he can't explain this whispering, he is certain there's a simple explanation behind it all. But Eric, he refuses to come back. On top of what he saw and experienced, he says he can't shake off an 'impending doom' feeling. It's too much for him."

"The animals, though ... Are they okay? Have any more gone missing since?"

"At the moment, they're all fine. No more have disappeared. Obviously, we are still having disturbances here. I even had trouble starting the car up this morning. I'm not sure if that's linked to all this or not."

"Listen, Bob ... We're coming up. Not Grant, he's too frightened, not that I blame him. But John and I, are. We're going to leave tonight sometime. Hopefully, we'll get there for tomorrow morning at dawn. I'm going to go and see my parents again tonight, say goodbye and we'll set off."

"David, I don't know ... This could be dangerous for you. Especially after what has happened down there with you three already."

"We both know that, Uncle. But the fact is, we're already involved and affected by this. Yes, whatever it is, is trying to scare us off perhaps and maybe we'd be fine if we just stayed away ... but I'm worried for you and Aunt Betty. It's just making me more determined to come up there. All of us need to investigate this ... what's actually going on, before anything worse happens."

"I'm touched by your concern, David. I'm sure your aunt will be, too. You're very brave, as is your friend. What about your dog? Would it be safe to bring him?"

"Brave or very stupid," David tried to joke. He heard his uncle laugh a little on the other end of the phone. "I wondered about Benji. Normally, it would be a lovely setting for him. He loves the outside, especially in the summer. I was going to leave him with my parents though, because it might have been safer for him and in case he wandered off into the forest. But with my folks going away to Spain, there isn't much else I can do. I don't want him in a kennel. He wouldn't know what had happened to him. He'd feel abandoned. So, I'm probably going to take the risk and bring him up there with us. I'll just have to make sure I take extra care of him."

"*We'll* take extra care of him. Very well. I appreciate the concern, David. If that's what you really want, I won't stop you. It will be lovely to see you again, albeit under such dire circumstances ... It's just, I don't want to feel responsible if, well, you know ... something happens ..."

"You won't be responsible for us, Bob. Me and John can take care of ourselves. Don't worry about that. We're going to be fine. *All* of us."

"Okay … Have you got a pen? I'll give you the directions to the farm. If you have satnav, it will only take you a certain way. You're going to have to go down a dirt track off a small country lane to get to us directly. That will take you straight up to our farm. There's a gate at the end. It will be open. We rarely have it shut …"

"Okay, hold on." David placed his phone on the table and fetched a blue biro from a smaller table in the corner of his living room, where he tore off a piece of paper from a pad. "Okay, what are the directions?" David put his uncle on loudspeaker and took all the instructions down.

"… as you come off that road, you need to take a second right. Then another right, and keep on going. By now, you're starting to head more into Rothiemurchus Forest," his uncle said, trying to give the directions in as much detail and as carefully as he could. "Then, follow that road up and you should see a small sign on the left saying 'Hamish Farm' on it, and an arrow pointing up. The sign and turning onto the lane can be easy to miss sometimes, as it gets quite overgrown around there …"

"Okay, Bob. I think I've got it all." David studied the directions on the piece of paper making sure he could read them all.

"Okay, my boy. There is another way to our farm. But that would take longer from the direction you'd be coming from. If there's any problems, don't hesitate to call me. If you're leaving tonight, although it's going to take a *long* time to get here, the roads and motorway may be quieter. I'm going to do the night shift with Gavin tonight. It was going to be Eric again, but obviously he's left now."

"Okay, Uncle. If there's any problems, I'll call you. I better get going. I need to pack and have a few hours shut-eye."

"You make sure John drives safely, okay?" Bob had just seen Betty come out of the store carrying a shopping bag.

"I will do. See you tomorrow!"

"Bye, David. You take good care!"

David got out a medium-sized rucksack from the bottom of his wardrobe. It had been hiding a pile of old comics he had collected when he was younger, which he'd been reluctant to throw out, in case they became valuable; they also had a sentimental value to him. He wasn't sure how long he would be staying with his uncle. At first, he just thought about packing a few T-shirts and a few of pairs of jeans. As it was summer, he wouldn't need coats or jumpers. But then he decided to take more clothes, just in case he needed them; summers up north could be unpredictable, so he grabbed his suitcase from the corner of his bedroom and threw it on the bed.

He packed all his underwear and toiletries in the rucksack including his hair wax, which he couldn't manage without; he always used just enough to still give his hair that 'natural' look. He packed the main and bulkier stuff in the suitcase, slipping his laptop into one of the small compartments together with the notes he and Grant had been threatened with. He then fastened the case back up and stood it next to the bed. Then he remembered to add some cans of dog food and a bag of dog biscuits for Benji to the rucksack. He then stripped down to his boxers and jumped into bed for some sleep.

# Chapter Eight

## 10th July, 2018

As soon as David woke, he phoned John to share the latest events at Hamish Farm. Shortly after, John arrived. With his rucksack over his shoulder, David wheeled his suitcase out to the car where John stood. John was smoking a joint and exhaling smoke rings into the air. The sun was gradually starting to set and it was beginning to cloud over.

"All packed, then?" John asked.

"Yep! Packed quite a bit. Probably won't even need most of the stuff, but you never know. Especially, when we don't know how long we're going to be up there for."

John walked round to the boot of his car. "I know what you mean. I didn't pack too much, really. Just the necessities. Oh, and some *rubbers*," he joked as he opened the boot, smiling.

"Jeez." David grinned.

John placed David's suitcase in the boot. "Jesus, what have you got in here? It weighs a ton."

Next to the suitcase was John's gym bag with his 'necessities.'

David laid the rucksack over his suitcase.

*****

"What did you tell your old man?"

"Ah, not much, really. I mentioned last week some time that we might be going up. I just said we were going away and helping out on your uncle's farm in Scotland, as he had some problems up there. I didn't really go into details. He said something along the lines of 'Make sure you get paid if it's work.' Typical Dad!" John overtook a parked car with hazard lights blinking on and off.

"You nervous?"

"A little, yeah. Probably will be even more so, by the time we get up there. You?"

"Same. Even more when we get there, like you say. I still don't know what to expect. I mean, maybe this is all a game, a joke, or there's some kind of rational or 'normal' explanation behind it all." David stared out of the car window.

"Yeah … Imagine if it's some kind of wind-up. Like hidden cameras or some kind of shit like that!" John made a slight laugh. "Honestly, I think this is real. Supernatural or not, something bad is happening." He stopped at some traffic lights.

"I keep going over things in my head. Part of me thinks there's a reasonable explanation, something sensible and I don't want to believe anything other than that. Yet, at the same time, we have to be realistic, and the things that have happened, that we've seen, to a certain extent go *way* beyond normal."

John indicated to turn right. "I'm with you, mate. We haven't seen anything *too* concrete, but things have happened that are *damn* hard to explain. Not just here, but at the farm. I mean, that cloaked figure that guy saw …" John shivered. "Normally, I would call it a load of bullshit, but what you saw and experienced, along with Granty, I believe it. Although, I guess having my car trashed, there's nothing exactly supernatural about that."

"I know, mate. Something has been messing with us either way. Human or not."

*****

They rolled up outside David's folks.

"You all right, Son?" Jason's cheerful voice answered the door in nothing but a beige towel; he was drying his hair with another towel.

"Put some clothes on, Dad. You always answer the door like that?"

John smiled next to David.

"Course," his father joked back.

"Where's Mum?" David asked as they walked in through the hallway and Jason closed the door behind them.

"Upstairs, giving Benji a bath. He rolled in something … Most likely belonging to a cat. I thought I'd get a shower in first." Jason flicked his hair up trying to get rid of any excess water.

"Nice," David said in a sarcastic tone.

"You all right then, John? Are you boys all packed? Seems a bit of a rush to get up there, doesn't it? You don't mind driving?"

John tried not to look at his best friend's semi-naked father. "Err, yeah. We're both packed, Jase. We didn't see any point in hanging about. It's not like we have anything better to do. And no, it's fine. I honestly don't mind driving us up there."

"That's all right, then. Seeing as silly bollocks here never learnt how to drive. Eh, David?" Jason joked, ruffling his son's hair up. "I know your mother's against you two going up there after what's happened, but I think Bob will appreciate any help."

"We're not going to make matters worse, Dad. If we feel we're intruding, we'll come home. I'm sure Bob and Betty will let us know if that's the case." David felt a pang of guilt about his parents not knowing about all the events. Even if his aunt and uncle wanted them to leave, he was determined to find out what was behind the strange occurrences on the farm and in the forest, even more so after what he and the others had encountered.

"I'm sure they'll be fine with it," Jason replied.

*****

They could hear a hair dryer from upstairs. Annette was drying Benji off. Benji really enjoyed his baths and a nice warm blow dry. The three men sat in the living room chatting. The television was on, but no one apart from John was really paying much attention to it. Jason was talking about Spain and how much he was looking forward to it.

They heard a clatter on the stairs and Benji's furry brown figure came charging in. All clean and fresh, wagging his tail, he jumped up to lick David's face.

"Hey, you! You been a good boy?" David asked.

"Oh, for Pete's sake, Jason. Put some something on." Annette frowned, entering the living room.

Jason sat in his favourite armchair still with only a towel around him. "You won't be requesting that later, dear," he jested, winking.

David pulled a face, cringing at the thought of his parents 'doing it.'

Annette shook her head, half-smiling. "You okay, boys?" she asked as she sat on the arm next to her husband.

"I'm good, Mum. We're both packed and are ready to head off in a little while."

"I can make you a quick something first, if you'd like?"

"Nah, it's fine. We'll stop off somewhere for a bite to eat on the way."

John nodded in agreement.

"Which route are you going to take, John?" Jason asked.

"I've looked into it a little bit. Best way is probably via the M6."

"Yeah, that's most likely the best way. That's the way me and Annette went. It was a long time ago, now. It can be a bit tricky to actually find the farm from what I recall. A few forest roads and bends. It might be easier now with satnav."

"We should be okay finding it. Bob said that the satnav only works to a certain point," David said.

"What about sleep? It's going to be a hell of a trek." Jason held Annette's hand.

"Might have to sleep in the car or a hotel. It's going to be awkward though, as we have Benji," David answered.

"It does seem a bit rushed, boys. Surely it would have made sense to wait until morning? Or even get a train up there. I don't see the rush, really," Annette asked the two.

"I know, Mum. It's just the way we wanted to do it. We can catch up on sleep once we get there. Chances are, it's going to be quieter on the way up there, too."

"Well, as long as you make sure you don't fall asleep at the wheel, John," Annette warned.

"Nah. I'll be fine, Mrs H. If I get really sleepy, then we'll just pull over."

*****

The time had come for the two friends to decide to set off. It was 21:33.

"You two try and have some fun and don't get in your aunt and uncle's way. If they decide you are getting in the way, come home!"

The two friends got up.

"I know, Mum. We will. You have a great time in Spain, won't you? We'll call you as soon as we arrive at Hamish Farm." David hugged his mum and gave her a peck on the cheek.

"Okay." Annette smiled and kissed him back.

"We will, David. You boys take care and drive safely. Send our love to my brother and Betty." Jason gave his son a hug.

David reluctantly hugged his half-naked dad back.

John shook Jason's hand and gave David's mother a hug too. She gave him a gentle kiss on the cheek.

The two friends waved as they left and John beeped the car horn.

"You know, I'm sure your mum likes me," John teased, smirking.

"Fuck off." David smirked back.

They looked at each other and both laughed. They were off. John drove down the end of the street in the setting sun and took a right, then headed towards the direction of the motorway.

Despite what they had experienced so far, they couldn't have predicted the sheer terror and horror that lay in wait up there …

# Chapter Nine

## 10th July, 2018

David yawned. He looked at the clock on the dashboard; 23:38. They'd been on the road for over two hours. It seemed like longer. The roads and the motorway were quiet. They decided to use the toll at Birmingham. It had just started to rain.

John turned the wipers on as a few spots of rain splashed onto the windscreen. "Only about seven hours or so to go," John joked, already feeling a little tired.

"Yeah, it's pretty tedious," David replied. He didn't like long journeys by car.

"It's worse for me; I'm the one driving."

"I know. I feel guilty about that." David looked over his shoulder at the back of the car. Benji was fast asleep on an old red and black, chequered blanket that belonged to John.

"So you should!" John joked and grinned, turning to David. "When are you going to take your test again?" John slowed down slightly. A large truck was changing lanes in front of him.

"Eventually … I just can't be arsed to retake it at the moment. I've already failed the theory test twice. It's also a pain having to pay again as well." David yawned and blinked to clear the tears from his eyes.

"Thick bastard." John glanced over and smiled.

David laughed. "Yeah, but when you took yours, it was easier."

"Maybe so, but that will teach you. You should have done all this years ago." John braked a little.

"True."

"I'm getting hungry, now. You want to get a bite to eat soon, seeing as we haven't eaten yet?" John patted his belly with his left hand, keeping his right on the steering wheel.

They hadn't had much of an appetite when they left.

"Yeah … I was going to say I'm getting hungry. When's the next service station?"

"According to my calculations, there are a couple not too far up ahead. Possibly another twenty minutes or so. I had a check earlier on, before I picked you up." John's attention was caught by headlights in his wing mirror.

"Your calculations?" David asked sarcastically.

John smiled.

They spotted a sign on the motorway which proved John's 'calculations' correct.

"Ahh. You see? I was right. About twenty minutes."

"How do you think Grant's feeling? We should give him a text in the morning. Maybe ring him?"

"I think we should. I'm sure he's going to be okay. Seeing as he's with his folks." John yawned.

The rain was coming down harder now.

"Great." John was annoyed. He switched the wipers on to full. Watching them was hypnotising. John shook his head trying to shake his sleepiness away.

"You all right?" David asked a little concerned.

"Fine, mate. Just the tiredness setting in. I should be all right after some greasy food."

"Me too."

"I'll put the radio on. That will help keep us awake," John suggested. He turned the knob on the old radio which made a slight clicking sound. He went through a few channels until he came across a station playing music. He didn't know the name of the song, but it had a good beat to it. He started tapping his fingers on the steering wheel.

A car speeding way over the limit overtook them, spraying a huge gush of water over the windscreen on John's side of his car.

David shook his head.

"Moron," John muttered to himself.

**11th July, 2018**

At midnight, John indicated left and pulled into the service station. It had stopped raining for now. He checked his petrol gauge and it was still virtually full. He had filled up before he picked David up. There were only a few cars in the car park. John reversed into an empty space near to the entrance of a fast-food outlet, Burger Boys. The emblazoned sign shone down on them.

Next to Burger Boys was a coffee house. A fried chicken outlet was slightly further down.

"I fancy a burger. Or do you want some chicken?" John asked, releasing his seatbelt.

"Burger Boys is good."

Since mentioning food, they'd grown very hungry over the last few miles.

"Cool. You want me to bring you something out, or shall we sit in and leave Benji here?"

"Benji will be fine here. He's still fast asleep." David looked back. Benji was snoring away on the blanket, his paws twitching in his sleep.

"Let's go!"

They shut the car doors as quietly as they could so as not to wake Benji. Empty coffee cups littered the ground, along with empty burger wrappings. The two bins either side of the skylight archway were filled to the brim.

John slipped on a half-empty ketchup sachet, managing to keep his balance by gripping a coffee house sandwich board. He cursed under his breath as David tried not to laugh. They pushed open the glass doors and walked left into the burger outlet. The smell of fresh coffee floated from the coffee house on the right. There were a few people sitting down inside. Some had already finished their food, but they were still sitting, chatting.

The pair walked up to the counter where they were greeted by a server.

"That a bloke, or a woman?" John asked keeping his voice down, leaning in as the server went to fetch their food.

"You know what?" David whispered back, "I don't know."

They both laughed.

"Hate it when that happens," John responded.

They smiled at the server as they came back and handed them their *Burger Boy's Monster* with fries, on a red plastic tray, together with two large Cokes.

"I'll get these, mate ..." David said, pulling out his wallet followed by his debit card.

"You sure?" John put the money he had half pulled out of his pocket back; he was hoping David would pay.

"Yeah, it's fine. Only fair. You've been driving us. I need to give you some petrol money as well," David stated as he put his card into the card reader and entered his PIN code.

John joked about him not covering it up, in case someone saw his PIN.

*****

They sat by the window on a pair of red seats across from one another. They could see the car just outside in the car park. A biker had pulled up next to it and made his way inside. His big, black boots made a stomping sound on the wooden flooring. He was carrying his helmet in one hand and sported a long, bushy beard. He was wearing a Union Jack bandana and all leathers. His jacket had skull and crossbones on the back of it.

John sat there, dipping fries into ketchup. David took a huge bite of his burger. He wiped a dollop of mayo from his chin with a napkin.

"I thought you were being careful watching what you eat? This is like what, three junk foods in two days?" John asked across the table, sucking on the straw in his drink.

"Something like that ... Well, there are exceptions. Everything in moderation." David winked. "Listen, I was thinking ..."

"You be careful," John replied sarcastically.

David smiled. "What if I take over and drive for a little while? You can get some sleep. It's going to be difficult getting a place overnight with Benj, and I don't fancy leaving him in the car all night. Plus, we would get to my uncle's quicker, as opposed to losing hours by both sleeping ..."

John had an unsure look on his face. "I know you can drive, mate. It's a good idea in theory. But it's a long distance and we can't afford to get caught with you having no licence."

"I know. Even so, the chances of us getting caught would be slim. Though, it might go the other way. The Old Bill might take advantage of people thinking they wouldn't get caught so late at night, even on a motorway." David considered, taking another bite from his nearly finished burger.

"We'll see how I feel in a few hours, maybe."

"And remember, too. If we get caught, my dad is a lawyer." David smiled.

"True." John grinned, taking another sip through his red and white swirl straw.

*****

John and David were the only two left in the building. They had just watched the biker parked up next to John's car get up and leave.

"We better think about setting off."

David nodded. He took the lid off his cup and swallowed the last of his drink. "We better go for a slash as well, before we go."

"Good thinking, Batman."

As David brushed down a few crumbs from his burger bun off his lap, his mobile rang. It was his mum. "All right?"

John mouthed he was going to the toilet and David signalled with a thumbs up.

"I'm just about to turn in. I thought I'd just see how you were getting on?" Annette asked on the other end. "We were up late watching a movie."

"Yeah, it's all good, Mum. We just stopped off for a bite to eat and are about to set off again. It's only been like three hours. No need to worry."

"I know, hun. I just wanted to make sure you were okay and safe."

"Aw, I know. We're good, though." David again felt the guilt, that his own mother had no idea what had been happening to him and the others.

"You and John are more than capable of looking after yourselves … It's just that I worry."

"I know, Mum. Listen, we'd better get going. I'll call you later as soon as we get to the farm … Promise."

A slight crackle came over the phone and the lights dimmed almost to off, before coming back on again. David could just about hear his mum tell him she loved him.

"I love you too, Mum … Bye."

David stood there in the outlet on his own, looking up and around, wondering about the lights, with his mouth slightly open. It was a little similar to what had happened in his living room and bathroom, but not as intense and without the strange pulsating humming sound. He swallowed slowly. Surely it was just a coincidence. *Not here, not in a fast-food joint.*

"Bloody lights have gone out in the bogs, ain't they!" came a shout from John in the toilet entrance, distracting David.

A worker who had started cleaning a table heard and looked up. John walked out doing his flies up.

David looked at John.

"What's up with you? Looks like you've seen a ghost."

"Nothing. The lights went funny out here, too … My mum just wanted to make sure we were okay and to wish us well."

"Oh, okay. I'm going to wait in the car. You still need to use the loo? We better crack on."

"Yeah, going to go now."

"Be careful in there though. The lights have gone out. I did consider taking a quick dump but didn't want to use my phone for light to wipe my arse."

David screwed his face up and shook his head.

John made his way to the exit, taking a detour to buy a coffee before he headed out towards the car. David pushed the wooden door into the toilets open. The only source of light was the green exit sign above the door. He could just about see his way to one of the urinals. He walked over, now desperate to go. Suddenly, he heard a noise to the right of him. It was the squeak of a finger running over a mirror or glass. He gave himself a shake and buttoned up his flies.

He made his way to the mirror over the basin. It was hard to see anything as there wasn't enough light. He pulled out his phone and used its light to see. Nothing. Almost instantly, it became very cold in the toilets. The temperature had dropped dramatically, all in the space of a few seconds. David started shaking. He could see his warm breath in the air, like on a cold winter's day. The mirror steamed up a little …

*"Turn … back!"* came a sudden, sharp whisper from above him.

Startled, David dropped his phone into the basin and then quickly gathered it back up, frantically using it to look around the dark toilets. His heart was pounding in his chest and he was breathing heavily. Behind him, he heard a crackling sound. He spun back round and saw the mirror freeze up. He stepped back carefully. As he did so, the mirror began contorting and twisting … Even in the low light, David could see that much. His back was now up against the far wall of the toilet … The mirror suddenly shattered, firing pieces of glass towards him. He instinctively guarded his face with his right arm, cowering down. Then, the lights came on.

David got up, slowly flicking the pieces of glass from his arms and hair. He made his way back to the mirror, broken glass crunching beneath his feet. Part of the mirror had remained, but it was now made up of a glass inverted pentagram, similar to the symbol on the note he had received. He was wary of touching it because of what had happened with the note; the nosebleed and pain in his head. But he couldn't resist. He ran his fingers over the glass symbol. It was smooth, yet cold to touch. It burnt his fingertips. He stood in amazement. Staring.

After a minute or so, he snapped out of his trance and took a photo of it. His heartbeat began to reduce a little. There was definitely no more doubt. Whatever was going on, *wasn't* normal. David really was starting to fear for their lives.

He exited the toilets, hurriedly moving past the counter towards the entrance. An employee, seeing David with a few spots of blood on his face, moved away quickly.

Outside, John stood at the side of his car. His hot coffee lay on its side, oozing fluid and steam from the small slit in the lid.

He was holding a note he had found from under one of his window wipers. At first, he thought it was a parking ticket. That was unlikely; he had a right to be parked there. It wasn't the note that had scared him. It was something else. His eyes were fixated on one of the car's rear door windows. Inside, Benji was still sound asleep. On the window were two large, frosted handprints, as if someone had pressed up against it, looking in. These were not normal handprints. These prints had five fingers and long nails or talons attached to them. The fingers appeared to be out of shape and bulging as if they were deformed. The two thumbs in particular, seemed fatter than the fingers, more bent and slightly curved round. There were long thick strands of grey-white hair stuck to the window.

John pulled them off, grimacing and flicked and brushed them onto the ground. A couple stuck to his fingers. *"Urgh."* He walked to the back of the car to check for anything else. There was a car park light near the car, which added visibility to that provided by the Burger Boys sign. He gagged at what he saw. Near to the exhaust pipe, was a pile of maggots wriggling all over one another. And the *smell.* John retched and coughed. He bent over spitting out a mouthful of bile that rose from his stomach.

There was a sudden gust of wind, blowing some of the maggots from the pile.

"Sweet Jesus!" John looked back at the maggots. He could hear them wriggling and glistening as they moved over each other. He then saw David rushing from the entrance towards the car.

"You wouldn't believe ... We have to get the hell out of here, *now*!"

"Woah ... What happened?" John placed his hands on David's shoulders stopping him.

David looked straight at him. "Something happened back there. I went to the toilet, I took a piss in the dark ... and then, then-"

"Take your time. It's all right," John said, trying to calm David.

David took a deep breath and started again. "Whilst you were in the toilet, I heard this crackle over the phone and the lights almost went off in the building. The same time the lights died on you in there."

"Go on."

"After you left to wait outside, I went in. I heard this noise on the mirror in there, like someone rubbing their finger over it. Then came a whisper, telling me, or us, to *'Turn back!'* And then, the mirror shattered!"

John could see the small specks of blood on David's face and the glint of small shards of glass on his shoulders.

"Then, when I looked at the mirror again, it had turned into *this*!" David pulled out his mobile phone and showed John the photo of the upside-down pentagram.

John's mouth opened and dropped. "There's something else ..."

David could see the fear in his friend's face. "Wh-what is it?"

"Look!" John showed him the weird handprints on the car. Some hairs still remained.

"Oh, my, God!" David thought of Benji and opened the door in a hurry. *"Benji! Benji!"*

Benji woke up startled. He was fine.

David hugged his dog tightly. "Whatever it was, was staring in at him!"

"I know, I know," John replied soothingly, trying to calm David. He looked over and saw a couple at the other side of the car park. They were staring, obviously wondering what was going on. "That's not all." John showed him the pile of maggots at the back of the car.

"Maggots, again." David tried to hold himself back from being sick.

"And here, look at this." John showed him the note he had found on his car: TURN BACK! LAST WARNING! There was no symbol.

"Is that blood again? That Biker? Could it have been him? Could it?"

"I don't think so. I know he was parked up next to us, but we saw him leave, remember? Besides, this most likely happened when the lights went out whilst I was in the toilet." John looked at David anxiously.

David stared back.

John walked back to the side of the car where the handprints were. David followed him. "What now? It's not too late to turn back, you know?"

"I don't want to turn back. I think it's going to get worse once we get up there. Maybe. I don't know. But there seems to be a reason why someone is stopping us from getting up there." David scrutinised the frosty deformed handprints. He let out a sigh.

John looked at him.

"If you want to turn back, I'll understand. I can go on alone. I'll find a way. A train, bus."

"*No*! We're in this together. This is the first thing I've seen which looks supernatural. I'm getting seriously worried now. The last thing we want to do is keep pissing these forces off, whatever or whoever they are. Unless someone's playing a prank on us, like wearing some kind of Halloween glove?"

"Always got to get a joke in, haven't you?" David forced a smile. "I'm going to take a photo of this." David pulled out his phone and took a photo of the strange handprints.

"You want to head off, then?" John asked, screwing up the note and placing it in his back pocket.

"I think so." David walked round to the passenger side of the car.

"Dropped me bleedin' coffee an' all, didn't I. Fucking scared me!"

"Benji must have been completely unaware of whatever it was; he surely would have got up and barked?"

"I know, mate. It's worrying. But let's do this. Let's try and find out what's behind all of this. Maybe someone up at your uncle's place knows something? Perhaps your uncle knows more than he's telling you?" John started the ignition.

"Well, we're going to try and find out. Scared or not," David replied, looking across at John and holding his fist up.

John bumped David's fist and they headed back onto the motorway, in spite of their fears.

*****

"Oh, yeah. I forgot to tell you ..."

"Tell me what?"

"You've got some speckles of claret on your face."

"Eh?" David pulled down the passenger sun visor and turned on the small light next to it. Examining his face in the small mirror, he picked off the tiny pieces of glass and rolled down the window to flick the particles outside. There was a half-drunk bottle of water on the floor, from which he poured a small amount onto his hands. He rubbed his face and used his T-shirt as a towel. "Think it's all gone." He checked his face from side to side in the yellowy light, noticing some faint dark circles under his eyes. He flipped the sun visor back.

"You know ... there's one thing I don't get?" John took one hand off the steering wheel as he scratched the back of his neck.

David looked over.

"These forces or entities, or whatever the hell it is, why not just, well, you know ..." He cleared his throat. "why not *kill us,* if they want us out of the way so much?"

"You know, John. I was thinking the exact same thing. Who knows? Maybe they lack the power to do so. Or they just want to scare us off for now? I've never been one to believe supernatural stories. Most stories I've heard have been hoaxes, but I'm seriously starting to believe in it all now."

"I know how you feel. I was the same. But if this is a wind-up, whoever is behind this, they're going to get it all right." John thumped the door. The sound woke Benji up who then lay his head back down on the soft blanket.

"The thing is, they must have been following us since we left?" David bit his lip.

"I was thinking that, just before you came outside. Or maybe, they're just watching us all the time?" John felt goosebumps thinking about it.

"Really is some scary, unexplained shit."

"You can say that again."

*****

It was pushing half past one as the rain started to fall again. The wipers drummed with friction as they moved back and forth. There were still many more hours and mileage to cover before they arrived at their destination.

David was struggling to keep his eyes open, looking up at the motorway lights to the left of him as they whizzed past with the rain coming down. His eyes began to feel heavy. He was startled for a moment as a motorbike roared past making him jump. He wondered if it was the same biker they had seen over an hour ago. He looked over at John who was concentrating on the motorway ahead. David still felt bad that John was driving them all the way to Scotland. It was a lot to ask. Especially during the night. He made a promise to himself that he would retake his driving test once they got back from his uncle's. His eyes widened slightly. *If*, they got back from his uncle's. They still had no idea of the potential dangers that awaited them up there. He started to get butterflies in his stomach from anxiety.

"You should try catching some sleep, mate," John suggested, his eyes still fixed on the motorway ahead.

"I might. I can still drive though, if you want? We can change over at the next service station."

"I really don't know. Tell you what. Try sleeping and we can decide after that." John really wished he hadn't dropped his coffee now. He questioned why he hadn't got another one before they set off again. He could really do with the caffeine kick right now.

"Okay," David agreed. He looked back at the window where the frosted handprints had been, wondering whether they were being followed. The rain had all but washed the prints off by now. He was glad he had taken a photo of them. "I see the prints have pretty much gone."

John glanced round. "Yep. I was thinking of washing them off, seeing as you have the pic. Guess there's not much need to now."

"I'll try and get some sleep, anyway." David tried to snuggle his head and neck into a comfortable position on the headrest. It was difficult to do so.

"Don't dribble on my seats," John joked.

David smiled. With his head facing away from his friend, he raised his hand giving him 'the bird.'

John laughed and shook his head, turning his concentration back to the motorway again.

# Chapter Ten

## 11th July, 2018

It rained heavily non-stop until 02:51. John was starting to feel exhausted. The tiredness was settling in further. He shook his head rapidly, forcing himself to stay awake. *Only a few more hours.* He slowed down for some motorway works ahead. The lane he was in was closed for the next mile or so according to an electronic sign, along with another lane to the left. Some blue signs with a white arrow pointed to a lane on the right which he needed to move into. That was also partially closed off.

He followed the way being the only car, driving between the row of numerous fluorescent cones. They were sandwiched between them. The headlights reflected off the cones. He looked over at the men to the left who were working through the night. Or rather, who were supposed to be working. A few were just standing on the wet surface, smoking and speaking. John saw one of them pick his nose and look at the contents on his finger, before flicking it aside. Another was in a digger, sat there reading a newspaper.

John shook his head. *Typical. All these cones and nobody working.* He looked over at David who had drifted off into a deep sleep. He was making the odd snort every now and then. John smiled and then yawned, before putting his foot down as the row of cones faded behind him into the distance, moving into top gear.

A nasty smell filled the car.

John sniffed. *What the?* John sniffed again. He looked at David and then at the back of the car where Benji lay. His legs were open, snoring lightly. He was making a small groan in his sleep. "Oh, you *dirty* little git," John said, squashing his face up. He quickly rolled down his window. "God, that's horrible. What's David been feeding you, boy?"

He gasped for air from the half-open window. The damp air was hitting his face and blowing through his hair. He rolled up the window as he drove under a bridge and glanced at the time; 03:00. He slowed downed and checked his hair in the rear-view mirror briefly. He then focused back on the motorway, quickly slamming on the brakes, abruptly awakening David and Benji …

"Wh-what happened?" David asked, still half-asleep. "I was having a nice dream about a dyed redhead." He then looked across at John in the driver's seat.

John had the steering wheel grasped in his hands. He sat there, frozen. His eyes stared ahead, his face tinted orange by the overhead motorway lights that were starting to dim and flicker.

"John? What is it?" David's eyes were still feeling heavy. He slowly turned his head to see what John was staring at. He had to rub his eyes to be sure of what he was seeing.

A huge, black-hooded figure hovered two feet from the ground wearing some kind of cloak. It was just about visible in the motorway lights and headlights.

David tried to speak, but he couldn't find the words. He and John both sat there mesmerised by it, both breathing heavily. The car with its engine running remained still, on a completely empty motorway.

A strange mist started to form around them, swirling in the beams of the headlights. It quickly became cold inside the car. John and David began to shiver. Parts of the mist flowed in through the air vents. Benji sat up and he too, saw the figure outside. He started to growl.

The dark figure eerily glided towards them slowly. A blue frosted breath came out of its unseen mouth. They couldn't see a face. No hands, nor feet. No form of a body was visible either, as the cloak moved and opened slightly. They could *sense* the figure begin to raise its invisible arm as if pointing at the three of them in the car, which began to shake.

*"Enough of this!"* John shouted and frowned aggressively. He got into gear and rammed his foot on the accelerator. The tyres made a screeching sound as they spun. The force pushed the three of them back further into their seats. The car hurtled towards the mysterious looking figure, still shaking.

*"Jooohhhhnnnn!"* David braced himself for impact.

*"I've got this!"*

As they made 'impact' with the cloaked figure, it just vanished, along with the mist. John hit the brakes bringing the car to a halt. The pair of them looked back over their shoulders.

"What the *fuck* was that?" David asked almost in a breathless whisper.

John swallowed. "I, I have no idea. But it was probably responsible for what happened back at the service station." John was still fuelled by the adrenaline pumping through his veins.

A pair of headlights came towards them at a fast speed as their engine stalled.

"Shit!" John tried restarting the engine.

"What is it?" David asked anxiously.

"Hold on ..."

After the fourth attempt, the engine restarted and the car accelerated away, just as a speeding van swerved past them. The driver angrily blasted on his horn. The van headlights illuminated the inside of John's car. The two friends released sighs of relief.

"Thank God, that wasn't a truck!" David reached his hand out behind him to pet Benji, who had calmed slightly, after the latest unexplained phenomenon.

Benji licked David's right hand. Nobody felt sleepy now.

"I still can't believe what we just witnessed. I'm glad you saw it, too. *And* Benji, for that matter. Otherwise, I would have thought I was losing my mind!"

David was shaking his head. His heart was still beating above average. "Now, we've actually seen *something* that had to be supernatural, together ... I'm sure it won't be the last time, either ... What the heck was that thing?"

David and John glanced at each other.

"I have no idea. It didn't appear to have a face. No legs, arms, hands. Was that even the same thing that put its prints on my car?" John focused his attention back to the motorway.

"And what about that mist that appeared?" David said, looking at the car clock.

"I know. The way it was just hovering there as well." John shuddered. "The way it started to come towards us. Looking straight at us with its empty, blank face. *Damn*! You could feel it pointing at us with no hand as well!" John looked back over at David who was still staring at the clock. "What is it?"

David still stared.

John took a look at his clock. He tapped the dashboard. The green digits flickered but the time was still stuck. "Useless thing. The clock's stopped."

David replied, his eyes still fixated on the digital time. "When we were at Grant's, checking on his place, whilst you were in the other room, when you fell over, I noticed his alarm clock in his bedroom."

"So? He has an alarm clock. It's not exactly unusual."

"The time on his clock had stopped and was blinking. It had also stopped at *three* in the morning."

John hit down hard over the dashboard clock. It still didn't restart. But the force he had made with his fist made the clock turn off for a couple of seconds before coming on again. "Well, so what? What's so significant about that time of hour?"

"I didn't think about it before … I now remember reading something. Something about *Witching Hour*, or *Devil's Hour*. Some people say it's midnight, but it's really 03:00. I just thought of it as folklore, you know? Just rubbish. Now, well, it's starting to make sense. It can't be a coincidence."

John began to feel unsettled. "I need to pull over," he said anxiously. He checked for any cars behind him and pulled over sharply onto the hard shoulder, applying the handbrake. He dashed out of his car door and ran round the side and threw up onto the grass bank. *There goes a good waste of a burger.* He wiped his mouth on his wrist.

David got out of the car. "You all right?" he asked worriedly.

John spat, trying to get rid of the acid taste in his mouth and throat. "I'm fine. I just suddenly came over nauseous. You have any of that water left?"

David rushed back to the car and grabbed the water bottle. "Here!"

John unscrewed the cap and knocked back the water. He sighed, then poured the last bit into his mouth swishing it about, before spitting it out onto the asphalt. Screwing the cap back on, he slung the now empty plastic bottle onto the grass and pulled out a stick of gum from one of his jean pockets. Throwing the wrapper down too, he placed the mint gum into his mouth.

"You sure you're okay?" David asked as they both got back into the car.

"I'm good. Probably a dodgy burger."

"You want me to drive? You can try getting some rest. I can wake you up once we get nearer."

"I don't know, mate. What if we get caught? It's the last thing we need."

"It'll be fine." David glanced at the clock again.

"Okay … But if we get caught, we'll just say I was unwell. Which isn't too far from the truth. I'm not sure I can sleep anyway now, after what's just happened. I guess it won't hurt to try."

They both got out the car again and switched sides.

"You sure you know what you're doing? Where to turn off?"

David smirked. "Of course. I'll just follow the satnav; at least that's working. We're not too far from the Scottish border." He turned on the car engine, put on his seat belt and took off the handbrake.

"Okay."

David hadn't driven a car since John let him the previous summer. He never had any difficulties driving. It was just that damn theory test he had problems with. Driving didn't faze him. He took to the wheel like a duck to water, even in spite of the scares they had experienced.

# Chapter Eleven

## 11th July, 2018

The dashboard clock was still stuck at 03:00. David took a quick peek at his phone. It was 05:34. John was asleep, as was Benji. David had a lot to tell his uncle. At least they were in Scotland now. Crossing the border earlier, there was a big blue sign with a large white *X* representing the Scottish flag which read *Welcome to Scotland* and *Fàilte gu Alba*. It confirmed that they were now in another country.

The sun had risen a little before five. It looked like another nice day ahead, with only a few clouds here and there in the sky. David checked the fuel gauge; it wasn't far off empty. There was still enough for a few more miles, but they would have to refill as soon as possible.

In spite of the scares and complications during the night, including the stop off, they were still pretty much on schedule to reach his uncle's in the planned time, albeit a little later. Seeing the cloaked figure would also have been highly unlikely, had they travelled up during the day.

David decided to wake John shortly after he left the motorway. They would need to refill and it would make sense to switch over.

*****

David drove past a sign and checked the satnav for the turning to leave the motorway. He slowed down indicating and drove down the small slip road, driving alongside a man and a woman in a black BMW. He looked over and made eye contact with the attractive brunette, who sat in the passenger seat. Her window was half down. He smiled at her cheekily and nodded his head slightly. She smiled back. The man in the driver's seat, most likely her partner or husband, happened to look over too. He looked serious and annoyed, with his naturally dark features. He sped up to get past David who laughed quietly to himself. *Miserable bastard.*

A groan came from John shortly after.

"John. John?"

John groaned some more.

"Wake up, bud. We're not too far now."

"Urgh, my neck." John tried moving his head and neck. "Wh-what time is it?" His voice was croaky and dry. His left cheek was slightly wet where he had dribbled onto the headrest. He let out a yawn.

David checked his phone again. "Just gone six." He placed his phone carefully back on top of the dashboard.

"Everything been all right? We're still alive? We didn't crash, then?" John was still moving his neck and head, stretching his arms.

"Yep. Nothing sinister happened."

"I really hope you went the right way."

"Check the satnav. It was all fine. I guess I'm a natural." David felt proud of driving all this way. Even if most of it was on the motorway.

"As long as we didn't end up in Wales. At least we made it through the night."

"Well, we're in Scotland now, Johnny ... We're going to need to get some more petrol and it would be best if we switch over. You drive. Then I can check the directions to get to Bob's farm. Go from there."

John looked at the fuel reading. "Yep. Going to need to top up. Still a little further to go yet."

"I'd say about an hour and a half. Maybe a bit more. Depending on any morning traffic."

"Go to the next service station, mate. We'll swap over there." John rolled down his window to breath some morning air into the car. He checked himself in the left wing mirror.

*****

David pulled into the next service station on the A9.

"You want anything from the shop?" John asked as he got out to refill his car.

"Get us a bag of wine gums and a Coke," David answered as he shifted across to the passenger seat. He could smell the petrol through the window and hear the hum of the petrol tank. The old car vibrated as John refuelled.

John walked casually over to the shop to pay.

"Feel better after that?" David called out and laughed as John scratched his right buttock, pulling the jeans out from where they had become wedged in his backside.

A couple of other drivers who were filling up their motors looked over.

John looked back and smiled, giving David the finger.

David laughed, shaking his head.

"They were all out of wine gums. I got you a bar of chocolate, instead. Here, catch!"

"No worries."

"Got your drink." John handed over the can.

"Is it me, or are these chocolate bars getting smaller?" David quizzed.

"Yep. It's called 'shrinkflation,' or some shit like that. Tight bastards. Same as you get a bag of sweets and the bag's only half-full. What's even more ironic, is the product gets smaller, but the cost goes up!" John pulled the ring on his own can of Coke.

"I've noticed that. The other week when I was with Granty, I got a bag of crisps. It said about 'sharing' on the packet, but there wasn't much to share." David unwrapped his chocolate bar. The chocolate appeared slightly white, where it had dried out from the heat Scotland too had been experiencing.

"It's a joke, mate."

"Speaking of Granty, I'll drop him a text message to see how he is and to let him know we've arrived in Scotland. I'll tell him we'll call him, once we get to my uncle's."

"For sure, mate."

From behind them, came a car horn. They both looked round. An impatient driver with a moustache in a red Hyundai Coupé, raised his hand at them, ordering them to hurry up and move away from the petrol pump.

"All right, all right," John said, placing his drink in the car's cup holder. He started up the car, raised his hand out of the window as a way of apologising to the driver, and left the service station, heading back onto the major road.

*****

As they came off the A9, it began to cloud over.

"Looks like rain." David looked up at the bleak sky.

What had appeared as another bright day earlier now seemed to be the complete opposite, even though it was still early morning.

"Mhm. Typical of Scotland." John noticed a few spots of rain on his windscreen.

They went over a slight hill and could see parts of a large forest in the distance on the horizon, along with some mountains.

"That must be Rothiemurchus Forest," David raised his voice in anticipation.

"Gotta be. Shouldn't be too far now."

It had been a long drive. Not to mention everything that had happened on the way. It was a nice feeling knowing they had almost reached their destination, regardless of the worries of what to expect once they had got there. They tried to blank that out for now, putting it to the back of their minds until they finally got to the farm.

"I think it's best if we pull over for a bit when we can. Even though we're almost there. Benji probably needs the toilet. I could do with a leak, too," David suggested.

"Good idea." John looked over his shoulder at Benji who was lying there looking up at him, with his big brown eyes and innocent face. "You been a good boy, haven't you, aye?"

"I was actually worried about him being in the car for all this time. He's been as good as gold. He hasn't wanted to relieve himself at all." David reached back and stroked his canine friend.

"He has been good. Considering what he's seen and experienced." More droplets of rain hit John's windscreen. "Though, the dirty lil' fecker dropped his guts whilst you were asleep. Not long before that thing showed up on the motorway. Perhaps Benj, knew in advance?"

They managed to find a place further up the road to pull over. It was a stark, yet pleasant contrast to the motorways and busy roads from the early morning rush hour. The views were becoming more scenic, with the forest growing nearer. There were fewer cars about as well.

They stopped at a layby surrounded by green overgrowth and bushes. Someone had dumped an old bed mattress there. Matted branches wrapped themselves around it. A gaping hole was in the middle. Numerous rusty bed springs protruded out and the worn-out material was stained.

"We might be able to fit that in the car, if you want?" John joked, unfastening his seat belt and opening his door. "Looks like it got a lot of use and wear. *And* some action!"

"Some people have got no respect. Just dumping it like that." David opened his door and tried to get out. For a moment, he was pulled back. He forgot to take off his seat belt. "Is that blood as well on it?" He walked over to the mattress.

"Possibly. I think it's safe to say it's probably seen better days."

David went to let Benji out of the car and put on his collar. They could feel spots of rain fall on their bare arms. "Looks like it's going to chuck it down any minute." David looked up.

"We better not take too long. I'm going to take a piss over here. Wouldn't want to damage the mattress any more than it's already wrecked."

"How thoughtful of you." David smiled.

"Well, you know me." John strutted off to the right.

"I'm going to take Benji this way. Let him stretch his legs too for a bit." David pulled slightly on Benji's lead.

John put his thumb up behind him as he relieved himself with the other hand.

It started to drizzle, which was quite refreshing. The petrichor odour permeated the air. David found a small opening in the bushes and led Benji up a slight bank into a green field. He walked a little further, then unhooked the lead to let Benji have a run about.

"There you go, Benj." David patted Benji who looked up at his master and then charged off.

He was watching Benji burrow with his front paws into the ground, when he heard a faint bleep and felt his phone vibrate in his pocket. It was a message from Grant. David wiped the precipitation away from the screen using his T-shirt and read the message:

> Hey, bud! Glad you arrived in Scotland okay. Feel a bit safer now I'm with my folks. Haven't actually told them anything though! I still feel bad about not coming up with you guys. :(

David looked up; Benji was still burrowing ferociously. He then replied to Grant:

> Don't worry about it, mate. You're safer with your folks! I'll give you a call once we've arrived and settled in a bit on the farm. x

Benji sniffed around. Squatting, he did his business.

"Guess you did have to go eh, boy?" David said aloud.

"You done?" John's voice came from behind him.

David jumped and dropped his phone into the damp grass. He spun round. "Jesus. You made me jump."

"Sorry, I didn't mean to."

David picked up his phone, wiping it this time on the front of his jeans and put it back in his right pocket.

It started to drizzle harder as the three of them made their way back to the car and past the old mattress.

"You're flying low, mate," David said, noticing John's open flies.

John looked down and did his zip up. "You shouldn't be looking!" He smiled.

*****

"Did you say it was the next turning, or the one after?"

They were now very close to Hamish Farm. Already it seemed a very remote area, even before they reached the outskirts of Rothiemurchus Forest. John wondered who would want to live in such a place. Bob had been right about the satnav. There was no signal now. They were going off the directions Bob had given David. The further they went in, the darker it became, particularly now the sky was clouding over more. John joked about needing to put his headlights on. It started to rain heavier, the car windows fogged up.

David looked down at the directions he had scribbled down. "It shouldn't be too far up ahead. There should be a turning on the left, going onto a country lane. It can be easy to miss. We need to keep our eyes peeled." David wiped clear his window again.

"Is it me, or is this road getting narrower? Let's hope nothing comes the other way; we wouldn't stand a chance of getting past." John was beginning to doubt whether this was the right road. He continued slowly. The overgrown vegetation reduced their visibility and the windscreen wipers were battling with the now persistent rain. "You're *sure* it's up here on the left?"

"Has to be. I definitely wrote down the directions as I heard them."

"It just feels like we've been driving up here for ages." John shook his head.

Just then, David noticed a sign to his left as the car drove past it. "Woah!"

John pushed hard on the breaks, bringing the car to an abrupt stop. "What?"

"Back up. I think I saw a sign." David wound his window down.

John reversed carefully back and they saw part of a sign, which had been hidden mainly by rain-heavy branches and overgrowth. David got out the car and pulled back the branches, squealing when a few drops of water trickled down his neck. The sign had a faded blue arrow on it and read *Hamish Farm*.

"Finally," John called out from inside the car.

Even Benji let out a bark, sensing they were happy.

Just as Bob had described, the country lane to the farm was barely visible it was so overgrown. David began to pull back more of the branches and twigs which had stretched across the opening to the lane from the bushes on either side.

"I'll give you a hand. Hold on." John dashed out the car, his face screwing up as the rain hit him. "Urgh."

Pulling back the twigs and branches, they broke them off where they could and stamped the firmer branches to the ground. Once they had made an opening, they could see the lane ahead was clearer, although still well shaded.

They darted back into the car, where John had to wind his window down and up to wipe the rain off. They crunched over stones and snapped branches beneath the wheels as they turned into the lane. Something even popped, which made them look at each other with anxiety. John turned his headlights on to give them a better chance of seeing where they were going.

"Definitely not much further now." John picked up a yellow cloth duster he had on the dashboard and wiped his side of the windscreen, trying to get rid of the condensation.

"Just a few more minutes." David wiped his passenger window with his hand again and looked out.

The lane narrowed due to hedge overgrowth. Overhanging branches pushed up against the sides of the car, clawing at the bodywork.

"Probably scratching the shit out of my paint work," John said to break any tense air in the car. He wasn't too bothered about his car; it wasn't in perfect condition and still had damage from the vandalism.

David wasn't paying much attention to what John was saying. He'd noticed how much colder it had become. Up until they had reached Rothiemurchus Forest, it had been raining but relatively warm. But now they were venturing further into the thick of the forest, the temperature was dropping. It had to have dropped by at least ten degrees; *is that possible?* "You feel that?"

"Feel what?" John turned his head towards David and then back to the lane.

"How cold it is?" David rubbed his arms for some warmth.

"Yeah, I was going to say. We are in Scotland, remember." John flinched slightly as a thick branch brushed noisily against his window.

The pair fell quiet. David was relieved they were nearly there but was beginning to wonder whether Bob and Betty were all right. Anything could have happened in the night. He should have called them once they were near to the farm.

Without warning, the car suddenly fell dead.

"What the?" John said, looking down. His foot pumped hopelessly on the accelerator.

"What is it?"

The headlights and dashboard lights had all failed.

"The car just died." John was alarmed now.

"What?"

John frantically tried to restart the engine. He twiddled the key on and off. "It's not having it."

"Well, we can't be far from the farm. We have to be almost there. I'll call my uncle."

"Bloody good idea." John was feeling increasingly uneasy. He looked out of each of the car windows in turn; first to the right, then to the back where Benji sat, then to David's side, and then back to the front. "Is it me, or does it look like evening?"

David pulled out his mobile phone. At least there was a signal. Just: two bars. Now one. Then back to two again. "Yeah, you're right." David swallowed. "It seems even darker now. I know it's raining. There's hardly any light at all coming through."

David wondered whether to ring the house phone or Uncle Bob's mobile. He decided on the mobile. He waited for the ringtone. After a few rings the volume began to fade slightly.

"Hello?" came the voice on the other end.

"Bob. It's me, David!"

"David? You okay? Where are ..." Bob's voice became inaudible and distorted. There was the interference Bob had mentioned at the farm.

"Bob, sorry, can you repeat that?"

John's frown was focused on David's call.

"David, I can't hear-" Bob's voice appeared to have been cut off.

David looked at his phone; the call was still connected but with no sound, until a crackle started, followed by a groan, and finally a high-pitched *screech*, unbearable to the ear. *"Argh!"* David winced, dropping his phone.

Even John winced. Benji cowered on the back seat. John and David both looked down at the phone by David's feet. They could hear static. Then, a sinister laugh. The pair froze.

David wasn't sure that the laughter was even human but it gave him the gumption to confront whoever or *whatever* was on the other end of the line. He retrieved his phone: "Who the *fuck* is this? What do you want?"

No reply came.

"Answer me, *dammit*! YOU HEAR ME?"

John had rarely, if ever, seen his best friend take the offensive like this; he was impressed. There was silence from the other end of the call.

Benji himself seemed taken aback by David's uncharacteristic behaviour.

David was breathing heavily, his nostrils flaring. He looked at his phone; the call had ended. "SHIT!" He threw the phone down to his feet. He leaned forward, turned slightly and thumped the headrest behind him, making Benji jump up and bark. The inside of the car fell silent.

"Wow; I've never seen you like that before, mate," John said softly. "I thought it was a bit of a turn on, if I'm honest." John tried his usual joke routine to lighten the atmosphere.

"This thing is messing with us. Whatever it is, or *they* are," David spoke quietly. He bent down to pick up his phone and checked it for damage. It was fine. He noticed there was no signal at all now. "Reception's gone. How about your phone?"

"Nothing."

"We need to get to the farm as quickly as possible. It can't be far. I remember Bob saying the farm was off a dirt track from this country lane." David looked back at Benji and stroked him. "Sorry, boy. Did I scare you?"

"Shit," John muttered, looking out at the rain again. "Do we make a run for it, or what? We can leave the luggage here in the boot. Come back for it later."

David nodded in agreement. "The most important thing is to get there. Sod the luggage for now."

"I'll try the car one more time." John tried the ignition several times to no avail.

"I need to get a jacket out first."

"Let's do this."

Keeping Benji close to him, David rummaged in the suitcase in the boot for a jacket. John retrieved his too. David swapped his trainers for his dark brown boots as the walk to the farm was likely to be wet and muddy. John had packed two extra pairs of footwear. The black trainers he was already wearing were the better option out of the three, with the others being a lighter colour. John slammed the boot shut. They turned their collars up, with grimacing faces.

"I wish we'd packed a torch; I can't believe how dark the forest is," John moaned.

"We can use our phones for light if need be," David suggested.

They both checked their surroundings and started walking up ahead. The overhanging green and wet overgrowth dripped onto them.

"You think we should make a run for it?" John asked.

"Maybe. It wouldn't be a bad idea. But let's just walk quickly for now. We might need to leg it later on."

John looked back at his car wondering if it would be okay. "I can't believe how cold it's got."

Lightning suddenly lit up the darkened lane, followed by the loud rumble of thunder. They cowered beneath the canopy of branches and leaves. The heavens opened fully. The heaviness of the rainfall permeated further through the canopy now; their jackets and jeans were becoming soaked.

"Jesus!" David shouted through the downpour.

They sped up their pace. The lane narrowed again. The vegetation filled their nostrils with its wet clingy smell. Benji's fur was drenched. It was impossible to sidestep the puddles. The overgrowth wiped its soggy wetness off on their bodies as they battled on.

The thunder and flashes of yellowy sheet lightning continued as they made their way up the enclosed country lane, hopefully to the dirt track that would finally lead them up to the farm. David checked his phone for a signal. There was still nothing. He asked John to check too, but his was the same.

They eventually got to the top of the country lane where with fewer trees and bushes, it was lighter and more open. The lane continued to the left. Straight on was a wet and muddy dirt track, with two tractor tracks filled with water.

"This has to be the dirt track leading up to the farm. I don't think we should go left," David said.

"You'd think there'd be another signpost, wouldn't you?" John said, with the rain trickling down his face.

"Sure is muddy."

"We've really got to go through that?" John already knew the answer.

The lightning and thunder repeated. Both men suddenly had the sensation that they were being watched. Benji started to bark.

"You feel that?" David almost whispered. He scanned around them, searching to find who was watching.

"Yeah … It's as if we're not alone. Like someone, or something, is watching us …"

Right then, they heard a distinct 'snap,' followed by another, the sound a twig would make if someone had walked over it. The sound came from somewhere behind them. Benji let out another bark. David and John looked at one another, their eyes wide.

*"Run!"* John shouted.

David yanked on Benji's lead as the three of them scampered over the dirt track, their feet splashing and squelching rapidly over the sodden surface.

Mud splashed as high as their faces. John felt his jacket get caught. It felt like an arm trying to hold him back. He daren't look back. They began to slip and slide in their haste … David eventually fell. He let go of the dog lead, just as his legs and backside flew up into the air. He came down with a splash, landing in a huge muddy puddle, covering Benji as he did so.

John heard the splash and stopped to look back. "You all right? *C'mon*!" he said anxiously, for once not finding a joke to add.

"Shit."

Behind David, John could see the huge branch that had caught his jacket. It wasn't an arm after all. He ran over to David who was sitting upright in the mud, which had softened his fall. John bent down and gave his friend a hand, helping him up to his feet. "You all right?"

"I'm fine. Even more wet. If that's possible." David picked up Benji's lead now covered in mud. "We need to move."

John nodded but couldn't free his foot from the mud.

"Come on!" David said. It was his turn to encourage them to get going.

"My foot's stuck!"

A splashing emerged from behind them. Someone was approaching. Because the dirt track was now following a horseshoe shape, they couldn't see who or what it was.

*"Come on!"* David tried to help John by pulling his leg and offering his shoulder as leverage and support.

John's foot freed, but left the trainer embedded deep in the mud. They both nearly fell as he came free. Whoever was coming was nearer, picking up pace.

John was about to retrieve his muddied trainer.

"Leave it! *Come on*!" David shouted again, watching the bend of the dirt track.

They began sprinting again, hopeful that the farm would soon be in sight. The rain continued to pour. Another flash of lightning and rumble of thunder suggested it would continue for a while. Along with the splashing behind them, came an inhuman *roar*.

*"Faster!"* David cried.

It was hard for John. His feet were now uneven with only one trainer, and he couldn't get a good grip with his sock-clad foot stepping on stones and in puddles. They were both trying to be careful not to slip over or get stuck again. They were also tiring and gasping for breath. They kept checking over their shoulders to see if their pursuer was visible yet. The next bend took them onto a final straight.

John caught sight of the top of a house. *"Look!"*

David raised his head and saw it. It was surely his uncle's farm.

Their legs ached, despite them being relatively fit. The mud and rain made progress harder work on their limbs. The house was getting closer. They saw a lawn ahead ... just a few more yards.

They came to an opening where an old white gate was fixed open. They moved from the dirt track onto the recently cut front lawn. There was a sound of crunching as they walked over a pebble patch edging. The house was to the right. They bent down trying to catch their breath. Benji was panting heavily, his tongue hanging out. The three of them were soaked through to the bone.

The rain stopped. Just like that. As did the thunder and lightning. Whatever it was that was pursuing them had also ceased. It was strangely quiet. John and David continued to bend down. They looked at one another but didn't say a word. David was hoping this *was* the farm.

"David?" came a gruff-sounding voice.

The pair of them looked up and saw a medium height man with short, grey and black hair, walking round from the left side of the farmhouse. Their reactions were slow from the exhaustion and fright, so it took a moment before his arrival registered with them. They were still getting their breath back.

Suddenly, David's eyes widened. *"Uncle Bob!"* he shouted with joy. It was such a relief to finally see him. A nice feeling. David dropped Benji's lead and ran over to his uncle, greeting him with a wet hug.

John smiled.

"What the heck happened to you? You're soaked through!" Bob asked intrigued, looking over David's right shoulder at John and Benji. He pulled away from David and placed his hands on both of his shoulders.

David waited to get more of his breath back before answering, "Our, our car ... It ... it broke down on that country lane back there ..." David pointed in the direction they had just run from.

Bob frowned.

David tried to compose himself some more before continuing. "Something ... something back there was chasing us. We could hear it coming after us. We couldn't see it. But we heard it. We sensed something beforehand. I think it's stopped now ..."

There was a pause before Bob answered him, "But you're okay? The three of you?"

David nodded. "Apart from being wet ... and John losing his trainer in the mud."

Bob smiled at his nephew and walked over to greet John. "You must be John?" Bob said warmly, giving a smile. He held out his right hand.

"Pleasure to meet you, Uncle Bob. We did meet once before."

"I recognise your face. It was a barbecue if I remember, at my brother's. A few years ago, now."

"That's right. The years go by so fast." John rubbed his nose and sniffed.

"They sure do. And here's that little fella, Benji." Bob crouched down and massaged Benji's wet ears. Bob remembered him from Christmas last year at David's parents.

"Oh, he loves that, Uncle Bob," said David, walking over to them.

Benji started to wag his tail and licked Bob's hands. But just as David and John were enjoying the relief of a slightly lighter mood, the atmosphere darkened again.

Bob stood up and cleared his throat. "It's good you boys came but I'm still not sure you should have." He walked to look down the dirt track. "This thing, or person that was chasing you. What happened exactly? What makes you think it was a thing?" Bob turned to face them.

Benji was now lying flat on his stomach, recovering.

"The car just conked out for no reason. It just died on us," replied John, looking straight at Bob and shrugging his shoulders.

"That's when I tried calling you. But I couldn't hear you properly. There was interference. And then ... then there was this horrible screeching sound. John and Benji heard it, too. Then this, well, *laugh*. I shouted down the phone asking what they wanted. I just lost it. Then the call went dead and so did the signal."

"Yes. I had interference too, David, when you called. I couldn't hear you properly. Then the call went dead, but that was it. There was no laugh or anything like that. What happened after that?"

"We left our luggage in the boot apart from our jackets. It started to piss it down and that's when the thunder started. It's pretty damn dark on that lane as well. When we reached the dirt track, we felt this odd sensation. Like there was something there, watching us. Whatever it was, I can't feel it now."

"Me neither," John confirmed.

"We've had a lot of that here recently, feeling like someone is watching us. It's a very strong sensation, I agree. Eerily strange. Nothing I've ever experienced before. And I know how dark those lanes can become, even in broad daylight. Not a lot of sun gets through parts of this forest. But then, some areas are fine and much lighter."

The dark clouds overhead began to break away and the sun came through again.

"Anyway," David said, "Benji started to bark. We then heard what sounded like a twig breaking. We made a run for it. We heard someone or something following us, and something roared!"

Bob could tell the boys were being sincere about it all, even if they were perhaps mistaken about what they had heard. "It's okay. I believe you. Whatever is happening here, to all of us, is getting worse. I can't help but feel this is only the beginning. We need to go inside and talk, as some other things have happened. I'll get Betty to make us some breakfast, if you boys feel like it?"

The two friends nodded. They didn't feel that hungry after what had just happened, but some greasy food might just make them feel a little better.

"What other things have happened?" David asked curiously.

"I'll tell you once we're inside and we've eaten." Bob smiled.

"What about my car?"

"It should be fine where it is for now. Hardly anyone uses that lane; it's only us. You two and Benji can dry yourselves off, have some breakfast and then we'll go and see about your car." Bob put an understanding hand on John's back and escorted them into the large old farmhouse.

# Chapter Twelve

## 11th July, 2018

After they had been greeted by Aunt Betty and had exchanged pleasantries, she went upstairs to fetch some towels for them to dry themselves off with. The old wooden staircase creaked with Betty's footsteps.

They waited with Bob in the large, but warm and homely, Victorian kitchen, dripping a little on the black and white, chequered floor tiles.

An empty wooden table with a white tablecloth draped over it sat in the middle of the kitchen. Around them were six wooden chairs, each with a white and grey patchwork cushion. An old inbuilt stove lined one wall of the kitchen with six hot plates; a kettle was steaming on one of them. The old kettle had a red button on the top of its handle which opened the spout; it reminded John of his grandmother's kettle. Behind the black stove, hung a few items of copper cookware. Around the kitchen were numerous shelves storing other forms of kitchenware, utensils and some books, as well as a couple of photos of Bob and Betty. The fridge hummed from a corner. A window looked over a couple of plant pots to a well-tended garden. Next to the back door, sat three cat bowls with names on them. They were full, except for one. Daisy's bowl was empty. David remembered the story Bob had told about her. Near to the back door on the wall was a calendar. The month of July showed a tractor.

The kettle began to whistle as Betty came back down with the towels.

Elizabeth (Betty) Hammond, née Peterson, and Robert (Bob) Hammond, were childhood sweethearts. They had started dating from the age of thirteen. They were now sixty. They were married when they were only eighteen. Bob was a few years older than his brother, Jason. They had one son, Darren, who was thirty-nine, fifteen years older than his cousin, David. He was currently away on service in the army. David barely remembered him, having only met him twice briefly, years ago.

Betty had miscarried when she was twenty-nine, which was tough on her and Bob. With only one child, she worried all the more when Darren joined the army. Darren always promised his mother he would return home safe and sound, and he always had. They hadn't seen him for almost a year now, although they had spoken to him on the phone a few weeks previously, not long before the strange occurrences on the farm began.

Bob and Betty had lived at Hamish Farm for almost twenty-five years. They bought the farm when Bob was working in real estate, thanks to an inheritance from one of his old bosses, Patrick Stevens, who sadly died from a car crash at the age of sixty-three. Bob was thirty-one at the time. Patrick had always liked Bob, who was his best employee. Bob helped Patrick make a success of his business and in return, Patrick wanted to leave him something in his will as a thank you; he didn't have family of his own.

Bob and Betty had moved from London to the farm, fancying a change. They had both loved Scotland since they first visited as newlyweds. Bob had wanted to be a farmer as a child; he always loved animals and had a fascination for tractors and combine harvesters when he was young. He came across the farm by chance in a property magazine. It wasn't too expensive at the time and needed little work. He had to take out a loan in addition to the inheritance money from Patrick. Betty's father, who was fond of Bob, insisted on lending him the money rather than him taking out a bank loan. Bob however, kindly refused.

Bob kept the name of Hamish Farm; they liked it. The land was a convenient opening, centuries old in the middle of Rothiemurchus Forest. The farmhouse was well over a hundred years old. The founder of the farm was a well-off Scot, Rupert James Hamish. He was rumoured to have built the house himself. When Bob saw the advertisement, the farm had been on the market for over three years. Bob was surprised at the lack of interest shown in it, despite the seclusion and even by the price. He expected it to be worth a fair bit more than what it was going for.

It took Bob a while to master the art of becoming a farmer, switching from being in the property business. He learnt from the best. Experienced farmers and workers helped him and he paid them good wages. It was perfect for them. But after everything that had happened recently, that love was now fast changing to fear and worry.

"Sorry, Aunt Betty. We're making your floor all wet and muddy," David apologised as he patted himself down and dried his hair.

"Don't be sorry, love. It's fine." Betty smiled. "And call me Betty, dear, now you're all grown up." Betty was an attractive woman, but this morning she had no makeup on. There were dark rings under her eyes and her greying dark hair hadn't been brushed. The strain of recent events seemed to be showing.

David felt for her. Bob had asked them not to mention what had happened on the dirt track, apart from the car breaking down; he felt they should discuss everything when they were alone. He was worried for her.

"Are you doing okay?" David knew she wasn't but felt he should ask.

Betty tried to put on a brave face. "I'm fine, David, thank you." She gave a half-hearted smile. "You're okay for a cuppa then, boys? I'll do you breakfast as well, if you like?" She walked over to the old kettle.

"If it's no bother?" David answered.

"Of course it isn't."

Betty pulled out three plain mugs from one of the kitchen cupboards and placed them on the worktop next to the microwave.

"You're perhaps wondering why we didn't modernise the kitchen too much?" Bob stood at the other end of the large dining table with his arms folded.

David tried to dry out the wet patches that he, John and Benji had made on the floor, wiping a towel around their feet and John's trainerless left foot. "A little." David rose back up. "But I like it. It has a warmth to it."

"Yeah, I like it a lot. Makes a change to be honest," John added, looking around the kitchen.

"Me and Betty decided to keep it as original as possible, like the rest of the house. We've refurbished some parts that needed doing and changed what we wanted, but we didn't want to go overboard and take away the foundations of it all. Isn't that right, darling?" Bob smiled and winked at his wife who in return gave a slight smile back as she poured boiling water onto the teabags in mugs.

"Sugar, boys?" Betty asked.

"Just one for me, please," answered David.

"Two for me, please." John held up two fingers.

"Have a seat," Bob offered, gesturing towards the chairs. He sat down himself.

David took a seat and pulled himself under the table. "We're making your seats wet."

"Oh, don't worry about that." Bob smiled, resting his elbows on the table.

Betty walked over carefully with the mugs of tea on a tray.

"You're not having one and joining us?" Bob asked Betty as she went to put the teabags in the bin and the teaspoon in the sink.

"I'm fine. I'll cook you some breakfast. You boys must be hungry after that journey?" Betty wiped the small tea stains from the worktop with a dishcloth.

"Erm, yeah. We kind of are." David still wasn't feeling overly hungry.

"You want a hand?" Bob offered.

"I'm good." Betty smiled as she placed two copper frying pans onto two different hot plates. She cracked eggs into one and placed sausages and bacon together in another.

Although they weren't hungry, once they smelt the sizzling food cooking, they soon regained their appetites.

"I've got some dog biscuits for Benji, here. We got them yesterday, once we knew you were coming up."

Benji's ears pricked up at the sound of the bag of dog biscuits rustling.

"Oh, you didn't have to do that, Auntie."

"It's fine, David." Bob smiled and winked as he softly blew on his tea, before taking a small sip from the mug.

Betty put the biscuits on the floor and Benji trotted over. She stroked his back a couple of times as he munched eagerly.

"He certainly likes them." David grinned.

Betty smiled and returned her attention to the frying pans.

"So, how long did it take you guys to get here?" Bob asked.

John looked at the ticking, wrought iron clock on the wall. It was almost eight. "We stopped off a couple of times. But it's taken us over ten hours in total." He sipped his tea.

"Not too bad," Bob replied. "The trip went smoothly, then?"

John winced as he burnt his lip on the hot tea. His face went red as he swallowed hard, burning his throat. He exchanged glances with David, both remembering the incidents at the service station near Birmingham and the cloaked figure on the motorway. David looked over at Betty and returned his gaze to give Bob eye contact.

Bob could tell something else had happened. He moved the conversation away from their journey while Betty was still there. "Those sausages smell good, dear."

Betty seemed in a world of her own. "Eh? Oh. They shan't be long."

"Great," Bob replied softly, banging the table and trying to sound enthusiastic about breakfast. He was eager to talk to the boys and find out what else had happened to them.

*****

They chatted casually over breakfast about business, the farm and in general. David felt good getting reacquainted with his uncle, who he'd always been fond of. Bob felt the same about his nephew. Betty eventually left to hang the washing on the line. So having finished their breakfast, the boys helped wash up and they could finally bring Uncle Bob up to speed on what had been happening. And vice versa.

"Okay … we need to talk about the current situation, boys. There's been some further developments around here since we last spoke." Bob checked that Betty was far enough away, looking out through the kitchen window to where she had started to hang out the washing.

"What kind of developments?" David frowned.

"You first." Bob smiled. "I know something else happened to you on your way up here by the way you looked when I asked how the trip went. Let's sit back down."

"It's going to sound crazy," John replied, shaking his head.

"Try me." Bob put an elbow on the table, placing his knuckles to his lips as if to prepare to listen.

John and David looked at each other. David took a breath and brought his uncle up to date …

Bob listened to it all and then picked up David's phone. He had also seen the note John had received on his car outside Burger Boys. Bob looked at the photo of the glass inverted pentagram. "This is the same symbol that was on Mandy's head. You know, one of our pigs that was mutilated?"

John and David looked at one another.

"I know, Uncle. If you swipe my phone to the left, you can see a photo I took of the handprints." David scratched his right cheek gently.

"My God," Bob muttered as he brought up the other picture on David's phone. "These prints … they look so *real*. And they aren't even humanlike." Bob swallowed.

Suddenly, they heard the front door close and the sound of someone with boots stomping on the wooden decking out in the hallway. A man entered with a twelve-gauge, single barrel shotgun, slung over his right shoulder. He was wearing a greenish tweed, tartan flat cap and a green quilted gilet over a white T-shirt. His dark brown boots added a couple of inches to his already towering height.

Bob smiled at his nephew's and friend's concerned facial expressions, when they saw this tall figure holding a shotgun looking down at them.

"All right, boss? Derek's turned up now, so I'm going to shoot off for a bit, if it's all right? I've finished feeding the animals and mucked them out." The full-bearded man looked down from his six-foot-four plus figure at John and David, with a confused expression of his own. He spoke in a Bristolian accent.

"That's fine, Gavin. Oh, and this is David, my nephew, and his friend, John. Remember, I said they were coming to stay with us for a bit?" Bob gestured towards the two friends sitting at the table. "Guys, this is Gavin. He was with me last night keeping an eye out."

Gavin held out his hand and shook John's, then David's. They winced at his grip. This was a strong man. "Pleased to meet you, chaps. We could perhaps do with the extra hand, especially now Eric has left. And of course, these bastards around here causing mayhem and upsetting folk means we've got to keep an extra eye out. I probably startled you with the shotgun. Can't be too careful around these parts at the moment. Don't worry though, I have a licence to use it." Gavin smiled to ease a little tension, showing his perfect white teeth as they all laughed.

Gavin Rogers was forty-four years old. He had been a farmer most of his working life and he enjoyed it. He had worked for Bob for almost twelve years now. His hours were sometimes random. He was the longest serving employee and also the foreman. He was naturally Bob's favourite and close with Bob and Betty. He'd do anything for them. He had been single for a few years and had never married. He was a happy bachelor. He lived about half an hour's drive away in a small cottage, but sometimes he would stay over for convenience. They loved having him there and he felt the same way.

"I'll see you in a few hours, boss." Gavin carefully placed the shotgun against the wall near the kitchen door before he left.

"He's a great guy, Gavin. He's a fantastic worker. Strong, too. I think the farm would fall apart if it wasn't for him. He'll do anything for just about anybody. Bloody big as well!"

"You can say that again." John smiled.

"Going back to what we were talking about … That *thing* you saw on the motorway. It's possibly the same thing that Eric saw yesterday morning, in the early hours," Bob said.

"Who's Eric?" John queried.

"You know? That worker that got freaked out and quit, because he saw some figure float into the forest," David reminded John.

"Ahh, sorry. I remember now."

Bob slowly got up and looked out of the window resting his hands on the kitchen sink. Betty was still hanging the washing out on the line. Bob bowed his head. "Well, thank God, you're all right. I have no idea what is going on. I'm hoping we can maybe find out. But at the same time, I still don't think you should have come. By coming, you're just getting yourselves more and more involved and endangering yourselves. You would have maybe been safer back home." Bob faced the two.

"I know, Uncle. I keep asking myself that. What if we had stayed home, or at least heeded the warnings and turned back. But I couldn't."

"It's not too late to turn back. We can get your car sorted out and you two and Benji can get away from here."

*"No!"* came a sudden and abrupt reply from David. "We may not see much of each other, Bob. But you're *family*. I *won't* leave you. Not now. Besides, it could already be too late to turn back. We could already have passed the point of no return. Whatever forces are at work, I don't think they'll back down now. We need to find out what the *hell* is going on around here."

Bob smiled and his eyes welled up. He turned and looked out of the window again so David wouldn't see him upset. He was touched by David's sincere words.

Betty picked up some more washing and used a few wooden clothes pegs to hang it up.

"You're very kind, David. Your parents must be proud of you. You're a brave man. You too, John. Sticking by your friend."

"He's always been there for me. Particularly when my mum died. To tell you the truth, I don't feel brave; I'm scared shitless! But I'm not going to turn my back on David. Not now. Nor you. I'm in this for the long haul. No matter what the cost."

"But that cost could be your lives?" Bob felt guilty that he had allowed John and David to get involved. He turned back to face them.

"I know, Uncle. But we need to stick together. Find out what's going on and stop it."

"Okay." Bob smiled.

"You mentioned something else had happened here, as we were walking up to the house?" David then asked. He was curious as to what else had been going on.

"Ah, yes ... It seems like we're not the only ones with animals disappearing or being killed. Angus, who owns the farm nearest to us, at the other end of the forest on the outskirts, came to see me this morning, about half an hour before you arrived. Early. He was a little distressed as you'd imagine. He's also had that strange interference and heard the odd whisper. His farm is quite a bit bigger than ours. Hence, he has more livestock there. I had already told him about our animals last week and wanted to warn him too, just in case.

"He noticed some chickens and ducks had gone missing early yesterday morning. We spoke in the evening over the phone. He'd found some blood and remains nearby. But this morning, he found one of his goats with one of its horns ripped out. That would take a *lot* of strength! There was quite a lot of blood. The poor thing was lying there in its pen, traumatised. The other three were unscathed. Angus mentioned some markings on its body, too. He had tried remaining awake during the night, but succumbed to sleep."

"Who are these sick fucks?" John asked in disgust.

"The little thing going to be okay?"

"I don't know, David. It lost a lot of blood. He dropped it off at the vets before coming here. The vet, Colin, knows quite a bit about goats. He's disbudded ours when they were kids. I didn't like the thought of a goat not having its horns. But when they're domesticated like ours, they don't really need them. They can be dangerous in the long run. They can hurt each other with them and get caught in fences. So, we decided it was best."

"Is it painful for them?" David asked.

"They were anaesthetised, so it wasn't too bad. Anyway, Angus wanted to warn me further, in person. He's now considering moving his animals to a secure location until the police catch whoever is behind it."

"What did the police say? Are you thinking of moving the animals to a secure location as well?" John asked, scratching the back of his head. His hair was still damp.

"He was going to call the police again as soon as he left here. I doubt they'll do much. They didn't seem to care overly, like with us. They'll do their so-called 'investigations,' but with no leads, what can they do? I guess you can't be too critical of them ... It being animals, they're probably not too bothered. I mentioned forensics when the police came here, but they said the case wasn't serious enough. After all, in their eyes it's just a couple of pigs and a few chickens. Obviously to us, they mean a *lot* more, not to mention the fear the attacks bring."

"Typical of the Old Bill. You'd think being 'pigs' themselves, they'd be a bit more cooperative and compassionate." John shook his head.

Bob raised a slight smile. "As for moving the animals to a secure location? It never really entered my mind until Angus mentioned it. I don't know really … After everything that you've told me, and now Angus, perhaps I should consider it? I think him and one of his workers are now going to keep watch during the night, until Angus decides on what to do."

"What's stopping you from moving the animals?" David asked. "It would be safer."

"True. It would cost money. Not that I'm too fussed about that. But we don't know how long they'd be away for. They're used to their surroundings up here. I don't know any place that could take them. I might look into it. Make a few phone calls. With a few of us keeping a lookout, we're not doing too bad at the moment."

"Do you ever think about installing cameras?" John asked.

"It's crossed my mind, John. I didn't think it would be worth it before. Maybe I underestimated the situation. I thought it was serious, but not to the extent it is now."

A flapping noise disrupted them making David jump. It was the clear, see-through cat flap fixed into the glass on the back door of the kitchen. A tortoiseshell cat casually climbed in and headed straight to one of the cat bowls on the floor. She was completely oblivious to Benji as she walked past him. Benji immediately got up to sniff around her as she prowled past.

"Oh, that's Josie. She's as laid back as they come. She's not fazed by dogs at all." Bob smiled and they watched her gobble down her biscuits before she went into the hallway and trotted up the stairs. Her tiny paws made a soft tapping sound on the wood.

Benji started to follow her. He stopped in the doorway of the kitchen and slumped down, watching Josie climb the stairs.

"She's probably gone upstairs to sleep on the bed with Sammy, our other cat, a black Tom. He's the opposite. A bit of a wimp. Just the two of them now. Because, you know …"

David smiled sympathetically as John looked at his trainerless foot.

"They miss Daisy. I buried her in the garden under her favourite shrub where she used to sleep. I saw Sammy and Josie both lying there yesterday. Very sad. Very sad indeed. It's hard for animals; you can't explain death to them … Awful." Bob shook his head from side to side. "Anyway, let's go look at your car, John. Then I'll show you around the farm and house: a guided tour, if you like."

"I was wondering something, Uncle." David felt a little reluctant to ask.

"What's that?"

"I know what happened to Daisy was tough. But how do you go about looking after Sammy and Josie?"

"It's kind of difficult with cats. They're not like dogs. Cats are more independent, so it's harder to keep an eye on them and to keep them in. Fortunately, although they used to venture into the forest before, more recently they've stayed in the garden or on the farm, close to the house. At night, we make sure they're in now. I think something in the forest startled them one night. I saw Josie and the other two jump at the bottom of the front lawn. Their fur stood on end. They were arching up their backs, doing that crab walk cats do when they're scared and stand on their side. They then charged back into the house and raced up the stairs. All three of them."

"Something isn't right about that forest," John said.

"I'm now inclined to agree, John. I'd forgotten about that incident until just now."

"There is something else too, Uncle ... When Grant, our other friend, was recorded sleeping on his own phone, his alarm clock showed the exact same time as when John and I encountered that figure floating in the middle of the motorway. Both clocks stopped dead on *three* in the morning."

"I do remember reading once, that that time of morning is also known as *The Demonic Hour*. Could your experiences be related to this? Ours? You know, me and your father use to go to a Catholic school as kids. I remember a teacher telling us about it. It's also called the *Devil's Hour*, or *Witching Hour* ... God. That was years ago. It's funny how you just suddenly remember things, isn't it?"

David and John nodded together.

"I read about it somewhere, too. And I've seen it mentioned in movies before. I was telling John about it."

"I used to think it was all mumbo jumbo, to be honest with you. Your father did, too. Even though your grandparents, may God rest their souls, were devoted Catholics. I wouldn't say they were strict, though. Your father and I always took the piss. We were both far from religious. I remember as kids we were always joking about it, even in church. I guess we should have paid more attention, eh?" Bob laughed nervously. "What size foot are you, John?" he suddenly asked.

John felt it was an odd question to ask until he realised. "Erm. An eight."

"Me too. I'll get you a pair of my boots to walk down in. Can't have you walking in just the one trainer." Bob winked.

Bob made his way across the wooden floor in the hallway to a white cupboard door under the stairs and pulled out a pair of black, steel-toe-capped boots for John.

Betty had just come in from hanging up the washing.

"We're going to check on John's car. We shouldn't be too long." Bob kissed his wife on the lips.

Betty gave a nod, walked into the living room and switched on the telly.

Bob then picked up his shotgun. "Just in case. Best to be safe," he said as David reconnected Benji's lead and they made their way outside, past the front lawn and towards the dirt track.

# Chapter Thirteen

## 11th July, 2018

Gavin's car was waiting for a part to fix the gearbox, so he had borrowed Bob's Land Rover. They therefore needed to walk back to John's car. John and David felt a bit uncomfortable walking back down the muddied track so soon. Bob insisted it would be fine. The day seemed more positive now that the sun was shining and it was warmer, with only a few puffy white clouds in the sky.

"I hope my car's all right," John said as they began walking down. "I'm not sure my insurance will cover me again. Not twice in as many days."

"I'm sure it's fine, mate." David looked back.

John was bringing up the rear as Bob led the way, his shotgun on a strap over his right shoulder. David and Benji walked behind him.

"Me, Gavin and Eric, a few weeks ago, trimmed back most of these trees and hedges on this dirt track to make it more accessible for cars and farm vehicles. That's why it's a little bit more open," Bob mentioned, looking about. "Even though we don't use this track a lot."

You could see the footprints that John and David had made and the pawprints from Benji, where they had run from their pursuer less than an hour earlier.

"You boys didn't get a look at whatever it was that was following you, then?"

"All we could hear was it running through the puddles after us. I didn't really want to look back. But when I did, I couldn't see anything."

David and John began to feel uneasy.

"Same here. Like David. I just heard the splashing, even above our own." John looked around feeling paranoid.

"Yeah. And that *roar* … I've never heard anything like it. There was just something about it. It wasn't human." David's feet slipped in the mud.

"Well, if it's still about, I've got my shotgun. Whatever it is." Bob tried to reassure his nephew and friend, tapping the shotgun with his left hand.

They approached the point where David had slipped over.

"This is where I went arse over tit. That puddle there. There's John's trainer." David pointed.

They briefly stopped and watched as John reclaimed his trainer, which made a sucking sound as he pulled it from the mud. "At least my trainer's unscathed."

They started to walk down the track again.

"See this branch sticking out?" John showed them, handling the leafless branch.

Bob and David stopped to look.

"I thought this was a fucking arm!" John laughed. "It caught on my jacket as we were running, when we heard those twigs snap. I didn't want to look back to check. It wasn't until you fell over and I stopped that I saw that it was just a branch."

They laughed nervously. After everything that had happened, a branch being an arm seemed so plausible. They walked nearer to the curve of the dirt track, the mud squelching and slurping underneath them.

"Do you drive, David?"

"Not legally." David looked up smiling. "I failed my theory test a couple of times and just never got round to taking it again. I plan on retaking it, though."

"I understand where you're coming from. Darren was the same, but he finally passed his test. You remember Darren, don't you?" Bob slipped a little on a dip in the mud.

"Yeah. Although only vaguely, if I'm honest with you. How is he? Is he still in the army?"

"Yep. He's still on active duty in Afghanistan, training some of their soldiers over there. We speak to him occasionally on the phone. It's always good to hear from him. It's been a while since we last saw him." Bob had a tone of sadness in his voice.

"Weren't they supposed to have moved our troops out of their ages ago?" John asked.

"Some, yes. But quite a few are still over there in the Middle East. The sooner Darren is home, the better. Even though he has his own place, he stays a lot with us on the farm. We miss him. We're obviously concerned for his well-being out there. Especially his mother."

"Understandable, Uncle."

Bob stopped, causing David to walk into him, instinctively holding his hands up to protect himself. The tip of his nose brushed against the butt of the shotgun. "What is it?"

"L-look," Bob said, pointing down at the mud.

The three looked down with open mouths, silent.

There in the mud and further down, were other footprints facing towards the farm. But these weren't ordinary footprints. They were similar to the handprints on John's car, back at the service station. Only bigger. They must have been twelve inches in length and about six inches in width. The outsides of the feet and toes appeared somewhat jagged. At the end of each toe appeared five sharp nails or talons.

"What the …" John muttered. "Is *this* what was chasing us?"

Bob walked slowly, following the bend where the trail had come from. He took the shotgun from his shoulder and held it in both hands, aiming it in front of him. Benji began sniffing the indentations. His growls turned into barks sensing something. David took photos to add to his 'collection.' Then they followed closely behind Bob. Nervously.

The stride of the footprints began to shorten. The first set they came to were inhumanly wide where the thing had obviously started to run. The dirt track straightened out as they continued to follow the footprints. They heard a rustling sound to the left of them in one of the overgrown bushes where the footprints had stopped. A strong breeze enveloped them as they stood staring at the origin of the rustling.

John started to speak.

"Shh," Bob hushed. He flicked the safety off on his shotgun and edged closer to the bushes. All of their hearts were pounding. Bob raised the shotgun.

Benji was still growling, John and David stood back.

*CAW.*

Four large crows flew out of the bushes at them. Benji barked. John and David jumped back. A few feathers floated down onto the muddy track along with a few leaves.

Bob fired off the round into the bushes; the shots forced him backwards and left a gaping hole. Numerous splinters of wood shot out. *"Christ!"* Bob shouted as he watched the crows fly off. He dropped the gun and bent down placing his hands on his knees. "I, I don't think I've ever been so scared in my life." He tried to calm himself.

John and David stared into the newly made dark hole in the bushes for a moment.

Bob picked up his shotgun and flicked it open. The empty red shell popped out. "Haven't fired this is in a while. I hope I don't have to, ever again." He hung the shotgun over his shoulder. "You guys all right?"

"Think I just soiled myself," John joked.

"I'm fine. I think," David replied, still startled.

"They probably heard the gunshot back on the farm. We should hurry. That was my only round; I should have brought more … We need to get to the car."

They started to jog and came to the other end of the dirt track and back onto the country lane. Bob's mobile started to ring. It was Betty. She had heard the gunshot and was naturally worried.

"Calm down, love! We're fine."

David and John could hear Betty's voice on the other end. Surprisingly, there wasn't any interference. They couldn't quite make out what she was saying, but she sounded a little frantic.

"I was just showing the boys the gun and how to fire it. That's all," Bob lied.

The other two stood listening.

Bob got Betty to calm down and promised he'd be back soon, before ending the call and putting the phone back in his rear pocket. "I'd appreciate it if you could keep quiet about these footprints for the moment, when we're around Betty."

"Of course, Uncle … I know it's not really my business in that regard, but don't you think she deserves to know the full extent of what's going on?"

"She does, David. All in good time." Bob tried to smile as he walked past David, placing a hand on the top of his nephew's shoulder.

Even with the sun high in the sky, it appeared fairly dark on the country lane surrounded by the trees and bushes of the forest.

"At least it's a *bit* brighter in here now, but it's still kind of darkish," said John.

"That's how it is in this forest. Some parts are well lit and some are darker. Some parts look wonderful in the sunshine. Saying that, perhaps it is just me … but the forest has seemed darker in the past few weeks or so."

"Can't deny that it's creepy," David stated.

"I'll give you that. You get used to it. Though, I'm starting to feel creeped out more now. Anyway, let's pick up the pace a little. We ought to get back. Just in case that thing is still about." Bob set a faster pace as the car came into view.

"There it is. Looks okay," John said, until he got closer. "What the fuck?"

On the bonnet, was an inverted pentagram. Only this time, it was made up of twigs and branches with a few green and brownish leaves. It was arranged immaculately. The circle itself was perfect. The three of them looked around, searching for anyone who could have done this.

"At least they didn't trash it this time," John half-joked.

"We still need to check the car. You two check inside and underneath. I'll check the back," Bob said.

David took another photo. Bob walked to the boot of the car and waited for John to open it. John placed his trainer on the blanket in the back.

"Eurgh. Yuck," John said, creasing his face up as he stood at the boot.

A pile of maggots wriggled on the ground at the rear of the car.

"Not again," David added. "What *is it* with these maggots?"

Bob opened the boot and all seemed fine. The luggage appeared to have been untouched where they had last left it. David checked his laptop in the compartment of his case. It was all good.

"I'll go check the front." John walked back to the driver's side. He leant in and popped open the bonnet. He swiped off the inverted pentagram with his right hand, then pulled out a few leaves and tiny twigs from under his windscreen wipers.

David pulled out the two notes that he and Grant had received which he had put in the compartment along with his laptop. "These are the notes Grant and I got." David handed them over to his uncle.

Bob studied them carefully, even holding them to the slight light the same way you'd check a bank note for a watermark.

"Mine was blank initially … then after the pain and nosebleed, it had this on it." David pointed at the symbol.

"You should have checked yourself out at the doctors or hospital," Bob replied with concern.

"It's all good in the hood," John called over, slamming shut the bonnet and then getting back into his car. "Let's see if we can get this heap started. Here goes nothing." John turned the key.

Bob and David waited.

The car refused to start. John tried again. The engine kicked in before shorting out. *"Come on!"* John thumped the steering wheel and inadvertently beeped his horn. He tried a third time. *"Yes!"* The engine had come to life. All of the car's gauges returned to normal. The car seemed fine.

Bob got in the passenger side as David and Benji climbed into the back. John revved the engine up a few times before driving up the country lane and then onto the dirt track, back up to the farm. John parked his car in an empty barn by the side of the house where the Land Rover was usually kept. It would easily house both and another. They sat in the car for a little while, talking.

"I will tell Betty everything. Just not now. Not after Daisy and everything," Bob said, looking back to David and then across to John.

"About the prints. Have you seen anything like them before around here?"

Bob sighed. "I've never seen *anything* like that before, David. Like all these other weird happenings. Up until a few weeks ago, everything was fine. There was nothing out of the ordinary happening here."

"Whatever was chasing us, it's footprints just seemed to stop. Yet, we could still hear it. It wasn't to be seen. I mean, is it the *same* cloaked thing we saw which didn't have any visible feet or hands, or something entirely different?" said David.

"Could it have been someone running through the mud with fake monster feet? Or like when people have those feet on a wooden stick. You know what I mean?" John asked, with a straight face and then grinning.

David gave him a friendly punch on his left shoulder, smiling.

Bob gave a slight laugh and shook his head. "I guess you're the joker out of the two, huh?"

John gave a slight pout and nodded, raising his eyebrows.

"Anyway, I'll show you around the farm now, if you'd like? It shouldn't take too long."

"Cool," replied David.

"We can make our way around. Remember, make yourselves at home. Our home, is *your* home."

# Chapter Fourteen

## 11th July, 2018

They stood outside the farmhouse, looking onto the green lawn and the outline of the forest just beyond it. The farmhouse was large, built of orangey-red bricks with a chimney. There were five bedrooms. Above the sturdy, white wooden front door with an antique brass knocker, was an archway porch made from red tiles. Not far from the front door was a green tin mailbox with a flap, reading *Hamish Farm*.

Over to the left of the farmhouse as they stood, was a field of barley that wisped in the gentle breeze. With its golden white heads, it was almost ready to be harvested. It was near to the muddied dirt track. Next to the field were two weathered steel tower grain silos, each with a conical roof that resembled that of a tin hat. Alongside the house was the barn where John had parked his car. To their right was another dirt track, another way out of the farm leading further into the forest. Unlike the other, this one was hard surfaced with a few weeds growing out from cracks and crevices.

The back of the house had a large garden with a small patio and wall. It was well looked after. Betty usually took care of the garden and sometimes parts of the paperwork, whilst Bob and his workers focused more on the farm itself. The lush back lawn had a patterned stripe to it. A small metal bench painted black, sat in one of the corners. In another, was a garden stone statue of Isidore the Labourer, who was the patron saint of farmers. At the back, was a cute bird table made from wood.

The garden had numerous shrubs and flowers as well as a few small trees, including a rather large apple tree to the left. Betty took great pride in her garden. She hadn't let recent events deter her. Looking after the garden was a welcome distraction from it all. It helped keep her mind occupied.

On one of the flower beds stood a garden gnome holding a Scottish flag with half of his face painted blue. It was a gift many years ago from Angus, to welcome Betty and Bob to Scotland. It was meant in good will, but with a little irony as they weren't Scottish. Not long after, they bought a gnome in return for Angus, with an English flag and its face half painted white.

Under an archway next to the garden on the left, was an area with very large fruit and vegetable patches. Something else Betty would attend to. They grew all sorts as the farm was mainly arable. They relied on its produce for the main source of income, and also on what some of the animals provided.

Bob and Betty didn't make too much, especially after paying their workers and their outgoings. But it was enough to live on and enjoy their quiet lifestyle. The farm was more of a hobby. They still had quite a lot in their savings, which they could fall back on if ever needed. Although they earned less than when Bob was in real estate, he and Betty never regretted the switch for a second. They were much happier, until recently.

Across from the garden and patches was the farmyard. A little further up were the chicken coop and animal pens. The pens themselves were made mostly out of wood with a tin roof, and either had wired or wooden fencing around them. They were definitely secure. Dried blood was still visible where it had soaked into the wood, from where the chickens had been taken and killed. Behind the coop, was a fenced off grass area for the chickens to free roam during the day. The animals were well looked after. Most had their own names and collars to help identify them. There were more animals and the farm was larger than David had expected.

Before the animal pens was the large, main barn. Numerous bushes and shrubs grew around it. It was where the farm vehicles were kept, along with machinery and agricultural equipment including the baler. Above the barn entrance was a light. The farmyard itself had half a dozen lights, each mounted on a high wooden pole. They provided adequate visibility at night.

Inside the main barn, along with other farming machinery and a trailer, were two tractors. One was green with yellow alloys and the other was identical, but blue with yellow alloys. The red combine harvester was parked next to them, a Case IH 2188 model. The combine was old, but still looked in good condition.

Behind and beyond the back of the farmhouse were three more fields, all next to one another. A small picket fence ran alongside them, along with a concrete pathway which was big enough to allow the farm vehicles to gain access to each of the fields, and down to the two dirt tracks. The smaller field on the left had the cow pen in it, with a straw yard where they slept. It had a red painted roof over it with half a dozen plastic skylights. Nearby, was a small, brick hut with a blue wooden door; inside was a stainless-steel holding tank for cooling milk. A few of the cows were grazing. The rest of the field was sectioned by wired fencing, so that the other animals could roam around freely when out of their housing pens, to get some exercise and graze. More wired fencing went around the rest of it, along with some rows of hedges and some trees.

The other two fields, larger in size, had crops in them; one again with barley, and the other wheat. The farm's three adjacent fields plugged the gap between the house and the north side of the forest.

After showing David and John around, Bob wanted to introduce Derek to them.

The two friends followed behind.

"With Eric getting scared and quitting, we're a man down. Of late, even during the day, one of us is keeping an eye on the animals almost all of the time. It's costing me a bit more as well, as I'm paying extra to have some of these guys work the nights, too, to keep an eye out. It gets a bit frustrating, especially when there's other work to be done.

"Gavin is here practically most of the time of late, since all the bad shit started. It's great having him around. But if one of us is on our own, we make sure we don't move out of sight of the animals for too long," Bob explained as they walked back to near the chicken coop. "Derek should be around here somewhere. Let's check the barn."

They made their way to the main barn.

"Derek?" Bob raised his gruff voice, "You in there?"

Derek came walking out hastily from the barn holding a pair of gardening shears in his left hand. "Sorry, boss. I wasn't away from the animals for long! I couldn't find the shears."

"That's okay." Bob smiled. "I'd like you to meet my nephew, David, and his friend, John."

"Oh, okay." Derek walked over to shake hands, wearing a pair of white gardening gloves. "I was just going to trim some of the bushes up."

"That's fine, Derek. Jack should be here any minute as well." Bob looked at his watch.

Derek Collins was a simple, yet quiet, Scottish man. But a very hard worker. He was the latest and currently the last, recruited by Bob. He didn't speak much and had never been in a relationship. He was only five-foot six and was bald, apart from the 'horseshoe' shape of hair on his back and sides. He was forty-four like Gavin but looked closer to fifty-four and spoke slowly in a light, Scottish accent.

Derek had been doing farm work on and off for almost ten years. He had worked for Bob for only four months. He didn't drive, but he did ride a moped that was perfect for his small frame, that was often parked inside the main barn next to the combine.

"Was that your gun that I heard going off a wee while ago?" Derek asked, scratching his bald head with his glove.

"It was. Just a false alarm, nothing to worry about," Bob replied with a smile.

"Oh, okay."

"Oi, oi ..." came a sudden shout from behind them. A cocky young guy came strutting up the dusty farmyard. He was wearing a grey singlet with sunglasses tucked down it, three-quarter length blue shorts, white socks and sand-coloured boots. On his head, he wore a back to front black baseball cap. He didn't look anything like a farmer.

"You're late, Jack," Bob said raising his rough voice slightly.

Jack shrugged his shoulders and held out his hands, as if to say 'whatever.'

Jack Wallace was twenty. He lived with his mother. His father had moved out around six years ago. His parents weren't divorced but separated. What started as a trial separation, soon became more permanent. He saw his father occasionally when he felt like it, but it wasn't ideal because he lived more than three hours away, in Ayr.

Jack had been working on the farm since the end of last year. He had turned up out of the blue one day unannounced and looking for work. He had no previous experience working on a farm, but Bob gave him a three-month trial.

Although he was a little brash and rough around the edges, Bob liked him from the start, as did his fellow workers. Despite his attitude and nature, he was actually a very good worker, apart from being late at times. So far, he had never taken a day off ill. He had even come into work one morning with flu, so Bob had tried to send him home. Jack was having none of it; "Nope, there's work to be done!" he had said with defiance. This was probably one of the reasons Bob was lenient with Jack's timekeeping.

Bob introduced Jack, to John, David and Benji. Jack crouched down and rubbed Benji's head with gusto. Benji, aloof at first, then licked Jack all over his face and mouth. Jack shook hands with John, surprising him by pulling him in for a hug. He then held out his fist to bump with David's. Once the introductions were done, Derek went to attend to the shrubs with his shears whilst Jack went to fetch the animal feed. Bob and the boys made their way back to John's car for their luggage. Next to John's car, was Jack's black Nissan Micra.

"Well, you've met everyone now on the farm," said Bob.

"What do they think about the things that have been happening around here? Derek seems quiet, and that Jack, he's a bit of a lad, isn't he?" David pulled his rucksack and suitcase from the boot.

Bob laughed. "Yes. Jack is a character, all right! I had my doubts when he turned up asking for a job, but there was something about him I liked and he's a damn good worker. Derek's the same. They all are. I've had numerous workers down the years, and apart from two, I never had to fire anyone. Derek is one of the quietest. Yes, he comes across as a bit simple. But he's a really sweet guy. You'll never hear him complain, either.

"As for what do they think about the events here? Not much. I mean, they haven't witnessed what you two have seen, which is ironic, as this is where the problems started. I'm going to have to talk to them about it and tell them. It's my duty to warn them. Whether or not they believe me is another matter. Gavin is the most rational one out of us here."

"Yeah, but when we show them the photos and notes, they'll surely believe us," John said, holding his gym bag.

"I think this is just the start. I can feel it, Uncle. It's like something *dark* is coming."

John and Bob nodded.

"There's a shitstorm coming, all right," John added.

"The most important thing for now, is that we watch out for one another and the animals. No one really does anything alone. Safety in numbers. I'm dreading telling Betty about it more. Sometime tomorrow, I'll hold a meeting and explain everything to everyone. I'll let you guys settle in first, get some sleep tonight and we'll go from there. You must be tired?"

"Yeah, we're pretty whacked, Uncle." David fought back a yawn. "I need to call my folks and Grant. Let them know we've arrived safely."

"I'll show you the rest of the house and your rooms. Then you can unpack." Bob smiled, leading them back into the house.

A muddied, light brown doormat that read WELCOME lay on the floor. They decided on taking off their dirty footwear. An old grandfather clock's pendulum was hypnotically swinging from side to side in the hallway. Upstairs, John and David's bedrooms were opposite each other at the end on the left. The house in general felt very cosy and snug. David guessed that in today's market, the house and farm would be valued for much more than they had bought it for. Not that Bob and Betty had any intentions of selling. Not at the moment anyway; they enjoyed working on the farm. At least, until of late.

John unpacked everything. He used the wardrobe to put most of his clothes in and a chest of drawers to put other things in, such as his underwear and socks. He almost knocked over the lamp that sat on top of the chest of drawers next to his bed, catching it in time before it fell onto the lime white carpet.

David decided to keep most of his stuff in his suitcase and just pull out what he needed, when he needed it. He took out his laptop and placed it on his bed, plugging the charger in. He then called Grant.

"Hello, mate!" Grant's voice answered. He sounded a lot better.

"Grant, how you feeling, matey?"

"I'm still a bit anxious, but I feel a fair bit better." Grant cleared his throat.

"You sound it! What did you tell your folks?" David walked over to the window that overlooked the back garden and fruit and vegetable patches. Beyond the fields, he could see the dense, green forest that was Rothiemurchus. It was a pleasant view. Although he wondered what horrible possibilities lurked within.

"Oh, nothing really … I just said that I hadn't been feeling too great. They're happy to have me here. Did you arrive okay at your uncle's farm?"

David wondered why the conversation was static free. There was no interference. It was the same as when Bob spoke to Betty earlier. "We did, mate. Safe and sound. My uncle's cool. As is my aunt. We've met the workers as well. They all seem like nice guys. Looks a really nice place, too. Even though it seems a bit of an odd place to have a farm."

"Nothing has er, happened, then?"

David paused. He wanted to tell Grant about the figure they saw and the prints and everything else, but he didn't want to worry him. Not now he was feeling a little better. He'd tell him everything once they got back. "Nah, everything's fine at the moment. Me and Johnny are going to help out on the farm as planned and check about the place. See if there's an explanation."

A shout came from the doorway of David's room, "All right, four-eyes?"

David handed over his mobile to John; they could hear Grant laughing on the other end.

"All right, buddy?" John asked.

"I'm just going to the loo," David said, heading for the bathroom.

When he returned, John was winding up the call.

"Okay, mate. We'll chat later … Will do. Laters." John hung up and threw David's phone back to him as he came into the bedroom. "He had to go; his mum was calling him. He wanted to tell you again, that he's sorry for letting us down."

"At least he sounded a little better. He asked if anything had happened. I didn't like keeping him in the dark. I reckon it's best if we tell him once we get back. Well, whenever that may be."

"I agree with you on that. *If*, we get back." John sighed.

"I'm surprised there wasn't any static. I guess it doesn't happen all the time." David walked over to the window again.

John sat on the edge of the bed. It squeaked under his weight. He looked down at the pale blue carpet. "What about those footprints, though?"

David rubbed his more than stubbly face and considered whether to shave. It had been over two weeks. He usually didn't leave it for over ten days. "I know. What the hell was that thing? How many are there? Those feet were *huge*. Was it even the same thing we saw on the motorway, or what?"

John shook his head and laid back onto the bed. He put his hands over his face and rubbed it. "Ugh ... God ... This is some heavy shit. I still can't get my head around it all. Floating figures, odd hand and footprints, whispering, which I haven't heard yet, mirrors breaking, strange symbols ... I mean, what the *actual* fuck?" He sat up and looked over to David who turned to face him.

David exhaled, pouting his mouth. He raised his eyebrows. "You know, I've still got a bad feeling about all of this. To begin with, I just wanted to get away for a while. I fancied a change of scenery and to help out on the farm. Now, all I can think about is why is this all happening? Where do we begin?"

"I hear you, mate. I'm with you on that. We should talk about it more tomorrow when your uncle tells everyone. Christ knows what their reaction will be."

"I'm worried about how my aunt's going to take it. She doesn't know the full extent of it. Even we don't." David bent down to stroke Benji who rolled over onto his back for his tummy to be rubbed.

"We definitely need to find out more about this area." John yawned.

"I'm dreading it ... We need to check out this forest. It has to be done."

"I was thinking the same thing. I'm not sure what good that may do? Didn't we read about there being certain activities around these parts? It's not like I'm interested in that. Certainly not now. But it just seems odd, you know? It comes across as a nice, peaceful area; then you've got all the other bad stuff happening."

"I know what you mean. Remember, this is a massive forest."

"Maybe one side is good and the other evil?" John semi-joked, although, they both considered it. "What now?"

"We should go back down and see my uncle. See if he needs a hand with anything. We still need to help with something; it's not fair he's putting us up and we aren't chipping in. Like I said, that was always the initial plan. We obviously need to find out what's going on around here, yet at the same time, we still need to work. I better call my parents, too."

John smacked his thighs and got up. "Yep, I agree. I'll take Benj back down with me and see you in a bit, if you want?"

"Okay," David answered as he rung his mum's mobile number. "See you in a bit."

# Chapter Fifteen

## 11th July, 2018

It was after four in the afternoon. It turned out to be a pretty hot day. John, for the past couple of hours had been helping a bare-chested Jack with some hedgerow trimming in one of the fields. It was the field with the cows in, which were now joined by some of the other animals for their daily run. They moved on to work on a tree; Bob wanted some of the branches cutting. John's mind was elsewhere.

"Pass the trimmer will ye, mate?"

"Huh. Oh." John handed Jack the trimmer.

"Ye okay? Ye seem miles away?"

"I'm fine. Was just thinking." John held the ladder firmly for Jack.

Jack started cutting the branches and when finished, handed back the trimmer. He climbed down and carried the ladder towards the next tree. John followed him.

"You enjoy working here, then?"

"Aye. It can be hard work. But it ain't rocket science." Jack knew that his accent was hard for non-Scots to understand.

"So, erm. What do you make of what's been happening around here, you know, with the pigs and chickens, and Bob and Betty's cat? And this whispering?" John asked, feeling awkward, not sure why.

Jack placed the ladder down at the next tree and rested his arm on it. The metal was warm to the touch. He puffed his cheeks out and exhaled. "There's some sick fuckers about, aye." He shook his head. "And what they did to that wee cat of theirs … sickening."

"Have you seen anything out of the ordinary, like that Eric did?" John wiped some sweat from his forehead.

"Nae. Apart from those whispers I've heard. As for what Eric saw, it was most likely his imagination, or lack of sleep. Failing that, some silly bugger playing games, dressing up! Cannae believe he left coz of that, aye." Jack snorted.

"Yeah." John half-laughed. *If only you knew.* "What about this whispering, what do you think that is?"

Jack picked his left nostril and flicked his finger. "Nae idea. Probably just the wind. Either that or we're going crazy. I haven't really heard them that much meself."

"You don't really believe it's the wind, do you? C'mon." John pushed.

Jack looked oddly at John. "How ye mean? It's probably just someone messing with us. Same bastards who killed the animals … if I catch 'em, I'll stick that trimmer right up their arse! Anyway, let's get these trees done."

John laughed.

Whilst John was helping Jack, David had been working with Gavin who had since arrived back at the farm; they were clearing up the piles of shrubs and bushes which Derek had cut. They put them in a heap ready for burning.

David was now helping Gavin shear the sheep, or at least he was watching how Gavin did it. Benji's lead was hooked to one of the wooden pen posts, with a bowl of water next to him.

Gavin turned one of the sheep onto its back and started to shear. The sheep was surprisingly submissive as it rested up against Gavin's firm legs. The sheep's own legs were twitching slightly as the buzzing shears did their work.

"It doesn't hurt the sheep, then?" David asked as he watched with interest.

"Nah … not unless you nick them or take a teat off!" Gavin joked slightly. "We usually shear them about once a year. Me or Bob. The older sheep get used to it, as you can see. They're pretty meek. It's only the younger ones that fidget, which makes it a bit harder." Gavin moved the tool, carefully shearing the wool.

"I wonder if they enjoy it?" David smiled.

"I think they tolerate it. But yes, perhaps some do."

"They'll be a lot cooler for it. I'm sure they'd appreciate that," David said. Then he looked over at Benji who was making a slurping sound with his long tongue, taking a drink from the bowl.

"Oh, for sure. Especially in this weather. That isn't the only reason we do it … you ever heard of Flystrike?" Gavin asked, looking up at David who shook his head. "It's where flies lay their eggs on a sheep's wool. Then after they've hatched, the maggots get under the wool and skin, eating away at it. It causes blood poisoning if it isn't treated, eventually killing the sheep."

David screwed his face up. "Nice," he said sarcastically. "That ever happened?"

"Once. A few years ago. Fortunately, it was caught early and we managed to treat it. The sheep was fine. Though, she died a couple of years later. Unrelated. We found her lying in the pen one morning. Died in her sleep. Sally, was her name." Gavin finished off the shearing.

"That's sad."

Gavin put the sheep back and rolled the wool up starting with the tail end, then placed it in the nearby wool sack along with the other fleeces, ready for transport in the morning to be cleaned and skirted.

"So, what do you make of what's been happening around here?"

Gavin tied the sack up. "Sickos. That's what! How anyone can do such a thing to those poor animals is beyond me. I know how much Bob and Betty love their animals. Me too. Betty was utterly distraught when she found Daisy on the washing line. Well, she still is. She hasn't said much since. I was here earlier with your uncle, when Angus turned up. Me and Bob were keeping watch last night and this morning."

"What about that chanting you heard and the fire?"

"Yes. Me and Eric were doing the nights. He was asleep. I suddenly heard a chanting coming from that side of the forest." Gavin pointed towards the south side of the dense forest. "I climbed up on top of the main barn to get a view. Parts of the forest around here dip down a little, you know? Anyway, I saw this glow. After a few seconds, the chanting stopped. The same with the glow, which I assumed was a fire; it went just like that." Gavin closed his fists and then opened his hands up, gesturing.

"I didn't want to concern Eric with it, and in all honesty, I was pretty shattered. The late nights are catching up with me. Then of course, not long afterwards, he supposedly saw that figure hover into the forest and felt something behind him."

"How far into the forest was it?" David asked. He felt a tingle on the back of his neck.

"Well, you see. That's the thing. It wasn't miles away. But it was a fair bit. I'm actually surprised I heard anything, if I'm honest with you. There was no wind, nor a breeze to carry the sound. Yet, I could still hear it quite clearly. Don't ask me what the chants were saying, though! I couldn't understand any of it. I thought it was strange that the fire just went out the way it did." Gavin looked pensive.

"What about what Eric saw? Have you heard this whispering or experienced the interference around here, like when you use your phone?" David was really intrigued now.

"I've spoken to a few people about that damn interference. Not everyone has it." Gavin scratched his black beard. "As for the whispering, I'm sure there's a reasonable explanation. Just don't ask me what! It isn't like we hear them a lot. But strange, yes. As for Eric, who knows? It could have been lack of sleep, someone messing about."

"Have you been in the forest lately?"

"In all honesty, I've been here a number of years and I can't say I've actually been into the forest that many times. No need to."

"I think Bob said something about stuff disappearing as well?"

"You sound like the police," Gavin joked.

David smiled. "Sorry, I'm just curious and worried."

"It's fine, really. You can ask what you like. It's only understandable you're concerned. Bob and Betty are your relatives, after all. To answer your question, yes. A few things have gone missing or been removed. Nothing major, just annoying."

"What sort of things?"

"A few hammers went. A ladder was moved from one barn to the other, even though no one had used it for a bit. A couple of shovels disappeared; we had to buy some more. Even a wheelbarrow was found on one of the barns where your uncle keeps the Land Rover. Things like that."

"How the hell did a wheelbarrow get up there?"

"Beats me. Perhaps they used the ladder? It's obviously just someone messing about and trying to scare us. Takes more than that to scare me, mind. I know we're quite a way from anywhere else. We're pretty secluded out here, but someone's responsible. I even thought I heard a young child's laugh a few days back. I was walking close by the forest and heard it, along with a rustle. Kids, eh?" Gavin moved his eyebrows and shrugged.

"Yeah," David said quietly, "Kids."

# Chapter Sixteen

## 11th July, 2018

It had gone eight in the evening. Gavin, Bob, John, David and Benji, were sitting in the farmhouse living room chatting. They were digesting the pot roast Betty had cooked them. Betty was outside watering the plants and the fruit and vegetable patches. She had also cooked for Derek and Jack, who were finishing off for the day and keeping watch before Bob and Gavin started their night watch.

"How long have you had Benji?" Gavin asked, sitting in one of the soft armchairs.

Bob was sat in the other one opposite, whilst John and David sat on the matching soft rose-patterned sofa, which was sprinkled with dark, purple cushions. Benji was lying on the twist pile, chestnut carpet at David's feet.

David noticed a photo opposite him on the top of the wall unit. It was of Darren, his cousin, and his aunt and uncle. The shaven-headed Darren was standing in between Bob and Betty with his arms around them. They were all smiling. Next to it, were a few more small, framed photos of his aunt and uncle, including a school photo of Darren as a child, grinning cheekily, with a couple of baby teeth missing.

There were three crystal cut decanters in a built-in glass cabinet, each filled with alcohol. There were some glasses and a silver engraved beer tankard that read *Happy 40th, Dad.* Bob had poured himself a glass of brandy; nobody else wanted a drink.

Above the sofa on the wall, was a large scenic painting of a forest, most likely Rothiemurchus. At the other end of the wall, hung a wooden crucifix.

"Almost three years now, Gavin," David answered. "He's still young … I thought you would have had a dog or two as well, Uncle?"

"Oh. We did, David. We've had two Border Collies since we moved up here," Bob replied, swirling his glass of brandy. "Unfortunately, they both died. One seventeen years ago or so now, and the other more recently; two years ago. Both females. The first one was named Bailey, the other was Bella."

"Sorry to hear that." David sensed his uncle's pain. "I think I remember about Bella, now."

"That's okay, mate. They had a good life." Bob sipped his drink. "When visiting down south, we would usually leave them with Angus or someone for the week. They would always get restless travelling long distances if we decided to drive and not fly."

"You ever thought about getting any more?" John asked.

"Sure. But me and Betty have decided not to get another one for the moment. We'd love to have a dog again; it's just the pain of when you lose them. I don't mean to worry you, David."

"That's fine. I know it must be painful to lose an animal. I sometimes think that about Benji. At least he's still young." David bent down and rubbed Benji. "What time are you two doing the night shift?"

"In about another hour." Gavin checked his watch.

"Yep ... me and Gavin, again ... it's a pain in the arse, but I really don't want to take the risk. We'd rather do it than the other guys. We'll start off together then one of us will take a nap in the barn, then swap." Bob took a larger sip of his brandy this time. "The old buddy system."

"Have you witnessed or heard anything since you've done the night watch?" John asked, sitting forward.

"Apart from what Eric saw and Gavin, there hasn't actually been anything. I did hear a whisper nearby a couple of times in the forest. Other than that, nothing. I'm still playing it safe. I don't want to let our guard down. Especially, after what you boys had happen to you ..."

Gavin looked over at John and David, then across to Bob. "Why, what happened?"

Bob breathed out. "Things are a *lot* more serious and dangerous than we first feared, Gavin. I'm going to tell everyone tomorrow. I'm worried about how Betty will react ... You may as well hear it now. I know you're a rational kind of guy, but this is undoubtedly going to challenge *any* rational explanation you might have."

"What the hell are you talking about, boss?" Gavin laughed slightly.

*****

The three went over what had happened. Gavin was shown the evidence, including the notes David had fetched from his suitcase. At one point, he had laughed and accused them all of winding him up. He didn't appreciate being taken for a fool. But then, remembering what had already happened on the farm, he had a rethink. He needed to assimilate all the information.

"I … I don't know what to think. *Surely* there has to be a reasonable explanation? *Something*?" Gavin got up and paced around the living room. "I mean … ghostly figures, monsters? Some kind of dark forces? Come on …" he raised his voice. He took off his cap and vigorously rubbed his head before placing the cap back on.

"I know it's hard to understand, Gavin. Believe me, I didn't want to believe it, either. These boys wouldn't lie. Not about something like this. I saw the prints, too. Something chased after them. I'd show you the prints myself; only they've gone … I went back later this afternoon. All the other prints and tracks are still there." Bob finished the last of his brandy, warming the back of his throat.

"Gone?" David asked.

"Well, that's fucking odd," said John.

"It isn't really odd, when you consider everything that's happened so far. That's normal compared to everything else," David replied, scratching his thigh.

"I'm still in shock. How can something like this even be real? Things like this *don't* exist … Now I know why you were asking me all those questions, David," said Gavin.

"It was the same for us too, mate," John said. "It's still hard to take in."

"It makes me even more worried about what to watch out for tonight," said Bob.

"Me and John are here to help. We can keep watch, too. At least for a bit, Uncle."

"We'd appreciate that," Bob replied. "We'll see for now."

"Are you going to install cameras around the yard, Bob?"

"I don't think it's going to make an awful lot of difference really, John. As long as we're keeping guard. I'm thinking about it. I don't know whether it would pick anything up. I'm still thinking about moving the animals to a safer location."

Just then, they heard the front door close and Betty walked in. "What are you gents talking about?" She smiled.

"Oh, this and that." Gavin smiled back.

Bob really wasn't looking forward to telling Betty about everything. She had a right to know. Perhaps it would be better to tell her now. He could tell Jack and Derek tomorrow. "Take a seat, love …" Bob said calmly to his wife.

John and David shoved up the sofa and made space for Betty to sit down.

"I have something to tell you." Bob tried to smile understandingly. He knew how all this would sound.

Betty's smile dropped from her face. She slowly eased down onto the soft sofa and listened, as Bob and the guys explained and showed her everything.

*****

Betty hadn't even been aware that Eric had left or why. She had also been in the shower earlier, when Angus turned up. She hadn't known about the goat incident, until now. She had started sobbing and held the silver crucifix on her necklace firmly in her grasp. David had a sympathetic arm around her shoulder. A few tears had dropped onto her pink gardening shoes. Gavin had fetched Betty a tissue.

"I, I don't understand." She sniffed again. "We've been here for years and everything has been fine. We've never had anything like this happen in all that time. We've even been for walks in the forest." Betty wiped her eyes with the tissue.

Bob was bent down in front of her. His hands were on her arms consoling her. "I know. But we, all of us, are going to find out what's happening and try to put a stop to it, okay?" Bob spoke softly. "I should have told you earlier, I know. I'm sorry … I didn't want to worry you more."

Betty nodded and raised her red eyes to Bob.

"We'll get through this. We'll be fine. I promise." Bob kissed her forehead.

"What are we going to do?" David asked.

"For now, we'll continue to keep a lookout and try to find out *exactly* what is going on," Bob replied. He wasn't sure himself what they were going to do. They lived in the middle of nowhere. He wasn't sure where to begin, who to ask, or what to do next. Like the others, he hadn't a clue of where to start.

"We're here for you, Aunt Betty." David squeezed his aunt's shoulder.

"As long as I'm around, you'll be all right," Gavin added.

"Yeah, no one's going to mess with the *BFG*," Bob joked.

Betty managed to laugh, sniffing.

"I'll tell the other two tomorrow. I'll let them finish off for tonight and go home," Bob suggested.

Betty looked down at Benji who was now fast asleep. She shook her head. "I, I just find it so hard to believe. It's unbelievable." A couple more tears ran down her face. To the others, she suddenly looked her age.

"We'll be okay, sweetheart." Bob gave her a hug.

*****

Bob had helped Betty do the washing up and then went upstairs to have a long soak before joining Gavin for the night watch. Betty had checked that their two cats were indoors for the night, propping a piece of wood over the cat flap and went up to read in bed. She found it hard to concentrate though; her mind was going over everything she'd learnt that evening.

David and John were sitting outside in the garden. They had watched on and off the World Cup semi-final of England's defeat to Croatia. "Typical England shit," John had said. Benji, was chewing on a bone.

"I really feel for your aunt." John shuffled in the plastic chair.

"I know. It's tough for all of us … seeing their cat on the line, must have made it even worse for her. Bob, too. Maybe we shouldn't have mentioned it yet, about that figure we saw?" David looked over at the clothesline. The washing was still hanging out. They could smell the sweet scent of the detergent.

"It's never nice keeping something important from someone. But yeah, maybe we should have been more tactful and kept it secret for now … I still have this feeling we're being watched."

"I know. I can feel it, too. I don't think it's paranoia." David looked around.

"How the hell, are we supposed to find out what's going on up here, anyway?"

"I really don't know. I think the first thing we need to do tomorrow morning is check out where that fire was that Gavin saw. I really don't fancy going into the forest; it's a case of having to."

"I hate to admit it, but I agree with you. I think we need to find out more about this place as well. That's a definite. I know we're in Bumblefuck out here, but there *has* to be someone who knows something, like the history of the place. Stories to tell. True or not. It may give us an idea."

"I'm thinking exactly the same thing, mate. We'll check with Bob and Gavin in a bit. I'm not sure I can stay up for much longer. I feel absolutely shattered. Headachy, too." David yawned.

John looked over at him and started yawning himself. He stretched. "I'm cream-crackered, too. I don't think I can sleep, though. Maybe not ever again, after these past couple of days!"

"I know what you mean. I don't fancy falling asleep, either."

They sat there for a few more minutes watching Benji chewing his bone and then got up. David looked up and saw Betty's light go off. He hoped she would be able to get some sleep.

"It's certainly a bit nippy once the sun goes down," John said.

"If it is to do with that." David remembered the coldness he'd felt when anything sinister had happened.

An unpleasant smell of vegetation reached their nostrils as they walked across the front lawn and took a right up to the farmyard where Gavin was standing. The shotgun was over his shoulder. The farmyard lights were now on.

"Gavin, you all right?" John asked.

"Good as I'll ever be."

"Are you the only with a shotgun?" David asked.

"Here, yes. I have one of my own. We just never saw the need for two. Even one. Until now, that is. I'll fetch mine tomorrow morning. Just to be safe."

"Where's Bob?" David looked around curiously.

"He's just checking on the cows, over there." Gavin pointed across to the cow pen as Bob came out. "Everything okay?"

"For now. You boys should really get some sleep. We're okay out here." Bob yawned.

"Looks like you need some sleep too, Uncle."

"Aye. But a farmer's work is never done. Right, Gavin?"

"Right, boss." Gavin smiled back.

"At least you've got a bit of lighting here," said John.

"True. It comes in handy when you're working early hours in the winter or at night." Bob looked up at the sky. "It looks like it's going to be a clear night."

"John and I are going to take a look in the forest tomorrow morning. I know it may be risky, but we believe it's something that needs to be done. We want to have a look around, and find where that fire was you saw, Gavin."

"I don't think that's a good idea."

"Maybe not, Uncle. But we need to start looking into all of this. I have absolutely no idea what we're looking for … but it could give us something to build on if we come across anything. We can't just sit around waiting for something else bad to happen. I believe we really need to start asking questions and research further into this place as well. Try and be proactive."

"Very well. I will go with you."

"No. I'll go with them, boss. I can show them where I saw the fire and where the chanting was coming from. I'll go home tomorrow morning and get my own gun. You can keep yours with you. You can keep an eye out here and make sure Betty's all right." Gavin was adamant.

"Okay. I need to talk to Jack and Derek anyway, bring them up to date. Though, I'd imagine Jack will think we're on a wind-up. We also have the wool being picked up in the morning."

"I can leave my phone with you, along with the notes to show them, Uncle? Help convince them," David suggested. "John's got his phone on him and Gavin will no doubt have his."

"Okay. Work still needs to be done here. I am running a business after all. But don't go venturing *too* far! The forest is very dense and vast. Particularly the more you go in. It's easy to get lost, even if you think you know the way you came."

"When was the last time either of you went into that forest?" John asked.

"Beats me. Not for as long as I can remember," Gavin answered.

"It's been a while for me as well. Me and Betty have been in numerous times. We'd usually drive down to a less dense part, if we fancied a walk or a picnic. It's such a huge forest. I don't even recall the last time."

"Did you ever experience anything odd back then? Or sense anything?" David wondered.

"There were a few times me and your aunt heard the occasional rustle in the bushes, or a few twigs snapping. And we sometimes felt we weren't alone. That doesn't mean it was anything supernatural, of course … saying that, there was one odd thing, now that I remember …"

"Really?" David asked.

Just as Bob was about to explain, the farmyard lights flickered and dimmed. Before anyone could say anything, the lights returned to normal.

"A power surge," Gavin said.

"Or something else," muttered David.

"I think we're okay." Bob checked their surroundings.

"What were you going to say, boss?"

"It must have been about seven or eight years ago now … me and Betty were taking a casual stroll one evening through the forest on the other side, with Bella. We'd been walking for a fair while or so, when we came across a slaughtered deer. Its innards were hanging out. Cut open. We thought poor thing and how awful it was. We carried on. Further up ahead, we came across two more. Exactly the same. Cut open with their innards and blood pouring out. It was recently done.

"I remember noticing a few carvings on a nearby tree there. I can't remember exactly what they were; just symbols. It's just suddenly come to me!

I can't believe I didn't remember that before now."

The others stood there and listened attentively.

"I do remember we turned back because it was getting dark early and more overgrown … Bella started growling."

"We could look into that area as well, maybe?"

"You could, David. But I don't think it would be worthwhile. It was years ago."

"First, let's check out where that fire was," Gavin said, swiping a couple of moths from his face.

"You boys should get some sleep. Feel free to watch some telly downstairs still, if you wish. We do get interference on the that too at times. It's the same with the internet and Wi-Fi. Speaking of which, if either of you want to use our computer or internet, or at least try to, feel free to do so. Upstairs, the signal can be a bit weaker at the best of times. The router is downstairs in my study. The password for the Wi-Fi is 'Hamish1,' with a capital 'H' and no space before the 'one.' So feel free."

"Thanks, Uncle. The TV was fine earlier during the football. I think I'll just go up to bed. You're sure you're okay out here?"

"We'll be fine, David. If we need any help, we'll come get you, or shout out. Don't worry!" Bob smiled.

The two friends, along with Benji, returned to the house, being careful not to waken Betty and taking off their footwear. Despite their cautiousness however, they couldn't help a few of the stairs creaking as they climbed them. One stair in particular made a large groan.

"See you in the morning, pretty boy," John whispered and winked as he closed his bedroom door. When he switched on the bedside lamp, he found one of the cats was fast asleep on his bed. He smiled, got undressed and climbed carefully into bed, trying not to disturb the cat.

David opened his bedroom window so he would hear if Gavin or his uncle called for help during the night. The cool, night air flowed in, along with a hint of pine. He stood staring out for a short while longer, before getting into bed. It was a while before he eventually got to sleep.

His and John's first day in Scotland and at the farm had already been a somewhat eventful one to say the least. There were definitely dark times further ahead for them all. They knew it. They could feel it. Something a *lot* darker was coming …

# Chapter Seventeen

## 12th July, 2018

A rooster crowed. David rubbed his eyes and yawned. He let out a slight groan as he pulled himself out of bed and checked his phone to see what time it was: 08:40. He had slept a solid nine hours. His legs ached a little, but he felt surprisingly refreshed. He stuck his head out of the window. It was a bright and clear morning. He wondered if anything had happened during the night. Betty was taking down yesterday's washing. She seemed calm. *Everything must be okay.* He watched as she folded a bed sheet. He smiled pulling his head back in, closed the window and bent down to stroke Benji who was still asleep. He pulled out a beard trimmer from his rucksack along with his hair wax and other toiletries, and then a towel from his suitcase. Stepping over Benji, he made his way out of the bedroom and into the hallway. John's door was still shut. David could hear him snoring.

Looking into the bathroom mirror, he decided that he definitely needed a shave. When he was all done and showered, he walked back to his room to get dressed and heard John's door open.

"All right, mate? You sleep all right?"

"Like a log, surprisingly."

"Yeah, I got off eventually. Slept fine. Even got a bit of pussy last night." John grinned.

David frowned, puzzled.

John pushed open the door to show David where Sammy the cat was, still sound asleep on the bed.

"You idiot." David laughed.

"I'm going to jump in the shower. I'll see you downstairs in a bit, yeah?"

"That's cool," David replied, tightening his loosening towel.

"Everything fine last night, as far as you know?"

"I didn't hear anything. I had my window open. Guess we'll find out in due course."

As they were going into the forest this morning, David dressed practically, putting some black jeans and boots on and a long-sleeved top. He left Benji sleeping in the bedroom and went down to the kitchen where Betty was ironing.

She looked up and smiled. "David, love. How did you sleep? Well, I hope?"

"I did, thank you. How about you?"

"I slept very well, thanks. I was a little worried for obvious reasons, and I still can't get my head around what you all told me last night. It's very difficult to believe. I do feel a little better this morning. It's a nice day out there, also."

David wasn't sure if she genuinely was feeling better, or whether she was just putting on an act, a brave face. Or perhaps she was in denial? He decided to play it by ear. "It's certainly been a nice summer so far. Well, weather-wise at least." David let out an awkward laugh.

"Would you like a cuppa, dear? The kettle has just boiled."

"Would love one, please."

"Just the one sugar, wasn't it?"

"Please."

"Your friend, John. Is he up yet?"

"He's just taking a shower. He should be down in a little bit."

"What do you have planned for today?" Betty asked, carefully handing over the hot tea.

David wasn't sure what to say. He didn't know whether or not to mention about the forest. "Erm. Just see what Bob wants done, really. We're here to help out where we can."

Betty smiled. "You know, you don't have to work all the time, David. You're under no obligation to whilst you are here. You're free to go out and do as you wish."

"I know Aunt Betty. But we still have to earn our keep, if we can." David blew on his tea.

Betty placed a hand on his shoulder. "It's fine." She returned to her ironing.

David frowned at his aunt. She was definitely acting strange. Something about her just didn't sit right.

"I can cook you up some breakfast, or there's plenty of cereal in the cupboard?" Betty offered, pressing one of Bob's white shirts.

"No, no. That's fine. Maybe later." David sipped his hot tea.

The conversation stopped as David drank his tea. He suddenly felt more uncomfortable. Betty started to hum a little as she continued ironing. She looked over and smiled again. He gave an awkward smile back. He wanted to finish his tea as quickly as possible, but it was too hot.

"Come on, John. Hurry up," he thoughtlessly whispered to himself.

"What was that, dear?" Betty asked.

"Oh, nothing. Just wondering how long John's going to take."

*****

John eventually arrived. "Morning!" He beamed to Betty.

"Morning to you! Would you like a tea, dear? The kettle's still hot."

Before John had a chance to answer, David caught his attention from across the kitchen. *No,* he mouthed, shaking his hand and head.

"Erm, no, that's fine, thanks. I'm okay." John frowned.

"Thanks for the tea. We should go see Uncle Bob now. I don't want to keep him waiting." David hurriedly put the mug in the kitchen sink.

"Okay, lovey. You boys have a good day."

David escorted John outside.

"What the hell was all that about? I really needed a cuppa," John asked as they crunched across the pebbles outside.

"Betty's acting really weird. Like nothing's happened. Like she's in denial. I just thought it was best we got out of there for a bit. It felt too uncomfortable. I had to disappear into the hallway for a bit."

"Is she all right? She seemed fine to me."

"I don't know. I'll tell Bob … Why are you wearing shorts? It would be better if you wore something to cover your legs up more. We'll be walking through the undergrowth in the forest."

"Fuck it," John said deadpan.

David shook his head. "Let's go see how Gavin and Bob got on last night."

They walked to the animal pens and saw Bob picking his nails.

"All right, Uncle? How did last night go?"

"Morning, David. John. You guys get much sleep?"

"We did, thanks. Surprisingly. How about you? Anything happen last night?" replied David.

"It went fine, actually. Gavin did say he heard some sounds and a bit of whispering in the night whilst I was having some sleep, but apart from that, nothing. Well, not that we noticed, anyway. I've checked the animals again as well."

"Where is Gavin?" John asked.

"He's gone home to fetch his shotgun. He should be back soon. Derek and Jack should be in shortly. As they've done a couple of nights, I thought I'd let them come in a little later. Bloody Jack still gets in late, though." Bob laughed.

"He's certainly a one, all right," John replied.

"Have you seen Betty this morning?" David asked curiously.

"Only briefly, when I went in to see if she was all right and to use the loo; why?"

"She seemed odd this morning."

"Odd? How?"

"I'm not sure. Happy … but it didn't seem right. Like it wasn't genuine, you know? Or she was in denial." David wasn't sure how to explain Betty's behaviour. Maybe he'd just interpreted it wrong.

"Uhm, she seemed okay to me. I'll go see her again in a bit. She might be putting on a brave face, David. It could just be her way of dealing with everything. She'll be okay." Bob smiled at his nephew, feeling his concern.

They heard a car engine coming from the hard dirt track. It was Gavin in Bob's Land Rover. When he joined them, he was carrying his own twelve-gauge single barrel shotgun. Around his broad but slim waist, he wore a camouflage shotgun shell belt, holding twenty-five red shells in it. A machete was fitted inside a leather sheath attached to the left side of his normal belt. On the right side hung a small black torch. The three of them couldn't help but laugh.

"Bloody hell, Gav. You look like you're ready for war!" Bob laughed.

"Yeah, you forgot the grenades, though," David teased.

Gavin's face suggested that he didn't share the joke. "Well, after what I've just seen …"

The others stopped laughing and frowned seriously. Gavin had everyone's attention now.

"I got back to my house, and there on the tarmac, was an upside-down pentagram drawn in chalk. A goat's head was in the middle of it!"

"What?" Bob said.

"Whoever these *bastards* are, they know where I live. The symbol was *perfectly* drawn as well. Even the circle."

"Did you call the police?"

Gavin shook his head. "I didn't see the point, boss. Not for now, anyway. I hosed down the tarmac and put the head into a plastic bag in my garage. I thought I'd bring a machete in case we need it in the forest. It's most likely going to be overgrown in parts. It will come in handy." Gavin looked down at John's green shorts; he didn't say anything.

"It seems we are all being targeted," Bob said. "I really need to warn Derek and Jack once they get here. It could be dangerous for them. Even bordering on negligence, having them still around. I'll talk to them." Bob scratched his rough chin.

"Perfectly understandable, boss. You don't want to feel responsible for anything. We can cope if you decide to give them temporary leave."

Bob nodded.

"I'm ready to go, boys. Ready when you are." Gavin looked at John and David.

"We're ready," David answered. "I'll bring Benji as well."

Gavin gave a nod.

"You guys be careful. If you come across anything bad, you come back to the house, as soon as possible. Okay?" Bob ordered.

Gavin gave a second nod.

David handed his phone and the notes over to his uncle, so that he could show them to Derek and Jack. The former had just turned up, waving on his moped.

At the forest outskirts at the bottom of the front lawn, Benji stopped. David pulled on his lead. Benji was having none of it. David tugged encouragingly. Still, Benji refused to follow. He began to growl. John and Gavin turned round.

"What is it?" John asked, just as he and Gavin were about to enter the forest.

"I don't know. He's refusing to go any further." David crouched down and petted Benji. "What's the matter, boy?" he said softly.

Benji continued to growl.

"He's not usually like this." John walked back and stroked Benji himself.

"Not normally. Apart from recently, whenever he's sensed something bad." David frowned, looking back at the dark edge of forest.

Bob came marching after them. "It's the forest," he called out. "Our cats refused to go in the forest, too. I'll look after him whilst you three are gone. Don't worry, David."

David handed the dog lead over to his uncle. He was reluctant to leave him.

"I'll make sure he's with me all the time, until you're back. Jack should be here any minute. I'll check on Betty, too." Bob grasped the loop handle of Benji's lead.

"Okay." David felt Benji would be safer with him, but he wasn't going to force him to do something he clearly didn't want to do. He watched for a few moments as Bob took Benji back up to the farmyard. Then he turned back to enter the forest.

The three of them moved through one of the forest openings, being careful not to hurt themselves on some of the sharp twigs and branches.

"How far in did you see the fire?" John asked, stepping over a fallen log.

The forest was pretty well lit with a pleasant shady light and fresh pine scent. Shafts of light entered between the thick of the trees, illuminating the green and brown mossy ground beneath them. From above, they could hear singing and chirping in the trees. Despite Benji and Bob's cats being afraid of entering the forest, the birds seemed unaffected.

Gavin, who was slightly ahead of the other two, cleared his throat. "It was a fair way. Some parts are going to be more overgrown, I'd imagine."

"I'm surprised you could even hear the chanting from that distance. Especially as you said there was no wind," David said.

"I know. It did seem strange."

"Seeing a fire seems pretty normal, compared to what David and I have seen, mate."

"Make sure we stick close together, boys. I know it's pretty light at the moment, but the deeper we go in, the darker it will get. I'm certain of it. Even more so, if it clouds over."

"It looks easy to get lost. There's so many trees," David said, looking around.

"The forest is supposed to cover around eleven and a half square miles, and has over ten million trees at least," Gavin stated.

John whistled, raising his eyebrows. The forest was larger than he'd thought.

"Rothiemurchus is renowned for its Scots pine. It's one of the few areas that still has the oldest pines. Some are well over three-hundred years old. If you look around, you'll see plenty of pinecones on the ground. You can obviously smell them." Gavin pointed to some of the surrounding trees and on the ground near to them. A crunch came from underneath his right boot as he stepped on a cone with the force of his size twelve foot.

"Have you ever thought that it's kind of strange, having a farm like my uncle's in the middle of a forest, in the middle of nowhere?"

"I guess I did to begin with," Gavin recalled. "I remember all those years ago, when I first started working with your uncle, it was quite an unusual area to have a farm. But it isn't actually as unusual as you may think. I've seen a few farms like this one. Albeit, on television. Hamish Farm is perhaps a bit odder, in how it's more closed in I suppose."

"You've never felt a presence, or that strange things were happening in all the time you've worked here?" asked John.

"Nope." Gavin pulled out his machete and adjusted the sheath. "Nothing at all."

The way was becoming denser with shrubs and bushes knotted together. The rays filtering through the forest were fading the further they went. John began to feel as if the forest was closing in on them. Suffocating them.

Gavin started to slash at the shrubs. "Careful," he warned the two friends, "There's a few thorn bushes in here." He started to hack a little faster, making a way so that they could walk through. The dampness was now noticeable, and there was a slight mildew smell.

*"Argh! Shit!"* John said and rubbed his right leg.

The other two looked round quickly.

"Bloody stinging nettles."

"I told you, you shouldn't have worn shorts," David said.

John grimaced. "Yeah, whatever."

After another few minutes of hacking and slashing, Gavin finally guided them out of the overgrowth. "Hold up for a bit," he said, rubbing the top of his aching right shoulder.

"You all right?" asked David.

Gavin nodded. "Just an old injury from my rugby playing days. I dislocated my shoulder. It still gives me gyp at times, even after all these years ... We just need to keep heading straight. It should be further up ahead. You see how much darker the forest becomes, now that we're heading in deeper?" Gavin looked around. "Of course, it depends on the density of the growth and trees. It may get lighter further on."

"It certainly seems creepier," John said.

"It's a good job it's a clear day. Otherwise, it would have been even worse. We better move on. The sooner we can check this out, the quicker we can get back to the farm. I'm not sure it's safe out here. I don't like it ... call me paranoid. But I feel like we're being watched."

"Oh, you're not paranoid, mate. You're certainly not alone there," David replied. "Me and John have pretty much felt it since we arrived here."

Gavin looked up at the canopy. A bird was flapping its wings above. Gavin's bearded face had collected small leafy debris.

"You think anyone else comes here, this deep in?" asked David.

"It's possible. Though this part of the forest is very remote. I'd say we're probably the only three in a long time. There's no real reason why anyone in their right mind would come here. Well, apart from whoever started the fire."

"Yeah." John looked around nervously.

*****

They walked on deeper, further into the confinement of the unending, green and brown mass of coppices. There was now a chill in the air; the branches started to sway as a strong breeze picked up, circulating the pine scent more. Dead leaves blew around them, swirling as if they were captured in miniature tornados. The trees creaked and groaned around them. The cracks and snaps of wood repeatedly startled them as they made their way. The rustling of leaves grew louder.

Suddenly, they heard a *thud* as something behind them dropped onto the dank earth. All three spun round, unnerved.

Gavin gripped his shotgun and swallowed hard. "It's probably just a heavy log falling and some cones … come on guys. I know some weird shit's happening. Still, we must stay realistic." Gavin tried to remain rational, but his voice sounded nervy. Even for him.

They were all tempted to go back. None of them suggested it. Each wanting to appear strong. Without words, they drew closer together and forged on.

"You think we're almost there?" David asked, his mouth slightly dry from nerves.

"We've been walking a fair while. I can't imagine it's much further," Gavin answered.

"God, it's cold in here," John said with a shiver, wishing he'd worn jeans.

"Keep close," Gavin advised, carefully looking about.

"How long have you lived in Scotland, Gavin? What brought you to the Highlands?" John tried to start a normal conversation to take his mind off the unsettling surroundings.

Gavin welcomed the distraction. He adjusted his flat cap which had dislodged on a hanging branch. "I've worked for David's uncle for pretty much twelve years now. I came up to Scotland from Bristol about four years before I worked on Hamish Farm. I'd recently lost my farming job, and an old school friend in Stranraer was working on a farm there. He got me a job working there with him. I didn't have too much to leave behind in Bristol, so I thought, why not? I'd never been to Scotland before."

"How did you end up at my uncle's farm?" David almost tripped over a twine of roots.

"To cut a long story short, I fell out with the owner and left. My friend had already left a year or so before, for the same reason, so I jacked the job in. Then, by chance, I was chatting one evening in a pub in Stranraer with another farmer, who was down there for a week's break, visiting his folks. He told me that he was working on some farm in a forest; your uncle's, near Inverdruie where he was renting. I'd never heard of it.

"Anyway, he was leaving at the end of the month. He fancied a change of career, nothing against Bob, or anything like that. He had nothing but praise and good words to say about your uncle. He said he'd recommend me, and I made him a copy of my CV to give to Bob. Bob contacted me and I drove up there. Took me bleeding ages!" Gavin laughed.

"How far is it to Stranraer?" asked John.

"Almost five hours. It's well over two hundred miles."

"Wow. That far," David said. "I don't know why, but I assumed it was closer."

"Yep. Thankfully, your uncle's worker, who was leaving, the one who recommended me, Clive was his name, put in a good word for me. And Bob liked my CV as well, so I started straight away, even before Clive left. Bob told me on the phone he'd give me a trial and go from there. Again, I didn't have much to leave behind in Stranraer, even less than Bristol, really. I was renting a furnished house, so I didn't have to worry about moving anything, just my personal stuff."

"You've never looked back, then?" David looked up at Gavin who was marching on in front of him.

"Nope. Clive had told me how beautiful the scenery was up here. He wasn't wrong! It was even more scenic than I imagined. I was sold straight away. Especially after meeting Bob. I obviously passed the trial and the rest is history." Gavin turned back to smile.

"What about your friend who got you the job in Stranraer, what happened to him? And what was wrong with the owner there?" John was curious.

"I haven't seen my friend for quite some time. We sometimes text randomly. He did a couple of odd jobs, before eventually moving down south. He ended up in a small town in Essex, a place called Saffron Walden. He runs his own cleaning company. He gave up farm work. He's doing quite well for himself … As for the owner? Well, let's just say he was an arsehole." Gavin laughed.

They all felt a little more relaxed mulling over Gavin's past.

That was until David noticed a goat's head symbol carved into some decaying bark of a tree. "Check this out," he alerted the others. He traced his fingers around the carving.

"A goat's head?" John said.

In the middle, on the top of the goat's head, was an upside-down cross. They searched around the tree, checking for anything else. There were three more symbols etched into the bark. One was an inverted pentagram. They were unfamiliar with the other two.

"John. Take a photo of these symbols. We might need them," David said.

John pulled out his phone and took some photos.

"We need to research these symbols and find out what they mean. It might give us an indication of what we're dealing with." David rubbed his left cheek.

"It's got to be witchcraft." John slipped his phone back into his shorts pocket.

A strong gust of wind swept through the forest, its force almost knocking the three of them over. They protected their faces with their forearms to deflect the leaves and dirt that flew at them.

*"Jeeez!"* David screwed his eyes closed.

Gavin's cap blew away and got stuck in a bush. He retrieved it and shook the debris off it and pulled it down on his head firmly. "Come on. We need to pick up the pace. I don't like it in here one bit."

"Here, here," replied John.

They walked on with more haste, ducking under along the way, until they reached a second tree with strange markings and then another. They seemed to be leading them to something. John recorded the symbols in photos on his phone.

"Look," Gavin raised his voice. He pointed towards a clearing, less than a hundred yards ahead. "That *has* to be where the fire I saw the other night was." Gavin was satisfied they had reached their potential goal.

They quickly made their way towards the clearing, where all three stood, staring. It was eerily quiet. There was an unnatural calm and silence. All they could hear was their own breathing. The birds no longer sang. There was nothing but dead silence. There was no grass at all, just a large oval patch of earth. There was no sign of a fire either. What caused them to stop and stare wasn't the clearing itself. It was what was in it …

A large, inverted pentagram of bones was centred perfectly in the clearing. Dead centre in the middle of it, stood an evilly warped tree, covered in green moss. Its huge roots twisted like tentacles and its body arched abnormally. The leafless branches reached out like clawed hands, ready to tear someone apart. Some stretched up to the sky as others wrapped around its own trunk.

"What the hell," David muttered.

"What is this? Are they human bones?" John asked, wide-eyed.

"Let's find out," said Gavin.

They edged slowly onto the clearing, catching a hint of sulphur and feeling static electricity. The hairs on their heads and arms rose, as did John's leg hairs. David recalled the same feeling from in his flat, three nights ago. There really was no doubt now that everything they'd experienced was linked.

"D-do you smell sulphur? Can you feel the static?" David asked. "I've felt this before, in my flat."

Gavin and John nodded.

"It's so quiet," John remarked.

"This whole area just seems dead. Nothing appears to be growing. Except for this creepy tree." Gavin held on to his shotgun tightly.

"Smells of eggs, too," John said, holding his nose.

"Yes, sulphur," Gavin responded.

They trepidly made their way to the tree and inverted pentagram, stepping over some of the bones. The static and smell grew stronger.

"What the heck?" John looked at the hair on his legs and touched his head. "I feel a presence here. Like we're being watched. Like we're not alone." John's eyes widened further. He gulped.

Gavin knelt down and looked at some of the bones, prodding them with the tip of his shotgun. Then he made his way around the rest of the occult symbol. John and David examined the tree, wary of the long, freaky branch-arms. There were no engravings on the bark. David held his hand out to touch it.

"You think it's safe to touch?" John tried to stop him.

David went ahead anyway. It was cold to touch. He could feel an incredible energy flowing through the tree. It pulsated through his hand and arm, then his whole body, which was so small compared to the overwhelming tree. "Touch it! Tell me what you feel?" David prompted John.

John touched it reluctantly. "My God. It's like there's some kind of life force flowing through it … Touch this, Gavin."

Gavin could also feel the strange sensation.

They started to feel and hear a slight humming sound as the energy grew stronger. They could feel a vibration underneath the soil through their feet. John and Gavin looked down. The earth began to shake the small particles of dirt and bones. John and Gavin instinctively took their hands away from the tree, but David's remained. He seemed to be in a trance.

*"David!"* John shouted. *"David!"*

David's head and face began to shake and shiver as the raw energy shot through him.

*"Gavin! Give me a hand!"* John called out.

Gavin dropped his shotgun and helped John try to prize David away from the tree.

"He's ... not ... budging," John said as he strained.

David's mouth opened. His eyes flipped to the top inside of their sockets, showing pure white.

*"Gavin! Help me!"* John pleaded again.

Gavin let go of David and retrieved his shotgun. He took aim near the top of the tree away from John and David and fired.

There was an inhuman roar as the contents of the shell pierced the tree with a bang, splintering the bark. John and David flew back onto the dirt and bones as the tree let go of its hold.

Everything stopped. The smell of sulphur vanished and the static died. All was quiet and calm again. Gavin rushed over to check on John and David, where they lay on the ground. David was still. John was moving. He shook his head and squinted.

"You okay, John?" Gavin asked concerned.

"Yeah ... I guess so," John answered, trying to get his bearings. "It ... it was like there was a power surge when you fired at the tree." He scowled as he sat up on his knees and looked at his lifeless friend, dormant on the ground. "David? DAVID!" he cried.

# Chapter Eighteen

## 12th July, 2018

"He's breathing. I just think he's unconscious," Gavin said, with his fingers on David's wrist. He checked for a pulse.

"DAVID, WAKE UP, MATE!" John persevered.

David made a slight groan and slowly opened his eyes. "Wh-what happened?" he asked, trying to get to his feet.

"Easy, mate." Gavin smiled. He and John helped ease David to his feet.

David stumbled slightly, but they caught him.

John gave his best friend a hug. "I thought I'd lost you then, for a minute!" he said gleefully.

David gave a half-hearted hug back, still feeling woozy. Looking around, he remembered where they were and what had happened. "Th-that tree. It was like it took a hold of me. It wouldn't let go. It felt as if it was draining something from me. *My life*. It was electric and then everything went blank." David slurred his speech a little. "The back of my head is killing me."

"You'll be fine," said Gavin, checking the back of David's head. There was no blood. "Oh, and those bones. They aren't human, you'll be glad to hear. They're animal."

"Really? Are you sure?" John asked.

"Positive."

"How do you know?" John asked again.

"Trust me. I know my animals." Gavin smiled. "Plus, there's a few deer skulls and others in there. See for yourself; they don't look human."

John and David checked briefly. They were happy to take Gavin's word for it. David then gently pushed past Gavin and John to stand in front of the tree. He daren't touch it again. There was something very evil about this tree. He felt faint and stumbled again. Gavin and John rushed to his aid.

"We need to sit down for a bit before we head back. We might be okay for now. Let's sit over there, on the edge of the clearing. It's best we get back to the farm as soon as possible, but David needs a moment." Gavin ushered them across to the edge of the clearing.

"What the hell is this tree?" John asked.

Gavin shrugged. "I have no idea. We need to find out. I'm sure someone is an expert in these things. We need to find out who is responsible for all these dead animals."

"Surely other people must have come this way and seen this, no?" John queried.

"It's possible. Remember though, we are pretty deep in and in a very remote part of the forest. We had to hack our way through some of the way." Gavin took off his cap and gave his hair a ruffle.

"You're sure this is where you saw the fire? I mean, there's no ashes." David started to feel a little better.

"Positive. I know there isn't any sign of a fire, but trust me, this was definitely the spot. I'm certain of it."

"What next?" David asked. "I wasn't sure what to expect in this forest. Now we've found something, what should we do?"

It still felt like someone or *something* in the forest was watching them.

"There has to be a group involved in this. The chanting I heard was from people." Gavin rationalised. He put his hand on David's shoulder.

"You think there's some kind of cult?" David rubbed the back of his head; the pain was easing.

"I've never heard of anything ... I'm inclined to now say yes." Gavin looked at his shotgun. "That noise the tree made when I shot at it ... it was as if it were alive ... this is so messed up."

"That's an understatement," John said quietly. "I'm going to take a pic of this clearing, and that tree as well."

"Good idea. Then we need to get back," Gavin replied.

*****

Ten minutes into their return journey, they were startled by a sharp whisper that came from all around them. There was a flicker in the light that was reaching them through the gaps in the canopy. They stopped dead in their tracks.

"What did that just say?" John asked, looking around.

"I didn't catch it. They're never clear what they say," Gavin answered.

"It was pretty hard to make out. It was-" Out of the corner of his eye,

David saw a figure to their right. He turned his head sharply to face it.

Standing in a darker part of the forest, next to a small shrub with white flowers, was a tall man wearing a hat. A ray of sun shone across him, lighting up where he stood. He stared blankly at David who stared back.

"David?" John asked. He then turned and averted his eyes to where David was staring. "What the?"

"Hey!" Gavin half-shouted to the man, seeing him too now.

The man turned his head and looked straight at Gavin, his face expressionless. He proceeded to walk towards them. He walked slowly with a slight bounce in his step. He appeared rigid, his unmoving arms at his skinny sides. As he came nearer, they could see his face in more detail; he was in his fifties at a guess. There were large black circles underneath his cold, staring eyes, one of which lazily drifted to the left. His pale, clean shaven face was gaunt and his cheek bones hollow. His forehead possessed a small scar. His short and greying, light brown hair was visible from underneath his beige, polyester campaign hat, ribboned in brown.

He was kitted in a forest ranger uniform. The trousers were olive colour. His grey, short-sleeved shirt that showed off his gangly, veiny arms had sweat patches on his chest and under his armpits. Stitched above one of the chest pockets in black, read *Rothiemurchus Forest Rangers.* Embroidered at the top of his right sleeve, was a pine tree. He wore black boots.

He stopped a few yards from them. "Hello … my name … is Harold … I … am a … forest ranger … here …" He spoke irritatingly slowly; his accent seemed robotic. He looked up and around towards the treetops, as if in a trance.

Something didn't seem quite right about him. He gave them the creeps. There was a brief silence as the three stood there staring at this unusual man, before Gavin spoke.

He cleared his throat. "Hi. What are you doing out here?"

"I … could ask you … the exact … same … thing …" this Harold replied with a wry smile.

David shivered.

"It is … my job … to look … after … the forest … here …" Harold took off his hat, revealing a large balding spot and thinning hair as he bent his head down to dab the sweat dry with a hanky. He placed his hat back on his head and stared at David.

David returned an awkward, false smile.

"I'll … ask you again … what are … you doing … out here?" Harold seemed more serious this time. He then fixated his stare upon John.

"Oh. You know. Just, erm, *enjoying* the forest and its scenery … what it has to offer," John answered sarcastically.

"You … shouldn't … be out … here …"

"Really? And why is that? Gavin asked.

"You … just … *shouldn't* …" Harold warned them.

Gavin didn't like being threatened by anyone. "Sounds like a threat, *Harold*?"

Harold gave off another wry smile as he returned his stare to Gavin. This time, it was wider.

"You know, it's a public place. We have the right to be here," Gavin challenged.

"Of … course …" Harold's smile fell from his face.

"So, where are you from? You don't sound Scottish … I'm over here, Harry!" John said sardonically, mocking Harold's lazy eye.

David nudged John; he didn't like John messing with this man. This so-called forest ranger unnerved him.

Harold looked back over at John, who gave Harold a cheeky grin.

"I didn't know this forest had any forest rangers?" Gavin quickly asked, trying to move the attention away from John. He too was unsure whether John's approach was helping.

"It … does …" Harold still looked straight at John.

"Anyway … we better get going. Right, guys?" David started to move.

"That's right," Gavin added.

"You're … staying at that … farm … aren't you?"

"Nah. Not us, mate," John answered.

"You … have a … nice … dog …" Harold smirked at David.

*"What?"* David stopped, turning back to face Harold. David felt his heart sink. He didn't like this creepy guy knowing where they were staying. He feared for Benji's well-being too.

John pulled him away. "Nice chatting, Hazza."

They quickly walked away. When they looked back, Harold began to laugh, just standing there in the forest, his hands by his side. It sounded twisted. Wicked.

"Who the *fuck* was that guy?" John asked as they made their way back through the forest. "What a *freak*!"

"You shouldn't have antagonised him," Gavin said sternly. "Especially as he knows we're from the farm."

"I didn't like the way he mentioned Benji. He sounded threatening,"

David said. An overhanging branch brushed his face with a large leaf.

"Yeah," John said.

"It certainly seemed like that," Gavin said.

"I've never seen anyone so damn creepy-looking." David shivered again.

"The way he just looked and stared at us ... he just seemed to appear out of nowhere, after that whisper!" John added.

"Something clearly wasn't right with him. He looked ill for starters. Good job we're keeping watch on the farm. Seems even more reason to now." Gavin sounded more than concerned.

"I can't get that laugh out of my head ... you should have shot him." John looked at Gavin.

"And get done for murder?"

"We could have said he came at us. I thought he was going to!" John continued, ducking under a thick branch.

"He must be spying on us and on the farm ... are there even forest rangers here? Is he for real?" asked David.

"I've never known of any forest rangers. But that doesn't mean that there aren't any. It makes sense, I suppose. I've never thought about it really," answered Gavin.

"Do you think he's behind what's been happening, or at least has something to do with it?" John queried.

"I don't doubt it for one second." David believed.

"We can't jump to conclusions. It is possible," Gavin added.

"He might be following us now." John looked back.

"Maybe." Gavin checked back over their shoulders too. "Let's get back pronto. Tell your uncle about everything and warn him."

"Shit," John said suddenly.

Gavin and David looked sharply at him.

"I've got bird shit on my top!"

Gavin shook his head.

# Chapter Nineteen

## 12th July, 2018

They arrived back at the farm as the gentle rain which had followed them since meeting Harold turned heavier. They saw Bob outside chatting to a man who seemed angry and distressed. He was speaking in a loud Scottish tone. Bob appeared to be trying to calm him down. A blue estate car was parked by the house.

"What's Angus doing here again?" Gavin said as they drew near.

"I know it's bad, Angus. I know what you're going through. But we *will* find who's responsible. That, I promise you!" Bob put a reassuring hand on Angus' shoulder. Despite his gruff and dry voice, you could distinguish the compassion in it. "You're back. Thank goodness," Bob called to the others as they approached.

"Aye. We have a lot to talk about, boss," Gavin replied.

"Angus, these two here are staying with us for a while. This here is David, my nephew, and John, his friend."

They both smiled at Angus who gave a slight acknowledgement in return. It was clear to everyone that this grown man had been crying. His eyes were red and bloodshot. Traces of tears were visible, disappearing into his gingery white, matted beard.

"Angus lost some more chickens and Jimmy, his beloved goat last night." Bob paused and looked at Angus who had his head down. "Jimmy's body was found mutilated. His head was missing. His other goat, the one with the horn torn out, had also passed away yesterday evening. He and a fellow worker kept an eye out during the night, but somehow, whoever was responsible, mysteriously slipped by them."

Everyone looked at Angus and could feel his pain.

"Poor things. I'm so sorry, Angus." Gavin then frowned. "It could be the head at my home, this morning …?" It suddenly dawned on him.

Bob's eyes widened. "Of course!"

Angus looked at his friend, puzzled.

Gavin walked over to Angus and led him a little distance away from the others with his arm around him. He told him about the head he'd found outside his home earlier that morning. Angus cried again. The others looked away, waiting for them to return.

"We're going to check if it is Jimmy. Angus would like to bury him. I'll let the boys here fill you in on everything. I'll be back later."

"Very well, Gavin," Bob said.

Gavin walked Angus to his car.

"And Angus?"

Angus looked back at Bob.

"We're always here for you. If ever you need anything. Day or night. Don't hesitate to call or come, okay?"

Angus nodded.

Bob felt for Angus who lived alone on his farm. His wife, Wendy, had died of a heart attack a couple of years ago. Angus had found her one morning on their kitchen floor. They had no children.

"Where's Benji, Uncle?"

"He's fine, lad. He's asleep in the living room. Betty's having a lie-down as well. She was complaining of a headache."

"How was she acting?"

"She was a little odd, I have to admit. Like you said. I'm sure she's fine. Or she will be, after she's slept off her headache. I think it's her way of dealing with things, you know? Oh, and here's your phone. You had a message on it, too. I didn't read it." Bob pulled out David's phone and handed it back to him.

Grant had asked how they were getting on. David would reply later.

"Did you speak with Derek and Jack?" David put the phone in his pocket.

"I did. I put the notes back upstairs in your case too, thanks. They took a little convincing."

"What did they say?" John asked.

The three stood in the rain.

"Let's get under some cover." Bob walked under the arched porch. "They couldn't believe things at first. The photos helped. I offered them full pay and temporary leave, but they insisted on staying and helping. I just hope they don't regret it ... Anyway, did you find anything useful from the forest? Anything that we can perhaps go on? Anything at all?" Bob looked hopefully at David and John.

"Perhaps we'd better go inside," John replied. "I could do with a cup of tea." He jokingly threw David a glare for having missed out on one earlier. He then smiled.

*****

"That's what the tree looked like ..." John showed Bob the photo. "I thought David was a goner!"

"Thank God, you're all okay," Bob replied.

They sat again around the kitchen table.

"Have you been that far into the forest, to that particular part? You've never seen that tree or the clearing before?" David asked, scratching his nose.

Bob shook his head. "I don't recall. Or maybe it wasn't a clearing at the time? I certainly would have remembered that tree, though." Bob tried hard to remember. Surely if he had come across such a clearing and tree, he would have remembered it. "Tell me more about that forest ranger that you spoke to."

"There really isn't much else to tell, Uncle. Other than what we've already said. He was just one scary looking guy. He knows about the farm and that we're staying here. It worries me."

*****

A while later, they heard Angus' car return to drop Gavin off.

Gavin pulled out a chair, turned it around and sat on it backwards, resting his strong arms on the top of it.

"How's Angus?" Bob asked.

"Pretty cut up, boss. It was indeed poor Jimmy. He recognised the markings on the back of his head. I really feel for the guy. Him staying on the farm by himself. It may not even be safe for him there. At least there's a few of us here. He said to tell you as well that he's definitely moving his animals to a safe location, and if you want to do the same, he'll help you out."

"I'm definitely considering it."

"I take it these two have told you about what we discovered in the forest?"

Bob nodded his head. "We were just discussing further about that forest ranger you came across."

"Harold? Yes, that was one strange looking bloke. The way he spoke as well. He seemed threatening towards us. I'm thinking we should call the police?"

"I don't know ... what do we tell them? That some creepy guy in the forest sounded threatening? It isn't enough to go on. They won't do anything, unless it's more substantial," Bob replied.

"I guess so." Gavin bit one of his dirty nails. "What did Derek and Jack have to say?"

"I think they believed it. Perhaps not completely. Jack as you know, thought it was a wind-up to begin with. He said he isn't bothered with it." Bob half-smiled. "Him and Derek, want to continue working."

"Typical Jack, acting the tough guy." Gavin gave a slight smile back.

"What do we do next? All this weird stuff is happening, and we have no idea who is behind it or why? It's like we're at a dead end already," David said, throwing his arms up in the air in frustration. They had only been at the farm for a day. Already, David felt annoyed that they weren't getting anywhere and had no leads to go on. He didn't want to wait for the next bad thing to happen; he wanted to be proactive, rather than reactive.

"I understand your frustrations and eagerness to get to the bottom of this, David. We all do. Rome wasn't built in a day. I think we already have something to go on with this Harold character. I can check online later, see if there is some website or information about these forest rangers. There has to be something. Even if Harold isn't his real name, it could be a lead … just that tiny bit of information could get us going." Bob tried his upmost to sound upbeat. "I'll make ham sandwiches for us all. Derek and Jack, too. Then I need to pop into Aviemore to do some shopping and pick up some stuff for the farm."

# Chapter Twenty

## 12th July, 2018

It was after half two in the afternoon. The rain had stopped, though the skies were still cloudy grey.

They had all eaten lunch apart from Betty, who was still asleep. Bob decided to let her be whilst he went to Aviemore.

Gavin was doing the daily mucking out. David had Benji by his side and was with Derek, who was milking a cow. John was with Jack again, burning some rubbish along with the tree and shrub cuttings from the previous day.

Jack had his T-shirt off revealing his white, untanned body. He walked towards the fire carrying a bundle of twigs and branches in his arms. He dumped the pile on the fire, prompting a puff of smoke and flames. Embers twirled above. "Ye cannae beat a burn up. That's for sure!" Jack said, brushing off some dirt from his bare chest.

"What does the tattoo mean?" John asked.

"That?" Jack looked down his left leg. The tattoo on Jack's calf was a burgundy heart shape. "That would be a tattoo of my beloved *Hearts*!"

"Hearts?" John sounded confused.

"Aye. Ye know? The Scottish football team … *The Mighty Jambos*."

"Oh. Sorry, mate. I think I've heard of them. I don't follow football too much. David does more than me."

"Ye what? Ye prefer netball, something like that?" Jack joked.

"I like watching football. Playing it, too. Like other sports."

"Ha," Jack said. He pulled out a large joint from his shorts pocket, flipping it into his mouth and lit it. His face and neck were red from the heat of the fire. "Ahhhh." He tilted his head back and exhaled. He blew some smoke rings into the air. The smell of the marijuana was strong. Jack took in another drag and held it in for longer before exhaling, spluttering as he did so. "Argh. This is some good shit … ye want some?"

"Sure!" John enthusiastically replied.

Jack handed the joint over.

John looked about in case Bob returned and saw them, before putting it between his lips.

"Don't worry about Bobby," Jack said. "He's fine with it. As long as I'm not out me head!" He grinned.

John took a few drags and coughed himself.

"Told ye it was good shit!"

"Aye." John nodded as he bent down coughing.

Jack laughed and John handed the joint back to him.

Jack smoked the rest, then threw the butt onto the fire that was beginning to die down a little. He picked up a few more twigs and branches, throwing them onto the flames. His eyes had become bloodshot and watery from the weed. "So, ye believe all this nonsense about what's going on around here?"

"You saw the evidence, didn't you? The notes and photos?"

"Aye. That I did. Don't get me wrong. I believe that something *is* happening around here. Some nutters for sure. But monsters, supernatural stuff? Nae way. Not possible."

John could understand in part where Jack was coming from. He supposed he couldn't blame him, but still, he felt a little annoyed. "Then how do you explain those prints in particular? What we saw on the motorway?"

"I'm sure there's something that could explain it, aye?"

"Like what?"

"I'm sure ye'll find out in due course." Jack shrugged.

John was tempted to tell Jack about the tree in the forest. He couldn't be bothered. He felt like he was wasting his time. He guessed that Jack would soon find out how extreme things were getting. As they all would. He stood staring at the dying flames, his face glowing with the warmth. He wondered how David was getting on with Derek, and whether he was as sceptical as Jack …

*****

The portable milking machine wasn't working correctly over at the cow pen. Derek had said it was the vacuum that wasn't working properly, so they had to milk the cow manually. David wasn't paying too much attention. He was thinking about Harold, the forest ranger they had seen. His creepy laugh was haunting David. He was worried for Benji. This Harold, could even be watching them now, from within the forest.

Derek had disappeared. After a short while, he came back carrying a metal bucket filled with warm, soapy water. A small cloth was floating on the surface. "Yeah, so it can be quite painful for the cows if the machine isn't working correctly."

David found Derek's simple Scottish accent, light and easy to understand, perhaps because of his monotone voice. He was still distracted; "What's that?" He stared down at Benji who was licking one of his paws.

Seeing the cows and other animals didn't bother Benji in the slightest.

"I said it can be painful for the cows if the milking machine isn't working right."

"Oh." David then looked down at Derek who had placed the bucket next to the cow.

"It takes a little while longer to milk a cow by hand as opposed to using a machine. It's always best to first clean the teats with either iodine or just plain soapy water."

David nodded his head slightly.

Derek swashed the cloth in the foamy water and then wrung it out. He then gently wiped the teats. He pulled out a dry cloth from his overalls and carefully dried the teats and udder.

The cow mooed.

"Warm water always helps to extract the milk." Derek then stood up. He placed another bucket, this one empty, under the cow's udder. It was swollen and looked ready to burst. "She's a good girl, this one. Candy's her name." Derek pointed to her blue collar with her name on it.

"I see."

"Bob took her in a couple of months ago, from a place where the owners were moving and selling what cattle they had. They were concerned that she might end up going to slaughter. She lost her calf not long after giving birth, but she's still producing milk. It's uncomfortable for her if we don't milk her."

"That's sad … Can you not tell the animals apart without the collar?"

"Some, you can. It depends on their markings. Sometimes it's easy to forget, aye." Derek smiled. He then sat on a small wooden stool. He lubricated his hands with some Vaseline to avoid friction and discomfort for Candy, then gripped the bucket with his legs to stop it from getting kicked over. He started to squeeze on a couple of the teats. After a few seconds, milk squirted out and splashed into the empty bucket.

The bucket was rapidly filling with warm milk.

*****

"… You should always check for mastitis, too … You seem preoccupied, David? Are you thinking about all this bad stuff that's happening?"

David wondered how Derek could appear so calm. But then Derek hadn't been through what he and the others had. "Yeah, I am, Derek. What do you make of it?"

Derek had almost finished milking Candy. Her udder now looked deflated. He looked round at David. "I've always believed in the supernatural; I saw a ghost once … I remember as a child, around eleven or twelve, we used to have a woods near where we lived. About a ten-minute walk. One day, I went with my friend, Freddy, his name was, for a kick-about there. They used to have this bit of a grassy patch there.

"Freddy was in goal; we used our jumpers as goal posts and I kicked the ball and it went into the woods." Derek laughed. "I went to fetch it and saw some little girl, just standing there in the woods in a yellow dress. No expression on her face. Just staring right at me. I picked the ball up, looked up and she'd gone. Just vanished."

"You sure it was a ghost?" David sounded doubtful.

"Aye. She looked pale, white looking. She just seemed to have vanished."

"I see."

"About what's been happening here and to you, it's hard to get my brain around it, you know?"

"That's understandable."

"I definitely agree that something isn't right. Like those whispers. Things disappearing and being moved … just a strange sensation." Derek got up from the stool. "I'm sure we will be fine. Your Uncle Bob will sort it out. Anyway, would you like me to show you how to milk a cow, aye?"

"Erm. Okay." David wasn't sure. He thought he may as well give it a try …

"You're doing okay. Always remember to squeeze the base of the teat. Then squeeze down. Don't loosen the grip at the base; otherwise, the milk goes back up to the cow's udder. You've definitely got the hang of it, I'd say. Makes your hands ache, doesn't it?"

"All right?" John interrupted, joining them. His face had a touch of black soot on it from the fire. He crouched down to watch David finish milking the cow.

"You stink of smoke," David said.

"I bet you're *well* tempted to suck on them teats, eh?" John joked.

David grinned back and squirted John in the face.

"Urgh." John laughed. He wiped his face with his top.

"Least that cleaned your sooty face up." David grinned.

Derek joined the laughter. His laugh sounded deep, dull and stupid. "I'll finish up here, David; I only need to put the milk into the holding tank."

"Great, Derek; thanks for the tutorial," David replied amiably.

John and David set off back to the farmhouse for a drink. The smoke from the fire lingered in the air as they walked.

"How much do you think we should give my uncle, like for food and stuff? He probably won't accept it, but I'm going to insist."

"We could give him fifty quid for now? Twenty-five each?"

"We should. Especially as we don't know how long we're going to be here for … What did Jack say about everything?"

"He wasn't buying it really … he knows things are happening, of course. But he doesn't really believe anything supernatural is going on. What about Derek?" John rubbed his eye.

"Derek isn't completely sure. He believes that something paranormal is perhaps happening. He's a nice guy. Although, I also think he's pretty gullible and would believe anything."

They turned the corner of the farmhouse and walked in through the front door. Benji slumped down in the hallway. They went upstairs to get some money each. As they entered the kitchen, Betty was just standing there, staring out the back door to the garden, humming.

"Hum, hum, hum, hum, hum, hum …"

"Aunt Betty? Are you okay?"

"Hum, hum, hum, hum, hum, hum …" she continued.

David walked over and placed a hand on her shoulder. "Betty?"

"Hum, hum, hum, hum, hum, hum …"

John frowned.

Her humming stopped abruptly. She turned her head slowly to the left and stared straight into David's eyes. Her pupils were dilated.

David felt a chill.

Suddenly, she snapped out of her gaze, shook her head and blinked her eyes. "Oh. Hello, David. And hello to you too, John." Betty smiled, giving John a nod.

"Are you okay?" David removed his hand from her shoulder.

"Why wouldn't I be, dear? I feel refreshed after my nap." She smiled again. It made David feel uncomfortable. She walked past them going outside through the front door.

John and David looked at each other.

"What the fuck was all that about?"

"I have no idea. She's been acting strange since this morning. Something isn't right. I'll tell my uncle once he gets back."

"The way she looked at you … *man*, that was scary."

"I know."

They rinsed out a couple of glasses and left the tap running to clear the hard, foggy water, before pouring some to drink.

John sighed in relief as he gulped down the refreshing drink in one go. He washed out his glass and placed it back onto the draining board. "So, what next?"

"I feel like I need to clear my head for a bit. Maybe take Benji for a walk. Somewhere different." David held the glass in his hand, taking his time with it.

"Like go for a drive? I'm up for that. Check out the area a little."

"It's best if we wait until Bob gets back. He should be back soon, I'd imagine."

They heard Bob's car outside.

"Speak of the devil," said John.

They went to greet Bob, who was carrying a couple of carrier bags. One had food in it. A loaf of bread was protruding out of the top. A hand fork had pierced through the other bag.

"Take these for us, would you, David? Just whack them in the hallway there. Be careful of that fork sticking out." Bob smiled.

David happily took the bags from his uncle.

Bob returned to his Land Rover for a new shovel and a garden tiller. He propped the tools up against the wall and hung his cap on the coat stand. "How's your afternoon been, boys?" Bob scratched the side of his head.

"It was good. I milked a cow for the first time in my life," answered David.

"Ah, that's good." Bob smiled again.

David checked outside the front door to make sure that Betty wasn't in earshot. She had now appeared on the front lawn with her back to them, staring aimlessly at the forest.

Bob saw David gaze past him. He turned and looked over his shoulder towards his wife and then back at his nephew. "What is it, David?"

"It's Aunt Betty. She's acting strange."

"Strange how?"

"We came into the kitchen just now and she was just standing there, staring out the door. Just like she is now." David nodded his head at Betty.

"Only she was humming. It was like she was miles away. When I approached her, she turned and gave me this ice-cold stare. Her pupils were dilated. Then she blinked and snapped out of whatever trance she was in."

Bob looked to John as if for affirmation.

"It's true," John replied, screwing his mouth up. "Something definitely seems up with her. It was like she was in a world of her own, mate."

Bob sighed. He turned back to Betty who was still just standing there. He shook his head. "I guess everything has affected her more than I thought. Perhaps we shouldn't have told her everything. Just kept quiet for now."

David sensed it was something else. Something darker that was changing her behaviour. But for now, he didn't feel like worrying his uncle. He wasn't sure what they could do about it if that were the case.

"I'll go see if she's okay," Bob said.

"Oh, just one more thing, Uncle."

Bob turned back round.

"I think it's only fair that me and John pay our way and chip in with things. For food and stuff."

Bob raised his hand. "I appreciate that, David. Honestly, you two don't have to do that. We appreciate having you both here and you're also helping out on the farm. If anything, I owe you. It really isn't necessary."

"Even so. We feel it's the right thing to do. I insist. Not taking no for an answer." David smiled.

"Okay. If you must." Bob smiled back.

John pulled out two crumpled notes and handed them to David. David noted their state and made a tut.

"What? You want me to iron them out?" John half-joked.

David added his own notes and handed them to his uncle who reluctantly accepted. "This ought to cover it for a bit."

Bob felt awkward accepting their money. As David was adamant on paying him, he put the money in his pocket.

"You don't mind if me and John pop out, do you? Take Benji out as well for a little while. It would be good to see more of the area. If you don't mind that is?"

"Of course I don't mind. Don't be silly. Just because you're staying with us, it doesn't mean you have to feel obliged to work here, and not be able to do what you like. You two can come and go as you please. As you see fit. Do anything you want, guys."

"I wouldn't mind a pint somewhere. I do fancy one," John stated.

"There's actually a nice little pub not too far from here as it happens. Well, it's not exactly close. It's near the outskirts of the forest. A twenty-minute drive or so. That's the closest pub to us. They do a really nice ale. The food is very good there as well. It's a lovely little pub. Me and Betty used to go once or twice a week. We haven't been for a few weeks, now. Alistair is the owner there. Goes by the nickname, 'Jock.' Friendly chap. Wicked sense of humour. You'd meet your match there, John. Well, if you can understand him, that is!"

John laughed.

"What's the name of this pub, Uncle?"

"The Auld Drongair Bàrd."

"Huh?" John looked puzzled.

"It means 'The Old Drunkard Bard.'" Bob smiled.

"Ah. Gotcha … What's a 'bard?'" John frowned.

"Don't you know anything?" David half-smiled, shaking his head. "It's basically a poet. Someone who sings. Stuff like that."

John pouted and raised his eyebrows, nodding.

"I'd happily join you two, but I've got work to do here. Plus, I need to keep an eye on Betty. I'll give you the directions."

"Sounds good," replied David. "Maybe we can ask about there, too. See if anyone knows anything?"

"You could. There are a few regulars who go there. It's their favourite haunt. A few get drunk. Their accents are even harder to understand after they've been drinking! Some can get quiet rowdy as well after work. Especially on a Friday and Saturday night. Nothing bad like. Usually just banter between the folk. Nothing to be worried about. It's a friendly pub, really. I imagine that it will be quieter on a week day after lunch. There's a couple of nice girls who work behind the bar there and they serve food, too." Bob winked at the pair.

John's eyes lit up. For David, women were the last thing on his mind. He couldn't allow himself to get side-tracked. There were more important things at hand. *Dangerous things.*

"Whilst you're out, I'll try and look into this 'Harold' guy as well. I already asked someone at the store who I see regularly. He wasn't too sure about there being any forest rangers here. He hadn't given it much thought, like myself. Though he did say, it seemed to ring a bell. I've never seen any rangers around here. I'll look after Betty whilst you're gone, David. She'll be fine." Bob put a hand on David's shoulder and smiled. "And tell Jock, I said 'Hi.' It's been a while!"

David took a leak before they left whilst John sat in his car waiting, along with Benji. David saw his aunt and uncle walking along the bottom of the front lawn. Bob had his arm around Betty and was speaking in her left ear, no doubt some words of comfort and support. Betty had her head down. She seemed unresponsive. Bob looked over and waved. David half-smiled, raised his hand and went up to the barn where John had pulled the car out and was texting someone on his phone.

"All right?" John said, looking over at David. "Granty just texted me."

"Cool. What's he up to?"

"Not much. He's still feeling bad about not coming up here. He said he's got someone coming over to his folks later. A friend of his dad's who wants help with his computer."

"If anyone can sort out a computer, it's Grant." David fastened his seat belt.

John snorted in amusement.

"What is it?" David asked curiously.

"Just a joke he's sent; 'What's the difference between marmalade and jam?'"

"Go on ..."

"You can't 'marmalade' your dick, down a girl's throat!"

David shook his head and laughed.

John was pleasantly surprised when his engine started first time without any problems. "Fancy that!" He was surprised again, pointing to the clock on the dashboard. It was now working fine, reading two minutes to three.

"Odd," David said.

"Maybe everything is going to be all right now, eh?"

Neither of them believed that.

John made his way across the back of the farmhouse to the dirt track opposite the one they had arrived on yesterday morning. He pulled up next to Gavin who was carrying a heavy bucket full of grain and bird seed. Some chopped up vegetables were also in the mix.

"All right, Gav?" John asked, sticking his head out of the window.

"You boys off out?"

"Yeah. We thought we'd take Benji for a walk somewhere. Check out the area a bit, you know? Go for a pint as well at the Old Bard," David replied.

"The Auld Drongair Bàrd, you mean?" Gavin smiled.

"That's it," David said back.

"Nice little pub that. Was there only last week for a meal and a couple of pints. I'd join you both but I have some stuff to finish off here before the night shift." Gavin switched the bucket to his other hand. His shoulder had started to ache.

"You and Bob doing it again?" John asked. "You ought to get a couple of security guards, instead."

"Yeah." Gavin half-laughed. "I'm probably going to have a nap at the house for a couple of hours or so before."

"Have you seen Betty much today?" asked David.

"Not too much, really. Why do you ask?"

"She just seems, well, sort of off." David scratched his ear.

"I see. Rest assured, I'll make sure she's okay and keep an extra eye out for her. It's probably the shock of these past couple of weeks. Especially, the last few days. I better go feed the chooks. I'll see you boys later on. Enjoy your pints."

"Will do. I could do with a drink or two after what we've been through. Even more so, after this morning!" David replied.

"See you later." John drove towards the exit. He beeped his horn at Derek and Jack who were in conversation near the pens. They both gave a friendly wave.

*****

"Blimey. Going this way makes you realise how enclosed the farm really is, doesn't it?" John looked across at David.

David was staring out of the window at the vast trees that surrounded them. He wondered what other dark things lurked within. He couldn't help thinking about that Harold in there. Watching them. And his aunt. Had something taken a hold of her? If so, what? "Huh? Oh. Yeah, trees, everywhere."

"You all right? You seem miles away."

"Just worrying about Betty and in general."

"Yeah … something isn't quite right with her. Maybe she's just feeling the strain after everything?" John eased off the accelerator, approaching a sharp bend.

"You don't honestly believe that, do you?"

"Why wouldn't I?"

"Am I the only one who think it's more than that?"

"What are you trying to get at, mate?"

"I know it's been tough on Betty … I'm just thinking that something has maybe taken a hold of her, you know?"

"What? You mean like possessed?"

"Sort of. Not so much possessed as such. Just. Well. I don't know. Something affecting her directly."

"I hear yer. I suppose after everything that's happened, I guess it's a big possibility. Normally, I'd say it was a stupid idea. But from what we've seen so far, if things were more normal, we wouldn't even be having this conversation!"

"I keep thinking about that Harold bloke as well."

"You too, huh? I mean, he was quite a *dish*, wasn't he?" John winked at David who managed to smile. "And that eye of his … oooo, baby. He was a dream all right."

They both laughed.

"You really are something else, John."

"Once we get out this never-ending forest, we'll find a spot where we can let Benji have a run. Then let's head on over to that pub. Get a couple of pints down us." John took his eyes off the road.

"Sounds good."

"Be interesting to see what these barmaids look like as well …"

*"John!"*

Benji's ears pricked up from the back.

"What?" John returned his eyes to the road and saw a red deer standing there. *"Shit!"* He pressed heavily on the brakes. It was like the figure on the motorway all over again.

The car screeched, gradually coming to a stop a few feet away from the deer who stood unfazed, staring at them. After a few seconds, it casually trotted off into the forest.

"Jeez. That was a close one." John breathed a sigh of relief. He rubbed his face with his hand.

Benji sat up in the back seat, his tongue hanging out.

"You really need to start paying more attention to the road, mate," David warned.

"Okay, *Dad*."

"That's the last thing we need. To write the car off or have an accident and be stranded out here." David looked at his phone. "There's no signal out here again."

Once they had composed themselves, John continued.

Further back down the road, a gangly figure stood, watching them drive off. It was Harold. David's paranoia had proved correct. Harold was indeed watching them. He was standing in the middle of the road, grinning widely, his hands by his side. Both were dripping with blood.

# Chapter Twenty-One

## 12th July, 2018

Once they had finally exited the thick forest, they let Benji out for a run a mile or so further on. They then followed Uncle Bob's directions, pulling into the car park at the rear of The Auld Drongair Bàrd, which was practically empty, apart from three other cars.

John parked up next to a yellow Lotus Elise. "Check out that baby." He looked with awe at the sports car.

"Nice."

David let Benji out of the back and they walked round to the front and stood there, looking at the pub and its black thatched roof and large chimney at the left side. The pub was fairly secluded off a country road, surrounded by a few unfarmed fields, some grassland and a small poppy field. Another part of Rothiemurchus Forest was in the distance, overlooked by beautiful green-brown hills and the Cairngorms mountain range. The crest appeared slightly blue on the horizon. Ben Macdui, the highest point, was also visible.

A few people were sitting in the small beer garden to the left on a patio under a black umbrella, each with their pints in front of them.

"I suppose it's all right to bring dogs in here?" David presumed.

"Bah. Course it is. If they let a bunch of smelly Jocks in, dogs would be a step up!" John joked.

At the front of the pub, the benches and tables appeared pretty stained and dirty. Some were damaged with missing chunks. A half-torn beer mat sat on one of the tables. Cigarette butts were squashed out on the concrete floor. They noticed more butt ends in the plant pots and wall-mounted, dented metal ashtray, shaped like a closed fist; it was full to the brim with ash. Someone had stuffed an empty crisp packet on top of it.

"You think that needs emptying?" John joked again, seeing the ashtray.

David smiled.

The pub looked like it was in need of a paint job. A yellowish stain looked as if someone had urinated or vomited there. David and John tried to hide their disgust. Above the tables and benches hung a sign that read *The Auld Drongair Bàrd.* It swayed and creaked in the gentle zephyr. The sign displayed a picture of an old man. He had a long, bushy white beard which matched his long white hair. He was sitting on a tree stump playing a lute. He wore a blue hat with a white feather, along with a loose, light green tunic.

"Guess that's the auld fart, eh?" John continued to joke.

They peered through one of the windows that had a half rubbed off *No Smoking* sign on the other side. It appeared quiet inside. The only person they could see was a man in a suit, who was sat at the bar reading a newspaper. He had a half-finished pint in front of him.

They made their way to the porch.

A pretty dark-haired girl walked out. She was wearing latex gloves, carrying a bacterial spray and a scourer in one hand, and a bin bag in the other. She made eye contact more with David. "Hello," she said in a soft voice and a welcoming smile. She sounded Irish.

John and David both smiled back. John stared at her pert backside in her blue Levi's. David gave John a firm nudge to warn him off staring.

"Ow! What's that for?"

The attractive girl looked back and smiled. She knelt down and squirted a few sprays onto the yellow stain. She had the cutest, perfect smile that David had ever seen. He smiled back. The girl blushed slightly, quickly turning her head and attempted to get rid of the stain. David thought she might have felt awkward cleaning up someone's vomit or piss in front of them, so he tried to usher John in. A window then opened above them; They looked up.

A man's head popped out and shouted down to the girl in a heavy Scottish accent, "Once ye done that, ye can go for your lunch, Emily. Take an extra half-hour, if ye want." The man looked over at John and David and smiled, nodding his head before slamming the window down.

"Okay, thank you," the girl replied. She looked over at David, smiling. She blushed again, before retackling the stain.

"Looks like somebody *likes yooou …*" John teased in David's ear.

"Shut up." David half-smiled.

They pushed open the red door and entered the pub.

The man in the black suit looked up at the two of them from the bar, giving a slight nod. He took a sip of his pint and returned to his paper, giving it a shake and turning one of the pages. He was indeed, the only one in here.

They walked slowly over to the bar making their way down a small step. Their feet making a slight, dull thump. Benji's small claws made a tapping sound on the hard surface. Scottish music was coming from somewhere in the kitchen with its flutes and bagpipes. It felt peaceful and serene.

The charming pub was quaint and cosy. The lighting helped provide a certain warmth to the place. It had a nice feel to it. A typical country pub feeling. Even though it had looked a little run down and dirty from the outside, inside, was quite a contrast. Even the wooden floor was shiny and immaculate.

At the end was a brick wall with a medium-sized fireplace. Above it, was a blackboard with the food menu written in perfect writing. John's stomach churned as he glanced over at the blackboard; *Jock's Special Burger - With Salad & Chips - Served With A Large Coke - £9.99*. He started to feel hungry again. Above the bar hung numerous pint glasses and above those, a collection of beer mats were fixed to the wall. A small plastic holder on the bar housed some taxi company business cards. A much smaller, propped up blackboard, also with perfect handwriting, displayed the drinks, beers and ale prices. Behind the bar, a signed football sat on the 'last orders bell' that was wedged in the corner against the wall. A green and white striped scarf that read CELTIC FC hung on the wall above several ale barrels. A sign below the scarf advertised as *Straight From The Barrel!*

John started to whistle quietly, tapping his feet and fingertips to the music whilst waiting to be served.

"Oi ... Jock. You out there? You've got a couple of customers."

John stopped whistling and tapping. Along with David, he looked across at the man in the suit who had called out.

He didn't look up. He placed his newspaper on the bar and knocked back the last of his pint. "That old Scottish bastard is busy doing something and neglecting his duties where it matters. Out here." He sounded English.

"It's er, okay if I bring my dog in here, isn't it?" David asked.

"Sure. Jock has a dog himself he lets wander around the place. Bloody old thing that is. Should have it put down." The well-suited man sounded abrupt, so it was hard for David and John to tell if he was joking or serious.

There were a few seconds of silence.

"That's not your Lotus parked out back, is it?" John asked.

"Yep. That it is," replied the man.

"Bloody nice car ... only thing is, I bumped it slightly, reversing in."

"You did what?"

"Ah. *Gotcha*! Only messing with you."

The man in the suit didn't respond. He continued to stare at John.

John dropped his smile.

"That's a good one!" the man then said, giving a nod. He smiled slightly. "Where is that Scottish git?"

"Aye, I hear ye! I'll be out in a minute," a voice shouted out from the kitchen.

"So, what brings you here, then?" the man asked.

"Like most reasons people come to a pub … for a drink!" John grinned sarcastically. "You a regular?"

"I guess you could say that. Been coming here for the past six or seven years or so on and off. The name's Simon."

"I'm John. This is David. We're currently staying at his uncle's farm for a bit."

"I see," Simon replied. "Well, it's good to have a couple more English guys about. I take it you're both English, like me, judging by your southern accents."

"That we are," David answered. "How about you? What brings you here? What do you do, if you don't mind me asking?"

"Actually, I do bloody mind! Hah. Only kidding. I'm a stockbroker. I'm currently up in this hellhole of a country on business. Several times a year, I have to come up here." Simon sounded like he didn't enjoy the trips. "Not to mention how long it takes."

"It's not so bad up here," David said.

"What? You have to travel all the way up here? Can't you just sit in an office all day and do things over the phone and the internet?" John asked.

"Hah. If only! There's more to it than meets the eye. I suppose it's not all bad. It gets me about. Good money, too. I have to travel about at times, seeing clients and what not. What about you two?"

"We, erm. We just got made redundant actually. So …" David felt embarrassed.

"Yeah. But we don't care. We've got enough to survive on at the moment. Right, Dave?" John slapped hard on his friend's back.

David winced.

"Bummer … never good to lose your job. Particularly through no fault of your own. Happened to me once. Years ago. Got a fair bit of redundancy, though. Every cloud has a silver lining, eh?"

"I guess so," David muttered.

"Argh … sorry about that, men. I was having a wee bit of trouble with me Wi-Fi. What can I do for ye?" Jock gave the two friends a friendly smile and placed his large hands on the bar. His accent was thick and hard to understand.

"I'll have another one when you've served these two lovers, Jock," Simon said, shaking his empty glass.

Jock looked across at Simon, then back at John and David. "Lovers, eh? We got a couple of poofters in here, aye?"

Simon laughed loudly.

David was about to speak, but John beat him to it. "Aye! We're on our honeymoon up here," John mocked in a reasonable Scottish accent. He always gave as good as he got. "We're here to see the bard, as well!"

Jock let out a huge laugh.

The girl cleaning the stain outside looked in through the window, curious to see what was happening.

"That's a good one, sonny," Jock said. "Well, ye'll fit right in here, then. We get a lot of your type in here. Don't we, Si?" Jock winked at Simon.

"Sure do."

"Argh. I'm only teasing ye both. Even if ye were, it wouldn't bother me, nae. Each to their own. Nae problem with any of that. Besides, Simon … I saw them out me window, checking out our Emily and her bahookie! Can't say I blame them, neither. She's a wee, good-looking little lass, aye?"

"Yep. Can't blame them for that."

The four men looked through the window at Emily, who was now removing cigarette butts from one of the plant pots. David again caught her eye. She smiled shyly.

"Aw. She's a little cutie that one, all right. Anyway, welcome to me humble establishment … what can I do for ye both?"

Alistair John McConalogue was in his early sixties, a well-built Glaswegian of five-foot ten and a half, and always game for a laugh. He had a full head of brown and grey hair with greying, bushy sideburns. He wore a black Celtic Football Club polo shirt over his blue jeans. On one forearm, was a faded tattoo of the Scottish flag and on the other, a small red heart with the word *Mum*, underneath. He had never married. He was a well-travelled man and fondly appreciated by his punters, who all called him Jock. They also believed him to be the epitome of a Scot.

"Just a lager tops for me, please mate," David replied.

"Make that two," John added.

"Coming right up." Jock grabbed a couple of fresh pint glasses from under the bar and pulled gently on the beer pump. "Do ye live around here, laddies?"

"Nah. We're staying on my uncle's farm for a while. Just erm, helping out, you know?"

"Aye. And which farm may that be?"

"Sorry. Say again?"

"What farm is that?" Jock spoke slowly in an English accent to help David to understand. It was a poor attempt, making them laugh.

"Hamish Farm. My uncle is Bob Hammond and his wife is Betty."

"Aye, I know them … lovely couple. Not seen them for a wee while." Jock poured some lemonade on top of the frothy beer heads.

"He recommended your pub to us. He said to say 'Hi,' as he hasn't been in for a while."

"Yeah, there's not many other options around here," John joked. "I suppose the pub is quite good."

"Ye cheeky sod. And ye bloody right it's good!" Jock joked back. "Tell them both I send me regards and to get their arses back down here." Jock refilled Simon's empty glass, looking up at David.

"That I will. How much do we owe you for the beers?" David asked.

"Argh." Jock motioned his right hand. "Put ye dough away. These one's are on the house … not making a habit of it, though!"

"You sure?"

"Aye."

"Kind of you, bud," John said, wiping the foam from the beer off his upper lip. "Surprising, for a Scot," he then joked.

"Ye cheeky bastard!" Jock laughed back.

"Add that last one to my tab will you, Jock?" Simon asked.

Jock carefully placed the refilled pint in front of Simon. "Ye already owe me fifty quid!" He pulled out a notepad from under the bar and added the pint under Simon's name, together with his previous orders.

"You know I'm good for it."

"Aye." Jock sounded annoyed.

David wondered why a man who possessed an expensive car and had a high paid job, so he said, would need a tab.

John took a larger sip from his lager and looked across at the blackboard. "Would it be okay to order some food?"

"We stop serving food at three, laddie."

"Oh." John was disappointed.

"What did ye want?"

"Well … your 'Special Burger,' of course!" John replied sarcastically. "Minus the drink."

"Good choice! Tell ye what … I'll make an exception for ye."

"Sweet! What's so special about it, anyway?" John cheekily grinned.

"Ye'll have to see …" Jock flicked his bushy eyebrows up and down.

"You're not going to spit in it, are you?" John joked again.

"Ha!" Jock laughed. "Ye ruined the surprise now, laddie."

"It is okay to bring my dog in here, isn't it?" David thought he'd better check with Jock.

"Aye. Ye can. As long as we've stopped serving food that is. Sometimes it's all right. Depending on folk." Jock disappeared into the kitchen to make John's burger.

Emily came back in. Benji began wagging his tail as she walked past them. She stroked him briefly and glanced over at David. She lifted up the bar flap and then she too disappeared into the kitchen. They could hear her tell Jock she had cleaned up outside and she asked if it was okay to have her lunch break, once she'd taken the rubbish out to the skip. Jock confirmed it was fine, and to take her time.

"You got much on this afternoon then, Simon?" John asked.

Simon didn't reply at first; he just stared into his pint. He looked troubled. "Huh? What's that?" He averted his eyes away from his temporarily untouched pint, towards John's direction.

"Have you got much planned for this afternoon?"

"Just business, really. This and that," Simon replied glumly. He looked down at his left palm, moving his wedding ring up and down with his thumb.

"What do you make of the area up here? You ever been in Rothiemurchus Forest? That's where my uncle's farm is," David asked. He felt a little uncomfortable as it now appeared Simon wasn't interested in conversation. His mind was clearly occupied elsewhere.

"A farm in the forest? Sounds a little peculiar." Simon finally took a drink from his glass. He swallowed. "Can't say I've ever been in that forest, if I'm honest with you. Sure, I've seen it, even driven through it, but not been in there per se. I'm not overly keen on Scotland. Though to be fair, these parts are nice, scenic, with the mountains in the distance as well. I've certainly been to worse places in Scotland, believe me!" Simon put his pint down on one of the green bar towels.

David took a swig of his. The glass was cold to touch and slightly frosted. The pint flowed refreshingly down his throat. "You, erm, you ever noticed anything strange around here at all?" David felt silly asking.

"Strange? In what sense? If you mean a bunch of smelly, foul-mouthed, drunken Jocks, then yeah, I have!" Simon laughed slightly.

A crash of pots and pans drew all their eyes towards the kitchen.

"Argh … bollocks!"

"You okay in there?" Simon called out.

"Aye. Bleedin' pots."

They could hear Jock banging them back wherever it was they went.

*****

John and David had taken their pints to one of the tables next to a window. Benji laid on the floor, half-dozing. There were a few spots of rain materialising on the windowpanes. The three were still the only customers inside, when Jock, with a blue towel draped over his shoulder, brought out his burger for John.

"Here it comes." John looked and licked his lips slightly.

"Here ye go, laddie. Get this down ye! I even threw in some extra chips for ye …" Jock placed the food in front of John.

"Nice one!" John replied.

John's mouth started to water. Chips and a side salad with beetroot were packed around the burger which was plump and juicy in a toasted sesame bun. A cocktail stick held the burger together with a tiny Scottish flag.

David looked on.

"That's the finishing touch, that's what makes it special?" John pointed to the flag.

"Aye." Jock grinned, his hands on his broad hips. *"Bon appetite!"* Jock returned to the bar, wiping his hands on the towel and poured himself a small Coke, which he sunk in one go.

John lifted part of the bun and squirted some ketchup inside. Using a fork from the table, he added some salad. "Don't know how I'm going to eat this … too big to get my mouth around." He took out the small cocktail stick and cut the burger in half with a knife.

David watched as John took a huge bite of the burger and chomped away. He wished he'd ordered one as well and pinched a chip.

"Jesus … this has to be the best burger I've ever had." John gave a couple of hiccups.

Jock looked over from across the bar and smiled.

John took a few more bites. He hadn't touched any of his chips, so David pinched a few more.

"I told ye it was a good burger, aye?" Jock said proudly, looking over.

John's face was flushed slightly red due to the heat of the burger. He finished another bite and sipped his pint before responding. "Honestly, mate … it's the best burger I've ever had. Straight up!"

"Aye, I heard ye say. Flattery will get ye everywhere. Apart from me bed!" Jock joked.

Simon raised his head and smiled.

"We have a chef here; he has the day off today. But the burger, that's my baby. I always make sure *I* make them."

"Why's it so damn good?"

"A hundred percent Scotch beef, laddie. Ground. That's just the part of it. There's a way of making and cooking it. It's a skill, ye know? Certain seasoning as well."

By now, David was more than curious. He asked John to cut a chunk from the untouched half. The burger was still hot as he popped the segment of meat and bun into his mouth and chewed. "Bloody hell … that really does taste fantastic. I'm definitely going to make sure I order this if we come in again."

"Oh, we'll be back, all right," John confirmed, just as a woman leaving the beer garden with her fella caught his eye through the window.

*****

When David and John had finished eating, they returned to the bar. A few more customers had arrived, mainly middle-aged. The pair ordered another two pints.

"How much do we owe?" John pulled out his bank card. "I'll get this."

"Call it nine pounds. This round is on the house, too. Seeing as ye first time punters. But seeing as I went out me way to do the burger, I'll have to charge ye for that. Business is business. I cannae let that one slide, nae." Jock winked and smiled.

"That's fine. Still really kind of you," John replied.

"Yeah, that's great. Thanks." David shifted on his stool. Part of the red cushion was coming away.

Simon, who still looked glum, finished his pint. "Put the burger on my tab, Jock. I'll be back tomorrow to pay it all off." He got up and tucked his stool under the bar and bent down to retrieve a long grey overcoat.

"I appreciate that, mate. Honestly, it's fine. It doesn't feel right to accept that." John was surprised at the gesture of goodwill, as was David and even more so, Jock, especially as they didn't know one another.

"Nonsense." Simon walked past the two. He touched Benji's head who tried to lick his hand in return. "I'll see you tomorrow, Jock. You boys take care, now." Simon gave a gentle pat on John's back, before heading out the front door and into the rear car park.

John raised his eyebrows and pouted. "I don't know what to do. He might feel insulted if I don't accept his generosity, but I want to pay."

"I am surprised. I've never seen him do that before, lad. Sod it. Take it as a compliment! I'll add it to his tab. He'll pay it. He always does. Not like he cannae afford it."

"What's up with him? He seemed sort of down and preoccupied," asked David.

"Aye. He's going through a rough patch. Some marriage difficulties. Been like that for a wee while now. Not good. He might be a little rough around the edges, but he's actually a nice guy. Don't tell him I said that though, aye!" Jock grinned.

"We won't." John smiled back, raising his hand.

"How long are ye up in Bonnie Scotland for, laddies?" Jock served a pint of beer and a glass of rosé for an elderly couple who came up to the bar.

There was an aroma of pungent perfume.

"We're not too sure, yet," David replied. "Guess we'll just have to see."

"Yeah," confirmed John, twiddling the cocktail stick between his teeth, "However long it takes."

The elderly couple paid for their drinks and went to sit down.

"Well, I'm sure ye'll find it a great place up here. There's plenty to do, aye. Walks, camping. Stuff like that. Lovely place. Though, it can get bloody *Baltic* during the winter!"

"I suppose so." David had no interest in any of the activities or the scenery up here. Normally, he would, in 'normal' circumstances.

"Ye should come to the disco we're having here, tomorrow night."

"Disco?" John queried.

"Aye ..." Jock leaned over the bar and pointed to a small flyer that was stuck onto part of the wall.

"Oh. Yeah, we might do," David responded, not exactly interested.

John paid attention as a blonde-haired girl entered, who was heavily stacked in the chest compartment. He tapped on David's shoulder eagerly for his attention. They both looked at the girl, who unbuttoned her jacket, hung it on a peg near the door and walked towards the bar.

Jock looked up. "Argh. Annabel, dear. Glad ye back. Could ye serve this gentleman here, please." Business was picking up.

"Sure … what would you like?" she smiled, asking the man in her pleasant Scottish accent.

"Your uncle was right. There are some *hot* girls working here," John said quietly in his friend's ear.

Annabel didn't hear John, but she looked up and half-acknowledged the two as she poured a pint of bitter.

David saw John staring at this Annabel's chest. He kicked him under the bar. John winced and dropped the cocktail stick from his mouth.

*****

They took their time with their final drinks. John needed to be careful as he was driving. Most of the customers had gone to sit outside, apart from the elderly couple. Annabel went around cleaning and wiping some of the tables. Jock was behind the bar taking a booking for a table for a group over the phone, for some time next week. David wanted to ask him more about the area and whether he had interference here on the phone lines.

"Okay, aye. We'll see ye all then, all right. Thanks." Jock placed the phone receiver back down and pulled out a booking diary from under the bar to write the details in.

"How long have you been here?" David asked.

"Since March, 1990; took over the pub not long after, in April," Jock answered proudly.

"Wow. Long time," John said.

"Aye, that it is! Don't regret it for a wee second. *Love it.*" Jock beamed. "Ye certainly meet some interesting characters as well."

"Have there been any weird things happening around the area since you've been here?" David asked.

"Ye hear all sorts of things down the years: people going missing, like in that forest. Just urban legends mainly. Myths, ye know? I doubt most stories are true." Jock stood with his arms folded over his slight belly.

"What sort of things? Care to elaborate?" John smiled.

"Argh. I cannae remember too much specifically off the top of me head … there is one though, I do recall, around the late nineties: a wee boy disappeared. He was never found, bless him. I cannae remember his name. Other peeps too, have disappeared. Supposedly. Others have reported strange sounds and fires coming from certain parts of the forest as well, aye."

"You haven't witnessed anything yourself, as such?" David shifted.

"Nae. Not personally. I do walk me mutt from time to time near the forest; Penny. She's an old lass. On her last legs, I think." Jock suddenly looked sad. "She never seems to like to go further in that forest. Nae idea why ... maybe because she's old and tired."

"You find anything creepy about the forest?" John asked.

"Me? Nae. I'm not scared of anything. I'm ex-army. The things I've seen!" Jock smiled, pulling up the top of his right sleeve to show another faded tattoo on his shoulder as proof. It looked like a silver eagle with the name *Waterloo* underneath it, and *Royal Scots Dragoon Guards* written on a scroll. "Though, it does sometimes feel like someone is watching ye in that forest. Nae doubt just paranoia, after all the stories ye hear down the years, aye."

"What about your phone, Jock? Have you had interference on the landline, the same as with a mobile?" David asked. "We sometimes get it on the farm."

"Not really, laddie. Sometimes the signal might go at times, like me Wi-Fi! But cannae say I've heard any interference or anything like that."

Annabel, who had finished cleaning the tables, couldn't help but overhear some of the conversation, along with the elderly couple who were sitting not far from John and David.

"Little *Charlie Begsbie* ..." the woman in her sixties suddenly said.

Everyone turned to look at her.

"What's that, dear?" Jock asked.

"That was the name of the little boy that went missing ... he was only nine. Coming on ten."

"Aye. That's right, lass! That was the name of the toatey bairn. I've remembered."

"It was the summer of 1999. He was with his parents, out camping in the forest when he disappeared," the woman continued.

Annabel lent up against one of the tables next to the couple, listening.

"What happened?" John's eyebrows lowered. He tried desperately hard to keep eye contact with the woman, rather than stare at Annabel's chest.

"It was the second night, I think ... he was the only child. Just him and his parents. They shared the same tent because he was still young. They heard some strange noises during the night that kept them awake. They were quite far into the forest too, if I recall."

"What kind of noises?" David asked.

"Whispering."

John and David's eyes became large.

"There were other sounds as well. The sound of twigs breaking, as if someone was walking around outside their tent, yet no one or anything was ever there. Laughter. Even some sort of chanting, moaning and groaning. They could smell smoke, but there was no fire …"

Everyone listened intently.

"And people still go camping after these stories?" John asked.

Annabel raised her eyebrows and joined in the conversation. "I guess some people are more naïve than others, or perhaps they haven't heard the stories, or don't believe them? Like Jock said, there's a lot of stories around these parts. People probably just write them off as scaremongering and myths. A lot of folk probably forget about stuff down the years. The forest is *very* large."

"That's not the only thing that's large," John muttered under his breath, getting David's attention. He was referring to Annabel's breasts. "Even so. I wouldn't want to camp out in that forest after hearing about that. That's a fact, Jack!"

"Me neither," Annabel replied.

"What happened after they heard these noises?" David rubbed his chin.

"Well, they managed to fall asleep, and they awoke the next morning to find Charlie was gone. No trace or anything. He had been sleeping between his parents. It was as if someone snuck into their tent and snatched him."

"Couldn't he just have got up and left the tent himself? Like maybe to take a leak?" John asked, slightly pricking the palm of his hand with his chewed cocktail stick.

"I guess it's possible, sure. Although, that might have woken his folks, seeing as they were all close together," the elderly lady replied. She seemed a local.

"Maybe something lured him out of the tent?" David suggested.

Jock looked on, listening keenly.

"You see, that's the strange thing. The father, William, said that it started to rain heavily and got ever so cold before they fell asleep. The ground was very wet when they woke. I think the noises must have eventually stopped for them to sleep. You'd think there would be some form of prints, wouldn't you?"

"Aye. Not unless they got rained away," Jock said.

"Maybe. Who knows?" Annabel replied.

"What did they do when they realised, he was gone?" David started to feel unsettled.

"You can imagine, the parents were distraught. Obviously. They called the police and a search went under way. But nothing was ever found. No trace. Apart from a dried pool of blood not too far from the tent. It was found a few days later. Whether it was poor Charlie's blood, I guess we'll never know. The mother hung herself a year or so later. Tragic it was. Janet, was her name. She was so overcome by the pain of losing her only child, she couldn't go on. She felt guilty, responsible for his disappearance. He was assumed dead."

"Why didn't they leave when they heard the noises?" John glanced quickly at Annabel.

"It's all well saying that in hindsight, isn't it? Remember though, it was the middle of the night. The father, William, wished they had, of course. He thought someone was playing a prank on them. Like I said, nothing was ever found, apart from that blood which may or may not have been the young boy's ... Now I come to think about it, a report did come back saying it wasn't human blood. Don't quote me on that, though. I'm not completely sure.

"I think there were stories at the time too, that the parents had problems and were taking drugs. So, a lot of what they were claiming got dismissed because of that. Some blamed them for their own child vanishing."

"What do you think? Do you think it was drug-related and they had something to do with their kid disappearing? Or do you think there's something up with the forest?" David asked the lady.

"I honestly don't know ... there's been a few stories down the years of noises, people venturing too far into the forest, never to be seen again. Things like that. To be honest with you, we stay away from it. We certainly wouldn't venture too far in. The place gives us the jitters."

"Such a sad story." Annabel looked at her cleaning cloth.

"I don't know what happened to the father. I think he moved away years ago," the woman added. "He probably couldn't deal with living around here after what had happened."

Her partner nodded his head as a few more customers walked in.

*****

"I'm surprised your uncle didn't mention anything about that kid going missing."

"Maybe they just forgot? It was years ago, although, it's not something you forget easily," David replied. "Anyway, I think it's time we started to head back."

"I hear you." John finished the last drop of his pint. "We'll see you soon, mate, yeah?"

"It's been a pleasure, boys. See ye tomorrow night, aye? And say hello to ye uncle for me!" Jock replied.

"Will do … Come on, boy!" David said quietly to Benji. He then turned to the couple. "It was nice meeting you."

"Take care." The woman smiled, along with her partner.

Just as they opened the door, John and David almost bumped into the other barmaid, Emily, as she came back from her lunch break.

"Oh," she flinched. "Sorry!"

"That's all right." David smiled. He found her even prettier up close. She had beautiful green eyes that sparkled.

They shared a short moment looking at one another.

"Ahem." John cleared his throat.

The pair let her pass.

She quickly turned around in a rush of unexpected confidence. "Are you, erm, coming to the disco, tomorrow night?" she asked in her soft, sweet accent. Her cheeks flushed.

"Erm. I-" David looked at John.

"He'll be here. We'll *both* be here. Count on it!" John interrupted.

"Great! I guess I'll see you then," she said pointedly to David.

The two friends left the pub.

"Told you, she likes you," John said. "I saw the way you looked at her, too. I'm more interested in that Annabel. I mean, she does have a lot of 'front.' Get it? Big tits?" John nudged David.

"Why did you say we'll be here tomorrow night? I really don't fancy going. Normally, I'd be up for it. Don't you think we've got more pressing matters to attend to?" David seemed slightly annoyed.

"Sure, I do! But there's only so much we can do at the moment. Besides, maybe someone at the disco will know more about what's going on around here? I know you're worried about your aunt. Who wouldn't be? She's acting strange … but it's not going to hurt to enjoy a night out, mate."

"I know. It's just I'd feel guilty. It's like I'm neglecting my aunt and uncle."

"Rubbish. We can get Derek and Jack to come along, too. It'll be a laugh. Get to know them some more. Maybe they know more than they're letting on and after a few drinks, they'll open up. What do you say, eh?" John said excitedly, nudging his best friend again.

"Okay." David sighed.

"That's the spirit! Get to know that Emily some more, too … David's in loooovvvveee, David's in luuuuuuuvvvveeee."

"Fuck off!" David tried not to laugh.

As they got to the car, they stopped dead. Tucked under the window wipers was what appeared to be another note. They both swallowed.

"Not again ..." said John.

They looked around cautiously in the car park. There was no one else about.

John walked slowly over to the windscreen and cautiously took out the note from under the window wipers. He unfolded it. "Oh, my, God," he muttered, looking up wide-eyed at David.

"What does it say?"

*"Sparkling Clean Windows."*

"Huh?" David swiped the note from John's hand. "Jesus!"

It was an advertisement for a window cleaning service. All the cars had them.

"I really thought it was another note then, and they had followed us here to the pub."

"Me too. Not to say they still haven't, though," replied John, taking the note back from David. He read it again then dropped it onto the ground. "Cheeky bastards, sticking these on our cars. We'd best get back to the farm, anyway."

As they left, they waved to Annabel who was smoking a cigarette outside the pub. She returned a wave.

"Seriously wouldn't mind giving her one ... I've got something she can have a drag on," John muttered quietly. He smiled and looked over to David.

David couldn't help but grin, shaking his head.

The return journey gave them another opportunity for a fantastic view of the Cairngorms and the forest below. It was hard to believe that such a beautiful place held so many dark secrets and unexplained phenomena.

# Chapter Twenty-Two

## 12th July, 2018

The late afternoon was pleasant by the time they returned to Hamish Farm. Jack was just leaving as they arrived. It was 17:53. They pulled up alongside one another and rolled down their windows.

"All right, Jack? Everything been okay?"

"Aye. Just off home now, John-Boy. Me mum's cooking some Scottish shepherd's pie; best damn pie ye'd ever have!" Jack's seatbelt was pulled over his bare chest leaving a red mark.

"Nice! Listen, me and David are going to a disco tomorrow night at Jock's pub. You know it? You fancy coming?"

"Aye. Could do. Nothing else much planned. Been there several times. He's a good fella, that Jock. Apart from the old git supports *Celtic*. Bah!" Jack spat out the window onto the ground.

"Sweet," John said. "We'll talk more tomorrow."

"Aye, will do. Gotta go."

"Same. I'm dying for a piss. Those pints have gone straight through me." John squirmed.

"See ye later." Jack sped off home.

"God, I bet he's a handful after he's had a few drinks inside him," David remarked.

"I bet he is as well. He's harmful enough, though. Be a laugh. I think we need something to lighten the mood. It'll be a good night. And I know, I know, it's not the reason why we're here, but we could do with a night out before the shit hits the fan some more … because you know, this is going to get *worse* before it gets better. *If* it does."

"I know … I'm just worried about leaving Bob and Betty on their own. And Gavin. Especially at night. I still can't help thinking about that Harold as well. I can't get that damn *creep* out of my mind."

"I know. There was something seriously off with him. No doubt about that. Maybe your uncle found out something whilst we were gone? At least it's a nice evening." John parked in the barn, locking the car up for the night.

Walking back to the house, Bob came out to meet them.

"I thought I heard your car … I'm glad you're back, boys. We need to talk."

"Everything okay? How's Betty?" David asked.

"She's fine. Well, I have to admit, she is acting a little strange, like you said. I'm sure she'll be okay after a rest. She said she was going for a lie-down, and to have an early night as she wasn't feeling too well."

"Again? I'm not liking this, Uncle. Something isn't right."

"We'll see how she goes. Come over to the animal pens. Gavin and Derek are there. I managed to find some things out about that guy, Harold, you met."

"Really? Like what?" John asked.

"Come." Bob led them both to the pens. "How was the pub and Jock?"

"Good. It's a really nice place. Quaint. Bit worn down from the outside, fine inside. Jock said to say 'Hi,' as well."

"You were right about there being a couple of smoking hot chicks who work there!" John added.

"I told you. We'll definitely have to go see him again soon, me and Betty."

"Great burger he does as well. Best I've had," said John.

"Okay … whilst you two were out, I managed to dig up some information online on your friend, Harold. There's a website with half a dozen forest rangers on it, along with their profile pictures. Oddly, Harold wasn't listed anywhere on it, nor his photo. Gavin checked. They had a number on there, which I called, asking if they had anyone by that name working for them; they said no. I even described his lazy eye, in case he was using another name. The guy said that he wouldn't have been able to disclose much anyway, for confidentiality reasons."

"Jeez. What about the uniform? Was that genuine? Is it what the rangers up here wear? Where would he have got that?" David asked.

"Maybe it's a mental or sexual thing … like it was his lifelong ambition to be a forest ranger, but he was rejected, so he pretends to be one?" John said tongue-in-cheek.

"It's definitely the same uniform. The guys on the website were all wearing the same outfit," Gavin confirmed.

"What a freak!" John squeezed his legs together. He really needed to use the loo.

"How did the guy you called, explain it?" David asked.

"He thought we must be mistaken, or else someone was messing about or having a laugh at our expense," Bob answered.

"Yeah, hilarious," David said sarcastically.

"We're no further." Bob shook his head.

"When we were at the pub, we learnt about a young boy, Charlie Begsbie, who went missing on a camping trip with his parents in the forest, back in 1999. The family heard sounds, whispering and chanting, before the boy went missing. They smelt smoke, too. Do you remember that, Uncle?"

There was a moment's pause. Bob looked so sad. "Ah, yes. That poor boy. He was such a sweet child, Charlie ... I can still picture his innocent little face, now." He averted his eyes from David and hung his head low.

"What? You actually *knew* him?"

"We, we both did, David. Your aunt and I. We knew his parents, William and Janet ... William worked for me for several months. He was a mechanic. I didn't really need anyone, but he was so desperate; he begged for me to give him a job. It wasn't long after Christmas. January, 1999. I felt sorry for him. He had no farming experience. He was only in his twenties, had racked up a fair amount of debt and was drinking heavily. He had Asperger's, too.

"Janet had become pregnant at fourteen with Charlie. She started to get bullied and dropped out of school. Not long after, William did the same. He tried to support them by working. One of his uncle's put him and Janet up, when their parents threw them out."

"That's pretty damn low. Throwing someone out when they're pregnant," said John. "Even more so, when they're so young."

"I know. I can understand their anger but they shouldn't have thrown them out."

"What happened after that?" David asked.

"Things did improve somewhat. William found numerous jobs but struggled to hold down a couple ... William's uncle eventually got him work in a garage and he did well there. His uncle died from a heart attack in the summer of 1998. They managed to keep the council house. Unfortunately, Janet then had a miscarriage and William lost his job. Everything all happened at once.

"William started to feel he was cursed. He began drinking more and Janet was prescribed antidepressants. She then started taking other drugs. But they *never* mistreated Charlie nor neglected him in any way. They were great parents." Bob felt himself well up, casting his mind back.

David wondered why his uncle knew all this in detail, yet hadn't mentioned it before now.

"Me and Betty got to know them well. We got close to them. We would sometimes help them out with money or at least offer. William hated accepting it. He wanted to provide for his own family. Or I would give William some 'overtime' that didn't need doing. He hated hand-outs. They both did. We even offered to put them up here for a bit, until they sorted themselves out. William got on quite well with our Darren, too. But then … Charlie disappeared …" Bob wiped tears from his eyes with one of his grubby thumbs.

"Wh-why didn't you mention this before, Uncle? Especially as they heard whispering and chanting? Amongst other things."

"I'm … I'm so sorry, David. The whispering and chanting I'd completely forgotten until a few days ago. At the time, everyone thought that it was to do with the drugs or alcohol. Some people thought they were responsible for poor Charlie's disappearance themselves. But they would never, *ever* have done anything to hurt their only child. Another reason is … your aunt and I felt, well, responsible. It's hard to talk about. It's why I didn't tell you all when I remembered it."

"Responsible? Why on *earth* would you feel responsible, Uncle?"

"We, we encouraged them to go camping, William and Janet, to take little Charlie. He always wanted to go. We thought it would be good for them. But Janet, well, she said she felt as if something was *drawing* her into the forest, like something was reaching out to her. We thought it was just her being paranoid with withdrawal. They were trying to turn over a new leaf, you see. We even bought them the tent and sleeping bags. After, we thought they maybe had a relapse. They insisted they hadn't …" Bob sniffed. "I, I didn't want to mention it before. I felt ashamed. Betty does, too. If we hadn't convinced Janet into going camping, none of this would have happened."

Bob put his hand over his face and rubbed it. He pinched the bridge of his nose together, as if to stop the tears from flowing. "There isn't a day that goes by, when your auntie and I don't think about the three of them."

Gavin put a consoling hand on Bob's shoulder.

"Back then, we didn't believe Janet. Yes, we've all heard stories of the forest maybe being haunted amongst other things. But no one ever really believed such things, until now. How wrong we were. I am so sorry I didn't tell you, David. *All* of you … I didn't mean to keep it from you like that. And if I'm honest, after Charlie vanished, there weren't any disturbances nor whispering.

"There had been other stories on and off down the years afterwards, along with local legends. Reports of people disappearing and that they were last seen in the forest, or people believing the forest 'took' them, but pretty much all those stories were made up. Some of these people did disappear, only to be found after, safe, or some weren't even near Rothiemurchus. It's hard to make out what is fact and what is fiction. When people hear stories, they jump on the band wagon and make things up."

"It's not your fault, boss. You shouldn't blame yourself. You weren't to know." Gavin sympathised.

"Myself, Betty, William, Janet and numerous others, including our Darren, searched for *weeks* after Charlie had disappeared. We found nothing. I only remember a pool of blood that got tested; it wasn't human blood."

There was nothing but silence for a moment. No one knew what to say. They were all shocked. Particularly David and Gavin. Gavin hadn't heard of the disappearance of Charlie Begsbie.

"I understand why you didn't want to talk about it," David said as Gavin looked at him and John.

"I'm ... I'm so sorry. Even your father doesn't know."

"It's fine, Uncle. This isn't your fault. None of it. You *have* to believe that." David felt upset himself. They had opened a can of worms. David could understand his uncle's reasons for not telling him and the others. But he couldn't help but feel surprised that he hadn't told David's father. After all, they were brothers.

"What happened to this William in the end? Is he still alive?" asked John. He screwed his face up, resisting the urge to urinate.

Bob reasserted himself, clearing his throat. He breathed out calmly. "After a few months, we finally came to the conclusion that Charlie would never be found. The official search stopped after about three weeks. There was nothing else to go on. No leads, no evidence, nothing. We assumed he was most likely dead. Your aunt used to have dreams about him ... he was standing near the forest on the farm, wearing his blue shorts and T-shirt, waving and smiling at her. She used to wake up feeling sad, realising it was just a dream. Sometimes, she'd stand looking at the forest, wishing her dream would come true.

"Billy, like us, blamed himself. Even more so. He felt a responsibility for Janet and his son. And he and Janet blamed themselves for not leaving that night when they first heard the noises and whispering. We tried helping them through it afterwards ... Eventually, it took its toll on Janet. She ... she ... hung herself in their house, one Monday evening, a year later. Billy found her ... just hanging there. He quit working and became a recluse. One day, he just upped and left. We never saw or heard from him again. Apart from a letter we received about a week later. I think Betty kept it somewhere. I haven't read it in years. Yet, I still remember word for word what it read:

*Please, don't blame yourselves after everything that has happened. I am to blame. Thank you for being there for me and Janet and little Charlie. He loved you guys and seeing you. You and Betty are two of the good ones. The only true friends we ever had.*
*Take care.*
*Yours,*
*B. x*

"He just vanished. He went off the radar. Your aunt and I tried to track him down and find him. We did searches online. Nothing ever came back. No addresses, other than the one we had already known about. Nothing at all." Bob shook his head again. "You know, it's almost to the date that Charlie disappeared; 21st July ... he would have been a grown man by now. Maybe, with a family of his own? Perhaps, he's still out there ..."

David walked over to his uncle and put his arm around him. "Everything's going to be all right, Uncle."

Bob half-smiled and nodded.

It made John feel sad too. He felt the pain of what William and Janet had endured. He may not have been as bad as those two, but he could definitely empathise in parts. It brought back painful memories of when his own mother died and he had turned to drugs and alcohol. Thankfully for him, he still had his father and David, and David's parents to help him through it.

"I'd like to stay and help tonight, Bob. If it's okay?" Derek offered, who had remained quiet throughout Bob's confession.

"That's kind of you, Derek. You honestly don't have to do that."

"I'd like to. I haven't done it for a while, and I don't expect you to pay me. I won't take no for an answer."

"Okay. But I'm still paying you." Bob smiled slightly.

"I really don't want to push you further, Uncle. I know it's hard on you. I've got to ask ... what do you think happened to Charlie? I mean, who do you think took him? Could he have wandered off by himself?" David hated asking.

"That's okay. Honestly? I don't know. At the time, we thought that maybe he wandered out of his own accord. Perhaps, he woke up in the middle of the night and heard something? Or maybe, something enticed him out? The same way Janet said something was calling out to her from the forest. Maybe he even drowned, if he wandered off and fell into the River Spey.

"Though, they were on the other side of the forest to where the river is, so that doesn't make sense. Plus, the river was checked by divers and no body was recovered … In my heart I like to think that he's still alive somewhere, but in my head, I know he's gone. May God, rest his sweet soul."

David was deep in thought as he listened to his uncle. "Look at the comparisons … when some of your livestock were taken and Angus,' there were no footprints, were there? It's definitely related. This hooded figure, or thing, possibly had something to do with it. There's inconsistency with the prints which we saw on John's car and on the dirt track. Why would there sometimes be prints and sometimes not? Is it possible it's some sort of creature?"

"And then there's the chanting. They claimed they heard it out camping. Like I did, when I saw that fire in the distance. There could be a group, a sect doing this." Gavin gave his two pennies worth.

"Right!" replied David. "There's no doubt it's all linked somehow. *All* of it. It would be *way* too much of a coincidence."

"I'm with you on that," John agreed. "Of course, there is another person who could be responsible for taking the kid."

*"Harold!"* David said at the same time as John.

"We can't jump to conclusions. We need more evidence and something concrete to go on," Bob advised.

"There has to be someone who knows more about these parts and the history of the forest? Like say, a naturalist?"

"We could start online, David. Someone might know more. We can't be the only ones interested," Bob said.

"I'll do some research later, Bob. I'll use my laptop. We really need to get moving faster on this," David said strongly.

"Okay." Bob smiled. "I'll look at getting us all something to eat."

# Chapter Twenty-Three

## 12th July, 2018

John was sat with David again in the back garden along with Benji, who was stretched out on the lawn. It was a perfect, clear night. The stars were out, twinkling and shining bright. Over to the west, there was a faint strip of orangey-red where the last remnants of the sunset remained. The chirping crickets were out in force. John looked up and saw a shooting star zip across the sky and disappear. He made a wish-prayer; *God. Let this shit be over with, already.* He was far from a religious person. He had even blamed 'God' for letting his mum die. Yet he prayed anyway. He was desperate. He used jokes to lighten the mood and for David, but underneath, he felt the darkness too.

The pair sat for a while in silence, listening to the crickets. An owl hooted close by. They could hear voices near the pens; Gavin, Bob, and then Derek's dull and monotone voice and laughter. David pulled out his phone and checked the time; 22:08.

"I still can't believe your uncle, kept all that from us about that Charlie kid."

"I know. I suppose his reasons were valid. If he did forget about the chanting and other things that the family had heard that night, it would make sense." David was still looking at his phone. The background had a picture of Benji.

"Would he ever have told us, if you hadn't asked him about it?"

"I was just wondering that. I'm certain he would have done."

"Maybe whoever is behind all this did something so he *wouldn't* remember?"

"Quite possibly." David yawned.

"What time's your folks' flight, tomorrow?" John then asked, remembering David's parents were off to Spain.

"I can't remember. My mum said she'd call from the airport just before they boarded."

"They'll probably have a better time than us, that's for sure."

David smiled slightly and looked at John. "Yeah. That's an understatement, for sure."

"You going to research online whether there are any naturalists about? As long as you don't look up 'naturists' by mistake," John joked. "I could check as well."

"I'll do it when I go up to bed. There's got to be someone, considering the nature of the place in general, with the forest."

"I think I'm going to turn in, mate. I'm shattered." John got up from his chair. "I'll see you on the morrow." He placed a hand on David's shoulder briefly and then made his way back into the house.

"Night, mate," David called after him.

*****

David sat alone. He heard the owl hoot again. It came from somewhere to his right, near the barn where the cars were parked. So much was racing through his tired mind; all kinds of thoughts and theories. He eventually went up to bed, again trying to be careful of the creaking staircase.

"I heard yer, coming up the stairs," John called out as David was about to open his bedroom door.

David shook his head and smiled, entering his room with Benji following him.

Sitting upright in the bed with his laptop on his lap, David first and foremost, looked up the disappearance of Charlie Begsbie. Surprisingly, there was only one main article on him. And even then, David had to search the website for it. It confirmed what they had learnt from the lady at the pub and from Uncle Bob. It mentioned the strange sounds they had heard and that *William Begsbie* and *Janet Durie* were both twenty-four, had financial difficulties and were drug users. There had been no trace of the boy, apart from some blood not too far from the tent.

A short paragraph at the end of the article mentioned that Charlie was not the first to go missing in Rothiemurchus Forest. There had been numerous reports of missing children and adults over the years; individuals who had 'ventured into the evergreen mass, never to return or be seen again.' A disclaimer stated that there was no evidence for many of these so-called disappearances, and that most accounts of them were based on hearsay.

Apart from young Charlie's name, no other names of missing persons were given. So, as Bob had said, there was no real evidence that these other strange cases of people vanishing were indeed valid. David scrolled down further.

A few burnt human skulls and bones had been allegedly found by a dog walker in the forest; there was no date. Again, this could be fabrication, nothing more. At the bottom of the article was the name of the author who wrote the report: *Marvin Aileanach*. Maybe this was a lead, so he added the webpage to his favourites in his web browser. Next, he wanted to check for a naturalist in the Rothiemurchus area. But the Wi-Fi connection went dead.

# Chapter Twenty-Four

## 13th July, 2018

David woke up in the middle of the night. He was lying on his back with Benji sound asleep next to him.

He noticed that the right part of the room had a white gleam to it. Still half-asleep, he thought it was the moon shining in through the window. Instead, it was coming from the floor at the side of his bed, so he looked down to check what it was; his laptop. He was certain he had shut it down before he went to sleep. He bent down and picked it up. It was not only turned on, but the webpage of the article he had been reading about Charlie Begsbie was also displaying.

"What the hell?" He rubbed his eyes and face with his right palm and fingers. He shook his head.

This time, he definitely made sure that he shut his laptop down. But not before he noticed that there was still no wireless connection. It was 02:59.

He climbed out of bed to go to the bathroom. It felt freezing, as if it was a cold winter's night. He rubbed the top of his arms with both hands, shivering. *"Jeez."*

David made his way to the bathroom down the hallway slowly in the dark. He was aided slightly by one of the lights from downstairs that had been left on again. His feet felt cold on the wooden floor.

He was about to enter the bathroom, when he heard a slight moan coming from Aunt Betty's room. He strained his eyes to make out the black outline of the door and heard a moan again. Then again …

He slowly walked over closer to the door and listened, with his head bowed … nothing. It was quiet. As he pulled away, it started again, louder. He put his ear to the door. It felt icy-cold against his ear. He could hear more groans and moans coming from inside the bedroom.

He was tempted to knock or call out to Betty, to see if everything was okay, but he couldn't bring himself to doing it. He felt so awkward. For all he knew, his aunt and uncle might both be in there. Bob might have left Gavin and Derek keeping watch and packed in early. He screwed his face up at the thought of it.

After a few more seconds, the sounds stopped, but he was sure he could hear someone talking in there. It was like a whisper ... he couldn't make out what was being said. It could even have been Betty herself, whispering and muttering in her sleep. Perhaps, she was having a nightmare.

He was beginning to shake more from the cold. He only had his blue boxer shorts on. For a moment, he thought he could hear footsteps from behind the door. Then, he heard a voice. It was definitely Betty's ...

"No. Noooo ... I won't do it ... please ... *stop*!"

David was worried now. Maybe Betty was just having a bad dream. Maybe she was sleep walking.

Without thinking, he instinctively tapped his fingers on the bedroom door and called out, "Au-Aunt Betty ... are you okay?" He slowly opened the door and peered in.

It was too dark to see anything. His heart was beating in his chest.

David instinctively felt the wall to the left inside the door for a light switch. He found it with relative ease. He swallowed again and closed his eyes, before opening them and pressing softly and reluctantly on the switch.

The room lit up and there lay Betty, sound asleep on her left side, wearing a dark blue, sleep mask. She was snoring.

David didn't enter the room but could feel the icy temperature hit his face and body. It was worse than his room or the landing. It was like being in a fridge freezer. He shivered again and looked around the room, confused. The window was closed. He knew he wasn't imagining what he had heard. Or maybe he was just tired and hearing things, after everything that had happened. But no, he quickly quashed that thought. He knew what he had heard; he wasn't hearing things. Frowning, he flicked the light switch off and carefully shut the door tight. He then went to relieve himself in the bathroom. Once done, he walked back down the cold landing and hallway and went straight back into bed.

*****

David woke up to a rumble of thunder and got out of bed.

Benji, who was still in a deep sleep and twitching, was now curled up on the bedroom floor next to the bed.

David walked over to the window and looked out at a gloomy morning. The skies were grey. There was a flash of sheet lightning, followed by another rumble of thunder. It looked like it was about to pour down. Betty, in her white nightdress, was hanging washing out on the line, in spite of the ominous weather. David thought perhaps he shouldn't be surprised, judging by Betty's recent behaviour. He watched a little longer as she hung the last item on the line. It was a white shirt. One of Bob's, presumably. As David expected, it started to rain.

A horrible sensation quickly washed over him. It was like he wasn't present, yet he was. He had a dreaded feeling of malaise and started to feel anxious. He looked round for Benji, seeking some comfort. Benji was sitting up staring into nothing. He appeared completely frozen.

David quickly bent down and touched his dog. Benji was cold to touch. "Benji? *Benji*!" David started to panic. He started to weep. *"Benji! Benji! What's wrong with you, Benji?"*

Suddenly, Benji's frozen body toppled to one side, exposing a huge gash straight down his belly. His intestines were seeping out of the gaping wound. Blood started to pour out, soaking the carpet and turning it from pale blue to dark red. The smell overwhelmed David, so that he could hardly breathe.

*"Oh my God!"* David was starting to get hysterical now. He jolted backwards and began to pace back and forth, his hand over his mouth. Tears were streaming down his face; he was sobbing desperately. He didn't know what to do. He held his head and pulled on his hair, his face screwed up, crying uncontrollably. *What the hell is happening?*

David heard a man's scream coming from out in the back garden. He quickly looked out of the window. David saw Betty there. She was standing with her back to him, next to the washing line. The white shirt that was hanging on the clothesline was now covered in blood. A man appeared from round the corner, dragging another man who was shirtless across the ground.

It took a moment for it to register with David, who wiped the burning tears from his eyes so that he could focus more. The shirtless man being dragged against his will, was his Uncle Bob. And the man pulling him, was none other than *Harold*. He was wearing his forest ranger uniform. David stared. He couldn't believe what he was seeing. First Benji, and now this.

Harold flipped Bob onto his back next to Betty, exposing what appeared to be a stab wound to his abdomen. David could hear his uncle begging Betty for help as he reached out to her. Expressionless, she just looked down at him.

David tried to run to the door and then downstairs to help his uncle but he couldn't move. His legs were completely frozen as if his whole lower body was completely paralysed. He started banging on the window. It wouldn't open. He began to shout. *"John! John, help me! Please, can you hear me? Fucking help! It's Bob … Harold has him!"*

John's room was only across the hallway but there was no response.

David frantically smashed on the window, repeatedly banging and punching on it. His hands grazed and turned red from the impact. He could feel a warm, wet feeling on his feet and heels. It was Benji's blood, flowing over the bedroom carpet. David helplessly watched, as Harold pulled out a large bloody knife from behind his back and handed it to Betty. As he whispered something in her ear, he looked up and saw David shouting and banging on the window from inside. He grinned widely. Deliciously evil.

David could sense the pure evil behind it. Betty crouched down over her husband and rested on her knees in her nightie. Bob was still pleading with her. She held the long and curved knife over her head. Without any hesitation, she plunged it straight into Bob's chest. Repeatedly. A crunching sound came from his broken ribs. Blood spurted out after each thrust, covering her face and nightie.

Bob cried out in agony as David screamed.

Burning tears continued to stream down David's face. He banged on the window until his knuckles bled. Blood stained the double-glazed window. It was impenetrable.

He was so helpless. There was nothing he could do. He watched his uncle's chest gush and bleed out. Uncle Bob was choking on his own blood, gargling. Choking his last few moments of life away. His arms and legs twitched. Then, he was gone.

Harold looked down at David's dead uncle, then back at David, still smiling. He tapped on Betty's shoulder and pointed towards David up in the window. She slowly turned her head and looked up with him. She stood in her bloodstained nightie, her face still emotionless but now painted with her deceased husband's blood. Murdered, by her hand. Her eyes were wide and as black as onyx.

A sudden crack of thunder was followed by an almighty flash of blinding white and yellow lightning that struck through the window, shattering it. It threw David against the other side of the bedroom, crashing him into the far wall above the bed, knocking the wind out of him.

# Chapter Twenty-Five

## 13th July, 2018

David shouted as he jolted upright. Then without thinking, he jumped out of bed. He was covered head to toe in sweat. He could taste the salt from it on his upper lip. He felt as if his heart was going to break out of his chest, it was so hard to catch his breath. He was panting heavily, checking his knuckles. They hurt but looked fine. He then darted round the other side of the bed to check on Benji who was on the floor, startled, but otherwise fine.

*"Benji!"* David said with joy, hugging him, squeezing his soft, brown body.

Still feeling panicked, David got up and anxiously looked out of the window. It was a glorious morning outside. The sun was beating down onto the well-kept garden.

It had been a bad dream. A nightmare. It had felt so *real* and *vivid.* He looked down at his knuckles again, rubbing them. He could still feel the pain where he had been banging on the window. Even his back hurt from crashing into the far wall.

He sat on the edge of the bed for a little while in silence, trying to calm down. He looked over his shoulder and saw a huge wet patch on the beige sheet, where he had been sleeping. He touched it with his hand. It was soaked. He had been sweating copiously.

He pinched himself a few times. He wanted to make sure he still wasn't dreaming. What if he still was? There was only way to find out, and that was to head on downstairs …

John was sat at the kitchen table eating a bowl of cornflakes when David came wearily through the kitchen. David was wearing a worn grey T-shirt over his boxers.

"Jesus. You look like shit," John said, putting his spoon down into the half-empty bowl of cereal.

"I, I had a nightmare …"

"You okay, buddy, you want to talk about it?"

David pulled out a kitchen chair and slumped into it. He sighed. He looked down at the two cats who were busily crunching biscuits from their bowls. He looked at his knuckles again, stretching his fingers. He opened and closed his hands, then looked up at John. His heart rate was only just returning to normal. He cleared his throat and shook his head. "You wouldn't *believe* the nightmare I've just had."

"Tell me about it!" John was concerned for his friend; he could see David's eyes were bloodshot and his face was pale.

David shook his head. "Something was up with Betty last night, too."

"Like what?"

David told John about last night in Betty's room, and how cold it was.

"You say you heard groans, coming from her room? You didn't hear a buzzing sound too, did you? Like a vibrator?" John tried not to laugh.

David didn't see the funny side to it. He was in no mood for his friend's jokes this morning. "Don't mate. Not now …"

"Sorry," John said as he took a mouthful of cornflakes, which were mushy from sitting dormant in the milk too long.

"*God*, it was so cold up there and in Betty's room. Freezing." David got up and poured himself a glass of water, then sat back down at the table. He took a few swigs from the glass. "And that's another thing … before I fell asleep, I looked up about that Begsbie kid. I turned my laptop off, put it on the floor and went to sleep. When I woke up later, my laptop was back on and it had this article I was viewing about him still there! I'm certain I turned it off."

"That's fucking well creepy, mate. This whole *shit fest* is."

"Tell me about it."

"What about this dream?" John asked. Milk was dripping down his chin and back into the bowl.

David was slightly annoyed, seeing him eat like that. If there was one thing he couldn't stand, it was noisy and messy eaters. That was one of his biggest pet hates. He took in a deep breath. He was tired. He recounted the terrible nightmare he'd had. He tried to overcome the emotion from his experience. As he told the story, he also tried not to look John's way too much, hoping to miss catching sight of his messy eating.

"I've never had any dream or nightmare like it … I was shouting. Calling out. You couldn't hear me …" David said again. When he finally did look

John's way, he was surprised to see how upset he was.

John sat gobsmacked. He didn't know what to say. He had listened, horrified by the details of David's nightmare. He thrust the chair out with his legs and back-end, making a scraping sound on the tiled floor, and moved round the table to give his best friend a consoling hug.

David was a little taken aback. Although they were extremely close, they rarely had intimate moments like this. Certainly not unless alcohol was involved. But he appreciated it; he felt the love of his best friend. He gave him a hug back and felt a warm tear, trickle down onto his shoulder.

John was crying. "I'm so sorry I couldn't help you when you were shouting out for me. I *promise* you, I'm here, I'm *real* ... you're *not* dreaming now!"

David laughed slightly with affection. He was welling up as well now. "It's all right, mate. It was only a dream ... you have nothing to be sorry for." He smiled and patted John's back.

They pulled away from one another and John stood up straight, wiping his eyes. "Jesus. Look at what you made me do. It feels like we're a pair of *gays*!" John quickly tried to divert the fact he was crying by making a joke, as he often did when he was in an awkward situation. It was in his nature. It was who he was. But behind the jokes and the sarcasm, there was a very caring and affectionate young man. John then went over to the tap and washed away his tears.

After emptying what was left of the cornflakes and milk into the kitchen bin, John washed and dried his bowl and placed it back in the cupboard.

David still sat at the table; his glass of water was now empty. "Where is everyone? What's the time?" He forgot about the clock on the wall.

John pulled out his phone from his shorts pocket. "Gone half-nine ... I think your uncle took your aunt to town. He said it might do her good to get away from the farm for a while. Gavin and co. are out back ... You going to tell Bob about the dream you had? Or *nightmare,* I should say."

"I think I have to. And about Betty in her room last night ... I don't know what good it will do telling him, but I'd rather not keep anything from him. We all need to know what we're up against. It was in no way an ordinary dream; there was something dark and sinister behind it. I just hope it isn't a premonition. It's best to warn him. Especially with the way Betty is acting."

"Yeah, I'm with you on that, mate. We all need to be honest and up front with one another. We need to make sure we've all got each other's backs," John replied. "Did you manage to find anything out last night before you went to sleep, about a naturalist? I was going to try myself but fell asleep."

"I was going to. But the Wi-Fi went dead. I'm going to look this morning. I did see an author name at the bottom of the article about that Charlie's disappearance, though. I added it to my favourites, so maybe we can get a hold of them? It could be something to go on. We've not much else to go on at the moment."

"Yeah, it could give us some details."

"I better go and get my phone. I imagine Mum might have rung or will do soon, if she hasn't already. They're probably on their way to the airport by now, if they're not there already." David got up from his chair.

"I'll wash your glass out for you. Where are they flying out from?"

"Stansted," David answered, leaving the kitchen.

David returned with his phone, which made a tune as it started up. John had opened up the back door to let some fresh air in.

John and David could easily have been forgiven for temporarily forgetting about past events, due to the wonderfully sun-kissed morning. The sound of the birds singing and chirping, sauntered into the kitchen. David had received a voice message from his mother, Annette:

*"All right, love? Just phoning to let you know that your father and I are at the airport. Give us a call when you get this message. Our flight is at twenty past ten. We will be boarding soon. Speak soon. Love you."*

"That from your mum?" John asked, looking round.

"Yeah. I best give her a call. Their flight is at ten-twenty." David deleted the voice mail out of habit.

"I should give my old man a call actually, later. Let him know I'm all right. Well, all right considering," John replied as David rung his mum.

The phone rang a few times before it was answered. His dad, Jason, answered, "Hello, Son! You okay? How's the farming going? Your mum has just popped to the toilet before we board. I think she spotted a handbag she liked, too," he half-joked.

"I'm good, Dad. Thanks," David lied. He was far from all right. He felt even worse than before he and John had driven up here. But there was no way he could explain everything now. Not over the phone, and certainly not as his parents were about to jet off on holiday.

"How's Bob? Everything okay with him and Betty? They feeling a little better now?"

"Erm. Yeah, I think so," David fibbed again, slightly screwing his face up. He so hated lying, something he was never comfortable with. Especially to his parents, who he looked up to and rarely kept anything from, unless there was a good reason. Protecting their happiness on their holiday was as good a reason as any. "They're doing okay, I think."

"Good!" Jason replied. "It's only been a couple of days I know, but what have you done so far? You enjoying it?"

"Yeah. Me and John are helping out here and there, chipping in, you know, when we can. I milked a cow, yesterday." David tried to convince his dad that everything was okay. He was a pretty good actor. Well, that's what one of his old school drama teachers reckoned, when he was in Year 8.

"Good! Bob will make a farmer out of you yet, boy, eh?" Jason joked. "How's Johnny? He okay?"

"Yeah, John's good too, Dad."

"I'm good, Jase. Hope you have a good holiday! Make sure you get some good photos of Annette in her bikini, yeah?" John called out. He could hear Jason laugh over the phone and David smiled.

"You fucking cheeky bastard!" Jason joked back. "Listen, your mum's coming back so I'll hand you over to her. You make sure you have a good time up there, okay? If you need anything, we're only a phone call away."

"I know, Dad. Have a good time and try not to work too hard."

"I won't. I'm not taking much work to Spain with me. Chat soon. Love you, Son."

"Me too, Dad."

"David? You okay?" His mum took over the call.

"I'm good, Mum. I just got your voice mail. You two have a good time over there."

"Oh, we will. How are you and John getting on? I hope you're not being too much of a burden for Bob and Betty? How are they? Are they coping well?"

"They're getting there. They both appreciate the help and support me and John are offering. We're not getting in the way or anything, if that's what you're worried about," David replied, looking over at John.

"Well, just make sure you aren't, love. And if you feel you are, or if Bob and Betty aren't comfortable with you two staying up there, make sure you respect their wishes and come home."

"Yes, we will, Mum." David rolled his eyes and shook his head, beginning to feel annoyed. Then again, his mum hadn't the faintest idea what was going on, so he couldn't expect her to understand. So long as his mum and dad were safe and away from it all, he was happy with that. That was all that mattered. David could hear the gate announcement.

"Listen, David, they're calling for us to start boarding. I'll text once we land and call when we've settled in. Remember, what I said about your aunt and uncle."

"Yes, Mum. I *know*!"

"Well, just make sure you do, honey."

"Have a safe flight, Mum. And be sure to give Aunt Sarah and her family my love."

"I will, David. You do the same from us to Bob and Betty, too. Love you!"

"Love you too, Mum."

"Have a great holiday, Mrs H!" John shouted.

"Bye, boys!" Annette hung up.

As it was a wonderful morning weather-wise, John and David decided to sit in the garden. David wanted to search for any naturalists in or around the Rothiemurchus area. Although it was still early in the day, the temperature had already risen significantly. It was going to be a blistering hot day it seemed.

They moved the two seats that they had sat on for the past two evenings onto the middle of the lawn so they could benefit from the sun as much as possible. They sat casually in their sunglasses.

David thought that it would be nice to get Benji to join them, when he had gone to fetch his laptop. But Benji was still fast asleep on the carpet. He had groaned when David tried to disturb him, so David left him be. He would take him for a walk around the farm later on, if the weather held up, which looked likely.

John rang his dad to let him know they had arrived okay in Scotland and that he was fine. Although it was two days late, better late than never. The death of John's mum had brought him and his dad closer, but their relationship was still a little strained, even after all these years. But ringing home was the least he could do; the right thing to do. He was his dad, after all. "You must hate lying to your folks, mate. I know you too well. It pains you to keep all this from them, doesn't it? I can tell you're eager to let it all out."

David was checking his emails. At least the Wi-Fi was working now. He had emailed a couple of companies with his CV well over a week ago, but had only just received responses. One said he wasn't suitable for the job, and another said the vacancies were already filled. He was disappointed. He shook his head. "Wankers … how can companies have the cheek to say there are no longer any jobs available, when they still advertise? And yeah, you're right, mate. I hate keeping things from my folks. Hopefully by the time they get back, this will all be over. Though, I wish I could believe that."

"I know how you feel. I felt a little awkward telling my old man I was doing good and that I was okay." John felt his face getting hot.

"I'm going to sit in the shade. It's getting too hot for me. The sun-glare is making it hard for me to see the screen." David got up from his chair and carried it, with his laptop in the other hand, to underneath the apple tree. Its ripe red and green apples looked ready to be plucked. The shade was perfect there.

He'd found the article again about Charlie Begsbie. Resting a piece of paper on the top of his right thigh, he noted down the name of the man who had published the article; Marvin Aileanach.

The article had been published online way back in 1999. David had only come across it by searching the stored archives of the website. The precise date of publication had been the 28th July, exactly a week after the disappearance. It appeared at least back then, that the local newspaper came out weekly, possibly on a Wednesday.

David saw that there was a 'Contact the Editor' email and phone number for a lady called *Deborah Goram*. Perhaps, she would know more about the disappearance and of this Marvin guy who wrote the report all those years ago. He jotted her name and number down too. He'd phone her rather than email; based on his experience with job applications, it might be quicker.

John came over, holding his chair to his backside and plonked it down under the shade next to David. His face was pink from the heat of the sun and he was sweating. "Ah … that's better. It's getting too fucking hot, now," he said. "What you got? You found anything that might help?"

"Here, hold this … I'm going to check for any naturalists in the area …" David handed the pen and piece of paper over to John.

"Marvin Aileanach?" John queried as he lifted up his sunglasses.

"Yeah. That's the name of the guy who wrote the article about Charlie Begsbie going missing."

"I see. And what about this other name and this website?"

"The website is where the article was published. Some local paper. It seems strange that no other mention of Charlie is anywhere else online. That's the name of the editor. She might know something about the area and also about this Marvin guy who wrote the article. He mentioned other disappearances as well …"

"Ah. Good thinking, Batman."

An apple fell from the tree dropping onto the grass and rolled towards John.

He bent down and picked it up, rubbing it clean on his black T-shirt. He took a bite with a crisp crunch. "Could be a good omen," he remarked, pointing to the apple. "What does it say about the other disappearances?" John asked, chomping away.

"Nothing much. It doesn't mention any names specifically. And no indication of whether it's true. I believe some are true. I mean, after what we've been through and the way this Charlie kid disappeared, why wouldn't others have vanished the same way? Of course, you're always going to get the bullshit theories and stories and stuff. But there's no smoke without fire."

"I completely agree with you."

"It even mentioned something about burnt bones being found."

"Shit. Really?"

"Yep. Skulls, too. Whether or not that is correct or not."

After John had bitten around the core of the apple and was done with it, he stood up and hurled it with his right hand over the garden shrubs in the direction of the nearby barley field. He rubbed his hands and sat back down in the chair. "Your uncle will probably get an apple tree growing in his field, now," he joked.

David continued looking at the screen. He smiled. "There's nothing coming up with regards to any naturalists in the area or even Scotland, period. I'm finding websites and people who wrote books et cetera, but again, nothing specific."

"I thought there would have been someone."

"Same. They must be about. I noticed a few websites that mention naturalists in general and all things related. Could always email them. I'll wait though, until I've spoken to the editor of the local newspaper. She could give us some much-needed information. She could even know someone who works in that field."

A few more apples dropped onto the ground around them. David's laptop screen began to flicker. Then suddenly, *all* the apples began to fall from the tree. It was raining apples.

*"Jesus!"* David said as the apples rained down onto his head and laptop. He quickly shut it and dashed out from underneath the tree.

*"What the ...!"* John said, following suit, covering his head and dashing out from under the shade, back into the hot sun.

They both stood looking at the pile of apples that had mysteriously fallen at once, both rubbing their heads where they had been hit.

They then heard a small child laugh and a cold draft swept past them.

They spun round, but whatever it was, had gone as quickly as it appeared.

"Okay. What the *fuck* was that?" John asked.

"I … I have no idea. It sounded like a child," David replied, still holding his laptop.

"Great … not only are we dealing with a strange entity or monster, a psychopathic, *freak*-wannabe forest ranger, amongst other things … we now have some spirit of an annoying *kid* to contend with!"

"It could be the same entity we've already encountered. It could be messing with us," David claimed.

"Well, you're not wrong there. We've certainly been messed with, that's for sure." John shook his head.

David suggested that they may as well pick up the apples as it would save Betty or Bob doing it. There was a fair load of them.

John fetched three large, steel buckets from under the kitchen sink to collect the apples in. Some of the apples had rolled out from the shade. They could feel the scorching sun on the back of their necks as they bent down to gather up the apples.

"You don't think that kid laughing, was maybe that err … *Charlie*, do you?" John asked, his back arched.

"The thought had crossed my mind … guess it's just pretty creepy. You'd think we'd start getting used to it by now though, wouldn't you?" David scooped up a couple of apples with both his hands and placed them carefully into the steel bucket, not wanting to bruise them.

"Well, I guess if it was his spirit or ghost … it pretty much confirms he's dead."

"I know … though, I think that was obvious. The burning question is *why* and *how*? Or maybe it wasn't his spirit, and he is still alive out there, somewhere. I just hope that we get to the bottom of it."

"You and me both." John sighed.

"It seemed pretty odd too, that my laptop appeared to be on when I woke up. Not just that, but the fact that the article of him was also somehow loaded up … maybe it *is* him and he's trying to tell us something?"

"Yeah, maybe. But we can't get too ahead of ourselves. Let's just see what that editor says. If she knows anything, that is."

John dropped the last few apples into one of the buckets and noticed a few of them were slightly bruised, no doubt from where they had fallen. *"Ugh!"* he said unexpectedly, dropping the last apple onto the grass and jumping back. It was crawling with maggots.

"What is it?" David asked, joining him and looking down. "Gross."

"They weren't there a minute ago. I'm telling you! I just noticed them as I picked it up … what the hell is it with us and maggots?"

A strong breeze swept right across the garden and with it, whispering flowed past them. Then, it was gone. Apart from the whisper they had heard in the forest with Gavin, this was the first time they had experienced this phenomenon on the farm. They looked around them.

"Did you catch any of that?" John asked.

"Uh-Uh …" David replied, looking around.

"This place is seriously fucked up, mate. All these weird goings-on. I'm surprised your uncle just doesn't up and leave."

"I actually think he most likely will, if we don't stop this. I have a feeling this is going to continue to affect all of us now regardless of whether we all just left … it's too late to turn back."

"Yeah. I guess we're going to be fucked, either way." John walked up and kicked the maggot infested apple into the bushes. He wiped his trainer clean on the lawn.

# Chapter Twenty-Six

## 13th July, 2018

They took the apple-filled buckets into the kitchen, placed them in a corner and sat chatting at the kitchen table.

"What are you going to say?" John asked.

David felt a little nervous, staring down at his phone. The pen and piece of paper with the names on were also on the table. "I'm not sure … I'll just go with the flow. See what comes out, I guess … feels a bit awkward, though. To tell you the truth, I'm worried about getting that damn static and interference. Sod it … here goes nothing …" David tapped in the editor's number and hesitated before he finally pressed 'dial.'

The phone rang on loudspeaker and David bit on his thumbnail. John watched him, smiling. David's pulse rose as a woman answered.

"Good morning, *Rothie Local News*. This is Sandra, how may I help?" She sounded as if she were in her early forties. Her accent was soft and easy to understand, thankfully.

There was a slight pause from David, before he answered. "Oh, yeah … *hi*! Erm … are you the editor?" He cringed at how timid he sounded.

John was trying not to laugh by biting one of his knuckles. He had rarely seen his friend so nervous talking with someone, particularly over the phone. Normally, David appeared confident with people.

"No, I'm sorry. That would be Deborah. I'm Sandra. I'm a reporter here. Deborah is currently out of the office; I'm just taking her calls until she gets back. She shouldn't be too long … may I ask who's calling? Is there something I can help you with? Or can I take a message for you and get her to call you back?" Sandra was polite and friendly, which made David feel a little more confident and at ease. He was relieved that there was no interference on the line.

"Erm … it's David …"

John managed to stave his laughter, but let slip a large snort he couldn't hold in.

David felt his neck and face grow hot. He looked over at John. *Fuck off,* he mouthed. He stood up, picking up the phone.

"David?" Sandra asked a little confused.

"David Hammond …?" David cringed again as he stamped his foot down onto the kitchen floor, annoyed at himself for sounding so weak and stupid.

Tears were rolling down John's face; he stood up and leant against one of the kitchen walls biting his arm to control his laughter.

"O-kay …" Sandra replied. "And what can I do for you, Mr Hammond? Is there something I can help you with?"

David heard the confusion and annoyance in her voice. He started pacing up and down. He was tongue-tied.

"Hello? Are you there?" Sandra asked.

Furious at John's laughter distracting him, he called out louder this time, *"Fuck off!"*

*"Excuse me?"*

David's eyes widened in shock that Sandra had heard him.

John couldn't contain himself any longer. He walked into the hallway and burst out laughing. Sandra could probably hear that too.

Finally, David managed to compose himself and started again … "I'm sorry about that. My name is David, and I wasn't swearing at you. I apologise. It was meant for my friend. He's being an idiot and making me laugh …"

"Oh, okay …" Sandra laughed herself a little. "Well, Mr Hammond, is there something I can do for you?" Sandra's voice held a little sarcasm.

"Well, basically this may sound a little random, but … I came across an article I am interested in on your website, and I would like to know more about it. Would it be possible to speak to the reporter who wrote it?" David felt his confidence return.

John walked back to the kitchen doorway still smirking. His eyes were red and moist from tears of laughter.

David raised his middle finger and stuck out his tongue.

"Oh, I see. Which article was it, and what was the name of the reporter?"

"Well, that's the thing and perhaps a problem you see, Sandra. The article was done way back in 1999. About a young boy who went missing, by the name of *Charlie Begsbie*. As for the name of the reporter, it's *Marvin Aileanach* …" There was a slight pause from the other end. David could hear the rustling of papers as Sandra went rummaging through some paperwork.

"Sorry ... bear with me one sec ... I'm actually fairly new here. This is only the end of my first week."

"That's okay, take your time." David wasn't exactly sure what Sandra was looking for.

"Ah. Here it is ... sorry about that. I know Deborah keeps a list of names and numbers of certain people. There's only me, Deborah, Jerry and another reporter, who is also a photographer, working here at the moment. There is no one by that name on the list. There are two others, but they're currently away on holiday. One is in Spain. They are called Kenny and Ian; I've never met them. I can ask about a Marvin, though?"

"Okay, that's fine. And thanks. My folks just jetted off to Spain this morning, too."

"Maybe they went to the same place?" Sandra replied with a little laugh, before clearing her throat. "Okay ... so I'm just checking for some other paperwork here ... no, I'm sorry, I can't see a Marvin, I'm afraid, Mr Hammond. I guess Marvin no longer works here. Perhaps for some time."

"Damn."

"Well, I can get Miss Goram, *Deborah*, to call you back? I don't know how long she's worked here, but I think it's been a number of years, now. She might know who this Marvin guy is, and about the article ... what's the name of the boy who went missing again?"

"That would be great. His name was Charlie Begsbie."

"And what's your number, Mr Hammond?"

"Call me *David*," he said cheekily. He looked at John who smiled back. David winked and made a cocky expression, like he was flirting with her.

They could hear Sandra laugh. David could hear from her voice that she was smiling as he gave her his number.

"Well, okay, *David* ... I'll make sure she gives you a call once she gets back. You have a nice day, now. Enjoy the hot weather. It's going to be thirty plus degrees today, they reckon."

"You too, Sandra. And lovely! Many thanks for the help. Goodbye."

"Bye."

"Oh my God. That was *so* fucking funny! I've never seen you look so uncomfortable," John said, walking back into the kitchen.

"Yeah, hysterical ... least you've not lost your sense of humour," David replied with a hint of sarcasm.

"I can't believe she thought you were telling *her* to *F-off!*"

"She said she'd get the editor to call me back. So, fingers crossed." David put his phone away.

"Yeah, I heard her."

"Guess we'll have to see. That's if she does. I'll call back if she doesn't."

They walked out the front and saw Bob and Betty return.

Bob drove the Land Rover up the side of the house to park it in the barn. Betty didn't look any better; she sat aimlessly in the passenger seat. Bob had to walk round and help her out. He opened up one of the back doors and took out a carrier bag of shopping. David thought about the nightmare he'd had again. It made him shiver.

"You going to tell your uncle about that dream you had?" John asked again, looking at David.

David thought for a second or two before answering, "Yeah. I should do."

Bob and Betty came over towards them. They had been gone a little while. "I'll make you a nice cuppa and bring it up to you," Bob said, smiling to Betty.

She walked past John and David and up the stairs, presumably back to bed. Bob stopped in front of the two.

"She going for another lie-down?" David was concerned again for his aunt's well-being.

Bob sighed. "She complained of feeling unwell and having a slight headache, again. I don't know what else I can do. I thought going for a drive and getting her out for a while might make her snap out of it, you know? We even went to a pond and fed the ducks. Well, I did. It's something she likes doing, normally. If there's no improvement, say, Monday, I think I better get her to a doctor. It's like it's some trauma ..." Bob sounded down.

"Did she say anything at all?" John asked.

"Not really. Only one-word answers. Two or three at the most."

"Not good, mate," John replied.

"I'll take a tea up for Betty and have a shower. Did you manage to find any naturalists in the area?" Bob asked, rubbing his neck. It was stiff from where he had fallen asleep in the early hours. "I've been meaning to check myself."

"No, nothing on naturalists, unfortunately. But I came across an old article about Charlie from the Rothie Local News. I'm waiting for the editor to call back to see if she knows the reporter who wrote it all those years back. Or to see what she knows in general. Hopefully, she'll call back soon. I was told she wouldn't be too long."

"Well, that's good, my boy. We normally get that paper once a week.

Either on a Wednesday or Thursday. Funnily enough, we haven't had it for a fortnight or so. Because we're out in the sticks here, one of their delivery guys drives out and drops it off. Well, usually."

"There's erm ... a few other things I need to talk about as well, Uncle ..."

"Oh?" Bob replied. "Listen though, can it wait for about half an hour? I want to make this tea for Betty and get into the shower." Bob sniffed his armpits. "Think I'm getting a bit ripe!" He smiled.

"Err. Yeah, sure. It can wait."

"Okay." Bob smiled again and made his way into the kitchen with his bag.

The other two followed behind him.

"I spoke to my folks earlier. They send their love. I spoke to them just before they boarded their flight."

"Oh, yes. I forgot they were flying out to Spain today. Well, I hope they'll have a great time." Bob unloaded the small bag of shopping with David and John's help, and then made a cup of tea for Betty.

Bob put the decorative flowered China cup on a matching saucer, followed by a couple of Rich Tea biscuits on the side. "She loves these." Bob smiled. "Hopefully, this we'll make her feel a bit better. You boys want a brew, while the kettle's still boiled?"

"I'm good, thanks," David replied.

John said the same.

As Bob picked up the saucer, he noticed the three buckets of apples in the kitchen corner. He looked at the two boys with a confused expression. "You guys took the apples down? I've been meaning to do that myself. I appreciate that!"

"Err. Yeah. Well, we kind of did ... it's one of the things we wanted to tell you about ..." David glanced over at the buckets.

"Okay ... you can in a bit," Bob said. "You two would love the cider I can make with those babies." He grinned at them. He carefully walked up the stairs holding the saucer, trying not to spill any.

"I'm going to go get Benji," David said, "Little mutt's been asleep for ages."

*****

David checked he hadn't missed a call from the editor, while he and John stood outside the barn where Gavin and Derek were doing some maintenance checks on the combine harvester. It was indeed, a blistering hot, glorious day.

Derek, who was holding a well-chewed pencil and a clipboard, was going around the combine ticking the checks off, whistling slightly. A large sweaty patch had formed on the back of his light grey T-shirt.

David watched Derek crouch down by one of the tyres to check it. David thought of the nightmare of Betty cold-bloodedly stabbing Bob. It was the most vivid and lucid nightmare he had ever had. Maybe this was *all* one big nightmare? He wished that it was, and he could wake up in his flat and laugh at it all. If only. Though 'laugh,' was a strong word to use. And probably not the right one.

"Me and Derek thought we may as well check the combine, get it out of the way. A 'service-check,' so to speak. We'll most likely start cutting a couple of the fields as of next week," Gavin said, his head in the combine cabin.

John was staring at the cutter bar, looking at how sharp the teeth and blades were on it as they shone brightly in the sun. They looked even more deadly close up. He was thinking how nasty it would be to get caught up in one of them.

"Was everything okay last night, out here?" David asked.

"Fine," Gavin replied as he pulled his head out. "Nothing out of the ordinary. Well, apart from still having that suspicious feeling that someone or something was watching us. It's come to a point now that it could just be paranoia."

Bob finally reappeared and strolled towards them. "Sorry ... I was just checking my emails and doing some things on my computer."

"Betty okay?" Gavin asked, climbing down from the combine.

"I don't know about her being okay, but I peered in just before I came back out and she's asleep for the time being," Bob replied. He was already perspiring in the heat, particularly on his forehead. "You wanted to tell me something, didn't you, David?"

"Yeah," David replied.

"Where's Jack?" Bob asked. "I'd like to see how he is this morning. I'd like to talk to you all."

"He's just fixing one of the fences, boss," Gavin replied.

"I'll go get him," David volunteered.

David found Jack, again shirtless, repairing a fence where some cows had backed into it a couple of days previously. It wasn't completely down, but it still needed to be sorted.

"Argh, *shit*!" came a slight cry from Jack as David approached him. He was banging a wooden pole into the dry soil and had accidentally whacked his thumb with the hammer.

"You all right?" David asked.

"Aye. I'll be fine … just hit me bleedin' thumb with the hammer." Jack tried to suck it better.

"Bob wants us over near the barn, mate."

"Aye … I'll just finish up here and be right over. Pretty much done now."

Once gathered, they stood near to the combine harvester talking again about the current predicament they were facing. Bob still felt uncertain, about having Jack and Derek still working. Even Gavin, for that matter. They remained adamant about working and watching each other's back and over the animals.

"Unfortunately, I think we're on our own with all of this at the moment. At least until someone can shed some light on it all," Bob said.

"I'm hoping this editor will call me back about the Charlie Begsbie article," David said, checking his phone again, although he would no doubt have heard it ring anyway.

Jack frowned. "Charlie?" His back was beginning to peel a little from the baking hot sun.

"I'll explain later, Jack …" Bob replied. He didn't feel like going through it all again at the moment. He was still raw from opening up to the others about it yesterday. "What was it you wanted to tell me, David?"

John and David looked at each other sheepishly.

Bob noticed and frowned.

"Erm … yes. Can I speak to you, alone?"

Bob was a little bemused. "Okay, sure …"

The two of them walked away from the combine and down to the front lawn, while the others returned to work. Benji stayed with John.

"What is it, David?"

"It's a little embarrassing, Uncle. Well. Not embarrassing as such. Just difficult to tell you, I guess. I just wanted to tell you first, alone …" David walked slowly with his head down.

Bob smiled. "After everything that you've told me so far, I don't think you ought to feel awkward about telling me anything further!" Bob affectionately patted his nephew's back.

David first mentioned about Betty and the sheer coldness in the early hours, then described his dream. "I'm telling you, Uncle Bob, this was no normal dream. I could feel, sense and smell *everything* in that moment. It was so tangible. I can't get that across enough!"

The pair stopped at the bottom of the front garden, not far from the forest boundary. At least they were a little in the shade as well.

Bob had listened carefully and to every word David had told him. He could tell by the way that his nephew described the exact details that this wasn't just an ordinary nightmare.

"I don't want to overreact or anything, and the last thing I want to do is worry you further. We already have enough going on, particularly you, with Aunt Betty … but I'm worried it could mean something. Or … or-" He was cut off by his uncle, before he could finish.

Bob finished his sentence for him. "You're worried it might be a premonition?" He half-smiled.

David blinked softly and nodded his head.

"I hear you. And I understand you," Bob said with sympathy. "I honestly feel for you; what you had to endure during that nightmare. I'm sorry. I agree too, it was most likely not a normal nightmare, so to speak … and it most likely is all related to what's been going on around here. It has concerned me. Even more so, after what you said you heard and felt in our bedroom … I'm glad you have warned me, David …" Bob held one of David's arms.

"I'm sorry."

"Please, don't be."

"Betty's behaviour, together with my dream; maybe she is under a dark influence? We have to stick together. Look out for one another."

Bob gripped both of David's arms now, giving him a slight shake with added reassurance and warmth. "We will … we're all going to stick together."

John, who was walking back and forth near the combine, was watching his friend and Bob having a heart-to-heart.

David sighed. "The thing is … something else happened as well … I don't know if it's a bad thing or not, though … Me and John were sitting out the back. I was on my laptop, looking up about Charlie and that. We decided to move underneath the old apple tree for some shade. All of a sudden, the apples just *fell* from the tree, all at once. They just came crashing down. And then … then we heard what sounded like a child's laugh and something cold went straight past us. We decided to pick the apples up. It would save you or someone else doing it. John even came across a maggot infested one. *Maggots*, again."

"I see …" Bob rubbed his bristly chin, which was mainly white, showing his age. "I don't know what that means. We've had certain things happen around here of late, like I said. Things being moved or missing. Not to mention these whispers. It's all very peculiar. And Gavin has heard a child laugh."

"You know, Uncle. I'm thinking, what if Charlie *did* die all those years back, and it was his spirit, trying to reach out to us? Last night, I turned my laptop off before I went to sleep, but it was back on when I woke up and the article about Charlie was loaded on the screen."

Bob let out a sigh and shook his head. "I honestly don't know, David. It's plausible, taking everything into account. But then, it could be this unexplained hooded thing or entity, that's trying to fool us and make us believe that."

It felt good knowing his uncle was on the same wavelength, thinking the same things that he and John had wondered.

After chatting a little more, they started to make their way back to John.

John was waiting patiently with Benji. He was replying to another joke from Grant. At least it seemed that Grant felt better now. John decided he'd give him a call later on.

"... Okay, that's fine. Let me know if that editor calls back, won't you? I've got some paperwork and other stuff to do this morning. At least the weather's more than nice today," Bob said to David. He smiled at John and made his way past the combine harvester.

"I will," David replied, bending down to give Benji a stroke.

"Well? How did he take it, about that dream and the apples?" John asked.

"Basically, he thinks the same as us; it could be Charlie or this *thing* playing games with us. He said he'll keep an extra eye on Betty. And to be careful."

"Well, at least you told him, mate. It does seem odd warning someone about their wife, who might end up killing them!"

"Tell me about it."

# Chapter Twenty-Seven

## 13th July, 2018

David took Benji up near to the metal grain silos. The ground there was flat and open. The green and brown earth was dry. It wasn't even midday, yet the temperature was rapidly increasing. It was thirty degrees already.

David wished he had brought his sunglasses; the sun was blinding where it reflected off the silos. He tried to shield his eyes with his right hand as he looked to the top of one of the silos, where a high-pitched chirping sound caught his attention.

On top of one of the silos, was an Osprey eagle. Although he knew little about birds, he recognised this particular eagle, having read about it briefly earlier in the week, when he, Grant and John were on his laptop in his flat. He recalled the distinctive greyish-white belly. He thought it was strange to see one out here on his uncle's farm. From what he remembered, they mainly ate fish and usually nested near water. He thought it was pretty cool seeing an eagle for the first time in his life in reality and wanted to take a photo.

The Osprey was staring down, probably at Benji, who was sniffing around the dirt at the base of the silos. Perhaps it saw Benji as a threat, although Benji didn't pay the eagle any attention.

As David pulled out his phone, the eagle took flight and soared over the fields, eventually disappearing into the forest. "Typical," he said to himself. He then looked up at the silos again and into the clear blue sky. He started to feel a little light-headed and dizzy; when it passed, he felt as if someone or *something* was watching him. Of course, it could have just been the paranoia of it all, as Gavin had mentioned earlier.

Walking further up, David turned to look down over the farmhouse and fields. It was a pleasant view, with the green of the forest outlining the farm; the silos overlooked the farmhouse, the golden fields soon to be harvested, the cows in the near distance grazing, and the hills and mountain range in the far distance.

It all felt very tranquil. If only for a moment. Then the harsh reality of the darkness they were experiencing hit him, and he wondered what secrets the forest surrounding them concealed.

David decided to take a photo of the scenery. As he took the picture and lowered his phone, he could see a shirtless figure that was Jack. David smiled to himself. *Does he ever wear a shirt?* Though it was understandable with this weather and temperature.

Just then, he felt his phone vibrate and ring. Hoping it was the editor, he noticed that his signal was switching between one and two bars. "Hello?"

"Is this David?" a woman's voice asked. Her accent was stronger than Sandra's, but understandable.

"It is, yes?"

"This is Deborah Goram, from the *Rothie Local News*; I was just returning your call. Sorry, you missed me, I had to pop out for a little bit."

"That's okay."

"I believe you wanted to ask me about Marvin and the disappearance of the young boy, Charlie, years back. Is that right?"

"Erm. Yeah. That's correct. I won't go into details, but I would appreciate it if you could shed any light on either of the two, preferably both. Is there any way I could speak to Marvin, directly?" David felt a little stupid. She must have been wondering why he was so interested in a reporter and a news article from so many years ago.

"I see … well, unfortunately, David, I don't think I can help you. You see, Marvin died. He's been dead many years now. In 2000, to be precise …"

"Oh," David replied, feeling frustrated.

"I'm sorry. It was most unfortunate. A freak accident …"

"Oh? What happened, exactly?" David was intrigued. He looked down at Benji who was burrowing into the ground with his two front paws and making a mound of dried dirt.

"He was leaving work one evening, in early January. It wasn't long after Christmas. He had been working late with something and offered to close the office when he'd finished. I only knew him for a couple of months. It's a small office here, so you get to know everyone who works here. I only started working here in November, 1999. It had been very cold and icy. Marvin, as he was walking down the steps to the pavement, must have slipped on one of the bottom steps. He fell backwards and cracked the back of his head. Such a freak and most unfortunate accident …" Deborah went quiet as she recalled the death of Marvin Aileanach.

"I am so sorry," David said. "How old was he? Were you close to him?" He could hear Deborah sigh on the other end of the line, just as he heard a slight crackle over the phone. He hoped the interference wasn't going to start again, just when he was potentially getting somewhere.

"He was fifty-two, David. Not old at all. I wouldn't say I was close to him. But, in the two months or so that I knew him, I got on with him. We all did. He was a friendly man and I liked him. He enjoyed his work and working here, too. There was talk about him becoming the next editor after Sue, the previous editor. I took over when she retired. Unfortunately, she died too, several years later. That was sad as well. She had cancer. She was a spinster and didn't have much family."

"What about Marvin? Was he married or anything? Any children?"

"He was married, yes … to Valerie. She never married again after his death. She was distraught, as you can imagine. I think she still lives around these parts. He didn't have any children himself, but Valerie had a son I think, from a previous marriage," Deborah answered. "There is something else as well …"

"What's that?" David asked as he tried to gently nudge Benji with his right trainer, to prevent him from burrowing further. It was as if he was trying to dig something up. He was starting to get muddy as the soil flicked over his fur.

"Well … somebody found him there. He died before the ambulance arrived; I'm surprised nobody found him sooner. He was drifting in and out of consciousness. Some woman found him. I don't know who she was, but before he died, his last words were something about hearing a whisper or whispering. I have no idea what he meant, and neither did the lady who found him. He was probably delirious, the poor man …"

When David heard Deborah mention whispering, he froze. The static on the line continued as David fell quiet.

"David? Hello? Are you still there?"

"Yes, I'm sorry. I'm still here. I erm, just got a little distracted for a moment. Do you know what Marvin was working on?"

"That's another strange thing. Before the rest of us left that evening, we saw on Marvin's desk the brown folder that he kept files in he was working on. Anyway, we assumed he took his folder before he locked up that night. It wasn't on his desk the following morning, nor on his body. It appeared that someone else must have come across his body and taken the folder. Most peculiar as to why someone would take his work. The woman who found him didn't recall any such folder."

"Could that lady have taken it, perhaps?"

"Well, I guess it's possible. But she didn't seem the type. She came in a couple of days after, with her condolences and a bouquet of flowers. That was very nice of her. She also said she was a regular reader of our paper and enjoyed reading it weekly. I honestly couldn't tell you what he'd been working on. Though, I do recall briefly overhearing him talking to Sue once about Rothiemurchus Forest and some disappearances. There were other assignments she wanted him to look into and he often said he was looking into something else, 'unofficial' so to speak ... he used to say that with a smile. I think it was to do with disappearances around here, but I don't really remember. I am sorry ..."

"That's okay."

"As for the disappearance of that young boy, Charlie, I never heard anything about him. Not until Sandra mentioned that you called, and I found it on our website archive; it happened a few months before I started working here ... I hope you don't mind me asking, David? Why are you so interested in Marvin?"

"No, that's fine. I don't mind you asking. Basically, I just wanted to ask Marvin if he knew of any other disappearances and about the area. I've heard a few stories and myths about the place. I'm ... erm, interested in things like that. Plus, I'm new to the area as well. I guess I am intrigued ..." David winced at his bullshit excuse.

"Oh, okay ..." Deborah sounded unconvinced.

David didn't want to go into *supernatural* reasons and explanations. One, she would probably think he was playing her for a fool and wouldn't believe him, and two, for the time being, he didn't feel comfortable telling anyone.

"Well, as I said, I'm not sure I can help you with anything, David. I've told you everything I know."

"I understand. This may be a bit random, too ... but, would you happen to know of anyone who might know about the area and er, about the forest at all? Like a naturalist, perhaps?"

"I don't, I'm afraid ..."

David stomped his right foot down in further frustration. Puffs of dried dust flew up from the ground. "That's okay. You've been a big help, Deborah. I appreciate you calling me back. I really do."

"You're very welcome, David. I'm sorry I couldn't help you more, but if you need any more assistance, I'd be glad to help. At least I'll try to." Louder, crackling interference accompanied her words.

David couldn't make out what she was saying. He was about to reply, but there was an even louder crackling sound and the call ended abruptly. David frowned and looked at his phone. His battery had been nearly full; it was now almost dead.

At first, he thought speaking to Deborah hadn't been much help, but at least now he had some more insight into Marvin, a reporter, who had died from a freak accident. And he had the first name of Marvin's widow, who according to Deborah, was still alive and lived in the area; *Valerie Aileanach*. That was of course, if she hadn't kept her maiden name or the name from her previous marriage. Maybe if he spoke to Valerie, she could perhaps give some details and insight into what her husband, Marvin, had been working on before his death.

Another thought came to David as he slipped his phone back in his pocket. His uncle had contacted the forest ranger committee about Harold. Surely, if anybody knew of any naturalists and about the forest, they would. They might also have experienced strange things too. He would ask his uncle. Benji was still burrowing ferociously. He was on a mission.

"C'mon boy. What you digging for?" David crouched down near the mound of dirt.

Benji resisted as David tried to prize him away. Benji had dug a fair chunk of a hole out of the soft dirt while David was on the phone. His head was bent down in the hollow.

After a few attempts, David eventually managed to pull Benji away. "Jesus, boy," David said, looking over Benji.

Benji's tongue was hanging out, panting. Flakes of dirt were over his eyes as well as his fur.

David looked back into the hole. Curious now, he started to dig himself with his hands. He was intrigued as to why Benji had been burrowing so enthusiastically. "God ... let's have a look at what you were so bothered about, eh?" David said aloud to Benji. Dirt was making its way underneath his fingernails.

Benji watched his master continue what he'd started.

David soon felt something small and metallic with his right hand, hidden in the dirt. He pulled it out and turned his hand over. A small pile of mud lay on his right palm. It had been deeper and was therefore moister. He removed the dirt to unveil a silver signet ring.

The tarnished ring had two small, engraved crosses on either side of it. David could just about make out the small marking of 925 on the inside of the ring that confirmed it was made of silver. The main part of the ring, the top, had a silver coin/medal set into it. David blew away the last remains of debris and tried to rub it clear on his blue T-shirt. The ring twinkled in the sunlight, now that it was a little cleaner.

On the inner part of the coin was the portrait of an elderly man with a long beard, wearing a robe. There was a halo around his hooded head. In his right hand he held a cross and in his left, an open book. Surrounding this image were some words that looked Latin: •EIVS IN OBITV NRO PRÆ SENTIA MVNIAMVR•

David had no idea what it meant. There were also other symbols and letters on the medal or coin. But they had since eroded or had perhaps been deliberately scratched away.

David turned the ring over and noticed there had been other inscriptions on the back too. He could see traces of letters and symbols, but nothing more. He did, however, notice on the outside of the ring at the bottom more unscathed lettering; VADE RETRO SATANA. Again, David had no idea what it meant, but assumed it was Latin.

He wondered how long the ring had been in the ground for.

David dropped the ring into one of his pockets and stood up, brushing down his dirty knees. He yet again felt he was being watched from somewhere. He checked around in all directions but could see nobody. A strong breeze came up suddenly. He appreciated the coolness as it swept across his face and bare limbs. He liked the hot weather but this was getting way too hot. He could feel the sweat from his upper back seeping through his T-shirt.

David gave Benji's fur a ruffle to shake out some of the dirt and they hastily headed back down to the farm.

John was outside the front of the house chatting to Gavin. "Ah … here he is, the man of the moment," John joked as David approached. "I've spoken to Grant. He says 'Hey' to you, bud. He still feels bad not joining us. I didn't like lying to him, but I didn't go into detail about what has been happening up here too much. I didn't want him to fret. As long as he's down there, he should be safe. Did that editor call back at all?"

"Yeah, she did."

"Well, what did she say? Did she give any useful info about the reporter?"

"I got that interference again; it even drained my battery. Unfortunately,

Marvin, the reporter who wrote the article about Charlie, died back in 2000."

"Shit," John said.

"I know. That's not all ... he supposedly slipped leaving work and cracked his head open."

"Talk about unfortunate," Gavin said.

"Yep. But check this out ... his last words before he died were something about *whispers* and none of his colleagues could find what he'd been working on. The editor reckoned that someone had stolen his folder from him, as he laid there."

John and Gavin looked across at each other, both with serious faces.

"Just when you thought this shit couldn't get any more serious," John replied.

"This is all pretty damn heavy. So basically, there's even more proof that weird stuff was happening all those years back?" Gavin said.

"Yep ... I found this too up in the field. Well, Benji did. He was digging away whilst I was on the phone." David pulled out the ring from his pocket and handed it to John who examined it, along with Gavin.

"A silver ring?" John said.

John handed the ring to Gavin to look at. He twirled it in his hand and held it up in front of him.

"Parts of the ring are damaged and worn off. The words are Latin I think," David added. "I can have a look online."

"It appears to be Latin." Gavin gave the ring back to David.

Despite the low battery and Wi-Fi signal on his phone, David then looked up online to see what the Latin meant on the discovered silver ring. The •EIVS IN OBITV NRO PRÆ SENTIA MVNIAMVR• translated to: *May we be strengthened by his presence in the hour of our death.* VADE RETRO SATANA translated as: *Step back, Satan.* The figure on the coin, was *St Benedict,* the patron saint of Europe. People believed that St Benedict would protect you from evil, as well as poison.

"Interesting ..." David said to the other two.

*****

David along with John, Bob and Gavin, were standing chatting near one of the fields. David had shown his uncle the ring he had found, just in case it belonged to him. It didn't.

"Maybe there's a shit load of treasure buried up there as well," John joked, grinning.

The others smiled.

"Do you own that piece of land further up, Uncle?"

"Actually, I don't. That particular sector is owned by the Forestry Commission."

A high-pitched whistling sound resonated above them.

They all looked up.

"I reckon that's the same eagle I saw earlier," David said, shielding the sun from his eyes with his right hand.

"Is that an eagle? I didn't know you had eagles in Scotland," John asked, risking sounding ignorant.

"Aye," Gavin replied, "It's an Osprey."

"I thought it was. They usually nest around water, don't they?" David asked.

John looked over at him; he seemed confused. "What do *you* know about eagles?"

David smiled. "I saw it come up the other day when you and Grant were round. Remember? When we were looking up the area. You were too busy on your phone."

"Oh."

"I've seen it before, too," Bob said. "I last saw it a couple of weeks ago on one of the barns. It's probably nested near the River Spey. It will have come from around that area, I would have thought."

They watched the eagle circle them, before it headed off back into the forest in the same direction it had flown earlier.

"That editor didn't give too much information, then?" Bob asked David.

"Only what I told you, Uncle … Like I said, maybe there is a way of contacting his widow somehow, to see if she can give any details? It might be awkward asking her about Marvin. Especially after all these years. It might be like opening up old wounds."

"Yes, I agree. It might be … if there is a way of getting hold of her, that is. I think it's a good idea to contact the forest rangers again. Someone may know a little bit more about the forest. I don't think there's anything more that we can do."

As the small group walked casually back towards the animal pens, they heard a slight rumble coming from their left. It was fast approaching. Before they knew it, a fighter jet roared over them, followed by another, letting out a large explosion of sound. It startled them as they cowered, especially Benji.

*"Jesus!"* John shouted as the jets disappeared into the distance as quickly as they appeared.

"Not seen any of those, for a long time!" Bob stated. "There's a few air bases up here in Scotland. Notably, RAF Lossiemouth. That's not too far from here. It's probably where they've headed to."

"Fucking loud enough!" John replied, making the others laugh.

Benji's ears were still pricked up.

"It's okay, boy. They've gone now," David said, stroking Benji's head.

# Chapter Twenty-Eight

## 13th July, 2018

Gavin went off to do some work while Bob, David and John, made their way to Bob's study. They saw Betty come down the stairs and the two cats darted down past her and into the kitchen. She smiled at the three of them and seemed more radiant. Definitely better.

"Good morning. What a beautiful day it is!" She beamed, stepping into the hallway.

"You look better, love! How are you feeling?" Bob asked. Seeing his wife looking better made him feel happier himself.

But David still wasn't so sure. There was an aura about his aunt, something that still didn't feel right about her. He remembered his nightmare again.

"I'm feeling a lot better now. It's just the past few days have been tough on me, you know? I'm sorry if I worried you all and scared you." She walked over to Bob and gave him a hug.

Over his shoulder, she looked straight at David and smiled. It made him feel uneasy, like she was acting. He sensed something aloof behind his aunt's eyes.

They watched as Betty walked into the kitchen. They could hear her open up the back door, no doubt to let the fresh air in. She then walked back out into the living room and proceeded to open the patio doors as well. Then stepped out into the garden.

"Well, I guess that's something," Bob said sounding hopeful. "She appears to have snapped out of her ordeal. Hopefully, I won't have to take her to the doctors after all."

"Yeah," David replied, raising his eyebrows. He didn't know what to think anymore. So much had happened.

The three of them and Benji walked into Bob's study.

"I wrote the number down of the forest rangers on a pad here. I don't think we'll need to use the computer. A guy I spoke to said his name was *Gareth.* He was the manager. He said to call back if I had any other queries. I'll put him on speaker phone so we can all listen," Bob suggested.

There were a few stacks of paperwork, folders and binders, stored neatly in his study on the shelves. It was the size of a small bedroom and kept tidy. A dust free, white wall desk lined the room. Bob sat down in a black leather chair and picked up the phone from next to a framed picture of him and Betty.

"*Rothiemurchus Forest Rangers*, how can I help?" someone with a northern accent, although not Scottish, answered immediately after the first ring.

"Good morning; is this Gareth?"

"Yes, it is."

"I spoke to you yesterday, if you recall? I enquired whether you had a forest ranger called Harold ..."

There was a slight pause from Gareth. "Ah, yes! I remember. *Bob*, wasn't it? Most peculiar; someone pretending to be a forest ranger and all kitted out. Christ knows where they got the uniform! Is there something else I can help you with, mate?"

"Yes, that's me. Well, I'm not sure if you can help, but there are a couple of other things. Basically, I was hoping that you might be able to tell us more about the area, and the forest in particular, or if you know someone who is a bit more of an expert on the area?"

"I'm happy to help, or at least try ... it depends on what you want to know, I guess? It's on our website, but to begin with I can give you a little background on what we actually do up here and what our job entails, if you like? I'll try not to bore you or go into *too* much detail!" Gareth laughed.

Bob wasn't too interested in the forest rangers per se, but he thought it wouldn't hurt. He thought it would be best to be polite, at least. And perhaps, the friendlier he got with this Gareth, the more chance he would help. He looked over his shoulder at John and David for confirmation. They both had their arms folded and nodded. "Sure, why not. It would be a start, to see what you guys do," Bob replied, though still a little reluctant.

"Cool. Our job, like most other forest rangers, is to look after and maintain the forest. We look after the well-being of the forest, but also the people that visit Rothiemurchus and the animals that inhabit it. We clear up litter, make sure there aren't any fires or arson, anything that can harm the environment as well as people."

"No shit," John muttered in David's ear, who smiled.

Bob heard too, looking round and cast John a smile.

"Also, any complaints ... to fishing regulations, regarding the *Spey* that flows through here ... there are obviously other things too, but I won't bore you with them ... I guess it's all pretty self-explanatory and obvious. Like I said, there's more information on our website. We are also proud to say that we hold the title as the 'longest serving private estate forest ranger service' up here in Scotland!" Gareth sounded proud.

To their surprise, Gareth started sharing a little more about his private life and how much he loved being a ranger. John mimicked a yawn jokingly.

"... so, I moved up from London a couple of months ago, where I was in charge of the forest rangers for Epping Forest. I actually prefer it, mainly due to the scenery and variety of wildlife. Oh, and I forgot to mention, we're government-funded a bit and we also do tours. Again, full details are on our website ..." Gareth finally finished what seemed like a mini-life story, which the three of them couldn't help but find slightly amusing.

Bob hadn't wanted to interrupt Gareth while he was waffling on. "I see. Well, thanks for the details on that, Gareth. There are only six of you, including yourself? It doesn't seem much for such a vast forest."

Gareth laughed. "Good point, Bob! It isn't many, of course. But if need be, thanks to the funding, we can get more temporary staff in and hire outside help. Particularly with the more 'nitty-gritty' stuff, like with the tree cutting and maintenance. Parts of this forest are owned by the government's Forestry Commission, as you will know. So, we all help each other out. We all do what we can, believe you, me!

"We sometimes get volunteers as well. Fortunately, it's pretty much well preserved for long periods and it's relatively well looked after by people who camp here and stuff. Apart from the pyromaniacs! It is enjoyable, even if it can be tough. Especially with these fires. But it's a good job and-"

Bob cut Gareth off. "Sorry, Gareth ... what was that about fires?"

"Huh? Oh, yes. It happened a few times last summer, too. The ones we're aware of. We've seen evidence of some fires. Certain trees have been burnt or singed; there are patches of ash in certain areas, things like that. Only small areas, but it's still a concern. We've contacted the local police. They've reassured us that it's fine and probably just isolated incidents. They are looking into the matter regardless and keeping an extra eye out to help us. I guess that's all we can do."

"Have you witnessed these fires, yourself?" Bob scratched his left cheek.

"You know what? I haven't. There's been a few people who have reported seeing flames, either in the distance or while driving past the forest at night.

One stepped out of his car to check, but as soon as he stepped into the forest, the fire went out.

"I've tried looking around at night a few times myself, to see if I could catch the culprits, but I've never encountered anyone nor any fire. Not that I've ventured too far in though, by myself. Just to be safe. There was even a couple who had driven through parts of the forest one night and 'pulled over in a layby,' like you, er, do! They said it felt as if they were being watched. They then heard some chanting. Then, they drove off." Gareth laughed. "We've checked on a few areas where people have claimed to see fires, but there weren't any signs of anything by the morning. Odd. That sometimes there was, sometimes there wasn't …"

Bob looked at his nephew and John. They were all intrigued. There were so many matching stories; the fires, the chanting … but what about this whispering and stories of disappearances and such? Bob pressed Gareth further; he was a talkative person and easy to question. "About the area though, Gareth. Have you seen anything? Anything like, erm, out of the ordinary? Like, have you heard any stories of disappearances, things like that?" As Bob asked the questions, a crackle came over the phone. Thankfully, it soon passed and Gareth answered.

"Well, we sometimes get a bit of that. Some sort of interference on our phones. Not an awful lot, but it can happen. Sometimes it's fine for a couple of weeks; then it plays up again. No one knows what it is. We've tried to contact the phone companies; they were vague about it. They said they'd look into it or there wasn't that much they could do about it. It isn't *all* the time though, so it isn't too much of a problem.

"It does seem to have been getting worse of late, for some reason. They said it's probably just the weather. How it can affect the signals and stuff … I guess it's just some part of the forest areas that get a poor reception? No doubt the mountains and hills affect the signal as well. To answer your question about anything strange … it's hard to explain. I'd say yes and no."

"How do you mean?" Bob asked, lifting his elbow, giving it a rub.

"Well, sometimes it feels like I am being watched, when I'm in the forest or near it. I've never actually seen anything or anyone. Sometimes I've felt a chill or heard a couple of sounds, like someone is whispering in the bushes! It sounds stupid, I know." Gareth laughed nervously.

Bob again looked at David and John, then focused back on the phone.

"Bearing in mind, I haven't been up here *too* long. It's funny, though … a few other people who come on our tours and go camping have said similar things and have had the same sensation. Not that it stops them, mind. But then, others haven't felt or said anything. Strange … I also came across a few strange symbols that were carved into a tree as well. Just minor things like that. Things that weren't there before.

"For example, I took a small group out to a spot to see some wildlife a few weeks back. I remember standing next to a tree as we were watching some deer, just ahead of us. We moved on and eventually came back the same way. I passed the same tree and I knew it was the same, but it had strange markings freshly carved into it!" Gareth laughed again. "I don't know what the symbols meant or what they were. It was starting to get dark and I wanted to make sure I had the group back by sunset … How about you? Didn't you say yesterday that you had a farm near to Rothiemurchus or inside the forest, itself?" It was Gareth's turn to ask Bob some questions.

"Yes, that's right … I have a farm here inside Rothiemurchus Forest."

"Wow. Seems a bit unusual to have a farm inside a forest, here."

"Not as unusual as you'd think, actually."

"It must be the other side of the forest to where we are, then? Must be a good few miles … I don't ever recall seeing a farm up here in the forest on one of my checks, or when doing a tour. Some manager I am!" Gareth laughed again. "I don't think the other rangers have ever mentioned anything, either. I guess it goes to show how big the forest is and how we as forest rangers, can't keep a close eye on and check every part of the *big old green mass.*" Gareth chuckled.

"Yep. It sure does." Bob assumed by Gareth's statement that he probably didn't know about Angus' farm either.

"To be fair though, the forest up here is a bit more isolated. It's cleaner than say, Epping Forest, which is near to London and more heavily populated. It's a different environment. Less fly-tipping for sure … Have you experienced anything similar to what I've described at all, anything strange or out of the ordinary, then? You said you've been here a number of years, didn't you? You probably know more than anyone!" Gareth laughed further. He seemed a friendly chap.

Bob didn't want to give too much away at the moment. He wanted to remain cautious and to keep his cards close to his chest. He still wasn't sure if he could trust telling Gareth everything, and he didn't feel comfortable giving too much away. So, he quickly diverted the question by asking Gareth another one. "Sort of the same, Gareth. What about other stories? Like have you heard of any disappearances or anything like that?" he asked quickly.

"Nothing too concrete. I mean, people talk, you know? When we take them on tours; they've heard certain stories about people going missing over the years. Even one about a little boy that went missing and was never found years ago. But if I'm Frank with you, I don't pay much attention; they're depressing stories. I doubt if many of them, if *any*, are actually true."

"Erm, yes, I can understand that," Bob replied in his gruff voice.

"I mean, I like to try and keep an open-mind about things, but I'm more of a 'seeing is believing' guy, you know? It's possible that maybe the forest is haunted, like I've heard people say, but who really knows? It still isn't enough to put me off. I enjoy my work up here, as do the other rangers, even though they've felt similar things. Or so they say … the only thing I'm really concerned about, is who's behind these fires, in case the whole bloody forest goes up. Especially, when it's summer and a hot day like this and everything is dry. We could end up having a bloody bush fire!" Gareth laughed slightly. "And that's another thing, Bob … if these stories are indeed *true*, even some of them, why do people still come on tours and camp here? Things can't be *that* bad."

"I guess that's true." Bob was thinking of poor Charlie. "I was wondering as well, Gareth. Do you know any experts on the area? Perhaps, a naturalist? Not that I'm saying you *aren't* an expert and your erm, team. No offence!"

Gareth chuckled. "None taken! There is someone, as it happens … I think they live not too far from *Rothie*. I've not spoken to him myself, nor seen him. I think he likes to keep himself to himself, you know? But my assistant, Danny, has a brother-in-law who's an ecologist near here. He might be able to aid you further. Danny's been dealing with him since before I started up here. He was looking into some things; some animals were found dead in a bad way and stuff … there were reports before I started; perhaps I should have mentioned it before, but I didn't think … hold on, I think Danny's about somewhere …"

Bob heard Gareth place the phone receiver down as he went to look for his associate. "Well, this could be something?"

"Maybe I should have Googled *ecologist*, rather than naturalist," David said.

They could hear Gareth's voice calling Danny's name, when a few more lines of interference came over the line.

Gareth came back to the phone and picked it up. "Sorry about that. Danny's busy, but I'm happy to give you a call back once I've spoken to him. I can try and get the name and number of his brother-in-law."

"That's great. Not a problem. My number is 01479 ..." Bob gave the rest of his number as well as his mobile one. Gareth made a note of it and promised to call back, regardless of whether he got any name and number from this Danny. And with that, the phone call ended. Bob sighed as he got up. "I'm not sure why I gave the area code." He smiled slightly. "Well, that was interesting ... hopefully we can get hold of this ecologist and he can tell us some more."

"Obviously nobody else has seen that inverted pentagram made out of animal bones that we saw, or that freaky fucking tree out there in the forest," John said.

"Yeah, maybe we should tell him, if he calls back?" David replied.

"I think it's best if we keep things to ourselves for now. Let us weigh up the situation some more. We need to work out who we can trust, if anyone, and who we can't," Bob said, folding his arms.

"True, I suppose. But at the same time, we can't expect people to help us if we keep everything to ourselves, Uncle."

"I know, David. The thing is, what if we tell someone and somehow make matters worse? Like with that tree you saw out there and those bones; what happened to you, when you touched it ... maybe you weren't supposed to have come across it? Perhaps, whatever is behind all of this or these people, don't yet know you were there? The last thing we want is to annoy them further. Maybe these are just warnings ... I honestly don't know what to think, anymore.

"Take that Gareth ... he seemed a pleasant sort of guy, but maybe he's part of all this? It's brought back even more painful memories for me, regarding Charlie. Like these awful theories of what really happened to him ... I dread to think how Betty would react if I told her more about all this, especially as she seems better this morning. Like with this Marvin reporter. I can't avoid telling her, but we need to know more first. Perhaps, when the time is right ..." Bob stared down at the black carpet floor, in thought.

"I completely understand, Uncle. But will there ever be a right time? The chances are, whatever that tree in the clearing was, 'they' already know we were there, and that Harold was watching us."

"Yep. It's highly likely. The thing is, so many people doubt the supernatural. I had my doubts until recently. But we have some evidence. What if we erm ... what if we went to the paper or the news, or at least the police? We could also get our 'fifteen minutes of fame,' if nothing else!" John half-joked.

Bob looked at John and smiled. "It's a good suggestion, John. But would the police and papers et cetera believe us, even with the evidence? They'd probably think it was an elaborate hoax. As I say, what worries me is that if we make it more public, we could make matters worse and risk our lives even more. It just feels like a whole bloody *catch twenty-two* situation."

"That's exactly what I think. Even before I came up here." David half-smiled back to his uncle.

"Take those notes, David, and the other warnings you guys had not to come up here. And that other poor friend of yours, Grant. Perhaps, you've angered them even more by coming?" Bob suggested.

"Like you say, *catch twenty-two*," David replied. "But by trying to scare me off, they just made me more determined to come. That's the irony. They started it. Now we have to try and finish it."

"One thing that has bugged me though, and I can't help but think ..." John said, "Why were they, whoever *they* are, so damn adamant to keep us away?"

"It's odd. To think that this hooded thing was not only on the farm, but possibly in my flat and Grant's. Not to mention John's trashed car and the service station and motorway incidents." David stared down at the carpet.

"Maybe they see you two as a threat?" Bob suggested.

John laughed. "*Us*? A threat to what? We're pretty much powerless against this *thing*. I'm surprised it hasn't taken us out already!"

They stood there looking at each other pondering, when the phone suddenly rang. It made all three of them jump.

Bob turned to pick it up. "Hopefully, it's Gareth. Hello ...?" There was nothing but silence. Bob frowned. "Hello ...?"

A slight static came over the line. It grew louder and then an unearthly cry came from the other end, causing Bob to drop the receiver in shock. It sounded like a low-pitched deep moan. *"Argh!"* Bob cried, holding his ear.

John and David could also hear the scream and Benji started barking.

*"Bob!"* David shouted.

The phone receiver swung back and forth on its twisted wire, smacking the underneath of the desk.

"I'm fine ..."

"What the hell was that?" John asked.

The three of them looked at the dropped receiver as it slowly came to a halt. There was no longer any sound coming from it.

David slowly reached out to the receiver with his right hand. He put his hand around it, quickly reacting on reflex to the static and dropped it, causing it to swing again. "Shit! I got a shock and it's so cold." He held his right hand in his left and winced. The palm of his hand and fingers were bright red.

John hesitated. He carefully picked up the receiver and held it away from his ear. Nothing. No static over the line; the receiver felt normal to touch. He slowly placed it back down on the phone base, turning to Bob and David who were watching him. "This is seriously starting to piss me off, now."

"You okay?" David asked his uncle.

Bob nodded. "I'm fine, David ... just startled. It was like a blast of icy-cold air firing into my ear." Bob held his palm to his ear.

"Let me take a look ..." David said as he looked into his uncle's right ear. "Jesus ..."

"What is it?" Bob asked; a look of concern fell across his face as he turned to his nephew.

Bob's right ear was red with frost particles around the inner hairs. As well as the vellus hairs.

"Your ear looks frosted," David answered.

John frowned and looked for himself.

Bob put the tip of his forefinger inside his ear and frantically wiggled it, trying to remove the particles and warm his ear.

"It's like those frosted handprints on John's car window," David said.

"Well, whatever it is, it's certainly a 'frosty' character," John joked.

"That's not 'cool,' John." Bob managed to give a smile, making a quip of his own.

The phone rang again and they all looked at one another.

"It could be Gareth calling back?" Bob said.

"Sod it!" David said. He reached over and picked up the phone and answered abruptly, "Hello?"

There was a pause.

"Erm. Hi. Is Bob there, please?"

"Hold on ..." David handed the phone to his uncle. He covered the mouthpiece and added, "I think it's Gareth. It sounds like him."

Bob gingerly took the phone from his nephew and placed the receiver to his left ear this time. "This is Bob."

"Hello, Bob; it's Gareth. I tried ringing just before, but you were engaged ... got some good news for you ... I've spoken to Danny; my assistant. He's given me his brother-in-law's number for you. You know, the ecologist? It's a mobile number and it's the only number Danny has. The guy's name is *Carl Graham*."

"That's great," Bob replied. "Thank you."

"Danny doesn't speak to Carl much, to be honest. And he probably won't be related to him for much more either, as his sister is divorcing him."

"Erm, okay."

"It turns out he doesn't actually live up here as such, but he's staying at some lodge or bed and breakfast in a small village not too far away, called Tomatin. I won't keep you, mate. I'll give you his number. If there's anything else you need, don't hesitate to call."

"Where is this Tomatin place?" John asked as they left Bob's study. "Do they specialise in tomatoes?" John smiled.

Bob laughed. "No. But there is an old distillery there. We've driven through it a number of times. It seemed a nice enough place. A little isolated."

"Sounds like another one going through a divorce or having marriage problems," David said.

"What's that?" his uncle asked.

"Oh, nothing. It's just there was this other guy, Simon, back at the pub yesterday, who was having problems with his marriage. He seemed a decent guy, though. He even offered to pay for John's burger."

"Yeah. Top man," replied John.

"That was nice of him." Bob folded the piece of paper with Carl's name and number on it. "I'll whip us up some sarnies, then get on the blower to this *Carl* fellow. Hopefully, he can give us some more insight. I'm not feeling too hopeful. It could just be a dead end." Bob scratched his head.

"We should try and contact Marvin's widow as well."

"Maybe, David. But we'll see how we get on with this ecologist first," Bob replied and they made their way into the kitchen.

*****

Bob had made his workers some corned beef sandwiches with horse radish, adding a little 'kick' to them. They were stacked on a large plate in the centre of the kitchen table.

Derek and the yet again bare-chested Jack had taken theirs outside, while the others remained seated in the kitchen. Bob was standing by the kitchen sink, smiling to himself. He was watching Betty water the back garden. She certainly seemed more like herself.

She smiled up at him as she watered one of the flower beds with her metal duck watering can. He smiled wider and winked.

There still wasn't a cloud in the sky and the temperature was steadily increasing.

"You said you spoke to this Gareth then, boss?" Gavin wiped his mouth with a tissue. Some breadcrumbs still remained in his beard.

John looked at him from across the table and slightly smirked to himself.

Even though Gavin was close to Bob and Betty, he still persisted a lot of the time to refer to Bob as 'boss.' It started off out of respect to begin with; now after all these years of working under Bob, it had also become an affectionate habit.

"What's that?" Bob replied, turning to face Gavin. He still looked a giant of a man, even sitting down. "Oh, yes ... I'll give this ecologist a call after we've done with lunch."

"You trust him, then?" Gavin took a bite out of one half of the triangular sandwiches.

"I guess. I'm not too sure who we can trust at the moment, as I was telling the boys." Bob walked over to the table and pulled out a seat to join the others. He reached out for a sandwich.

"How's the ear?" Gavin asked.

"Pretty much fine, now," Bob answered.

They had informed Gavin and the other two about what had happened in Bob's study.

*****

Once lunch was done, Gavin went back to work outside while the remaining three sat around the table still.

Bob decided to use his mobile to ring Carl rather than return to his study.

"What are you going to ask?" David queried.

"I'll just see what comes out. To be honest, I'm not going to go into details. Not over the phone. We don't know who may be listening in ... plus, it would be easier to explain things in person. We'll have to get a rough idea as to what this Carl knows to begin with. Let's see ..." Bob dialled and waited. After several rings, the call cut into an answer phone:

*"Hi, you've got through to Carl. I am away until the sixteenth of July, so feel free to leave a message and I'll get back to you then. If you have my other 'non-work' number and it's unrelated to business and urgent, please call that."*

Bob ended the call.

"Answer phone, eh?" John asked.

Bob nodded. "Aye. Away until Monday."

"You're not going to leave a message?" David asked a little surprised.

"I don't know. The answer phone message wasn't exactly welcoming. He mentioned if anyone had his 'non-work' number and it was urgent, then to call that."

"I know. But we are kind of desperate and it is *urgent*," David replied, trying to encourage his uncle to at least call back and leave a message.

"I know … I guess it wouldn't hurt to leave a message," Bob said.

"Even though we don't have his other number, he may still have this other phone on him, mate. He might call back sooner than Monday, if he gets a message beforehand," John added.

"I suppose it's worth a try." Bob listened and waited for the answer phone greeting to finish, before leaving a message for Carl. "Hi. My name's Robert Hammond. I own a farm here in Rothiemurchus Forest, and was just wondering if we could speak at all, about what you know about the area? That is, if you can help at all … I hope you don't mind me calling out of the blue like this. I erm, managed to get your number from the forest rangers who work here. I spoke to the manager, Gareth, and I think Danny, your brother-in-law, passed on your number for us."

Bob felt a little stupid. So, he decided to finish off. "It's, erm, important. I won't go into details over the phone. But if you could please call me back as soon as you can, I'd very much appreciate it. Many thanks … oh, and my number to call back on, is either my landline or mobile …" Bob gave both his numbers and finished the call. "Well, let's hope he calls back Monday, if not before. Failing that, I guess we'll just have to try again."

"I suppose there isn't much more we can do at the moment," David replied.

"I know we've already been over all this, but you've been on this farm for years, Bob. It's odd that apart from the events of the Charlie boy, you didn't come across anything bizarre before?"

"What are you insinuating, John? Are you calling me a liar?"

David was a little shocked by his uncle's response.

John didn't know where to look. He felt his neck go hot. "I … sorry, mate … I didn't mean for it to sound like you were lying."

Bob smiled. "Only messing with you!"

"Oh, you *bastard*!" John grinned back. "You had me going there for a moment! I thought you were being serious."

They all laughed.

"In all honesty, in all the years we've lived up here, we've never come across anything out the ordinary. Apart from what I already told you. I know it sounds strange, as we are inside the heart of the forest … I do remember now, overhearing people when out and about, talking about fires in the forest, when they were driving past at night. I remember someone saying that it was probably a tramp cooking some sausages!

"I think snippets were mentioned about how anyone caught for arson would be dealt with, but I don't think it was the Rothie Local News. We used to get two other papers, but they've long since gone, the companies who printed them. It's funny how you forget and then it just suddenly *pops* back into your head."

"We believe you, Uncle. I just hope this Carl comes back with something."

"Me too. Fingers crossed, eh?" Bob said, flicking the outside of his mobile phone on the table, spinning it round. "John mentioned that you two are going to that disco tonight, over at the pub? It should be good. Get your mind off things for a bit."

"Yeah. I'm not sure it's a good idea, though."

"Why not? It would be good to have a few drinks, to try and forget about things for an evening. Don't be worried about us, David. Betty seems on the mend and we'll be okay with Gavin. Take Jack and Derek with you. Go and enjoy yourselves."

"I don't know." David still sounded unsure.

"C'mon, bud … that Emily will be devastated if you don't show up! Besides, once the booze starts to flow, people open up more. We might overhear something. I know we should all stick together, but there will be a group of us. Safety in numbers."

"Okay … I suppose it won't hurt."

"It's going to be a blast. You'll see!" John put his arm around David.

"Get off," David said, trying not to smile.

"I take it there's a taxi service around here?" John asked, looking over at Bob. "Obviously, I won't be driving if there's alcohol involved."

"There's a few, sure." Bob smiled. "I don't know about picking you up; it will be late and obviously me and Gavin will be doing the late one again. I wouldn't want to leave Betty, especially late at night. But I could drop you boys off?" Bob offered.

"Thanks, Uncle. But we'll taxi it. It's best if you stay here, just to be safe. I mean, it's not like it will cost too much, I expect. And even if it did, we can split it between us all."

"Okay. As you wish." Bob smiled again.

"Jack said he was up for it. I'll double check with him. I haven't asked Derek, yet. I mean, would he come? He doesn't exactly seem the disco or sociable sort."

"I think he'll go, if you ask him, John. I agree, he is a little, how do you say, introverted, but it will do him good," Bob replied.

"Yeah … I'll try and fix him up with some of the local totty, get him smashed!" John laughed. "I'll be focusing on my *own* needs and wants mainly, though."

David shook his head, half-smiling.

"Ha … as long as you don't get him too plastered. I want him back in one piece come Monday," Bob joked back.

"You're okay to look after Benji for the night? I'm not sure how late we're going to be or when the pub shuts. I don't want us to be too late, though."

"Of course. It's fine. He can help us keep watch tonight. I'll make sure that Betty is okay, too. Pop in and out of the house. I feel better though, now that she's feeling more like herself." Bob rose from the table, scooping up his mobile and dropped it into his back pocket."

# Chapter Twenty-Nine

## 13th July, 2018

"What do you say then, Dezza? You up for coming tonight? It will be good!" John asked Derek as they stood with David next to the cow pen.

Derek was chewing hungrily on one of the corned beef sandwiches that Bob had made earlier. It had started to dry out a little, where it had been left out in the hot sun.

It was even hotter now it was past midday. The wheat and barley fields looked like a fluffy sheet of gold with the sun radiating down upon them.

"I don't know ..." Derek answered. He waited until he had finished his mouthful of sandwich before answering fully, "I was thinking of helping Bob and Gavin again, tonight."

"Ah. They'll be fine. Besides, Bob said it would be okay for you to come. So, how about it? We've just confirmed with Jack. He's up for it. We're going to get a taxi and pick him up at his. We can do the same for you. We'll all chip in. Not that it's going to be much." John was excited.

Derek clicked his tongue as he thought it over. "I guess, it's okay. I'm leaving a little earlier today, too. As I helped last night."

"Great!" John said, slapping Derek on the back. John grimaced, feeling the sweat on Derek's T-shirt. He wiped his hand on his shorts. "We erm, can pick you up at say, seven or something? Let us know your address later, mate, just before you finish for the day."

"Okay," Derek replied, clearly lacking the eagerness John was showing.

"I thought he may have taken a little more convincing to join us," David said as they left Derek. He screwed his face up in disgust, noticing a cow defecating in the field.

"Yeah. I know you're worried about leaving the farm tonight, but we can't remain cooped up here all the time. Not that we've exactly remained in, during the time we've been here. It's only our third day. Your uncle and co. have been all right so far during the night," John said, looking over at the chickens. "They have their shotguns, too."

David gave a slight nod.

"You could argue that if something drastic was going to happen further, it would have done so by now." John tried to sound rational.

"I honestly believe that this is just the beginning. Maybe *they* or *it*, are just biding their time, you know? Perhaps they want to lure us into a false sense of security?" David swiped a few midges away that were buzzing around his face.

"That makes sense, too." John stopped and bent down to scratch his left leg. He had what appeared to be a small bite on his shin next to the bone. "Been fucking bit, as well."

David stopped too and looked down at John's fine-haired legs. "You need to shave them," he joked.

"Yeah, yeah … you're the ape!" John joked back, making David smile.

"You shouldn't scratch it. You'll just aggravate it further and make it worse."

"Yeah, but it feels *so* damn good. Bitter sweet!" John scratched hard on his leg with his nails making a rasping sound back and forth over the bite. The small red lump started to bleed from his aggressive scratching. "That's what I hate about wearing damn shorts," John responded, seeing what he'd done.

"We'll go see if Bob has some ointment," David suggested.

Making their way back into the farmhouse, they mentioned about it being 'Friday the thirteenth.'

*****

John was in the shower getting ready for tonight at The Auld Drongair Bàrd, while David was patiently waiting for him to finish. It seemed as if John had been for ever in the bathroom.

David was on the phone to his mother, who had called to let him know they had arrived safely at her sister's home in Spain. "Okay, Mum. Well listen, you make sure you take care and have a great time, okay? Send my love to Dad … Okay, I will … Love you too, Mum. Bye, bye." David threw his phone on the bed and went to knock on the bathroom door. "You done in there yet? You've been ages!"

"Almost done, mate! Just doing my hair, then need to brush me teeth. Won't be more than a few minutes."

David returned to his room to wait.

They had booked a taxi for ten past seven. The company couldn't do seven on the dot or just before. The disco itself, from what they recalled from the flyer, started at eight-thirty. They were to pick Derek and Jack up along the way and hopefully arrive at the pub for around eight, give or take. Derek's address was in the other direction, though not too far, whereas Jack's place was nearer to the pub.

Finally, John finished in the bathroom.

"About fucking time," David said.

"Bite me!" John replied as he entered his room and closed the door.

David walked into the steamy bathroom and showered.

*****

With the towel wrapped around him, David happened to pass Betty as she was coming up the stairs, just as he came out from the bathroom opposite. Her smile seemed genuine enough, but he still felt there was something different about her. Upon entering her bedroom, she turned her head over her shoulder and smiled again, letting out a weird murmur and then closed the door behind her.

She had made David uncomfortable again. He debated whether or not to go out, but he didn't want to let the others, particularly John, down. And he felt safe in the knowledge that both Bob and Gavin would still be holding the fort with their shotguns.

"You got any of that Armani aftershave with you, Dave?" John asked, taking David by surprise.

"Huh? Yeah, I brought a couple of bottles of aftershave with me."

"Sweet. We'll be needing to smell nice and fresh tonight for the ladies." John smiled. "I'll come use it in a bit … you okay?" John frowned.

"Just thinking … I'd better get dressed. The taxi will be here soon."

It was a fantastic summer's evening as John joined David outside the farmhouse, waiting for the taxi to arrive. There hadn't been a single cloud in the sky all day.

Benji was sprawled out on the front garden lawn. He looked up, when a bumble bee caught his attention.

John was looking his best in a short-sleeved white shirt with black jeans and a pair of blue suede shoes. His favourites. David wore a short-sleeved dark navy shirt, a pair of dark grey slim-fit jeans and a pair of beige suede boots with a small heel.

"*Jesus*! How much of my aftershave did you put on?" David asked. "What did you do? Douse yourself in it?"

A strong breeze ruffled Benji's fur and further spread the aftershave's sweet scent.

"Something like that …" John said sarcastically, smiling. "You know me. I like to smell *fresh*," he joked.

David couldn't help but smile, shaking his head. "You better not have used it all?" He had used a subtler amount than John. Another brand.

"Relax. There's plenty left."

"You know, it's not supposed to be too obvious you're wearing aftershave," David advised.

"Whatever … yer *dick*." John grinned and lightly kicked the back of one of David's muscular calves.

David grinned too, kicking back on the side of John's leg.

"You're all ready to go then, boys? *Phew*! You certainly smell like it," Bob said, coming out of the front door. "You going to paint the town red, aye?"

"Something like that …" David replied. He was still not overly enthusiastic about leaving the farm and going out tonight.

"Well, you both look smart. You'll be fighting off the ladies!"

"If he doesn't *fumigate* them, first." David laughed.

"Listen, I know you're worried about going, David. But we'll be fine. You're not exactly too far away if we need you, and we can call you if need be. Just promise me you'll try and have a good time, okay?" Bob placed a hand onto David's left shoulder.

"I promise, I'll try," David replied. "I've just got a bad feeling. Well, I've had a constant bad feeling since this all started. Even more so, since we arrived up here."

"We can't keep living in fear. We still need to live our normal lives, David. Do what makes us happy and human … If something *is* going to happen, then it's going to happen. But at least for tonight, just try and have some fun, okay? Try and take your mind off things. Have a few drinks … and on me …" Bob pulled out a fifty-pound note from his pocket and handed it to David.

"We can't take that, Uncle. We wanted to give you the fifty." David felt awkward.

"Just take it," Bob insisted.

David reluctantly took the note. Bob was basically returning their money.

"Thanks, Uncle Bob!" John said appreciatively.

"No problem." Bob smiled.

David walked over to the lawn and bent down to stroke Benji, saying cheerio.

"He is concerned, isn't he?" Bob said to John.

John nodded. "Yep. You could pick anything out that's happened since the start of the week to understand why. We all are. But ... I think what topped it, was that nightmare he had, you know? It's totally freaked him out. I know he's worried about you all and the farm."

"He's a great boy. Very true-hearted and loving. I'm surprised he's single, not least because he's a good-looking boy. He takes after his parents, that one. You're not so bad-looking too, you know?" Bob smiled and winked.

John grinned and nodded his head. "Flattery will get you *everywhere*, Bobby!"

Bob laughed out loud.

"He's kind of fussy, when it comes to the ladies, though."

"Well, John. He's going to make a woman *very* happy one day, I'm sure of it. A lot of nephews wouldn't even have considered coming up here, with all the current dangers. It proves how much he cares."

"I know, mate. I thought the same thing. But you're family. His words. In part, he's doing it for himself too, because he feels threatened by all of this. But overall, he's looking out for you and Betty."

Bob smiled to himself and looked at David and Benji. "He's a very brave boy. You are as well John ... He totally adores that dog."

"Tell me about it. That's another reason he wanted to help out. He loves animals and was concerned about their well-being up here," John replied, then checked his hair in the reflection of his phone screen. He was concerned the breeze had displaced it. "He's all heart."

"That he is," Bob said as David rejoined them.

Crunching of gravel signalled the arrival of their taxi; a black saloon car with *Rothiemurchus Cars* embossed along the side.

"Well, looks like that's our ride!" John said, rubbing his hands together.

"Just make sure you boys have a great time, yes?" Bob said. "And David, don't worry about Benji. I won't let him out of my sight." Bob smiled reassuringly.

"I'm riding shotgun ..." John said as they got to the taxi doors.

"Be my guest," David replied, not fussed about sitting in the back.

"All right, mate?" John said, opening the passenger door and climbed in.

"Yeah ..." came the rough reply of the taxi driver. He was wearing tinted glasses and a black leather cap. He must have been in his late fifties. He didn't even look at John. According to the ID that hung around his neck, his name was Mick Diver.

David's "Hello" to the cabbie received no acknowledgement.

John texted Jack and Derek to let them know they were on their way, then gave the driver their addresses. He then tried to make small talk. "So … erm … been busy?" he asked, glancing over at the driver, Mick.

"Yeah …" came the reply. "Ticking over …"

"You're English too then, judging by the accent?" John asked.

"Hah! That obvious, eh? Indeed I am … I moved up here a decade ago with my wife … she's Scottish, you see … she wanted to be closer to her family."

"Where did you come up from?" David asked from the back.

"… Peterborough … I was a cabbie back down south, as well." There was sometimes a slight delay when Mick the driver replied or spoke.

"Oh, right. And how do you like it up here? It's certainly nice scenery," John replied.

"That it is …" said Mick as they drove on through the forest either side of them, with the sun shimmering through the trees. "And how about you two? How long have you lived up here?" Mick asked, adjusting his leather cap.

"We've only been up here for a few days. We're helping out on my uncle's farm." David looked out of the window. The forest looked unnaturally dark, even with the evening sun shining bright.

"Yeah," confirmed John, his pungent aftershave was filling the taxi.

Mick wound his window fully down, even with the aircon on.

"We live down south in Hertfordshire. St Albans to be precise," John continued, pulling the sun visor down and admiring himself in the small mirror on the flap.

"… Ah. St Albans. Nice place that … I used to have an old aunt we visited there. Many years ago … I remember the countryside there. *Very* nice."

"Yep. It's a nice place for sure," David replied.

For a few minutes, nothing else was said, until John broke the silence. "So … *Mick* …" He decided to take the piss a little, pausing himself when speaking to imitate Mick's slow speech.

Mick looked across at John, frowning. "Ah … you saw my ID tag, then?" He laughed.

"Yep!" John laughed. "If you don't mind me calling you by your first name?"

"… Well, it *is* my name." Mick smiled.

"I'll take that as a 'yes,' then ... You live near Rothiemurchus? Or not too far?"

"Not too far ... I live in a small village called *Laggan* ... not too far away. Lovely area, too ... Like most places up here in the Highlands ... Lovely scenery."

"What about erm ... this forest, here?" John asked, gesturing to the vast woodland as they went through it. "Ever been in there?"

"... Why do you ask that?"

"Oh, just curious. It's erm, pretty big."

"I went in once with me wife ... not long after we moved up here ... but never again. Not after what happened to me in there ..."

John spun his head round to catch David's eye. David leant forward, eager to hear more.

Mick could see their interest and wasn't sure what they were expecting. He decided to humour them a little. "You see. Me and *Claire*, that's my wife ... we decided to go for a country drive ... we heard about Rothiemurchus Forest, so thought we'd check it out some ..." He looked back at David, then at John, then ahead to the road. "So, we're walking through the forest ... it had been raining, so it's a little muddy, you know? When suddenly ..." Mick shook his head.

"Wh-what happened?" John asked impatiently.

"*Suddenly* ... my bloody feet gave way and I go arse over tit, and landed in a freaking pile of *horse shit*!" Mick burst out laughing.

A bewildered John looked back at David who was shaking his head.

"I'm sorry, lads! It was just your faces ... especially, *yours*," Mick said, looking at John. "Honestly though, I wouldn't say it's the main reason I haven't been back ... but my whole back was covered in a streak of *shit*! I thought it was mud at first ... until I took my T-shirt off and saw that it wasn't ... Needless to say, we didn't last long in the forest."

"Well, what's the main reason you didn't go back?" David asked, sitting back a little on the seat.

"It's never crossed our minds to go back in there ... plus, my wife said she felt a little uncomfortable there, too. Like someone was following and watching us ... I didn't feel that, but then, I was preoccupied with having a whole load of horse crap on my back!"

"You didn't believe her?" asked John.

"Nah ... maybe there *was* someone following us ... maybe they were one of those *doggers*! Hoping me and me wife would 'get it on' ... *Ha*! Chance would be a fine thing. That will be the day; when she puts out! The silly mare was just being paranoid and over cautious … she gets a bit like that." Mick checked one of his dashboard gauges.

"Yeah," John replied under his breath as he looked out of the window. Little did Mick know.

*****

They arrived at Derek's who met them at the top of his road.

"Derek, my man!" John called out of the window. "Get in, mate!"

Derek was wearing a light blue shirt that appeared too long and too big for him, and a pair of dark green corduroy trousers. On his feet were a pair of newly polished black clodhopping shoes.

David felt a little sorry for him. He opened the passenger door and shifted over so that Derek could get in. He caught a scent of Old Spice as Derek joined him. "You look smart," David said, trying to give Derek some confidence.

"Thanks," Derek replied sheepishly, shutting the door after him.

"You looking forward to tonight then, Dez?" John asked, turning his head.

"I suppose."

John laughed. "Don't sound too enthusiastic eh, mate! Have you ever been to The Auld Drongair Bàrd pub, Mick?"

"A few times, yeah. Been a while, though … it seemed a nice enough pub, if a little run down from the outside, if I recall … They do some good food as well … I had some really nice curly chips there," Mick answered, while checking his wing mirror as a car was preparing to overtake.

"Are you self-employed?" David asked.

"Aye … Obviously I work for the company, but I am self-employed, yes … there are two owners: Lionel and Bernard …"

"What are they like as bosses?" asked John as he again checked himself in the sun visor mirror.

"They have their moments, I guess … they're not too bad, apart from the fact they're always bickering about something or other … silly bastards!" Mick gruffly laughed.

*****

There was some traffic on the way to picking up Jack. By the time they pulled up outside his house and Mick gave a toot on the horn, it was almost eight already. They waited a few minutes and then John reached over to press the horn again. A little to Mick's surprise.

"Where is he?" John said annoyed.

*"Oi, oi!"* Jack called out. He strolled out of his terraced house and made his way to the taxi. He was wearing a white V-neck T-shirt, light blue jeans and green suede Adidas trainers. "Budge up, aye!" Jack said, climbing into the taxi next to Derek.

*"Christ!"* David said. "How much aftershave have *you* got on, Jack?" He put the back of his fingers to his nostrils.

"I put on a couple of squirts, aye." Jack grinned.

Even John found it hard to bear the scent and unwound his window all the way to the bottom. David did likewise.

"And I thought *yours* was bad, John." David shook his head.

*****

When they arrived at the pub, they each handed over their share of the fare to John, who in turn gave it to Mick.

"Don't worry about the odd fifty pence, mate. Keep it. Call it a tip," John said.

"Fifty pence is fifty pence," Jack said in the back.

John laughed. "Ha. Typical Scot. Fussed about a few pence; you know why a fifty pence coin is shaped the way it is? 'Cos you need a *wrench*, to pry it from a Scottish man's hand!"

"Aye … ha … bleedin' ha … that's an old one." Jack's tone was sarcastic as he rolled his eyes.

The others laughed, including Mick.

"What time do you boys want picking up?" Mick then asked.

"Not sure yet, mate. Depends on when the pub shuts or if we've had enough. We'll be sure to call you though, when ready," John answered as he opened the taxi door to get out.

"Fair enough," Mick replied. "You boys have a great time … doesn't exactly look busy as of yet."

"Still a little early," David replied.

"Yeah. The disco itself doesn't start until eight-thirty, we think," John added. "Hopefully, it will be heaving!"

"For your sakes, I hope it is." Mick laughed as the others climbed out.

"Aye, it wants to be!" Jack said.

"See you later, boys." Mick smiled.

"Hope it *was* worth it," said John as the four stood there. "Quiet at the moment; are they even open?" John walked over to one of the square pane windows and peeked in.

Apart from a couple of old men sitting at one of the tables in the corner, near to the fireplace, there wasn't a soul in there. There wasn't even anyone behind the bar. There was no sign that a disco was being set up.

"Well?" asked David.

"They seem to be open." John's breath fogged a patch on the window. "I can't see anyone, apart from two old men sitting in the corner." John pulled his face away from the glass. "There certainly doesn't appear to be any sign of a disco. It's probably been cancelled. Seeing as it's supposed to start soon." John sounded disappointed.

David would feel relieved if it *was* cancelled. It would give them an excuse to head back to the farm.

"Fuck's sake," John muttered to himself. "Well, we may as well go in. Have a few drinks and see what's what."

"Aye, let us have a check," Jack agreed, leading the way as they walked over to the red door and entered the pub.

# Chapter Thirty

## 13th July, 2018

They made their way down the step and towards the bar, catching the attention of the two old men who appeared to be in their late seventies. One was wearing a green deerstalker cap.

David heard the one with the cap, mumble something imperceptible under his breath.

"At least the flyer's still there," John said sarcastically.

They heard a scraping of a chair to their left on the floor and watched as the man wearing the cap got up and grabbed his wooden cane and slowly made his way up another step to the gents. He walked with a slight stoop. There were a few dominoes lined up and scattered on the table, which the two had obviously been playing.

"Looks like disco night has been cancelled in favour of *Old Farts' Dominoes Night*, eh?" John muttered quietly to the other three.

Jack couldn't help but laugh.

The other old man who was seated turned round and shot the group a dirty look. It was unlikely he had heard John's comment but knew something had been said to make Jack laugh. The old gentleman reverted his eyes to his pint and swigged back several large gulps of his bitter. He had a longer white beard than his playing companion.

"Well, it doesn't look like any disco is on tonight," David said quietly.

A couple of minutes later, they heard a few stomps from upstairs. Then shortly after, the sound of someone coming from the kitchen.

Jock made his way out into the bar area and greeted the four of them. "Argh, Gentleman! I'm glad ye could make it," he said cheerfully.

"Where's the disco, mate?" a confused John asked.

Jock laughed.

"And where *is* everyone?" John gestured with his hand, looking around.

"Ye'll be pleased to know that the disco is still on, aye! Reggie, the DJ who does it, he phoned me to say he's running late."

"Great! At least it's still on, then." John grinned widely.

David was disappointed.

"Why's it so quiet, though? Surely people would have turned up for half eight, aye?" Jack asked.

Jock again laughed, just as the old man returned to his seat from the toilet, walking steadily with his wooden cane. "It usually is to start off with. But after an hour or two, it picks up. Ye will see!"

"What time is the disco due to start now?" David asked. Part of him hoped that the DJ would call again, saying he couldn't make it.

"He told me around nine, nine-thirty at the very latest … *argh*. Bloody DJ … *hah*!"

"Just hope it does pick up," John said.

"Aye …" replied Jock, wearing the same black Celtic polo that he had worn yesterday. "I'm gonna move the tables and chairs in a wee bit. It will definitely pick up. Not unless these pair of miserable sods scare the folk off." Jock laughed and looked at the two old men who had restarted their game of dominoes in the corner.

They looked over at Jock and the capless one gave him a glaring look.

"They're harmless enough, though … they just take their game of dominoes very seriously, ye know, aye? They've been coming here ever since I took over …"

"I take it they're not going to stay for the disco?" John joked.

"*Hah*! Now that would be a miracle. But nae, they're usually gone by the time it kicks off. They don't like things too loud … especially that one there …" Jock laughed again, pointing at the capless old gentleman. "Never mind those pair of grumpy old bollocks, though … ain't that right, Ralf?" Jock called over to the table where the two old men were sitting.

The one without the deerstalker hat turned his head to the bar. He made an utterance and waved his hand in the air, before returning to his game.

Jock laughed yet again. "That one there … he's Ralf … the other old sap, wearing the cap, that there, is Samuel … Name ye poison, laddies!"

John bought the first round; pints for Jack and Derek and double shorts for John and David; a Jack Daniels and vodka, respectively. No ice.

John knocked his back within twenty seconds. The other three looked on. "What?" John said. "Hit me again, Jock!" He put the empty glass down on the bar.

"Aye. Ye in the mood tonight, eh?" Jock smiled, refilling the glass.

"That I am! So, Jock ... those two fitties working behind the bar, tonight?" John asked, paying for his second drink.

Jock grinned. "Ha! Ye mean my Annabel and Emily, aye?" Jock poured himself a pint of Guinness. "I gave 'em the night off."

"Oh ..." John said, feeling disappointed. He took a sip of his drink.

"Fear not, though ... they both wanted the night off to enjoy the disco." Jock smiled as John's eyes lit up.

"Great!" John replied, glancing at David.

They took their drinks over to sit at a table near to Ralf and Samuel.

"Don't mind us," John joked as he sat down.

The two old men looked at John blankly.

"Miserable cunts," John said as the others sat down.

Jack grinned.

"Well, here's to a good night, *aye*?" John raised his glass.

The others did the same, splashing a few drops of alcohol onto the table. They heard an utterance of annoyance.

They sat for a few minutes, taking their time with their drinks. None of them saying too much.

"On the pull tonight then, Derek?" John smiled cheekily.

"Huh?" Derek replied, looking up from his yet to be touched pint.

"I asked if you were on the pull, tonight?" John heard a disgruntled mumble behind him.

"Oh," Derek answered. "I, I don't know."

"I'll look after you, bud." John winked at him.

John thought that if Derek got a few drinks inside him, he might feel more confident. More outgoing. Plus, John was interested to see what Derek was like inebriated.

David checked his phone for any missed calls or messages; there were none. He was still worried about something bad happening back at the farm. He sipped his vodka and Coke. "You been here before, Derek?"

Derek finally touched his drink. "A couple of times, aye. Not for a long time, mind."

"How about you, Jack? When was the last time you came here?" David asked.

"Think the last time was about six months ago."

"Where's your local haunt?" John asked.

"Anywhere, really. Wherever me mates decide to go, ye know?"

"How long have you both lived around here?" John asked.

"Six years for me. Moved up from Edinburgh with me mum after she and Dad split up ... was tough on us both. Mum thought it seemed like a nice area."

"It must have been tough for you. Sorry to hear that," David said.

"Don't be sorry. Me da was an arsehole, aye!" Jack smiled.

"Fair enough." David smirked back, taking a larger gulp at his drink this time. "How about you, Derek? What's your story?"

"I've pretty much lived here all my life ... born and raised in Dunfermline, but moved up here when I was nine, with my folks. Moved out though, about four years ago," Derek answered.

David thought that it was better late than never for Derek to have finally moved out from his parents' home.

A tut came from behind them again. John was getting slightly annoyed by the two old men disapproving of their chatter but he bit his tongue. "Bet you moved out because your folks didn't like you bringing all those ladies back, eh, Dez?" John teased and grinned.

Derek smiled awkwardly and his cheeks turned a deeper shade of red.

*****

A few more people finally arrived. The newcomers ordered their drinks and proceeded to tables inside and out in the beer garden.

"At least a few more people are arriving," John said a little sarcastically.

Another tut came from one of the old men.

This time, John had finally had enough. He necked his drink back and slammed down the empty glass on the table. He spun round in his seat and stood up to confront the two old men. "Seriously, what the fuck is your problem?" he raised his voice.

His voice caught Jock's attention from behind the bar.

"You object to people coming into a public place and chatting, because it disturbs your shitty game of dominoes? If you're that flamin' bothered, play that *crap* in your own homes! That way, you won't be disturbed."

"Calm down, mate," David said, feeling a little embarrassed and looking around the pub. He placed a hand on one of John's shoulders to push him back down to his seat.

Jack started laughing and Derek sat sheepishly, staring at the table.

The two old men looked at John completely expressionless, apart from a grunt from the capless one. They returned to their game.

"Unbelievable ..." John lowered his voice, shaking his head.

Jock came over and was trying not to laugh. "There any trouble here, lads? Ye two causing problems for these young gents? I won't have ye upsetting folk, now," he said sarcastically to the old men, with his hands firmly on his large hips.

"Sorry, mate," John said, looking up at Jock. "Just tired of these two miserable old gits, tutting at everything we say. We're only having a drink and chatting."

Jock smiled understandably at John. "Ye not the first one to complain, aye. Though, no one has ever had a go like ye just did, ha! I'm going to be moving the tables and chairs soon ... so ye two better finish ye game off," Jock said to Samuel and Ralf.

There was another grunt.

Jock went back to the bar to serve a couple of regulars who had walked in and he chatted amicably to them.

"I can't believe you just did that," David said quietly.

"I couldn't help it. They just pissed me off," John replied, looking at his empty glass. He needed a refill.

"It was funny as fook." Jack grinned.

John smiled back. "I need another drink." He headed for the bar.

"You have any more thoughts about what's been happening on my uncle's farm?" David asked Derek and Jack, tapping his nails on his glass.

Derek and Jack looked at one another.

"Aye ... still don't know what to think, if completely honest with ye ..." Jack replied. "All this talk of weird happenings and supernatural shit."

"Well, it's happening, mate. I sincerely hope you and Derek don't encounter anything me and John have. Believe me, things *are* happening."

"I don't know what to think either," Derek replied. "We can't deny that something *is* happening."

"You've heard the whispering, right? Gavin definitely heard that chanting and saw the fire as well." David looked over to the bar where John was getting another drink. He was laughing about something with Jock.

"Aye, that whispering is pretty hard to explain, I guess." Jack frowned.

"I know you both find it tough to believe. But you *must* be careful and watch yourselves," David said cautiously.

"Watch ourselves how?" Jack asked confused.

David was about to answer but saw Derek staring at the two old men, Samuel and Ralf, behind him. He turned to see the two men watching them.

David felt awkward, he didn't know what to say. "Hi …"

The old man in the deerstalker eventually said, "Whispers …" His voice was breathless with a slight Scottish accent.

David's eyes widened. "You've heard them, too?"

The other old man moved a white domino piece and grunted.

"In the forest, we saw them …"

David felt a sudden tingle of fear.

"Saw who?" David asked.

*"Them!"* the old man replied. "They were-"

Before the old man could finish his sentence, his opposite cut him off. "Enough of that *crap*, Samuel! Back to the game. We need to finish up soon, aye …"

Samuel bent his head and returned to their game.

"Woah. Hold on a sec … you can't just leave me in limbo like that. What did you see?" David asked eagerly.

Samuel ignored him as he played a domino piece with six spots on. Two diagonal threes on each side. His head down, like a child who had been told off by his teacher.

John finished his conversation with Jock and was surprised to see David talking to the old men on his return.

"*Please* … what did you see? It's important."

"What's going on here?" John asked, holding his JD and splash of Coke.

Ralf raised his white-bearded face. "Huh? Oh, it's ye!" He then made a grunt.

"So, you can speak, eh?" John replied.

Ralf grunted and turned his head away, back to the lined-up dominoes.

"They overheard us speaking. Samuel here, said something about whispers and seeing something in the forest," David explained to John.

Ralf looked up and tried to make eye contact with Samuel. "Ye see what ye done, now? Ye silly old *coot*!" Ralf gave Samuel a firm slap across the top side of his head, dislodging his deerstalker cap. Samuel barely flinched. He took the hit like a scared child.

"Hey!" said John. "Don't hit him."

"Argh. Ye want one too, eh?"

John laughed. "Why don't you try it, *old* man?"

Just as Ralf got up and squared up to John to confront him, somebody called out behind them, walking out of the kitchen. "Oi. What the hell is going on?" A man walked over to the group to mitigate the confrontation.

"Argh … nothing." Ralf aggressively threw his right arm in the air and sat back down.

"Who are you?" John asked abruptly and took a swig.

Jack smiled at the way John asked. He was loving the whole situation. He gulped at his beer. Derek continued to sit quietly.

"I'm Nigel …" the man in his early thirties replied, with his blonde moptop hairstyle flopping over his forehead. His accent sounded Welsh. "I work here. So, what's this all about? Jock mentioned there was an argument already."

"Yeah, it was me," John replied. "I didn't like their attitude. Mainly, *his.*" John pointed a finger at Ralf.

"Well, just watch it, yeah? It's a decent pub here. We don't want any fights. And Ralf, you're more than old enough to know better … you two had better finish up your game in a few minutes, anyway. Me and Jock have got to move the tables and chairs to make room for the disco."

"Argh. Whatever, ye *sheep shagger,*" Ralf muttered.

"What did you say?" Nigel frowned.

Ralf ignored him as a few more people walked into the pub and made their way over to the bar.

"You've got about *five* minutes to finish up your game," Nigel told them firmly, giving Ralf a stern look as he went to serve the new customers.

"Listen, Samuel … I need for you to tell me what you saw in the forest. You're talking about Rothiemurchus, right? Please, we're already in danger." David sounded desperate.

"He didn't see *anything,*" Ralf interrupted. "He's losing his marbles." Ralf tapped the side of his own head firmly.

"He wasn't speaking to you," John said to Ralf.

Ralf gave John another dirty look.

"*Please,* Samuel," David asked again. He moved his chair next to him. He wanted to hear as much as he could from him, before they finished their game and left. There wasn't much time.

Samuel slowly raised his head to David and looked him in the eyes.

David hadn't noticed until he sat closer to Samuel that the whites of his eyes were slightly yellow. As was his face. Although his face was mostly covered by his white beard, David saw yellow pigment on his upper cheeks and around his wrinkly eyes. David wondered if it was jaundice. He remembered visiting the grandfather of a school friend, who had had liver problems and had the same appearance.

Samuel's hat was still lopsided on his head from where Ralf had slapped him. "We saw them in there."

John got the impression that Samuel was disabled in some way. He pulled up a chair and sat on the other side of him. Ralf glared at him but John ignored him.

"Yes," David replied, "But *who*?"

*"Them!"* Samuel said with more force.

David exhaled, trying to remain calm. "Who do you mean by 'them,' Samuel? Talk to me ..."

Samuel blinked his pale-yellow eyes a few times. "A fire ... chanting ... blood ... there was *so* much blood."

David and John's eyes became larger as they looked at one another. Jack stopped grinning.

"What else did you see?" John asked. He placed his drink down on the table, being careful not to disturb the set of dominoes and not wanting Ralf to kick off about anything else.

"They were wearing robes ... masks ... hoods ..." Samuel breathed in with difficulty. "Chanting ... and that scream ... *no, no, NO!*" Samuel put his yellow wrinkled hands against his ears and bent his head down, shaking it.

"Ye fools, don't ye see what ye've done? Ye've set 'im off ...! Come, Samuel. We're leaving. We'll call it a draw if we leave now. Otherwise, *I'm* the winner." Ralf picked up a small black pouch from underneath the table next to his feet and scooped the dominoes into it. He almost knocked John's drink over as he reached to claw the dominoes over from Samuel's end of the table. Ralf pushed his chair out forcefully with his backside, scraping the wooden floor.

*"Wait!"* David was getting more desperate. "Who were *they*, Samuel?"

Samuel was whining slightly, his hands still over his ears.

*"Don't you tell them, Sam!"* Ralf shouted.

The whole pub went quiet and looked over. John gave an awkward smile back, while Derek turned a shade of red.

"We saw that *thing*, too." Samuel was almost crying now. It was hard to make out what he said, unless right up close to him.

"What *thing*?" David pushed.

"The thing that resides in the forest."

Ralf reached over and pulled Samuel up from his seat, just as Jock and Nigel came over.

"Ye've said ENOUGH!" Ralf shouted aggressively.

The rest of the pub must have wondered what was going on.

"Nothing to see here." Jock smiled over at the other customers in his pub. "Come on, aye. What's this all about?" Jock asked calmly.

"*Argh* … nothing. We're leaving. Ye got ye crappy disco, soon."

"Ye want me to call a taxi for ye?" Jock asked.

"Aye. Do it, *now* … I don't want to wait in here any longer, with these *degenerates*. We'll be waiting outside," Ralf snapped as he pulled Samuel with him towards the door to the beer garden, pushing past Nigel as he did so.

"What an *arsehole*," John remarked, swallowing another mouthful of drink.

David got up. "Wait," he called out.

Nigel placed a firm hand on his chest.

"I need to find out-"

"Let it go for now, mate," John said.

"Need to find what out?" Nigel asked curiously.

"Nothing … doesn't matter," David replied.

"What did you guys do to set them off like that?" Nigel asked.

"Nothing," John replied, screwing his mouth up.

"Well, you must have said something?"

"We, erm. We just asked if they wanted a game of dominoes some time and asked how long they've lived around here … then that Ralf went off on one," John replied, knowing it sounded like bullshit.

"Yeah, right." Nigel laughed.

"What's up with them two? Particularly Samuel? I mean, is he all there?" David asked.

"They've been coming here for as long as I can remember, lad. Ralf has always been tightly wound. But he seems to have gotten even worse down the years … as for Samuel, he has always been the more passive one out of the pair. He lost his beloved wife about twenty years ago … he has progressive dementia, jaundice, *and* chronic bronchitis! Safe to say, he's been through a lot, aye," Jock answered.

"And what about Ralf?" John asked. "Is he married?"

Both Jock and Nigel looked at one another and laughed. *"No!"* they said simultaneously.

"There's a surprise," John said, twirling his glass around on the table by the rim.

"That's the first time I've seen Samuel flip out like that, though," Nigel replied. He noticed that Samuel had left his cane behind. "He's forgotten his bloody cane as well. I'll go take it out to him."

They looked out of the window to see Ralf and Samuel in deep conversation. Ralf was giving Samuel an earful about something. Samuel had a brief coughing fit.

Ralf then walked over to the window and tapped hard on the glass with the knuckle of his index finger. He gestured angrily with his hand to Jock to call his taxi, using his pinky and thumb of his right hand.

"Aye, the miserable bugger … I best call his cab, then get these tables and chairs moved …" Jock went to make the call behind the bar, while Nigel took the cane outside. Ralf snatched it from him and forced it into Samuel's hand.

John necked back his third drink. The other three had still barely touched theirs. "Come on, boys … drink up." John tried to encourage them.

David had lost the will to enjoy the night after Samuel's words.

"Ye believe what that old guy just said?" asked Jack, swallowing hard on his now lukewarm pint.

David nodded. "I do, yes. Okay, so he might not exactly be completely 'all there,' but then, maybe that's to do with what he witnessed in the forest? Don't you believe him?"

"Aye, maybe. I don't know." Jack frowned.

David looked out of the window to where Samuel and Ralf were still standing.

Ralf seemed to have calmed down but was still speaking to Samuel. David considered opening one of the pub windows to eavesdrop, but the taxi showed up. It was surprisingly quick, seeing as Jock had only just phoned for one.

Jock walked over. "They said it would be any minute … must have been in the area already, aye."

"Jeez. That Ralf is a prize prick," John said, watching them leave through the window.

Jock smiled and went back behind the bar.

"What do you think?" David asked Jack and Derek.

"I don't know," came Jack's reply. "He probably saw something. But considering his state of mind, it's hard to say."

"I don't know either," said Derek.

"Jesus, guys … I still can't believe you doubt this? I know you haven't seen what we have, but Samuel described similar stuff and others have encountered it as well," David raised his voice slightly. "Chances are, it's the same thing what we encountered on the motorway *and* chased us up here; don't you think?"

"I do, mate. I agree with Jacky-Boy, that this Samuel is a couple of beers short of a six-pack, but like you said, maybe what he encountered affected him. I believe he came across something terrible. And this *Ralf* may or may not have been there, too. Either way, they know about it. He seems concerned about Samuel opening his mouth about it," John said.

"Exactly. Ralf was reluctant to let Samuel spill the beans … if only I could have got Samuel alone or had a few more minutes …" David sighed and shook his head.

"Aye … it's pretty messed up. Maybe I have been naïve about it all?" A serious looking Jack stared into his pint.

Derek gave a slight nod.

John noticed a couple of attractive young ladies in miniskirts enter the pub and make their way to the bar. "Yeah, well you can't ask that Samuel now, Dave … they've gone and we probably won't see them again … I need another drink." John hastily walked over to the bar with his empty glass to where the two females stood.

David was annoyed John had changed the subject and was more interested in the women at the bar than what he could have found out from Samuel.

John subtly tried to check out the ladies' backsides. He started laughing and joking with them and pointed over to where David and the others were sitting. One of the ladies looked over at David and smiled flirtatiously, but he seemed distracted. Just as John thought he may have been getting somewhere with the women, two men, one tall and stocky, came up to the bar and kissed the girls.

"You aareet, mate?" the tall stocky one said to John. He sounded northern and appeared huge now he was standing close. He had a tribal tattoo from his wrist up to his neck. John at five-foot nine felt like a dwarf.

"What's up?" John replied, raising his eyebrows, feeling a little insecure.

"Well, it was nice chatting to you, John. Have a good evening," one of the women said, as the four of them made their way outside into the beer garden.

The one who had smiled at David did so again as she walked past. Her assumed boyfriend nodded at him. He was the big one.

John watched them go outside and turned his nose up in disappointment; he knocked back half his drink. "You win some and you lose some, eh?" he said over to the table where the other three were.

"Aye." Jack grinned back. "That ye do."

# Chapter Thirty-One

## 13th July, 2018

The DJ still hadn't turned up, but he had called Jock a few minutes before they shifted the tables and chairs.

The time was getting on for nine, by the time Jock and Nigel had finished moving the last of the tables and chairs to make space for the disco, the light in the pub had gradually started to fade as the fine summer evening drew in.

A few tables were piled up in the corner, while a few other smaller tables and chairs were stacked out the back next to a blue tarp. There was still seating available at the end of one side of the pub. David and the others decided to move out into the beer garden for a while.

"Well, one thing's for sure; it's certainly a pleasant view up here in the Highlands." John stood, appreciating the scenery. He was now at the end of his fourth drink with a fifth sat on the table from David's round. The others were only on their second drink.

The sun was starting to set in the west, creeping its way behind the mountains. The temperature was still high, but more bearable. They watched as some cars drove past. A few taxis stopped off outside the pub, dropping people off.

David sat quietly looking over to Rothiemurchus Forest in the distance.

"Ye okay, Dave?" Jack asked, wiping his mouth with the back of his hand. "Ye look lost, mate."

"I'm fine, Jack," David replied, not breaking his gaze. "Just thinking."

"Let's just enjoy tonight. Put everything else to the back of our minds, yeah?" John put an affectionate arm around his friend's shoulder as he sat down next to him.

David sighed. "Okay, fuck it! It's only one night." David knocked back his drink and quickly started on his other.

"That's the spirit," John replied.

"I'll get the next round in," Jack offered. "Derek can get the next one."

"Sure. We may as well scrap the rounds after that. Just get our own drinks in," David suggested.

"Aye, makes sense," Jack agreed as Derek gave a little nod in agreement.

"I need the loo." David got up.

It was starting to get busy. On the way back outside, David almost bumped into the flirtatious smiler. He stepped to the side and let her pass. She thanked him and gave another seductive smile. He checked her out as she made her way to the ladies. Her huge boyfriend was still outside in the beer garden.

"Think one of those birds fancies me. She keeps giving me this look and smile," David said, sitting back down.

"Which one?" John asked.

"One of those you were speaking to at the bar. Her fella's the big fucker with the tats."

"Oh, her … lucky bastard." John laughed. "Wouldn't want to do anything to piss him off."

"I know." David smiled.

"Aye. I'd bite his ankles, if he started any shit!" Jack joked, making the others laugh. Jack was the same height as John.

*****

A short while later, they saw a fairly large silver panel van pull up outside the pub. On both sides of the van it read *Reggie's Mobile Disco* in white lettering printed on a black oval background. To the left of the background was an image of a DJ's decks with two large speakers either side. *Let the partyin' begin!* was printed in black underneath, along with a mobile number. A sticker of the Jamaican flag had been stuck above the petrol cap.

"Looks like the DJ has finally shown up," David said.

"Aye, 'bout time," replied Jack.

"He's got to set up yet, too," John added. "Probably won't take him long."

They watched as the DJ began carrying his equipment in. Jock came out to help him.

"I'm sorry I'm late! I had problems with me van starting. Then there were some road works that held me up further," the DJ, Reggie, said. He was black with a short goatee beard and thin moustache. He had long dreadlocks and spoke with a Jamaican accent.

"So, how do you fair with the ladies, Jacko?" John asked. "Anyone in your life, right now?"

"I do all right, aye. Nae seeing anyone at the moment, mind."

"I won't bother asking you, Dez. I know you're a 'sly fox' and do all right," John joked affectionately.

Derek went red again and smiled awkwardly.

They were distracted by the sound of broken glass.

The big boyfriend with the tattoo, who was sitting a few tables down, had accidentally dropped his glass. "Shit," he said in his northern accent. He bent down and picked up the shattered pieces of glass and put them in one of the black ashtrays.

His girlfriend advised him to be careful and not to cut himself. After he was done, he brushed his hands together and went inside, presumably to order another pint. He ducked his head as he went through the door frame.

*****

It took a little while for the DJ to finally set up. He had stopped occasionally to chat to Jock and other people and ordered himself a pint.

The pub was starting to fill up so there wasn't much space to dance. John and David weren't bothered as they weren't keen dancers. John just liked the atmosphere and the women. For him, there was more of a chance to 'get lucky' than in a quieter pub. He enjoyed the way some women became more flirtatious after a few drinks at discos and how they danced, grinding themselves up against guys, provoking them.

The small group of four had moved to a corner not far from the bar. The red, green and blue disco lights shone and flickered on and over them.

They had come across a couple, Anthony and Melissa, both in their late thirties who were also from down south: Loughton, not too far from London. They were in Scotland for the week, staying in a small bed and breakfast in Aviemore as it was Anthony's younger brother, Lee's, wedding the next day. Although they were not from Scotland, Lee's fiancée, Vicky, had opted for a wedding up in Rothiemurchus. She had fallen in love with the area and its scenery a couple of years back, when they had visited for a week's getaway. It had also been when Lee had proposed to her.

"... so, yeah, it was her idea to get married up here. Our old man was a little annoyed though; he didn't fancy the drive up to Scotland. But we told him he could fly up here instead and then rent a car. And that's exactly what some of us did. Though, a few still decided to drive up," Anthony said, with his pint in one hand and his other arm around Melissa's waist.

"How long was the flight?" asked David.

"An hour and a half, give or take," Anthony answered. "We flew out from Luton. We preferred Stansted ideally, as it's closer. But Luton and Gatwick were the only airports near to us that flew to Inverness. Luton, obviously being the closest."

"Yeah, I remember seeing Inverness Airport when we looked up how to get up here," David mentioned. "It would certainly have been a lot quicker."

"Why didn't you fly, then?" Melissa laughed.

"I have a fear of flying," John said raising his voice slightly over the music, which appeared to have grown louder.

"Oh," Melissa said, "That's a shame. But yes, it would have shed a few hours off the journey!"

"Do you fly back on Monday?" David asked.

"Yep. Late morning," Anthony also raised his voice.

"What time's the wedding, tomorrow?" John asked, his face started to feel a little flushed from the alcohol he had drunk.

"Not until two," Anthony replied, having a drink of his pint.

"It's a lovely little church," Melissa said, affectionally rubbing Anthony's hand on her waist. "Lee and Victoria came across the St John the Baptist Church in Rothiemurchus when they first came up here. The wedding reception is being held next door in their community hall. We visited the church the other day. It's surrounded by a nice little woodland, too. It's very pretty, isn't it, Anthony?" Melissa looked at her husband as they shared a quick kiss on each other's lips.

"I'm sure it is," John said.

"It's known as the 'little white church on the ski road,'" Melissa stated.

"How about you fellas? How long are you staying up here? On a farm wasn't it, you said?" asked Anthony.

"That's right. On my uncle's farm. We're erm, just helping out for the summer. We're not sure yet how long we're going to be up here for. Derek and Jack work there," David replied, motioning towards Derek and Jack.

Derek smiled shyly and Jack raised his pint, giving them a cheeky wink.

"So ye getting on it, tonight?" Jack grinned.

Anthony and Melissa both laughed.

"Unfortunately not, no," Anthony answered. "We'll stay for a couple and a little while. We drove here and parked out the back. So, no heavy one I'm afraid for us two … plus, we don't want to be hungover for the big day tomorrow. We'll save the booze for that, won't we, Mel?" Anthony looked lovingly at his wife and gave her an affectionate squeeze on her hip.

"Oh, for sure." Melissa smiled. "We weren't sure about coming. Everyone else invited to the wedding was having a quiet one tonight. We were going to do the same, but the big guy behind the bar persuaded us to drop in tonight, when we came for lunch here earlier on."

"That seems about right." John laughed.

The DJ was playing some music with a heavy bass to it, although no one had started dancing yet.

"Well, it was nice chatting to you guys. We're going to sit in that side bit over there. It's getting a little too loud for my liking; call me old fashioned ... you're welcome to join us, of course," Anthony offered.

"Cool," replied John. A short, dark-haired girl had just caught his attention. "We can later, before you go. But if you'll excuse me, some girl just looked at me. No offence." John beamed.

"None taken. See you later, maybe?" Anthony laughed.

The couple walked over to the quieter seating area and John approached the girl, leaving David and the other two.

"I'll be back in a bit," David said. "I just want to get a bit of fresh air. It's getting too loud, too." He had to shout the last sentence.

"Aye. Nae probs, chap," Jack replied, glancing around.

David made his way out into the beer garden where a few other people were standing. Some were puffing on their cigarettes. Once finished, they returned inside. The broken glass from earlier had since been swept up.

*****

David stood alone, admiring what was left of the sunset over the mountains and the red, orange and slightly pinkish sky. The scorching hot day was now almost at an end.

A young woman came up from behind him, standing next to him. "It's certainly a beautiful view, isn't it?" she said in her soft Irish accent.

It took David a second to turn his head.

"It's going to be a lovely clear night. Perfect for seeing the stars." She looked up above them.

"Oh ... *Hi*," David replied. "Sorry, I was miles away." He recognised Emily.

"That's okay," she said with her perfect smile. "I hope I didn't disturb you? I saw your friend in there, the one you were with yesterday. We were erm, coming outside. Me and Annabel. She is getting the drinks."

"It's fine. You didn't disturb me at all." David smiled back.

Emily looked amazing in a black dress with a mesh see-through top panel that extended over her petite shoulders.

David caught the aroma of her perfume on a stroke of breeze. Seeing her again made him feel better. He temporarily forgot his problems. "You, erm … you look amazing."

Emily blushed. She bit on her lip, feeling embarrassed. "Thank you … you do, too … I thought I might have been over dressed for a disco." She laughed slightly.

"Don't be silly. You look lovely … it's always good when someone makes an effort … you've got the night off, then? Well, obviously!"

Emily chuckled. "Yes. Jock said Annabel and I could take the night off. Let our hair down. It was nice of him … I'm glad you came, too." She smiled again.

"Me too …" David smiled into her green eyes.

"And here they are!" a buoyant John interrupted. He was starting to feel the alcohol flow through his veins. He walked out into the beer garden with Annabel, Derek and Jack.

"What happened to that girl you were going to chat with?" David joked.

"Ah … she had a boyfriend. *Typical*!"

"Or she said that because she wasn't interested?" David replied, grinning.

Emily smiled.

"Yeah, yeah," John replied, taking a seat on one of the benches.

The others followed suit.

Annabel handed a bottle of orange alcopop with a red straw to Emily and started sipping from her own purple alcopop.

"A straw?" John half-joked.

"Well, we don't want to smudge our lipstick now, do we?" Annabel smirked.

"True … though I can think of better ways to smudge your lipstick," John joked, flicking his eyebrows up and down.

The group smiled and David shook his head.

"This is Jack and Derek, who work at my uncle's farm," David then said.

Jack nodded his head and Derek smiled.

"I'm sure I recognise you two?" Annabel replied. "I think I've seen you before."

"Aye, it's possible. I've been in here a few times. Not for a wee while, though," Jack replied with a cheeky grin.

"I've been in here a few times," Derek replied.

"How long have you both worked here?" John asked the ladies.

"Almost ten years now," Annabel answered, sucking on her straw.

"Just the four years, for me," Emily said, with eyes only for David.

He didn't notice as he had his head tilted back to finish his drink.

*****

As the sun finally set, the beer garden was lit by a couple of wall-mounted lights. The disco lights also filtered through the windows.

The group spent the next half-hour or so of shooting the breeze, trying to get to know one another and having a laugh. There was plenty of banter. In Emily and David's case, they were only interested in getting to know each other. John was hoping he could 'have his way' with the busty Annabel.

Supernatural events were not mentioned and the conversation was all light-hearted. Derek was also making an effort to join in, relaxed now by the alcohol. John and David were glad to see this.

"Do you have any plans to move up here?" Emily asked David.

"I don't think so. My home remains back south, in my flat. I've got a few other friends I hang out with there. It's my home, you know? Obviously, I don't have a job at the moment. But hopefully, that will change when I erm, get back." For a moment, David hesitated. He suddenly remembered why he was up here. If things got worse, he might never return home.

"Yep … plus he still lives close to home, so his mum does his dirty washing for him and stuff," John joked.

"Well, at least I live alone and have my own place," David retorted, smiling.

*"Touché!"* John laughed.

The others laughed too.

"You live with your folks still, then? I'm the same. Well, I don't actually live with my folks. I lodge with an elderly couple, but it's the same as … I've been meaning to move out for a while. It's just too *darn* expensive," Annabel said.

"I know. Tell me about it … I live with my dad," John answered.

"Your parents divorced?" Annabel asked.

"No." John paused. "My mum died of cancer when I was sixteen."

"Oh … I'm so sorry." Annabel sounded saddened.

"Don't be sorry. It wasn't *your* fault." John smiled.

Annabel smiled back. "It's such a horrible disease, though. It's about time they cured it."

"Here, here," John said and finished his drink. "I'm going to get another drink. You ladies all right for another? Dezza? Jacko? Dave?"

"No thanks. We're fine at the moment." Emily smiled.

Annabel said the same as did the rest, Jack gestured with his hand.

"You should slow down a bit, mate," David suggested.

"Ah, rubbish!" John laughed and made his way back inside.

"Well, your friend's quite a character," Annabel said to David.

"You can say that again."

The DJ came out for a cigarette, having left a track playing.

"You okay, Reggie?" Annabel asked.

"Hey, gyal ... how you doing?" Reggie walked over to give Annabel and then Emily, a welcome kiss. "Thought I'd come out for some fresh air and a cig. Getting pretty hot in there." He put one of his cigarette papers on the table, along with a green packet of tobacco and sprinkled some into the open paper. He rolled it up and licked to seal it, then popped it in his mouth. "Ah ... shit ..." Reggie said, frisking his own pockets of his loose jeans. "Think I left me lighter at home."

"Nae worries. Here ..." Jack said. He pulled out a silver Zippo lighter from his pocket and threw it to Reggie. Jack rarely smoked cigarettes, only pot when he could.

"Cheers, man." Reggie lit his roll-up and handed the lighter back to Jack.

"This is Reggie, by the way. He does our discos a couple of times a month or so," Annabel said.

Reggie reached his right hand out and clasped Jack's, Derek's and then David's hand. "Good to meet you all ..." he said as he puffed on his cigarette.

"Likewise," David replied. "You're from Jamaica, then?"

Reggie laughed. "Yeah, boy. Was it that obvious?" he joked.

"No, not at all." David smiled, being sarcastic. "What brought you to Scotland? You're a long way from the Caribbean."

"Aye," Reggie replied and smiled, taking his cigarette from his mouth and flicking some ash into the ashtray. "I came over about six year ago. Well, I've been to Scotland before. I used to live in London, too. My father was actually born in Scotland, in Perth. I was born in Jamaica, meself."

"Aye. I can see why ye would swap the weather of Jamaica for Scotland," Jack joked.

Reggie grinned, revealing a gold tooth in the low light. He flicked more ash into the tray. "Well, if the weather remains the same as it was today, you won't hear me complaining!" Reggie looked up at the now dark sky. The stars were beginning to shine brightly. He then looked through the window. He noticed a few more people were now dancing; *"Dem bashment gyal ... "* he said to himself.

The others frowned at what must be Jamaican slang.

"It was nice meeting you guys. I'm sure we'll speak more later. But I best get back to me decks; they won't play themselves." Reggie laughed.

"No worries, Reggie," Annabel said.

"Just make sure you get those sweet tooshies up dancing." Reggie winked and joked at the girls, stubbing his cigarette out in the ashtray.

They all laughed as he turned and made his way back inside. A woman strutted past. "Damn, gyal," he said to himself, checking her out.

The woman heard. She looked back and smiled.

John returned carrying his drink.

"Oh, and that's John ..." David said, "He's with us, too."

"That's Reggie, the DJ," Emily added.

"Yo," Reggie said, giving John a shug handshake.

"Sup?" John replied, being careful not to spill his latest drink.

Reggie went back to attend to his decks and John rejoined the group.

"Seems a friendly guy," John said.

"Oh, he is." Annabel smiled.

*****

By eleven, the disco was in full swing and the pub was packed to the rafters.

More people were starting to become intoxicated. Numerous spills and splashes of booze reached the wooden floor as folk danced into one another.

All three bar staff were being kept busy; Jock, Nigel and a young local called Craig, who hadn't worked there long according to Emily.

Crowds were now gathered outside the front of the pub as well as in the beer garden, vying for fresh air. Although the temperature outside had dropped, it was still fairly mild. Inside, sweaty bodies raised the temperature. Those with more energy were dancing the night away.

"*Jesus,* it's fucking hot in there!" an inebriated John remarked, coming out to the front, where David, Emily and Derek were standing.

They had recently been rejoined by Melissa and Anthony who they had met earlier in the evening. Annabel and Jack were both still inside, chatting to each other as well as others.

David smiled. "I know. It's too small in there. Not sure it's ideal for a disco."

Emily chuckled. "You're not the first to say that. Though to be fair, although it gets busy, I don't recall it ever being as manic as this."

"Well, that's because we're here," John joked as the others smiled. John's face was covered in beads of sweat. His earlier neatly brushed back fair hair was now messed up and wet from perspiration. He had even been dancing, which was unlike him. Sweat patches and beer spills had dampened his white shirt.

"Yeah, I saw you dancing in there." David grinned.

"Yep … I don't normally dance. The *power* of alcohol, eh?" John sounded a little out of breath.

"Do you dance?" Emily asked David.

David laughed. "Nah … there's not enough alcohol in the world to make me dance."

"Well, we'll have to change that, then," Emily challenged with a seductive look in her eyes.

David felt a tingle. "Are you and Annabel working tomorrow? There'll be a lot to clean up."

"Oh God, I know … I've already seen the trampled-out cigarettes in the beer garden. Even out here … and the spillages inside. There's even loads of crisps on the floor," Emily replied. "Me and Anna don't work until a bit later on, though. So that's okay. I get to have a lie-in. Hopefully, I won't be too hungover." She giggled. Emily then saw that Anthony was staring at her. She had noticed it earlier but brushed it off. This time, she felt uneasy.

Melissa looked at Emily too and smiled. She felt herself quiver a little. They had seemed pleasant enough at first, but now they seemed a little creepy to her. The others didn't seem to have noticed anything. She turned her head away from them.

"When are you guys off?" John asked Anthony and Melissa.

"Oh, we'll probably be going soon. Make sure we get some sleep ready for the big day tomorrow," Melissa answered.

"Sleep?" Anthony replied. He had his hand wrapped around his wife's waist again. "Not if I can help it …" He made a slight roaring sound and nuzzled Melissa's neck playfully.

The others found it a little cringing but laughed, apart from Emily who just looked on.

"At least stay for one more?" John suggested. The alcohol was pretty much in full flow inside him now. When sober, he was a naturally outgoing, friendly and confident person, just like David. But when he was drunk, it brought his personality out even more. It enhanced it. And his sarcasm.

Melissa and Anthony looked at one another and smiled. "I guess one more drink won't hurt. We don't have to be up *too* early, tomorrow," Anthony said.

"Great!" replied John. "We may as well sit out here." There was an empty table outside the front. "I'm going to cool off a bit, before I go back in there."

They sat down outside on the two benches.

Emily however, didn't. "I'm going back inside to check on Annabel." The others noticed a concerned look on her face in the low light.

John frowned. "You all right?" he asked, sitting on the end of the wooden bench.

"Yeah." Emily tried to smile.

"Actually, I'll come with you. I need to take a leak ... I'll see how Jack's getting on as well," David mentioned, getting up.

"Jack's okay. Annabel is, too. They're inside chatting," John said.

"I'll be back in a bit," David said as he and Emily made their way back in.

"I think they like each other ..." John beamed at Melissa and Anthony.

They smiled back at him.

"You okay?" David asked concerned. They stopped just outside the beer garden door.

"Yes," Emily replied unconvincingly.

"You don't seem it." David smiled softly. "What is it? Tell me."

"I ... I don't know. It's just that couple you were talking to."

"What, Melissa and Anthony? What about them?"

Emily sighed and shook her head. "They just ... I don't know ... they just, don't seem genuine to me."

"In what sense?" David frowned.

"They just seem *odd*. I don't know. Like they're phoney. And the guy, he kept staring at me. It just creeped me out."

"Aw," David replied sincerely. He instinctively placed a hand on Emily's shoulder.

She smiled at him.

He pulled his hand away, feeling awkward. "I thought they seemed fine to me. They seem like a nice couple."

"Maybe it's just me and the alcohol." Emily laughed nervously.

David felt bad that he may have given the impression that he didn't believe her, when that wasn't the case. "I hadn't noticed anything, but you've obviously sensed something ... anyway, there's nothing to worry about. It's not like you will ever see them again. They're going back Monday and I imagine they'll be off soon tonight, because of the wedding tomorrow."

"True. I don't want to talk to them again, though."

"That's all right. Let's get another drink."

David stayed with Emily, Annabel and Jack, inside for the next twenty minutes or so.

Jack was chatting to a couple of people he knew from his school days who had turned up. Annabel and Emily chatted to a few regulars they knew from working at the pub. David chipped into the conversation every now and then; he didn't want to seem too much like an outsider.

John and Derek joined them inside briefly. John was even more generous when drunk and had come in to buy a round for a group outside. He had got chatting to a few more people out front. Derek joined him to help carry the drinks back out. Although John was interested in Annabel, he felt the night was still young and Melissa and Anthony would be leaving soon anyway. He considered it would be rude too, to just leave them, particularly when he had persuaded them to stay longer.

John said he would be back later for Annabel, which made her laugh. She seemed to like his cheeky personality.

David wasn't too near the window that was now open, but he could still see through the crowd of people and dancers, outside to where John and the others were. He saw Melissa and Anthony laughing and joking. He was surprised that Emily had felt uncomfortable around them. To him, they seemed the perfect couple.

"How are you feeling?" David asked into Emily's ear.

She just about heard him over the music.

Reggie was in the corner with his headphones on, moving to his tunes.

"Better." She smiled. "Just as long as I don't have to speak to *them* again." Emily glanced over through the window to where Melissa was sitting with Anthony, still in conversation with John and Derek, and some others.

"I'm going out to join the others," Jack said, after catching up with his old friends.

"Okay, mate," David replied. "I'll be er, out there too, in a bit." David wasn't sure about rejoining Melissa and Anthony.

"Aye, okay." Jack took his pint with him. He accidentally bumped into a couple of guys who were dancing, but they didn't seem to mind.

Reggie took off his headphones and made his way through the cluster of people up to the bar to order a drink.

On his way back outside for another ciggie, he stopped by David. "All right, matey?"

"Yeah, good," David raised his voice.

"You're not one to dance then, no?" Reggie grinned, with his white teeth and gold tooth.

David laughed. "Nah. Like I said earlier to Emily, there isn't enough booze to get me up on the dance floor, I'm afraid."

"Shame, my man … it's always good to boogie. The women love it." Reggie grinned again, taking a sip of his pint and wiped his lips. "What about you, Anna?" Reggie called over to Annabel. "Why aren't you dancing yet, gyal?"

"All in good time, Reggie." Annabel smiled.

Reggie looked at her tight, black ribbed top that showed off a hint of cleavage. He turned to David and gave him an acknowledging expression, screwing up his face, implying *phwoar*. He held out his hands in front of his own chest, slightly moving them up and down with his pint in one of them.

Annabel hadn't noticed.

David smiled. He knew that Reggie wasn't the only one. John felt the same. No doubt other men in the pub too, for that matter.

"I expect you to dance too, you know?" Reggie said to Emily who smiled back.

"We'll see," she said.

"I'm going to get some fresh air, Em," Annabel said to Emily. "I might go check on your friend as well." She smiled over at David.

"Be my guest." David grinned.

"You coming?" Annabel asked them.

Emily looked at David and then outside to where the others were. "Erm. In a bit." She didn't want to go outside until the couple had gone.

Melissa happened to look in and caught sight of them inside. She smiled and waved. David smiled back, feeling a little funny because of what Emily had told him.

"Who are they?" Annabel asked.

"Just a couple we got chatting to earlier. I think they're leaving soon. They're from down south, too. They're up here for a wedding tomorrow," David answered, just as Reggie put on another track before heading outside.

"Oh, cool. She seems nice," Annabel said over the music. "See you in a bit …"

"You don't want to go outside, then?" David joked slightly.

"I think I'll pass, thanks." Emily raised half a smile.

"Do you want to go and sit down? We can go in that other bit. It might be a bit quieter and less packed."

"Sure," Emily agreed.

They agreed on getting another drink first and then made their way up the step, squeezing through people and past the main entrance into the side bit to the right. There were a few other people sat there, but a few tables were still vacant. It was a little cooler, better lit and less noisy.

A fairly large Royal Arms of Scotland shield that featured the red lion and its blue tongue was mounted on the wall. There were a few pictures of Jock in his younger days when he was in the cavalry regiment. In one, he was wearing his army fatigues playing a set of bagpipes. Another was a group photo with his regiment, posing in their uniforms with their rifles; they stood in front of an army vehicle with a large machine gun mounted to it. Jock was holding a blue Scottish flag with another soldier at one end.

"Do you clean the picture frames?" David asked Emily.

She looked a little confused. "Yes, at times … why do you ask?"

David smiled and pointed to a dusty cobweb attached to one of the frames, which reached to the artexed ceiling that looked like it needed a coat of paint.

She turned round and saw the cobweb. "Oh … I only gave them a wipe yesterday. There must be a spider around here somewhere." She turned back to face David and smiled.

"Yeah, yeah … that looks like it's been there for a while." He laughed.

"Okay, I guess I missed *that* particular one, but they can keep coming back the next day." Emily giggled.

"It's okay. I believe you." David grinned.

Emily got up and swiped the cobweb away with her hand and sat back down. "Better?" she joked back.

David laughed. "*Much* … So, how long have you been up here for? Tell me more about you?" David took a small swig of his vodka and Coke.

"Okay."

David thought how cute she looked as she sucked on her straw, hollowing out her cheeks slightly. He was warming to her.

Emily Ailise Berne was twenty-three years old. She was born in the spring in Cobh, a small seaport town on the south coast of Ireland. Her middle name of *Ailise*, was the same as her grandmother's. Emily was extremely close to her mother, Eleanor. Emily's father had walked out on them before she was born. She had never met her father, and he had never made any efforts to contact her over the years. Her mother used her maiden name of *Berne*, rather than using her father's name.

After the death of her grandmother, Emily's mother decided there was no reason to remain in Cobh. She had few friends there and had dated on and off a few times, but nothing ever came of it. She had devoted her life primarily to bringing up her daughter and caring for her mother, who sadly died of Alzheimer's, and she thought it might be best to start anew somewhere, once Emily had finished school. Emily had been sixteen, when they moved across the Irish Sea.

Eleanor had come across a job online in Manchester, caring for elderly people who were suffering from Alzheimer's. After about a year and a half in Manchester, Emily and her mother moved up to Aviemore, Scotland, where they rented a small cottage. Eleanor was offered an opportunity in a newly built care home and was eventually promoted to supervisor. Emily still returned to Ireland when she could or her Irish friends would visit her, although one of her closest friends had moved to America, and another had married and moved to New Zealand.

"… and that's about it." Emily sipped another mouthful from her bottle of drink via the red straw.

David yawned as a joke. "I'm sorry." He then smiled.

Emily gave him a friendly slap on his right hand.

"Seriously, though. I'm sorry about your grandmother. I've read how awful Alzheimer's is. Horrid way to go. Must have been tough for your mum and you."

"It most certainly is. I was really upset when she went. My mum certainly was. As you could imagine. It's not just the death itself, but also the suffering that comes before. I remember my gran used to fall over a lot and hurt herself. She was always bruised. One time, she twisted her ankle and even broke her ribs. Having to watch someone you love suffer is awful. You just feel so helpless, you know? Towards the end, she didn't always recognise us. I was really close to my gran as well …" Emily had to stop.

David could see Emily's eyes start to well up. "What about your grandfather?"

"Oh … he died a fair bit before I was born. I never knew him, unfortunately."

"Same. My grandads both died before I was born, too. One of my grans died when I was ten, from a heart attack and the other, when I was thirteen, again, from a heart attack. I think one of my grandads died from one, too. I can't remember. Sometimes, when I was younger, it seemed boring like a chore, visiting my grans. Maybe a bit depressing too, as one of them lived in a dark old flat." David laughed a little. "The thing is, I wouldn't feel like that at *all* now, you know? I'd love to visit them." David stared blankly at the table.

Emily put her hand on his and smiled.

He looked up at her. He wanted to tell her how beautiful she was. But for now, he held back. The reality suddenly hit him. *Hard.* Now wasn't the time to start getting close to someone. The last thing he wanted to do was get close to somebody with all that was happening around the farm. Besides, he wasn't sure he wanted to fall for someone who lived hundreds of miles from his home. He pulled his hand away slightly, making out he had a scratch on his nose.

"What about your, erm, other grandparents? Your father's side? I don't mean to pry. I know it must be difficult to talk about it. Why did your father walk out? Do you mind my asking? I can't believe anyone would do such a thing. Some people don't deserve kids."

"Don't be silly … I don't mind. He basically told my mum that he wasn't ready to have children. He didn't just get up and leave straight away, though. He left after about three weeks, I think. He was with my mum for almost three years. He just couldn't do it. Be a father. And he wasn't sure he loved my mum, anymore. If he ever did," Emily answered in a sad tone.

"Bastard …" David replied quietly.

Emily smiled.

"I just can't believe he upped and left … fair enough, he might have been scared and needed to clear his head for a while. That would have been somewhat acceptable, perhaps."

"I know. There was talk that he ran off with another woman. But to be honest, I stopped caring and asking questions by the time I was eleven or twelve. Asking questions all the time would have brought back painful memories for my mum. I had my friends, mum and gran around. That's all I ever needed. I suppose it would have been great to have a dad. I guess you can't miss what you've never had."

"Well, if he *was* seeing someone else, that's even more appalling. Did you ever think about trying to find him, to see what he had to say?"

Emily sighed. "It crossed my mind a few times. It's only natural. Easy to search with the internet, I suppose." She laughed a little. "If he ever contacted me out of the blue, I wouldn't decline meeting or speaking with him. But as far as I'm concerned, it's in the past and I don't care anymore … I'm not sure I'd even want anything to do with him …"

"I don't think anyone would blame you."

"As for my dad's parents … I never met them either unfortunately; they lived in Belfast. They sent me birthday and Christmas cards a couple of times when I was young. Along with some presents. They both died, though. When I was three and four. Both in the space of a few months. Very sad … In fact, they didn't even know I existed until I was three. My so-called father rarely saw his parents and he never mentioned he had a baby until a few years after.

"My mum never knew them, neither. I think they were ashamed of their son, walking out on us both. But like I said, I haven't asked such questions for many years now. You just … move on, you know?" Emily's smile looked a little sad. "If they hadn't both died, they probably would have come and seen me, or us, them. My mum did plan on doing so. She regretted it, after they passed … It obviously didn't help, them only knowing I existed when I was three. They had my dad late in life, so they were a bit older and I don't think they were in the best of health."

"I'm sorry; sad that our grandparents died so early."

"I know."

"Change of subject … how about relationships? Or is that a tender topic, too?" David joked, trying to lighten the mood a little.

*"Erm …"* Emily's face cringed and she smiled. "Not *too* great. I've had numerous dates, but there was only ever one guy I can say that was serious …" Emily felt a little uncomfortable.

"Bad subject?" David joked again, sensing her awkwardness.

"I met someone not long after I moved to Manchester, with my mum … we were together for just over a year. It didn't work out."

"What happened, if you don't mind me asking? You don't have to say."

"It's fine … let's just say he was cheating on me. I'm well over it now, though. It's funny, too … *now*, I don't even know what I saw in him! Maybe because I was a little younger at the time, I was naïve. I was only sixteen when I met him. He was a year older … but he definitely hurt me. I'm certainly more careful now."

"I'm sorry. Well, he's an absolute *moron* to cheat on someone as lovely as you. Anyone who cheats is an arsehole, period."

*"Aw …"* Emily blushed. "Thank you … I er, think you are, too …" She reached out to touch David's hand again.

David realised he wasn't keeping to his intention of playing it cool, so again, he pulled his hand away, reaching for his drink. "So, erm. Has there been anyone since?" he quickly asked.

"No … although it was years ago now, it took me some time to get over my ex, but it helped that we moved up here for a fresh start. I've been on dates, but nothing came of it. I guess I'm just fussy. There wasn't any spark."

"Wow," David said. "You've been single for like, almost six years?"

"Yeah." Emily embarrassed, reached out for her drink.

"I'm amazed. I'd expect them to be queuing up!"

Emily looked up at him and gave an uneasy smile. "Like I said, I guess I'm just fussy. I can't just be with anyone for the sake of it, you know? How about you?" she asked. She was interested to know about David's past relationships.

"I'm the exact same as you. I've had a few dates here and there and had some casual relationships. I've been single for two years. That was the last serious relationship I had. It just ran its course though, eventually. I've just not met anyone and felt that 'click,' since. I agree, I can't be with someone just for the sake of not wanting to be single. I've known a few people who go in and out of relationships and as soon as they break up, they jump to someone else!" David laughed.

"I know! If you truly love someone, you'd think that it would take time to get over that, before going straight back into a relationship with somebody else … I guess everyone is different?" Emily laughed too.

*****

They continued laughing and chatting together. David opted not to mention anything about what had happened to him and John on the farm. At least for the time being.

Emily had her arm propped up on the table, her soft chin resting on her knuckles. She was fixated on David's face as he recalled a funny story from his childhood:

"… so, me, another friend, *Daniel* and John, are racing on our bikes across this big green common … Dan's in front of us and me and John are at the back, slightly behind …" David swallowed before continuing. "I start doing these *bunny-hops* on my mountain bike and John sees these girls over to our right and starts doing the same, trying to show off, you know? Just as he overtakes me, his front wheel comes off! And the way his head just *sunk* down, into the ground underneath his chest, when the bike collapsed …" David gave an impression of it.

"I mean, I was pissing myself. I don't think any of the girls were paying any attention, so I was the only one who saw it … I couldn't stop laughing. I shouldn't have laughed, as John could have got hurt … thankfully, he was fine. Well, apart from a bruised ego." David laughed.

Emily giggled. "Oh my God … I shouldn't laugh. He could have been really hurt. Or worse."

To David, she seemed like the absolute, perfect package. Beautiful, funny, great smile and laugh, cute, sexy; she had it all. He felt like he had known her for ages. The feeling was more than mutual.

"I know … but what made it even more funny, was how the front wheel just kept on rolling! Daniel saw this wheel go past him. Oh, man. I was dying … Johnny was so annoyed; he just walked right over the common, picked up his wheel, hand-screwed it back on and cycled home without a word."

Emily found the story hilarious; she could picture John doing this and she was really enjoying David's company.

"There you are." John came round the corner. "I was just wondering where you guys were." His words sounded slightly slurred.

"Yep, we're in here … we're having a *wheely* good time," David joked. He was getting tipsy too.

Emily giggled again.

"Eh?" John asked confused.

Emily cleared her throat. "David was just telling me about that time your wheel came off on your bike …"

"Huh?" John replied and then remembered. "Oh. Yeah … erm, well, whatever." He grinned. "You guys coming back out in a bit? That Melissa and Anthony are going soon." He gestured outside with his left thumb.

"Erm, yeah … we'll be there in a few minutes," David replied.

Emily's face fell.

"No worries." John winked back.

"We can go back out later, after they've left, if you like?" David could see Emily was still worried about going back outside.

"Okay."

"Melissa and Anthony said that Jock mentioned the disco to them earlier, when they were here for lunch. Did you see them then?"

Emily frowned. "No, I didn't. But I was helping out in the kitchen during lunch."

"Ah, okay. I was going to say, too … you've still kept your Irish accent, despite being over here for a few years."

"Yeah … it hasn't grown *Scottish* yet." She tried to smile.

"And what's Cobh like? I'm not sure I've ever heard of it."

"Oh, it's *lovely*!" Emily beamed, showing her perfect set of natural, white teeth. "It's a little quiet. A very quaint place. Charming, if you like. Very friendly, too. It's on an island, named *Great Island*, which is part of Cork Harbour."

"Is there much to do there? Like what's the nightlife like?"

"It isn't too bad. There's a few nice places and pubs there. One of my old school friend's dad used to run a pub called *Top of the Hill,* when I was younger. We used to get free food and drinks, though nothing alcoholic, as I was still young." Emily laughed. "But it was great ... some people might find it boring perhaps, but I loved it. My mum paid for me to go back to visit; she felt bad for moving me away. She sometimes went with me too, if she had the time off work."

"You soon got settled in over here, though?"

"Yes, eventually."

"You still miss it?"

"A little. Like I say, my closest friends have moved away since, so it doesn't matter too much now."

"You're glad you're here, up in the Highlands and Bonnie Scotland, then?" David smiled.

Emily looked into his eyes and smiled back. "I am now ..."

David cleared his throat, feeling a little awkward. "How about, er, work? What did you do in Manchester and up here, prior to working in this place?"

"Oh, this and that ... nothing too great, if I'm honest. I never felt like going to university, college or even sixth form. I considered it, but I wasn't sure what I wanted to study or do. My first job was in Manchester at a laundry company. I absolutely hated it. Washing other people's dirty clothes and stuff. The manager wasn't very nice, either. I only lasted a couple of months. I then worked in a department store, serving customers, doing this and that. That was a little more enjoyable. It was good meeting new people and having a laugh at times.

"That's where I erm, met my ex, too ..." Emily cringed a little. "Then, when I moved up to Scotland, I got a job working in sales for a picture framing place. That was easy enough. Unfortunately, the company went under. Then I ended up working for Jock. I saw an advert in the window here. I've been here ever since. The last four years have flown by. I think they do, as you get older. I have to say though, I do enjoy it. It's only bar work, but I like interacting with people. They're mainly friendly folk that come here. Jock pays well, too. He respects his workers and we are all very fond of him."

David found Emily a sweet, mild-mannered girl. Warm-hearted and genuine.

"You followed your mum twice, then? First from Ireland, and then from Manchester to up here?"

"Yep."

"Some people wouldn't have done that twice."

Emily laughed. "I know. I guess I didn't have much choice. Not the first time. I suppose I could have opted to stay in Manchester, but for obvious reasons, I wanted to get away and I didn't fancy renting my own place. It would have been expensive. Lonely, too. I mean I had friends there, I still see them on the odd occasions, but I'm not so close to them."

"I know what you mean. It can be expensive. When I first moved into my flat, I felt a little lonely. But having my folks not too far away certainly helped. Obviously, my friends as well. Particularly John and Grant who are often popping round. Especially, John! Getting Benji was a big plus, too."

"*Aw* ... Benji; cute name."

"I moved out on my own about four years ago and I got Benji a year after. He helps with the lonely nights." David laughed.

"That's so sweet." Emily looked straight into David's blue eyes. "I'd love to meet him properly. I saw him briefly yesterday, when you came in."

"Erm, sure ... I think me and John will be up here for a little while yet. So yeah, why not?"

"You'll obviously need another job, too. Will you struggle now, with your flat and rent?" Emily asked. She pulled the straw out and drank the last of the bottle by mouth, before placing the straw back in the empty bottle.

"I don't think so. I have a bit saved up. I guess I've always been prudent with my *wonga.*" David grinned.

Emily chuckled back. "That's good, then. I'm sure you'll find another job soon enough, once you, erm, go back down south." Emily hoped that David would stay up in Scotland rather than finding another job back home. Perhaps it was the alcohol? It seemed silly. She had only just met David but she felt like she had known him longer than just tonight. She felt a chemistry between them. She could also sense that David was attracted to her and seemed comfortable in her company, but he seemed a little reserved.

"We should get back to the others. I can check if that couple have gone yet, if you like?"

"Sure, okay. I can get another couple of drinks in for us both, if you want? Seeing as you got the previous ones."

"Sure. I'll have the same. I'll go check if the coast is clear."

"Okay."

# Chapter Thirty-Two

## 14th July, 2018

Emily took her time waiting at the bar, chatting with a few customers and with Jock. It had gone midnight.

David returned to where the others were sitting outside. Melissa and Anthony were ready to leave.

"You're off, then?" David smiled at them both as he approached.

"Yep. We best get going. Get some rest for the big day." Anthony checked his watch. "You need to go to the loo before we head off, love?" he asked Melissa.

"Yes, I'd better."

"You two still up for fishing Sunday, yeah?" Anthony asked Jack and John.

"Yeah, bud. For sure," John answered.

"Aye. Sounds cool. Never been fishing before." Jack grinned. "I'll let ye know, mate."

David looked on, a little confused. "Fishing?"

John looked round at him. "Yep … Ant's going fishing on Sunday, before they head back on Monday. He asked if we would like to go along."

"Since when did you like fishing?" David smiled slightly.

"There's a first time for everything, aye," John replied slightly slurred. "You should come, too."

Anthony smiled. "Yes, you should! The more the merrier … how about it?"

They all looked at David. It made him feel uncomfortable. "Erm. I don't know. I'll think about it … I've got some things to do. What about you Derek, are you going?"

"I wouldn't mind … but I'm going to me ma's for Sunday lunch," Derek replied, his eyes weary from alcohol.

"Come on, mate … it will be good. Get away from the farm for a bit."

John tried to encourage David. He tried to raise his eyebrows inconspicuously, to remind David of the problems that they needed to get away from.

"I'll give it some thought. My uncle's erm, busy and might need my help," David lied. He was thinking of what Emily had said about the couple, and fishing wasn't his thing anyway.

"Well, you've got my number, boys … give it some thought, Dave." Anthony smiled.

"I best go take a quick *Jimmy Riddle*," Melissa joked, making her way inside.

"Okay, honey," Anthony replied.

Inside, Emily asked Jock to put the drinks under the bar while she went to the ladies. After she had washed her hands, she replied to a text from a friend who had moved from Manchester to Cambridge. She didn't fancy going back outside to join the others whilst the couple she didn't like were still there.

She could feel and hear the vibration a little from the bass of the music coming from Reggie's speakers. It moved over the walls and white cubicles. She could also hear the sound of a slight rummaging, as someone in the far left cubicle went through their handbag. Whoever it was dialled someone on their mobile; Emily could hear it ringing at the other end. When someone answered, there was terrible interference on the line for a few seconds. Even though the cubicle door was closed and the phone was not on handsfree, it was still hearable. Emily then recognised Melissa's voice.

"It's me …" Melissa said, not sounding as friendly and polite as she had earlier. "We're off in a bit … Yes … We managed to get possibly one of them, to come on Sunday …"

Emily frowned. She could barely hear the voice on the other end, but it sounded slow and was definitely male.

"Him? I don't know. Anthony's probably trying to convince him further as we speak …"

Emily could hear the person on the other end of the line talk some more and then heard him laugh maliciously. Melissa started to laugh with him. Emily's earlier suspicions of the couple not being genuine now seemed all the more credible.

*"Co-dhiù, bidh togail againn ri d' fhaicinn an ath-oidhch',"* Melissa said encouragingly. *"I can't wait!"* she added passionately. She gave a final laugh before ending the call.

Emily heard Melissa flush the toilet and undid the latch. Without thinking, she quickly darted back into the far right cubicle and closed the door. She had no idea why she didn't just exit the toilets. Melissa came out and started to hum to herself and washed her hands. Emily heard Melissa's heels on the hard floor as she was about to leave the toilets. Melissa stopped humming when she reached the door and halted. She then turned and approached Emily's closed cubicle. A slight shadow appeared underneath the door.

Emily started to breathe a little heavier. She instinctively cupped her hand over her mouth to prevent herself from making a sound. Emily sensed that Melissa was *looking* straight through the door. A loud burst of music then sprang into the room, with two girls laughing and chatting.

*"Hello,"* Melissa said to them, her polite and friendly tone returning as she moved away from the cubicle door.

The girls replied, "Hello" and began chatting amongst themselves as one powdered her nose and the other put on some more lipstick in front of the mirror.

Emily was relieved to see that Melissa's shadow moved away from underneath the door and the sound of her dark heels disappeared out into the crowded pub.

David, meanwhile, had forgotten he was supposed to be letting Emily know the coast was clear, although Melissa and Anthony had recently left. "You're honestly thinking of going fishing?"

"Sure, why not?" John's rapid drinking earlier was now catching up on him.

David smiled and shook his head.

"What?"

"Nothing. It's just you've so often said how boring you thought fishing must be."

"Yeah, well. You know, it might be fun. Anthony seems a pretty cool guy. Plus, the scenery's nice." John's eyes were beginning to look bloodshot from the booze.

"How about you, Jack? You said you'd not been fishing before?"

"Nae. But I'm willing to give it a go, aye. Plus, Anthony said he'd bring a crate of beer." Jack took some ready salted peanuts from a split open bag on the table and popped them in his mouth.

David smiled. "That's your main reason, huh?"

"Aye. A bit," Jack said with a grin as he washed down the nuts with a swig of his pint.

"They were certainly a nice couple," said Annabel. "I doubt I'll see them again. I should have asked for Melissa's number."

"I'll ask Ant on Sunday, if you'll give me *yours*." John grinned at Annabel who couldn't help but smile.

"Maybe later, if you're lucky ..." Annabel smirked.

Emily appeared from the beer garden, holding a bottle for herself and another drink for David.

"You okay, babe?" Annabel asked.

"Yeah."

"You don't look it." Annabel frowned.

"I'm fine," Emily replied, with a less than convincing smile.

David frowned too. He sensed something had happened. He decided to wait to ask until they were alone again.

"Here, have a seat, Em." Annabel squeezed up on the bench. "Think I'll get Jock to sort these benches out. I just felt a splinter on me bum."

"That wasn't a splinter!" John winked, flicking up his brows.

Annabel laughed. "Well, whatever it was, it wasn't very big. Just a *little* prick," she joked.

Everyone laughed apart from David, who smiled and Emily, who didn't react at all.

Emily handed over David's vodka. "Sorry, I took my time. I got chatting to some other people and erm, I had to go to the loo."

"That's okay. Thanks for the drink."

"Cheer up, lass!" Annabel said to her friend.

"Sorry. I just have a bit of a headache."

"Aw," Annabel said, putting a comforting arm around Emily's shoulders. "Reggie's beats will do that to you!"

Annabel Fletcher was half-Scottish from her father's side, twenty-five and her accent was more Scottish than English. She lived a good twelve miles from the pub where she worked, in a small secluded village called Nethy Bridge. She lodged with an elderly couple who were old friends of her parents and were also her godparents. She had known them her whole life. Her parents had moved eight years ago to Newcastle, due to her father's work. Her godparents had never had children of their own and the three of them became very close.

*****

With the exception of David and Emily, the others went back into the packed pub. John wasn't much of a dancer, but he decided to at least try further and 'bust a few moves' to impress Annabel. At the worst, he would make her laugh. And he did. He also insisted on trying to get a 'bird' for Derek, as he had said he would at the start of the evening. A couple of women also caught Jack's attention.

Emily preferred to stay outside because it would be 'better for her head' than going back into the loud music and hot cluster of people.

"So," David said. "Did something happen back in there, earlier? You can tell me. You haven't got a headache, have you?"

Emily looked up at him. She had hardly touched her drink. "No. My head is fine."

"You still feel uneasy about Melissa and Anthony? They've gone now; it's fine. It's not like you'll see them again." David gave an understanding smile.

Emily didn't say anything.

"Please, tell me. You seemed better before you went to get the drinks." David placed his hand on Emily's and looked at her.

She welcomed it and smiled back at him. "Maybe it was nothing … I'm probably just being paranoid."

"Maybe you aren't?" After the week's events so far, David knew how confusing reality and paranoia could be.

"Okay. After I got our drinks in, I went to the loo …" Emily began to tell David what she had overheard.

David listened carefully.

"Maybe I'm just being paranoid. I don't even know who she was talking to. I couldn't hear the voice on the other end properly. But I'm certain it was a male. I heard some crackling sounds, too. It certainly didn't appear to be a clear line. But the way I heard them, *laugh*. Both of them. *Ugh*." Emily gave a shudder as she looked at David. A strong breeze suddenly came up and blew her long, dark brown hair. "The way she stood outside the cubicle door as well … it was like I could *feel* her looking through the door."

David's blue eyes widened in shock.

Emily frowned. "Wh-what is it?"

"I think Melissa was talking about *us*!" David said a little frantic.

*"Us?"* Emily asked worried.

"Not you, but *me and the guys*!"

"I don't understand. Why would she be talking about you?"

"While we were inside, Anthony invited John, Jack and Derek, to go fishing on Sunday, before Melissa and him go back on Monday …" David paused and exhaled. "He asked me if I wanted to go, but I said I'd think about it. Your feelings about them had got me worried. But to be honest, I'm not interested in going fishing, anyway. I have erm, other things to do."

"I thought *I* was being paranoid … you really think she was talking about you? She's only just met you," Emily half-joked. "Maybe it was a coincidence? Maybe I was just being silly."

Alarm bells rang for David with Emily's description of interference on the call, a 'slow sounding speech' and the 'dark' laughing. There was no chance it was a coincidence. This all sounded *way* too familiar. He remembered the spine-chilling laugh they had heard in the forest, when he, John and Gavin had found the creepy, weird tree, and how *Harold*, the supposed forest ranger had laughed too. Could Melissa have been talking to their forest ranger? He wasn't ruling anything out at this stage.

David wanted to open up to Emily about everything, but he didn't want to get her involved. He just couldn't. "I'm going to have to warn the others. Tell them not to go."

"What will you say? They'll probably think I'm being silly." Emily sounded a little anxious.

"Trust me, they won't," David replied with a knowing smile. "I'll think of something."

"I feel bad, though. Maybe I am just overreacting? What if she was just confirming with someone else from the wedding, who say, liked fishing and was going, too?"

Under any other circumstances, David would have found Emily's suggestion plausible. But he sensed something wasn't right. "Perhaps you're right. We don't know anything about this couple. Maybe they are genuinely nice people … but I don't think you were mistaken."

"Oh. That's another strange thing," Emily said.

"What's that?"

"As she ended the call, she said something in a foreign language. Then she said in English, *'I can't wait!'*"

"That's odd … maybe they were just sharing a harmless joke and that's why they laughed the way they did?" David tried to make light of it.

"When are you going to tell them?"

"I'll talk to them later. I'll let them have some fun, first." David could see John's pathetic attempts at dancing through the window and thought he would probably be too drunk to listen to anything right now anyway. David's evening had lost a little of the sparkle he had enjoyed earlier, but he couldn't do anything at the moment, so he thought he may as well try to enjoy the rest of the night too.

*Sod it.* He looked straight at Emily, knocked his drink back and stood up sharply. He had an incredibly beautiful woman in his presence who liked him and the feeling was mutual, despite how hard he fought it. He held out his hand to Emily and said, "Let's go back inside. Let us at least *try* and enjoy the rest of the night! Try and forget about that Melissa and Anthony for now. Yeah?"

Emily smiled and took his hand as she too got up taking her drink and they made their way back inside.

*****

By two in the morning, the packed pub slowly started to clear and people gradually left. The floor was sticky with people's drink spills and somebody had dropped another packet of crisps, which had been scattered and trampled across the wooden floor.

David and the group were seated outside in the beer garden, winding down. They were all drunk, but calm. The stars above them were twinkling away.

"What time does the disco end?" John slurred.

Annabel was seated on John's lap with her arm around his shoulder. "Reggie, normally stops around two-ish." She checked her watch; she was starting to feel tired.

"It would probably be a fair bit earlier if the pub was closer to people's homes," Emily added. She had said earlier that her 'headache' had now gone.

"Yeah. That's about right … there's always pricks like that. *Killjoys*, who stop others from enjoying themselves. Especially on a weekend," John said drunkenly.

Emily and Annabel smiled at his remark.

"True," David said.

"*God*, I could do with one of Jocks burgers right about now … I mean, why does booze always give you the munchies?" John asked.

Annabel smiled. "Good luck with that. I don't think Jock will fancy cooking at this time of night … maybe if it was a little earlier, he'd have made an exception. He usually goes up to bed at half two. He lets one of us or whoever is working close up the pub. Sometimes he might clean up a bit first."

"Yeah. Have you seen the state of the floor? Have fun clearing that up," David joked. He was feeling tired also.

"I might have to get a bag of crisps before we leave," John said, tapping his stomach. He was finding it hard to keep his heavy eyes open. "Listen, Dez.

I'm sorry I couldn't find you a woman, mate. I did try."

"That's okay," Derek replied. He had a large beer stain and sweat patches showing through his light blue shirt.

David smiled. He was glad Derek had made an effort chatting and joining in their fun. Having a few drinks had obviously helped bring Derek out of his shell.

"What about you, Jacky-Boy? How did you fair with those two girls you were chatting to?" John asked.

"Aye, not bad … I pulled one of 'em … got her number as well." Jack grinned as he pulled the left side of his T-shirt away from his shoulder, revealing a large love bite.

"Jesus," John replied. "She a *vampire*? Why did she bite your shoulder?"

*"Aye!"* Jack laughed as the others joined in.

Derek's laugh was even deeper and louder now he was intoxicated. It made the others laugh even more. Emily giggled heavily, trying to cover her mouth.

David looked at Emily. *God. You are just too damn cute.*

"I need the loo," Annabel said.

"You need a hand?" John joked back.

"Cheeky." Annabel smiled and gave him a playful slap on his cheek as she climbed off his lap.

As Annabel went back in, Reggie was coming out for his final smoke break. He walked over to their table.

"Great disco, mate," John said.

Reggie grinned, wiping sweat from his forehead. "Cheers, man. Some nice moves I saw from you!"

"I try," John replied, too drunk to notice the sarcasm.

Reggie pulled out a large joint from the back pocket of his jeans. "Thought I'd smoke this bad boy, before I finish."

"Fuckin' 'ell. Big enough ain't it, aye?" Jack watched as Reggie grinned, popping the joint in his mouth.

"Can I borrow one of your lights again, bredrens?"

"Aye. If ye give me a puff on that." Jack laughed.

"Sure," Reggie answered.

John also had his eyes on the joint.

Reggie lit it and handed Jack his lighter back. He tilted his head back and exhaled, puffing out three smoke rings. The smell of marijuana was strong. "*Irie*. Dis is some *good* shit … I don't make a habit of smoking it. It just helps me relax and wind down after a good night of jamming. Here …" Reggie handed the joint to Jack. "Remember to puff, puff, pass." He smiled.

After Jack was done, he handed the joint back to Reggie.

"Anyone else?" Reggie asked.

"Let's have some," John asked eagerly.

Reggie gave the joint to John who took numerous drags making him cough. "*Jeez*! This is some good shit, all right."

Reggie laughed, just as Annabel returned. "I'll have some of that." She smiled.

"Sure thing, gyal."

Annabel stood casually with one arm across her midriff below her large bosom, smoking the joint with her other hand. "Emily?" Annabel asked, holding out the joint in front of her towards Emily.

"What is this? Pass the puff?" David joked.

"Oh. I don't know," Emily replied. "I've never tried it. I've never even tried a cigarette."

"A drag won't hurt, honey." Annabel smiled.

"Okay, why not ..." Fuelled with courage from the alcohol, Emily didn't want to appear weak in front of the others. She took the joint and had a long drag on it. She exhaled, coughing. "Bloody hell ... that's strong! I don't get how people like that." She screwed up her face and swigged the remains of her drink, trying to get rid of the taste. She handed the joint back to Reggie.

The others watched and smiled.

"I don't like it, either. It's bad enough when he smokes it in his car or in my flat," David replied, pointing at John.

John stuck up his thumb sarcastically.

"May I have some, please?" Derek asked.

Everyone was surprised but Reggie handed Derek the joint. He took several large drags and then exhaled, spluttering and coughing.

Reggie and John laughed.

David patted Derek on the back. "You all right, bud?"

Derek nodded. "Aye ... I think so." Still bent over, Derek's face was red, his eyes watering. He gave the joint back to Reggie to finish off. He sat back up and wiped away a couple of tears. "Don't think I'll try that again, though."

The others laughed, especially Jack.

At that moment, the lights both inside and in the beer garden began to flicker. The music started crackling and jumping. Then, the power went off.

The whole pub became dark as the music abruptly came to a halt. A few ironic cheers came from the remaining customers inside. The sound of a dropped glass breaking on the floor caused another louder cheer.

"Looks like you've knocked out the power and used up all the electricity," John joked to Reggie who was still enjoying his joint.

*"Raas,"* Reggie muttered, fumbling on the table for the ashtray to stub out the joint. "I guess that's me cue to finish up for the night … I was going to make that me last tune, anyway." Reggie placed what was left of his joint back in his pocket.

"I don't think we've ever had a power cut here before," Emily said.

"Oh, it's happened a couple of times. Not for a long time, mind," Annabel replied.

"I better go back in," Reggie said, just as the power came back on and the music stuttered back into life.

"And we're *back*!" Jack said.

*****

It was quarter to three in the morning by the time the last of the customers had eventually left. Only David's group still remained and a couple of locals remained at the bar talking to a tired Craig and Nigel.

Taxis had come and gone. The car park which had been full earlier, was now empty. Reggie had moved his van close to the front door to load up his gear. Jock offered to give him a hand again.

"Well, I suppose we'd better get a taxi soon. That's if they're still working … maybe we should have booked in advance?" David said.

"You should be okay," Annabel replied. "They usually work all hours. Which taxi firm did you guys use?"

"Oh, erm. Rothiemurchus Cars?" David replied.

"Ah. Yeah, they're okay. We normally use Highlander Cabs. We know a couple of guys who work for them."

"Highlander?" John asked.

"Yeah." Annabel laughed. "We actually pre-booked one for around three. We'd offer for you to jump in with us, but there's not enough room."

"We've got Nigel jumping in with us, too," Emily replied.

"What's that?" Nigel asked looking up, hearing his name. He had started to sweep the pub floor with an old broom.

"We were just saying there isn't any room left in our taxi." Emily smiled.

"Oh."

"You don't have to sweep that. We can do that later, when we are in," Emily added.

Nigel laughed. "Yes. But didn't Jock say you two could come in a bit later, after tonight? We'll be open before then."

"Oh, yeah … I didn't think about that." Emily giggled.

"You're right, we didn't." Annabel laughed.

"I better get our taxi booked," suggested David, now feeling very tired.

Derek was nodding off in the corner.

David pulled out his phone and looked at his call history for the taxi number he had dialled earlier. His signal was intermittent. "Anyone else get problems with the signal in here?"

"Aye," Annabel replied. "It's sometimes like that in here. Most of the time it's fine, though. You can use the phone here, if you want? Or try outside: you'll most likely get a better signal out there. Or there's that old phone box across the road still." She gave a slight laugh.

"Nah, that's all right. I'll try outside." David smiled.

"I'll come outside with you," Emily said, getting up.

David smiled at her. "Okay."

David managed to get a taxi 'for as soon as possible,' but it wouldn't be until just after three, so they had at least another twenty minutes or so to wait.

"When are you going to tell the others or warn them about Sunday?" Emily asked a little concerned.

"I'm not sure. I don't think John's going to pay much attention at the moment, seeing as he's drunk. He'd probably forget as well. It's best to wait until the morning. Same with Jack. I don't think he works weekends on my uncle's farm. Well, not usually. But I can call him later on. He might change his mind about going." David put his phone away.

"Maybe we're just worrying over nothing?" Emily smiled at David and placed a hand on his shoulder.

"Maybe." He smiled back at her.

For a moment, they stared into each other's eyes, but were soon distracted by the slamming of Reggie's van doors.

"Well, that's me done for the night. Or should I say, *morning*." Reggie smiled as he walked over to the pair. "I'll see you soon, Emily. Probably in another couple of weeks." He kissed her on her cheek.

"Okay, Reg. Will do. You take care."

"I will, gyal … it was good meeting you, friend," Reggie said to David, shaking his hand.

"You too, mate. I might see you around." David smiled.

"I'll just go in and say goodbye to Anna and the others … and to collect me *coil.*" Reggie grinned, making his way back through the front entrance.

"Coil?" David asked Emily.

"He means money … Jamaican slang."

"Oh," David said, "Of course."

Emily chuckled. "Will I, erm, see you again?" Emily asked, biting her lip.

"I, I don't know. Possibly. I'm going to be up here on my uncle's farm for a little while yet. I dare say me and John will pop in again, before we eventually go home … I am interested in having one of Jock's burgers." David tried to laugh.

"Ah, yes … his famous burgers. They're most certainly popular amongst the folk up here!"

"I'll bet."

"I hope. I mean, it would be nice to see you again, but if you don't want to, erm, it's okay."

"Oh. It's not that. I would like to see you again. It's just, I'm busy helping my uncle out and I have things to do." David saw Emily frown.

"Well, we can still chat or text? We can see, if you're not too busy. I can give you my number, if you'd like?"

"Sure. I'm happy to do that."

They both pulled out their mobiles and exchanged numbers, just as Reggie came back out.

"I'm off, guys. Either of you need a lift?"

"Nah, we're cool thanks, Reggie," David replied. "We've got a couple of taxis coming."

"You could have hopped in the back of me van." Reggie grinned, getting in his van.

"*Now* you tell us." David smiled.

"Me beds crying out for me. You take care, guys. *Peace*!" Reggie raised his two fingers doing the 'peace' sign.

"See ya," David said.

"See you soon," Emily added.

*"Likkle more,"* Reggie called back as he drove off, beeping his horn and waving from the window.

*****

After John had thanked Jock for a good night, he and the others went outside to wait for their taxis. Emily disappeared inside to talk to Jock and go to the ladies.

"So … how's it going with you and Emily, then?" John asked, gently nudging David's side, swaying slightly.

"Okay," David replied, half-smiling.

"Just okay? Yeah, yeah." John winked back. "And Annabel, darling … do I get a kiss goodnight and your phone number? I think I've been a 'good' boy and deserve it."

"What makes you think I *want* to give my number to you?" Annabel laughed.

"I don't think. I *know*!" John grinned.

Annabel shook her head, smiling. "What's yours? I'll call you."

"When?"

"Give me your number and you'll see." Annabel smirked.

"Ah, okay." John staggered slightly over to Annabel where he gave her his number. "And how about that kiss?" he asked, leaning in to kiss Annabel on the lips.

She leaned back slightly, trying to avoid contact. "All in good time …" she said with a smile and then quickly pecked him on the cheek.

"What? That's *it*?"

"For now. All in good time," she repeated.

They were suddenly all lit up by a taxi's headlights as it approached them.

"Ah, good timing," Emily said as she came back out.

Annabel said her goodbyes to everyone and she and Nigel got in the taxi.

"Well, I had a good night, tonight," Emily said to David.

"Me too." David smiled.

"I really hope we can see each other again, soon." Emily touched David's left hand, kissed him on the cheek and joined Annabel in the back of the taxi.

The taxi driver looked austere and stared at the four men standing there. David thought there was something familiar about him. Whoever he was, he didn't seem friendly. Emily waved as they drove off and Nigel raised his hand half-heartedly. Annabel blew a kiss to John.

"Fucking prick tease," John said annoyed.

"Who, that Annabel?" Jack asked.

"Yeah," John replied, throwing his hand up in the air. "Acts all interested and sits on me lap, and that's it."

"Relax, mate. She probably just respects herself. Besides, she said she'd call you," David replied.

"*Bah* … maybe. But she didn't exactly want me to have her number."

"Did anyone recognise that taxi driver? I'm sure I've seen him before somewhere …"

"Nae. I don't think so?" Jack answered.

"Mhm, mhm, not me," Derek replied.

"Can't say I did. I wasn't paying much attention to be honest. He looked like a miserable fucker though, whoever he was. Besides, what was that with you and Emily?" John asked.

"How do you mean?"

"Well, you sort of seemed uninterested. Are you *mad*? She's *gorgeous* and obviously keen on you … you're not into her?" John was staggering on the spot. He'd no doubt feel the consequences of his heavy drinking later when he woke up.

"It's not that I'm not interested. It's just I've got more important matters to worry about at the moment. I think we all do!"

"Ye mean about what's happening on ye uncle's farm, aye?" Jack replied.

"Yep … *and* there's something I need to tell you guys. But it can wait until morning."

# Chapter Thirty-Three

## 14th July, 2018

Their taxi arrived just after five past three in the morning. It was a different driver to Mick, who had brought them. The driver told them it was his last job before retiring for the night, and the fourth time he had picked someone up from the pub that night.

"Ah, shit," John said, sitting in the back between Derek and Jack.

"What is it?" David asked, turning from the front to face him.

"I forgot to get a bag of crisps before we left. I'm bloody *Hank Marvin*! Hey, cabbie. Any takeaways around here?"

The taxi driver turned his head slightly. "A few, but they'll all be shut now, I'm afraid."

"Typical," John replied frustrated.

"Ye could have asked that Annabel for some of her milk, aye?" Jack joked, referring to Annabel's more than ample breasts and making Derek laugh again.

David smiled and shook his head.

"Ha! Yeah." John laughed, resting his head on the leather headrest. "Ah, Annabel …"

David was feeling hungry too. "We can get a bag of crisps or something when we get back in?"

"Yeah, whatever," John replied sleepily.

*****

By the time the others had been dropped off and they were heading for Hamish Farm, John had dozed off.

"Was a good night, then?" the driver asked David who was also struggling to stay awake.

"Uh? Oh. Yeah. It was good, thanks." David yawned. "I just want to get back to bed, now."

It was nearly four.

"Me too," the taxi driver replied.

"You live around here?" David asked.

"Not too far."

David looked out at the surrounding forest. He couldn't see anything, other than the dark outline of the trees and the headlights on full beam towards the road ahead. It felt eery. John began to snore.

"You come this way much, through the forest?"

"Not if I can help it." The taxi driver laughed. "There's a few times I have done. You can't get away from it, if you're a cabbie … I don't ever recall coming this far in before. It's a fair few miles in this way, to your uncle's farm, did you say?"

"Yep, that's right," David replied with another yawn.

"To be honest, this forest gives me the creeps," the driver said as he took a turning that would eventually lead up to the farm.

"Oh?"

"Yeah. I don't know. It's just something about the place, I suppose. I wouldn't want to live here."

"Yeah."

As they got closer to the farm, they could see a faint blue light flickering above the treetops.

"What the hell's that?" David asked. "I think it's coming from the farm!"

"It looks like an ambulance or police light … only one way to find out." The taxi driver put his foot down to accelerate.

Getting nearer to the farm, the blue light grew brighter and the taxi headlights seemed to dim. An ambulance was parked outside the house as the driver had predicted, with its blue lights swirling around.

*"John. Wake up!"* Before the taxi could stop completely, David jumped out and started running to the farmhouse. His uncle came out of the house with a male paramedic.

"Wh-why you shouting?" John woke up feeling half-asleep and still drunk. "We back yet? What's with the flashing lights?"

*"What happened?"* David demanded, sprinting up to his uncle.

Bob greeted him with a smile. "Everything's fine," he said calmly, putting a hand on his nephew's shoulder.

"What's with the ambulance?" David asked frantically.

Bob looked over to the paramedic and smiled. He walked David away and explained to him, "Listen, your aunt is fine. She had a slight seizure; they're going to take her to hospital and run some tests overnight. But they reckon she's fine."

"A seizure? Well, how? Has she ever had one before?"

"No. Your aunt is a diabetic. She hadn't been taking her medication, which probably explains her strange behaviour of late. Coupled with the stress of what's been happening, it's no doubt resulted in the seizure. The paramedics have said she's fine. She was fortunate, but they're going to take her in, just to make sure."

"She's a diabetic? I didn't know. Well, I suppose I wouldn't," David replied, calming down. "But how do they know she's going to be fine? I mean, what if she isn't?"

"We'll know for sure later on or tomorrow. The paramedics have checked her over and she seems fine at the moment. Apart from having another headache. It explains a lot and makes sense, her not taking her meds, David," Bob explained further. "One of the female paramedics is helping her get dressed to take her into hospital. She's adamant she's fine and doesn't need to go. Typical Betty." Bob tried to laugh. He was still a little worried himself.

"Yeah, but they're just paramedics, they could be wrong. What do they know?" David tried to keep his voice down, but the paramedic standing outside the front appeared to overhear and looked a little embarrassed, diverting his head.

"What's with the ambulance?" John groaned, making his way out of the taxi towards David and Bob. "The taxi's still waiting for the rest of his fare."

Bob could smell the booze on John's breath.

"Here," said David, pulling out a note and some change from his pocket. "This should cover it. Tell him to keep any change."

John staggered back towards the taxi.

"You boys ought to get some rest. The sun will be up soon ... I take it you had a good night?" Bob asked.

"It was okay ... I'm going to the hospital, too."

"There's no need right now, David. I'm going to go with her, just to be there for her. You and John need to get some sleep. You both smell like a brewery," Bob joked.

"But I want-"

"No, David ... please, sleep. You can come see her tomorrow. She's fine."

"Anyone going to tell me what's going on?" John yawned.

"Betty had a seizure," David replied a little annoyed.

"What? She going to be okay?" John swayed and looked like he was about to collapse himself.

"She's going to be fine. She wasn't taking her meds. We're just taking her to hospital to make sure," Bob answered.

"I *knew* I shouldn't have gone out tonight ... I had a feeling something may happen." David shook his head.

"Don't be silly ... it wouldn't have made any difference had you been here or not. She still would have had the seizure. It's *not* your fault."

"Yeah. Don't blame yourself, mate," John slurred.

They heard Betty as she made her way out of the front door. She had a blanket draped over her. The other paramedic was helping her out of the door to the ambulance. "I'm telling you, I'm *fine*, dear! I feel a bit headachy, but other than that, I'm perfectly well ... I don't need to waste people's time going into hospital. There's others that need more help than I do."

"It's just precaution, Mrs Hammond. We have to make sure. It's our job," the female paramedic replied. She looked up at Bob and the boys and smiled. She wore the green paramedic uniform like her colleague and was in her late thirties.

"She ain't too shabby," John whispered in David's left ear.

David shot John an angry look.

John held his hands up in defence.

The paramedic helped escort Betty carefully to the back of the ambulance, where her colleague opened the two large doors.

"Is this necessary, love?" Betty looked to Bob.

"It's just to make sure. They'll just run a few checks. You'll be back later on or tomorrow at the latest." Bob was starting to doubt if she was okay. She looked fine, although a little tired. Perhaps there was a more serious reason behind the seizure? Not taking her insulin must surely be the reason though.

As Betty was helped into the ambulance, Gavin appeared from the side of the house, carrying his shotgun. He looked exhausted with dark rings under his eyes. Working these long nights were becoming a burden. "How is she?"

"I'm okay, Gavin ... I don't see the need to go into hospital," Betty called from inside the ambulance.

Gavin smiled. "I see you two are back. How was your night?"

"It was okay. Until we got back," David replied. "When did she have this fit?"

"A little over an hour ago," Gavin replied. "I went into the kitchen to get a drink and found her on the floor shaking. She was foaming from her mouth. Pretty scary stuff."

"Thankfully, she didn't hit her head when she fell. She came down for a glass of water. After that, she doesn't remember anything," Bob said as he climbed into the ambulance. "She was like that for almost ten minutes ... she'd recovered by the time the paramedics arrived. Isn't that right, love?"

"Well, you folks did the right thing, calling us out. Particularly as it was her first seizure," the male paramedic commented. He hopped out of the back of the ambulance and made his way round to the driver's seat. His colleague stayed with Bob and Betty.

"Give me a call, boss. When you're finished at the hospital. If you need picking up."

"I will do, Gavin. Thanks. Hopefully, we won't be too long." Bob nodded. "See you soon, David. Don't worry. You two get some sleep!"

"I hope that it's nothing more serious," David said as they watched the ambulance drive away.

"I'm sure she'll be fine. It certainly explains her odd behaviour," Gavin replied. "We had to leave the pens unguarded for a period. I better get back there now. Just in case."

David still wasn't convinced. His aunt not taking her medication and being stressed could have been the cause, but he sensed it was something more. Something darker. "Where's Benji?" he suddenly asked.

"He's in the living room. The cats are in there, too. Benji followed me in when I found Betty."

"Everything else been okay, while we've been out?" John asked, feeling hungrier than ever. His head was beginning to throb.

"Apart from Betty, nothing out of the ordinary." Gavin yawned.

"I'm going to get something to eat, then bed. I'm famished. Don't worry, Dave. I'm sure your aunt is going to be fine." John stumbled inside and made his way to the kitchen.

"Someone's certainly drunk." Gavin smiled.

"Yeah. He often gets like that ... I'm going to get Benji, then head up to bed. Well, if I can get any sleep after everything. It just seems like one damn thing after another."

Gavin patted David's back. "I know, mate. Try and get some sleep. I wish I could. But I'm going to keep watch for a little while yet. At least until the sun comes up. I'll be out here, if you need me, okay?"

"Sure, Gavin. Thanks. Or I can stay out with you?"

"I'll be fine. I've got this ..." Gavin smiled and tapped his shotgun.

David went to see Benji and gave the two cats a stroke. He decided to stay with the cats for a short while before he took Benji up to his room. He didn't like the thought of Sammy and Josie being on their own downstairs, so he waited until the sun came up, before finally going upstairs to bed. As David went up, John came down again to fetch another bag of crisps. He said he couldn't sleep.

In his bed, David still felt a little drunk. He dreaded sleeping after his awful nightmare the night before. He was even more worried about his aunt. He hoped the alcohol would help him to sleep. He shook his head as the breaking dawn lightened the room. It felt strange having a night out and coming home when the sun was rising.

It was still hard to believe everything that had happened. He did however smile, when he thought of the time he had enjoyed talking to Emily and getting to know her. It still felt warm in his room, so he dangled one of his legs out of the side of the bed trying to cool himself down.

He heard John stumble up the stairs and a rustling sound outside the door. He heard John rip the packet open and curse as crisps fell onto the carpet.

David eventually drifted off to sleep.

# Chapter Thirty-Four

## 14th July, 2018

It was a quarter past eleven when David awoke from his drunken slumber; his head ached, but not as bad as he'd suffered in the past with a hangover.

His top lip was slightly stuck to his upper gum where his mouth had become dehydrated. He looked down at Benji and called his name. Benji rolled over and grunted.

David sat on the side of the bed and stroked Benji's soft belly gently with his foot. He remembered the gaping gash from his nightmare and was relieved not to have had any bad dreams during the night.

He got himself out of bed and checked the time on his phone. There weren't any messages or missed calls. He went to look out of the bedroom window. It was overcast. He pulled up the window to let a soft breeze in and stuck his head out for some air. It was much cooler today. He left the window open, enjoying the fresh air. He then made his way to the bathroom. He noticed a few crumbs of crisps outside John's bedroom on the floor.

In the bathroom mirror, David noticed a faint, red lipstick mark on his left cheek where Emily had kissed him the night before. He smiled at his reflection and felt a tingly feeling thinking about her. But now wasn't the time to start a relationship.

He suddenly remembered the taxi driver who had picked up Emily, Nigel and Annabel. He could have sworn he had seen him somewhere before, but he couldn't place him.

David hurried downstairs in his grey boxers, hoping that Bob and Betty were back. He checked the living room and the kitchen. No one was about. He was about to walk outside when Gavin came through the front door. "Gavin," David raised his voice. "Have you heard anything from my uncle, yet?"

"I have. I was due to pick him up shortly but he insisted on getting a taxi back. He wanted me to stay here; Betty's going to stay another night in hospital. They just want to make sure she's definitely okay. They ran a few tests and she had an MRI scan. They all came back clear, so they believe she's fine. Derek's turned up, too."

David frowned. "Derek's in? He never said anything about working today? I thought he might have been a bit hungover, anyway."

"He doesn't look too bad." Gavin laughed. "He's not long been here. He wasn't meant to be working. He said he was just concerned about us, so came in. I've just come in to get us a coffee."

"I guess that's nice of him."

*****

After a quick shower, David joined the other two outside. "Derek … I didn't think you'd be in today. How are you feeling?"

"Hi, David. I'm okay, thanks. Bit tired."

"Not too hungover, then?" David laughed slightly.

"Nae. I took some painkillers earlier. I don't mind helping out for a wee while. Just hope that Betty's okay."

"Yeah, me too, mate … You enjoyed last night, yeah? It looked like you were having a good time. You came in okay on your moped, too?"

"Aye, it was good. And yes, I came in on my moped. Was just careful, because of last night." Derek started to laugh. "I think I'm still over the limit."

David watched as Derek fed some of the farm animals. "What did you make of that couple, last night?"

"Huh, couple?" Derek looked up.

"You know? Melissa and Anthony?"

"Oh, them," recalled Derek. "They seemed okay. Nice couple. Shame I can't join them fishing tomorrow … why do you ask?" He threw a few apples into the pen for the pigs. "They love apples." He smiled.

"I just wondered. Emily thought that something was perhaps off about them and that they didn't appear genuine."

Derek looked at David and frowned. "Really?"

David nodded.

"Strange. I thought they seemed nice."

"I did too," David replied, watching as the pigs chomped noisily on the apples. He didn't feel like going into detail about what Emily had overheard; there wasn't much point, as Derek wasn't joining the fishing group. It was

Jack, who he was worried about. He would contact him later. He was possibly in bed and probably nursing a hangover. He may have already changed his mind or he may not even remember. John would most likely be easier to convince, once he got up.

*****

Over a couple of hours passed and David was surprised that Bob had not yet returned. It was still overcast. He was throwing a stick for Benji in the back garden.

He received a text from Emily, saying how much she had enjoyed last night. She said she felt a tad hung over, 'lol,' but could still go in to work.

David replied, saying he enjoyed last night too, and added a smiley emoticon.

*"Urgh,"* came a groan from behind David.

He looked round to see John, coming out with just a pair of shorts on, holding his head.

"It awakens," David said in a sarcastic tone.

"My head's killing me … what time is it?"

"Gone half one," David replied as he threw the stick further up the garden for Benji to chase.

Benji rolled on the floor chewing on it, wagging his tail.

"How much do you remember from last night?" David smiled.

"Urgh." John took a seat. "I remember a fair bit. I didn't make an arse out of myself, did I?" John was often paranoid after a night out, worried that he had said or done something he would regret; *hangxiety*.

"Nah. Not overly. Well, apart from that shit you call dancing," joked David.

"Shit. Yeah. I remember that, unfortunately … Oh, shit, how's your aunt? *Jesus*, I only just remembered the ambulance."

"Bob wanted Gavin to stay here, rather than pick him up. He was going to get a taxi back from the hospital; I thought he'd been back by now … Derek came in as well. Even though he wasn't supposed to. He said he was concerned because of everything; he says he's fine, too. Betty had a scan and got the all clear. They reckon she's okay, but I'm not so sure." David sat down next to John on the patio.

"She'll be okay, mate. I'm sure she is. At least the scan came back all clear. I can't remember fully … wasn't it something to do with her not taking her meds?" John winced from the pain in his head. "I'm still a little surprised

Derek came in, though. Guess he doesn't feel as shitty as I do."

"That's what they reckon. She's diabetic and hadn't been taking her insulin. Probably because she's been stressed, too; that's what caused the seizure."

"You don't believe that?"

"After what's happened, I honestly don't know." David looked around the garden. "Do you remember telling Anthony you would go fishing? And Jack saying he would go, too?" David looked at John, who appeared to be in some discomfort.

"Fishing? Oh, wait. Yeah, I remember. Something about going down to the river here … erm, I may do. Fishing isn't exactly my thing, though."

"That's what I said last night."

"Well, I'll try anything once." John smiled. "They were a good couple."

"I need to talk to you about that …"

"Oh?" John asked confused.

"Yeah."

"Shit, hang on." John suddenly got up and threw up at the side of the garden. His head pounded more from the retching and bending down. "I'm glad I didn't take any painkillers yet." John sat back down. "What did you want to tell me, about that Melissa and Anthony?"

"I don't think they're as they seem."

"In what sense? From what I recall, they seemed genuine and polite; friendly enough."

"I thought so, too. Perhaps that's the impression they like to give."

"Why the suspicions, then?"

"It's what Emily said … Anthony was giving her these creepy looks."

"Maybe she was just misinterpreting it? I mean, we were all drunk. Obviously, me more than anyone," John joked.

"Nah. Even if that were true, something else happened after."

"What?"

"She basically didn't want to go back outside until they were both gone."

"That's a bit extreme, isn't it?" John laughed slightly.

"No," David said, defending Emily.

"What's happening with you two? She clearly likes you, bud. You're a fool if you don't pursue it. Even if it's just a shag, she's probably well up for it."

"What? *No* … she isn't like that. But listen, something else happened."

"I'm listening. Get to the point … I need to take something for this sodding headache."

David hurried to update his friend; he could see he was suffering. "… what's even more concerning, is what Melissa said to the other person, 'We've got at least one of them possibly coming on Sunday, and I'm not sure about him yet, but Anthony is trying to convince him to come.'"

It took John a few seconds for everything to sink in. "Shit … you think she was talking about *us*?"

"Yep … I mean, I could be wrong. It's possible that the person they were trying to convince was me, because I was reluctant to join. You'd already said yes, and Jack was up for it. She could have been speaking about any of us. Though, Derek said he couldn't go, as he was going to his mum's … You know what else?"

"What?"

"The way Emily described the voice over the line and the laugh, it reminded me of that Harold freak we saw in the forest a couple of days back … maybe I'm jumping the gun a bit. She even said she heard her say something that wasn't even in English. And something about 'not being able to wait.'"

"Fucking hell … you think it might be him?" John looked worried. "I wonder what she meant?"

"I know … Melissa freaked Emily afterwards, waiting outside her cubicle, when she ran in there."

"*What*? Jeez."

"I hadn't even told Emily anything about why we're up here or what's been happening. I don't want to get her involved."

"I was all up for it, but I was drunk. Now after what you've said, I really don't want to … If they were discussing us, were they talking about the actual fishing or something, well, something *else*?" John felt sick again and took some deep breaths.

"I don't know, mate. But we need to warn Jack and let him know."

"For sure. Better to be safe than sorry … maybe they were going to cut us up and use us as fish bait?" John was trying to be funny. Neither of them laughed.

"You've got Jack's number, haven't you? And Anthony's?"

"Yeah. I've got both. We can call Jack later. I need another lie-down to get rid of this headache. As long as we notify Jack before tomorrow, we should be all right. That's if he's still going ahead with it."

"Sure, we'll call him later."

John took a couple of painkillers for his head and went back upstairs to sleep off his hangover, but he ended up tossing and turning. He'd brought a plastic bucket from under the kitchen sink and placed it next to his bed, in case he was sick again. It would save rushing to the bathroom and he didn't want to throw up on his hosts' carpet.

David felt pretty much fine physically. He sat in the living room with Benji, waiting for his uncle to arrive. He was beginning to worry that perhaps Betty had had another seizure. He was also texting Emily:

> You feeling hungover this morning? x
>
> Not too bad. John's pretty bad. Gone back upstairs to bed. Self-inflicted, so no sympathy! Lol. How are you and Annabel? x
>
> Oh, poor him! Me and Anna not too bad, thanks. Jock wasn't too bothered if we didn't come in anyway. Lol. x
>
> Sounds like a good boss! x
>
> Yes! We don't take advantage of his good nature, though. Did you tell the others about that couple? It's still freaking me out! :( x
>
> Aww. I mentioned it to John. He's not going. I mean, he doesn't even like fishing. Derek wasn't going and we're going to tell Jack later. He's probably still in bed. x
>
> I hope they don't think I'm being stupid! :( x
>
> Nah. Believe me, they won't! John didn't. x
>
> Okay. :) You any plans for today? x
>
> None. Waiting for my uncle to return from the hospital. There was an ambience here last night. My aunt had a seizure. :( They ran some tests though and she's going to be fine. I hope! x
>
> I am so sorry. :( I'm sure she'll be fine if they say so. What did you mean by an 'ambience?' x
>
> Sorry. Lol. Bloody predictive text. I meant ambulance! x
>
> Ha ha! x

David got up as he heard a car outside. He hoped it was his uncle. Indeed it was. He could see him through the window in a red taxi.

I've got to go. My uncle has just got back. I'll text you later. x

Okay. I hope so. :) Hope your aunt is okay! x

Thanks. Me too! Talk later. xx

Byeeee! xxx

David hurried out the front door to meet his uncle.

Bob was carrying some bags in. "I'm a bit late; I did some shopping." Bob smiled.

"How is she?"

"She's fine, David. The cause of the seizure was her not taking her meds and being a little stressed. We didn't go into detail though, about everything up here, although we mentioned about Mandy and Daisy. They're keeping her in, just for another night for observation. She'll be home tomorrow. How are you feeling, after last night?"

"I'm good. John isn't too great. He's gone back to bed."

"It must have been a good night, then?" Bob laughed.

"I'll give you a hand with putting the shopping away, if you want?"

*****

Bob decided on taking a shower before putting the shopping away. David had already offered to start doing it, but Bob insisted it was fine and to wait for him.

David noticed a large bruise on his uncle's upper chest/right shoulder region near his armpit, when he returned in his vest.

"Don't worry about that ..." Bob smiled, looking down at it. "It's from the other day. When I fired the shotgun into those bushes. The gunshot forced the gun back onto me. It's not uncommon. Especially when you don't fire them often. It aches a little, but I'm fine ... So, anything happen last night, meet any nice girls?" Bob grinned as he and David put the groceries away.

"There was one, who works at the pub."

"Which one was that? Was it that little brunette one? The one with an Irish accent, was it?"

"Yep, that's the one." David couldn't help but smile.

Bob could see a twinkle in his nephew's eye. "Ah. She's a pretty little thing."

"She sure is ... we texted a little today, but I'm not sure about it. I don't know if it's worth it. I mean, on top of everything that's happening around here, she lives up here and I live down south. Perhaps if she was closer ..." David stacked a couple of tins of baked beans into one of the kitchen cupboards.

"I understand your concerns, David. But if you like her and she does you, then maybe give it a shot?" Bob stretched up to one of the cupboards and made room for some bags of flour. He winced a little at his sore shoulder.

"I honestly don't know, Uncle. I mean, we have all this other shit going on; the last thing I want to do is involve someone else in it all."

"That's true; did you tell her about any of it?"

"No ... but something happened last night that I believe is linked."

"What?" Bob looked concerned.

They continued unpacking the shopping and David told Bob about Melissa and Anthony and Emily's concerns.

*****

"It's all very odd. *Disturbing*," Bob said.

The two of them sat at the kitchen table with their mugs of tea. Neither of them had yet touched their brew.

"You don't think that maybe Emily is somehow part of this, David? I don't mean to put you off ... perhaps she was lying? For whatever reason ... after all, you've only known her a few hours."

David puffed his cheeks out and shook his head. "Nah, I don't think so. Not Emily. We had this connection, you know? It felt like we had *so* much in common, as if we'd known each other for a long time. I know it sounds silly."

"No, it doesn't." Bob smiled at his young nephew.

"I believe she's genuine, Uncle."

"Either way, you should still be careful. Trust your gut."

"I will. I'm not sure if I'll see her again. I guess we'll see. There's just so much going on and now with Betty having this seizure."

"I understand," Bob said, picking up his cup of tea. He blew on it and sipped carefully, trying not to burn his lip. "You think it could have been this Harold chap, on the other end of the line that Emily heard?"

"Possibly. We need to tell Jack ... If my suspicions are right, what the *hell* were they planning on tomorrow? Surely it wouldn't have been fishing?"

"We'll have to make sure we stop him from going. You say this couple are up for a wedding today, and returning home on Monday?"

"That's right. So they said. It's just all a head fuck. This Melissa and

Anthony seemed fine to me. Well, to all of us, except Emily." David rubbed his face with his right hand.

"Drink your tea. It will get cold otherwise." Bob smiled.

"How far is the hospital where Betty is?"

"A fair bit. About fifty minutes, depending on traffic."

"I do hope she's okay," David said, finally having some of his tea.

"Me too. She's in good hands," Bob replied, giving David's hand a firm grasp.

"I hope this Carl bloke gets back to us on Monday," David added, suddenly remembering the ecologist Bob had contacted.

"Fingers crossed."

"I wonder how that other farmer, Angus, is getting on? It must be hard on him, losing his goats and animals like that."

"Yes. Bless him. He's had it tough as well. Make no mistake. Especially being alone on that farm since his wife died ... Did you get to ask anyone last night about the area?"

"I don't think we did. Other than a taxi driver saying the forest creeped him out, and one saying his wife didn't like going in there because it felt like they were being watched."

"Well, I'm glad you had a good time." Bob smiled again.

David's eyes became large as he suddenly remembered Ralf and Samuel. He told Bob about them. He couldn't believe he'd temporarily forgotten.

"Good God ... I wonder what it was that he saw? Who on earth did he mean by 'them' and this 'thing?'"

"I think it might have been what John and I encountered, and your ex-worker, Eric." David shuddered.

Bob swallowed. "It's possible. But that thing you saw on the motorway ... you weren't even in Scotland, and certainly not the forest, here!"

David shook his head. "I don't know what to think. Perhaps it can manifest itself wherever it chooses? Like in mine and Grant's flats. Jesus ... this is all too much. Maybe if we could somehow get in contact with this Samuel, he could perhaps tell us more. The Ralf guy, who I assume was his friend, gave him a slap for daring to speak to us about it. Total arsehole."

"Yes, he seems it ... I think we could be onto something."

"Maybe I can find out where he lives? I'm sure someone at the pub will know. I can check with Emily and Jock."

"I wonder what he meant by robes and masks? This thing that you saw was wearing a cloak or robe. The same as what Eric saw before he quit; the cloaked figure that floated into the forest."

"That's right. It seems that there's some kind of cult around here … like some Satanic sect? Don't they sacrifice animals and wear hooded cloaks or gowns?"

"I think they do," Bob answered, not completely sure. "Though, I've certainly never heard of any talk about a cult up here … of course, there have been accounts like with, erm, Charlie. Obviously of late, there have been things happening and possible signs, like Gavin seeing and hearing that fire and chanting. But why is it so much worse now? What with what's been happening to us and Angus. I don't know what to think, anymore."

"It certainly messes with your head," David replied. "Not to mention physically … you look awfully tired, Uncle. Gavin, too. Doing these night shifts can't be good for you."

"It certainly isn't … I don't recall the last time I had a good night's sleep. Perhaps we don't have to keep watching the animals, but I don't want to take the risk. Maybe they've seen us keeping guard and we've scared them off." Bob laughed a little nervously.

"Maybe it's time for me and John to start helping?"

"What – doing the night watch?" Bob finished his tea.

"Sure. Even if it's only for a couple of nights. It will give you and Gavin a chance to catch up on some much-needed sleep. Neither of us know how to use a gun, but as long as we're on the lookout."

"I don't know. I wouldn't expect either of you two to do that, David. Besides, sometimes Derek and Jack help out."

"But it makes sense. I mean, we're staying here and it's not like we have any daytime commitments or anything. We could sleep in afterwards. I'm sure I can get John to agree."

"We'll see. I would definitely appreciate the chance to get some sleep. I'm sure Gavin would as well … me or him, could do it with you. I wouldn't want to take the risk of it just being you and John."

"You don't have to worry about that. If anything *did* happen, all we'd have to do is shout out or run into the house to wake you both."

"I'll have a talk with Gavin." Bob smiled.

They continued chatting about Betty.

David wanted to visit his aunt, but apparently, she was adamant she was fine and didn't need any visitors. She was due home tomorrow anyway. Bob would however, speak on the phone to her later.

*****

It was evening by the time John got up. He had slept on and off during the day and still felt a little worse for wear. The painkillers had helped.

David insisted that John join him and Benji for a walk around the farm, citing the old 'the fresh air will do you good' cliché.

They chatted about events; Samuel and Ralf, the girls, Betty, 'going fishing' and how David had informed his uncle of what Samuel supposedly saw.

"I wonder if Emily or Jock might know where this Samuel lives? I want to know more about what he saw."

"Same. It might be a bit awkward turning up at his house to ask. You saw the state he got in as well, when you pushed him on it. Even if that dick, Ralf, wasn't there, he might not have said much more."

"I still think we could have pushed him further, had it not been for Ralf."

"Yeah. Fucking *Wreck-It Ralf*!" John joked.

David smiled, lobbing a stick for Benji to fetch. "I suggested to my uncle that we help out nights. I don't think it's right that he and Gavin are doing so much. Bob looks exhausted."

"Yeah, I noticed that. I don't mind doing it. Not tonight, though; I want to get an early night. I'm still recovering." John laughed.

"That's fine, mate." David smiled.

"Annabel never called … probably won't, either. Bitch!" John grinned.

David laughed. "It's only been a day. Not even that. Besides, she's probably busy working, like Emily is."

"True. But Emily texted you." John gave a wry smile.

"That's true."

"What's happening with you and her?"

"There is no me and her."

"You know what I mean … it's clear she likes you and you must like her? She's gorgeous, mate. Annabel's hot too, not just because of her breasts. Well maybe but, erm, you know." John laughed. "I'm not sure I have a type. But if Emily asked me out, I'd jump at the chance. It's obvious she likes you."

"You'd jump at the chance to get her in the sack, eh?" David half-joked, looking across to John.

"Yeah. But in general." John grinned. "I'm more into Annabel for obvious reasons. Well, I'd like to be into her, *period*." John winked.

David tried not to laugh. "You're unbelievable."

"She likes you a lot. Even though she's only just met you. Annabel said herself that she does. I don't think she just wants to get inside your pants either, bud."

"No, she's not like that."

"Yes or no, though? Do you like her like that or feel something, a spark, for example?"

They both stood for a moment; they weren't too far from the north border of the forest.

David moved his head, trying not to make eye contact with John. "Okay. I do. Satisfied?" David tried not to smile.

"Attaboy." John gently punched his friend's shoulder. "Go for it!"

"But with all this crap happening, it might be too risky to get her involved. And even if it were under normal circumstances, she lives here in Scotland and I'll be hours away. It's not practical."

"I know that … I'm sure you could work something out. Where there's a will, there's a way."

David sighed. "I don't know. I guess we'll see. I'm just going to play it by ear for now. It's secondary. We need to figure out *what* and *why* things are happening up here, first … and that reminds me. We still need to tell Jack!"

David had tried ringing Jack from his uncle's study numerous times during the day, but his phone had been switched off. He had left a couple of brief messages, saying they needed to talk.

"We ought to." John took his phone out and dialled Jack. Still, his phone was switched off. "I'll send him a text to see if he's still planning to go. At least when he turns his phone on, he'll get these messages."

"How was it being arranged?"

"How do you mean?"

"Well, you obviously have that Anthony's number and he has yours. Same as Jack. You've not heard from him? Are you supposed to contact him?"

John stood for a moment thinking, holding his phone. "I can't honestly remember … I might have said I'd confirm today or perhaps he said he'd phone Sunday morning. He has his brother's wedding today, remember?"

"Yeah, he's probably too occupied with all that … that's if there even *is* a wedding …"

John frowned and gave a slight laugh. "What, you think they were making it all up?"

"I don't know. It's possible."

"Yeah. But it all sounded pretty genuine, like about the church, flying up here et cetera, et cetera. Why would they make it all up, in some fabricated lie?"

"I don't know. It's probably a stupid suggestion. Chances are, there is a wedding … or, perhaps it's all part of a bigger plan. Like trying to get us to go tomorrow … making them seem more convincing to us?"

"Well, there's only one way to find out," John said. He looked up Anthony's number and dialled on speaker phone.

"What are you doing?"

John raised a finger as they heard the phone ring. Not for the first time, there was some static on the call.

*"John-Boy!"* came Anthony's voice sounding chirpy. "How are you, mate?"

"Hey, Ant! I'm not bad, ta. Bit better now, but was hanging out me arse, earlier!" John could hear Anthony laughing.

"Good night, though!"

"Yeah, mate." John gave a phoney laugh. "How goes the wedding?"

"*Good* … plenty of booze and food. I'm just outside enjoying a cigar."

"Listen, Anthony, I'm not sure I can make it tomorrow for the fishing. I erm. I might have to help David on his uncle's farm. One of the other workers isn't well."

There was a slight pause from Anthony as a crackle of interference swept through the call. "Oh. That's okay. I can ring tomorrow to double check whether you're free, that's if I'm up to it myself, after tonight." Anthony's laugh didn't sound real. He also sounded annoyed by John's rejection. "It won't be until after lunch."

"No worries. Yeah, give us a bell tomorrow. I might still be able to make it."

"Will do … that Jack fella. I've not heard from him, yet. I wonder if he's still interested in coming? He's probably hungover and forgot." Anthony laughed some more. "Listen, John. I'd better get back to the reception. You have a good evening."

"I will, thanks. Talk later."

"Sure." Anthony ended the call abruptly.

"So, what do you think?" John asked, putting his phone away. "He sounded a little pissed off."

"So I heard. It could be nothing … he was outside, right?"

"That's what he said."

"Well. Don't you think we should have heard people talking or music at a wedding reception in the background?"

"He could have been a bit away from the reception? I know that look … what are you thinking?"

"Oh, I don't know. I just thought …"

"Yeah. Go on ..."

"What if we took a drive down to where this church is to see? It can't be *too* far. I mean, didn't Melissa say the wedding reception was being held opposite the church or next to it? Like the community hall?"

John laughed. "You want us to spy on them, to see if they were being honest about the wedding?"

"Sure, why not?"

"Well, what if there *is* a wedding on and they see us?"

"They won't see us. We can just drive past and see."

"And what if Emily's the one who's being deceitful?"

"I honestly trust Emily's word ... if there is no wedding, it proves Emily's theory."

"God, I don't know ... what if the three of them are all in it together?"

"There's only one way to find out. We can go check and then contact Jack."

"Okay. But I still feel a bit shitty, bud. Not to mention the fact I'm probably still over the limit."

"We can wait a little while. Failing that, maybe Bob or Gavin can take us. Or I can drive again ... If there is a wedding reception on, it'll last well into the night." David started to feel a little excited but also nervous about checking up on Melissa and Anthony.

"You're probably right. I'm starting to feel hungry. Wouldn't mind popping to a takeaway."

David smiled to himself.

"What?"

David raised his brows. "Nothing. Just you and your food. Even though you don't feel great."

"Well, I am a bit of a foodie," John joked. "Been a bit of an unhealthy week this week, in more ways than one ... I'm sure one more bit of junk food won't hurt."

They made their way back to the pens and mentioned their idea to Gavin and Bob; they weren't keen on the idea. For obvious reasons.

"You know of this church, then?" John asked.

"I sure do. It isn't overly far. It's on the B970. We've been in there a couple of times. Not for many years, mind. Nice church, in a nice location," Bob answered.

"The only thing I'm concerned about is if Melissa or Anthony see us," said John.

"We could just say we were driving past and thought we'd check out the nice church they'd told us about?" David said confidently. "If they are genuine, there's no reason for them to get suspicious."

John snorted. "Okay."

"Just make sure you watch yourselves, okay?" Bob asked. "Get back before dark."

"We will Uncle, we will," David reassured him.

# Chapter Thirty-Five

## 14th July, 2018

"You're sure you're in a fit state to drive?" David asked as he, Benji and John got in John's car.

"Ah, I should be okay. I'll be better after I get a bite to eat," John replied, turning on the ignition. "At least the clock is still working." John pointed to the car clock. "Do you feel a little nervous?"

David looked at him. "A little. I don't know why. We're only going to check the church."

John took the handbrake off and slowly drove out of the barn.

They had found the location of the church online so John tapped it into his satnav.

*****

"I forgot to ask your uncle about takeaways around here," John said, always thinking about food.

They both laughed as they heard his belly growl. Even Benji's ears pricked up in the back.

"That was a corker!" John laughed further.

David checked on his phone for nearby takeaways. It took a little while to load up due to the poor signal. He was hungry too, after not eating much all day. "There's a few about. Depends on what you fancy, though. Pizza?"

"Yeah, I'm inclined to go for that."

"Likewise. There's a pizza place in Aviemore … that's where Emily lives as well."

"Bet you wouldn't mind a 'pizza' her, eh? Come to think of it, I wouldn't mind, either. A *big* piece," John joked.

David smiled. "I thought you were more interested in Annabel?"

"Yeah, but seeing as she hasn't contacted me yet, I won't hold my breath, mate." John turned on his window wipers to wash a large bug off his window.

"You want to go now or after we've checked the church?"

"I'm a bit anxious. Perhaps we'd better wait until after we've checked the church?

"Yeah, okay." David laughed slightly.

"We're going to have to pass the church first anyway, the way we are going ... next right should take us onto the road before the one with the church on." John glanced at his satnav.

They were glad to have driven out of the forest and their nerves had dropped a little. Now getting nearer to the church, they started to become a little more nervous again.

They drove past a couple of road signs that read *Inverdruie* with the speed limit of *40* on top and *Please Drive Carefully* below. The area generally appeared very scenic and peaceful.

*****

"Any second now," John said.

"Yep. I can't help feeling a bit nervous."

"Chickenshit." John looked over and smiled. "Nah. I feel the same, mate."

David gave an anxious smirk.

A few scattered spots of rain fell onto the windscreen. Sitting on a grassy bank to the left, was a *Men at Work* sign which looked like it had been left there for a while.

Further up on the right, they drove past the visitor centre and an Aerial Adventure Course. A little past that, was a white building with a small funnel-like bell tower, familiar to them from the photos of the church online.

"Shit. There it is," John said softly and swallowed. He started to slow down as they approached, pulling over to the left.

Like other parts at the side of the road, the church was surrounded by a small woodland and trees.

They both sat there for a moment in the car, across from the church, their anxiety increased.

John rolled down his window. Apart from a few cars passing on the other side of the road, it all sounded pretty quiet. "You hear that?" John looked and listened out of the car window. They could see a small wooden building near to the church, which they assumed was the community/church hall.

"Hear what?" David swallowed. "I don't hear anything."

"Exactly." John glanced at David. "I don't hear or see anything that resembles a wedding reception; they lied."

"I'm going to take a look," David said, unclipping his seatbelt.

"What if they're in there?"

"You just said they lied and that they weren't in there?"

"Yeah, well, what if I'm wrong and they see us?"

"Sod it …" David said as he got out the car. "It looks like no one is here, anyway."

"Shit," John said, getting out too.

Benji was left in the back.

They waited until a large truck went past and crossed over the road.

They stood at the top of the short steps which had a wooden railing going down and a gate at the bottom. A wired fence ran along the top at the side of the road.

A very faint sound of thunder came from behind them, way off in the distance.

"Well, that's a good sign," John joked.

"If there is a wedding going on, it must be the quietest and most boring wedding I've ever come across," David said sarcastically, looking at the building and church.

Perhaps ironically, everything was exactly how Melissa had described it.

"Let's go take a look. Just to be certain," John said as they made their way slowly down the small steps.

"Stop."

"What is it?"

David was reading the white notice board on the left of the steps. There was no notice of any weddings, only certain religious dates and times, along with a couple of random notices, including a church jumble sale the following weekend. "There's no notice of any weddings."

"May as well check in the church."

"Why? Probably locked, anyway."

"Just for the hell of it." John walked over to the black doors. He gave them three firm thrusts. "Yep, locked."

"Pretty damn obvious."

"Might have been open."

"I doubt it; not at this time of evening." David turned his attention toward the wooden community church hall. There weren't even any cars parked next to it.

They followed the short path over to the wooden building. Some headstones rose up from the ground to their right, along with a few large trees. Despite it being a small church, numerous people appeared to be buried here.

As they reached the building, John checked the doors, which were also locked. David peered in through one of the windows. John then did the same, looking through another. Inside was completely empty. The inside of the building reminded David of his pre-school years, where he used to go as a child.

"I think it's safe to say those pricks lied," John said, pulling his face away from the window.

David did the same, shaking his head. "I can't believe they lied."

"Why on earth would they, though?" John scratched his right temple.

"Like we talked about earlier, to sound genuine."

"Yeah, but *why*? People might lie about something like a job, because they're embarrassed about their real job, for example. Or about something small. But a wedding? And the details of it? It doesn't make sense, unless, we got the wrong church," John said, looking around.

"Nah. This is definitely the place. They named and described it perfectly. No doubts."

"Seems a bit small for a wedding reception."

"Not if you moved the tables and chairs. There's outside here as well." David looked up to the top of the road and saw an ice cream van shoot past.

"Jesus," John said. "They must have lied about Anthony's brother and fiancée. That must have been bollocks as well?"

"It's fucking odd … unless, it is all part of their plan to seem genuine."

A man's voice called out, startling them. He appeared from the left side of the church. "Can I help ye boys?" The man was casually dressed in a light blue T-shirt and trainers. He was wearing dark green cargo pants and was clean shaven; he looked to be in his early forties and his black hair was tied back in a ponytail. "I'm sorry … I didn't mean to startle ye both. I thought I heard voices." The man smiled as he came closer.

John and David looked at one another, unsure of how to reply.

"Hi!" John said.

The man stopped just in front of them, his hands on his hips. He was slightly shorter than the two friends.

"We were just having a look around. We have a friend who's getting married next year and we're checking places out for him."

"Yeah, that's right," John added. "He's a fussy bastard and can't make his mind up! We were driving past and thought we'd have a look and take some photos for him … as long as we aren't intruding or anything?"

The man with the ponytail smiled. "Ye aren't intruding … me name is Marcus. I'm the church sexton here. I was just doing a bit of pruning out back and I heard voices. Unfortunately, the church is locked in the evening, unless you book an appointment."

"No problem; he can make an appointment if he likes our photos." David tried to smile back.

"Failing that, ye can have a look online: there's a website," Marcus replied, trying to help.

"Oh, sure. We can get him to do that," David replied. "Do you er, get a lot of weddings, here?"

"Aye, we do get a few!" Marcus answered. He noticed a bit of dirt on one of the windows and walked over to wipe it off with his T-shirt.

"Any lately?" John asked.

"There hasn't been a wedding for a good few weeks. There is one booked at the end of August."

John and David again looked at one another.

"Wouldn't happen to know their names, would you?" John asked, laughing a little awkwardly.

"Their names? Funnily enough, I do, aye … they're good friends of mine! Gwen and Steven."

"Oh, right … I only ask because we got chatting to some folk recently, who said they were getting married somewhere around here. I thought it might have been them, but it's not." John laughed.

"Yeah." David laughed too, just as another rumble of thunder sounded. "Well, it certainly seems a nice little place. We'll be sure to let our friend know. We better head off; I can feel a few spots of rain."

"Yeah, I'm starving as well," John mentioned.

Marcus laughed. "Aye. I'm pretty hungry meself. I better finish off in case it starts to chuck it down … be sure to tell ye friend about this church, though. I'm sure he'd appreciate getting married here, along with his other half. It was nice meeting ye both."

"Likewise," David said back.

Marcus turned and walked back to behind the church, leaving John and David to themselves again.

"He seemed like a friendly guy," David said.

"We thought that about Melissa and Anthony … I'm in two minds to give the lying shit a call." John frowned.

"No, don't do that. We need to let Jack know. Let's get back to the car."

They made their way back up the steps to John's car, just in time, as it began to rain quickly and heavily.

"Chances are, Melissa and Anthony somehow *knew* we were going to be at the pub last night. That's if those are their names? And they deliberately tried talking to us and made up all this shit, to dupe us into believing they were genuine, like we said, to gain their trust."

"How would they know we were going to be there?"

"I can't answer that. Your guess is as good as mine. Maybe they were checking us out, too … they wanted to see if we would say anything about what has been happening up here, which we didn't, as far as I can recall, although, we were both drunk."

"You mean checking us out, as in joining them for a gang bang?" John joked.

David didn't laugh.

"Sorry," John said. "I don't think I mentioned anything about what has been happening. If I did, it was probably very brief. I don't really remember too much."

"I'm pretty sure I didn't mention anything to anyone … I don't recall you saying anything. There's definitely a reason they were there last night."

"You're probably onto something there, mate."

"What if their plan was for us to take a liking to them, like we did, and lure us into a trap? A false sense of security? What if it *was* that Harold freak on the phone to Melissa?"

John stared at the steering wheel, thinking. "Yeah. It makes sense. They'd obviously want to come across as being nice people so that we'd go fishing with them."

"Exactly … I could be wrong but something clearly isn't right with them. To lie about a wedding, coupled with what Emily overheard."

"Then again, they didn't have to say anything about a wedding, did they? They could have just said they lived up here or they were up here on a holiday?"

"Perhaps Anthony's brother *did* get married up here or is planning to, although obviously not today. A half-truth can sound more convincing and believable." David looked back over at the church.

"What a couple of headfucks," John muttered. "What would they have *done* if we did agree to go fishing?"

"Christ knows … but we need to tell Jack."

"I'll call him now," John said, getting out his phone ... "Typical. No answer. I'll leave a message." John waited for Jack's cocky answer phone message to end and then left a message; "All right, fella? It's John. Listen, mate. Can you give us a call as soon as possible? It's urgent. I know David already phoned you earlier on ... it's about going fishing tomorrow with Anthony. We don't think you should go. But give us a call. It's important. Talk to you later." John put his phone on top of his dashboard.

"I hope we can get a hold of him before tomorrow," David said.

"Me too."

As John was about to switch on the engine, there was a tapping on his window. It was Marcus, his face and long hair wet from the rain. He startled them again. This time, he was wearing a rucksack.

*"Jesus,"* John said, and wound down the window.

"I'm sorry for startling ye guys again! I couldn't possibly ask for a favour, could I?"

"Erm. Sure?" John replied.

"Me mate was due to pick us up after work, but he's having problems with his car. Can I ask where ye guys are heading? I saw ye sitting in your car."

"Erm. We were going to get a bite to eat in Aviemore." John felt the rain on his face through the open window.

"Would it be okay to give us a lift? It's on the way to Aviemore. It isn't far. Well, it's actually just past Aviemore. Normally, I'd walk if I couldn't get a lift, but it's starting to tip it down, aye."

John looked at David who just raised his eyebrows and shrugged.

"Er. Sure. Hop on in. Never mind the dog," John said.

"Great!" Marcus opened up the back door and got in. "Hello, boy," he said to Benji, giving him a stroke.

Benji who was half-asleep, seemed to back his head away as Marcus touched him, making a slight whimper.

"I guess he doesn't like being disturbed." Marcus smiled. "I appreciate this, guys. Sorry, if I've made ye back seat wet."

"Don't worry about it, bud," John said, looking again at David.

The three of them sat in the car, awkwardness in the air. David and John felt a little nervous. After meeting Melissa and Anthony last night, they were now even more paranoid about who they could trust.

"You don't drive yourself then, Marcus?" John asked.

"Nae. I used to do lessons years ago. But at the time I lost me job and couldn't afford them anymore. After that, I lost me confidence." Marcus laughed. "I do appreciate ye doing this though, guys. I don't mind a bit of rain, but not when it's pissing down like this."

"It's fine, mate. It isn't a problem," John replied, looking at Marcus in his rear-view mirror, checking on him. He, like David, was a little edgy.

"You worked at the church, long?" David asked, looking round.

"Ten years or so now. I'm a one-man team most of the time. I have a couple of guys who help out once or twice a week, if need be. It's not exactly a big church or grounds, aye."

John's phone started to ring and made a buzzing sound. It was Jack calling back. John didn't want to answer it until they were alone; he didn't want Marcus to overhear the conversation. He let it ring off and then put it back on the dashboard.

"Who was that?" Marcus asked. "Not one of those annoying calls, was it?" He laughed.

"Yeah. Like those old PPI calls, no doubt … wankers can't seem to take a hint," John lied.

"Aye, tell me about it!"

"Yeah," David added.

"Where did you say you needed dropping off, mate?" John asked.

"It's just up on the left, mate. In fact, ye can drop us off here, if ye want? I can dash the last bit."

"No, it's fine," John replied. "Just say where."

"Oh, okay. Cheers."

A couple of minutes later, John pulled over.

"Listen, guys. I know it wasn't that far, but I appreciate the lift."

"No worries." John smiled.

"I might see ye around?" Marcus got out the car.

"See you later," John and David said in unison.

Marcus shut the door, waved and then lifted his rucksack over his head to shelter from the downpour and ran off to wherever it was that he lived.

"He seemed like a nice bloke."

"Yeah. But I'm not so sure I trust anybody, anymore," John replied.

"I know the feeling."

John rung Jack and again reached his voicemail. "Bloody voicemail, again! If we can't get hold of him, maybe we can go see him?" John suggested.

"We could, but hopefully he'll call us back."

"You still want to grab something to eat?

"For sure," David agreed.

# Chapter Thirty-Six

## 14th July, 2018

John found a car park where they could park up to feast on their large deep pan, twelve-inch pizzas, topped with pepperoni, bacon and onion. They opted for some burger sauce on top. Benji sat upright in the back, patiently waiting for some of his share.

Once David had finished his, he placed the open box in the back of the car for Benji to feed on the few leftover crusts. David then took the empty greasy boxes and two empty drink cans and hurried to a nearby bin, scurrying in the still heavy downpour. There were a couple of rumbles of thunder.

"I'll try Jack again," John said, picking up his phone with his greasy fingers from the pizza.

"John! I was about to call ye."

"*Jack* … glad you picked up. How are you feeling, after last night?"

"Better than earlier … I was a bit crappy." Jack laughed.

"Me too, mate. Listen. We need to talk."

"Didn't ye say something was urgent?"

"Yeah. Are you still going fishing, tomorrow?" John could hear Jack laugh.

"Aye … why not? It will be a laugh. Cannae say I've been fishing before. But I'm up for it, for sure. Anthony already texted me earlier from the wedding."

"What? Listen, Jack. *Don't* go. You could be in danger."

"Danger? What ye on about, ye silly bugger?"

David snatched the phone from John's ear. "Jack, it's David. This Anthony and Melissa; they're *not* who you think they are." Static interference fizzled over the line.

"What do ye …"

David couldn't make out the rest of what Jack was saying. "Jack. *Listen* … there was no wedding. They *lied*, Jack …" The line went dead. David felt an electric shock go straight up his arm, causing him to drop John's phone. He held his arm with the other. "*Shit*! I just got an electric shock again." David picked up the phone. The signal had completely died.

John grabbed the phone from David and checked for himself. "It feels cold," he said, examining it. "What did Jack say?"

"I don't know. I couldn't hear him because of the interference."

"Let's go to his house and warn him. I think I remember the way. You keep trying to reach him." John threw his phone into David's lap and started the car. The ignition failed the first few times, but eventually fired up.

*****

"You sure you know the way?" David asked. "You might want to slow down a bit; it's not like he's going tonight!"

"I think once we get off this road, I'll remember the way easily from where we picked him up in the taxi. Still no signal on either phone?"

"Nothing."

The sun was gradually starting its descent behind the mountains, which looked even greener now wet. The rain was now a light drizzle.

"He'll probably think we're a couple of nutters, turning up at his house." John swung his car sharply around a bend on the wet tarmac.

"Jesus, mate. Steady."

"I still can't believe that those two bastards lied. I should give *Anthony* a piece of my mind. Find out what they're playing at," John said, pushing down hard on the brakes.

"Maybe it's best to play dumb for the moment. We don't want to make matters worse. Though, they are probably already aware we know. That static interference on the line again, was no doubt intended to stop us from warning Jack."

"That's what I don't get, though. If these *forces* can do all this supernatural stuff, then why not just kill us? Why beat around the bush? It's like in a movie, mate … you hear all this crap or even in so-called real-life documentaries of hauntings and stuff: why dick around? Just *kill* someone already …"

"Maybe it's like a game to them? Or maybe there are certain things they *can't* do. I don't know. But for now, we need to warn Jack." David suddenly thought about the taxi driver from the night before, who had picked up Emily, Nigel and Annabel. He remembered where he had seen the moody looking bloke. "Shit …"

"What?"

"I don't know if you remember, but last night, the taxi driver who picked up the girls and that Nigel … remember, I said I recognised him from somewhere?"

"Yeah, the miserable twat who gave us a dirty look."

"I've just remembered where I've seen him … it was when we first came up here and I was driving; I had just come off the motorway. There were him and a girl in a car. He was driving. She smiled at me and I smiled back. He gave me a dirty look back then."

"A dirty look because you smiled at his bird? Ha … no wonder he was pissed off when he saw you again last night, then." John smiled.

"It just seems a bit coincidental, a bit weird, I suppose. To randomly see someone briefly and then again, a short while after in a different place."

"Maybe. Or maybe he was just working and taking this girl somewhere?"

"Possibly. I didn't recall it being a taxi they were in, though."

"I doubt it means anything. It happens all the time. You bump into people when you least expect it … I remember someone telling me once they were catching a bus in Australia and in the middle of nowhere, East Bumblefuck or somewhere. A neighbour from back in the UK was at the same bus stop! Chances of that, huh?" John took a left.

"Yeah, maybe it's not *that* weird. But still strange-ish."

"Before we got to that church, we went past a visitor centre. Might be worth going in there and asking about?" John said, looking over at David.

"Perhaps. We can't just start asking questions about supernatural entities and cults, though," David replied.

"Why not? Sure, we can."

"They'd think we're nuts … at the moment, I think we should focus more on the ecologist who we *hope* is going to ring Bob, trying to question Samuel and tracking down that reporter, Marvin's widow."

"*And* Emily." John smirked.

David smiled and shook his head.

"How are you going to get information from Samuel? We don't even know where he lives."

"I'm not sure," David replied. "Perhaps, Emily will know?"

"Maybe," John replied, taking a right.

*****

John took a wrong turning on the way to Jack's place, but eventually pulled up outside his house. "God. I'm going to feel a bit stupid turning up at his doorstep unannounced." John looked over at the front door of where Jack lived.

"I do a bit, but it needs to be done." David handed John his phone back. Neither phone had any signal. "Well, let's go talk to him."

Jack's car sat on the small driveway and they could see a light through the frosted, diamond shaped window of the black front door.

David pressed the doorbell and they heard it ring inside.

Jack's mother opened the door, wearing a light blue dressing gown and a green face mask. She looked a little confused, to see two young men standing there outside her door at this time of evening. "Yes?" she asked. "If ye selling something, I'm sorry, but ye wasting ye time."

"Sorry to disturb you, but is Jack about? We work with him. We tried phoning but we had no signal," David said politely, feeling awkward.

John bit his lip, trying not to smirk. "Yeah, we'd like to talk with him, if he's about that is?"

"Hold on. He's upstairs ..." Jack's mum looked a little dubious. She left the front door ajar and walked to the bottom of the stairs. "*Jack*! There's a couple of English lads at the door for ye ..."

John and David could hear a reply from Jack but couldn't make out what he said.

"Well, she seems nice," John said sarcastically, smirking to David. "Typical ... my phone signal's back, now." John looked at his phone.

David's was too. "Always the way."

"He's just coming," Jack's mother half-shouted out to the two outside.

Jack arrived and also looked surprised to see the two standing at his door. "All right, guys? What are ye doing here?"

"We tried to phone you, bud. But both our phones went down. We need to talk to you," John answered.

The three of them moved to the bottom of Jack's driveway and David and John tried to explain their concerns. Jack had said he got no missed calls from David earlier that day, only a text message and John's voicemail.

"Ah ... *C'mon*, guys," Jack said, smiling. "I admit that something *odd* is happening around here, like. But ye honestly think that them two are a part of it?" Jack found it hard to believe and thought they were just being paranoid.

"Even if they aren't, explain the wedding, mate? Why on earth would they lie about something like that, unless they had a hidden agenda?" John asked.

Jack sighed, scratching his left cheek. "I dunno ... maybe ye got the wrong church or something, aye?"

David shook his head. "Listen, Jack! Whether you believe us or not, *please*, don't take the risk."

"But I already said I'd go, now … Anthony said he's going to call me tomorrow to arrange picking us up."

"*Something* was even trying to prevent us from telling you; we couldn't get through to you on a decent connection." David felt like he was trying to convince a brick wall.

"Please, don't risk it," John said firmly.

"What if I call him, now?" Jack suggested.

John and David both looked at one another.

"And say what?" David asked.

"I'll tell him about ye concerns and ask him why he lied … hear it from the horse's mouth, so to speak, aye."

David and John felt a little uneasy.

"It had crossed our minds to phone him," David replied.

"If ye claim something was trying to stop ye both from calling me, they probably already know they've been rumbled."

Jack, in his black shorts, got his mobile out and called Anthony. Jack raised his eyebrows for a moment and gave a wry smile as he held the phone to his ear. They could hear the phone ringing.

David felt his heart begin to race.

"Argh, crap," Jack said. "Nae answer."

"Didn't it go to voicemail?" David asked. He and John felt a little relieved.

"Nae. It just cut out. Maybe he's busy with the wedding? I'll try again later." Jack slipped the mobile back into his pocket.

"Jack …" John said. "There *is* no wedding. Wake up!"

Jack half-laughed.

"I just don't get why you find it so *hard* to believe what's going on, mate? Anthony and Melissa are *liars*. We've proved that. And Emily's suspicions were spot on," David said, trying to convince Jack further.

Jack stood there thinking it over. "Aye, ye probably right … it's not like they're me mates … if he calls me up tomorrow or before, I'll tell him I can't make it. Fuck him." Jack laughed.

After Jack had gone back inside, the two friends sat in the car for a few minutes before heading back to the farm.

They caught a glimpse of Jack's mum, peering out from behind the living room curtains.

"Did you buy any of that about him not going tomorrow?" John asked.

"I don't know. I'm not convinced. I sincerely hope he doesn't."

"I'm not sure, either. It just frustrates the hell out of me that he has a hard time accepting it all."

"Same. But then, if it were the other way around, I'd probably think we were paranoid, too … talking about all this shit we've experienced. He hasn't been through what we have," David said, glancing over at Jack's house where an upstairs light came on.

"I feel a bit worried, Jack will tell Anthony about us going to the church."

"Me too, but what difference does it make?" David put his seat belt back on.

"It's certainly some frightening shit. I feel like we're being watched now. I don't even know what's real or just paranoia, now." John checked behind him, before pulling the car out.

"That's exactly how I feel."

"Let's get back to the farm, before it gets dark." John looked at the car clock. It had gone half-eight.

*****

The sunlight was diminishing further by the time they got back to Hamish Farm.

David had received another text from Emily.

"Who's that from, *Lover Boy*?" John teased. "Emily, I presume?"

"You presume correctly." David smiled as he read the message.

"What's she saying?" John still hadn't heard anything from Annabel.

"She wants to meet for lunch, tomorrow," David answered unenthusiastically.

"And? Do it … you're a fool if you pass up the opportunity to meet her again."

"Maybe." David was still thinking about Jack, but he texted Emily saying it sounded great, but he would let her know tomorrow.

She tried to start up another conversation with him. David said he'd text back later as he was going to have a bite to eat. He didn't feel like texting her; his mind was too occupied. He put his phone away.

"Well, what did you say?"

"Huh? Oh, I said I'd let her know. I've just got so much crap on my mind at the moment. I'm still worried about Jack."

"Understandable … you should still go and meet her. Maybe I should give Anthony a call, demand answers?"

"I think we should leave it for now. Just in case it makes matters somehow worse."

Making their way to the farmhouse, Bob came out holding a beer can. He and Gavin hadn't long eaten. He greeted the two as he stood at the top of his front lawn. "You're back. You okay? I was getting concerned. What happened with that couple?" he asked with intrigue.

"They lied," David answered.

The two explained to Gavin and Bob about that evening. They expressed their concerns about Jack going fishing the next day.

"I hope he doesn't go, Uncle. He said he wouldn't, but I'm not convinced."

Bob sighed. "He can be stubborn, Jack. But he isn't stupid." Bob finished the last of his beer and gave the can a shake. He then crushed it in his right hand.

"What if he does go?"

"We'll just have to make sure that he doesn't, David. We'll contact him in the morning."

"What about Aunt Betty too, are you picking her up tomorrow morning?"

Bob smiled. "I spoke to the hospital. You'll be pleased to know that she's *definitely* coming home tomorrow. She's going to be just fine." Bob smiled again, with added reassurance.

"That's great to hear. I just hope everything is going to be all right with her … About tonight … I'm willing to help keep an eye out. You two need a good night's sleep." David looked at Gavin and then at his uncle.

"What do you think, Gavin?" Bob asked.

"Well, I could do with a good night's kip, boss."

Bob smiled. "I tell you what. You sleep proper tonight, Gavin. Me and David can keep watch."

"If you're certain?" Gavin replied, holding his own can of beer. He appreciated the offer of getting a good night's sleep.

"I think it's best if one of us does it with David. I don't feel comfortable otherwise," Bob mentioned.

"I wouldn't mind helping out, but I still feel tired from last night. Don't mind if I sit this one out, do you?" John asked, scratching his backside.

"Up to you, mate. I was only speaking for myself. Not both of us. You can maybe help out another night," David replied.

"It only needs two of us," Bob added.

"Cool. I might actually hit the sack soon, if that's the case. Unless you need extra help?" John checked.

"You're all right." Bob smiled.

"We've got Benji. I'll keep him out here with us. He'll hopefully sense any danger, like before." David believed.

# Chapter Thirty-Seven

## 15th July, 2018

David looked at his phone to check the time. It had just turned midnight. He was doing the first shift, and his uncle would do the second. Bob was asleep in the barn on an old mattress and pillow next to one of the tractors. The mattress reminded David of the one that he and John had seen fly-tipped by the side of the road, when they had first arrived up in Scotland. A duvet was crumpled in a heap on the floor next to it, in case it was needed.

His uncle's shotgun lay next to the mattress on the concrete ground beside him.

Bob had informed his nephew to wake him *immediately*, if anything happened and to wake him up anyway, at around two in the morning.

David had been texting Emily on and off, but she signed off at about ten-thirty to get some sleep. He hadn't told her he was on a night shift.

The air had become chilly in the last hour. David was wearing a light grey jacket to protect him from the night air. There wasn't a sound to be heard. It felt too quiet for David's liking. The animals had also stopped making any noise for the last hour or so; it was dead quiet.

The silence made David feel tense. Benji hadn't appeared sleepy. He kept joining David wherever he walked as he patrolled the farmyard. Once Benji was tired enough, David would leave him tied up next to his uncle in the barn. It was almost as if Benji was on edge. Every now and then, his ears would prick up and twitch and he would turn his head towards a lit or darkened area, curiously. David wondered if Benji's sixth sense was making him nervous. Perhaps Benji knew that someone or *something* was out there in the dark, watching their every move. David could feel it too.

David heard a rustling to his left in the black outline of the forest. There were a few small snaps of branches and the sound of something falling down onto the dark ground. Benji turned his head in that direction as David slowly swallowed. He used his phone as a flashlight and shone it over to where the sounds came from.

He moved his light source quickly over the area and although there were a few more sounds, nothing appeared. Or at least, he couldn't see anything. Then there was silence again. Benji bowed his head back down and David let out a sigh of relief. "Fuck doing this every night, eh boy?" he said, looking down at his furry companion.

David then looked up at the dark sky. At least it wasn't raining. It was, however, a cloudy night. Every now and then, David could see the quarter moon shine in the north-east whenever there was a break in the blackened clouds. It was about half an hour since he had last seen it. He didn't know why, but seeing it made him feel better, perhaps because of the light it cast.

David continued to pace up and down the farmyard, when he heard his phone. It was a text message from Emily, asking if he was still awake:

> Hey! Hope I didn't wake you? Are you still awake? I can't sleep. :( x

David smiled at the text message.

> Hey! No, you didn't wake me. I can't sleep either actually. Why can't you sleep? x

> I'm not sure. I'll try again shortly. I still feel tired! Still thinking about that couple isn't helping. :( x

> Aw. Do you want me to come tuck you in? :p x

David thought he'd flirt with her a little. He couldn't deny their mutual attraction anymore, and it would keep his mind distracted from the darkness that surrounded him in the yard.

> I wouldn't mind! ;) Hee hee! It's cold tonight as well. I'm trying to be all snug! x

> Lol. Yeah. It is a little nippy tonight! What are you wearing? ;p x

> Just my skimpy nightie. ;) x

> Ha ha. No wonder you're cold! x

> Yeah, lol. Could do with some extra bodily warmth! ;p x

> I'll be right over! Ha ha x

> Oooo. ;p ;p x

David was suddenly distracted by what felt like a few pebbles being thrown at the back of his neck. Startled, he spun round, accidentally kicking Benji who looked up at him. *"What the fuck?"* he whispered, before swallowing. He walked slowly down past the barn, where his uncle was still asleep. As the farmyard lights slightly dimmed, he felt a cold burst of energy whizz past him and heard the laughter of a small child.

Benji's fur stood on end, his eyes wide and his ears pricked up fully. Surprisingly, he didn't bark.

David quickly switched on the camera flash on his phone and ran with Benji to the end of the farmyard, following the child's giggles.

He went down to the bottom of the lawn and shone his light. Whatever it was, had gone. David called out softly, "Ch-Charlie? Is that you? Talk to me, kid ..." David wondered if it was the same presence that he and John had encountered, when the apples fell from the tree in the back garden.

There came no reply.

"Jesus." David breathed out. His heart was beating ten to the dozen. He stood for a few minutes. He then looked at his phone. Emily had texted a string of messages:

> Hopefully, we can do lunch tomorrow. Or later, seeing as it's already Sunday! :) x
>
> I should get some sleep. Can't stop yawning. x
>
> You've probably fallen asleep, ha ha! Well, message me later. Goodnight! xx

David texted a response:

> Sorry! Dozed off. Yes, I'll message you tomorrow. Or in a few hours, depending on which way you look at it. Lol. Night. xx

Emily didn't text back. She had probably turned her phone off, intending to get some sleep.

The temperature dropped considerably further.

David felt himself shiver. He looked up and could see some moonlight trying to shine through the blanket of dark clouds.

As he turned to make his way back up to the farmyard, he heard heavy breathing several yards behind him over the pebbled edging, in the trees and bushes. He froze. His eyes enlarged as they moved side to side. Almost too scared to turn round, he forced himself to.

He stared into the mass darkness and slowly raised his phone up to light up where the breathing seemed to come from.

Benji started to growl.

The young child's laughter came again, along with heavy breathing. There was that static feeling again too. *Energy.*

David's pulse increased and he edged forwards. He tried to swallow slowly again but his mouth was dry, hurting his throat. "Wh-who's there?"

Benji let out a couple of warning barks.

David could see his own warm breath in front of him as he held the phone close to his face. "What do you want?"

A few rustles came. The child's laughter was heard again. It then sounded darker, like a more demonic laugh, mocking him.

Benji cowered down and started to whine as David stood there, frozen.

Whatever it was, could sense his fear and was feeding on it.

"Wh-what do you want?" David asked again in a whisper.

The laughter stopped abruptly and the silence resumed; whatever it was had gone.

David stood there, his hands and feet cold and numb. He could hear and feel his pulse throbbing in his ears.

"David?" came Bob's voice from behind him.

David's shocked involuntary reflexes threw his phone up in the air. He turned to see his uncle. The lower half of Bob's black jeans were lit up by the fallen phone still emitting its light as it lay on the lawn.

"Are you okay?" Bob frowned, yawning. He walked over and picked up the phone and wiped it, before handing it back to David. "I didn't mean to scare you, boy."

David slowly took the phone from his uncle. "Th-that *thing* was just here, in the bushes and trees," replied David, shaken.

Bob gently retook the phone from David and shone it into the forest boundary. "What happened?"

"I had these small stones thrown at me and I felt a rush of energy. There was a child laughing. I followed it down here. I thought … I thought it might have been Charlie. There was heavy breathing too, and this child's laughter became demonic," David explained to his uncle in a hurry.

Bob continued to shine the light over the trees and bushes of the forest, he was still half-asleep.

"Did I wake you?" David asked.

"No. I just happened to wake up and I wanted to see how you were getting on. I came out of the barn and saw you and Benji standing down here, shining your light … I shouldn't have agreed to you working the night, David. I'm sorry." Bob turned to his nephew and handed back his phone. "It feels so cold as well."

"Don't be silly. You've got nothing to be sorry for. It was my decision."

There was another rustle.

Bob instinctively put a protective hand over his nephew's chest.

Benji, who was still a little on edge himself, slowly walked over to where the sound was coming from.

*"Benji!"* David whispered sharply.

David and Bob slowly walked with Benji as David shone his light ahead.

Bob had left his shotgun up in the barn where he had been sleeping. "Careful."

A ringing sound came from where the rustling was. Followed by a faint whine.

Benji barked and started to sniff the bush as David pulled him back. "What the hell is that?"

"I, I don't know," Bob replied sounding worried.

Before they could step back, a small frog hopped out from a gap at the bottom of the bushes, making the pair of them and Benji jump back.

*"Jesus!"* David raised his voice in alarm.

Benji sniffed the frog before pulling his nose back.

"It's just a frog," Bob said, breathing a sigh of relief.

"I didn't know they made such sounds?"

They watched as the frog hopped away into the hydrangea in the middle of the lawn. David followed it with his phone flash.

"I don't think I can get any sleep, now," David said as they made their way back up to the pens in the farmyard.

*****

They chatted for a little while sat on a pair of old white, partially rusted garden chairs. David didn't want to leave Bob by himself. David had mentioned about meeting Emily for lunch and how he still had doubts. Bob told him to do what he felt was right and to follow his heart. They then got back onto the darker topic of discussions.

"It was the same child's laughter John and I heard when we picked up those apples. Maybe it was this thing all along, playing with us?"

"Maybe we should go to the police?"

"The police? What will they do? They didn't do anything when you reported the mutilations."

"I know, David … it's just we're desperate for answers. We know absolutely *nothing* about what's been happening around here, who is behind all this and what this *thing* is … it sounds nuts."

"Exactly … it does sound *nuts*. The police will think we're bonkers if we explain all of this … even if I showed them the photo evidence of the prints and that."

"I know. We'll get Betty back home from the hospital, and we'll start to look into things some more. I'll try ringing that Carl guy, again." Bob yawned. "You need to try and get some sleep. That mattress may be quite old, but it's pretty comfy … I'll be fine on my own. I have my gun."

David refused at first but his Uncle insisted on David getting some sleep. "Okay," David replied reluctantly. "I'll at least lie down. C'mon Benji." David slowly took Benji into the barn where the mattress lay. David felt bad about leaving his uncle on guard on his own, but he was feeling tired and his uncle had a shotgun after all.

"I'll be fine," Bob called out reassuringly as Benji and David entered through the opened barn doors. Bob felt uneasy. All this was happening on and around his farm, but he hadn't experienced anything like the events his nephew and John had experienced.

David must have been exhausted because he got off to sleep with relative ease. The old grey mattress was pretty comfortable to sleep on, just as his uncle had told him. Benji lay on the floor next to him.

# Chapter Thirty-Eight

## 15th July, 2018

David awoke and looked at his phone; 07:48. He could hear the noises of the farm animals stirring. He rubbed his eyes and yawned, making his eyes water.

It was a clear and bright Sunday morning.

David soon realised that Benji wasn't there. "Shit." He got up and made his way out of the barn. The sunlight hurt his eyes and made his brow ache. He looked to his left and to his right, up and down the farmyard. No one was in sight. David felt panic creep in. He quickly made his way to the farmhouse.

As he was about to enter through the front door, Benji came out with his uncle who was holding a cup of fresh tea.

"Thank God, for that. I thought Benji had gone!" David said, feeling relieved.

His uncle smiled at him. "I'm sorry! I saw Benji sitting up and thought I'd bring him in for his breakfast. You were still asleep."

"That's okay … did anything else happen last night? I dozed off pretty quick, surprisingly."

"I saw that … to tell you the truth, I dozed off for about an hour in the chair, just as the sun was coming up, but everything seems okay. I checked on the animals as soon as I woke. Everything was fine during the night, too. There were a few sounds, like in the trees. Other than that, nothing happened, thankfully … it looks like it's going to be a nice day as well." Bob drank some of his tea and looked up at the clear sky. "There's a pot of tea in the kitchen."

"Is anybody else up, yet?"

"Not yet. I'll let Gavin sleep in some more."

*****

David sat at the kitchen table, thinking about last night and the demonic laughter he had heard, when he suddenly remembered Jack. He'd call him shortly.

John came strolling into the kitchen. "Hey!"

David looked up at him.

John was shocked when David told him what had happened in the night. "You think it was the same thing that knocked all those apples from the tree the other day?"

David let out a sigh. "It might have been Charlie's spirit the other day, and again last night. But there was heavy breathing that didn't resemble that of a small kid. Then I had that horrible other laughter. Whatever this thing is, it's clearly fucking with me. Well, us. I sense it's enjoying doing so."

"I just hope we can get some answers. Sooner, rather than later."

"I know. I'm glad you're up. We need to give Jack a call, in case he's still thinking about going fishing today." David drank his tea.

"Shit, yeah … I forgot about that. I'll go grab my phone. He probably isn't up yet, though." John fetched his phone and dialled. It went straight to answer phone. "All right, mate? It's John. We hope you aren't planning on going fishing today. It isn't worth the risk. Give us a call back when you can." John hung up. "His phone was off. Surely he can't be stupid enough to take the risk."

"You wouldn't think so."

"I'll try him again in another hour or so, if he hasn't called back. We've got a few hours yet. Didn't he say it was this afternoon?"

"I think so."

"I'll give Grant a call later too, to see how he's getting on. It's been a couple of days," John added.

*****

Just after eleven, Bob left to fetch Betty from the hospital. Gavin, who'd appreciated the long lie-in and good night's sleep, had been up for around an hour and was outside in the farmyard. He had been told about last night. John and David were watching boring Sunday telly in the living room.

"Another text from her?" John smiled, sitting in one of the soft armchairs.

"Yeah … she still wants to meet later on this afternoon."

"You going to? At least she's interested in you … I've heard nothing from Annabel."

"I might meet Emily later. I said I'd let her know. I want to see Betty first, see how she is."

"That's understandable, mate. Where does Emily want to meet you?"

"Maybe at the pub or somewhere. She isn't working today; she offered to come pick me up here."

"Cool ... or I can drop you off, mate? I don't mind."

"I'd appreciate that. I'm not sure I like the idea of her driving through this forest by herself. I don't feel comfortable with that. I don't even like the idea of you doing it."

"I can certainly see where you're coming from. Don't worry about me," John replied, just as he heard a text alert from his own phone.

"That might be Annabel, now," David teased.

"Ha. I doubt it ... it's from Jack." John sat up.

"What's he say?"

John read the text out loud, "Hi Johnbo! Thanks for the concern, lol! I had a long lie-in and had me phone off. That Anthony texted me this morning and apologised for not being able to go fishing after all. Maybe he's hungover aye, from that fake wedding! Ha ha! Don't worry; I didn't say anything about ye guys. Me phone will probably be turned off again soon, as I'm going to help me ma do some shopping, then back to bed! See ye both tomoz ... He put a smiley face at the end." John then showed David for himself.

David looked blankly at the text.

"What do you think? I wonder why they changed their minds? Maybe because they know we suspect something? Or they wanted all three of us, together?"

"I don't know. I've still got a funny feeling about it all."

"In what sense?"

"I don't know. Just a bad feeling."

"You don't think Jack's being straight with us?"

"What if it wasn't him that sent the text?"

"Who else would have sent it?" John frowned.

"I don't know. Maybe whoever is behind all of this? Or even, Anthony."

"God. Now you're really worrying me. Well, there's only one way to find out. I'll call him. Hopefully he hasn't turned his phone off yet."

"John ... ye okay? Didn't think ye would call again."

"Sorry, mate ... we just wanted to make sure that it was *you* who texted us." John had the phone on loudspeaker.

Jack laughed. "Who else would it have been, aye? Ye don't have to worry about me now though, mate. I've gotta go; me mum's waiting in the car."

"Okay, Jack. See you tomorrow," John said and turned to David. "Well, at least that's cleared up."

"Yeah. Hopefully we don't have to worry about this Anthony guy for a while now ... I wonder if they even live down south or up here?"

"Who cares, mate. At least we don't have to worry about Jack." John slumped back down in the comfy armchair.

"True ... I don't think it's the end of it, though. It's just the beginning."

"Yep. I'm not sure we've seen the last of *that* couple."

A programme came on television presented by an attractive blonde-haired woman.

"That's the presenter I mentioned to you, a few weeks back, remember?" John suddenly perked up.

"What, her?" David replied. "I vaguely remember."

"Yeah. She's *fit as*! Not a bad set of 'fun-bags' by the looks of it."

David couldn't resist smiling at his friend.

*****

It was a quarter to one by the time Bob returned home from the hospital with Betty.

She was adamant that she needed no help. "I'm fine," she said, but Bob gently took her arm as she climbed out of the Land Rover.

John and David went out to greet her and Gavin came down from the yard.

"Before you all ask, I'm feeling fine," Betty said a little sarcastically and smiled.

Bob bent down and picked up a small carrier bag with some of her things. He smiled at the three, closing the door as Betty started to make her way indoors.

"How is she?" David asked.

"She seems fine. The doctors said the same thing." Bob waited for Betty to go inside, before asking about Jack. "Did you manage to get hold of Jack?"

"Yep. He said that Anthony cancelled, anyway," answered John.

"That's good. I'm glad that's sorted ... I'm going to pop the kettle on for Betty, though, she's probably already beaten me to it." Bob smiled again and made his way inside.

"At least she's home," David said.

"Yep. She certainly looks better," Gavin noted.

David heard his phone go again; it was another text from Emily asking if his aunt was home yet. She seemed eager to meet him this afternoon.

"Emily, again?" John grinned.

David smirked. "She wants to meet at the pub for around two and then go for a walk afterwards, seeing as it's a nice day. She says to bring Benji as well."

"Sounds like someone's keen, eh?" Gavin smiled.

"I can take you, if you like? Betty seems fine. You don't have to worry about me. I'll just be bored and lonely on me tod," John joked, pulling a sad face.

Gavin and David both smiled.

"Aye ... but you can help me out with some stuff, if you like? I've got some shit needing to be shovelled." Gavin grinned.

"Gee, nice. Thanks." John laughed.

David gave it a few seconds' thought and decided to take Emily up on her offer. After all, he liked her and his aunt seemed fine. "If you don't mind, taking me? It will be a good opportunity to ask her and maybe Jock, some more about that Samuel and Ralf."

"Good idea. But don't give her the impression that that's the only reason you're meeting her, bud," John advised.

David then went and had a quick shower to freshen up. He changed into some soft light blue trousers and a white scoop neck T-shirt with slightly rolled sleeves. After splashing on some aftershave, he skipped down the stairs wearing a pair of dark blue canvas trainers. It was only the second time he had worn them. He saw his aunt come out of the kitchen.

She looked at him and smiled. "You look nice, dear. You smell nice, too. Bob says you're meeting a girl?"

David hesitated slightly, before replying, "Erm. Yeah." He still felt awkward around his aunt.

"Well, she's a lucky girl to have you."

"It's only lunch and the second time I'm seeing her."

"Well, you have a good time, love. I'm sure you will." Betty winked.

David stood in the hallway. Something still didn't seem right with her. He joined Bob and John outside.

John let out a teasing wolf-whistle. "Here he is. The *Lover Boy.*"

"Yeah, yeah ... you're just jealous." David tried not to laugh.

"You're going to the pub again, then?" his uncle asked.

"Yeah. She said something about maybe about a walk after as well. She wanted me to bring Benji, so she can meet him properly."

"Sounds like it's getting serious, mate. Wanting to meet your dog, already," John joked.

"She's seen him before. When we first went to the pub, remember?"

"Yeah, but that doesn't count." John grinned.

"Just make sure you have a good time, David. Be *careful.*"

"You sure you'll be all right?" asked David.

"For sure." Bob smiled. "Don't worry about us. Just enjoy yourself."

As Bob walked away, David had a quiet word with John. "Try and keep an eye out on Betty, if you can."

"Why? She seems all right now."

"I've still got this *feeling*. Maybe I'm just being silly … I don't know."

John smiled at his friend. "I'll keep an eye out, mate. Gavin wants some help with some stuff when I get back, though. If you need me to come pick you up, just give us a text or call … I'll go bring the car round."

*****

David felt excited as he waited outside the pub for Emily. He had arranged to meet her just after two and was a little early. He considered going inside and waiting for her but thought it would be more polite to greet her outside.

He slowly paced up and down, admiring the view. He took off his sunglasses and looked across at the green valleys in the distance. Sunlight focused the verdant fields. The occasional dark shadow appeared, when a cloud slowly moved in front of the sun.

"Ye all right, laddie?" came Jock's voice.

David turned to see Jock in the pub beer garden, collecting a couple of empty glasses. "Hey, Jock. I'm fine. I'm just waiting for Emily," he called back.

"I see … why not come inside and wait?" Jock smiled.

David walked over with Benji to where Jock was standing.

Jock moved to just behind the small, black wooden fencing that went around the edge of the beer garden.

"I thought it would be better if I met her outside."

"Aye. I see. What time ye meeting her?"

"Just after two."

"She'll be here soon then, lad. She isn't one for being late."

David was about to ask Jock about Samuel and Ralf, but before he could, there was a toot of a car horn and Emily arrived, right on time.

"I'll be with you in a sec. I'll just park my car around the back," Emily said out of her passenger window. She was driving a white Mini Cooper with a black top.

David smiled at her.

"And there she is, aye." Jock smiled. "I'll see ye both inside." Jock gave David a wink as he made his way back inside the pub.

Emily looked amazing again. She was wearing a navy-blue top with short sleeves and a black pair of jeans, with a pretty pair of open-toed pink sandals. Her dark hair was tied back in a ponytail. She walked over to David and smiled. She smelt fantastic too. "You look nice," she complimented him.

"Thanks. You do, too."

She lent in to kiss him on his stubbly cheek, catching scent of his aftershave. She felt a tingle. She liked a man who looked and smelled nice. "And this is obviously, *Benji*." Emily knelt down to stroke Benji's head; he tried to jump up at her and lick her hands.

"Come on, Benj. No jumping or licking," David said, smiling. "Not on a first date," he joked.

Emily giggled. "I'm glad you could make it." She smiled again.

"Same," David replied. Not only did she look beautiful, but cute too. David had to resist the urge to give her a cuddle. "Shall we go inside, then?"

"Sure … I haven't eaten much all morning. I'm pretty darn hungry," Emily answered as they went inside the pub.

They decided to sit in the same area as they had two nights before, in the small side room to the right of the pub. They decided on two large Cokes, each with ice and a slice of lemon.

There were a few other customers, but not many.

Although animals weren't usually allowed in during lunch hours, Jock insisted it was fine, as long as they sat in the side room and nobody else joined them. Failing that, they could sit outside as the weather was nice.

"So, how are you feeling?" David asked.

"Better." Emily smiled. "Though, I still keep thinking on and off about that couple … Did Jack go fishing in the end?"

"Thankfully, no. Well, I certainly hope not. We spoke to him this morning; Anthony had cancelled, anyway."

"Oh. That's good, then. Maybe he was too hungover from that wedding they went to, yesterday."

"Erm, yeah."

"Is there something else?"

David thought he may as well tell her about yesterday and be as honest as he could. "Yesterday, John and I went to the church where the wedding was supposed to be."

"Why would you do that?" Emily half-smiled, curiously.

"John called Anthony, saying that he couldn't go fishing. Anthony said the wedding was going good and how he was outside getting a breather and having a cigar."

"O-kay?" Emily replied still confused.

"Well, we couldn't hear any background noise, like a wedding reception being on. So, we, er, decided to take a drive down there to see if they were being legit or not, about a wedding." David smiled awkwardly.

"Oh my God." Emily giggled. "And what happened, did they see you?"

"Nope ... there was no wedding."

"Oh my ... why on earth, would they lie about something like that?"

David let out a large breath. "I don't know ... but it gave us the creeps, to say the least."

"I can imagine ... it has me."

"We definitely got the church and location right. We even bumped into the sexton there, who was working. He wanted a lift because it started to rain and he told us that there have been no weddings for weeks, although two of his friends are getting married there in August."

"That is so weird ... what would you have done, had Anthony and Melissa caught you there?" Emily laughed nervously.

David grinned slightly. "I don't know. We probably would have just said we were driving past and checking out the church ... John would probably have blagged his way out of it."

Emily chuckled. "Yeah. But it could have been embarrassing ... it's so strange, that they would lie about something like that."

"I know ... let's try not to think about it. What do you fancy having to eat?" David smiled, changing the subject. He picked up and scanned the menu.

"Erm. I'm thinking of having the honey roast ham baguette. It's filling and comes with salad ... I think my tummy just made a slight rumble," Emily joked. "I already decided before I got here."

David loved the way she giggled. It was so natural and genuine. Just like her. "Good choice ... decisions, decisions ... I think I'll go for the *auld Scottish sausage with caramelised onion*," he said in a fairly decent Scottish accent, tapping his stomach with a smile.

Emily laughed. She looked straight at David, never taking her eyes off him. "Ah. Another popular choice with the regular folk up here ... you stay here, I'll go order." Emily got up and made her way to the bar.

David smiled to himself and down at Benji. He felt himself warm even more to this attractive, young lady.

After a few minutes, Emily came and sat back down. "Shouldn't be too long." She beamed. "So, is your aunt going to be okay?"

"I hope so. She's just been a little stressed lately and hadn't been taking her meds for diabetes."

"Oh, that's not good. I'm sure she'll be okay if the doctors say so, though." Emily tried to reassure David.

"Is Annabel not working today? I didn't see her."

"She has the day off, like me. She also has tomorrow booked off. I think she has a couple of appointments, one being the dentist in the morning," Emily replied, sipping her Coke. "We don't usually work too many Sundays, anyway. If we do, it's only for a few hours."

"John's a bit pissed that she hasn't contacted him."

"Has she not contacted him, yet? She said she liked him and that she was going to message him last night."

"No, she hasn't. John would have called her, but she didn't give him her number." David laughed.

"She's normally good to her word. She isn't one to lead somebody on or anything like that. I'm sure she'll contact him."

"How long have you had your Mini?" David asked, drinking his Coke.

"About two and a half years now. It's second hand but was in great condition. It still is. It wasn't too expensive, either. Though to be fair, my mum helped me a little. I've always been careful with money, though."

"Me too. I'm the same. I don't understand how people waste their money so easily or don't budget their spending before their next payday."

"Oh, I know. I never spend beyond my means. Do you think you'll take up your driving lessons, again?"

"Yeah. I can drive, just not legally. It's just the theory test I struggle with. Of course, the longer you leave it, the tougher it becomes."

"I know. Fortunately, I passed my theory first time round, and it only took me two attempts to pass the practical."

"Well done you," David said with a little sarcasm.

Emily laughed.

After a short wait, a middle-aged woman wearing glasses appeared, carrying a couple of plates with generously filled baguettes. She smiled as she approached them. "Here you are," she said, carefully placing the two plates on the table.

"Thank you, Beitiris." Emily smiled.

"You're welcome. Enjoy your lunch!"

David smiled politely and nodded.

"That's Beitiris. She's worked here for some time. She works in the kitchen, mainly. She's really nice," Emily said, cutting her baguette in half.

*****

They continued to chat and laugh, getting to know each other further over lunch. Eating didn't prevent them from chatting.

Benji looked up at them both and let out a slight whine.

"Aw. Poor baby wants some," Emily said, feeling sorry for the dog. She broke off a piece of her baguette and dropped it for Benji who scoffed it quickly down and then looked up at Emily again.

"He's often like that," David said. "He gives you that sorrowful look with his brown eyes. He already had his lunch before we came out. Didn't you, eh, boy?" David smiled lovingly at his dog and bent down to stroke him. "I suppose I better leave a bit for him, too." David gave the last of his baguette to his canine companion.

Emily looked at them both, smiling to herself. She could tell how fond David was of Benji.

"You don't have any pets, then?" David asked.

"Me? No. Well, we did have a cat once. *Bertie* was his name. A ginger Tom."

"What happened?" David wiped his mouth with a red napkin.

"He was only a few months old. We got him not long after me and my mum moved here. He disappeared for a few days and one morning, my mum found him dead at the front of our house." Tears suddenly filled Emily's eyes.

"Oh, I'm so sorry," David replied sincerely. He reached over and touched Emily's hand. He thought about mentioning his aunt and uncle's cat but thought better of it. At least for now.

"That's okay." Emily tried to smile.

"Do you know how he died? Was he hit by a car or anything like that?"

"We don't know. We had a vet who lived a few doors down from us. He's moved now, but he had the week off at home at the time. Poor Bertie was already dead, but my mum went to fetch the vet, anyway. He examined Bertie but couldn't find what killed him. He assumed it was a heart attack. Perhaps he was frightened by something? I don't know. I remember the vet … he took the body away for us. It was all very sad. He was only young. Sorry." Emily sniffed.

David took a clean napkin from the table and handed it to Emily.

She smiled as she wiped her eyes. "We had him cremated and buried in our back garden with a little wooden headstone."

"That's so sad. Animals are so innocent, you know? It's dreadful when an animal or pet suffers."

"I agree."

"Are you okay?

"I'll be fine. I guess it still makes me sad, when I think about little Bertie. He was only young and very affectionate."

David tried to cheer Emily up and skimmed through the menu again. "I know what will make you feel better ... how about that chocolate sponge, with chocolate sauce and ice cream? My treat." He grinned.

Emily chuckled back. "That's one of my favourite desserts here."

"I thought that would put a smile on your face." David grinned again. "I'll go order. I'll be right back." David got up from his seat and went to order the desserts.

Emily watched him as he did so. She hadn't noticed it before, but she thought David had a cute bum. She reached down and petted Benji on the head.

*****

Once they had eaten their desserts, David noticed that Emily had a small spot of chocolate sauce on her left cheek, next to the corner of her mouth. He looked at her and smiled.

"What?" Emily smiled too, confused.

"You've, erm, got a bit of chocolate on your cheek," David said, pointing to his own cheek, to show where it was on hers.

"Oh." Emily blushed a little and felt embarrassed. She tried to use her tongue to get it, but felt even more awkward when she couldn't reach it.

"Here ..." David laughed. He got another clean napkin and wiped it clean for her. He found it cute.

"Thanks," she said sheepishly.

David was enjoying chatting with Emily. He thought it would be as good a time as any, to ask her what she knew about Samuel and Ralf. "Do you see much of those two old men, at all? Samuel and Ralf? Do you know them?"

"I see them quite a bit. I know Samuel has problems with his lungs and health. He lives alone somewhere in one of the villages around here. He has a carer who looks after him and drops in a couple of times a day. Ralf lives by himself too, as far as I'm aware. I don't know where, though. Why do you want to know about them?" Emily gave a confused frown and smile.

"Oh, I was just curious. John had a bit of a run in with them. Well, mainly with Ralf, before you came in the other night. They weren't happy that we were chatting while they were playing their dominoes."

Emily laughed. "Yeah, that sounds like Ralf. He's the temperamental one. You weren't the first. And probably won't be the last. They usually come in two or three times a week to play their game. Always on a Tuesday afternoon at least."

David decided not to push it any further. Beitiris came and took the empty bowls away for them.

"Did you want to go for a walk?" Emily asked, looking out of the window to her left. "It's still a nice day. Perhaps, we could take Benji somewhere?"

"Sure. I'm up for that. Do you know of anywhere?"

"We can have a drive, and see?"

"Okay. I can pay for lunch. I know I said about the chocolate sponge being my treat, but I'd like to pay for all of it. It's the least I can do for you being such great company." David smiled sincerely.

"Aw, bless." Emily blushed again. "But honestly, I don't think I can let you pay for all of it." Emily took some money out of her small purse. "That should cover it. Put any change in one of the charity boxes at the bar ... I'll go and bring my car around the front."

Emily told David that Jock would probably claim lunch was on the house. She told David to decline the offer. She didn't want to take advantage of Jock's good nature.

Jock indeed, insisted on the meal being on the house.

David was having none of it. "I appreciate that, Jock, but we're paying and that's that." David grinned.

"Aye. If ye insist, laddie. It's nice to see Em on a date ... don't think she's been on many since she started here, which is a surprise. She's a beautiful and sweet little thing."

"That she is," David agreed.

"Aye. I don't blame ye for checking her out the other day. I knew ye weren't a bufter!" Jock laughed.

David gave a confused smile. He had no idea what the word 'bufter' meant.

"It means homosexual," Jock told him. "Not that I have anything against it! Each to their own." Jock smiled.

"Ah, I see." David tried to laugh.

As Jock was working out the price on the till, David saw a fairly large old dog come out of the kitchen area, and out from behind the bar. It looked like it was struggling to walk. "Hello, you," David said as the dog walked slowly over to greet David. He ruffled the long white and grey fur on the dog's neck.

Benji started to wag his tail as the two dogs sniffed each other; both then wagged their tails excitedly.

"Ah, ye just met me *Penny*," Jock said. "I've had her since she was a wee pup. She's almost ten, now."

"What sort of dog is she?"

Jock handed David some change, most of which was Emily's. "She's a Scottish deerhound, laddie. She's getting on a bit. She suffers a bit from arthritis in her legs. A small amount of paracetamol helps her, though."

"Paracetamol? Is that safe?"

"Aye. Well and nae. It depends on the dosage. Me vet works out the correct amount and says it's safe," Jock replied, looking down at Penny. "Isn't that right, girl?"

Penny looked up at Jock, continuing to wag her tail. David put the change into one of the charity boxes as Emily had requested.

Emily then came back into the pub, having parked her car at the front.

"Ye okay, Em? Enjoy ye lunch?" Jock smiled.

"It was great, thanks. As always. Hello, Penny." Emily bent down to stroke Penny and then Benji, so he didn't feel left out.

"I put the change in the box, here." David pointed.

"Cool, okay." Emily smiled. "Are you ready to go?"

"Sure."

"What ye both got planned now?" Jock asked, folding his large arms.

"We're going for a walk somewhere, seeing as the weather seems nice," answered Emily.

"Well, ye both take care now, aye? See ye soon."

"We will," Emily replied.

"Thanks for lunch," David said.

"Anytime, laddie. Anytime." Jock beamed warmly as he watched the two walk out of the pub and get into Emily's Mini Cooper.

# Chapter Thirty-Nine

## 15th July, 2018

"So, where shall we go?" David asked, sitting in the passenger side in Emily's car. The interior was spotless, even the mat on the floor. A fruity smell came from a car air freshener that resembled an ice-lolly as it dangled from the rear-view mirror.

"You obviously know the area better than me." David smiled, putting on his sunglasses.

"I wish I'd brought my sunglasses, now," Emily said, looking over at David.

"Not to worry. You can share mine," joked David.

Emily gave a laugh. "I do have one place in mind, where we could take a nice stroll. Though, you're spoilt for choice up here. There's so many lovely places around."

"Where did you have in mind?"

"We don't have to walk the whole way, but there's a walk people do. It starts at Coylumbridge, not too far from here. It takes us to an iron bridge. I think Benji would enjoy it, too. It's very scenic. Me and my mum have walked it a few times before. It's been a few months since we last did it. It can take a good couple of hours or more. Depending how far you wish to go. Seeing as it's a nice day and not too hot, I think it would be a nice walk … if you feel up for it, that is?" Emily turned the key and started the engine.

"It sounds great. It'd be a good opportunity to burn off lunch too, eh?"

Emily giggled. "Yeah."

"Do we er, need to walk through the forest?"

"For sure, but it's not too enclosed. It's scattered and open, and mostly on a footpath."

"Oh, okay." The thought of the forest made David feel uneasy, but as it wasn't too enclosed and daytime, he thought it should be okay.

"So, what do you say?" Emily faced David.

"Let's do it."

"Cool," Emily replied sounding exited. "We can probably find a place to park, near to the campsite." Emily checked the road in front of her, before setting off for the short drive to their destination.

*****

"This should be okay," Emily said, parking her car under a large tree at the side of the road.

David was a little surprised to recognise that they were on the same road as the church they had visited. He waited for a car to pass, before getting out and putting Benjie on his lead. A warm breeze skimmed across his face. "You sure it's okay to park here?"

"Yes. It should be fine. I've parked here before." Emily opened the boot of the car and went round to it. "Ta-da!" She grinned as she held up two bottles of chilled water.

David smiled, walking to the back of the car. He saw a third bottle along with a blue cat bowl, in a blue, small drinks cooler.

"I thought I'd come prepared … the bowl belonged to Bertie."

David didn't know what to say. It was a small gesture, yet at the same time, it meant a lot to him. "Aw. That's really thoughtful." He smiled. "Thank you."

"I, I thought of it this morning. And popped to the shop before the pub." Emily looked a little embarrassed.

David thought even more how damn cute she was.

They made their way past the caravan site to their left.

A couple of children were playing badminton, laughing while their parents sat by them reading. This normality gave David a slight surreal feeling. It was like watching something uplifting or real for reassurance after watching a horror movie as a kid. Like seeing the news afterwards, even though he didn't like the news. Seeing the two kids playing was peaceful and realistic, but paradoxically it depressed David. It contrasted too strongly against the horror of his recent experiences, which were *real* and not a horror film.

He shuddered, thinking how close the children were to the evil potentially surrounding them in the forest.

"Are you okay?" Emily asked. "You seem distracted?" Emily had been chatting about something, but David was miles away. He hadn't heard a word of what she had said.

"Uh? Oh, I'm sorry," he quickly said. "I was just thinking about something. I didn't mean to be rude."

"That's okay. What were you thinking about?" Emily smiled.

"Oh, nothing much. I was just watching the kids playing. It, er, brought back memories of when I was younger." He was worried that Emily would think he was nuts if he told her the truth.

"Oh, okay."

"When was the last time you came up here?"

"Back in January; me and my mum came. It had been snowing. It took a while longer as it was hard work in the snow." Emily laughed. "You should see the scenery and the mountains when it's snowed, though ... it's a beautiful sight. It isn't just in the summer it looks amazing. Autumn too, when the leaves turn brown and fall."

David could tell how much Emily appreciated the environment up here and the wonderful scenic views it had to offer.

"You're a bit of a naturist, then? I don't mean that in a *naked* sense." David laughed.

Emily laughed too.

"Well, that wouldn't be a bad thing, I suppose." David couldn't resist pursuing the humour.

Emily laughed again. "Cheeky! But I do love nature, yes. I think at times, you just have to stand back and admire nature for what it is and appreciate it. That includes animals, too ... I like taking pictures when I can, as well. I might even take some today, though I do have enough of this particular area on my laptop, already."

"You can never have too many."

"True."

As they walked a little further, David could see a few tents. They followed the path making their way into the woodland some more but didn't see the tent owners anywhere nearby.

He wondered how people could still camp here, after what had happened to Charlie all those years ago. And possibly to others. People obviously weren't aware of the dangers. Or perhaps they just forgot with time. Perhaps this part of the forest wasn't so bad; it was a little less dense. Regardless, it was certainly a beautiful setting.

"Do you go into the forest, much?"

"Sometimes, I do. I don't tend to go too far in, though. Especially, if I'm on my own." She laughed a little. "I'm usually with my mum or someone else.

A few other friends and people I know. Annabel and I have done a few walks, too. We had a picnic once, just the two of us, a couple of summers ago now."

"You're good friends with Annabel, then? Why don't you like going too far into the forest?"

"I've known Anna since I started working at the pub. We're good friends. Pretty close. We do a few things together. Girlie nights in and stuff." Emily giggled. "As for going too far into the forest, I don't know. I guess it can sometimes be a little spooky if you're on your own. Some people claim it's haunted, like a lot of forests and woods, I suppose. It sounds silly, but I get worried about getting lost, too." Emily gave an awkward laugh.

"Nah. There's nothing silly about that … I'd probably feel the same way on my own. I certainly wouldn't want to get lost in there."

"At least it isn't just me, then." Emily smiled.

"Have you ever heard anything else about the forest?"

"Erm. What like?"

"Anything? I've heard people say it's a little spooky as well. Like they're being watched. Even of people disappearing, like a young boy, once."

"I've overheard a couple of people in the pub talk briefly about hearing strange noises at times, or how some people have been starting fires. But nothing about any disappearances. I don't read too much into stories like that, if I'm honest with you. There's all sorts of stories about haunted places, forests and what not."

"You don't believe in such things, no?"

Emily let out a sigh. "I do and I don't … I'm open-minded, I guess. But I'm not sure I buy into all that about monsters and stuff. I'm a 'seeing is believing' kind of girl. Saying that, I think we do have a spirit or a soul and there is something when we die. Well, at least I hope there is! If there isn't, I guess we wouldn't know any different, when we finally go … how about you? Do you believe in those sorts of things?"

"Me? I er, I guess I'm like you in that regard. Seeing *is* believing," David tried to joke. "There's something else, I want to ask you."

"What's that?"

"Do you know that taxi driver who picked you three up the other night, at the pub? He looked pretty moody."

"What, you mean Zac? Yes, he does have that look about him, doesn't he?" Emily chuckled. "I don't know him personally. Annabel does a bit, I think … why do you ask? Did he scare you? To be honest, he does me, a little. He doesn't say much."

"I thought he looked a little creepy," David said. "When we arrived up here, I saw him in a car with another woman. She smiled at me and I smiled back. He glared at me. I didn't think much of it, until I saw him the other night when you got in the taxi. I just thought that it was a strange coincidence."

Emily frowned. "That is a little strange. But maybe not, if you think about it. Being a taxi driver, he probably gets about."

"I suppose." David felt sweat build up on his lower back from walking in the warm afternoon sun. He then heard his phone, which was vibrating in his pocket. It was a text message from John asking how his big date was going. "It's John. Asking how I'm getting on."

Emily smiled. "Aw. Your best mate checking up on you, making sure I'm not leading you astray, eh?"

Even though she came across as bashful, David could see a playful glint in Emily's green eyes. "Something like that." He laughed, popping the phone back into his pocket.

*****

They walked on, along the dusty footpath, chatting and laughing.

Every now and then, a soft breeze would kick up, picking up the smell of fresh pines and blossom. They occasionally stopped for a little respite, to admire nature's creation and to drink their cold water. Intermittent openings in the top of the trees revealed the mountains in the distance. They had passed nobody.

David felt tempted at times to take Emily's hand in his, but perhaps it was too early. He was still holding Benji's lead and the bowl. Benji didn't seem to mind this part of the forest. "I might let Benji loose for a bit, if we come to a bit of an opening."

"There are a few places up ahead where he'd probably love to run about. The only thing is, you're supposed to keep dogs on a lead as some of the birds up here nest on the ground."

"Oh?"

"Yeah. The capercaillie."

"Caper what?" David smiled.

*"Capercaillie."* Emily laughed. "It's a type of bird. I remember reading about it online somewhere, when me and Mum first moved up here. We looked up some possible walks that we could do together."

"I see." It was obvious to David that Emily was close to her mother, by the way she often spoke about her and how they did things together. Having only the one parent, it was completely understandable.

They had been walking for almost an hour and had passed a couple of signs advising dog owners to keep dogs on a short lead because of the birds, when they finally saw two joggers; a male and female. The female smiled but her male companion just continued past, straight faced. They stopped a little further on and checked their pulses and sports watches.

"I've never been one for jogging. It makes me laugh when you see these stick figures jogging. They never look like they need to exercise, although perhaps that's why they're so slim. I guess it isn't just about looking slimmer but being healthier in general."

"Me neither. I tried a couple of times, but I gave up in no time." Emily grinned.

"Well, for what it's worth, I think you look fine as you are," David said sincerely.

"Aw. Thank you … I do like my takeaways. All in moderation though; I'm careful with what I eat. I could probably eat pizza every day, if I knew for certain I wouldn't gain any weight!" Emily giggled.

"Yep, me too. I don't think I would ever get fed up with *pizza*. It's always good to treat yourself. It's just annoying that most favourite foods are bad for you, eh?" David laughed.

"Oh my God, that is so true."

They decided to stop further up ahead for another breather. They took a few swigs of water and David placed the blue bowl on the ground for Benji, who noisily lapped the water up, moving the bowl around with his long tongue.

"Looks like he's enjoying that." Emily smiled.

"It was a nice gesture to bring the water, Em. Thoughtful to think of Benji, as well. I didn't even think of it."

Emily felt her face go a little hot again. "You're welcome … and *aw*, you called me *Em*."

David raised his eyebrows quickly. "Well, you know …" He smiled.

A couple of young lads zoomed past them on their mountain bikes.

One almost came off of his bike as he skidded on the footpath, throwing up small particles of dust and tiny stones. *"Fuckin' 'ell, mate. Almost come off me bike!"* the lad behind shouted as the other one laughed.

"Ha-ha. Keep up, ye wanker!" The other lad quickly looked round.

David and Emily watched them both disappear and then looked at one another and laughed.

*****

"This would be a good spot to let Benji off the lead," suggested Emily.

They had come to a large clearing with light green grass. The rest of the forest could be seen in front of them; it seemed to be denser further on, with the mountains beyond.

"I don't think there will be any nests on the ground here. It should be fine," Emily said, standing with her hands on her petite hips. She too, could feel the sweat building up on her lower abdomen and back. "Phew … I feel a bit warm, now." She pulled her top away from her sticky skin.

"Same."

Emily felt some of the long grass poke between her painted toes. "Perhaps, I should have worn better footwear." She half-laughed.

"At least it isn't raining."

"True," Emily replied as David let Benji roam free.

"How far is it to this bridge?"

"Oh, not too far now." Emily took another swig of her water bottle.

David smiled as he looked at her.

"What?"

"Nothing," David answered. "It's just you look sweet, standing there drinking your water."

Emily gave a cute laugh back. "Really?"

"Really."

Emily stopped smiling and could see the sincereness in David's handsome face, now that he had taken off his sunglasses. She felt a tingle, but averted her eyes away from his, feeling a little shy.

There was a moment of silence between the two, when they heard a slight fracas. They quickly looked to their left, where Benji was wagging his tail and barking at a large bird.

"Benji, get here!"

"Oh my," Emily said. "It's one of those capercaillies."

They rushed closer. The bird had raised its black tail which was speckled with white. It was challenging Benji and trying to defend itself.

As David grew closer, he could see its brown wings, black and green breast and red markings over its eyes, like thick red eyebrows. The capercaillie was both chirping and croaking; it reminded David of the noise made by rubbing a stick across the ridged back of a wooden frog he had played with as a child.

"Stop it, Benji!" David pulled Benji away.

Benji barked.

David moved Benji away from the capercaillie, but the bird followed them.

David started to run with Benji and Emily did the same. They started to laugh nervously at the way the bird still came after them, before it finally stopped and gave up.

Benji sat looking over at the bird, his tongue out, panting.

"Bloody hell," David said. "I've never seen a bird go after someone like that!" He started to laugh again.

"Me neither … it's my fault. I shouldn't have said it was fine."

"Don't be daft. It's not your fault." David put Benji's lead back on. "Better keep him on this until we get back. Shall we get going?"

"If you like."

*****

A little while later, they eventually reached the iron bridge, where both the path and area were more open.

"I was expecting the bridge to be much bigger." David laughed. "I thought it was going to be something more like the Golden Gate Bridge," he joked, gazing at the small steel bridge.

Emily laughed back. "Sorry. I didn't mean to get your hopes up for some marvellous construction! It's all about the walk and taking in the scenery, really."

"I know … *and* the company."

The two of them rested their arms on the metal bars, looking over into the river below. They gazed down at the rocks beneath the shallow water. It felt peaceful listening to the water. They didn't say a word for almost a minute. They just looked around and below them, and smiled at each other.

David felt that this part of the forest might not be affected by any dark presence, unlike his uncle's farm. It seemed so different.

"This river is called the Am Beanaidh," Emily finally said as they stared down at the swirling water.

"You've done your research, then?"

"Yeah. I read that the bridge is known as the Cairngorm Club Footbridge after the climbers who built it."

"Impressive," David said sarcastically, making Emily laugh.

They stood on the bridge for a short while longer.

"Which way shall we go back?" Emily asked. "We can either go back the way that we came, or a different way. Either way, we end up back where we parked the car. It's the same direction, just on a different path."

"I don't mind. It would be good going on the different path. Let's check out that way."

"Good call. It's what I'd prefer. I obviously know the way, so we won't get lost."

"Okay. I was thinking about how long it would take to get back to my uncle's farm if I walked … I think it's that way," David said joking and pointing. "I think the forest would be way too thick though, and I'd most likely get lost." Just the thought of having to trudge through the thick forest worried him.

Emily laughed. "Shall we go, then?"

"Sure."

Coming off the iron steps of the bridge, Emily accidentally caught some dirt and twigs in the sandal of her right foot.

"You okay?" David saw Emily pulling something away from the sandal.

"Yeah." She smiled. "I just got something stuck in my toes. It's my fault for wearing sandals." She walked carefully down the riverbank near some rocks and took off her right sandal. She swished her foot and let the cool water trickle over it, removing the dirt.

David walked over to her and held her arm, so she wouldn't slip.

She looked at him and smiled.

"Wouldn't want you to fall into the water, now." He winked and smiled.

After she was done, she shook her foot dry and slid her sandal back on.

As David helped her up the bank, she noticed a wooden beaded rosary a few feet away, on one of the large grey rocks that sat at the side of the riverbank.

She walked over and picked it up, examining it. Some of the wooden beads were broken or missing. The wooden cross had a chip missing at the bottom.

David then noticed a few stains of faded, dried blood on one of the other rocks.

"Is that blood?" Emily asked, still holding the necklace.

"It looks like it. I don't think it's recent, though. It's faded with the weather most likely." David bent down closer to examine the stains.

"I certainly hope that this person was all right … I wonder if this rosary belonged to whoever's blood this is?"

"Maybe. I'm sure they're probably all right. There isn't much blood. Besides, it could even be a wild animal's blood," David suggested, trying to reassure Emily. "Let me have a look at the rosary."

Emily handed it over to him.

Taking it from her, some beads dropped onto the ground, uncovering the frayed brown string that threaded through them and connected the cross at the bottom of the chain. "I think it's seen better days. I don't think it's worth keeping. Not unless, you want it?" David said joking a little, holding the rosary up.

"Perhaps, if it was in better condition." Emily smirked.

"Are you a religious person?"

"Sort of. I was baptised a Catholic. I don't practice it though or go to church." Emily giggled.

"Shame on you," David joked.

Emily laughed.

David didn't find it too funny though. He wasn't religious himself but wondered if now was the time to start. He tossed what remained of the rosary into the river. It barely made a splash as the river whisked it away upstream.

They started their return journey on the path alongside the river. David spotted a worm that was drying out on the footpath. It seemed to struggle. Emily was touched when David picked it up, dropping it onto wet muddy soil where there was some grass.

Emily offered to take Benji's lead as David had been holding it on the way out, but she struggled, whenever Benji pulled.

"I can take him, if he's a bit too much for you? I know he can be a bit of a lump at times."

"That's okay. He's not too bad."

"If your arm starts to ache, let me know."

*****

They came to another clearing, around half an hour later. The tall pine trees around the outskirts of the wispy dried grass, emanated a sweetness in the air. The wind had picked up, forcing the dry grass over to one side like a side parting of a hair style.

"Maybe this is a perfect time for a selfie moment." Emily giggled.

David laughed. "I can take a pic for you, if you like, with the mountains in the background?"

"Well. I was, erm, thinking of maybe both of us in it, together. And maybe Benji," Emily said shyly.

"If you like." David walked over closer to Emily as she took her phone out and brought the camera screen up.

"Hold on ..." David took off his sunglasses and tucked them down his T-shirt and then picked Benji up, still with his lead on and the three posed for the camera.

"Say, *cheese* ..." Emily smiled as she pressed the shutter button.

David was close enough to smell the freshness of Emily's hair as his own brushed against hers.

They laughed at the photo. Benji's face looked in shock.

"God, look at my smile ... talk about *cheesy*," David said.

"Nonsense. You have a *great* smile."

"Not as lovely as yours ..."

The pair looked into each other's eyes for a moment.

# Chapter Forty

## 15th July, 2018

They heard thunder from the Cairngorms. They looked over into the distance to see some menacing, dark clouds quickly loom over the mountains. The clouds appeared to come out of nowhere. Another couple of rumbles sounded from the horizon.

"That doesn't look good," David said, feeling a little tension.

Emily felt the same.

"It sure looks black over there." David swallowed.

The clouds seemed to be fast approaching. Neither of them wanted to be stranded out in the open in a thunderstorm.

David looked over at Emily with a concerned look on his face.

"What is it?" Emily asked nervously.

"We need to get out of the open," David said with alarm. "Your hair's standing on end!"

"So is yours!" Emily replied somewhat shocked. Their mood of laughter and romance seemed to have vanished. "Benji's fur is, too!"

They quickly moved from the opening back onto the footpath, which was more covered. David felt tingling in his arms and started to feel nervous. "My arms feel tingly."

"Mine too."

"Shit." David laughed nervously. "Usually, when your hair stands on end or you feel tingly, it means there's going to be a strike of lightning."

"I've heard that as well."

"It might mean we're getting charged up … how far is it back to your car?" David sounded a little frantic.

"I, I don't know. Maybe another half an hour." Emily looked worried, looking around.

"I think we need to move. It's going to rain any minute. Let's try running."

"Okay."

More dark clouds threatened overhead. The middle part of a cloud rose up like a huge anvil.

"Let's move!" David said. "I'll take Benji." He took the lead from Emily's hand.

They started to run along the footpath, which was difficult for Emily in her sandals. She still held the blue bowl. The empty bottles of water were disposed of in a bin earlier.

They heard a few more rumbles of thunder followed by a bright yellow flash of sheet lightning, making them jump.

"Which way do we go?" David asked as they came to a fork in the footpath.

"Take a left. We just need to stay on that path and follow it all the way back." She puffed, a little out of breath.

The rain arrived. Running in the rain was déjà vu to David; a repeat of when he and John had been chased up to the farm. There were a few more flashes of lightning and the rain started to fall heavier. The dusty footpath became sodden.

"I, I need to stop," Emily said. She came to a halt and bent down slightly with her hands on her now wet thighs.

David stopped with her. "You okay?"

They flinched in response to another rumble of thunder. This one louder.

"I just need to catch my breath."

"Same," David replied as yellow forked lightning cut across the sky. "At least we have a bit of cover here."

They had stopped under the shelter of a few well-leafed branches, which prevented some of the rain from reaching them.

"How long do you think this storm will last?"

"Not long, hopefully." David smiled reassuringly. He looked up and then across the sky. There was nothing to see but dark grey.

The wind was now blowing rain onto their faces.

"I'm pretty sure they didn't forecast this … it was supposed to be nice all day." Emily's voice faltered. "I've never liked thunderstorms. Certainly not being stuck outside in one!" She cowered as there was a crack of thunder.

David put a comforting arm around her wet shoulder.

She looked up at him and smiled. It made her feel a little more protected.

"We'll be all right." David smiled. The branches above had started to droop with the weight of water which was now pouring through. "I think we need to move."

"We're still a fair bit from my car, though ... I have an idea."

"What's that?"

"There's an old, abandoned cottage, well, what's left of it, not far from here. If we run, it would probably only take us a few minutes. We can take shelter there until the storm passes."

David didn't feel too keen. He wanted to get back to the car as soon as possible, but in the circumstances, it probably made sense. "Okay. Lead the way!"

They started to run again. Benji was soaked. The rain was hitting them square on. They left the footpath cutting through another clearing. This time much smaller and overgrown with dandelions.

The deserted cottage was about twenty metres away. Emily was right. It took them less than five minutes to reach the derelict cottage. "It's over there!" She pointed.

They clambered through the overgrowth, some of which was waist high. Emily carefully avoided some stinging nettles. Her feet were already filthy from the rain and mud; her sandals weren't holding on well. She stumbled slightly and David grabbed her arm.

Seeing that she was struggling, David offered to give her a piggyback. "Hop on," he said, arching over.

"Huh?"

"Get on my back ... your sandals are barely holding together in this."

"Are you sure?"

"Yes!"

Emily climbed onto David's back and he carried her through the overgrowth. "Almost there ..." he called, still holding Benji's lead in his hand.

Half of the brickwork of the deserted cottage had collapsed. What was left of the stone roof tiles left huge gaps for water to pour inside. Thick, dead branches covered the top of the building over the roof. Some stacks of rotten wood were piled to the left, next to a thorn bush.

David looked into one of the splintered window frames. The glass had long since gone. "Yeah, this will probably keep us sheltered. There's a bit of cover." He noticed a dead sparrow on the ground.

Emily saw it too. "Aw. I hate seeing dead animals and alone like that."

"I know. Poor thing," David replied sadly.

They walked through the opening where the door used to be.

"You know, it's ironic that we're seeking shelter when we're already soaked," David joked.

"I know. But we need to get inside from the storm; it isn't showing any signs of stopping."

The thunderstorm was all around them, casting its darkness into the cottage.

"I can't believe how cold it is." Emily started to shiver. She sat down and huddled up on a small pile of wood.

They positioned themselves in one of the most protected corners, which sheltered them from the elements outside.

The inside had been completely stripped. The fireplace partly remained but the chimney was no longer there. A few old wooden beams still held across the roof, well-decayed. A musty smell filled the dampness.

"I wonder how old this building is, and how long it's been like this?" David said, looking around.

"I don't know … I first came across it a few weeks after I moved up here, with my mum. It wasn't actually as bad as it is now. It's worse now. We saw a few kids up here once, kicking and smashing the walls with a sledgehammer. They had a wheelbarrow, too." Emily tried to laugh.

David laughed. "Kids, eh?"

Emily cowered down again as more thunder and lightning came.

David looked over at Emily in the low light of the building. "We should be fine here. Are you okay?"

"Yeah. Just a little cold and wet … and scared."

"Aw." David wished he had a coat or a jacket to put over Emily's shoulders. "Budge up." He grinned at her.

Emily shifted up on the stack of old wood, allowing David to sit next to her.

He put his right arm around her and gave her a rub, trying to warm her up. He pulled her into him.

"Thanks." She looked up and smiled at him gratefully.

"I don't know if I'm helping or making it worse," David joked. "I'm as wet as you are."

"That's okay. I don't mind," Emily replied, looking up at him.

Benji lay at their feet, soaking wet.

"I guess you were right about wearing something better on your feet." David smiled.

Emily laughed nervously, looking down at her feet. "Yep … the sandals will be all right once I've given them a wash."

"There we were, saying we didn't like jogging … well, I think it's safe to say that we became sprinters this afternoon."

Emily laughed again, but soon stopped, when another loud crack of thunder came, and lightning lit up the inside of what was left of the old building.

*****

The pair of them sat there, waiting out the storm.

"Haven't seen any more flashes of lightning for a few minutes ... the thunder seems to be dying down, too. I think it's blowing over."

"I hope so," Emily replied.

Just as David was about to say something else, they heard a sound from outside, close to the building, like someone walking past. Although the ground was soft and wet, they could hear mushy thuds and squelches.

Emily looked up at David, concerned.

The footsteps stopped for a few seconds and then started again.

David and Emily froze still.

"Perhaps, it's just a dog walker going past?" Emily whispered.

"Maybe," David replied cautiously. He wasn't so sure. He wondered who would be out in this weather, although someone might be stranded like they were. He got up slowly, letting go of Benji's lead. "I'll go check ..." He carefully stepped between the rubble on the floor, trying not to make a sound and leaned to look out of one of the window frames.

A tall thin person wearing a long blue raincoat with its hood up stood with their back to David. They stopped, as if they knew David was watching, then started whistling quietly. Whoever it was then carried on walking ahead.

David looked at the large boot prints in the mud, relieved that at least this was a person, and remembering the unnatural footprints he had seen on the way up to his uncle's farm. David watched until the person turned a corner and disappeared out of sight.

He then jumped as his phone sounded and started vibrating. It was a text message from John again, asking when he'd be back and whether he'd 'gotten lucky.' David returned the phone to his wet pocket.

"Well ... was someone outside?"

David nodded. "Someone in a blue raincoat."

"Where did they go?"

"I don't know. They headed off in that direction, somewhere," David said, pointing.

"Thank God ... I was getting worried for a moment."

David tried to smile.

Emily had no clue about everything David had been through, so it was normal for her not to think too much about a stranger passing. But David still felt something was odd about it.

After another few minutes, the rain eventually stopped and more light filtered through the remaining clouds. The interior of the derelict cottage felt less dark now that the storm had finally passed.

Emily stood up and joined David as he watched out through the empty doorway. They could still hear a faint rumble of thunder in the distance.

"I'm so glad that's over," Emily said, before her own phone started vibrating … "It's my mum, texting to ask if I'm okay." She texted a response to her mum and then wondered why David was watching her. "What is it?"

"It's your eyes. Your mascara has run … it looks like you've got a couple of black eyes," David joked.

"Oh." Emily laughed. She turned her phone camera into selfie mode to take a look and stepped outside. Her wet fringe had fallen onto her pretty face in strands, curling slightly.

"You look sexy." David smiled.

"Stop it, you!" Emily smirked, embarrassed.

David suddenly wanted to kiss her but resisted. "We should erm, make a move and get back … just in case another storm comes."

"Best, yes," Emily replied, seeing David's hesitation and disappointed he hadn't made a move.

*****

It took under half an hour to get back to the campsite. The skies were still grey, but at least there had been no more rain.

They walked back past the tents in their wet clothes and saw no one on the way.

"You don't mind us getting in your car with these wet clothes on?" David asked. "I guess we don't have much choice."

"Not unless we take them off." Emily giggled cheekily.

"Well, there is that." David laughed. "My nipples are already coming through, like a wet T-shirt competition."

Emily laughed. "I used to have a couple of towels in the boot, for when me and mum or Annabel went on a walk, and they forecast showers. We never needed them. Typical that I don't bring them and we *do* need them." Emily chuckled. "We'll just have to whack the heating on."

David smiled.

A large puddle was at the end of the path. David looked at Emily's soaked sandals. "Hop on, again," he commanded.

Emily climbed onto David's back for the second time and the pair of them laughed. She put her arms across his neck and David felt her wet body press against his.

David jolted a little, to prop her up and held onto Benji's lead and the bowl.

Emily could smell David's wet hair and aftershave. His hair smelt sweet like coconut; she liked it. She liked the way David took pride in his appearance without seeming vain.

David made his way through the water which just reached his ankles and put Emily down carefully near her car.

Benji shook wildly, trying to dry his fur.

Emily whacked on the car heaters for them all. She laughed again as she looked at her eyes in the rear-view mirror. "At least no one gets to see me like this, until I get home." She giggled. "Well, apart from you."

"You're all right … look at me." David pulled the top of his T-shirt away from his toned chest. "You can still see me pokies."

They both laughed at David's nipples showing through.

"Well, you can't see mine." Emily giggled further.

"Well, if we had a fairer competition, you'd win!" David grinned.

"Oi, cheeky!" Emily laughed. "It's strange, the way that storm appeared out of nowhere …" She rubbed some of the condensation off her windscreen with her hand.

"I know." If Emily thought that was strange, David wondered what she would think about everything else that was happening. But she was right. That storm had appeared out of nowhere.

"At least we're safe now … I was worried when our hair stood on end. I thought we might be struck by lightning!"

"Good thinking about that old cottage, *Batgirl*."

Emily grinned. "At least it protected us from the storm for a while."

"Yep … I'm going to take a nice shower when I get back," David said, looking at Benji in the back seat.

"Oh, me too … Do you want me to take you back to your uncle's farm? I honestly don't mind."

"It's okay. You don't have to do that. I can give John a call. I'll get him to pick me up from the pub again, if you want to drop me off there? You've already done enough." David looked at Emily. He laughed again at her smudged makeup.

She gave him a playful slap on his arm.

"Ouch," David joked. He then texted John asking him to pick him up at The Auld Drongair Bàrd.

*****

"John's picking you up shortly, then?" Emily asked as the pair of them sat outside the pub in Emily's car.

"Yeah. He said he was going to have a quick bite to eat and then come fetch me. He probably won't be too much longer."

"It's great that you two are so close. You obviously have a great relationship."

"Totally … he's like a brother to me, you know? I love him to bits. But boy, does he piss me off at times." David laughed.

Emily laughed too. "That's the case with most close friends. Even family."

"Is Annabel your closest friend?"

Emily gave it a few seconds thought before answering. She had to think. "I would say so … I have a few friends, here. Annabel, I spend quite a lot of time with. She has other friends though and is sometimes busy doing her own thing. She's very close to her godparents. I don't know them all that well. We are close and I like her a lot. But maybe we lack that bond you and John have. I had that with friends when I was younger and back in Ireland. But those friends have since married and moved, as did I."

"Aw. Yeah. It must be tough to lose friends. Especially when you're so close. I've been fortunate. I have a few friends back south, like Granty, who I told you about."

"Yes. Is he the one who works with computers?"

"That's right. I would say Grant's a best friend, too. I know him through John, but I'm closest to John. I've known him much longer. Grant knows that as well, but we all get on well. We all live close to each other."

"It certainly sounds convenient."

"Oh, for sure … I never take them for granted." David remembered that he wanted to ask Jock about Samuel and Ralf. "I might get a bag of crisps to keep me going until I get back to the farm."

"Sure, okay. I enjoyed today. Even with the storm." Emily giggled shyly.

"I enjoyed spending the afternoon with you as well, Em." David leant forwards to kiss her.

Just as they slowly leaned into each other, a car beeped its horn.

It was John. "Hope I wasn't disturbing you?" he shouted out, teasing.

Emily smiled sheepishly, blushing. David shook his head.

"I'd better go. But honestly, I had a great time, today."

"Same ... I hope we can do it again, *soon*. Not necessarily a walk. But something."

"For sure." David smiled.

They instinctively leaned in again, giving one another a quick kiss on the cheek, knowing that John was watching and waiting, with a huge grin on his face.

"You take care," David said.

"You too."

David got out the car and let Benji out.

"Bye, Benji!" Emily said.

David smiled at Emily again, closing the door.

"I thought you'd be a bit longer than this," David said to John.

"Thought, or hoped?" John teased.

David smiled.

"I didn't bother getting anything to eat. I was going to wait until I picked you up. Your uncle was going to make some salad for dinner."

David turned to wave to Emily, who started up her car, waved back at the two and drove off.

"*Ooh*, Davey-Boy ... looks like you're in *lurve*! That smile on your face ... looks like you two were about to 'get it on' as well, had I not turned up," John teased his friend some more.

"Eat shit!" David tried not to laugh.

"Why are your clothes damp, mate?"

"We went for a walk on the other side of the forest and got caught up in a thunderstorm."

"Thunderstorm? There wasn't any storm back at the farm."

"Really? Strange ... it certainly came on unexpectedly. How's Betty?"

"She's fine, mate. She seems chatty and stuff."

"That's good to hear."

"I take it your date went well, then?" John asked, grinning.

"It did. We had a great time. Apart from that storm and some weird guy in a raincoat."

"Huh?"

"I'll tell you about it in a bit. I was going to go inside the pub and get some crisps and take a leak. I wanted to ask Jock about Samuel and Ralf, see if he knows anything about where they live. Em didn't know too much."

"*Em*, eh?" John smiled, teasing David for using a pet name for Emily.

David shook his head.

"Oh, I spoke to Grant earlier on. He's fine; nothing going on there. I told him you were on a date with some hot Irish chick. He said to say 'Hi.' I didn't tell him anything else. I didn't want to worry him."

"At least he's doing okay, still."

John joined David in the pub.

There were a few customers in there and music was playing. John stood at the bar, while David went to the gents. John ordered a couple of pints.

A middle-aged man, who John hadn't seen before, served him.

"I got you a bag of salt and vinegar, mate," John said as David came out of the toilet.

"Cheers. They'll do. Any sign of Jock?"

"Nah. Not yet. Another guy served me. Not seen anybody else."

They stood at the bar to drink their pints.

"I wonder if Annabel's working?"

"Nah. She isn't working today. According to Emily, she's supposed to be contacting you."

"Really? I haven't had a message from her."

"Emily said Annabel's usually pretty good at keeping her word. Apparently, she told Emily that she likes you."

"Hah. Funny way of showing it." John tore open his pork scratchings, releasing a spicy smell. "You want one?" John offered, holding out the bag.

David wasn't overly keen on pork scratchings and declined. "Excuse me, mate," David said to the man behind the bar, "Is Jock about?"

"Jock? Nae. Well, he is. But he's finished for the day. He's gone for a lie-down."

"Oh."

"Anything I can help ye with?"

"Nah, it's fine," David replied as the man went to serve another customer.

"Guess we'll have to hold off on asking about those two old gits for now," John said, crunching on a pork scratching.

David shared the events of his afternoon with John, telling him about the walk, their hair standing on end, the storm, the old cottage and the person in the blue raincoat he had seen.

*****

When they had finished their pints and snacks, they set off for the farm. David was drier now; only his canvas trainers were damper.

"At least your date went well, mate. I'm pleased for you … you were certainly gone long enough. You going to see her again, soon?"

"I hope so. I still feel a bit reluctant. Again, for obvious reasons. She offered to take me back to the farm, but I didn't want her driving back by herself through the forest."

"Ah. Makes sense, bud. But it's okay for me to do it on me own, eh?" John teased.

"Well …" David half-smiled. "You say we've got salad for dinner?"

"Yep. Your uncle and the rest have probably already eaten."

"What did you do while I was out?"

"Me? I just helped Gavin clean out some of the pens and stuff. Nothing too hectic. I tell you what though, those animals sure shit a lot," John semi-joked, making David laugh. "We were talking about tonight, too … I offered to help with Gav, tonight, whilst your uncle gets some sleep."

"You're up for that, even after what I heard last night?"

"Sure. Well, erm, sort of … I was thinking you might do it as well?" John replied, taking the road into the forest.

"Maybe. Although, I'm starting to feel a little tired. That walk was draining. Especially when we had to leg it. Maybe I'll have a quick nap after I've eaten." David yawned. "Hopefully no more storms. I'm getting tired of them. It was like when we first ran up here, when we were chased by that *thing*."

John turned to face David. "How could I forget?"

David screwed up his face, pulling away from John.

"What?"

"Your breath. Those pork scratchings *stink*."

John grinned and breathed out nearer to David's face, tormenting him.

David leaned further away, annoyed.

*****

John had parked his car in the barn at the farm. "I haven't had salad for God knows how long," he said as they approached the house. "Hope it hasn't got cold," he joked.

"Me neither. I don't remember the last time. Probably when I was still living back home with my folks."

They walked into the kitchen and saw Bob and Betty there. Two plates of salad were on the kitchen table with a sheet of tin foil over them, ready for the pair.

"David!" His uncle smiled. He was drying his hands with a white kitchen towel. "How did your date go? Ah. I can tell from that smile that all went well."

"It went good, thanks, Uncle. We had a nice time. Apart from getting caught up in a thunderstorm."

"You went for a walk, then? We didn't have any thunder here. Where did you go?"

"We went for a walk to an iron bridge; I don't know if you know it? We parked near to a campsite and walked up from there."

"Ah, yes. I know it. Me and Betty have been there. A *long* time ago."

Betty was doing some washing up. She looked over and smiled at David.

"I caught them about to do some kissing action when I arrived to pick up Lover Boy."

Betty shook a wet dish onto the draining board. "Oh, leave the boy alone!" She smiled. "He obviously likes this Emily. It's sweet."

David was surprised that Betty knew Emily's name. Perhaps his uncle told her. "Thanks, Aunt Betty. And yeah, I definitely like her … How's things with you? Are you feeling okay, now?"

"I'm well, dear. It's good to be home, even though it was only a day in hospital." She took her yellow rubber gloves off and placed them next to the kitchen sink. "I think I'll go and watch some telly before an early night." She smiled at the three of them, before making her way into the living room.

"I might join you in a bit," Bob replied. "You don't mind working through the night?" he asked John.

"Nah. I'm cool with it. I want to be of some use up here. It's why I came up with Dave, mate. I am a bit nervous though, with everything that's happened, but I'll be fine."

"I might stay up for a bit as well," David said.

Bob smiled at them both. "I appreciate it. The animals have been fine since we started keeping watch. Whether or not that's because of us or just coincidental, I don't know. I don't want to take any risks, though. We can't be too sure."

"Completely agree, Uncle."

"Yep, better safe than sorry," John added.

"Hopefully that Carl will get back to us tomorrow and can fill us in some more," said David.

"We can only hope, my boy … I'm going to see Gavin for a bit. You two enjoy your salad. Some nice pork pies, too."

# Chapter Forty-One

## 15th July, 2018

David showered and then took a nap before joining Gavin and John for the night shift. He was sure he wouldn't sleep through, and he didn't.

He awoke just after ten. He switched his mobile phone on. He had a couple of text messages from Emily, saying again how much she enjoyed his company and looked forward to seeing him again soon. Also, that she was having an early night. She had also sent the selfie with Benji from when they were in the clearing, just before the storm hit.

David smiled to himself viewing the picture. He texted her back, even though she was possibly asleep. There was certainly no doubt that he was developing feelings for her. He looked outside the window and then opened it. It seemed dry. The night air felt cool and he could hear John and Gavin talking.

He turned the light on to get dressed. He pulled on a pair of grey tracksuit bottoms and an old top and jacket. He considered leaving a sleepy Benji in his room but didn't want to leave him on his own. He felt Benji was safer by his side.

"It's awake …" John saw David and Benji walk up the farmyard towards him and Gavin. "How was your nap?"

"Good. The hot shower made me a bit sleepy. How's it going, anything happen?"

"Negative," Gavin replied. "At least not yet."

"Bit nippy," John noted.

"I'm just about to get some sleep in the barn. John offered to do the first half. I told him to wake me in a few hours," yawned Gavin, holding his shotgun.

"Any news on when your car's getting fixed?" David asked.

"We were actually just discussing that. The part is supposed to be coming in tomorrow. So hopefully, tomorrow sometime. Most likely in the afternoon, if all's well. I'm gonna get some sleep anyway, boys. If anything happens, you make sure you wake me."

"Will do," John said and they watched Gavin walk towards the barn with his shotgun.

*****

An hour or so after Gavin had fallen asleep, John was already bored. He and David sat on the chairs Bob and David had used the previous night. Benji lay at their feet.

"God, fuck doing this every night," John said, shaking his head. "These bastards taking the animals could probably just sneak past us, anyway. I don't get why your uncle doesn't just move the animals like that other farmer, Angus, decided ... it would make sense. It would save on having to stay up all night. Failing that, hire a couple of security guys."

"No one asked you to do it, mate."

"I know. But I'm just saying. It would make better sense, wouldn't it?"

"I suppose so, but I'm sure my uncle has his reasons. To hire security guards costs a lot and you need to be able to trust them."

"True ... although I'm sure your uncle could probably afford it. But then, I suppose we don't know how long they'd be needed for."

"Exactly. Plus, it could be too much hassle to move the animals. Bob might lose money; he'd be losing the produce of the animals, if he moved them. We don't know how long it would be for or how much it would cost. Perhaps, he feels safer them being here, where he can keep an eye on them. Especially as he's so attached to them."

"I can understand that," replied John as he let out a loud yawn, squinting away the moisture in his eyes. "I know it's night-time and all ... but is it me, or is it really quiet out here? Just seems, I don't know, *strange*."

"It's definitely not you ... I feel it."

"I feel like someone, or something, is like, watching us ... like our every move."

"Yep." David looked around.

"Fucking creepy."

"Tell me about it."

"Anyway, let's talk about something else. When are you going to see Emily, again? I still haven't heard anything from Annabel."

"I guess we'll have to see. It's still difficult because of what we're dealing with here, and of course, the distance, too." David looked at the photo of him and Emily again and smiled to himself.

"Yeah, I know what you mean. Long distance relationships are hard." John looked at David and glanced at the picture on his phone. "Nice pic." He grinned. "That just before the storm?"

"Yep ... literally just before it came over the mountains ..." David frowned as he looked further at the photo.

"What is it? You shocked at seeing your ugly mug? Get used to it, as you're stuck with that face for the rest of your life," John joked.

David used his thumb and forefinger to zoom in on his phone. He zoomed in on an area just over his own head in the picture. Behind them was mainly trees and bushes. He frowned but didn't say anything.

"What is it, mate? I was only joking. You don't look that bad," John joked again.

"What do you think that is?" David asked, pointing to a small blue part of the photo. "I only just noticed it ..."

"What, that?"

"Yeah ..."

"Erm ... I don't know. Somebody standing there, maybe?"

"Exactly what I'm thinking ... it looks like the person in the blue raincoat we saw, while we were in that old cottage."

"It's probably just someone out for a walk, like you and Emily were. Perhaps, they just got caught up in the storm? Same as you guys did."

"Maybe ... but what if they were following us?" David zoomed in further.

"Creepy, if true," John said, looking around the yard. He started to feel uneasy. They could hear faint snores from the barn where Gavin was sleeping.

"Look here ..." David showed John the photo.

John leant over.

"It looks like this person is holding their hand up ..."

"Maybe they're waving and photo-bombing you," John half-joked.

"See here ... look at these lines coming from their fingers ... it looks like ... *electricity*." David slowly ran his own fingertip around the part of the photo in question.

John frowned.

Yellow sparks of electricity seemed to be emanating from this figure's fingertips. You wouldn't see it unless you zoomed in. And even then, the lines were very faint.

David swallowed. "You agree?" he asked almost whispering.

"I don't know … it does look like it."

"I have an idea …" suggested David. He used one of the settings on the photo editor to reverse the colours of the photograph. Most of the picture turned dark turquoise and the previously faint lines turned black.

"Shit …" John muttered.

"Shit, exactly … that *definitely* has to be electricity coming from their hand …"

"Who the hell can do shit like that?"

"I have no fucking idea."

"Could it be what we saw before, or that Harold guy?" John asked.

"I don't think it's what we saw before, no. The hand appears human. It's too far away to see the face, but it does look human. Harold's a possibility. But how could he do something like that? It could be anyone who's linked to all of this."

"This shit just keeps getting stranger and scarier." John thought he heard a noise to his right. "It's started to get colder as well …"

# Chapter Forty-Two

## 16th July, 2018

David had been walking up and down the farmyard, trying to keep awake and checking on the animals, making sure he didn't stray too far and keeping Benji and John in his sight. By midnight, John had fallen asleep in his chair. David let him be for a bit, even though it was supposed to be John's watch. Benji, who was sound asleep at John's feet, twitched his ears and opened his eyes as David sat down.

David was starting to feel tired. He pulled out his phone and looked again at the photo Emily had taken of them. He zoomed in on the person with the 'lightning' coming from their fingers. He still couldn't explain it. He put the phone back into the pocket of his tracksuit bottoms and sat there for a couple more minutes; his head was starting to drop as he struggled to remain awake. His eyes briefly closed as he fought the tiredness.

A noise stopped him from drifting off. He sat upright. It took a while to realise what he was hearing: *chanting*. He slowly got up from his seat. It seemed to be coming from deep within the forest, from behind the large barn where Gavin was sleeping. It was faint, but he could still make it out. He swallowed slowly, standing still. He wasn't sure what to do, so he woke John.

John groaned as he opened his eyes. "What?" he asked as he saw David standing over him, shaking his shoulder.

*"Listen!"* David hissed sharply, holding his index finger up.

John frowned, his neck feeling a little stiff.

They both listened.

"Is that … chanting?" John rubbed his neck as he got up.

David nodded.

They couldn't understand the words; it was either too far, or not in English, or both.

"It's coming from over there." David pointed behind the barn. "Different from when Gavin heard chanting and saw a fire over there." David pointed again, to the south this time.

"Shall we wake Gavin?"

*"Listen!"* David hissed again.

The chanting grew faster and louder. They could hear some moans and groans.

"Let's get on the barn roof and take a look!"

Before David could answer, John was already jogging over to the barn.

David followed.

It began to rain lightly. John propped the ladder against the side of the barn; it thudded as it hit the wood.

"I thought you didn't like heights?" David said as John climbed the ladder.

"I don't!" John replied, looking down at David. "I want to see what's going on, though. Hold the ladder, mate."

"Be careful!" David held the ladder steady and glanced over to check on Benji who had gone back to sleep. The ladder jarred in his hands slightly from the force of John climbing.

John stepped off the ladder and carefully climbed the sloping metal roof of the barn. His trainers slipped a little.

David couldn't see him. "John?" he called out as loud as he could whisper. "What can you see?"

John stood on top of the barn, just as the chanting ceased. The rain began to fall more heavily, so he started to make his way back down the ladder.

"What did you see?" David asked again as he held the ladder tight. His hands were getting cold.

John slowly descended, careful not to slip on the now wet metal rungs of the ladder. "Nothing. As soon as I reached the top, the chanting stopped. I couldn't see anything. No fire, nothing. Nothing but darkness." John jumped down missing the last six rungs.

"Like Gavin, then," David replied.

"Yep!"

"Like Gavin, what?" Gavin surprised them by suddenly appearing in the dim light at the side of the barn, holding his shotgun. "What are you boys doing?" he yawned.

*"Fucking, Jesus!"* John said. "You scared the shit out of me!"

"Sorry … I heard footsteps on the roof, so I came to see what was going on."

"We heard some chanting," David answered.

"Really? Did you see anything? A fire?"

"Negative," John replied.

"But I want to show you something." David pulled his phone out and showed Gavin the photo.

"That your girl?"

"Erm. Yeah. That's Emily. I wouldn't say she's 'my girl,' though."

"Not yet!" John winked.

"Ah. That's a lovely looking lass! I've seen her in the pub. Cute little thing." Gavin smiled.

"Yeah, she is. But look at this ..." David showed Gavin the raincoat-clad figure, then the sparking fingertips in the reverse-colour photo.

"Strange ... I can't explain that."

"It's fucked up, that's what it is," John remarked.

"Good Lord. There really is some crazy shit happening of late," Gavin replied.

"That's an understatement," David said. "What do you want to do now? You want to go back to sleep for a bit?"

Gavin sighed. "Nah. I'm up now. I probably won't get off again. You boys can have some sleep, if you want. You can go back inside. Don't worry about sleeping in the barn. There's only one mattress there."

"I'm not sure it's safe you being out here on your own, Gavin. Shotgun or not."

Gavin understood David's concerns. He smiled. "Don't worry about me. If anything happens, I'll fire off a round or two. That will wake you!" Gavin could see the two boys were tired and he wasn't afraid.

Eventually, David relented. He fetched Benji and he trundled back to the house.

John decided to stay out with Gavin. He would feel bad for leaving him, especially when he offered to help during the night. He insisted.

# Chapter Forty-Three

## 16th July, 2018

It was quite early when Bob opened his eyes, feeling refreshed after a much welcomed, good night of sleep. He stretched his arms and checked the alarm clock on his bedside table. It had just gone eight. He looked over at Betty, who was still sleeping in her blue sleep mask. It was good to see her more back to her normal self after the hospital. Although he felt a little guilty for not telling her everything, he believed it was for the best for her well-being.

He yawned and climbed out of bed, in only his flimsy vest and pyjama bottoms. The two cats were stirring from their slumber at the bottom of the bed. He tutted to get their attention, feeling sorry for them missing their companion, Daisy. He made his way to the bathroom.

Downstairs, he made himself some toast and glanced at the buckets of apples that John and David had gathered a few days earlier. He planned to make some home-made cider and would do it soon. Glancing out of the window, he could see it was another nice morning. He removed the board he had set against the cat flap to prevent the cats from going out in the night. Josie, the tortoiseshell cat, trotted into the kitchen, closely followed by Sammy, the chubby black Tom, with his tail up. Bob poured some biscuits into their bowls and the cats ate passionately. Sammy, the greediest, lapped up the extra biscuits which had spilled onto the floor.

"Morning, boss!" Gavin said, coming in and taking off his tartan flat cap. He gave his dark hair a ruffle and placed his cap on the kitchen table. He yawned widely, revealing fillings in his back teeth. "Has the kettle just boiled? I could really do with some tea … Derek and Jack have just got in."

"Just boiled. Was everything okay in the night?"

Gavin told Bob about the chanting David and John had heard and the photo David had shown him. The two sat at the kitchen table eating breakfast together.

*****

Bob went to his study to do some paperwork, but was interrupted by a call. "Hello?" he said cautiously.

There was interference on the line and a brief pause before the answer came. "Hello?" the voice said.

"Hello?" Bob repeated.

"Is this Robert?" the caller asked.

"Yes?"

"This is Carl. *Carl Graham*. You left me a message on my phone the other day. I'm just returning your call. You said it was important?"

It took Bob a few seconds to recall who Carl was. "Oh. Right, yes!" he replied, putting a hand to his head. "I'm sorry. I was miles away."

"That's okay … how can I help?" Carl sounded English and quite well spoken.

Bob felt flustered; his mind went blank and he didn't know how to start to explain everything.

"Are you still there?" Carl asked as the silence stretched.

"Sorry, I'm still here, yes … Erm. It's a bit hard to explain over the phone. But, erm, you're an ecologist, right?" Bob asked, clearing his throat.

"That's correct."

Bob sensed that Carl was friendly, although he sounded a little abrupt, which made him feel awkward. Not having expected the call, Bob felt unprepared. A draft came from behind him as the study door opened and Sammy came in. Bob swivelled on the leather chair, moving the casters across the carpet to close the door, and then slid back to the desk.

Sammy jumped onto the desk, purring, and rubbed his head on Bob's hand affectionately as he held the phone. The cat tried to play with the cord of the receiver, so Bob gently pushed him away.

"I was just wondering what you could tell me about Rothiemurchus Forest?" Bob asked.

"What would you like to know? Didn't you say you had a farm in the forest? You probably know more than me about the area!" Carl laughed.

Bob felt patronised and he didn't like it, so he dived in to ask what he wanted to know. "Okay. Basically, some strange things have been happening around here of late. This is going to sound stupid, but we're looking for information. Well, *explanations*."

"What kind of things?"

"It's pretty awkward to explain over the phone. Plus, this interference makes it so hard to hear you. It's got worse since we started the call."

"Yes. I can hear it too, but what sort of things have been happening?" Carl asked again calmly.

Bob breathed out, blowing inadvertently onto Sammy's black fur as he sat purring in the loaf position. "Unexplainable things," Bob answered. "This is going to sound crazy, but possibly *supernatural* things." Bob didn't want to go into too much detail over the phone. He felt silly. Plus, he didn't know whether anyone was listening. He was especially nervous after what had happened last time he was on the phone.

This time, it was Carl's turn to be silent.

"Are you there?" Bob asked.

"I am. Sorry. It's probably best if we speak in person. You can explain in more detail then. Can you meet me this afternoon, around two?"

"Erm. Sure. Where?"

"I'm staying in an old bed and breakfast in Tomatin. But I've recently rented out an office for my work, to have a little more privacy. It's not too far from the bed and breakfast." Carl cleared his throat.

"I can meet you there."

Carl Graham gave the office address, which Bob noted down. Bob knew of Tomatin.

"I'll be bringing my nephew and his friend too, if that's okay? They, erm ... they have evidence of things that *can't* be explained. They're the ones who have witnessed these things more than anyone."

Carl paused again. "I understand. Bring what you have. It's important that we meet. I don't wish to alarm you and I don't like to discuss much more over the phone. These people can listen in. You could be in grave danger."

The interference grew louder.

"*People*? What people?" Bob asked anxiously.

"Please, just meet me this afternoon. Goodbye." Carl ended the call abruptly.

Bob slowly replaced the receiver. He lowered his eyebrows. Betty entered making him jump in his seat, startling the cat.

"Bob? Sorry, love! I didn't mean to startle you. I know you're busy." Betty smiled. "But I was wondering if we could go into town? I fancy getting out of the house this morning."

"You're fine. You just made me jump." Bob smiled, rising from his chair.

Sammy jumped off the desk and ran past Betty.

"That's great you want to go out. The only thing is, I've got some things to do, and I have to pop out this afternoon. Just work-related."

"Oh," Betty responded disappointed.

"No matter. I can get Gavin to take you, if you like? We can cope without him this morning. He won't mind."

"That's good, yes. I don't mind going with Gavin."

"Just as long as you take your insulin this morning." Bob kissed her on the cheek.

"Already done it!" she replied, patting his behind.

*****

Bob checked on Jack and Derek and then waved Betty and Gavin off, just as David came down. "Morning, David. I've got some news; the ecologist phoned, Carl!"

"What did he say?" David was eager to hear.

"We didn't talk much because of the interference and Carl was worried about discussing too much over the phone. He said 'these people can listen in.' I told him we had these unexplained things happening here and he said we could be in danger. He wants us to meet him this afternoon, at two."

"So, we could be onto something?"

"We shouldn't get our hopes up too much. We'll have to see. I told him that you have photos we could show him."

"This could be a start. Do you think we can trust him?"

"What choice do we have? Something or someone has been slaughtering my animals. Angus' animals, too. I'm sure we're not the only ones. Not to mention the other weird things going on."

"Not much choice about what?" John joined them, wearing only his pale pink boxer shorts.

"We're meeting the ecologist this afternoon!" David told him.

"Really?" John said.

"I haven't told Betty this, by the way. I don't want her to relapse."

"You're doing the right thing, Uncle; don't feel badly about it. We'll see what this Carl has to say, first."

Bob smiled at David.

"I wonder if we can trust him?" John pondered aloud. "Better bring your shotgun, just in case! What about Gavin; was he okay after I left him? He sent me up to bed not long before the sun came up."

"Gavin's fine ... I'll get him to join us as well, just in case we do get into any trouble! He may be a bit of a friendly giant, but no one in their right mind would mess with him. Besides, it's best he knows what's going on. Jack and Derek will be fine on their own. We can fill them in later."

*****

Whilst John was in the shower, David showed Bob the photo that Emily had taken.

"Just when you thought things couldn't get any stranger, eh?" Bob said as they stood out the back.

"Just coming in for a drink of water," Jack interrupted them.

Bob smiled.

"You're all right then, mate? Didn't go fishing!" David asked.

Jack gulped a full glass of water in one go before replying, "Nae. That Anthony couldn't make it as I said, aye. But I wouldn't have gone, anyway."

"Well, you made the right choice," Bob said. "Listen, Jack … we've got an important meeting this afternoon with this ecologist, so you and Derek will need to hold the fort until we get back. Don't mention anything to Betty; don't want her worrying."

"Aye. Nae worries!" Jack poured himself another glass of water and stood at the kitchen sink. "Where ye meeting this fella?"

"Tomatin," Bob answered.

"Aye. I know the place," Jack replied and gulped down his second glass of water. Some drips flowed down his chin, which he wiped away with his hand. "Well, best get back to work."

"He's kind of blasé about everything, isn't he?" David commented.

"I think he still thinks this is some kind of a sick joke being played on us all."

*****

"Well, would you look at that." John smiled as the three of them and Benji got inside Bob's Land Rover.

David sat in the front and John in the back with Benji.

Bob decided it would be best for Gavin to stay back at the farm, just to be safe, as he was still worried about Betty. He was also concerned at leaving just Jack and Derek by themselves, in case anything happened. Bob put his shotgun in the boot, although he didn't have any intention of using it.

"Look at what?" David asked, fastening his seatbelt.

"Ha!" John said. "That Annabel has finally got back to me. About fucking time! Maybe she isn't a bitch after all," he joked.

David tried to smile, but his mind was on their forthcoming meeting. He was already a little nervous. In fact, they all were. He had been texting Emily on and off all morning. He said he was busy this afternoon. "What does she have to say?"

"Sorry for not messaging sooner … and she wants to meet up tomorrow evening."

"That's all right, then."

"Yeah."

"What does she want to do?"

"I'm asking her now." John texted back.

Bob started up the old Land Rover. Betty stood outside the farmhouse waving them off. Bob waved back, feeling guilty for keeping her in the dark, but also finding it a little odd that she hadn't asked where they were all heading off to. He had told her he was going to show the boys around the area some more.

"She wants to go bowling," John said and laughed.

"Bowling?" David asked.

"Yep!"

"When did you last go bowling? Is there even a bowling alley around these parts?"

"There's one. It's actually not long been open. It opened just before Christmas last year, if I recall," Bob replied from the driver's seat.

"It's a few years since I went bowling," John said. "I wasn't that bad, either! I had to wear these crappy bowling shoes. Not my style."

Bob laughed.

"I don't remember that?" David replied.

"Well, forgive *me* if I don't tell you everything! I'm sure I did, anyway?" John retorted sarcastically. "I went with that Greg."

David tried to remember who Greg was.

"You know, that other guy I sometimes hang out with? The one with the long hair … dyes it black?"

"Oh. *Him*. Yeah, I know. Bit of a cocky bastard. Likes to wear that long leather trench coat a lot."

"Yep. That's him. Annabel's going to let me know for sure tomorrow, after she's finished work. She'll probably cancel, knowing my luck."

"At least she got back to you. Emily said she was true to her word."

"Yeah, but it would have been nice had she messaged me sooner," John replied, putting his phone away.

They drove through the forest and the afternoon sun filtered through the trees.

*****

"It certainly looks a nice morning, again," Bob said.

"I just hope we aren't being set up," John said from the back. "At least you've brought your gun," John joked, looking in the boot.

"Yep. But I don't intend using it. It might act as a deterrent, if anything. Hopefully not even that." Bob looked back at them over his shoulder. "That's the Tomatin Distillery just there," Bob mentioned as they drove past the renowned distillery. "You can't beat their whisky." Bob smiled, looking over.

John and David read on the wall sign that the distillery had been established way back in 1897.

"Gavin loves their whisky, too. He asked me to stop off there on the way back so I can pick up a bottle." Bob grinned.

"If we're fortunate enough to get back," John muttered under his breath. Only David heard him.

The three were starting to feel a little anxious, now that they had arrived in Tomatin.

"It looks a nice little village," David said, looking about. "Though, quiet. Doesn't seem much to do here."

"Yeah, like where's the pubs?" John asked.

"I think there's one here," Bob replied, preoccupied.

They went past a few houses and a school, then a large bed and breakfast.

"That must be where Carl is staying." Bob checked the paper on which he had written the directions.

"She ain't bad!" John said, staring out of the window at a woman in her late thirties, pushing a pram with a small child.

The others looked to see who had caught his attention.

"There should be a turning just down here on the right. Then the offices should be a little further down on the left. Just past a newsagent," Bob stated, slowing down a fraction as he saw the turning.

The small block of offices came into sight, with a white and green *To Let* sign at the front. A fire escape with metal steps came down from the left at the top. The car park was practically empty apart from a couple of cars. Bob parked up.

"Well, it seems all right so far," David said, opening the door and putting one of his legs out onto the concrete below.

"Unless they're waiting to ambush us inside," John said.

A helicopter flew over them as they all piled out of the Land Rover.

"Leaving your gun eh, Bob?" John asked.

"I can't exactly walk into an office block with it. Might give the wrong impression!" Bob tried to laugh to ease the tension.

"It might give the *right* impression. It might be too late, once we're inside," John replied.

David was quiet.

"You all right?" John asked.

"Yeah. Just a little worried. Not so much about whether we can trust this guy, but about what he knows." David looked up at the office windows.

"I know what you mean," John replied.

"Well, let's go inside and find out," Bob said, making his way to the entrance.

The others followed behind, along with Benji.

"It doesn't look like anybody else is about. I can't hear anyone," John said as they climbed the stairs. "Not always a good sign," he added, holding on to a red plastic railing.

"I think we'll be fine," Bob said. "I've got a hunch he's genuine."

They could smell a faint hint of tobacco as they stopped on the dark blue carpeted hallway. They heard someone sneeze in one of the offices to their left. All the doors were closed. They then walked slowly down.

"This is his office, I think," Bob said quietly as they stood outside the door.

The smell of cherry tobacco was now strong.

"I may as well knock," Bob whispered.

"Here we go," John joked nervously as Bob held his fist up for a second and gave two firm knocks.

A couple of coughs came from inside the office.

"Come in; it's open," said the voice.

Bob slowly pulled down on the silver door handle and gently opened the door. The smell of cherry tobacco grew stronger as the door opened.

The three men and a dog stood in the doorway. A man in his fifties with dark and grey hair with a neat side parting, stood over a desk leaning on his hands, reading from a folder and smoking a pipe.

He looked up, took the pipe from his mouth and checked a gold watch on his left wrist before speaking to them. "Ah. You must be Robert. I'm Carl. Come in. Please." Carl gestured them into his office. "We have *much* to discuss."

The office itself, although large, was quite bland with a plywood desk situated in the middle. There was a small bookcase stacked with numerous books to the right, flush against the wall. An oversized book stuck out: *Natural Wonders of the Earth*. A small fan was fixed to the ceiling. A framed ecologist certificate hung on the wall and in the corner stood a water dispenser.

"Please, sit. Sorry, there are only two chairs." Carl smiled, motioning to the two plastic chairs in front of his desk. He sat in a large brown, leather swivel chair.

The three of them, still wary, checked around the room as though it might be a trap.

Carl could sense their tension and was feeling cautious himself.

Bob and David sat and Carl wafted some of the smoke from his pipe away, then tapped the remaining tobacco out of his pipe into an ashtray. He picked a plastic cup up from his desk, poured water onto the smouldering tobacco and then dropped the cup into a small bin underneath his desk.

"It is okay to bring my dog in here?" David checked.

"Of course. I'm staying in a bed and breakfast, but I'm here on business. I wanted to have a little more privacy for my work, so I found this office ... You'll have to excuse the smoke. We're not supposed to smoke in here. But a few of us do, and nobody has complained, yet." Carl gave a smile and walked over to open the window. "I can tell from the looks on your faces that you're worried."

Bob and David glanced at each other.

"I wish I could say that there's nothing to worry about, but I'm not going to lie to you. There's a lot of awful things happening and it's only going to get worse. I know you don't know me from Adam, but you *can* trust me. I hope I can trust you all as well." Carl sat back down on his swivel chair. "Anyway, I'm Carl Graham." He reached out to shake Bob's hand and then David's, followed by John's.

"This is my nephew, David, who I mentioned over the phone and his friend, John," Bob introduced his entourage.

Carl sighed. "Before we get down to things, without boring you with too many details, I'll explain what I do."

John looked at the closed office door, still feeling a little nervous and half expecting Melissa and Anthony to suddenly barge in, along with Harold.

"Basically, I've been an ecologist for over thirty years now; forestry ecology is my main field. My job is to study the environment and relationships between animals and wildlife in areas, such as forests and woodlands. I get sent to various places around the UK and even abroad occasionally. I shan't bore you with the *precise* details. I know that's not why you're here." Carl laughed, trying to ease the tension.

"I've lived in Scotland for five years now. I used to live in Aberdeen. Well, technically speaking, I sort of still do. My wife's living in our house, there. *My* house! The job has put a strain on my marriage, along with other things. The wife was never too happy with moving up here from down south — we used to live in Bedfordshire.

"Sorry, I digress! Anyway, for the past year, my company asked me to focus on the Rothiemurchus area. I have to handle other projects, too. Danny, my brother-in-law, as you know, happens to work for the forest rangers up here, so he's been informing me about certain things regarding the animals. However, we don't speak too much. I think he blames me for the marriage difficulties. Perhaps, he's right!

"There have been reports of animal and wildlife mutilations inside the forest and others around here. People claiming their beloved pets have gone missing and some have been found horrifically mutilated: cats with their heads cut off, gutted and being left on the doorstep. Gruesome things like that and *much* worse ... but it's really hard to know where to begin. Perhaps, it would be better if you started? Tell me about what you've experienced. Did you say you had evidence of some sort?"

The others looked at each other.

"Try to tell me everything, no matter how crazy it sounds." Carl had a serious look on his clean-cut face. He rested his elbows on the desk and clasped his hands together.

Bob let out a sigh. "You're right. It's *really* hard to know where to begin ... It started a few weeks ago on my farm." Bob swallowed before continuing. "We've been hearing strange whispers, things have been going missing, animals have been killed and mutilated, and my poor cat." Bob hung his head.

"I'm sorry. I know it's not much consolation, but you're not the only one."

"I know. Another friend of mine, who's also a farmer, Angus, he's had similar things happen. He's moving his animals to a safe location. I've considered doing the same. But for now, we're taking it in turns to keep watch during the night. We haven't had too much sleep of late," Bob explained.

"That's sensible. I know it must be tough on you. But let's start from the beginning, and why you ended up contacting me ... I'm going to record our conversation for reference. It also saves me from writing everything down.

Don't worry. Speak *freely*." Carl pulled out an old cassette tape recorder, ready to record.

*****

It took a while for Bob and the other two to explain everything. They showed Carl the photos and notes and once they had started, they couldn't stop.

Carl barely said a word. He just sat taking it all in, listening intently. When they had finished, he got up and looked out of his office window with his back to them and his arms crossed. He stood in silence. His light blue, short-sleeved shirt was tucked into his beige pleated trousers.

Again, the others looked at each other.

"I can't explain everything, but we do have possible theories and some answers. You asked me, Robert, why these things are happening now. Or why they seem to have become worse of late. Well, like with that poor boy, Charlie ... the fact is, that these things have been happening for *many* years now. It's just that you don't hear about them, or they're not always documented. The forest is several miles across. You're pretty much bang in the middle of it. But as the forest is so big, it's basically very difficult to know about everything and everyone that has gone missing.

"But for you to know truly what you're up against, it's best if I start from the *very* beginning. I'd appreciate it if you held any questions until after I've finished." Carl turned to face them again and then walked back to his desk. He stood over his chair, looking at the three of them and at the notes of warning. He breathed in, and then began telling what he knew.

"I'm not sure if you've ever heard of the Grey Man of Ben Macdui? It's basically Scotland's answer to Bigfoot. There have been many stories over the years of sightings by climbers on Ben Macdui; it's the highest peak of the Cairngorms. Of course, people write this off as myth and fabrication, like all sorts of stories and folklore fabricated to scare people. But, what if I told you that this *Grey Man* exists, but not in the way people might expect?"

The three of them sat there, looking puzzled. They knew nothing of a 'Grey Man' in Scotland. They waited for Carl to continue.

"*Am Fear Liath Mór*, which is the Scottish Gaelic term for the Big Grey Man, first came about in the 1800s, when a scientist and enthusiastic climber, John Norman Collie, had a frightening encounter. Since Collie's account, there have been other reports, but this is what he said himself, about his experience ..." Carl pulled out a sheet of paper from his folder. He read out the climber's report and then showed the three for themselves:

> *I was returning from the cairn on the summit in a mist when I began to think I heard something else than merely the noise of my own footsteps. A strange sensation washed over me, a static like feeling enveloped me.*
>
> *For every few steps I heard a crunch, and then another crunch as if someone was walking after me but taking steps three or four times the length of my own. I said to myself this is all nonsense. I listened and heard it again but could see nothing in the mist. As I walked on and the eerie crunch sounded behind me, I was seized with terror and took to my heels, staggering blindly among the boulders for four or five miles nearly down to Rothiemurchus Forest. Whatever you make of it I do not know, but there is something very queer about the top of Ben Macdui and I will not go back there myself, I know.*

"There have been many other reports from people claiming to have witnessed hearing or seeing something. Many are lies, complete fabrications, or people just being paranoid. One climber even claimed to have shot at some creature with his revolver. I'm sure you can Google online and find similar accounts. Some have even drawn what they believe to be the Grey Man, like here ..." Carl pulled out another couple of sheets of paper with drawings on them and a few blurry copies of black and white photographs.

Some were artists impressions of what the Grey Man supposedly looked like from eyewitness accounts. Most looked similar to illustrations of Bigfoot. One difference though, was the grey hair this creature was meant to have. There were claims that the monster was at least ten feet tall. Some had reported seeing fangs.

Carl laughed as he pointed at one of the drawings where the Grey Man wore a top hat.

The others didn't laugh.

"These drawings aren't what this Grey Man looks like. Even the photographs are fakes; they've been checked professionally." Carl pushed the papers to one side. "But this ... *this* is what the Grey Man looks like." Carl whipped out yet another piece of paper and showed the three men. "To a certain extent ..."

David turned to John behind him who was breathing heavily over his left shoulder. They were both shocked. For on the piece of paper were some drawings, including three coloured photographs paperclipped together. They were of a hooded figure wearing a black cloak. One of the photos was a little blurry, but you could still make out its grey and jagged hands with black talons or claws. It was hovering above the ground without feet and the face couldn't be seen.

"No fucking way," John whispered, looking up at Carl.

Carl gave a slight nod of understanding. "I do believe this is the *same* entity you encountered on the motorway up here. And possibly in your homes back south. No doubt behind your experiences on the farm, too."

The three felt a cold shiver. This was the first time Bob had been able to visualise the entity David and John had spoken of. And of course, Eric.

Carl cleared his throat before continuing. "I know you're eager to ask me questions but please, bear with me ... Other people down the years, have claimed to have seen a cloaked figure disappear behind trees, or a slight glimmer of something resembling that of a cloaked figure in the Rothiemurchus Forest or near to Ben Macdui. Some say it glided above the ground. Some could see a greyish colour on its feet and hands. Or they saw just a greyish shadow. Even grey and white hairs have been found ... There are some conflicting stories, for sure. But this is no Bigfoot or man. This, quite simply put, is a *demon* ... an evil and malevolent entity."

Although they had expected it to be a demon, the three of them were spooked to hear Carl say it.

"Believe me, I doubted this at first. I couldn't believe this was real." Carl swallowed; he looked a little unnerved himself now.

The others looked straight at him.

Carl tapped on the photograph that showed the hands. "This particular photograph was taken by *Marvin Aileanach* in October 1999. Your reporter you queried about."

David started breathing heavily.

"Marvin was researching disappearances in the forest. After Charlie Begsbie had disappeared, he wanted to investigate further stories of Rothiemurchus Forest, prior to his untimely death. He took this photo one afternoon." Carl let the others take in this information and process it, before continuing. He got up briefly and sprayed a plant before returning to his desk.

"That night in early January 2000, he was working late and due to meet one of my colleagues. I was working in Canada at the time. Anyway, my colleague, Scott McGuinness, was to meet him in a pub. It was unofficial. Scott wasn't assigned to be up here. Marvin had contacted him a couple of weeks prior. The pub was less than a ten-minute walk from the office.

"After almost an hour of waiting, as the pub was about to shut anyway,

Scott decided to walk to the newspaper's office to see if Marvin was still there. That was where Scott found him … He'd supposedly slipped and cracked his head open. Scott was shocked, of course. He checked Marvin's pulse and he was already dead, or so he thought. Scott noticed a folder on the ground next to Marvin's body, so he took it. He assumed it was what Marvin wanted to show him. He then heard some whispering and laughter. Underneath a dimming streetlamp, he saw this *thing*, hovering there in a hooded cloak, with its abnormal hands and talons. He could see these talons or claws, extend."

"Jesus." John stood and stared.

"Having no signal on his mobile, he found a phone box, but couldn't get through to the emergency services nor police: the line was dead. He eventually got through to the police from another phone box. They asked him to come down to the station in the morning and said they would send an officer and an ambulance to collect Marvin that night. He also heard laughter in the background over the call … Scott was so terrified, he rushed home.

"In the morning, the police were nonchalant about it all, and certainly didn't believe the story about what he'd seen. Scott decided not to show them the folder. He said that something appeared 'off' with the police officers."

"So *that's* what happened to the file, then?" David said. "But it still doesn't make sense. This woman who came across Marvin said there was no folder and that he was *still* alive. He mentioned hearing these whispers … I guess she found Marvin *after* Scott, and he *wasn't* dead when Scott saw him?"

Carl breathed in deeply and exhaled. "You're right. Marvin *wasn't* dead when Scott left him. Apparently, his pulse was weak, due to the cold weather and his head injury. Scott always felt terrible about that; he would have returned if he'd known, in spite of this *thing*. Scott found out about all of this afterwards.

"The woman also called an ambulance and had no problems getting through, but unfortunately, Marvin succumbed to his injury." Carl bowed his head a little. "The police obviously never sent an ambulance that night, although they had told Scott they would."

"And this is how you got Marvin's photo, from your colleague?" Bob asked curiously.

Carl looked at him. "Scott? No … he was overcome by guilt. He blamed himself for Marvin's passing because he waited too long for him in the pub. If he'd gone to the office sooner, Marvin might have been okay. He also blamed himself for failing to find Marvin's pulse and then not going back and rechecking it … he felt ashamed that he'd rushed away in fear." Carl lowered his head again.

"What happened?" John asked.

"A week later, Scott took his own life. He sliced his wrists in the bath one night." Carl shook his head, remembering.

"I'm so sorry," Bob said. "That's terrible."

"It's okay. I wouldn't say we were close, but we got on. Anyway, his wife, Phoebe, contacted me a fair while after … *Eight* years later in fact! She was going through some of her husband's things one morning and she came across a large envelope with my name on it. It had a brief note saying if anything happened to him, it should be given to me. She'd been too grief-stricken to go through all of his belongings earlier and had never paid much attention to his paperwork.

"Inside were some information, which I'll get to, and some photos, including this one here." Carl tapped on the photo again. "Not long after, I was officially sent up here to investigate the area that Scott had been looking at unofficially. Animals were still being mutilated. Other things were happening that the police were reluctant to investigate or didn't have an answer to.

"I've been up here for a quite some time now, in Scotland. With all my other commitments, the work's certainly taken its toll on me. It's been stressful. I mean, look at my hair! I didn't have any grey before." Carl laughed, pointing to his head.

"The thing is, I was taken off researching Rothiemurchus and the surrounding area after just a couple of months. In fact, less than that, much to my annoyance. Another tinpot company had taken over, and I was assigned elsewhere, including abroad at times. But I still felt as if I owed it to Scott, and even Marvin, to investigate, and not least, because I was curious! But I was scared and I still am. Even more so, now. Back then, I had no leads and no one to turn to or trust. So, I let things be.

"At the time, I hadn't really come across too much myself, apart from a few strange markings carved into trees, like symbols, things like that. I always felt someone or *something* was watching me, though. I also came across some mutilated animals … My boss, also thought the photos Scott left were fake. He never really believed the other reports, neither.

"Then, just over a year ago, we got a new boss. Some people contacted us about some animal remains, saying the police weren't doing much about it and there were reports of fires in the forest. We also had a new guy, *Brad*, a weird looking bloke! I met him a couple of times. He seemed strange, quiet. Anyway, he was sent up to investigate part of Scotland and of course,

Rothiemurchus. He claimed that everything was fine. Then, after a couple of months, he rung our manager saying that he'd found another job and wasn't coming back, so the investigation soon fell to me. After all those years!"

Carl pulled out another sheet of paper with more photographs on it. "These are some photos taken over the years of hoof prints that people believe belong to the Grey Man. In some photos, it has four legs. But again, this isn't correct ... These photos are what this *thing's* feet look like." Carl showed on the paper, a couple of photos of some abnormal footprints in snow. They were practically the same as those John, David and Bob had seen in the mud, although smaller.

"These photos were taken in 1998 by someone out walking their dog in Rothiemurchus Forest. They enjoyed taking photos of the scenery. Scott tried to follow up with this guy, but unfortunately, he was long dead from a stroke." Carl then showed another photograph. "Look at the footprints in this photo. They're a fair bit bigger ... I took this photo last winter, in December snow. Look at how much bigger they are." Carl compared the sizes in each photo with those on the mobile phones. "It's basically grown!" Carl stated.

Carl offered everyone a drink, but they were fine for now. He had one himself from the water dispenser, before walking back over to his desk.

"There's been a cult around here for many years, now. A Satanic one. Evil. They call themselves The Acolytes of The Grey One ... or, in their more preferred terminology, in Latin form, *Famuli Cani* ... They have been slaughtering and mutilating your animals. They are also responsible for the disappearances of children and others. This has been happening for *many* years ... for the past few years or so, things have been getting worse. Their evil is getting stronger; hence the increase in the feet size. I was assigned up here because wildlife has been sacrificed and mutilated in and around the forest. Remember, you said you saw that evil and twisted looking tree, David? And the inverted pentagram of animal bones? These are prime examples of their work.

"We don't yet know how many there are of them in this cult. They kill animals and murder people, usually torturing them first for their own sick and twisted pleasures and agendas. The demon *encourages* them and feeds off energy from the souls of the dead. Good-hearted people, animals and particularly children's souls, give the entity and its followers more power and potential for growth. The more innocent, the *stronger* the sacrifice." Carl drank some more water.

The three of them listened with their mouths open. They weren't sure what they expected but hearing this was terrifying.

"We believe that the whispers you've been hearing are not only of this demon, but are also from the trapped spirits of its victims, including young children, who have been sacrificed down the years. You see, this demon has a hold on their souls. They are bound to it and vice versa. They can't cross over whilst this entity has a hold over them. We also believe that the demon mimics its victims, making child-like noises. That's possibly what happened to you two, under the apple tree."

John and David looked at one another with fear in their eyes as Carl singled them out.

"As for the interference, that static you've been hearing, you aren't alone experiencing that. It's the energy of the spirits and of the cult interrupting the signal. Sometimes it can be strong, sometimes it's weak or missing altogether. Sometimes, the static is caused by the entity being near. It's usually more in and around Rothiemurchus Forest. But it's more consistent and stronger, the further into the forest you go. Particularly, of late." Carl finished his plastic cup of water and threw it in the bin. He cleared his throat again.

"I know it's a hell of a lot to take in! The cult initially started out sometime in the $14^{th}$ century. We are looking into how and why it began. Some cults form from bad people trying to worship the Devil, making sacrifices and/or using ouija boards and things like that. People start to join them, forming a cult and making an oath, a blood oath."

"Jesus. This is *too* much," John said, shaking his head.

"I know it's difficult. I had a hard time taking it all in too, believe me! They believe they are appeasing Satan and this Grey One. They get joy out of seeing an innocent animal or human suffer and being tortured. They believe that the more they worship Satan and his demons, the more they will get what they want in return. Some might sacrifice an animal, or even a human to get rich. It can start off small. It can begin with a dog, a cat, a chicken. Even a rat!"

David felt saddened at the thought of innocent children being tortured and murdered. It was cold blooded murder. And also, defenceless animals. He leant down and stroked Benji. As he did so, he noticed a black laptop bag lent up against the desk.

"These Satanists believe that the more they sacrifice, the more they get. So, they turn to bigger things ... sacrificing humans, *babies* even. They'd sacrifice a baby even whilst it was still in the womb. They consider abortion a sacrifice to their God."

There was silence for a few seconds.

"This cult first summoned this demon many centuries ago. Most likely using sacrifices and dark magic to conjure it. It's possible that they did this on Ben Macdui during a celestial alignment."

"Sorry, but you keep saying *we*. Who do you mean, exactly?" David frowned.

Carl smiled. "I'm working with a demonologist I met last year, Arthur. He filled me in with all this stuff."

It was beginning to get a little warmer in the office. Carl got up and flicked a switch on the wall next to the door and the ceiling fan whorled into life.

"In the 14$^{th}$ century, there was a fierce warrior who was chief of the Clan Shaw. Well, back then, it was the Shaw branch of the greater Mackintosh family. He went by several names. But the most common were *Seath Mór* or *Shaw Mór*. Or just *Sgorfhiaclach*, which means 'bucktooth.' He fought in The Battle of the North Inch, also known as The Battle of the Clans, where he fought for victory at Perth in 1396. Clan Chattan were the victors.

"He died in 1406 and his grave lies in the Doune of the churchyard of the old Rothiemurchus Parish Church. The Shaws have much history across the centuries in this area and are a *very* respected clan. It's all online, and if you are interested, you can research for yourselves ... but what you *won't* find, is how they fought this cult and demon, stopping them for several hundred years. Their success was led by *Seath Mór*."

Carl's audience turned to look at each other.

"The information we have is still limited and a little sketchy, I'm afraid."

"If this is true, with people being sacrificed ... surely people, the police and the media would know about it?" Bob asked, scratching the crown of his head.

Carl let out a forceful sigh. "There are possibly a *lot* of people involved in this cult. These people can come from all walks of life, from the police, lawyers, judges, the media, freemasons, influential business people, even *priests*. They help cover it up. Even the supposed 'Holy Men of God.' Most of the time, they cover their tracks well. If something comes out, they use their power and resources to cover it up. And when I say power, I don't necessarily mean in a supernatural sense, but simply through their authority in society.

"They may leave traces. For example, people, such as your good selves, hear chanting and see fires, but again, reports come out that it's just arsonists or druggies. Anything reported about the cult is made to sound like they are just crazy people on drugs doing weird things. When people report their animals being slaughtered, it's played down.

"We also believe that the cult *wants* people to see and hear things, to frighten them. So, they sometimes reveal themselves deliberately. Sightings have been reported for years. People don't believe it and just write it off as myths and folklore, like the Loch Ness Monster. When people *do* investigate, they usually end up vanishing or dead, like Marvin ... That's why I tend to keep my head low, if I can help it." Carl could feel his mouth and throat begin to dry up again.

"I have to be careful; they no doubt already know about me ... I honestly hope that we can trust each other. These people are humans like you and I, but can possess unnatural powers, having dabbled in the occult and black arts, although their power still has its limitations."

A cool chill flowed from above as the ceiling fan spun around over them, slightly lifting sheets of paper on Carl's desk.

"Seath Mór, ending the cult back then, also stopped the demon. With no one to make sacrifices, the entity lost its power from feeding on souls of the victims. We believe that this demon became dormant somewhat, before being resummoned. Or, it perhaps 'died' to a degree.

"John Collie's experience and account, we believe, was the first genuine and recorded encounter of this demon since the cult was stopped all those centuries ago. Collie stated that he never actually *saw* anything, but there have been sightings of a cloaked figure near Ben Macdui and the forest since. Until this demon returned fully again, it wasn't as strong. It had lost its power and was weak. It could only appear and manifest itself occasionally. These accounts of what people saw, were most likely your more basic apparitions and perhaps remnant residue sightings ... Arthur, knows more."

They heard someone outside in the hallway open and close a door.

"We believe this entity came back into full existence on the 1st March, 1996 ... *St Eichatadt Day.*"

"What day?" asked John, frowning.

"St Eichatadt Day is a day in the Satanic calendar involving blood rituals, where the blood of humans is drunk for vigour and strength, and to pay homage to demons. Once the cult ended, things were fine for many, many centuries. But around the mid-1990s, the cult and demon were reborn so to speak, most likely by the work of descendants of Famuli Cani ... discovering their ancestors' past."

"How do you and this Arthur know all these things?" Bob asked.

"One of the cult members came forward."

"They *what*?" David asked.

"He never gave his name but contacted Arthur some time last year."

"What made him come forward; wasn't it a risk to him?" David asked further.

"Yes. A fortnight later, he was found with his throat slit and his fingers and toes smashed. He had been tortured and executed. His body was found near the River Spey, north of Rothiemurchus. There was no media coverage." Carl shook his head in dismay. "He was frightened and wanted out, which considering what these sick people are like, is highly surprising. They are *very* selective as to who they take in."

"Why does the demon, wear a cloak?" John asked.

"I'm not sure. Arthur would probably know. He has been studying this cult for years now, trying to find out more about them. Other stories no doubt got lost down the years. Mixed in too, with the false accounts. The Grey Man name is in reference to its skin and hair. Our 'friend,' the now dead cult member, confirmed this." Carl scratched his lower back.

"Shit," John said and the others looked at him. "I remember at the service station, those prints on my car. I remember pulling off a few strands of grey hair from the window!"

"Arthur believes this cult has a hidden lair, where they perform their most horrific and special rituals. Unfortunately, the cult member never managed to disclose where this was."

"Why are *we* being targeted, like on the motorway on the way up here? After all, it's my uncle's house that's in the forest. Our own homes are way back down south!" David looked at Carl.

"I don't know. The demon and its cult obviously went out of their way to prevent you from coming up here. And it is strange that they revealed their powers. We've never had anyone experience this before. Well, not that's on record, anyway. They're obviously keeping you alive for now. That perhaps includes myself."

"Gee. Guess that makes us *special*, then," John said sarcastically.

"What about the dream I had?" David asked.

"An example of what powers they have. They wanted you to experience pain and suffer mentally: it's a form of black magic."

"If this demon has arms and legs, why have these two seen it hovering above the ground?" Bob asked, pointing at his nephew and John. "One of my workers, Eric, saw it gliding in the forest, too."

"Being a demon and a powerful entity, it can manifest itself pretty much as it likes. Like when you saw it in your flat, David, with your dog. You said you saw a flicker, or a shadow outside, then went back in and your lights started flickering and you heard a humming sound, but couldn't see anything, right?"

"Erm. Yeah. It was terrifying!" David answered.

"Basically, this entity can change from a solid figure, to just a shadow or even become invisible. Arthur also believes that this entity likes to feel human at times."

"What if what we experienced at home and on the way up here were different entities entirely?" John asked.

"I don't believe that is likely, John. Arthur has also experienced things, too."

"He's seen it as well?" Bob asked.

"Oh, yes. He's seen it in the forest. He believed that it was toying with him, *stalking* him there ... He's heard the chanting and smelt the burning fires during the cult's rituals. But he's never seen them, surprisingly! Like me, I've heard the same. But it's like whenever someone hears them chanting, or sees their fire, it suddenly stops. A fair few people have also mistaken optical illusions for the Grey Man." Carl pointed out a few pictures of this illusion. It was basically a circular rainbow and yellow halo, surrounding a blurry image of someone.

"I've seen this illusion a number of times myself. Not just up here in Scotland, but in other countries and places, too. Especially, on mountains and ridges and when misty. It is somewhat of a phenomenon but there's nothing supernatural about it. It's basically caused when the sun, or the light is behind you and projects your shadow through the clouds, distorting your shadow and image. The light hitting the water droplets forms the halo. Naturally, people think it's a spectre of some sort. But it's just a natural thing. In fact, this photo here, was one I took on Ben Macdui earlier this year." Carl smiled, showing another photo.

"Because most people who see the illusion are climbers, fatigue can add to their belief that it's something more sinister. Tiredness can do a lot to the mind and play tricks on it." Carl helped himself to another cup of cold water from the dispenser. "Oh, there's something else ..." Carl walked over to his bookcase and retrieved a book. He dropped it heavily on the desk, startling Benji, and turned to a page which had its corner folded over. He pointed out an extract and spun the book round so they could see:

*In a remote corner of Rothiemurchus Forest is the burial site of Seath Mór Sgorfhiaclach, a chief of the Clan Shaw, who was alive during the 14th century. Shaw had a reputation for being a formidable warrior, being well over six feet tall, with a twisted smile that struck terror into the hearts and souls of even his own followers. Over the centuries, people travelling through the forest have spoken of encounters with a gigantic figure challenging them to a battle. If they accepted his offer, then no harm would be done to them and the scary figure would disappear. But if anyone showed fear when they crossed paths with him, they would perish, never to be seen again.*

John and David both recognised the extract.

"We came across this last Monday evening, at my flat, when we were looking up the area on the internet," David added.

"That's right. God, that seems so long ago, now. And this is that Seath Mór guy, who took down the cult all those centuries back?"

"That's correct, John," Carl answered.

"Is this relevant in any way?" David asked.

"It's possible that it's just another myth … but there have been reports over the years of people claiming to have had encounters, much like that of the Grey Man. But certainly nothing in recent years. The jury is still out on this particular claim."

"Then why show us? You must have a theory?" John wondered.

Carl looked at John and swallowed. "Smart boy … It is just a theory. But Arthur, well, he thinks it could be possible that now the cult and its demon are back, so is the spirit of Seath Mór. Or that Seath Mór could never rest in peace, believing that *they* would return one day."

David looked at the page opposite the extract. It had more information about the Clan Shaw and some photos. It told about the history of the Shaws and their origin. It mentioned nothing about their fight with this Satanic cult, which he found strange.

Carl slammed the book shut, again startling Benji, who stared up at the desk. Carl walked over to the bookcase, replaced the book and sat back down to take another sip of his water.

"It seems strange that the cult is never mentioned in this clan's history?" David asked.

Before anyone could ask any more questions, the phone on Carl's desk rang. The group all looked at one another. Tension crept into the room as the phone continued to ring.

"Hello?" Carl answered. He breathed a sigh of relief and shut his eyes for a second.

The others could hear a man's voice on the phone.

"Sure ... Okay ... That's not a problem," Carl said as he pulled his wrist up to check the time. "Okay, I'll see you soon. Yep. Okay. Bye." Carl put the phone back down. "Listen, I have to meet someone and report back to him about my work. Nothing related to any of this. He's an impatient sod and wants to meet me in half an hour. Now, I know there's still many things you need to ask me, and I promise we'll talk again." He turned the tape recorder off, ejected the small tape and slipped it into his trouser pocket.

"I'm going to meet up with Arthur in a couple of days and pass on everything you've told me. I'll be in touch as soon as I can. Hopefully, our next meeting will be with Arthur. He can fill you in more."

"But what do we do now?" Bob asked concerned.

"Just keep doing what you're doing. Look after those animals and yourselves! *Don't* contact anybody else, and do *not* trust anybody! The chances are, they already know you're here. They have people, their minions, everywhere." Carl rose from his heavy leather chair and pushed it towards his desk. The chunky leather arms made contact with the desk. "If you could send me over the photos you have on your phones, that would be great. I'll take the notes too, if that's okay?"

"That's fine; it's not like we need them," David replied as he and John blue-toothed the photos over. There was a strange, black mark covering half the photo that John took of the creepy tree and the clearing, which hadn't been there before.

Carl walked over to his window and closed it. Back at his desk, he picked up the folder and scooped the papers back inside it. After turning off his ceiling fan, he politely showed the three of them out of his office and locked the door after them. "Probably a waste of time locking my office. I'm sure they could break in, if they wanted," he half-joked. "There isn't really anything they'd be interested in there, anyway. It's in here and elsewhere." Carl patted his folder and tucked it under his arm.

# Chapter Forty-Four

## 16th July, 2018

"Well, he left pretty sharpish in his posh red Audi, didn't he?" John commented as they all climbed back into the Land Rover.

"That he did," Bob replied, putting his key in the ignition.

"You think we can trust him, Uncle? We never even got to discuss about that tree."

"What choice do we have? I believe we can. Maybe he is one of them, and he was feeling us out, trying to find out what we knew? But I think he's legit. What about you?"

"I think he's all right," David replied. "I'm just freaked out even more by all this."

"I suppose he confirmed what we already kind of knew, though. But sacrificing people, animals and even babies … what kind of human beings do this?" Bob shook head in disgust.

"Sick fucks, that's who!" John retorted.

"I think it's even more disconcerting that only John and I have encountered this demon. It didn't even wait for us to come up here to Scotland. It seemed pretty damn adamant it didn't want us up here," David said.

"I know, bud. Hopefully that demonologist guy, Arthur, can fill us in," John replied. He saw a man further down the road staring at them. He was wearing jeans, a black vest and a pair of sunglasses, and was smoking a cigarette. "Is it me, or is that guy staring at us?"

"Who?" David asked.

"Him, over there." John pointed as the others looked across at the man.

David checked the other way to see if the man was focusing on something else, but there was only them in his line of sight.

"I think he's looking at us," Bob said.

"What's his problem?" John asked.

"Could be one of them," David suggested.

John wound his window down, leaned his head out and stared back at the man. "You all right, mate?"

The man said nothing. He stared for a few more seconds, before flicking his cigarette out in front of him, releasing a few embers as though he was dismissing them. He then turned his back and cockily walked off, out of view.

"Fucking weirdo," John said, winding his window back up.

"Perhaps it was one of them spying on us?" Bob said.

"Maybe we should go ask him?" John suggested.

"No. Let's leave it. The last thing we want is to piss them off even more," David replied.

"David's right," Bob said, turning his engine on. "I think it's best to get back to the farm. See if everyone is okay!"

*****

Bob had stopped off at the old Tomatin Distillery to pick up a bottle of their finest whisky for Gavin, before returning to the farm.

Betty was outside at the front of the house, watering the pink hydrangea as they walked round. "You're back." She smiled.

Bob smiled back. "Has everything been okay? Everyone all right?"

"They're fine. I just made them a brew. The pot's still fresh, if you want one?" Betty finished off her watering.

"That sounds great," Bob replied, holding the boxed bottle of whisky.

"I'm going to go and water the back garden," Betty said.

"Okay, love."

Bob stood at the kitchen window watching Betty in the garden. He turned around, blowing on his hot tea, before taking a sip. He looked at the buckets of apples in the corner of the kitchen. "I think I'll mash some of those apples up, tomorrow. Make some of my cider." He smiled at David and John, trying to introduce a lighter tone. "You boys drink cider?"

"I can't say I've ever tried it," David replied.

"Me neither, actually. Usually shorts for me or a pint of beer," John answered.

"Well, you'll like my cider." Bob winked. "We're going to cut one or two of the fields this week, too. We normally do the barley towards the end of July."

"I wouldn't mind taking a spin in that combine of yours!" John grinned, making Bob laugh.

Gavin then came in through the front and into the kitchen. He was eager to hear about the meeting. "All right, guys? You're okay, then? I tried calling but couldn't get through. What did this Carl say?"

The others then filled him in on everything, trying to remember what they could from their meeting with Carl.

Gavin wasn't affected by most things, but this got to him.

*****

After Betty had cooked them all dinner, with a little help from Bob, she decided to take a long soak in the bath. The rest went to watch the TV and weather forecast.

"I guess Scotland does get hot days and heatwaves, then," John joked.

"Aye. That we do," said Bob. He was stroking Sammy who was sitting on his lap, purring.

"What about Jack, Gavin? Did he believe what Carl told us?" David asked.

Gavin was holding his bottle of whisky and took out a lowball glass from the cabinet. He blew in the glass, to clear any dust that had settled in there.

"I don't think you'll find much dust in my glasses." Bob smiled.

Gavin set the glass down. "Force of habit." He smirked and poured himself a generous shot. "I think Jack was a little freaked out to tell you the truth … he's starting to see that there's something seriously wrong, here."

"About time," John replied.

"Derek was shocked, too. I need some ice …" Gavin left for the kitchen.

"I hope we can meet with this Arthur, soon," David said.

"I hope so," Bob replied. "We still need more answers."

"You're sure you don't need me or John tonight?" David checked.

Bob smiled. "It's fine. You can stay up if you like, but we'll be okay. We'll have our two guns again, especially after what we've been told!"

Gavin returned holding three ice cubes in his right hand. He walked over to his whisky-filled glass and plopped them in. Two were stuck together. "Whisky's even better on the rocks," he claimed, rubbing his hand dry on his worn jeans. He shook his glass lightly and gave it a swirl, before letting the ice settle in his drink. "You sure you guys don't want any? It's a bloody good Scotch. *Strong*!"

"Actually, yes, pour me a glass," Bob replied.

"Yeah, sod it. I'm game. Make that three! May as well try it," John replied as Gavin reached into the cabinet and pulled out two more lowball glasses.

John choked as the whisky burnt his throat. "*Fuck me* ... that is strong."

Gavin grinned. "Told ya. I love it!"

Sammy suddenly leapt from Bob's lap, startled by something. He started to lick himself frantically.

"What's up with him?" John asked.

"He often gets like that. It's probably a flea. One minute he's sitting there all calm, then he suddenly jumps up," Bob replied.

"Do you treat them for fleas?" David asked.

"We do. They don't scratch as much. Poor Sammy; sometimes he loses some of his fur on top of his head, and it can get a bit scabby. Mites, apparently, according to our vet. Josie, on the other hand, is fine."

Gavin sat down. He moved his shotgun and propped it up against the armchair.

"Don't suppose you've ever shot anyone with that?" John smiled.

Bob laughed. "He's not in the army."

Gavin laughed too. "That's a negative. Although, sadly, I've had to put some animals down with it. One of which, was a calf, years ago, before I started working here. It was all caught up in some barbed wire fencing. The poor little mite was in pain, all tangled up."

"You couldn't rescue it?" David asked.

"I don't think so. It had obviously tried wriggling itself free, but at the same time, just got more and more entangled. The wire had dug in deeply and he'd lost a lot of blood. It was too difficult to free him, so I had to put the poor thing out of its misery. I felt really bad about it. There were other times as well. Had some cattle maimed by foxes and had to do the right thing then, too. Always tough." Gavin scratched the left side of his bearded cheekbone.

"Can imagine, mate," John replied.

"There wasn't a vet nearby, either. Though it wouldn't have made any difference," Gavin added, adjusting his flat cap.

*****

Gavin and Bob had relieved Jack and Derek earlier in the evening, whilst John and David continued to watch some TV, before going up for an early night.

John was looking forward to tomorrow evening and his first date with Annabel. He hoped she wouldn't cancel before then, but he was feeling optimistic. He went to lie on his bed and sent texts to Annabel and also to Grant.

He was still careful not to mention too much to Grant, similar to how Bob was towards Betty. Sammy and Josie were at the bottom of John's bed, stretched out.

David, also in his bedroom, was checking his emails on his laptop, and clearing out his junk folder. He rarely signed up for anything on the internet and yet he constantly received spam and porn emails. He was sure John had signed him up for some porn sites as a joke, although John always denied this with a wry smile. When finished with his emails, he thought he'd have a search on the internet about everything Carl had told them. Nothing came up about the cult or demon they were dealing with, which wasn't surprising. He only found the 'basic' information Carl had mentioned, such as about the Clan Shaw, the Grey Man and Seath Mór.

He then typed in 'Satanic cults.' A few mugshots were returned of convicted people, who had been charged for murder or assault for rituals they had performed. They claimed they had heard voices telling them to commit these foul acts. Numerous images came up of symbols, including Baphomet, the goat-headed figure, of which there were numerous illustrations and photos. He read a few articles about rituals and sacrifices. Some were allegedly true accounts of activities while others were more general, about what certain cults do, regarding their beliefs. David shuddered. The reality of what they had been experiencing with this secret cult frightened him.

His phone lit up with a message from Emily, asking if he wanted to meet up again soon. He wasn't sure what to reply, not wanting to risk involving her in everything that was going on. Before he answered, she sent a second text, joking about going bowling with John and Annabel, but then added that as it was their first date, they should let them go alone:

Lol. Yeah, it's probably best if they go on their own! x

What about dinner? :) x

Dinner? Maybe! x

I know a nice little Italian restaurant just outside Aviemore. It's not too far from my house, actually! x

We can do! Don't think I've ever had Italian food before! Well, apart from pizza and pasta, ha ha! x

It's really nice. I've been a few times. I took my mum there for her last birthday, and she did the same for my latest one. The staff are really friendly and the food is great. So what do you say? :) x

David hesitated for a moment.

> Okay, I'm sold! Why not? x
>
> Great! Do you want me to pick you up from your uncle's farm? I'm sure I can find it! x
>
> You don't have to do that. Maybe John could drop me off if he's meeting Annabel tomorrow evening? I'll check with him in the morning! :) x

They said goodnight to each other and David turned off his phone. Although worried for Emily's safety, he really wanted to meet with her and he could tell Emily was keen. He certainly didn't want her driving through the forest to meet him though. He stroked Benji, put his laptop on the floor and decided to get some sleep.

**17th July, 2018**

In the middle of the night, David woke and couldn't get back to sleep. The moon was shining brightly into his bedroom. He got out of bed and looked out of the window; he could see the moon light up the northern side of the forest. He wondered how his uncle and Gavin were getting on. As he watched, a strange mist slowly appeared and settled over the forest. It started to weave in and out of the trees. He could see parts of it twirl up and twist, as if dancing. David started to become nervous. This was unlike any mist he had seen before. There was something eery about it, the way it moved, the way it flowed. He briefly opened the window to see if it was windy out. There wasn't so much as a breeze.

Benji was half-lying on David's jeans, so he carefully pulled them out from underneath him, trying not to wake him. Benji let out a soft groan. David quickly got dressed and headed for the stairs, deciding not to wake John.

As he went down the first stair, he heard something from Betty's room. David froze. He listened in silence, staring at Betty and Bob's closed bedroom door. Nothing. He moved down another stair and heard another sound. He stopped again. It sounded like a laugh. There was a TV in the room, so perhaps she was up late watching something.

He waited a couple more minutes but there were no more sounds, so he rushed downstairs, forgetting to miss the 'noisy' stair. Outside, the still air felt cold. The moon was so bright, it was like someone was shining a torch down from the night sky.

An owl hooted as he made his way up towards the main barn. He couldn't see Bob or Gavin anywhere. There was no one in the barn. The mattress looked as though someone might have slept on it, but David was starting to feel a little worried, so he continued on up past the barn. The moon was illuminating the fields and pens, but he halted when he saw the mist, a twirling cloud of white and grey, in and around the trees, covering the forest in the moonlight.

The mist slowly spread down the other side of the forest to his left. The farm animals were now disturbed, making grunting noises. David turned, hearing a clambering sound from the top of the barn. Gavin was on top looking down. For a moment, they both startled one another.

"David?" Gavin said, looking down.

Bob appeared beside Gavin on the roof.

"What are you doing up?" Gavin asked.

"I woke and saw this strange mist. I came to warn you," David said worriedly.

"That's why we're up here. We heard the chanting. We couldn't tell which direction it was coming from. It's like it was coming from all over the forest," Bob said concerned.

"This mist is spreading all across the forest, although there's no wind." Gavin looked around.

"Maybe we should all get inside?" David suggested.

"I'm not leaving the animals on their own, David. Besides, I don't think this mist is coming away from the forest. It seems attached to it. It seems to be speeding up," Bob replied.

"What do you think it is?" David asked.

"Well, it's a mist of some sort, but it doesn't seem natural!" Bob answered. "I've never seen anything like it."

Bob and Gavin both stood for a while, watching the blanket of mist sweep across Rothiemurchus Forest, before they climbed back down the ladder.

"Bugger me, it's cold!" Gavin said, shivering as he and Bob joined David. "Even the animals seem unsettled by it. They're normally fast asleep by now."

"What time is it?" David asked.

Gavin looked at his watch under one of the farmyard lights. It flickered but he managed to make the time out: "Just gone twenty past two."

In less than a few minutes, the whole of the forest surrounding the farm was completely immersed in the mist.

Apart from the animals grunting restlessly in the yard, the night held an eery silence. The chanting restarted.

"It's hard to pinpoint exactly where it's coming from." Gavin checked around.

"It's like an echo." David wondered if the others could hear the tremble in his voice.

They could now clearly hear what was being chanted.

*"Cane! Cane!"*

Bob hung his shotgun over his right shoulder as the chanting turned to a distinctive moaning.

Suddenly, an unnatural roar emanated from deep inside the forest.

*"What the hell was that?"* Gavin asked.

"You think it's close?"

"I don't know, David," Bob replied, looking around cautiously. It was the first time he had heard the chanting.

The farmyard lights flickered, dimmed and returned to normal brightness.

"I really don't like this, Uncle."

"Me neither," Bob replied.

*"Cane! Cane! Cane!"* The chant grew louder and stopped precipitously. All became silent.

The three men looked at one another. The scream of a woman came from within the forest, followed by another roar.

*"Was that a woman?"* David asked, frantic now.

"I … I don't know. It sounded like it!" Bob replied.

The brightness of the moon was temporarily shut out by a passing cloud.

"We should go to check!" David suggested.

"You want to go into the forest at night with this mist, and *them* in there?" Gavin replied. "Besides, we don't know exactly where the scream came from!"

"What if she's in trouble?" David said.

"It could even be a trap," Bob replied. "There isn't anything we can do, David."

"Let's call the police!" David looked around, not understanding why everyone was holding back.

"And say what? That we have a weird mist and heard chanting and a scream? I doubt they would read much into it. Certainly not during the night. It would take them a while to get out here, anyway. And Carl told us the police could be involved in this." Bob swallowed, just as the moonlight reappeared and the mist began to fade quickly away.

All was quiet, even the animals.

"Wow," Gavin said, "that mist is receding fast!"

"It still doesn't feel right," David said.

"There's no reason for all three of us to be out here." Bob looked at David.

"We should all stay on watch," David replied.

"We'll be fine; we've got guns," Bob reassured David.

"If anything comes, at least we're prepared!" Gavin said, pointing to his own shotgun and lifting up his padded green gilet to reveal his ammo belt full of cartridges.

Eventually convinced somewhat that they would be okay, David made his way back to his bedroom. Benji was safely still asleep, snoring at the side of the bed. It was a good hour, before David finally closed his eyes and fell asleep.

# Chapter Forty-Five

## 17th July, 2018

"You awake, mate? I'm coming in!" John knocked again on David's bedroom door.

David squinted, rubbing the corner of his right eye with his forefinger. "I am now," he replied dryly.

"Sorry, mate. Gavin and your uncle told me about last night. Why didn't you wake me?"

"Yeah. It was fucking creepy!" David replied croakily. "What time is it?"

"Just gone ten. Anyway, on a lighter note, Annabel texted me. She's working at the pub today, but she's okay to go bowling tonight!"

David could see the excitement in his friend's eyes. "Yeah. I'm going for dinner with Emily tonight, too. Can you drop me off first?" David yawned.

"Sure. See you downstairs when you're ready. I'm hungry."

*****

At breakfast, David shared with John how guilty he felt not going into the forest to check whether anyone was hurt.

"I wouldn't beat yourself up over it, mate. Bob seemed to think it could even have been a trap and it's not like you could have done anything. Sounds like you didn't even know where the scream came from."

"I know. It just freaked me out. Well, all of us." David looked up from the kitchen table; Aunt Betty came in through the back door.

"Morning!"

"Morning." They smiled back.

"You feeling okay, today?" David asked.

"I'm well," Betty replied, emptying the kitchen bin and noticing the empty cereal box on the worktop.

"Oh. Sorry about that. I was going to put it in the bin after breakfast," David said.

"That's okay, love. No problem!" Betty put the box into the bag and pushed it down. She put a new bin bag into the bin and took the full one outside.

"At least she looks better."

"Yeah," David replied sounding unsure.

"You don't think?"

"I don't know what to think, really. Last night, when I woke up, I thought I heard laughter coming from her room. Similar to last week."

"Really? Maybe she was watching TV or just dreaming. I wouldn't dwell on it too much."

"I know. I still don't think everything is right with her. Just a hunch."

David got up to wash the cereal bowls just as Bob walked in. They heard someone go upstairs in their boots at the same time.

"Morning, David. You okay?"

"Fine. How did the rest of the night go?" David asked, drying his hands.

"Nothing else happened. I managed to get a few hours kip in. Gavin's gone up for a few hours now," Bob replied. "You managed to sleep okay?"

"I did, surprisingly after last night."

Betty returned so they stopped chatting, but she'd already heard David's words. "After last night? What happened last night?"

David turned to his uncle for guidance.

"Oh, nothing," Bob said. "David woke up during the night and came to see if we were all right."

"Oh." Betty smiled. "I don't know why you still keep watch to be honest, love? I think we're okay, now. The animals have been fine for a while."

At first, Bob was surprised by her response, but then realised, of course, that she didn't know the full extent of everything as they'd kept things from her. "You're probably right," Bob lied. "But it's just to be on the safe side for a while." He walked over to the sink and poured himself a glass of water.

"Do you want me to make you any breakfast?" Betty asked. "I think there's some bacon in the fridge."

"I'm fine, love. I'm not too hungry at the moment. I'll wait until lunch."

"Okay. Well, if any of you need me, I'll be in the living room catching up on some of my soaps." She laughed, before making her way across the hallway.

Bob drank from his glass of water. He looked at the apple bucket. "I think I'll crack on and make some of my cider later on, try to get my mind off other things." He finished the glass of water and rinsed the glass out.

"Do you need help with anything today?" David asked.

"I don't think so, really. We've got it covered." Bob smiled. "You're welcome to help out with things if you like, though?"

"I can cut the fields, if you like? I don't mind getting on that combine!" John semi-joked.

Bob laughed. "I'm sure you wouldn't mind!"

*****

Later, after Betty had watched her soaps, she fancied going out, so Bob suggested a drive and maybe some shopping. He let everyone know that he and Betty were going to stop off somewhere for a spot of lunch too. Bob had also spoken to Angus over the phone, who had informed him that his animals had been relocated yesterday, near to Kilmarnock. Angus had sounded dejected.

"You just cutting the one field today, then?" John asked as Gavin climbed into the combine harvester.

Despite only getting a few hours sleep, Gavin didn't feel too tired. "Aye. It will take a little while. But for today, just the one."

"Well, if you need a break, I'm more than happy to take over for a bit," John replied tongue-in-cheek.

"Nice try!" Gavin laughed as he started up the combine.

It purred into life, giving off a puff of black smoke from the exhaust funnel on top.

John watched Gavin drive off, making his way to one of the barley fields to harvest, shielding his eyes from the sun with his hand. He noticed the post van arrived and David was chatting to Jack. John walked over to join them. "Guys. What are you chatting about?"

"Same old, same old," David answered.

Jack laughed. "Aye! About those wackos murdering folk and killing the wildlife."

"You don't believe it?" John asked.

"I didn't say that!" Jack replied.

"You don't sound like you believe it," John said, finding it hard to keep his annoyance out of his voice.

"It's just that I've lived here for a wee while now, and I haven't heard anything before. It's such a quiet and scenic area. It's difficult to believe!"

David and John glanced at each other. His naivety annoyed them. Before they said anything further, Derek appeared. He was wearing a white backpack sprayer and some safety goggles. When he took the goggles off, they left a couple of red marks underneath his eyes.

John laughed. "You look like someone from *Ghostbusters*, Dez! Very appropriate, with everything going on up here!"

Derek laughed back with that laugh of his. "Aye. Just been getting rid of some of the weeds around here. They always seem to come back quickly, though! Hopefully not this time. Been using some more powerful industrial weed killer." Derek raised the long black sprayer up to them. "It's supposed to be pretty strong." He made out to spray them and they all laughed.

*****

After a while, John and David went to stand near the two grain silos along with Benji to watch Gavin in the combine, harvesting the bigger barley field behind the back of the farmhouse. The cutter bar rotated as clouds of yellow and white dust spewed up.

Gavin raised a hand and waved to them both. It was beginning to feel muggy.

"It looks like fun," John said, "Driving one of those things."

"Yeah. It's clever how they work," David replied, looking up at the sky.

"What's on your mind?"

"Everything."

"I know," John said, still watching the red combine. "You still up for tonight, with Emily?"

"I suppose. I'd feel more enthused if we didn't have this other stuff to contend with, obviously. But I don't want to let her down. I really like her. But after the meeting with Carl, I feel even more worried than before." David kicked half a flint of stone on the ground as he looked down.

"Yeah, I know; me too. But I'm not going to let it ruin my evening with Annabel!" John held out his hands in front of his chest, mimicking Annabel's breasts, which made David smile.

"I don't think she's the sort to put out on a first date, mate."

"Maybe so. But I like a challenge!" John replied, with a wry smile on his face. "We need to sort out a time to go this evening, and where you need dropping off. I'm sure we'll both have a good time, regardless of everything." John scratched the underneath of his chin where it was sore from shaving.

"Hopefully," David replied. "You going to say anything to Annabel about what's been happening?"

"Nah, I don't think so. At least not yet, anyway. Besides, I wouldn't want it to get in the way of anything. Well, you know? Of anything *sexual*, so to speak." John smirked. "How about you? You going to tell Emily?"

David let out a small sigh. "I don't think so. Not for now. I'm not even sure of what to say. I can't even get my own mind around it all."

Just then, they heard a loud sneeze from the dirt track behind them. They both turned but could see no one. Trees and bushes blocked the view. Another sneeze came, and then another.

"Who do you think that is?" John whispered.

"We should go check." David started to walk back past the side of the farmhouse and John and Benji followed.

They made their way down to the gate and to the end of the dirt track, where they heard another sneeze. To John and David's surprise, a little down the dirt track, were an elderly couple.

The elderly man was bent down, his hands on his bony knees. He was wearing beige shorts and a blue checked shirt. His dark socks were pulled up from his brown shoes. The woman was wearing a dark red jacket and a pair of light blue trousers. Some dried mud had congealed on her white trainers and she had her right hand on his back and a cane in her left hand.

"This *darn* hay fever," the man said.

"Aye, I did tell you to bring your nasal spray, dearie!" the woman replied.

They were both Scottish.

The man with his white thinning hair and the woman with her fluffy white head of hair, appeared both in their eighties; they looked up and saw John and David looking at them. The old man raised his head. His eyes were red and puffy. He took out a hanky from his shirt pocket, shook it and blew his nose before wiping it, screwing up his nostrils as he sniffed.

The couple then smiled at them both and slowly walked towards them.

"Hello!" the elderly woman said.

"Hi," David replied, feeling a tad awkward.

John raised a reluctant hand.

"We're just out for a walk," the elderly lady said, walking steadily towards them with her cane. "We parked the car further down." She pointed behind her. "We didn't know there was a farm up here."

"Yes, me and my wife, Ilene, we do like our walks!" The old man smiled, before letting out another sneeze. "I still drive, even at my age! At least the weather has held off, too. Just as well, really. The rain can sometimes make my hay fever even worse." The man laughed and coughed.

"As I said, Gerald. You should have brought your spray. It does help!"

"It's probably worse too, as the fields are starting to get cut," John replied.

"Ah, yes. We thought we heard a combine," Gerald said.

"Gerald, here, used to work on a farm and drive a combine harvester himself. That was many moons ago, though!"

"Indeed, it was." Gerald laughed as he wiped his nose again.

They made small talk for a few more minutes. The elderly couple asked about the farm and John and David told them how they were up visiting David's uncle, but not why.

Ilene told them she was eighty-four and her husband Gerald, had just turned eighty.

John joked that she must like younger men and that she only looked sixty. "Or sixty-four, max!" He grinned cheekily.

"Oh, stop it!" Ilene laughed again as she rested her gaunt fingers on the top of her wooden cane. Her bulgy, blue veins were profound in her old age.

Gerald, with his thinning hair, showing several liver spots on his scalp, looked up. "I can feel a few spots of rain, Ilene. We should start to head back in case it buckets it down." He again, wiped his nose with his hanky, before putting it away.

"Yes. I can feel a few spots too, my love. We've got a bit of a walk back to the car." Ilene too, looked up at the sky, before looking back at John and David. "Well, it was lovely chatting to you two boys."

"Likewise." David smiled.

Ilene turned her attention to Benji who was sitting quietly. David had told them his name, but neither she nor Gerald had paid much attention to the dog. "Goodbye to you as well, Benji." Ilene smiled as she held out a shaky arm to touch him.

David noticed that her finger was swollen around a silver wedding ring, despite her bony and lean fingers.

Benji was subdued as Ilene petted him. Normally, Benji greeted people wagging his tail, but today he seemed particularly unresponsive. Benji looked up at her aged hand as she wiggled her fingers out to him.

"Hello, you! *Trobhad, fhir bhig*," Ilene said as she stroked underneath his brown chin. "Coochy-coo. You're a wee handsome boy, aren't you, little one. There's a good dog."

Benji started to growl and suddenly snapped at Ilene's hand. Although old, her reflexes were sharp and she instinctively pulled her hand away. Benji continued to growl and started to bark, baring his teeth.

*"Benji!"* David shouted, bending down to hold onto him and stop him potentially leaping towards the old woman. "I am so sorry! Are you okay?"

Ilene looked a little shaken and glared at Benji.

*"What's gotten into you!"* David shouted to Benji again. "Did he bite you? I am so sorry. He's never done anything like that before!"

Ilene didn't say anything. She continued to glare at Benji.

John didn't know what to say either. It was completely out of character for Benji.

Finally, Ilene responded, "I'm fine. *Thankfully*, he didn't get me."

"Come! We should get back to the car," Gerald said to his wife, putting a consoling arm around her. He gave the two men a stern look. "You should look out for that dog. He could be dangerous!"

"Again, I'm so sorry!"

"*Hmph*! Good day to you!" Gerald said as he and Ilene slowly walked back down the dirt track.

Benji was still growling.

Gerald and Ilene gave one final glare back to them.

*"Bad boy!"* David chided Benji.

Benji grew calm and licked David's hand. A few more spots of rain fell on them.

"I honestly don't know what made him do that!" David said, shaking his head. "He's *never* gone for anyone like that before."

"I know. Totally out of character! He seems fine now, though." John knelt down to stroke Benji who licked him.

David sighed. "What if they go and report him? I can't bear to lose him!"

"You'll be fine. It's not like Benji attacked her or anything. Nor does he have a record or past history of doing it. I don't think they put dogs down just for biting once. Anyway, he didn't actually bite her."

"What if it becomes a habit, though? *Shit*!"

"Maybe he just doesn't like old people, or the smell of her perfume?" John tried to joke.

"Jesus, John. No jokes now, please."

"Sorry. Bad timing. What I did find weird was how Benji was so quiet while we were talking to them. I know he doesn't always jump up, but you know what I mean?"

"I know. I thought that."

*****

When Bob returned in the afternoon, he, John and David started crushing up the three buckets of apples outside on the garden patio. They could hear the hum of the combine where Gavin was still harvesting the field. They each had a bucket and were releasing the juices by smashing the apples. David and Bob were using pieces of wood, while John had a long metal rod from one of the barns. They had discarded the few mouldy and bruised apples they found.

"It will be fine, mate. The worst you'd get, would probably be a warning. Benji just isn't that sort of dog. We all know that." John enthusiastically mashed up his bucket of apples. He liked the sound of the wet, crunching noise. "At least there's no sign of any maggots!"

"John's right," Bob replied as he gave his arms a break. "It will be fine ... you said this couple were quite elderly?"

"Yeah. She was eighty-four and her husband had just turned eighty. They seemed pleasant enough," David replied.

"Yeah. Until they gave us the 'evils,' when Benji went for that Ilene!" John said. "You often get people walk up this way, Bob?"

"At times we do. Though it's kind of rare, seeing how deep we are in the forest up here. I think some people see the dirt track and just follow it up to see where it leads. They don't always see the sign." Bob laughed. "I recall one time, when we let a young couple walk through to the other side. That was a good few years ago, now."

"How often do you make cider, Uncle Bob?" David asked, taking a break from pulping the apples.

"Every year, if I can. It seems a waste of good apples if we don't do something with them! There's far too many to eat before they go rotten. Sometimes, we might give some away. We don't have neighbours, as you know. But Angus would sometimes take a bucket or even two off our hands, when his wife, Wendy, was alive. Especially, if I didn't fancy doing any cider.

"She used to love making her apple crumble! It tasted great as well. They would sometimes bring one round to thank us for the apples. It was even better than Betty's home-made crumble, but don't tell her that!" Bob laughed. "Another guy I knew too, had a couple of horses he'd take some apples for. Old Fred, his name was. I don't know what happened to him. He moved further up north a few years ago. He was a cheerful fellow. He might not even be alive now, for all I know; he was getting on a bit back then."

"Betty didn't want any apples then, for apple crumble?" David asked.

"I did ask, but she said the more apples, the more cider for me. Hah! She's not overly fond of cider, herself."

David could see that Uncle Bob enjoyed making cider. It was nice to see him relaxed. David felt good sharing this moment with him.

"So, what's next?" asked John, "After we've finished bashing these apples?" He wiped away a small piece of pulped apple that had splashed up onto his forehead.

"The apples need to be pressed. I made my own press. You'll see once we're done here."

"Right," John replied.

*****

When they finished breaking up the apples, Bob fetched his home-made press. They put the apples into a dark blue mesh bag, which they placed in a large white plastic box with a hole drilled into it, for letting the juices out.

Bob placed a board over the mesh bag to press down onto the apples with an old car jack he had fitted to the frame to apply the pressure. "That always does the trick!" Bob grinned as the three of them started to see the effects of the press.

Light, brown-red liquid began to fill the white tub at the sides of the press.

"Sometimes, I might add some sodium metabisulphite to kill off any bad moulds or bacteria, but that's only if there are a lot of bad apples. These look fine to me. If we did that, you'd have to wait twenty-four hours before applying the yeast, which you do afterwards, or it would be killed off as well … I'll go fetch the yeast now."

"A few of those apples were bruised, though," David mentioned.

"Not too many. It doesn't matter. Besides, some bruised apples can actually make the cider taste sweeter!" Bob cleared his throat and went inside.

"You all right?" John asked David while Bob went to fetch the yeast.

"Yeah. Just thinking. So good to be doing normal things, like helping make this cider, but hard to get all the bad stuff out of your mind."

"Yep … you're not alone in this, though." John put a hand on his friend's shoulder.

"True," David replied. "Hopefully, we can all get through this, somehow."

"I've found the yeast," Bob said, reappearing and walked back over to the press. He tore open a small sachet and poured the contents into the rising juice. "I've got some fermenting bottles we'll pour this into. The yeast turns the sugar into alcohol. I usually let it sit for around three to four weeks. You have to be careful, as sometimes it can turn into vinegar!" Bob laughed.

*****

Once all the juices from the pulp had been extracted, Bob went to fetch a couple of fermentation bottles. They poured the apple juice through a sieve into the fermentation bottles, carefully avoiding any spillage. Bob then secured the tops with a fermentation lock, to prevent oxidation.

"That's it, then?" David asked.

"Aye!" His uncle beamed. "That's all there is to it. It tastes fab, once it's fermented!" Bob winked.

"Where do you store it, whilst it ferments?" John asked.

"It needs to be in a place where the room temperature is steady and away from direct sunlight. I usually opt for the cupboard underneath the stairs. It's cool, but still at room temperature. We can store the bottles in there out of the way."

"We might not get a chance to taste it, if it isn't ready for another month or so," David said solemnly.

"You two are *more* than welcome to stay for as long as you like!"

"Thanks, Uncle ... but that's if we survive everything." David looked down.

"Stop that talk, David! We're all strong. As long as we all stick together and try and work this out, we'll be fine! We just need to meet with this demonologist." Bob tried to sound upbeat but was feeling despondent himself.

David sighed.

Bob then carried one of the heavy glass fermentation bottles and John carried the other. They made their way back indoors to the cupboard under the stairs. Just as John placed his bottle down and closed the door, they heard the phone ring in Bob's study. Bob rushed to answer it.

Bob returned soon after. "It must have been a wrong number. There was nobody there, they just hung up." He then went into the kitchen.

John's own phone then rang. "It's Annabel. Hope she isn't pulling out of tonight!" John went outside to answer the call and returned a couple of minutes later, all smiles.

"I take it the bowling is still on for tonight, then?" David asked.

"Yep! She wants to meet around half eight. I said I'd be dropping you off on the way."

"That's good," David replied. "I can let Em know what time to book a table for."

"It's all good, mate. I'm going to have a wee nap, now. Charge my batteries for tonight, in case I need them!" John smirked.

David smiled and shook his head at his friend.

"I'll see you in a couple, or a few!"

"No worries," David replied. He went into the kitchen and saw his aunt and uncle standing outside in the garden with a glass of wine each, smiling. He wanted to join them, but he could sense it as a special moment from the way they were chattering and laughing. He hoped he would have that when he was their age. But he still sensed something not quite right about Aunt Betty.

*****

Emily booked the table for eight-thirty. On the drive over, both John and David had felt that they were being watched as they made their way through the forest. Although it was nothing new. David was pleased John had taken his advice and not overdone the aftershave this time.

At eight-fifteen, John pulled into the front car park of the Italian restaurant on the outskirts of Aviemore; it was raining quite heavily. "Seems like a nice place," John said, peering out through his fogged windscreen with the window wipers still going.

A red and white canopy protected a few tables from the rain at the front of the restaurant. Hanging down, were the colours of green, white and red, representing the flag of Italy. Lights from inside promised warmth inside.

"Giuseppe's Grande Ristorante, eh?" John said. "I wonder if he knows Gino," he joked.

"Yeah!" David gave a laugh. He was feeling nervous. "I wonder how he's getting on?"

"I'm sure he's doing fine."

"It really does seem ages since we saw him, but it's only been a week."

"I know. So much has happened since then."

"That's an understatement," David replied, looking out of his window. He watched the rain come down and looked to see if Emily's car was there yet. He couldn't see it.

"You sure you don't want me to wait here with you? Annabel won't mind if I'm a bit late."

"Nah. I'm good, cheers. She might be inside already, but I can't see her car."

"Or you could wait underneath that canopy?" John suggested, pointing.

"True. But I think I'll go inside and wait. I can get a drink first and look at the menu. She'll probably be here soon, anyway. I don't think she's one to be late. I've still got over ten minutes." David opened the passenger door. "Shitty weather!"

"Aye, that's Scotland for ye!" John replied in his attempt of a Scottish accent. "Let me know what time you need picking up, yeah? Although, you're on your own if Annabel invites me back!" John smiled confidently.

"Yeah. Good luck with that!" David smiled, beginning to get wet. "I'll let you know when. You have a good time. Remember, don't throw those balls *too* hard!"

John laughed. "You have a good time too, buddy. I'll see you later!"

David closed the car door and made a dash inside the restaurant as John gave a toot on his horn and drove off. The bowling alley wasn't far.

# Chapter Forty-Six

## 17th July, 2018

As David opened the door, the smell of freshly cooked food hit him. It instantly made him hungry; his belly rumbled.

He checked the reservation Emily had made at reception and was shown to his seat by an attractive dark-skinned woman, wearing a white top and black skirt. She asked if he'd like anything to drink, with a twinkle in her dark brown eyes. He opted for a large vodka and Coke. Her accent was Italian with a hint of Scottish.

David, for some reason unknown to him, felt a little anxiety about the date. Perhaps it was due to current circumstances or because he had never been in an Italian restaurant before. Or maybe, it was because he was meeting the most beautiful woman he had ever seen and he really liked her. He texted Emily to tell her he was already seated and then picked up the menu.

He wasn't sure what to order, let alone how to pronounce some of the names of the dishes on the menu. He wanted to order something he hadn't tried before, something classy. The attractive, olive-skinned woman returned with his drink and placed it on a white coaster by his phone. She smiled again and told him to let her know when he was ready to order.

David took a long swig of his vodka and Coke. He accidentally swallowed some crushed ice. He dabbed his mouth with a white napkin. He looked around the restaurant. A family with two young children, both boys, sat a few tables down from him. His table was positioned near the back, by a large scenic oil painting that depicted a table with a vase of flowers on a flowery balcony looking out to sea. It looked tranquil. David wondered if the painting was imaginary, or if the place actually existed. Regardless, it was an excellent painting by someone highly talented.

After he had examined the painting, he turned his attention back to the menu. Still debating what to have, he happened to look up and saw the waitress smiling at him. He returned the smile. Another waitress carried food out from the kitchen and he could hear a conversation in Italian from inside.

At half past eight, Emily came through the door, looking as radiant and beautiful as ever. David gulped and took another sip of his drink. She wore a red dress, a small black leather jacket and black heels; her hair was loose.

Emily felt nervous herself as she greeted the male receptionist who was in his forties. He obviously knew her as he moved forward to kiss her first on her left cheek and then on her right. She seemed a little embarrassed as she caught sight of David sitting at the back, watching. The receptionist placed his hands on Emily's forearms and asked her how she was in his thick Italian accent. He told her she looked "Bellissimo!" and then took her jacket and hung it up. Emily was led to the table by the same waitress who had seated David.

"You look absolutely amazing!" David said as he got up to greet Emily. If it wasn't for the waitress standing there between them, he would have kissed her, though not on her cheeks where the receptionist had.

"Thank you. You look fantastic, too!" She looked David up and down in his grey shirt, slightly open at the chest and his blue slim-fitting jeans.

The waitress pulled out the chair for Emily to sit and asked if she wanted a drink. She ordered a glass of red wine.

David waited for the waitress to leave, before commenting again on Emily's appearance. "I'm speechless. You really look so lovely, Em!"

Emily averted her eyes a little. She felt embarrassed taking compliments. "Thank you. You look very handsome, yourself! But then, you will always do."

"Flattery will get you everywhere!" David joked, trying to make Emily laugh and feel more comfortable. "Honestly, though, thanks! That's a great compliment coming from someone as beautiful as you."

"You're too sweet and kind," Emily replied, smiling.

"It looks like I may have some competition, though," David joked, nodding his head towards the man who had kissed her. He was talking to a middle-aged couple, who had just walked in out of the heavy rain.

Emily turned around and laughed. "Oh, that's Luigi. He's sweet. He always greets me and my mum like that! We sometimes see him about in town, as well as here … not as sweet as you, though."

The waitress came over and carefully placed the glass of red wine in front of Emily. "Let me know when you're ready to order," she repeated, acknowledging both of them, before going to greet the couple who had just entered.

"I'm sorry I didn't text back. I was driving and was pretty much already here when I got it," Emily said, placing her white handbag on the floor.

"That's okay. I would have waited outside, had it not been for the weather."

"Yeah, it's tipping it down out there. I would have got here earlier, but someone's car had broken down." Emily had a small sip of her wine and smiled at David.

"Do you normally sit here?" David smiled back.

Emily shook her head. "Not usually. We sit anywhere, really. But it's my first time at the back."

"Oh, really? Well, I'm flattered!" David laughed.

"Oh, I'm sorry. I didn't mean it to sound like that!" Emily felt embarrassed, realising what she had just said and how it could have been misinterpreted.

"Ha. Don't be sorry. It's just my dirty mind!" David grinned.

Emily giggled back.

"I was just looking at the menu before you came in. I honestly don't know what to order. Plus, I don't really feel comfortable trying to say any of these names."

They both laughed.

"Oh, that's all right. They don't mind if you pronounce it wrong. They find it funny. But I know what you mean; we're spoilt for choice, really. But it's all top-quality food. You certainly get your money's worth!"

"What do you normally have?"

"Well, we've been here a few times. I usually like to try a bit of everything. Experiment!" Emily laughed.

"That's not one of your innuendos again, is it?" David grinned.

"Oh, no, no, no." Emily chuckled. "I remember I went for the chicken scallopini last time out. It was real yummy!"

"It certainly sounds nice."

"Oh, it was delicious!" Emily smiled.

"I worry about choosing something and not liking it. I don't want to seem rude by not eating it," David said, still trying to make up his mind on what to have.

"I know what you mean. I'm the same. But the best thing to do, if you feel like that, is to go for something you would usually like."

"What? Like a pizza?" David laughed.

Emily laughed. "If you like! Their pizzas are really nice. But like I said, all their food is."

"I did think about going for a pizza. What about you? What are you having?"

"I thought about going for the pepperoni bread as an appetiser. As for the main course. Erm … I'm going to go for … for spaghetti and handmade meatballs. Yummy!" Emily said, putting her menu down.

David looked up from his menu and saw her smiling back at him. His fondness for her seemed to be growing; she looked so cute and excited about her order.

"I might have the same. I like meatballs. Sod it. It's a bit of a safe bet maybe, but the hell with it!" David smiled back at Emily. "Great minds think alike, eh?"

"Oh, they sure do," Emily replied, with a twinkle in her eye.

The waitress pulled out an order pad and flipped it open. She wrote down Emily's order first.

"And the same for me please, including the pepperoni bread," David said as the waitress jotted his order down too.

She looked at him again after finishing taking the two orders and smiled.

"I think she likes you," Emily said teasing as the waitress disappeared into the kitchen.

David laughed. "You jealous?"

"I would be, if you were with her tonight and not me," Emily replied, looking a little shy. "I certainly couldn't blame her for liking you."

David reached over to her left hand and held it. "That's sweet." Pulling his arm away, his elbow knocked his drink over, spilling it onto the red and white gingham tablecloth.

Emily quickly jumped up to save it from spilling on her dress.

*"Shit!"* David said and leapt up too.

A few customers looked over from their tables.

Emily laughed as David looked at her.

"Did any of it go over your dress?"

"I'm fine. Don't worry about it!" She smiled.

A male waiter came over to help clean it up.

"I'm so sorry," David said as the man knelt down and wiped up the drink.

"It's fine. It happens." The waiter smiled kindly. "Move over here to this table. I'll change the cloth on this one. This table's free tonight."

"Okay, thanks," David replied, and he and Emily changed tables.

"I'll get you another drink. What was it?"

"A large vodka and Coke, please," David answered.

*****

Their main course was well worth the wait. The portions were generous. Emily had been correct when she said you certainly got your money's worth.

They laughed and chatted about things and talked about when they had been caught in the thunderstorm. David avoiding talking about any of his worries. He wanted to enjoy Emily's company and the evening. Nor was anything said about the kiss they would have had, if John hadn't interrupted them last Sunday. The restaurant became pretty busy and some soft piano music floated from speakers in the background.

David felt a little full. The pepperoni bread had been filling and he still had a fair bit of spaghetti and a few meatballs left on his plate.

Emily had gone to the ladies and he was wondering how John's date with Annabel was going. Without Emily with him, he started to dwell on the situation in the forest again. He looked around the now packed restaurant. It was certainly a popular place. He wondered how many people in here knew about Rothiemurchus Forest and the evil within it. They were all laughing and chatting and enjoying their meals. Or, for all he knew, maybe some of them were members of the 'cult.' He shuddered at the thought of it. He even considered whether Emily could be trusted. He felt terrible for doubting her; she seemed so sweet and innocent. She couldn't possibly be part of something so twisted and evil. She was putting on a fantastic act, if he was being played.

He started to feel depressed. He remembered Benji snapping at the elderly woman earlier that day. He took a large swig of his drink; it was his third, or fourth, if you included the nearly full one he had spilt. He had switched to singles after the first finished double. Emily was on her second glass of red wine. She vowed not to have another because she was driving.

David picked up his fork and started prodding at the remaining spaghetti. He heard a vibrating sound from Emily's phone in her bag underneath the table.

"Gotcha!" came Emily's voice, having snuck up behind him. She lightly pinched his sides.

David jolted, banging one of his knees on the underside of the table and rattling the plates. A few customers looked over to see where the noise came from.

"Jesus!" David said, holding his chest.

"I'm sorry!" Emily said sheepishly.

David looked at the two drinks on the table that were swaying in the glass. "Could have knocked the drinks over again." He smiled.

"Oops! I should have realised that. Sorry," she apologised again and sat back down, seeing other customers looking at them. She felt a little awkward. "It's just you looked distracted, sitting there playing with your food. You kind of looked so sad and deep in thought … It's not, erm, me, is it? You're having a good time?"

"No!" David replied strongly. "I mean, yes, I'm having a good time. I meant no, as in not at all because of you! I was just thinking about something. It's not you at all, Em. Far from it. I'm having a really great time with you."

Emily smiled and took hold of his hand. "Is there something you want to talk about? You seem troubled. I've noticed it before. Sometimes, you seem deep in thought. Distracted. Sometimes it's better to talk about the things that are bothering you. A problem shared is a problem halved."

"It's nothing. Honestly," he lied. There was no way that he wanted her to share his problems; far from it. He did consider telling her, though, just for a second.

"Sure?"

"Sure! Now let's finish our meal, although I'm so full; these meatballs are the size of tennis balls!" David grinned.

Emily laughed. "I know! But they taste great, don't they?"

David managed to finish everything and was surprised that Emily had no problem whatsoever finishing hers. He joked about how much she could eat and yet still stay slim. She laughed, claiming she was still careful about what she consumed, to avoid piling on the pounds. They both waited for the main course to settle, before moving on to a dessert.

"Oh, I forgot to tell you, your phone went while you were gone."

"Let me have a look." Emily bent down and took out her phone from her handbag. "As I thought. It's my mum, bless her. Seeing how the date is going." Emily chuckled to herself.

"I'll let you text her back. I need to use the little boys' room."

"Okay." Emily laughed.

While David was in the toilets washing his hands, he heard whispering and laughter coming from behind him. He turned to face the four cubicles. They were all open, bar one, on the far right. He swallowed and slowly walked towards it. He paused and heard the sound again. He crouched down to check under the door whether anybody was in there; no one.

Getting up, he heard the door unbolt and slowly open, but the cubicle was empty. David could feel a presence. Suddenly, there was a foul smell of excrement coming straight from the cubicle and the lights began to flicker. He quickly covered his nose and mouth with his hand. A man then entered and frowned at David, walking over to the urinals. The lights had returned back to normal and the smell had disappeared instantly.

David felt embarrassed, with the man looking at him. He took his hand away from his face. "I just, er, smelt something bad," David said to the man, feeling stupid.

"Well, we are in the toilets!" the man said sarcastically in his heavy Scottish accent.

David watched as the man washed his hands, shook his head and left. He stood there looking at the cubicle for a short while. The presence had definitely gone. He slowly walked towards the exit, looking back again at the empty cubicles.

"You're back." Emily smiled. "You took your time. I thought you'd escaped out of the toilet window!" she joked.

"Not a chance." David tried to smile and appear okay.

Emily could see he wasn't. "Please, David," she pleaded with him as he sat back down. "Are you okay? Is it me? Honestly? It's just that we get on really well, and then you look so down, or like your mind is elsewhere."

David smiled gently at her. "I'm sorry. I do have stuff on my mind right now, things going on. I'll be honest about that. But please believe me, it's *not* because of you. You make me feel better and I really do like spending time with you. You are a pleasant distraction!" He smiled widely at her.

"That actually sounds wrong. You're *more* than a distraction! I really do like spending time with you. I really like you. You're smart, beautiful, cute. You make me laugh. You're even cute when you're not trying to be, and you don't know it." He took both her hands in his from across the table and they looked into each other's eyes. "You are perfect in every way … I swear to you. It's not because of you. I love spending time with you, Em. I really do."

Emily smiled back at him. David's tender and honest words struck a chord with her. Her eyes welled up. She could tell from his face and tone that he was being sincere. She believed him. "I, I feel exactly the same way …"

As they started to lean in towards one another, they were stopped by the waitress who asked if they would like to order dessert.

"Erm. We haven't decided yet," David said. "Could you come back in a couple of minutes?"

"Okay," she said rudely this time and walked off.

"She seemed a bit off?" David said, slowly letting go of Emily's hands.

"They're usually friendly here. I haven't actually seen her before. Perhaps, she's jealous?" Emily replied half-joking.

"Jealous? Of what?"

"That she's not with you and I am. I've seen the way she looks at you. I think she likes you."

"Oh, well. In that case, I'd better go and get her number!" David joked, making Emily laugh again.

The moment for their first kiss had passed. It would have to wait, for now. The waitress was also watching them both.

Although David had lost his appetite somewhat, after the incident in the toilets, he decided to try a dessert. "I don't want anything too rich. What about you?"

"Oh, I'm ready for something filling!" Emily replied. "And that *wasn't* another innuendo." She giggled.

"Hah!" David replied. "For someone so slim, you certainly have an appetite!"

*"Guilty!"* Emily laughed. She looked at the menu. "I'm going to go for the Tiramisu. I've had it before, but I think I'll go for it again."

"What happened about going for something different each time?" David joked.

"Oh, well."

"I think I'll go for the cannoli with ice cream."

"Wise choice." Emily smiled.

"I'm glad you approve!" David laughed. He held his hand up, signalling to the waitress who was standing over near the bar; she strolled over to take their final order and left. "I wonder how Annabel and John are getting on? I'm surprised he hasn't texted me, asking me how my date is going."

"Perhaps he's thinking the same thing about you? What would you tell him anyway, if he asked how you were getting on with me?" Emily rubbed her chin with her finger, looking at David with a seductive look. She then began twirling her hair.

David felt a tingle. He found her so beautiful. "What would I tell him about how our dinner date is going?"

Emily nodded.

David breathed out. "I'd probably be blunt and tell him I was hating every minute of it," he said sarcastically.

Emily sat back, her mouth open, pretending to be in a state of shock. "Well, I never … how *rude*!"

They both laughed.

"I was thinking of texting him earlier on. He's not bowled much before.

I've only been a couple of times before myself."

"Me too. Not for a long time, though … maybe that could be our next date?" Emily half-suggested. "Or even a double date?"

"It could well be." David smiled back. "I think John's kind of hoping for something more after the bowling as well."

Emily giggled. "I think it's wishful thinking on his part! She isn't the sort to go that far on a first date, regardless of whether she likes the guy."

"That's exactly what I said to him. But that's John. Confident and cocky as always! At least what you see with him, is what you get. Even if he is sometimes a little forward and direct."

"And besides, I don't think the old couple who she lives with, would appreciate her bringing him back to theirs! Unless he intends on taking her back to your uncle's farm? It won't happen anyway; she just isn't like that."

"I don't think my uncle would mind too much. I think he's pretty laidback. Have you met the old folks Annabel is staying with, then?"

"I have, yeah. Only a few times, mind. I wouldn't say they're odd, but they don't say much. They're getting on a bit! I think they just like keeping themselves to themselves. Nothing wrong with that."

"True."

On the mention of elderly couples, David told Emily about Benji earlier in the day.

Emily reassured him that it would be fine and it wasn't anything to worry about. "So, that's what's been troubling you, then?" She smiled sympathetically from across the table.

"Erm. Yeah," David replied. He wasn't exactly lying; he had been thinking about what happened with Benji at the dinner table, but amongst all the other concerns too.

"Aw. As I said, David. He was fine with me. I'm sure it was just an isolated incident." Emily held his hand again but pulled away just as the waitress returned with their desserts.

"Enjoy," the waitress said, with a smile this time.

# Chapter Forty-Seven

## 17th July, 2018

At McLintock's Bowling Alley, John was still surprised at how well he was playing and hoped to win the last frame.

John and Annabel had enjoyed a meal together in the café prior to playing.

*"Strike! Get in!"* John fist-pumped and then raised his hands aloft, making Annabel laugh.

"Well done!" she said. "You don't play too badly, for someone who doesn't bowl regularly."

John laughed. "Well, what can I say, Annabelly? I guess I'm just a natural." He held his hands out and pouted with pretend arrogance across his face.

Annabel laughed, shaking her head.

Another man with his wife next to their lane looked over and smiled.

"Well, if you don't knock down all those pins, I guess I've won *again*! No pressure," John teased Annabel as she prepared to throw the final ball.

She tried to ignore John's comment but couldn't help but smile as she ran up and released the bowling ball.

They both watched as the green ball flew into the gutter.

Annabel hung her head. *"Shit!"* she said annoyed with herself.

John got up and sarcastically applauded, holding the score sheet in his teeth. "Shit, indeed!"

"Yeah, yeah, you lucky bastard." Annabel smiled. "Let's have a look at that score sheet." She snatched the sheet from John's mouth and double checked it.

"It's no use. You lost! I would have won overall anyway, if you add all the frames up," he bragged. "*And,* if I recall, at the start of the evening, you promised me a *kiss* if I won." John flicked his eyebrows up and down.

"Yes, yes, I did," Annabel said, shaking her head, trying not to laugh.

"Well, here I am!" John beamed, holding his arms out.

Annabel walked over to John, raised herself up on her tiptoes and placed her hands on his shoulders. She kissed him full on his lips twice. "There," she said, smiling.

"Well, I was hoping for a longer kiss," John half-joked.

"Don't push your luck, Mister." Annabel smiled.

*****

After their game, they had moved over to the bar for a while.

"Well, it feels good to get out of those ridiculous shoes," John said.

"Aw. I thought they suited you," Annabel replied sarcastically.

"They'd look better kicked off at the bottom of your bed!" John joked.

Annabel couldn't help but smile, again shaking her head.

"Honestly, though. You play a good game!"

"Thanks! I've played a few times. More so when I was younger. I've had a bit of practice, but obviously, I'm not quite the natural like you," Annabel said jokingly.

"That is true!" John replied, checking the clock behind the bar. It had just turned eleven. "Excuse me, mate?" John said to the bartender. "What time do you finish up?"

"Finish up?" the bartender replied.

"I don't mean what time do you personally finish, I mean the bar. I'd like another pint, please."

Annabel laughed at John's remark, but the bartender didn't see the funny side. "We close at eleven-thirty, sir. Would you like the same again?"

"Please," John replied. He got a buzz out of making Annabel laugh. He hoped that making her laugh as he'd done throughout the evening, would get him somewhere. He would like to laugh her into bed. "Actually, seeing as you're shutting soon, just make it a half."

The young bartender poured the half-pint for John and took a sneaky look at Annabel's large breasts, before quickly averting his eyes.

"I wonder how David and Emily are getting on?" John asked, paying for his drink.

"I'm sure they're getting on really well. It's obvious they like each other. Em talks a fair bit about him at work. I think they're a good match! Meant for each other, even though they've only just met," Annabel replied.

"I was going to text him. I'm going to have to anyway soon, to see when he wants picking up … unless you wanted to do, erm, something else?" John hinted.

"I don't think so, John. I'm pretty beat. Plus, I have work tomorrow."

"Well, that's okay. I can come back and tuck you in, then?" John grinned.

"Nice try, Mister! Listen … I've had a really good night, but I don't want to rush things."

John was disappointed. He glanced up and saw the bartender smiling to himself as he washed out a glass. John was irritated to think the spotty lad had overheard Annabel's words. *He'd be lucky if he ever got laid.* He watched the lad pull out his mobile phone and begin texting.

Apart from two other couples, the bar was now practically empty. The whole bowling alley was beginning to wind down and empty out.

*****

John popped into the toilets before leaving. Coming back out to return to Annabel, a man, who must have been in his forties, started to say something as he passed him in the corridor.

*"Chaidh rabhadh a thoirt dhut cumail air falbh … Cha tug thu aire air an rabhaidhean sin … Agus airson sin pàighidh tu … "*

"Huh?" John asked as he stopped and looked around. "What did you say, mate? Were you talking to me?"

The man didn't say anything in response; he just whistled to himself and stopped at the toilet entrance. He then spoke again, without turning his head. "You were warned to stay away. You didn't *heed* those warnings. And for that, you shall *pay*!"

John gulped and froze on the spot. "Wh-who are you?"

The man still stood with his back to John. He stood tall and suddenly motioned his head around in a circle, as if he was exercising his neck muscles; then he started whistling again. Suddenly he stopped whistling and began to laugh, giving John the chills.

John slowly backed away as the man entered the toilets. *"Argh!"* John jumped as he backed into Annabel. He felt the softness of her breasts and turned to face her.

"You okay?"

"Sorry! I, erm. Yeah, I'm fine."

"You don't look okay?" Annabel frowned.

"It's nothing. You just made me jump; that's all."

"What's the matter? Did you see a big spider in the toilets?" Annabel joked.

John laughed nervously.

"They've shut the bar for the night. They'll be closing the bowling alley, soon."

"Okay."

"You sure you're okay?"

"Yeah," John said. "Let's just get out of here."

As they walked off, John looked back to see if the guy was following them. He wasn't.

John walked Annabel to her small, purple Peugeot.

"I've had a really enjoyable evening." Annabel smiled. "We should do it again some time. Well, not necessarily bowling."

"Yeah. That would be good." John tried to smile.

"Well, don't be *too* enthusiastic." Annabel laughed.

"I'm sorry. It would be great, honestly! Just drop me a message or something. I'm up here for a while, yet." John saw a man and a woman staring at him from across the parking lot, before getting into their car and driving off.

"Well, good night, John!" Annabel smiled as she planted him a smacker on his lips, which caught him off-guard.

John half-smiled at her. "Chat soon. Drive safely."

"You too!"

Before returning to his own car, John waved Annabel off and stood alone in the car park, looking around. He sensed he was being watched. He then quickly dashed to his car to avoid any further encounters. The car failed to start a couple of times, but when it did, he soon spun out of the car park.

# Chapter Forty-Eight

## 17th July, 2018

Emily had struggled to finish her Tiramisu. It had sat in the bowl for well over an hour and a half.

"I guess your eyes were bigger than your little belly, eh?" David smiled.

"Aw. That's not fair. I've eaten most of it!" Emily laughed.

"Seems a bit strange, you ordering a coffee too, when Tiramisu tastes like coffee."

"I do like my coffee." Emily smirked. "Help me finish it ..." She held a spoonful of Tiramisu towards him.

David leant over and took it in his open mouth.

"Nice, isn't it?" Emily smiled, with her hand under the spoon, in case any fell.

David wiped the cream from his mouth before answering, "I have to admit, it is good! I'm not sure I've even had it before. I've always liked the smell of coffee, but I never really liked the taste of it, until I got older."

"I've always liked it."

David used his own spoon this time to help finish the dessert. After they'd finished, they settled the bill. They had a debate over who was going to pay and eventually each paid half and left a ten-pound tip between them. David received a text from John:

> Hope you had a good night, mate. We need to talk! I'll assume you want picking up and I'll be there shortly.

"That's a serious face," Emily said, noticing David's frown.

"Huh?" David replied, looking up. "Sorry. John's going to pick me up in a bit."

"Everything okay?"

"Yep." David smiled.

"Well, we should go then. I'm going to use the loo quickly first. I'll meet you outside. It looks like it's stopped raining."

It was getting on for midnight and the rain had passed. David saw Emily chatting to Luigi who fetched her jacket and helped her on with it. She threw David a look through the glass door, gesturing that she wanted to leave, but didn't want to offend Luigi.

John pulled up, not too far from the entrance.

"Everything all right? How did the date go?" David walked over and asked impatiently.

"The date went fine, but something else weird happened." John stopped when he saw Emily approach.

"Sorry about that," Emily said, walking towards John's car. "Luigi always likes to chat."

"Who's Luigi?" John asked.

"He's the greeter at the restaurant; Em knows him."

"Hi, John!" Emily smiled. "How did your date go?"

"Great! We had a really good time, thanks. Annabel's pretty good at bowling, though, not as good as me. Needless to say, I won." John grinned slightly.

Emily laughed. "Well, I'm glad you enjoyed yourselves! We had a fab time as well, didn't we, David?" Emily had a seductive look in her eyes.

"For sure." David smiled back at her.

"Would you like to walk me back to my car?" Emily asked innocently.

"Of course."

John waited anxiously while David escorted Emily to her car. He tapped his fingers on the steering wheel. A man had come out from the restaurant wearing a chef's outfit and started smoking a cigarette. He nodded to John in the car who nodded back. He was no doubt enjoying a smoke after a long shift.

John watched as Emily put her hand on David's arm and rubbed it affectionately. They kissed on the cheek, before hugging each other goodnight. David opened the car door for Emily, then walked back towards John. Emily waved to them both as she drove off home.

"What? No kiss on the lips?" John half-joked.

"Not whilst you're watching," David replied, closing the door. "So, what happened?"

"I'll park over there and tell you."

They drove past the waiter who had smoked his cigarette and put the stub out on a wall-mounted ashtray before returning inside.

John told David that his date with Annabel went more than fine. Then he told him about the man who had threatened him with some strange language, and about the couple in the car park staring at him. "… Annabel wondered why I was spooked when I backed into her chest, though, you can't exactly miss it."

"Shit. It's like we're being watched all the time … I had something happen as well," David replied, then told about his experience.

"Where do we go from here? We're stuck out there in the forest in the middle of nowhere, surrounded." John shuddered. "Being threatened like that really shocked me. You think it's too late to head home?" John said half-serious.

"That's up to you, but I'm staying. I'm not leaving my uncle by himself. Certainly not now. I know he's got Gavin. But even so. I'm still concerned about him and Betty."

"You're right. Sorry to suggest it. You can count on me. Besides, I have unfinished business with Annabel. Let's get back to the farm!" John said, starting the engine.

**18th July, 2018**

Making their way back to Hamish Farm, John turned the radio on for some music. Although they were chatting, John felt nervous and wanted a normal feel in the car. It had since gone midnight and theirs was the only car on the road. David felt the same. The night seemed creepier than normal. A couple of miles or so into the forest and the radio began to crackle and lose its signal. David was drifting off to sleep with his head against the window, but the crackling woke him. The green radio digits displaying the frequency of 107.1FM were flickering on and off.

"You hear that?" John asked. "The radio was working fine, until we came into the forest."

"I know … *Woah*! You see that!" David said, sitting forward in his seat.

"See what?" John replied, feeling the tension.

"The radio frequency just changed to *666*!"

"What?" John looked at the radio.

"I swear it changed," David said as crackling completely drowned out the music they had been listening to.

"Why does your uncle have to live all the bloody way out here!"

The crackling was now replaced with chanting, growing louder and louder.

"What the fuck?" John said, glancing at the radio, but quickly back to the dark road ahead.

David turned the tuning knob on the radio, but the chanting continued. "It's on *every* frequency!"

"It sounds like Latin ... *Turn it off!*"

David turned it off. "No signal on my phone, either."

"Sounds about right," John replied nervously, swallowing.

"Why are you slowing down?"

*"I'm not!"* John pushed his foot all the way down on the accelerator.

*"Shit. Not again!"*

They sat in the car surrounded by total darkness, deep inside the forest. Even the headlights failed. Both their hearts began to beat harder.

"I really don't like this," John whispered. "This could be it. *We're done for!*"

Everything was oddly quiet, apart from their breathing. Then the temperature fell. They sat waiting. A few minutes passed. The radio turned on by itself and the chanting began again. Then laughter from both men and women, and possibly children too. It wasn't the same demonic laughter that David had heard before, but still it sounded wicked and mocking.

David and John both swallowed, their mouths dry.

*"What the fuck are we going to do?"* John started to panic as the laughter intensified. *"Shall we get out?"*

"And go *where*? Into the forest? That's probably what they want!"

There was nowhere to run. The forest was all around them. They were still a few miles from the farm, with nobody in sight.

The laughter increased and a stronger chill filled the car. They began to feel the car roll forwards, slowly at first, then with increasing speed.

"Is that you doing that?"

*"How the hell can it be! Can you hear the engine? I'm not doing anything!"* John shouted above the laughter.

As the car moved on, the pair noticed a flame appear in the middle of the road up ahead. It grew into a circle, lighting an inverted wooden pentagram; they were heading straight towards it.

"Is that a head of some sort?" John asked as they approached closer to the flames.

"It's ... it's a goat's head."

The car came to a halt.

The flames swirled out from the inverted pentagram just above the car windscreen. The goat's head was in the middle of it. They could hear wood crackling from the heat.

The laughter from the radio started to subside and a dark voice could be heard. *"Soon!"*

Then, without warning, the severed goat's head from the centre of the inverted pentagram shot forward, hitting the windscreen. David and John instinctively covered their faces to protect themselves. The goat's head rolled off the bonnet, onto the road. The burning symbol collapsed and fell to the ground and its flames vanished. Everything went quiet for a few moments, until John's engine suddenly came back on, and the headlights flashed onto the road ahead.

John swallowed. *"Is ... is it over?"*

*"I don't know! Let's just get the fuck back, in case something else happens!"* David looked across at John who appeared frozen. *"John! Come ON!"*

*****

Uncle Bob tried calming the two young men down. He had made them all hot chocolate, while Gavin stayed on guard outside.

"H-honestly, I thought that was it," John repeated for the third time.

"I knew we shouldn't have gone on those dates, knowing about coming back through the forest at night." David shook his head.

"At least you're safe now," Bob said reassuringly.

"Are we really, though?" John replied. "If they can do things like move my car, and Christ knows what else, we are completely powerless!"

"You're right. But whoever these cult people are, apart from the thing that they summoned, the rest of them are still human. They are probably watching us here, too. But I don't think they'd necessarily risk taking us on here, since we're armed. Maybe that's why they haven't done too much of late?"

David looked at his now barely warm, untouched, hot chocolate. "Perhaps you're right, Uncle. But John's warning tonight at the bowling alley, and the presence I felt at the restaurant ... that voice saying *soon.*" David shook his head. "I get the impression they're biding their time. Playing us. Until they strike. And it's *always* John and me. I mean, what the *hell* did we do? Sure, we defied their warnings. But it doesn't make sense? It's like they were on to us before we even got here."

"Too damn right," John agreed.

"But this started with the mutilations of our animals, and goes back years before, going back to poor Charlie."

"I know. I'm sorry. Of course, you've been affected too, worse with your animals and cat," David replied.

"Don't be silly. No need to apologise! I know what you meant. You two have definitely had more things happen to you. But we are *all* in this together." Bob smiled understandably.

"It's certainly taken a shine off the evening with our dates that went so well," John said sarcastically.

"Yeah. I had such a great time with Emily. It's like that lovely feeling has all been taken away now." David took a sip of his chocolate.

"Let's hope Carl and his demonologist friend can help us," said Bob.

John laughed ironically. "What can they honestly do to help? Sure, they have information and claim to know stuff. But so what? If these things have been happening for decades, centuries or whatever, what are *they* going to do to stop them now?"

"I … I don't know, John," Bob replied. "But we have to *hope.* Carl said he'd get back to us before the week is out. One step at a time."

John looked down, shaking his head. "If only Annabel had taken me back to hers, perhaps we'd have been all right!" John joked.

Bob and David had to laugh.

"Maybe. But I'd still have needed to get back home," David replied.

"True," John said. "Maybe we'd have been better off getting a taxi."

"Benji was okay, then?" David asked, looking down at Benji sleeping in the corner of the kitchen.

"Good as gold!" Bob answered. "He's been completely fine, David."

They heard footsteps coming down the stairs.

"Damn," Bob said. "It sounds like your aunt's woken up. We can talk about this more, later. Let's not say anything whilst Betty is about … We didn't wake you, did we?" Bob smiled.

Betty yawned. "I don't think so." She smiled back. "I had a bit of trouble getting off, and thought I'd come and make a nice cuppa; has the kettle already boiled?"

"It might need boiling again … Their dates went well."

"Of course! I almost forgot. You had a great time, then?" Betty made her way over to the kettle.

"Really well, thanks," David replied.

"Mine too," John added.

"That's great news," Betty replied. "Think I'll have some of my favourite biscuits."

"Allow me, darling." Bob opened the cupboard and handed her the pack of Rich Tea.

"Actually, I fancy some Digestives, instead. Do we have any left?"

"Here." Bob swapped the biscuits.

"I'm going to watch a bit of late-night TV downstairs, whilst I have this. Hopefully, it will make me sleepy!" Betty smiled as she made her way across the hallway, biting into a biscuit.

"Night," John said, and then waited until he could hear the TV on. "I still can't get that laughter out of my head from the radio. I don't think I'm going to get much sleep tonight. Maybe I wouldn't have done anyway, had I been in Annabel's bed," he joked.

Bob and his nephew shook their heads, trying not to smile.

"What?" John said, with a slight grin on his tired looking face.

*****

John and David spent some time in John's bedroom, before they attempted to sleep. It was so difficult after tonight's events. They didn't make it any easier by searching on David's laptop for demons, Satanists and the Grey Man again. Sammy, the black cat, was lying on the carpet near the door.

"Yep. Everything we've already heard about," John commented. He was laid back on his bed looking at his phone.

"I know. Ironically, I never used to believe in this stuff."

"Yep. And now it's real and it's happening to us!"

"Perhaps that's what you get for being naïve … I never thought I'd be affected by something like this; who does?"

"I know, mate." John yawned.

David checked his emails. There was nothing of note, apart from an email from his mother, sharing a selfie-stick photo with his father and his mum's sister, Sarah, somewhere on a beach in Spain. He replied, saying how the weather looked fine, and they looked to be having a great time. David then shut his laptop.

"Your mum didn't send any photos in a bikini, then?" John smirked, lying on his bed.

"Perv." David smiled, bending down to pick up a small cushion from the carpet and throwing it at John. "At least they're having a good time. More than can be said for us."

"At least we have Annabel and Emily as pleasant distractions."

"I guess so," David said, getting up from the bed.

They heard a slight scratching underneath the door.

"That's Josie, I bet. Those pussies certainly know where to come, eh?" John smiled and David opened the door.

Josie, the tortoiseshell cat, strolled in and jumped up onto the bed.

"At least they're not fussed by Benji," David said.

"That's because Benji's a big softy, ain't ya, pal!" John leant down and petted Benji.

"People might think differently, if they'd seen him earlier," David replied.

"I told you, mate. Don't worry about it."

"Yeah … night. C'mon Benj."

"Sweet dreams. Don't let the bed bugs bite!" John said, throwing the cushion back at David, hitting him in the lower back and making Sammy jump.

# Chapter Forty-Nine

## 18th July, 2018

David tossed and turned before drifting into a dream … He was standing in the large forest clearing where they had found the bones shaped into an inverted pentagram with the sinister tree. But this time, there was no tree nor bones. He was all alone.

He couldn't remember how he got there. Or whether he was dreaming. He pinched himself on the arm. Although he felt the pinch, it was still like a dream. The ground was damp on his bare feet. He looked down, confused. Why wasn't he wearing any shoes? He was in a pair of his blue jeans and an old grey T-shirt.

The moon was full; freakishly big and bright, but there were no stars, despite it being cloudless. It was eerily quiet.

He started to look around. He scratched the back of his head. "What the …"

He started to hear faint chanting. Distant at first, it then began to edge closer and surround him. There was no indication of where it was coming from. He started to panic. He spun around in the clearing. The chanting grew faster and became deafening.

*"Ave Satan! Ave Cane!*
*Ave Satan! Ave Cane!*
*Ave Satan! Ave Cane!*
*Ave Satan! Ave Cane!*
*Ave Satan! Ave Cane!*
*Ave Satan! Ave Cane!*
*Ave Satan! Ave Cane!"*

David crouched down, clutching his ears, wincing.

Then, the chanting stopped.

He gradually stood up and took his hands from his ears. All was quiet again. He looked at his hands in the moonlight. They had blood on them. He was bleeding from his ears. He noticed the cold night air on his bare chest and torso. He looked down at his naked upper body. He was no longer wearing his T-shirt. On his chest, was a bloody inverted pentagram with an upside-down cross in the centre. The warm blood trickled down his stomach onto his jeans.

He watched, as a ring of fire surrounded him at the edge of the clearing. The flames moved inwards, eventually forming another inverted pentagram.

He heard a rumbling sound from underneath him. The ground shook and he could feel the sweat on his body turn cold, as if it was freezing.

A crunching sound reverberated from the ground, piercing through the damp soil. Numerous thick and long roots sprouted up in front of him and the tree shot up, appearing in all its full evil glory, towering above David who watched in frightened awe.

The clearing, illuminated by the brightness of the full moon, now began to change to a bright red.

David turned to look at the moon, which was also blood red. The tree began to make a groaning sound. Creaking at its centre, it began to vibrate and peel its bark back, opening up. A blinding light shone out of it, so that David had to shield his eyes with his forearm.

Static electricity hummed through him as though he were being charged up.

He removed his arm to squint at the tree, which he felt lured to. He looked down and felt his feet and body rise slowly off the ground, levitating. He was hovering a few feet in the air and suddenly, he was pulled in towards the tree. He tried to shout, but he couldn't. All he could do, was blink and breath as the tree pulled him closer in. Slowly at first, then without warning, he sped up, ploughing into the bright yellowly, white light.

David bolted upright in his bed, gasping for a huge intake of air. He was covered in sweat. His heart was palpitating, as though he was going to hyperventilate. His ears hurt and were ringing. After several minutes, he managed to compose himself.

The glimmer of dawn was emerging, which made him feel more comfortable. Eventually, he managed to fall back to sleep. Surprisingly.

*****

David woke a few hours later to a tapping sound. Through his open window, he could see a song thrush trying to break open a snail's shell on one of the stone turtles on the back garden lawn. A couple of knocks then came from the bedroom door.

"All right, mate? You're awake, then." John poked his head in.

David frowned. "You all right?"

"Yeah. Can you do us a favour?"

"Depends on what it is?"

"There's a *fucking* great spider in my room! You couldn't get rid of it for me?"

David couldn't help but smile. "No worries."

There had been a few times over the years, when John had asked David to remove spiders for him. He had a horrible phobia of them. When he was eight, a friend who collected them had left a box for John to open as a joke. The friend found it hilarious, but John had frozen.

"You want to hold it?" David joked as he raised the glass he had caught the spider in.

*"Get that fucking thing away from me!"* John shrieked, backing off.

David safely disposed of the arachnid in the garden, where he noticed that the song thrush had given up on the snail. He then headed back upstairs. "The spider won't be bothering you, anymore."

"Thank fuck for that. Cheers, bud."

"Anytime." David smiled. "It was certainly a whopper!" He then told John about his latest nightmare.

"Fuck. I'm sorry, mate. It seems strange that you're the only one getting these nightmares!"

"I know …" David looked out to the front lawn from John's window. He could see his aunt outside with an extension cable and a lawn mower. She seemed better now. He then decided on a shower.

He rested his hands on the cream wall tiles and closed his eyes, letting the hot water trickle over him. He thought about his nightmare; he felt targeted more than the others.

Exiting the bathroom with his towel wrapped around him, David saw his uncle come up the stairs.

"David … Carl has just rung."

"Oh?"

"He wants us to meet him tomorrow morning with his demonologist friend. Same place, at ten."

"Okay. I just hope they have some way forward for us; I had another nightmare last night."

"I know. I'm sorry. I was just speaking to John downstairs when the phone rang. Are you okay?"

"I guess. At least for now." David then described his nightmare.

*****

"Okay, we'll see you tomorrow!" John said sounding excited as he got off his mobile. "Good news." He smiled at David who had come downstairs.

"What's that?"

"Annabel wants us to double date tomorrow. At least she wants to see me again. I'd rather it was just me and her, though."

"Double date?"

"Yeah."

"Emily hasn't said anything about it. In fact, I haven't even heard from her since last night."

"I'm sure you will! Annabel said to tell you Emily will message you soon about it. They're busy at the pub this morning; something about having to make a shitload of sandwiches for a work buffet lunch. She didn't use the word 'shitload,' though." John smiled.

"What do they plan on doing?" David asked.

"Guess!" John smiled again.

"I dunno … bowling?"

"Think outside the box. *More* outside!"

"Jesus. I don't know. Tennis?"

"*Tennis*? What the fuck!"

"I don't know. Just *tell* me!" David wasn't in the mood for guessing games. His mind was distracted.

*"Quad biking!"* John grinned widely, holding his hands aloft. He dropped his phone onto the wooden hallway floor. "Shit."

"Quad biking? What the hell."

"Yep! Quad trekking. She said she'd phone again later after work to talk more."

David looked serious.

"Cheer up, pal. It'll be fun!"

"Maybe, if all this other stuff wasn't happening," David said glumly. "I'm not sure that it's a good idea."

"C'mon mate. You said the *exact* same thing about the disco and you had a good time. Especially with Emily! I don't mind if it's just me and Annabel, though. But she might lose interest if you and Emily don't go."

"I don't know. Besides, we've got to meet Carl again tomorrow morning."

"I know," John replied. "But it won't be until around three or four that we go with the girls. That Jock gave them half a day off."

"Don't you have to book in advance for that sort of thing?" David asked.

"Usually. But Annabel has a friend who works there. Probably helps when you have big titties! So, it's all good!" John replied, rubbing his hands.

David was impressed that John was still trying his best to make the most of things. Obviously, Annabel helped too. "I'll see what Emily says, if she contacts me."

"I'm sure she will. She likes you a lot!"

David tried to smile.

# Chapter Fifty

## 18th July, 2018

Gavin had decided to cut the other remaining barley field and John and David could hear Betty still busy with the lawn mower, but out at the back now.

"I haven't seen this shit in ages," John said, shaking his head. "It's still the same old crap, with people trying to prove their innocence to their partners."

They were sat in the living room with morning TV on, a tabloid talk show.

David was texting Emily who had followed up with him on the quad trekking idea. "It's the same with a lot of other programmes. I don't know why you don't just turn it off. It's always the same old rubbish in the mornings."

"What I find ironic is how the host chastises most of his guests, yet if it wasn't for these people, he wouldn't have a show. Seems hypocritical to me. He's still the same arrogant twat."

"True. But you can say that about a lot of things. People making a living out of bad people and stuff," David replied, scratching his forehead.

"Yeah, but all this guy seems to do is moan and criticise people! I feel like a stay-at-home mum watching this crap during the day."

"Turn it off, then!" David laughed. Emily had made him feel better. She had apologised for not texting earlier, but she was busy at work. She had also dropped her phone into a salad bowl whilst texting him, covering it in mayonnaise, which made him smile.

"Nah. Going to wait for the lie-detector results!" John said, looking over at David. "At least you look happier."

"Emily's making me smile."

"Definitely love!" John grinned.

"Eat shit," David replied, giving John the finger.

John smiled to himself and went back to watching the show.

The lie-detector results soon came through; John was right. Despite the man on the show protesting his innocence and getting angry about the accusations, he had cheated numerous times on his overweight girlfriend.

"Told you!" John said as the host walked over to show the results to the guilty guy, who still denied the allegations. "The teeth on him as well. Surprised anyone would wanna shag him!"

Just as David was about to comment on this, Derek rushed in, out of breath.

"Where's Bob?" Derek panted.

"What is it, Derek?" David asked as they both got up.

Derek swallowed, before answering, "It's … it's one of the cows … I think she's giving birth!" He pointed out towards the pens.

John and David looked at one another.

"That it?" John said to Derek. "You seem a bit concerned. You must be used to seeing that?"

"Normally. Aye. But we didn't know she was pregnant!"

Bob had come downstairs and entered the room.

"Boss!"

"Is something wrong, Derek?"

"No. Well, maybe, I don't know!"

"Well, what is it?" Bob asked concerned.

"It's one of the cows. I think she's giving birth!"

"What?" Bob smiled, confused. "That's impossible. None of the cattle are pregnant."

"Come see for yourself, boss!"

Bob and Derek hurried outside and John switched off the TV, before they too scuttled after Derek and Bob up towards the pens.

The group, along with Jack, stood in the cow pen watching as the black female bovine, Clarabelle, lay on her side.

"What do you think, boss?" Derek asked, scratching his bald head and perspiring in the summer heat.

"I don't know," Bob said. "Perhaps, she's just unwell?"

"Aye. But she seems to be pushing!" Derek replied.

"Why the surprise though, Uncle? It's normal for a cow to give birth, isn't it?"

Bob took a moment to reply, "Normally, of course. But not in this case, because apart from cows, we only have a few oxen," Bob answered.

"Oxen?" John asked.

"It means the males have been castrated," Derek explained.

"We don't breed cows, anymore. We haven't for a number of years, now," Bob added. "And even when we did, the calves were born in the spring, never the summer." Bob walked closer to Clarabelle and knelt down, stroking her stomach. He muttered some consoling words to her.

He started to press. He could feel some contractions and cramping. He looked up at the four men looking down at him. Shock stared out from his unshaven, tired face. "Derek is right; she's about ready to give birth! How is this possible?" he said, getting up. "I can't understand it … she never even appeared pregnant. We surely would have noticed it?"

"How long does it normally take for the calf to come out?" John asked.

"It can take a few hours. But I think she's close," Bob answered.

"Do you need to do anything? Can we help?" David asked.

Bob shook his head. "There's nothing that we can do, really. We must just let nature take its course."

It took Clarabelle sixteen more painful minutes to finally give birth. She moaned and writhed in a fair amount of discomfort and pain. A concerned Bob tried to console her, by stroking her as she lay and pushed.

John felt sick and joked about being mentally scarred for life from the birth as he started to see two small, wet-hooved feet and legs come out of the cow's vagina.

Bob pulled gently on the legs to help as Clarabelle appeared to be struggling.

Jack looked on with a strange smile on his face.

The baby calf finally oozed out onto the straw, covered in blood and a white, slimy, wet sheath wrapped over its small body.

The calf remained still to begin with, not moving until Clarabelle rose, wobbling and started to lick her new-born clean. She removed the covering gently with her teeth and large pink tongue.

*"What the heck is that?"* John asked alarmed as the black calf emerged from the sheath.

The group stared down at the mother and new-born calf with *two* heads.

"Is it alive?" John questioned further.

"I … I think it is," David replied. "You can see one of its eyes blinking." He looked over at his uncle to gauge his reaction to this abnormal birth. Bob just stood there, ashen-faced. He then knelt back down and examined the calf.

Clarabelle's wet and rough tongue touched his hand. He didn't say anything at first. He was still in shock. His other hand covered his mouth as he frowned. He was deep in thought.

The two-headed calf gradually came to its senses and began to stand up. It too wobbled as it tried to find its balance.

Bob eventually spoke, rising to his feet. "I … I recall many years ago, reading a story of something similar. I think it's extremely rare."

"It seems okay, though," David said.

They watched the mother and calf share a tender moment. Clarabelle was still affectionately cleaning her calf.

"Aye, it does," Derek said.

"How on *earth* did Clarabelle get pregnant in the first place? This doesn't add up! Surely, we should have noticed? It's like it's happened almost immediately!" Bob rubbed his rough face again. He had no answers.

John couldn't help but make a joke. "You haven't been having your way with these animals, have you, Dezza? Eh? You crafty so and so!" He winked.

Derek laughed.

Bob and David gave John a stern look.

John held his hands up as if to say 'sorry.'

"It's certainly a strange one, aye!" said Jack, who had remained quiet during the birth. "Not something I've seen before … guess there's a first time for everything!"

"I think I'll call the vet out. Just to get him to have a look at the calf."

"That's a good idea, boss," Derek agreed.

*****

It took well over an hour for the vet to arrive. Colin Roberts had known Bob for a number of years and had often dealt with Bob's animals when they needed treatment, occasionally having to put an animal down for him, which was one reason Bob had called him. Although the calf seemed fine, if it was in pain, something might need to be done.

Gavin had since stopped harvesting and joined the group before the vet arrived. He too had no explanation for how Clarabelle got pregnant.

"Well, its vitals seem to be okay," the vet, Colin, said. He took the stethoscope from his ears, placed them in his black vet's bag clipping it shut and stood up. "You know, it is *extremely* rare for something like this to happen, but it isn't completely unusual."

"You've seen something like this before, then?" David asked.

"Personally? No. But I have read of it happening. I think I read once that it happens every three or four hundred million times. As I said, extremely rare!

Unfortunately, though, the offspring don't usually live for long."

"You say it's fine, though?" Gavin asked. He had since taken off his flat cap to give some air to his sweaty head.

"Yes, it appears to be from what I can tell. Its heart rate seems perfectly normal. As does its breathing and internal organs."

"But how on earth did she even get pregnant?" Bob asked. "We should have been able to see, surely?"

Colin smiled. "Sometimes an animal can be pregnant without it being detectable. As for how your cow got impregnated in the first place, I can't answer that. It's very strange, I admit. But perhaps there's been a rogue bull up here somewhere, which managed to get in and mate with your cow? As you're aware, animals have been disappearing, and in yours and Angus' case, a lot worse. I'm sorry to bring that up."

"That's okay," Bob replied. He sighed. "Maybe you're right. But I don't see how a bull could have got in."

"Sounds like 'bullshit' to me," John muttered.

Only David and Jack heard. Jack prevented himself from laughing.

"What do we do now?" Bob asked.

"Just treat the calf as you would any other animal. I don't see any reason for it to be euthanised. It's not in any pain and it seems in perfectly good health. As I said, though, the life expectancy isn't long, I'm afraid. Only time will tell," Colin replied.

"Seems a bit contradictory. You say it's fine, but at the same time, you don't expect it to live long. What might cause it to die?" David asked, looking first at Colin and then at the calf.

"Animals born with this rare condition are weaker. It's a condition called polycephaly. It's where an embryo starts to split into twins, but the split doesn't fully develop. It's only one animal, not two." Colin smiled, trying to explain the strange abnormality.

"Pretty damn disturbing, whatever causes it," John remarked.

"I understand your concerns." Colin smiled again, rubbing his neck. "But it isn't anything to be alarmed by in that sense. I know some people believe it is a 'bad omen,' but that's a silly old wives' tale. Hopefully, everything will be okay, but don't hesitate to call me, if you're worried about anything, Bob." Colin gave a friendly pat on Bob's right shoulder.

"A bad omen, huh?" John said as they watched Bob walk Colin back to his silver Volvo.

"Aye. I wouldn't read too much into it," replied Jack.

"Normally, we wouldn't," David said quietly.

"At least the calf appears fine," Gavin said. They watched it roll over to get closer to its mother. "We'll just have to keep an eye on him and take extra good care of him."

*****

That evening, after Betty cooked a steak and chips dinner, she went for a long soak, followed by a read and an early night.

With the exception of Jack and Derek, the others were out talking in the cow pens.

They were looking again, at the two-headed calf that was asleep with Clarabelle. None of them had mentioned anything to Betty.

"You obviously love animals, Bob, and you don't send them away to a slaughterhouse. I'd have thought you perhaps would have been a vegetarian?" John asked.

"It may sound hypocritical, but I believe you can still love animals despite eating them. The same as vets. Many aren't vegetarians or vegans. To be honest, me and Betty did go a fair while without eating meat but we kind of relapsed so to speak, a few years ago.

"To be fair, though, we tend not to eat too much meat if we can help it. Regarding the farm, we've never sent animals away to a slaughterhouse. We always wanted animals to live a happy and safe life up here. They're all part of the family, really! More than just pets. We like to think of them as companions."

"I've often considered giving up meat. I love animals and it seems wrong – innocent animals being born, just to be killed and eaten. But then, killing innocent animals humanely for food is better than for rituals or sacrifices!" David said.

"It makes me laugh, when you get these so-called vegetarians or vegans, wearing leather and stuff. So hypocritical!" John said. "I've been thinking. Perhaps this calf was some kind of immaculate conception," he half-joked.

"What if it is some kind of bad omen? Although, it's not like bad things *aren't* already happening." David shook his head.

"Or maybe it's all a strange coincidence? She got pregnant and we just never noticed."

"You don't really believe that do you, boss? Even I find that hard to believe," Gavin said. "There is no way in hell she's been pregnant for nine months or so! We would have known. You know that."

No one said anything for a moment.

"I guess I'm trying to convince myself that this is somehow normal." Bob walked over and gently petted the calf first and then the mother. "We'll have to come up with a name for him!" Bob smiled, looking around. "Though I guess, we'll have to see how he goes."

*****

The evening grew darker into the night with cloud cover. There were a few rumbles of thunder. David once again offered to help his uncle and Gavin, but Bob insisted they'd be fine, so David and John finally went up to bed.

"What another fucked up day," John said as he and David stood outside their rooms.

Benji made his way into David's room.

"Shh! Keep your voice down. Betty's only down the hall," David replied, frowning.

"Shit. *Sorry*! I'm not sure how much longer your uncle can keep all this from her, though."

"I know. But he's doing what he thinks is best for now."

"Yeah. Going to be an interesting day tomorrow seeing Carl and the demonologist. Hopefully, they can help with all this. Then, of course, we've got the quad biking with the girls!"

They heard a door open from down the hallway. Betty came out in her nightie. She stopped for a moment and stared at them, before going into the bathroom.

"Bit strange. You think she saw us?"

"Of course she did. It isn't that dark. She probably heard us talking." David swallowed. He was a little concerned.

They could hear Betty humming in the bathroom.

"She's doing that creepy hum again," John whispered.

David didn't say anything.

"I'm sure she's okay, mate. Don't worry about it," John said, opening his bedroom door.

They heard the toilet flush and the bathroom door open. Betty walked slowly back to her bedroom without acknowledging either of them. She closed the door.

"I'm not convinced," David replied.

"Try not to worry about it. I'm going to crash." John gave an affectionate slap on David's back and then turned the light on in his room. The two cats were back on his bed. He smiled at them. "I'll see you in the morning."

"Night," David replied, still looking down the hallway.

John lay on his bed before falling asleep, thinking about everything. He felt concerned, like the others, but he found some comfort in thinking of Annabel and tomorrow's double date quad trekking.

**19th July, 2018**

It was now John's turn to dream …

He was standing in the bowling alley. He was almost naked, except for the Union Jack boxers he had worn to bed. He began to shiver as the coldness of the bowling alley enveloped him. He could feel his bare feet on the hard, cold floor.

*"What the shit!"* he said to himself. His hands began to freeze and he started to tremble. He walked over to some mirror on the wall with *McLintock's Bowling Alley* printed on it. His feet left frosted prints. His soles were beginning to burn with the cold. *"Ow! Shit!"* He tried rubbing his feet warm.

The corners of the mirror began to ice over. His upper body began to tense with the bitter cold. He saw his pale face and body, his lips blue. His reflection disappeared as the whole mirror became covered in ice. John then watched as his legs, followed by his arms, became blue from the unnatural cold. His body was starting to freeze. The end of his toes and fingers became black and blue through frostbite. He wanted to scream, but his mouth and throat were too cold and frozen. It felt like ice was coursing through his veins and blood vessels, freezing them in the process.

His upper body became white and frosted and his eyelashes hardened. It was becoming harder to even see. Down the bottom of one of the bowling lanes, he saw a cloaked figure hovering, massive and daunting. *"Mmmfff. Mmff. MMFFF!"* John tried to call out but his mouth and throat were completely frozen.

He could sense this cloaked entity was laughing at him.

There was another voice. *"Chaidh rabhadh a thoirt dhut cumail air falbh … Cha tug thu aire air an rabhaidhean sin … Agus airson sin pàighidh tu!"* It kept repeating as if on a loop.

John recognised the voice of the man who had threatened him at the bowling alley. Suddenly, the walls and floor of the bowling alley began to fold away and disappear. He was floating in darkness, completely frozen. He could no longer see the cloaked figure, but he sensed it was still there with him. It had blended into the blackness and this chanting seemed to come from all around him now:

*"Canus, Canus, Canus, Canus, Canus, Canus."*

He quickly dropped through the emptiness to the ground and seemed to be in a small clearing in the forest, lit by the full moon. He slowly got up, no longer frozen. He covered his nose from the foul stench of something terrible, which made him feel nauseous. He looked around at nothing but darkness and the outline of the trees, except for the cloaked figure, hovering on one side. John's heart thumped in his chest. He must run, but where? The cloaked figure glided towards him, its grey hands held out, black talons stretched. But before it could grab him, John opened his eyes and gasped aloud. He sat bolt upright in the bed, startling both Sammy and Josie, who both jumped off the bed in the moonlight.

"David. *David!*" John tried to shout to waken his friend. His heart was still beating nineteen to the dozen. His hands and feet were still cold and sore.

"What time is it?" David groaned, opening his eyes, still half-asleep. "Why's the light on? Not another spider?" David noticed his friend was caped in sweat. "What is it?"

"I … I had a dream. A *nightmare*. I can't breathe." John's voice trembled.

It took a few seconds for David to respond. He tried to calm his friend down and told him to sit down and breath slowly, in through his nose and out through his mouth.

John explained the nightmare. He had managed to calm down, but his hands were still shaking. David put an arm around John's shoulders to reassure him.

"It felt so real, and I *felt* everything."

David smiled with sympathy and understanding. "I know, but you're fine now."

John sighed and looked at David. He was near to tears. He shook his head. "I don't think I can sleep, now. What time is it?"

"I'll have a look." David got up and turned his phone on, checking the time, before turning it back off. "Just gone half-three. The sun will start to come up soon. You can stay in here, if you want, mate?"

"I don't know. Sounds a bit gay!" John tried to joke, causing them both to raise a wee smile.

"I'll lie on the floor next to Benji. You can have the bed. We can get a few more hours in at least before the meeting."

John agreed and David moved onto the floor next to Benji.

David soon fell back to sleep, but John lay in the bed, dozing in and out of consciousness until dawn.

# Chapter Fifty-One

## 19th July, 2018

John sat alone at the kitchen table. He wasn't hungry but tried to eat a small bowl of cereal before their meeting with Carl and Arthur. He was staring blankly, watching milk run off his spoon, when David came into the kitchen with Benji.

"Hey. You all right? Did you sleep okay, after what happened?"

John looked up. "No. Not really, mate. I dozed on and off but couldn't get off properly. I feel like crap. I'm not sure I'm up to going out with Annabel later."

"I'm having second thoughts as well. Even though I'd really like to see Emily."

"You can go. I don't mind taking you. I'll see how I feel after we've met with Carl and his friend. Although, we'll probably feel worse! Shit … I'm not even hungry." John threw his spoon into the soggy bowl of cornflakes and pushed his bowl away.

"Where is everyone?"

"Your uncle's upstairs in the shower, Gavin's still outside. I've not seen your aunt, though. Bob said she's upstairs watching TV."

"Ah, okay. I might have some breakfast, before we head out."

"You can have mine, if you like? I haven't touched any of it," John offered.

David pulled up a seat and took John's bowl of cereal. "How about the baby calf? Is he fine this morning? Something else to tell Carl."

"Didn't see him myself. But they said he was okay, still."

"That's good, then."

"I'm going upstairs until your uncle is done. Check my messages, too." John got up from the table, looking glum. He walked past David placing a hand on his left shoulder.

*****

Gavin stayed behind with Jack and Derek again whilst the others went to Tomatin. Bob told Betty he was going to show David and John around a bit more and do some shopping. Betty didn't question anything.

John was subdued on the way to Tomatin. He and David texted Annabel and Emily, saying they'd confirm later, as John wasn't feeling too good. When they arrived in Tomatin, it started to rain. There seemed to be more cars parked up than the last time they were there. They couldn't help but feel that it was a pointless exercise attending a second meeting but they were desperate for any help they could get.

"Well. Here we are again!" Bob said, unfastening his seatbelt.

"For what good it will do," John muttered.

"We have to at least try," replied Bob.

"I know," John said back.

The three of them and Benji climbed out of the Land Rover. Bob had left his shotgun in the boot again. He had taken it just in case. They made their way to the entrance of the building, where a ladder was propped up outside.

A man wearing a blue cap with a window squeegee was cleaning the windows. "Good morning," he said as the three entered the building.

They walked past the other offices, where David made eye contact with a seated woman who smiled at him.

"I'll knock," John said as they came to the office door of Carl.

They heard Carl clear his throat from inside.

"Come in ... Ah. I'm glad you could make it." Carl smiled. "Arthur is running a little late. He should be here in a short while. Please, sit."

Whilst they waited for Arthur to arrive, they told Carl about the incident on the road with the goat's head, their nightmares and about the two-headed calf. They waited nearly twenty minutes for Arthur to arrive. A knock on the office door was followed by an elderly man walking in.

"I'm sorry, I'm late," Arthur said, closing the door after him. He carried a brown leather satchel over his right shoulder. He was tall, slim and dressed in black jeans and a tucked in black shirt. Around his neck hung a large, chunky, silver cross.

Arthur Dooley was seventy years old and looked it, with long white hair tied back in a ponytail, and a bushy, white goatee. He was half-American from his father's side and born and raised in Philadelphia. His parents had divorced when he was seventeen, after which his English mother returned home. After his father died suddenly of an aneurysm, Arthur and his wife, Mary, now deceased, moved to England to be near his mother in Cambridge, where he taught religious studies for twenty years before taking early retirement. Arthur had been a 'self-styled' demonologist for over sixteen years, but was well-qualified with a PhD in theology, religious studies and religious sociology; he could also speak and read in Latin.

*****

After Arthur had greeted the group and spoken briefly about his work, including challenging demonic activities and hauntings, the others brought him up to date on all their experiences. Bob mentioned Betty too. Arthur then reiterated the historical explanations Carl had already given them.

"But why do John and I experience the worst of it all? For example, why are we having these nightmares?" David demanded. "Things were happening to us *before* we even came here. We just don't get it."

Carl had borrowed a chair from another office so Arthur could sit.

Arthur cleared his throat before explaining further. He had long since lost his American accent so he sounded English. "Perhaps, they felt you were some kind of threat and wanted to stop you from coming. Punishing you for going against their warnings ..."

"A threat to what? Why would *we* be a threat? We're just human beings. What could *we* do to threaten them?" John laughed at the irony that they might be frightening the cult.

"There are some things in this world, which we will never fully understand, if at all. It's also feasible that these people and the entity they worship 'likes' something about you. Perhaps, they are testing you?"

"Testing us how?" David asked.

"Your resolve. Especially, after you ignored their warnings. You said you planned your trip around two weeks prior to coming, after you had lost your jobs? It's quite possible that they were watching you or knew about your plans somehow. And your other friend's plans. Grant, was it?"

"Look, it's obvious that these people are evil. But why not just kill us; why are we still here? Others have died before, just for knowing about them. I'm sorry, but it just seems contradictory," David said.

Arthur smiled understandably. "Killing people is too easy for them ... They don't always target bad people, or people who are already sinners. It's more often the good people in this world they target. Although some believe that God uses Satan, the Devil, whatever you wish to call him, to punish wicked unbelievers and that demons can't do anything unless commanded to do so ... Personally, I don't believe that.

"Regarding *Famuli Cani*; the demon encourages them to kill and sacrifice people and animals. Evil also tries turning good further and further away from the light and God, until the point at which they can't be saved, destroying their faith." Arthur asked Carl if he could fetch him some water.

"This cult gets sick fun out of terrifying people and playing with them. They want to break you. Make you suffer. Before they end up killing you. If you just died straight away, there would be more chance your soul could be saved. You may not have lost all faith in God. It's possible they're just biding their time. They're waiting for their moment. They no doubt have plans for you both. *All* of us." Arthur swept his hand around the room, motioning to them all.

"Take the other night you were telling us about ... when you were in the car and you heard chanting over the radio and saw the goat's head and inverted pentagram of fire. They could no doubt have killed you then ... but the torment and suffering are more enjoyable to them. It's what comes *before* death. Famuli Cani, particularly The Grey One and demons in general, feed on people's fear, emotions and negative energy. It gives them more power. Especially the sacrifices. They clearly don't wish you dead, *yet.* Myself included. They could be weighing you up. It senses you are *good* people. They find you a challenge, perhaps."

"Well, at least that's something, then. At least we're 'nice' people and may or may not go to Heaven, eh, when they *do* eventually decide to kill us!" John replied sarcastically.

David and the others looked at him.

"Unless, they break us so much that we lose what little faith we *do* have and go to *Hell* instead? It's nice to know that 'God' is willing to let it happen and potentially punish us for doing so." John sounded a little abrupt.

"I'm certain you are some of the good ones." Arthur smiled and tried to reassure. He sensed good in these people. "Some believe that demons are on a leash as well. Basically put, demons can only go as far as God allows and permits them. Although I'm religious, I don't agree with all views and aspects of religion. But if there are demons and evil spirits, then surely it is proof that there is a God."

"God has a funny way of proving he's about. There's more horrible shit happening in the world than good," said John, annoyed.

"I understand. I ask myself the same thing at times — like we all do. Eternal life comes into it, too. Many people believe that demons want to lure our soul to their dark side, lead us away from salvation and to hurt God also, by doing so. And in this case, *The Grey One* offers rewards for certain sacrifices."

"You're basically saying that it's possible that if we lose faith in God, whilst suffering and being tormented, our souls may be punished for eternity?" David asked sounding confused. "And how does this demon communicate with its people?"

"It is one possible explanation, yes. But I don't really agree with it. As I say, I'm somewhat religious. But that doesn't mean I necessarily agree with everything that is in the Bible or all this nonsense about the *wrath* of God. The Old Testament is full of things like that. For me, if anything, God is good and about love." Arthur stroked his white beard. "As for how the demon communicates with its cult, it may be telepathic. Some demons aren't capable of speech, which is why people hear voices inside their heads.

"Your accounts are unique; I have to admit. I've spoken to people over the years who have claimed to have seen a hooded, cloaked figure in the forest. But you're the first I've come across with all these varied experiences. Sometimes, demons don't like showing themselves, because it may encourage non-believers to turn to God, which is something they obviously don't want. That sounds contradictory, I know. You've seen this demon, albeit, not its face."

"I guess we really are 'special,' then," John again replied sarcastically.

"You spoke of rewards The Grey One gives in return for sacrifices ... what sort of rewards?" Bob asked.

"For example, drinking the blood of victims can increase life span. Or taking the blood from a baby or child that has been sacrificed — their youth can make *them* young again. The spillage of such innocent young blood is the ultimate sacrifice." Arthur looked down at the desk, saddened.

"What kind of sick fucks sacrifice babies and children?" John asked.

David shook his head. "It's disgusting."

"That's one way of putting it ... but that's what we're up against. It's what these people, Famuli Cani, are about. They enjoy the torment and killing. They perform numerous rituals."

"What about this tree? What the hell is that thing? We could feel this energy pulsate through it." David asked. "And the smell of sulphur."

Arthur exhaled. "The cult member that came forward, before they were tortured and killed, spoke briefly of a sinister looking tree, somewhere in the forest. He didn't go into too much detail, but claimed the tree had been formed from sacrifices down the years. The energy from the poor, lost souls, along with dark magic, helped it to grow; witchcraft and Satanism combined.

This deceased member said something about how it helps the demon transport or teleport to wherever it wishes outside the confines of the forest."

"Teleports? It's starting to sound a bit far-fetched," John replied.

"Maybe. But remember, it *was* in my flat. And in Grant's place, too." David looked at John who looked back.

Arthur nodded. "The smell of sulphur is usually associated with demons. The smell of rotten eggs, excrement. Basically, bad odours and foul smells like that. Maggots are a representation of death and decay."

"Surely, if we came across this tree, then other people will have, too?" David asked.

"Our source from the cult claimed the tree could disappear underground. It wasn't always visible. Perhaps, you weren't supposed to have seen it that morning? Or maybe, it was part of *their* plan to allow you to come across it deliberately? I don't know. People have mentioned symbols being carved into the trees. Most people don't pay too much attention to them. But the cult is marking their territory, where they perform their sacrifices. Some believe that Rothiemurchus Forest also has ley lines running directly underneath it. Other forests in these parts, too." Arthur had a sip of water from his plastic cup. His mouth was becoming dry from all his talking.

The others waited for him to continue.

"Despite its supernatural powers, this entity doesn't have the power to kill by itself. Because the cult summoned it in the first place, it's linked to them, and has to rely on them. It's powerless without the acolytes. Well, less powerful. Just as they are powerless without it, to a certain degree. They both feed off one another … The more the sacrifices happen, though, the higher the chance that this dark entity will be able to do more things. We already know it's grown from the footprints." Arthur drank some more.

"How often are these sacrifices performed? Not just the animals, the human ones?" Bob asked.

Arthur finished his water. "Most Satanists stick to the *Satanic calendar*. Famuli Cani are no different …" Arthur pulled out a couple of sheets of paper from his brown leather satchel and placed them on the desk for everyone to view. He also put on a pair of round glasses from his satchel. "There's a lot that goes on within this cult. They aren't just about sacrifices. They do many things. They have meetings, get togethers, things like that. Usually, dark things, mind. They also have orgies."

John looked up from across the desk at Arthur. "*Orgies*? Maybe they aren't too bad after all," he joked.

Arthur raised a smile. "As you can see, the calendar is quite detailed."

The three of them scrutinised this calendar, or Satanic 'holidays.'

Carl was standing near the window. He opened it, lit his pipe and wafted out the match.

"Satanic Revels? Sounds like they have some fun," John said sarcastically and pointed to a date: 3rd August. "Sexual rituals? Anal, oral, vagina? That's not too far from now!" John pretended to act excited.

"Yes," Arthur replied. "Now, I'm not saying all cults do all of this. But regarding Famuli Cani, they most certainly do. That's the thing too, Robert …"

Bob looked up at Arthur.

"You've been at your farm for many years, yes?"

"That's correct."

"You said you've never had any experiences, until the past two or three weeks?"

Bob nodded. "Well, apart from … from Charlie."

"Right. So it wasn't always every night that these things happened. Plus, Rothiemurchus Forest stretches over a huge area. That includes other forests around here, too … The cult might not even have known about your farm until recently so it's feasible you wouldn't have heard or seen things all the time down the years. Especially, as things have also been covered up. Just because you're in the middle of the forest and things are happening, it doesn't mean you're always going to be aware of them all.

"Famuli Cani has always been careful about exposing itself. Yes, there have been reports of fires, but like we've already stated, they're protected by the authorities and such events are passed off as arson or nothing major." Arthur got up himself this time to pour another cup of cool water and walked back to the desk to sit down.

"For many years, they always stuck to the calendar. But their thirst, quite literally, for blood and power, has grown stronger and more sadistic. They have added their own additional sacrifice and ritual dates to those on the traditional Satanic calendar. They no doubt have increased their numbers, becoming more powerful."

"What's so significant about the dates on this calendar, anyway?" Bob asked.

"The Satanic calendar lists dates which are 'unholy' days, in the same way that Christians have certain special holy days. These dates are more potent to them for their rituals and killings. For example, celebrating Christmas or

Easter on other days, say in January or during the summer would lose the significance and have no meaning. It isn't the same. But keeping to the tradition, it means more and is stronger.

"The Grey One holds influence over its followers. Now that the group has more members, it's more powerful and stronger. More power creates *more* power. Regardless, they enjoy these rituals and killings. The calendar and dates are based on numerology and astrology. You can see some details overleaf; it's made up of four periods of thirteen weeks each. The number thirteen is held in *very* high regard with occultists and Satanists, and deemed a strong and powerful number."

"Unlucky for some," Bob said to himself as they turned over the sheet of paper, reading some more information about the calendar.

It mentioned how many rituals and occult activities were held during a full moon or certain moon phases and how cults could move around undetected.

David saw more of the titles and dates of certain rituals and their descriptions. He was horrified by what he read. "They even *eat* humans, including infants? I thought sacrificing them was bad enough!" He felt sick.

"I'm afraid so, yes," replied Arthur.

"It also says here that they have intercourse or sexual relations with demons?" John asked, seeking confirmation.

"I am not sure Famuli Cani participates in that particular ritual ... demons don't necessarily have reproductive organs. But they can still feel sexual pleasure. The cult can also wear masks, sometimes the skin of the victims they've sacrificed."

"That's fucking sick!" John shook his head.

"Remember that Samuel in the pub? He talked about masks," David reminded John.

John nodded.

Arthur shared that he had also received warnings over the years and that the now deceased ex-member of the cult had approached him randomly in the street one morning in the small village of Carrbridge. Famuli Cani leant towards the *theistic* Satanists, who believe that Satan is a deity. Arthur was also concerned that the two-headed calf could well be a prophecy that something terrible was about to happen. Arthur also showed them photos of mutilated animals and symbols of the occult used by Satanists and Famuli Cani.

"Such awful things, eh?" Carl said, finally finishing his pipe.

"It's still odd that the cult wants to remain secretive but displays powers sometimes, or leaves mutilated animals to be photographed. It doesn't make sense," David said. He fetched himself a plastic cup of water.

"Get me one too please, mate," John asked.

"They want people to see what they're capable of. To frighten us, if not to warn us. They wish to hurt people. Not just physically, but psychologically as well. Mentally and emotionally scar them. They're still careful not to reveal themselves, fully. And the things they do leave behind, such as the slaughtered animals, are deliberate. They *want* you to know that they are about. Perhaps, the same way a serial killer leaves clues and bodies. An ego thing as well," Carl said; he then walked over to his wastepaper bin and emptied out his pipe. He sat down next to Arthur.

"There are so many of these bastards involved. Even if not directly, they're on their payroll and paid to keep their mouths shut or face the consequences! Those people in themselves are no real threat, but they can disappear if they don't cooperate." Carl opened one of his draws and placed his pipe in there.

"Why haven't you gone to the local or national press? Maybe we should. Expose this cult and go out and prove demons and stuff actually *exist*!" said John passionately. "And at the same time, protect ourselves."

"Oh, John, my dear boy." Carl smiled. "In theory that's a great idea. It's just not a practical one. Perhaps, it's because we've not gone to the press that we're still alive? We want to expose this cult for what they are; murderous, vile, sick and twisted bastards. And to prove that *evil* entities exist … but it just isn't that simple.

"They no doubt watch us and have informants, like that guy you mentioned earlier, who you saw watching you leave here the other day. But if you go to the police now, the press or whoever, with the evidence you have so far, your photos and the notes, you will no doubt be stopped … we *are* in grave danger. It's highly possible that they have something in store for us."

"As mentioned, I've received notes like you in the past, warning me to back off … I even went abroad for a few years. I eventually came back. I had this strange feeling that I needed to return; like I was *supposed* to come back."

"How do you mean?" David asked Arthur.

"I don't know. *God*, maybe … I know it sounds silly, but maybe it's my job to help expose them. Or stop them. But only at the right time."

David and John looked at each other. They found it hard to believe Arthur was 'chosen' by God.

"Maybe we are chosen, too?" John joked.

Arthur smiled. "You never know. I do find it unique that you two have encountered what you have. But demons alone, can choose whom they wish to afflict. It can be random. Other times, they can sense something about you."

"I'm not sure I even believe in God," John said.

"But if there's evil, and demons, surely there is a God too, no?" Arthur asked.

"Maybe." John shrugged.

"You say that maybe you're only still alive because you backed off or haven't reported all of this. But why did others die who knew? Like that reporter, Marvin? Or why isn't that Samuel who we told you about dead?" David asked intrigued.

"Maybe they have bigger plans for me. For us ... it could even be that they're keeping us in a false sense of security. It certainly isn't nice, even unbearable at times, knowing that they know we know about them," Carl explained.

"Mine and Angus' farm obviously haven't been the only ones targeted over the years, then?" Bob asked.

"There have been numerous ones. You're not alone in that sense. I doubt it's much consolation for you, though. Others have lost pets, like yourself," Arthur answered. "Not long after I returned from abroad, there was a small farm near Abernethy Forest, not far from Nethy Bridge. The farm is no longer there. But the farm was run by an elderly couple and their two grown-up sons.

"Like you, they had a cat. It had gone missing for over a week. It was unusual, as it was more of an indoor cat. One morning, the housekeeper awoke in the early hours and heard this terrible screeching sound. She went downstairs and found the poor cat totally skinned and cut open on the back lawn. Its intestines were pulled out and laid out onto the grass. A Satanic symbol was carved into its body. Shortly after, they discovered several ewes out in the field, with their legs hacked off and bodies cut open. Their innards had been used to paint a perfect inverted pentagram on the grass."

"Dear God!" Bob exclaimed.

"Two days later, another farm not too far from there, suffered a similar fate. This time, it was chickens that had been hacked and torn apart. They also had a pet dog that was mutilated, its eyes gouged out. They had a stallion; again, slaughtered. Its genitalia cut off and stuffed into its mouth. Strange occult markings were sliced into its skin and nobody heard anything." Arthur swallowed.

Bob listened nervously.

"What happened to them? The ones who ran the two farms?" David asked.

"The elderly couple retired a few months later. They sold off the farm and the land, which has been built on. They didn't have many animals. As for the other farm with the horse, a similar thing. They didn't have many animals, neither. But they ended up losing more in the weeks that passed. The farmhouse is still there. But it isn't really a farm as such anymore. It isn't active. It's just a whole lot of empty land, really. Within a year, the family who ran it, still traumatised by what had happened, packed up and moved abroad. It never got any mention in the press. The victims were too scared to make it public knowledge, in case there were ramifications."

"What did the police say?" Bob asked Arthur.

"The usual stuff, really. Basically, that they'd look into it. They classed it as 'inflicting needless suffering on a defenceless animal.' In other words, they weren't too fussed. The police also believed that it was better not to inform the papers, because it would encourage other 'disturbed' people to follow suit … I think we know the main reasons why the stories are often hushed."

"Remind me, what were the origins of this demon?" Bob asked.

"The Grey One, or *Canus*, the Latin name for it, was summoned and arose during the winter solstice on a snow-capped Ben Macdui. Hence the ice and coldness you have experienced. I believe Rothiemurchus is a dark forest, and was reported as haunted long before the cult came," Arthur explained. "That may have attracted the demon, further."

"What about the chanting? What language is that?" David asked. "It sounds like Latin to me."

"You're correct." Arthur smiled.

"Can you speak it?" John asked.

"Yes. I studied it many years ago, like my wife … One language I can't speak though, is Scottish Gaelic; apart from a few words or phrases. That's another language that this cult uses. Not so much during their rituals, but in general or when discussing their matters with one another, along with their dark secrets."

"Are all these cult members Scottish?" David asked.

"Not at all. The cult originated mainly from Scottish nationals, but as the cult grew, members of any nationality or race could join, so long as they took the same blood oaths, served their *Master* and shared their sick creed," Arthur explained. "Although, they are usually pretty strict on who is chosen to join them. There are initiations that these new members have to go through, according to the ex-cult member who contacted us. We believe that the demon was summoned fully again on Saint Eichatadt Day."

Bob sneezed. "Excuse me!"

"Bless you." Arthur smiled.

"Think we can all do with that. A blessing!" Bob said as the others smiled slightly.

"Amen to that!" Carl half-laughed.

"Saint Eichatadt Day is a significant day in their calendar. It's a day of blood drinking and honouring demons. What better way to honour a demon, than sacrificing, summoning and affiliating yourself to it … Demons are the Devil's minions and they, Famuli Cani, also honour and thank Satan, for giving them Canus."

"Famuli Cani is the Latin name for this cult, then?" John asked.

"That's right; their preferred form. It basically means servant, and an attendant to a god. It comes from the word 'Famulus.' As for Cani, that comes from 'Canus,' which can mean 'frosty' or 'hoary white,' to describe hair and old."

On the subject of Latin, David remembered the silver ring that he had found, which he'd brought with him. He took it out of his jeans pocket and handed it to Arthur who confirmed what David already knew; the ring had St Benedict on it and could supposedly protect against evil.

"Perhaps, you should wear it. It might protect you," Arthur suggested.

David looked briefly at the ring and returned it to his pocket. "What about the person in this photo with electricity coming from their fingers?" David asked suddenly, getting out his phone.

"Again, black magic; witchcraft. It appears that whoever this person was, they were most likely following you. Be careful. Just because people appear normal, it doesn't mean that you can trust them," Arthur warned, looking at the photo of Emily and David.

"Are you referring to Emily, the girl I was with?"

"Yes. I'm not saying she's one of the cult members. I'm just saying you need to be careful, and not trust anyone. Well, apart from us. The same goes with you, John. All of you."

"But Emily is fine. She's sweet. I thought about the possibility. But no … there's no way she would join a cult," David said.

"I hope you're right. But I advise you to keep your distance from any new contacts in the meantime," Arthur advised.

"I'm with David on this. Annabel, the other girl, there's no way she's part of all this … Anyway, we've heard a *lot* of talk, but not much about how the *fuck* we stop all of this." John sounded a little angry.

Carl and Arthur sighed.

"That's the sixty-four-thousand-dollar question," Carl said.

"We, we don't really know," Arthur replied, hanging his head and sighing again. "Unfortunately, we don't know who they are or how many of them there are."

"And that's it? Jesus!" John said. "I knew this meeting would be a waste of time. It hasn't helped us at all!"

"There's nothing else we can do?" Bob asked.

"I am afraid not ... I'm still looking into other leads. I don't wish to say too much yet, though."

"Where do we go from here?" David asked. "It feels like we're sitting ducks. We can't just sit around, knowing they're a threat to us, whilst they keep on murdering innocent people, kids and animals ... *surely*, we must go to the police?"

"Bad idea," Carl said.

"Why? It's crazy not to! There might be someone on the force who *isn't* part of it all," David tried to insist.

"Because it's too risky; that's why," Arthur explained.

"Well, if they're likely to kill us anyway, it could be worth a shot," John said.

"We advise you *not* to go to the police!" Carl insisted assertively. "It isn't only us we have to worry about. It's our families, too. I'm in the process of going through a divorce, and boy, does that woman piss me off something chronic! But, I still love my wife. I couldn't risk anything happening to her *or* my children."

"If you're worried about your families, why not drop it all? Why make matters worse by pursuing it and talking to us?" John asked.

"They will grow more powerful and dangerous if nothing is done. And I owe it to Scott and Marvin. We just need to be careful and play it safe," Carl answered sadly. "Remain patient."

"Maybe it's best if you and John return home, David. It's too dangerous for you up here."

"*What*? Not a chance, Uncle!" David said firmly. "Besides, it could be too late now, anyway."

"I am afraid that David is most likely right ..." Arthur said as Bob and David turned to face him. "This entity and its worshippers may already have attached themselves to you all ... it could well be too late. Even if you go home, they will find you and torment you, regardless. That's what they want. We are all in great danger."

"So, what do you recommend?" David was looking for answers.

"Yeah. Hang crosses all over the house?" John said impatiently, looking at Arthur's large cross dangling around his neck. He doubted it was real silver.

"For now, we must protect ourselves," Arthur stated. "Bide our time."

"For fuck's sake!" John raised his voice, standing up. *"Argh!"* He ruffled his hair in frustration, pacing across the room.

Benji looked up, startled.

"Please, you need to calm down," Arthur pleaded.

"How can I? There's no fucking solution!"

"Please, John, sit down," Bob said calmly.

John exhaled. His nightmare seemed to have pushed him a little over the edge. He managed to sit back down.

"I do have experience in supernatural phenomena," Arthur said.

The others looked at him.

"This is by far the worst case I've come across … but there is one thing you can do, to try and prevent their dark energies and black magic from entering your home. Whether it works or not, depends on how powerful they are." Arthur looked across at the group.

"Well, how can we do that?" John asked, frowning.

"Salt Crystals," Arthur suggested.

*"What?"* John said completely flabbergasted.

"Salt can protect you against evils spirits and demons …" Arthur explained.

"Oh, c'mon! *Seriously*? You're having a laugh, mate!"

"John, let him finish!" Bob said, trying to calm him again.

"I know it sounds silly, but it serves as protection to ward off not only evil entities, but black magic, too."

"How, exactly?" David questioned.

"Basically, salt is pure and absorbs dark and psychic energy, purifying it. It can act as a barrier to prevent evil entities from entering somewhere. They can't get past it. It can help prevent people from being affected by dark influences. It can also have the same effect on benevolent spirits, too."

"This can work?" Bob asked.

"Yes. I'm not saying for certain in this case, but it's worth giving it a shot. It certainly won't hurt." Arthur looked serious. "At least until we find out what to do next."

"Maybe we should just plaster the *whole* damn forest with it, then!" John added sarcastically.

"I know it sounds dumb, but trust me, it may help. Especially in crystal form."

"You've seen proof of this?" Bob asked.

"I have. There was a case I was helping out with in southern Portugal. A family there, had problems with a haunting in their new home. Things were being moved around and items were disappearing. The wife was targeted the most. She'd be attacked in her sleep without realising it until the morning, when she woke with scratches on her arms and legs."

"What happened?" John asked.

"A priest came to bless the house and the house was cleansed."

"What's that got to do with salt, then?"

"If you let me finish, John." Arthur smiled. "Because the spirit was already in the house before they moved in, it was difficult to remove it. But we found that lining the rooms and beds with salt prevented the attacks. At least, for a while."

"At least for a while? The salt didn't really help, then?" John asked, shaking his head.

"Because the spirit in question fed off the family's fear, it drew more energy from it. The salt lost some of its potency. The root of the problem always needs to be erased. Thankfully, the priest's efforts worked."

John shook his head with a wry smile on his lips.

"What do you suppose we do, exactly? Cover the whole farm in salt?" Bob asked.

"What if we got a priest to bless the house?" David asked.

"A medium or priest won't work. It isn't like this demon is residing in your home. For the salt, I can help you out with that. I know someone who sells the salt crystals you need. It incorporates additional minerals and is blessed with holy water," Arthur explained. "You don't have to worry about the cost. I can sort it out. Leave it to me."

"Like that's going to work." John gave a look of disdain.

The others looked at him.

"It won't hurt, mate. We need to do something," David said.

John shook his head.

"I can get it delivered to you within a day or two. You need to mark lines of it around your home and the animal pens," said Arthur.

"It's certainly worth a shot," Carl advised.

"I don't know if you're religious people, but now might be a good time to find some faith. Praying can help," Arthur added.

John snorted. "Yeah, right!"

After further discussion, David mentioned that he and John were due to meet Emily and Annabel. Arthur and Carl tried again to dissuade David and John from trusting new acquaintances. Before they parted, Carl and Arthur promised to contact them soon as they were still looking into a few things.

"A waste of fucking time!" John said as they all got back into the Land Rover.

"Maybe. But there was no need to have been so dismissive with them, mate," David replied.

"I mean, *salt*, really?" John protested.

"John, he was only trying to help. Even if it doesn't help, it's worth a try. We don't have any other ideas and at least it's not going to cost anything." Bob turned the key to start the engine.

"How can we be sure we can trust them? Arthur looked more like a damn hippy, with that long hair of his." John shook his head.

# Chapter Fifty-Two

## 19th July, 2018

The two friends couldn't decide whether to see Emily and Annabel. Emily had texted David, asking if they were still on for later.

"Maybe it would be good to go and take our mind off of things?" John suggested.

"There's no way Emily or Annabel would be part of a cult," David said.

"You're probably right, David, but you're best to keep your distance for now," his uncle advised.

"I know, Uncle. It's just hard … I really like her."

Bob looked back at his nephew and smiled. "I know you do."

*****

Back at the farm, getting out of the Land Rover, they heard a loud scream, coming from behind the farmhouse.

"That sounded like Aunt Betty?" David said concerned.

The screams continued as they hurried to the source in one of the barley fields recently harvested by Gavin. Betty was screaming with tears running down her face and by her stood Derek.

*"What is it!"* Bob shouted frantically.

Strewn over the barley stalks were the remains of the new-born calf and Clarabelle. Both animals were completely disembowelled and decapitated, with their limbs severed. Flies were buzzing around the dead flesh and innards, which were carefully arranged in the shape of a near perfect, inverted pentagram, with the calf's two heads placed in the middle. The hearts of the animals lay on top of the two points and the three other points also had organs placed on them.

Bob was too aghast to say anything or even comfort his wife.

"Oh my God!" John spoke quietly.

"Unc-Uncle?" David said softly.

Derek was in tears. "I'm. I'm so sorry." He sniffed. "I tried phoning you, but there was no signal. I came over really odd and sick. I had to rush inside and use the downstairs loo. Then I heard the phone ring in your study, so I answered it, like you always asked of us." Derek started to weep harder.

"Betty was in the shower. When I picked up the phone, I heard this whispering and laughter, and someone saying my name over and over again. Then the line just went dead and I must have passed out. I was out for about fifteen minutes, I think. When I came back outside …" Derek sobbed into his hands.

"What about Jack?" David asked. "Where's Gavin?"

"J-Jack had to rush home. His neighbour called and said his mum had fallen. I'm … I'm so sorry, boss." Derek was now crying uncontrollably. "They were lying down together in the pens …"

David looked over at his aunt who was shaking. At least she had stopped screaming. Then he looked over at his uncle and back to Derek. "But what about Gavin?"

"Ga-Gavin told me to stay near the pens. We heard someone crying out for help. In the direction of the dirt track past the silos … just before I came over ill."

"They did this in around fifteen minutes, whilst you were out cold? You didn't hear anything?" John asked Derek.

Derek turned and looked at him, his eyes red and watery. "N-not a thing … I heard absolutely nothing." He wiped his nose on his cuff. "I'm sorry," Derek repeated, hanging his head.

"It's not your fault, Derek. You're not to blame. As long as you're all right." Bob put a consoling hand on Derek's shoulder, before walking over to his wife. "We need to find Gavin."

Betty turned to him; her own eyes red. "I … I came out to see if the boys wanted a cup of tea," she said, starting to cry again.

"It's okay," Bob said, hugging his wife and closing his eyes. He fought back his own tears.

Just then, Gavin came running up behind them. He had heard Betty scream. He wondered what they were looking at. When he saw, he realised their shock. He was speechless and in total shock himself, close to tears.

Gavin explained that after Jack had left, he and Derek had heard a woman's voice screaming for help. He had run all the way down the dirt track and beyond with his shotgun, past where John's car had broken down. The screaming continued, leading him further away from the farm. He then came to a tree with a note on, where the screaming had turned to laughter. He showed the others the handwritten note:

*Hope you enjoy the little surprise back at the farm!* ☺

*****

It had begun to rain heavily. Some of the blood seeped into the wet soil under the bloodied stalks. Bob had since taken Betty inside, whilst the others went to take shelter in the cow pens. David and John told Gavin what Arthur had explained to them.

"These fuckers must have been waiting for us to leave this morning. They obviously knew we were going to that meeting and they wanted you three out of the way," David said.

Gavin nodded. "It appears so. It's almost like they're toying with us. Trying to break us. Exactly as Carl and that Arthur warned."

"I bet they're still out there now, watching from the forest." John looked around.

"What are we going to do about the remains?" asked David.

"We can clean it up once it's stopped raining," Gavin answered.

"I dread to think of the pain they went through," David said.

"If only Jack had been here," John said. "I hope his mum his okay."

Gavin put his arm around Derek's shoulders and smiled. "Don't blame yourself, Derek. This wasn't your fault. Far from it. I shouldn't have left you. Maybe if you were outside, perhaps it still would have happened and you'd have been hurt too, or worse. As long as you're all right. Maybe you should go to the doctors, just to be safe?"

"I'm fine … I shouldn't have left them alone."

Gavin affectionately squeezed him. "Look at me!"

Derek reluctantly looked up at Gavin. He was close to tears again.

"It was not your fault, okay? It's all on them."

David pulled out the St Benedict ring. He didn't usually wear jewellery, but he put it on his right ring finger. It was a bit of a squeeze and the dent didn't help, but he managed to push it on.

John watched him. "You're going to wear that?"

The other two looked.

"May as well," David replied. "It can't hurt."

"Be about as effective as that salt when it arrives," John mocked.

Bob rushed up to them in the rain.

"How is she, boss?" Gavin called out.

"Not good. She's having a lie-down … I told her *everything*. Including about Angus and his animals being moved. She's in a bad way. She didn't need to see that." Bob wiped away a few tears. "The phone is working now. I just spoke to Jack."

"Is his mum okay?" John asked.

"She's fine, apart from a sprained ankle and headache. Jack insisted on coming back this afternoon. I told him to take the rest of the day off."

"That's good, then. At least she's all right," David said, looking again at the silver ring.

"I've been thinking, too. We're going to move the animals to a safer location."

"Really?"

"Yes, David; we should have done so from the start. I should have done it when Angus told me about his troubles."

"Where to, though? And won't it be costly?" John asked.

"It might be. I'm going to ring Angus to see if there's a place he can recommend, and ask him about the place he had his animals moved to. We need to do this as soon as possible. I don't care about the cost. We need to think about the animals' well-being, and our own. I wish I'd done this earlier."

"Maybe, boss. But you weren't to know how bad things would get," Gavin said, trying to give some words of comfort.

Bob shook his head. "As soon as you boys arrived and told me what had happened to you, I should have acted. We would certainly have had more sleep … Me and Betty are even thinking of getting away for a while, once the animals have been relocated."

"But remember what Arthur and Carl said? It may be too late for that now, Uncle."

"What about the animals, boss? We can't move them away for good." Gavin scratched the back of his head.

"Maybe we can? Perhaps, it's for the best. I love all our animals here. They're part of the family. But they're not safe here. And we don't know how we can keep them safe. We can't go on like this. Doing these nights."

"How do you know they'll be safe anywhere else? Temporary or permanent?" John asked.

"There is that, too, John," Bob replied. "We'll have to see. But for now, at least, moving the animals is the best bet." Bob hung his head.

"Whatever you decide, boss. I'm with you all the way," Gavin said.

Bob looked up and smiled. He could always rely on Gavin. Not only had he always been his best and longest serving worker, but also a true friend as well. Loyal as ever.

Bob then looked at Derek who was still staring at the ground. He walked over and hugged him. His body felt limp. "Please, don't blame yourself, Derek. You're not to blame for any of this. If anyone is, it's me. Please, don't feel guilty."

John and David decided to cancel their quad trekking date, giving illness as their excuse. They were in no mood right now and didn't want to leave the farm. Emily seemed the more disappointed out of the two.

# Chapter Fifty-Three

## 19th July, 2018

Bob sat alone in his study with the door shut and cried. After a few minutes, he wiped his eyes and phoned Angus. At least there was little interference this time. Angus gave Bob the number of the large farm sanctuary near Kilmarnock. Bob waited a moment before contacting them and tried to compose himself.

Apart from the distress from the day's events, Bob's emotions weren't helped by an old polaroid photo turning up in one of his desk drawers of William, Janet and little Charlie. They were sat on a tractor all looking so happy. Betty had written the date on the back of the photo. Although the ink had faded, it was three weeks before Charlie had disappeared.

Meanwhile, as the rain had eased, Gavin and the others started to clean up the remains of the animals. They wore latex gloves and took large yellow refuse bags with them. The rain had further rinsed some of the blood into the ground.

David picked up one of the calf's tiny legs and carefully placed it in one of the bags, along with some of the other parts. He felt sickened, like they all did. "What will happen to the remains, Gavin?"

"In the past, we've sent them away to be cremated. Colin the vet usually helps with that." Gavin looked at Clarabelle's decapitated head with her green collar and name disc; her dead eyes stared blankly, lifeless. He felt his own eyes begin to well up.

"How did they manage to get Clarabelle into this field from the pens?" John asked. "Obviously the calf could have been carried."

Gavin wiped his eyes on his forearm before turning to John. "What's that? Oh. Yeah. They obviously lured her."

John screwed up his face as he picked up one of the hearts. "Sick fucks," he muttered to himself.

"I'll hose away the rest of the blood. We've a hose on the tap just over there," Gavin said, nodding to his right.

"Least it's eased off," David said, looking up at the grey skies.

"So much for going quad trekking," John said. "Not that I'm exactly fussed about it."

Jack drove past, heading up to the barn to park. He gave a brief wave.

"I thought Bob had said he needn't worry about coming back for the rest of the day?" David said.

Gavin smiled. "That he did. But that's Jack for you!"

Once Jack had parked up, he jogged over to join the others. He was wearing a grey hoodie. "I'm so sorry about what happened!" Jack said sincerely. "If only I hadn't been called away."

"Don't you start, Jack!" Gavin tried to smile. "Derek's already beating himself up, like myself. As is Bob, for not moving the animals sooner."

Jack turned towards Bob who had come back out after his call.

"I'm sorry, Bob. I really am," Jack said.

Bob smiled. "I said you didn't have to worry about coming back, today! How's your mum?"

"Good, aye! If she wasn't, I wouldn't be here," Jack tried to joke.

The others smiled.

"It's nice of you," Bob replied. "Thank you."

"Did you get through to Angus, boss?" asked Gavin.

"Angus?" Jack asked.

"Yes, I did. I spoke to Angus, Jack. I wanted some advice on moving our animals to a safer location."

"You're going ahead with it, then?" Gavin asked.

"Yes. I think it's for the best. I've got my mobile on me. I got through to a gentleman who dealt with Angus' animals, who's going to call me back. Angus is planning on going away until this is over."

"Over? Good luck with that," John said. "It's probably only just beginning!"

"Angus said the police were looking into the matter and will inform him," Bob added. "I didn't tell Angus about the extent of it all. There's no point concerning him, even if he believed me. At least him and his animals are safe now."

*"Phhhh."* John scoffed at the police.

*****

Soon after, Cedric who owned the animal welfare sanctuaries, rang Bob to confirm that he would arrange something for Bob's animals. Angus' animals were located near to Kilmarnock, but Cedric had no more availability there. However, he assured Bob that the animals would be well looked after and fed, and safe from the 'sadistic bastards' Bob had described, wherever the location. A couple of other places were available near to Glasgow and further south in Carlisle. Although more expensive, Bob felt the animals would be safer further away. There were no guarantees and he wished he didn't have to resort to such measures, but he didn't have a choice.

Cedric said that he would have to make another phone call or two, and he would call back later on.

"How much is that going to set you back?" John asked. "I bet this Cedric bloke, isn't short of a few quid!"

"Not as much as I first thought. But enough." Bob smiled. "It seems fair. I suppose they're doing us a favour to a certain degree, and not just the animals."

"Do they get picked up by the sanctuary's own transport?" David asked.

"They're not going to travel there by themselves, are they?" John said teasingly.

"Shut up," David replied, holding back a smirk.

"They provide the transport at no extra cost. Cedric said that because I was a friend of Angus and with everything that's happened, he'd not charge for the pick-up. He's known Angus since his school days, apparently. Money isn't the issue here, anyway. It's all about the animals' safety!"

As Bob finished talking, a few whispers emanated from the northern end of the forest. They looked across as the trees and bushes blew in the wind. They couldn't make out what was said, but it was fairly loud. A chill swept in between them, rustling the bags which held the remains of the two animals.

"Fuck, that's cold!" John said.

It made them shiver for a few seconds, before all went quiet.

"I think that's the first whisper I've heard in days," Jack commented.

"We better finish up here," Bob said.

*****

Nobody was hungry at dinner and shortly after, Bob received another call from Cedric. They arranged for the animals to be picked up on Sunday morning. That was the soonest Cedric could help. A call would be made when the trucks were near to the farm. Bob also rang Carl to let him know what had happened and their plans for the animals.

There was some slight positive news for Gavin. His car had finally been fixed after a delay and was delivered back to the farm late that afternoon.

David and John went up after dinner and researched the animal sanctuary in Carlisle on David's laptop.

"It looks a nice enough place. It's certainly big. It says there are a few hundred animals there already."

John was looking out of the window of his room. "Yeah, it does. I just hope they can be trusted. Imagine if the sanctuary was run by that cult."

"I think they'll be fine. Carlisle's a big city. I'm sure people would know if there were sinister goings-on." David tried to sound positive.

"Let's hope so … I reckon your uncle is making the right call. He can't keep on guarding them every night … I'm dreading even closing my eyes tonight."

"I'm the same. Maybe this ring will help protect me. Maybe you should get one."

"Ha! Yeah, right, mate. I doubt that's going to have any effect on the *forces* at work up here … I'll give Granty a call in a bit, anyway. See how he's doing. Good thing he never came up with us!"

"Yep. At least he's safe down there."

John turned and saw David on his phone. "You texting Emily, again?"

"I'm just apologising again about not going today. She's asking how we are."

"It would have been good on the quads. It would have been a laugh, I reckon. Especially with Annabel going up and down!" John grinned.

"I repeated again that we were both tired and had headaches."

"Annabel hasn't texted me asking how I am. How inconsiderate!" John joked.

"I really want to see Emily again, but the last thing we want is to put them at risk as well."

Jack knocked on the door and joined them. "All right, boys? Thought I'd just let ye know I'm off now. Mum needs some help. I think she's going to milk her sprained ankle for a wee while yet, aye!" Jack smiled. "Derek's gonna help out tonight."

David and John smiled.

"Okay, buddy. See you tomorrow," John replied.

"Aye, ye will do!"

"Night," David said.

*****

At half eleven, John and David were outside their rooms, talking quietly.

"I'm so worried about falling asleep," John said worriedly.

"Me too. Try not to think about everything. I know it's easier said than done."

"At least Annabel texted to check I was okay. Proves she cares," John joked.

David smiled back. "Yeah."

"Well, wish me luck," John said quietly, entering his bedroom.

"Good luck!"

"You too!" John replied, closing the bedroom door.

# Chapter Fifty-Four

## 20th July, 2018

The next morning, while dressing, John glanced out of his window and noticed a small white courier van outside. Gavin, Bob and Derek seemed to be carrying large blue bags in from the back of the van. John realised it must be the 'magic' salt that Arthur had promised. "What a crock," he said to himself.

David knocked and then entered John's room.

"Morning. You all right?"

"Yeah. I'm good. I slept fine, surprisingly. How about you?" David rubbed the right side of his face.

"Dreamless. Looks like the salt turned up!"

"Same. What, already?"

"Yep. For what good it will do. Let's go look!"

Downstairs, there were numerous bags piled up inside the front door.

"Well, that's the last of it," the courier driver said as he placed the final bag down carefully on top of the others.

David counted thirty bags.

"Have a great day," the driver said to the others, taking Bob's signed receipt with him.

"That was quick," David said as he and John joined Bob and the others outside.

"I know. Arthur said a day or two. I was expecting it more tomorrow," Bob replied, scratching his lower back.

"What do we do with it now?" asked David.

"It needs to go all around the house and pens. Even though the animals are going Sunday, it's still best to be safe than sorry. It hasn't cost me anything. Arthur said he'd take care of it." Bob stretched his arms.

"Just as well, Bob. It would have been a waste of your money because this isn't going to help," John said cynically.

"Maybe, John. But let us remain positive." Bob watched the van drive off.

"It's worth a shot," Gavin said.

"I'll give Arthur a call in a bit. Let him know it's come." Bob yawned.

*****

"Where's this stuff come from?" John asked as he and David each poured a bag of salt around the back of the house.

The white crystals were quite large yet light. They had a slight hue of pink-purple to them.

"I don't know. Maybe from one of Arthur's 'witch doctors,' perhaps?" David replied.

"I honestly can't believe we're doing this … that cult must be laughing their arses off at us." John emptied another bag.

When Bob returned from phoning Arthur, Gavin took off his flat cap and slapped some dust off it, before pulling it back over his head. "That's the pens covered, boss."

"That's good. Best to be safe."

"Yep. David and John have just about finished around the house. The garden and patches have been outlined as well."

John approached them, carrying an empty bag of salt. "That's the house done, Bob. David's going to take Benji for a walk around the farm."

"That's good. Are there any bags left?" Bob asked.

"Nah. We've used them all up," replied John.

"We've covered some of the fields a little, too," Gavin added.

"And the garden." John pointed towards the lawn.

"Arthur ordered just enough, then." Bob nodded.

"My damn back aches from bending over!" John said, screwing his face up and flexing his back.

*****

David headed up to near the silos again, which now had barley stored in them. He made sure Benji didn't venture too far away. While Benji was trotting around, David heard his phone ring.

"Hiya!" Emily said cheerfully. "What are you up to? You doing okay?"

The call caught David by surprise. They had been texting on and off earlier, but he had explained he needed to help his uncle with something. "Hey! I'm better, thanks. I'm just taking Benji for a walk."

"Aw, Benji!"

David could sense her smiling at the other end of the call. "That's my boy!" David tried to smile back. "How's work?"

"I'm about to leave in a bit. Jock said I could start later, remember? I told you in my text." Emily laughed.

"Oh, yeah. Sorry." David laughed.

"That's okay." Emily giggled.

There was a moment's pause.

Emily sensed that David seemed occupied. "I'm not distracting you, am I?"

"Of course not!"

"You seem busy. Distracted."

"No, it's fine. I'm just keeping an eye on Benji. I don't want him to run off into the forest. I don't fancy chasing him." David tried to laugh.

"Yeah, I can just imagine you running after him!"

"He's normally a good boy, though. Aren't you Benji?" David replied as Benji finished his business and casually walked back over.

"Aw. I'm sure he is."

"Well, when he's not going for old people," David joked.

Emily giggled again. "True! I wanted to see how you were doing. But, erm, that wasn't the only reason I phoned."

"Oh?" David frowned.

"I was wondering if you'd like to meet up tomorrow night? Well, when I say meet up, I mean, would you like to come over?" Emily felt a little shy over the phone. She didn't want her offer to give the wrong impression.

"Come over?"

"Erm, yes. My mum is going away in the morning. It's short notice, but she's been asked to cover at another care home for a week out of town. They're short-staffed with holidays and a couple have gone down with gastroenteritis."

David wasn't sure what to say. "Maybe?"

"We can order a takeaway and watch a movie? Or I could cook you, us, dinner?"

"Dinner, huh? I'm flattered!" David said sarcastically. He still didn't know what to say.

Emily laughed. "If you want? If you've made other plans, I understand." Emily's voice fell.

A few crackles of static came over the call.

She tried to lighten up the tone a little. "We've been on a couple of dates already, and I think I can trust you in my home!" She laughed. "You can bring Benji, too."

David laughed. "You can trust me, Em! Don't worry about that."

"I, I know. I was just teasing. So, what do you say?"

"Sounds great … but can I let you know later on?"

"Oh, okay. Sure. That's cool."

David saw Benji's ears suddenly twitch as they heard a noise in the nearby bushes. David stared towards where it came from. Benji started to growl and cower.

"Listen, Em. I'm sorry, but I have to go," David said quickly.

"Is everything okay? Is that Benji I can hear growling?" Emily asked with concern.

"Yeah. He's seen another dog," David lied.

"Oh."

"I'll talk to you later, okay?"

"Okay, bye."

David had that uneasy feeling that he was being watched. He knelt down and put Benji's collar back on. Benji stopped growling but let out a couple of barks.

Whatever was in the bushes began to move, disturbing the branches and leaves in the undergrowth.

Benji let out another couple of barks as something began to crawl slowly and then pick up pace, moving upwards and away from them. Within a few seconds, it dashed away.

David felt relieved; kneeling down, he stroked Benji's soft head. "It's gone now, boy."

Benji looked up at him and licked his wrist.

"Good boy." David smiled at him, standing back up.

"All right?" John's voice came out of nowhere.

*"Fuck!"* David said startled.

"What?"

"You scared the shit out of me!"

"Sorry." John frowned. "You okay?"

"I guess." David sighed. "We heard something in the bushes and Benji started to growl and bark again."

"I thought I heard him bark. Did you see anything?" John looked over at the now still bushes.

"No. Just a few rustles."

"Maybe it was that *Grey Man* and the salt scared him off, eh? Made him do a runner." John smirked.

David turned to face him. He couldn't help but raise a smile at his friend. He told John about Emily's invitation as they returned to the farmhouse, carefully stepping over the line of salt crystals. David had to place a little back in place, where Benji's back legs disturbed it.

"Really? That's great. Get in there!" John nudged his friend.

"It's nothing like that. She's being innocent."

"Maybe ... but remember the third date rule; anything goes!" John grinned.

"I don't think so. I don't think that's her intention at all. Besides, I'm not sure I'm even going to accept her invitation."

"Look, mate." John turned to face David. "I know there's all this shit going on, but what else are you going to do, if you don't go? Just sit around here worrying? You may as well have some fun. We don't know how long we've got left! I can look after Benji. At least Emily's interested. Annabel's gone a bit quiet."

"I don't know what to think. Arthur warned us not to trust anyone."

"I wouldn't worry about what that old hippie thinks! I know we both lost some interest, yesterday. But if it were me, I'd definitely go."

David smiled. "I know. I really do trust Emily. My gut instinct tells me she's fine, but what if it's a trap? And regardless, I don't want to get her involved in any danger."

"I think you should go, if you really like her. You could even tell her about it all? Come clean!"

"I want to, but I don't want to scare her. I might see her and say it's best if we take a break for a while, that I'm busy with the farm and not ready to commit. I'm not sure it would ever work, anyway. The distance and that."

"That's up to you, buddy. I think you should go, though. We can't stop doing the things we love, just because of these crazed, sick fuckers up here!"

"I guess." David tried to smile.

John put his arm on David's shoulder and shook it gently. "You can always take a wee bag of salt crystals to help?"

They both smiled and glanced down at the line of salt again.

*****

David's parents rang him that evening. It had gone seven; he didn't speak to them for long. They were heading out to dinner. After he had wished them well and vice versa, he turned his attentions to Emily. He had a feeling that she might be a little disappointed that he had ended the call abruptly and that he had been reluctant to meet her tomorrow night. Since her call earlier, however, John and Bob had persuaded David that he should go, so he decided to call her.

"Hey, you!"

"Hey! Are you okay?" David replied, sitting on the edge of his bed.

"Kind of. I've just got out of the shower. I had a feeling it might be you!" Emily chuckled.

"Aw. Why 'kind of?' You okay?"

"Better now. I went to work but got a really bad headache. Jock paid for me to take a taxi home and leave early. We were a bit busy. He wouldn't take no for an answer!"

"You're okay now, though?" David was concerned.

"I'm fine, thanks. I took some painkillers and had a bit of a lie-down, and it's pretty much gone now. I thought a shower might help, too."

"That's good! What about your car? Is it still at the pub?"

"Yeah. I left the keys with Jock. He said he'd bring it back later for me and get a taxi back. He said he planned on doing some shopping in Aviemore, anyway. It's really nice of him. I could have just got a taxi tomorrow morning."

"He certainly seems like a nice boss to work for."

"Oh, he is!" Emily smiled.

"I'm sorry about earlier, by the way. When I had to go. I hope it didn't sound rude?"

"Rude? Oh, don't be silly! It's fine. Was Benji okay?"

"Erm, yeah. He was. It was nothing, really. The reason I called though," David quickly changed the subject, "I would like to take you up on your offer of hospitality tomorrow evening," David teased with his formality.

"That's great!" Emily giggled.

David laughed himself. "So, what's on the menu?"

"You'll have to wait and see!"

They spoke a little more, arranged a time to meet and said goodbye for the night. Just as some interference came over the call. Emily and her mother were going to have a 'girlie' mother and daughter night in, just the two of them, before her mum left for a week.

David was looking forward to seeing Emily and headed back downstairs after his call.

"Well?" John asked as David came into the living room. "You going?" John was sat drinking a can of beer and holding another unopened one in his other hand.

"Yep. She said to get there for around seven-thirty. Dinner will be about an hour later."

"Try not to look too enthusiastic about it," John said sarcastically. He handed the other can of beer over. "Your uncle said we can have a couple more, if we like."

"Cheers. Benji still with my uncle?"

"They're outside doing something. Derek and Jack have only just left."

"What about Betty?" David opened his can up.

"Doing the dishes." John nodded towards the kitchen.

"I was going to ask if it was all right to take me, tomorrow night. But after our last experience in your car, it's too dangerous. I'll get a taxi."

"Up to you, mate. I don't like the idea of driving back alone, after what happened last time. But I'll take that risk for you."

"Don't be daft, mate. I'm not having you risk yourself for me. It's risky enough as it is."

"Aw. That's so *sweet*!" John grinned, teasing.

"Wanker!" David grinned back. "Heard from Annabel?"

"Nope … but I might text her in a bit. Let's join the others outside. I'll grab a couple more beers."

*****

"You're going to miss these animals, aren't you, Bob?" John asked, feeling the sensation of a few beers in his head.

"That I am! I still think it's the right decision, though. The sanctuary seems really nice and safe." Bob sank back the remainder of his beer.

"Yeah, it does, Uncle, from what we've seen online," David said, reassuring his uncle, then looked at his phone. It was almost midnight.

John was a little peeved that Annabel hadn't replied to his last two messages. He wondered if she was annoyed about them not going quad trekking. He finished his last beer off and placed the empty can on the ground. He stamped on it and crushed it flat, briefly startling Benji. "I'm going to head off to bed, guys."

"Goodnight, 'John-Boy!'" Gavin joked. He had enjoyed a couple of beers, himself.

"Night, mate. I'm going in a bit too, I think," David said.

John raised his hand and walked down from the farmyard towards the house, carrying the squashed beer can.

"You sure you don't need me to help tonight, Uncle?"

"It's okay. After tonight, we'll only have to worry about doing this one final time."

A sound came from their left in the trees, like something was flapping. It soon stopped.

"Probably a bat," Gavin said.

"Maybe." David yawned.

"You should go up to bed, David." Bob smiled.

# Chapter Fifty-Five

## 21st July, 2018

The next day, John and David helped out with a few things on the farm, including baling the hay, until it was time for David to get ready for his date.

David intended to book a taxi, but Gavin insisted on taking him in his car with his shotgun to be extra safe. Gavin was glad to have finally got his blue Vauxhall Astra back. He'd had it for six years. He also wanted to check on his own place. John had decided to go along too, for 'extra security.' Bob remained back at the farm with Betty and Derek, who happened to turn up late afternoon. He still felt guilty about last Thursday's incident and had wanted to come in.

"You about ready to go, then?" John asked. The work out in the fields had made him thirsty and he was drinking a cold glass of lemonade.

"Yep. Just about." David poured himself a lemonade too.

"You're taking Benji with you?"

"Yeah … Emily wants to see him, again."

"Ah, right. He's outside with your uncle."

"You heard back from Annabel?"

"Yeah, she got back to me just now. I asked her when she would be free and she said she'd let me know. So, fingers crossed."

"Cool."

"You looking forward to tonight? Remember, it's the *third* date!" John winked.

David ignored the gesture. "I am." He sighed. "I just don't want to involve her, you know?"

"I know, buddy … but she'll keep your mind off things, if nothing else. Do you good to have a break. You ready to go? I'll go get Gavin."

"Let me just finish this."

John went and got Gavin who brought his car round.

David rinsed their glasses and made his way outside.

"David, you look smart!" Bob smiled.

David smiled back.

Betty turned to look at David in his dark green, short-sleeved shirt and black jeans. "Yes. You look *very* handsome, David!"

"Erm, thanks," David said, still feeling unsure about his aunt.

"Have a great time. And don't worry about us. We'll be fine." Bob smiled again.

"I'll try!"

Approaching the car, David looked back at his aunt. She turned towards him and waved, smiling. It made him feel uncomfortable.

*****

"I've just thought ... maybe I should have brought a bottle of wine?"

"You thinking of getting her drunk, eh?" John joked from the back seat.

Gavin smiled. "We went past that small shop a couple of minutes back. Want me to turn around?"

"I think I should. It would be polite ... if you don't mind going back?"

"It's no bother, mate," Gavin replied, turning the car back around to the small convenience shop.

"You really didn't have to come, either." David looked over to John.

"Anything for a bestie!" John grinned.

Gavin pulled up just shy of the small shop.

"What did you get?" John asked as David got back into the car carrying a bottle of wine.

"Just a bottle of red."

"How much that set you back?"

"Fifteen quid. Not bad, I suppose."

John frowned. A man caught his attention from across the street. He was standing at the end of an alleyway smoking a cigarette.

"What is it?" asked David.

"That bloke over there. See? He's standing there watching us."

David and Gavin peered across the street.

"He looks like the same guy who was watching us after our first meeting with Carl! He's even wearing the same clothes."

"Definitely looks like him," David replied.

"I'm going to get out and have a word!" John said, unfastening his seat belt.

"Don't!" Gavin reached over, pulling John's arm back as the man turned around casually and walked off down an alleyway, out of sight.

"Yeah, you keep walking, pal," John said to himself, annoyed. "Fucking creep!"

"Can't be a coincidence. They're definitely watching us. Maybe we should turn back?"

"Don't let them put you off, mate. Fuck 'em! You can't let Emily down. Not now."

"I guess. Maybe I should just come clean with her tonight. I really don't know."

"See where the mood takes you. Maybe it would be good to tell her. That way, perhaps she could find out more about that Samuel and Ralf and what they saw, seeing as she works at their local."

David exhaled. "Yeah, we'll see."

*****

Emily lived in a quaint cottage, smaller than David expected. There was a small pebbled driveway and a rockery at the front. The shrubbery must have been a scented variety, because it could be smelt even in the car. A wrought iron bench sat under one of the windows and on the front wall, hung a large green, metal shamrock. Emily's Mini, sat outside the red garage.

"Nice house," John said, scratching his ear.

"Pleasant enough," Gavin replied.

"Yeah. They don't own it. Emily told me they rent it."

"Have a good time, mate. Don't worry about us. Just enjoy yourself!" John said warmly.

"I'll try!" David replied, opening the passenger door. He let Benji out too. "Thanks again for the lift, Gavin. Stay safe on the way back!"

"No worries." Gavin smiled.

"Give us a call if you need picking up later. Or tomorrow morning!" John grinned and flicked his eyebrows. He got into the vacant passenger seat.

David shook his head. "Dick." He tried not to smile.

"Good luck, mate," John called out as David made his way to the front door with Benji. "Did you take your rubbers?" John deliberately raised his voice.

David scowled over his shoulder, carrying the bottle of red wine by its neck. *"Shut up, you idiot!"* he hissed back quietly.

John and Gavin laughed. John beeped the horn as Gavin reversed back and swung the car round, before heading off to his own place.

David pressed the doorbell and heard a pleasant melody from inside the hallway. He waited for several seconds before the door opened and Emily greeted him with her pretty face and warm smile.

"Hey! How are you?" She felt her cheeks glow a little. "I'm glad you came! Did you find it okay? And hello to you too, Benji!" Emily knelt down and stroked Benji who in turn licked her face.

"Hey, yourself!" David smiled back. He noticed Emily's breasts held in a black bra as she bent down in her loose T-shirt. "Yeah, it was fine. Sorry if I'm a bit late."

"Late? Don't be silly! I said from half-seven. It's great you've come early!" Emily seemed really pleased to see him.

"I, er, got you this. I actually forgot until we arrived in Aviemore. I got Gavin to stop at a shop we passed. I know you like red wine." David handed the bottle over to Emily.

"Aw. That is so sweet!" She kissed him on the cheek, smelling his aftershave and looked briefly at the bottle. "Come in. Dinner should be ready about eight-thirty, as planned. Actually, my timing may have been a bit off. I think it might be sooner." She grinned warmly.

"It's certainly a nice place you have here," David said, wiping his feet on the mat.

"Oh, you should see the back garden. We only rent, as you know. But it's still *our* home. We love it!" Emily gushed.

"Shall I take my shoes off?"

"Oh, it's fine. As long as they're not dirty."

"Nah, they're fine." David checked the soles of his brown boots, smiling.

Emily giggled.

David could smell a mixture of whatever was cooking in the narrow hallway, as well as a fresh and clean scent. It smelt great.

"Come. We can sit in the garden for a bit if you like, before dinner? It's a nice evening. You'll have to forgive me, though: I'll need to keep an eye on dinner and I still need to get changed."

David and Benji followed Emily. David checked out her backside in her jeans as he followed her. This beautiful young lady really was perfect in every sense. "Go and get changed? You look fine!"

"Aw, thank you. So do you!" She turned back smiling. "But I like to make an effort for my guest."

David noticed the twinkle in Emily's eyes again.

The smell of whatever was cooking became stronger as David entered the kitchen. He caught glimpse of a cookbook open on the worktop and some dirty pots and spills, indicating she'd been busy preparing the meal. The back door to the garden was open. "Is that chicken I can smell?" David asked as they entered the garden.

"You smell right!" Emily chuckled. "It's a 'quick roast chicken with root vegetables.' I hope you'll like it."

"Oh, I'm sure I will. It sounds great."

"Well, this is the garden." Emily stood on the patio with her hands on her small hips.

David thought she looked sweet, standing there. He really was starting to fall for her. "Wow," he said, admiring the garden.

Numerous tall trees stood at the back of the house, shading part of the garden. Flowers and shrubs lined the rectangular lawn. The garden was obviously well looked after. A green summer house was tucked to the left and on the right sat a bench. Emily guided him to the back of the garden, where a small iron gate led to a huge and recently cut field with wildflowers all along its border. Beyond the field, you could see the Cairngorms in the distance.

David expressed his admiration again as he appreciated the view, listening to the birds and savoured the flower scent.

"I did say wait until you see the back!" Emily smiled, clearing her throat slightly.

"Yep, you did. You show off!" David joked and gave her an affectionate nudge as they both looked at one another.

"It's great when it snows up here. It's still just as beautiful, but different, you know?"

*Not as beautiful as you, though.* David thought to himself.

Returning to the patio, Emily suggested they dine 'alfresco,' which for some reason made them both laugh.

David sat down on one of the white iron chairs with Benji at his feet.

Emily went inside and reappeared a couple of minutes later, carrying a large plate. "I know dinner won't be too long but I thought we, or you really, could do with a little appetiser in the meantime."

"Aw. You've really gone out of your way with all this! It would have been less hassle for you, if we'd just got a takeaway."

"Don't be silly. I enjoyed making it all. It was no hassle. And besides, I, I think you're worth it." Emily could feel herself blush slightly in the warm evening sun.

"That's really sweet of you, Em ... but you would have been enough of an appetiser!" David joked.

Emily giggled again.

There was something about her giggle that made David's heart melt.

"These shouldn't be too filling. They're a toasted ravioli. Crispy and baked. I made the breadcrumbs myself."

"Now you're bragging!" David joked again, beaming.

Emily laughed. "Really, I'm not! Though, I can't help but feel proud of myself just a *teeny* bit. I don't cook too much … I'll be honest. I didn't make the marinara sauce."

"I'm flattered. I really am, that you've made so much effort with all this."

The ravioli tasted great. Benji liked it too.

Emily and David once again chatted and laughed. Emily attended to the dinner every now and then. David asked if she needed any help, but she declined and repeated that David was her guest and that she had it all covered. After a while, Emily excused herself to get changed and prepare the Dijon cream sauce.

"You okay, Benji?" David said, looking down at Benji who was munching away on a few leftover crispy ravioli.

*****

Eventually, Emily returned with her hair tied back, a black dress and some sparkling earrings. She had also retouched her red lipstick.

David thought she was beautiful as she was, no matter what she wore. But seeing her in her black dress enhanced his desire for her. "Oh, wow … you look amazing!"

"Aw, really? I don't know why, but sometimes I feel a bit insecure in this. I think it makes my bum look big."

"What? Are you kidding! You look amazing … you look lovely, Em, whatever you wear. Though, when you dress up, it brings out your beauty even more, if that's possible!"

"You're too kind," she said, managing not to blush this time.

"Do a twirl for me," David said cheekily as he dipped his last but one ravioli in the marinara sauce.

Emily smiled and slowly turned round.

"Oh God, *yes*! Your arse looks *massive*!" David joked.

"How mean!" Emily giggled.

"Honestly, you look great. I don't know why you think your bum looks big. It's perfect. Just like the rest of you."

This time, Emily did blush again. "You really are full of compliments tonight, aren't you?"

"I'm only being honest." David smiled. "You'd look great wearing a bin liner!"

Emily laughed as they looked at each other.

Just then, the telephone rang indoors.

"I bet I know who that is." Emily smiled. "My mum, no doubt. She said she'd phone. I better go answer it and I'll be right back with the dinner!"

David could hear Emily inside on the phone with her mother.

"Yes, Mum … I know. Listen, I've got to go. The dinner is ready … I love you, too. Bye. Byeee! Sorry about that," Emily called from the back door. "I'm just about to dish the dinner up. She does go on sometimes, bless her! She wanted to make sure I'd closed the kitchen door to the hall whilst cooking, which I didn't."

"Oh, you rogue!" David joked.

Emily stuck her tongue out at him.

*****

After they had finished their meal, David praised Emily on her cooking skills and for being a fantastic host. She had learnt from her mother who was a good cook, and self-taught from books and cooking programmes. David loved that Emily was so humble and modest about everything. She had also bought some special treat biscuits for Benji, so that he wouldn't feel left out.

"More wine?" Emily offered.

"Sure." David smiled back.

"I hope you've got room for dessert!"

"I have." David grinned. "What have we got?"

"Chocolate chip ice cream!"

"Don't tell me you made that as well?"

"Actually, no," laughed Emily.

"What, I wasn't good enough for you to make it for me!" David pulled a sad face, jokingly.

"*Aw*! No, it wasn't that. I just thought it would be easier I guess, and less time-consuming."

They both laughed.

"Maybe next time, I can make you some, though." Emily winked.

"Lovely." Smiled David.

Emily went in to take the ice cream out of the freezer to thaw it; she returned and they carried on chatting.

The evening with Emily had taken David's mind off all his recent experiences completely. They spoke some more about how lovely the area was around the cottage.

"Sometimes, deer look over the fence." Emily smiled. "They're so cute but they're easily scared if you approach them, even with food."

"It's certainly a fantastic place up here. I knew that from photos and programmes I'd seen about Scotland," David replied, drinking up the rest of his wine.

"Maybe you should move, then," Emily hinted.

"You never know!" David smiled. "Is it okay to use the bathroom?"

"Of course. It's just upstairs. First door on the right."

"Be back in a jiffy." David winked, getting up from his seat.

"Okay. I'll go and serve up the ice cream." Before Emily got up herself, she turned and watched David walk inside, checking out his body. She smiled to herself, resting her elbow on the table, biting gently on her red varnished thumbnail.

Before returning downstairs, David noticed a small cabinet with a couple of photos in silver frames. One was Emily as a child, probably around six or seven, and the other was Emily most likely with her mother, a dark-haired woman; they had their arms around each other. He could see similarities between the two; Emily's mother was also a very attractive woman.

"Hey," Emily said as David returned to his seat outside, "There you are. Ice cream is served!"

"I saw a couple of photos upstairs on the landing. I take it they're of you and your mum?"

"You did, did you?" Emily smiled. "Yes. The one of me on my own was when I was seven and the other was taken last summer with my dear mum."

"I can see the similarities between you two. She's a good-looking woman. You've got great genes."

"People sometimes joke that we're sisters, rather than mother and daughter." Emily giggled again.

"I can see why!" David picked up his spoon. "It's certainly a nice evening," he said, looking up at the clear sky.

"Indeed, it is. Great evening, *great* company." Emily's green eyes sparkled seductively as she looked across the circular wooden table at David.

David looked straight back at her, his desire growing.

"There was another reason why I thought it would be good to bring Benji this evening … I thought we could go for a little stroll after we've eaten, across the field out at the back. Benji will like it." Emily took a small mouthful of the choc-chip ice cream.

"Sounds great. Benji can stretch his legs."

"Ow!" Emily quickly said. "I've got that darn brain freeze." She grimaced and giggled at the same time.

"Aw." David laughed. "I hate that."

*****

When finished, they left the dishes to soak and took Benji out through the gate. The sun was setting as they walked casually across the field.

"It really is a wonderful sight, isn't it?" Emily said, looking at the remains of the sunset over the Cairngorms.

Part of the sky was orange-red, along with some streaks of violet and blue. A few bright stars had already begun to twinkle in the soon to be night sky.

"It really is. You see things in photos and on TV, but to appreciate it fully, you have to experience it all first hand," David replied.

"Yes. You do."

They both stood in the middle of the open field admiring what was left of the sunset.

David felt Emily place her hand in his. He turned to face her. He could just about see her green eyes in the twilight. His urge to hold her was stronger than ever. He instinctively placed his hands either side of Emily's soft face. "You're so beautiful, Em. You're perfect in every sense. I think it's rare that you find someone so amazing and cute, as well as beautiful and caring. And sexy. Everything about you is perfect. Even the way you giggle." David gently stroked Emily's face with his thumbs.

She closed her eyes for a moment and smiled, savouring his tenderness, with her head slightly tilted. "I feel the same, David. I haven't felt like this about anyone before. Not only are you so handsome, but you're kind, funny, warm … I love everything about you."

"I thought that you were so cute and lovely, the very first moment I set eyes on you. I've never felt anything like this, either. I can't help it. I'm falling for you."

"I'm falling for you, too."

They looked deep into each other's eyes and lent in to kiss each other passionately with their warm and eager mouths. David then moved his hands and wrapped his arms around Emily's petite body, pulling her tightly to him. She wrapped her arms round David's toned frame. Their heart's raced as they held each other. Sexually charged energy flowed through them, each desiring the other's body. A shooting star flashed overhead.

*****

Later, with her warm naked body wrapped around David's, Emily nestled her head into his neck, kissing him. David held her tightly.

"What happens now?" Emily smiled as she rubbed her warm hand over David's hairy chest and less hairy torso. She preferred hair on a man. She believed a man should look like a man.

David moved a few strands of her dark hair from across her forehead. "What do you mean?" he asked, looking into her emerald eyes.

"About us … I'm worried I won't see you again after you've finished at your uncle's and gone back home." Emily lowered her eyes.

"I … I don't know, Em."

"You want to be with me, though? I really want to be with you. But … but I don't just want a fling, you know?"

David held her face and gave an understanding smile. "Of course, I do. I'm crazy about you. I'm sure we can work something out. We don't have to worry too much about it at the moment, though. I'm not going back anytime soon."

"I really am falling for you." Emily's eyes welled up a little.

"Aw." David smiled lovingly and they kissed passionately again.

They chatted for a short while holding and playing with one another's hands, when they heard a scratching at the bedroom door.

"Aw. That's probably Benji," Emily said.

"I hope so!" David replied. "If it isn't, we should be worried," he half-joked.

Emily chuckled. "Yeah! I feel bad we left him in the other room."

"Nah, he's okay. He was falling asleep anyway, when we left him. He's probably just woken up and feels a bit lonely and confused about where he is."

"Aw. I'll go let him in."

"You stay. I'll go." David smiled, not too shy to show off his toned physique.

Emily was surprised that David didn't work out at a gym. He had made her laugh, when he joked that his body was just a 'natural' temple.

He put his blue designer boxer shorts back on and went to open the bedroom door. Benji sat wagging his tail and jumped up at David, accidentally scratching his stomach, before jumping onto Emily's bed. Emily helped him up.

"Aw. Hiya, Benji!" Emily giggled as Benji licked her face.

"Stop licking, Benji!" David smiled as he too received licks on his face. "Come on, boy. On the floor." David noticed a few bits of dried mud from Benji's paws on the bed cover.

"It's okay. He can stay on the bed." Emily ruffled Benji's fur. "He can sleep with us, tonight."

David got out of bed again to use the bathroom and texted John to let him know he was staying at Emily's for the night; he didn't want everyone worrying about him. John responded that all was fine at the farm and teased David about the 'third date rule' being proven. David turned his phone off and got back into bed with Emily.

# Chapter Fifty-Six

## 22nd July, 2018

"Morning, handsome!" Emily said to David. She opened the light pink curtains. "Rise and shine!" she joked.

The early morning sun flooded the room and straight onto David's face. He shielded his eyes, screwing up his face. Emily walked over and kissed him.

David groaned and yawned. "What time is it?"

"Aw, little sleepy head!" Emily giggled. "Just gone nine."

"Ah, okay." David sat up and stretched. He rubbed his eyes and looked at Emily in her white bathrobe with damp hair. Even without makeup, she was a natural beauty.

"I was going to wake you earlier, but thought I'd let you sleep. You looked so cute and innocent lying there." Emily grinned. "Would you like a shower?"

"Yeah, I might do in a bit."

"You could have joined me." Emily winked and jumped onto the bed to cuddle David.

"Well, you should have woken me, then." David beamed. He could smell her fresh damp hair. "Where's Benji?"

"He's fine. He's downstairs eating treats."

"He certainly likes them."

"Do you want me to take you back to the farm? I honestly don't mind. I can make us breakfast first, though. Unless, you're in a rush to get back? I'd like to see your uncle's place." Emily looked at David, leaning on one elbow.

"You don't have to do that. But we'll see."

*****

While David showered, Emily cooked a full breakfast of waffles, bacon, beans and eggs. "Almost done!" she said, looking over her shoulder.

David joined her in the kitchen and gave Emily a hug from behind and kissed her cheek, looking over her left shoulder. "Smells great!" He smiled, kissing her neck. He gently smacked her bottom.

"Take a seat." She smiled happily. She was buzzing from last night. She hadn't felt this strongly about anyone before and it felt great.

"Yes, sir!" David teased, pulling up a seat at the kitchen table.

Being caught up in the moment with Emily the previous night had taken his mind off things. Now, dark memories returned to plague him. He took a sip of the orange juice Emily had placed on the table and checked his phone. John had texted to ask if he needed picking up, so he answered that he wasn't sure yet.

"Here you go ..." Emily placed a warm plate in front of him.

"You really are spoiling me!" David touched Emily's lower back affectionately.

"Anything for my new man," she replied tongue-in-cheek, resting her hand on his shoulder before sitting at the table with him.

*****

After breakfast, they did the washing up together. Emily giggled as David flicked foam into her face and she then retaliated. Even Benji got some on his fur. Then they went to sit in the garden, chatting together for a while.

Feeling so at home with her began to make David feel guilty for not being open about why he was in Scotland. He hesitated to talk to her about everything because he didn't want to put her at risk. He also hesitated because he still had a lingering doubt over whether she could be trusted, which made him feel even worse, considering they'd slept together.

"... so yeah, I rarely do Sundays," Emily said.

They were sat on the wooden bench at the bottom of the garden.

"What's that? Oh, that's good."

"You okay? I'm not boring you, am I?" Emily smiled.

"Don't be silly! I'm just thinking about something."

"About us?" Emily smiled again, gripping his arm.

"Sort of." David could tell how happy Emily was.

"What else? You can tell me."

"I ... I wanted to tell you about this before."

Emily's smile disappeared. "Please, don't tell me you're seeing someone back home?"

"No! Nothing like that." He squeezed Emily's hand. "I was planning to come to my uncle's farm after I lost my job, but the real reason I decided to come is that my aunt and uncle have been having problems …"

Emily frowned. "Like marriage problems?"

"No. Though, maybe that would have been easier to resolve …" David breathed in and out, trying to work out how to explain everything to Emily. "My … my uncle's been having problems on the farm … someone has been mutilating his animals. One of his cats was strung up on their washing line, skinned and gutted."

"*What?* Oh my. That's *awful*, David!"

David looked at her face. She sounded sincere. "I … I know."

"Who would do such an awful thing?" Emily squeezed David's hand.

David swallowed. "We were looking into that, and-" Before David could answer, the phone rang inside.

"Ignore that. Tell me." Emily smiled caringly.

"Anyway … we started looking into things and-" Again, David was cut off. This time by Emily's mobile phone, ringing on the bench.

"Drat!" Emily said. "It's Jock … I'd better get this."

David sighed as Emily took the call and waited for her to finish.

"I'm so sorry! That was Jock. Annabel's not feeling good. Jock asked if I'd go in as soon as I can to cover for her. Sunday's always busy with Sunday roasts and that. I don't want to let him down. He said he'd pay me overtime, which is good!"

"Oh, okay," David replied. He was disappointed not to be able to tell Emily everything, now he'd started.

The situation then became more awkward when Annabel rang. David began to feel frustrated while Emily talked to her.

"I'm really sorry! I hope you don't think I'm rude?" Emily said, feeling bad.

"Not at all. It's fine." David half-smiled.

"Annabel just wanted to apologise, bless her. It's not her fault … Jock had told her he'd phone me."

"What's wrong with her?"

"She says she had an upset stomach, perhaps a dodgy takeaway from last night … We've got a bit yet though, before I go in. It's so awful about your aunt and uncle. What was it you were going to say?"

"We were basically looking into it. My uncle contacted the police."

"What did they say?"

David hesitated. "Not too much, really. Just that it was possibly drugged up sickos, something like that. We've been watching the animals at night, taking turns. Well, I say 'we.' More my uncle and his workers, one in particular; Gavin, who brought me last night with John." David had lost the momentum to explain everything. Emily was also going into work soon, so now no longer seemed the right moment to explain what had been going on.

"Oh my. That's terrible. Your poor uncle and those animals." Emily gave David a warm hug. "No wonder you've appeared distracted at times."

"Yeah," replied David, hugging her back. He thought about the animals being relocated this morning, but he would have to tell Emily another time.

*****

David decided on a taxi to take him back to the farm. He didn't want to put any of the others out or put them at risk. When the taxi arrived, he and Emily tenderly kissed each other goodbye and said they would see each other soon. Emily apologised for cutting their morning short and said she was so sorry again for what was happening on his uncle's farm.

"You … again," came the greeting from the taxi driver. He was chewing gum and wearing dark tinted glasses.

David got in the back of the taxi with Benji and recognised Mick Diver, who had driven them all to the disco. "Oh, hi, again!"

"How have you been? I see you haven't wasted any time with the lasses up here!" He winked over his glasses, chomping away on his chewing gum.

David could smell the mint from his gum. "Erm, yeah. She works at the pub."

"Yes, I thought I recognised her … beautiful young lady! Fine figure on her as well, you lucky bastard." Mick laughed.

David smiled. "Yeah."

*****

Mick took a wrong turning inside the forest, which David didn't notice as first, because he was texting John.

Mick turned the car around and retraced back to the correct turning. "Sorry about that … I thought the road looked a bit different!" Mick laughed. "There's something weird about this forest, even during the day."

"That's all right," David replied. "It happens. You can just take some of the fare off," he joked.

"Yeah, right … cheeky bastard!" Mick grinned, checking his wing mirror. "So, how you finding it up here, anyway? The young lady aside!"

"Erm, it's good. A bit quiet, I suppose. But I expected that, anyway."

"And that friend of yours? He okay …? He was a cheeky little shit … the one with the over-powering cologne, if I recall."

"John? He's doing okay, too."

"Good, good."

As the taxi approached the farm, a large truck was leaving. Mick wasn't too sure what to do, so David opted to get out, so Mick could reverse back and turn around where there was a slight opening on the side of the dirt road. David paid Mick the fare and made his way to the farm with Benji. He watched at the side of the dirt road, holding Benji by his lead, as the silver truck slowly drove past him. He could see some of the cows inside through the open grates and hear their confused grunts along with some of the other animals.

Another truck was parked up by the barn and David could hear talking.

"It's a very well-run place. Your animals will be well looked after. You don't have to worry about that," a man said from behind the truck.

"Here he is!" John said, noticing David. John was stood in a pair of Wellington boots. He'd been helping with the animals and clearing the pens out.

"All right! The animals are on their way, then," David replied.

Bob came to stand by David and they watched as the two truck drivers helped a couple of pigs up a ramp into the truck. They must have wondered what on earth the lines of salt crystals were for.

*****

"And we're done!" one of the drivers in a yellow cap said, closing the ramp. "That's all three trucks loaded."

Gavin put his arm briefly around Bob's shoulder. They were both going to miss the animals. Even Derek had turned up again to help and see the animals one last time. The last truck made its way carefully down the side of the farmhouse just as Betty came back out to join them.

Bob smiled at her sadly and put his arm around her. "They'll be fine, love," he said, kissing her firmly on her cheek.

Dark grey clouds eased over the sky, promising rain.

"You still not going to go into details, then?" John nudged David as they stood in the now empty animal pens. "I told you about the three-date rule! I was right, eh?"

"So you keep saying," replied David, a little annoyed. He was used to John fishing for details, but because of his feelings for Emily, it annoyed him more than usual. He wasn't one to kiss and tell: period.

"It was just a great evening. That's all."

"God, you're no fun!" John joked.

"I've just thought," David said, changing the subject, "I wonder what my uncle's going to do now with Derek and Jack, now there are no animals here? I imagine Gavin will stay here, but I wonder if there'll be enough work for them all now?"

"Nice change of subject there, David! But yeah. I guess there will be less to do around here, now."

"I guess we'll see." David looked down at Benji who was chewing on a bone.

"When are you going to see Emily again?"

"Soon, maybe. I'm not sure. I need to tell her about everything. Especially now our relationship's moved on."

"Hah! You did do the *deed*, then!" John grinned and nudged David.

"Shut up!" David tried not to smile.

John shook his head. "You devil, you!"

*****

It felt strange that evening. They didn't need to worry about the animals anymore. Bob, Betty and their staff had looked after them for years. Feeding them, mucking them out, checking on them. Now they all felt empty.

"At least the animals have got one another," Bob said. He was holding a small glass of brandy. "They assured me that they would all be kept together. So that's something."

"It's certainly going to take a heck of a lot of getting used to, not having them around. That's for sure," Gavin replied. He got up to pour himself a drink.

"What about Jack and Derek, Uncle? Surely there will be less work now the animals have been moved?"

"Me and Gavin were speaking about that. There are still things to be done, but obviously less now. I'm going to give both Derek and Jack indefinite leave. Me and Gavin can handle things from here on in. More importantly, I think it's perhaps safer too, for them not to be around here. Derek was starting to feel uncomfortable, driving through the forest by himself on his moped, like he was being watched. Jack, too."

"What about financially? With the animals going, is that going to hit you?" John asked.

"We're fine. We still have all the fruit and vegetables out the back for starters! Also, the barley has been cut, and the wheat will be soon." Bob smiled. "I think that's the least of our worries, though."

"Don't forget me and John can help out when needed, Uncle. You know that! We're *not* going anywhere."

"I know, David." Bob smiled again, looking at his nephew. He drank some more brandy.

"Maybe next week, we will have some more answers," Gavin suggested, sitting back down.

"Hopefully. Perhaps now, we can look forward to getting a proper night's sleep for once!" Bob said, finishing off his drink. "I might sleep down here, though. Just in case something happens."

"Well, you don't have to worry about that entity, Bob. We've got *salt* now," John joked sarcastically.

The sound of Betty slamming her book shut, startled them all slightly. "Think I'm going to go to bed," she said, getting up.

"You feeling okay?" Bob asked.

"I'm fine. I just have one of my headaches coming on."

"Oh, okay. I'll come check on you in a bit," replied Bob, then looked at the others, raising his brows.

"Night," she said to the others, leaving the living room.

"She okay?" David asked.

"I think so. Probably upset her with the animals going. She's still taking her meds which is good."

**23rd July, 2018**

Earlier, Bob had checked in on Betty who was sound asleep and had put his old long johns on and returned downstairs to sleep on the sofa. He had made sure the back and front doors were locked and went into the living room. After getting used to the night shifts, it felt odd not doing it anymore. Bob felt like the animals must still be out there, all by themselves. He laid under an old yellow blanket. The two cats, Sammy and Josie, were asleep at the end of the sofa.

Bob awoke, when he heard what he thought was a child laughing. He listened and heard it again. He carefully swung his legs out onto the carpet, careful not to wake Sammy and Josie.

The left on light in the hallway dimmed a few times.

Bob heard the laughter again and began to feel a little uneasy. He walked slowly out of the living room and towards the front door and heard it again. He placed his ear to the front door; it felt cold. He fetched the front door key from his study and unlocked the door. Taking his time, he dropped the key into one of his pockets and opened the front door.

The child's laughter seemed to have stopped. He grabbed a small torch from the pocket of his coat which was hanging nearby. The light in the hallway dimmed again. Shining the torch through the open front door, he could see the drizzle falling on the front lawn. He nervously moved the beam around as he shuddered in the doorway. The temperature had dropped. The light of the torch moved over some of the salt crystals lined up outside. Hints of pink and purple reflected from the crystals. There was no laughter, only silence, until the hydrangea in the middle of the lawn started rustling. He heard the child-like laughter once more. Giggling.

"Hello? Who's out here?" Bob asked nervously.

Bob saw the shrub move and shake in the light of his torch and someone or something dashed out from it but he couldn't see what. The sound zipped to a few feet away from him to the right. Then to his left. Bob thought that maybe this was Charlie. In spirit. Surely he wouldn't play games like this? Bob swallowed.

A huge gust of ice-cold breath hit him full on in the face forcing him backwards, causing him to drop the torch. He heard the hard exhalation. Without thinking, he shut the door forcefully. He bolted it quickly and with shaking hands, he locked it as fast as he could. Breathing fast, he stood staring at the door for a moment. He could feel his face cold and burning. He then walked hurriedly to the downstairs toilet and looked in the mirror. His eyebrows and eyelashes were frosted over. He turned the hot tap on and splashed warm water over his face and rubbed it in. This *had* to be this entity. He made his way back to the sofa. The cats were still asleep. He turned the living room light on and gripped his shotgun.

# Chapter Fifty-Seven

## 23rd July, 2018

Throughout the night, Bob drifted in and out of sleep. He rose early and made himself a cup of tea and unlocked the front door. Everything appeared normal. Bob returned to the kitchen and removed the wood which closed the cat flap. Then he opened the back door and stepped out into the garden.

Standing there with his hot cup of tea, Bob felt a strong wave of melancholy wash over him. Losing some of their beloved animals and cat, Daisy, had been awful, but everything that had happened had taken its toll on Bob. Up until a few weeks previously, everything had been fine and they had been happy. He thought about going out to feed the animals and then remembered the reality; they weren't there. They had fed them and mucked out the pens for almost twenty-five years. Now, he'd have to let Derek and Jack go too.

Bob watched some morning TV until the others got up. Gavin, was the first. He could hear the TV and made his way into the living room. Soon the rest joined them, including Betty, who seemed quiet. While she was in the kitchen, Bob told the others what had happened in the night.

"Told you, didn't I? That salt was a waste of fucking time," John said. "That *thing* is still about!"

"Maybe the salt prevented it from entering?" David suggested.

"Yeah, right," John replied.

"Did anything else happen?" asked David.

"Only what I told you. There was nothing more after I closed the door."

"You're definitely all right, though?"

Bob smiled. "I'm fine, David. You boys slept all right?"

"Fine," John said. "No nightmares, thankfully."

"Same, Uncle."

"That's good," Bob replied. "I think I'll give Arthur a call later. Tell him what happened and see if there's any news."

"Yeah. Tell him what a waste of time the salt is," John said.

"Are Derek and Jack in yet?" David asked.

"Not yet. I told them to come in later, as there's less to do. I'm going to let them know I'll pay them holiday pay whilst this is going on. Knowing them, they'll probably still insist on coming in."

*****

Later that morning, as Bob suspected, Jack insisted on working, the same with Derek.

"It feels wrong. Getting paid for doing nowt!" Jack said. "There's still stuff to be done, Bob. We've still got all that trimming and cutting to do, aye?" Jack was more adamant than Derek.

"I know, Jack ... I think it's too risky. It's not like you're losing your job. If this ever stops, the animals will be back, and things can go back to normal again."

"It doesn't feel right. I have to admit," Derek agreed.

"Just think of it this way. It's no different to having normal holiday. There are other temporary jobs out there you can perhaps apply for, and still get paid for here, too. It could be good for you."

"Aye, but it still feels wrong. I'd rather take unpaid holiday," Jack replied.

"Me too, boss. It's not fair to keep getting paid. We don't even know how long it's going to last." Derek scratched his back.

"That's kind of you. But I'm going to pay you, regardless. You're damn fine workers and have always been reliable. It's the least I can do! You can stay for the rest of the day if you wish, or head on home."

Although Derek and Jack insisted on staying for the remainder of the day, they finally agreed to take paid leave.

*****

Around noon time, Bob called the animal sanctuary to make sure that his animals had arrived safely, which they had. They were already settling in well and they were altogether, which gave Bob peace of mind. Cedric offered to send some photos later by email, to reassure Bob.

At the now empty animal pens, John and David were chatting with Jack who was hosing them out.

"What do you think you're going to do, now?" John asked, hands on his hips.

"Cannae say for sure. I'm sure I'll find something until this blows over," Jack answered.

"Blows over?" David said. "You think?"

Jack shrugged his shoulders. "Maybe … I don't know."

"You going to look for other work?" David asked.

"Aye. I don't know about other farm work, but I don't like sitting around doing nothing all day."

"We can call you and Derek for a drink and a catch-up?" John suggested.

"Sure, aye! We'll definitely see each other again, ye can count on that, and soon!" Jack grinned cheekily.

*****

By three in the afternoon, Bob had received photos of the animals from one of Cedric's employees. It made him feel happy and sad, knowing that his animals were safer but so far away. He went outside to the front, not really knowing what to do with himself. David joined him on the front lawn. They both stared at the hydrangea. What had previously been a vibrant shrub with bright pink flowers was now dead. Brittle, light brown heads flaked onto the grass as Bob touched them.

"That thing, from last night?" David asked, looking at his uncle.

Bob nodded. "I believe so … there's no other explanation. They were all fine and out in bloom yesterday, as you know."

David shook his head. "Yeah."

"I'm going to give Arthur a call."

David watched his uncle go back inside.

A few crackles of interference came over the line. Bob called Arthur and it took a few rings before anyone answered.

"Hello?"

"Arthur? It's Bob."

"Mr Hammond! How are you?"

"I'm not too bad, considering," Bob replied.

Bob explained what he had heard and experienced in the night and what had happened to the hydrangea. He also mentioned that his animals were now safe.

"I was going to call you, myself. We may have some news … Not much to go on at the moment, but a small development, perhaps."

"Really?"

"Yes. I'd rather not say over the phone. If it's okay, can I come to your farm, along with Carl, to discuss things in person?"

"That's fine. I'll give you directions."

"If you could, please. I'd like to see the farm for myself."

"When's good for you?" Bob asked, scratching his neck.

"I've still some things to do. But tomorrow morning, say around nine?"

"That's fine. We'll all be here."

"Very well. I can hear this static is getting worse."

Bob had to shout the directions over the phone to Arthur because of the interference and then ended the call.

*****

At the end of the day, Derek grew emotional saying his goodbyes to Bob and the rest. Jack in his usual way showed no emotion. Bob told them both that if he needed something doing, he wouldn't hesitate to call them in.

After they had left, John joined David for an evening walk around the farm with Benji. "You going to tell Emily about all this now?"

"I'm going to have to. I would have yesterday, if the timing had been better. I wanted to see her tonight, but she's working, covering again. Someone else is ill, now," David replied, keeping an eye on Benji.

"It's getting serious then, with you two?"

David sighed. "Yeah. But I don't think I can let it develop further with what's going on. It just isn't right. I don't want her getting hurt."

"She's no doubt going to get hurt, though, if you call it off."

"That's what I'm worried about. But perhaps it's the lesser of two evils … How's Annabel?"

"She's better. Back in work tomorrow. At least I don't have to worry about cooling things with her, seeing as there's nothing to cool!"

"It's for the best, perhaps," David said, throwing a stick.

"I guess. I know we've only been here for two weeks almost, but it feels weird not hearing the animals. One of those goats made me laugh. That *Vinny*."

"I know. I feel the same … it just feels odd."

"Must be so tough on your uncle. And Betty. First the mutilations, now sending your animals away."

"At least they're safe, now. It will be interesting to see what Arthur has to say."

"Probably not a lot. Old duffer!" John smiled.

David shook his head, smiling. "You shouldn't be so harsh … he's trying to help."

"I know. It's just depressing as well as frustrating. Finding more information is one thing. But stopping this cult and demon is an entirely different thing altogether … what the hell are we supposed to do about it?"

David felt his friend's frustration. "You're preaching to the choir on that."

# Chapter Fifty-Eight

## 24th July, 2018

Betty, who seemed chirpier this morning, insisted on washing up after breakfast, whilst the other four stood outside waiting for Carl and his associate to arrive. A few minutes later, a red Audi appeared round the corner of the hard dirt track, driving slowly, parking up next to the farmhouse.

"Morning. Sorry we're a bit late," Carl said out of the window. "We got a bit lost! Can we leave the car here?"

"Sure." Bob smiled. He then introduced Gavin to Carl and Arthur.

Arthur wore the same black attire and silver cross. He looked at the line of salt crystals around the house and up to the pens. He nodded. "Good. You've lined it out correctly."

"What's he on about? It's not exactly hard to put out, is it?" John whispered quietly in David's ear.

"It could be doing its job. Shall we go inside?" Arthur suggested.

"Of course, if you wish," Bob answered.

They made their way inside. Arthur stepped carefully over the salt crystals. Betty came to greet them.

"You must be Mrs Hammond?" Arthur said, holding out his hand to greet her.

Betty smiled. "I am. But please, call me Betty!" She smiled, admiring his large cross.

"We're sorry for your losses and what you've been through," Arthur said tenderly.

"We know it's awful, but we're hoping to help," Carl added seriously.

"Thank you. It's kind of you to say." Betty offered a small smile in return.

Bob showed them into the living room where he politely asked them to sit and Betty joined them.

"It's a lovely home that you have here." Arthur smiled.

"We like to think so, don't we, love?" Bob smiled over at Betty.

Betty smiled back.

"I'll get straight to the point," Arthur said. "We can discuss other things afterwards. The main reason I'm here, is-"

"Oh, I'm sorry, but would you two gentlemen like a cup of tea or coffee?" Betty offered.

"That would be lovely, thank you. A tea for me, two sugars." Arthur smiled back.

"The same for me, please. Only one sugar," Carl added.

Betty smiled as she got up. "Shan't be long!"

Arthur looked at her curiously as she made her way to the kitchen. He was glad she had left the room. "As we mentioned before, Seath Mór defeated Famuli Cani many centuries ago. I was mainly unsuccessful in tracking down and contacting his descendants from the Clan Shaw, until a couple of weeks ago. It wasn't from the want of trying! Although some contacted me back, they couldn't, or refused to help. Most no longer live in Scotland, or the UK for that matter. They emigrated long ago. Some also changed their family name, which made it so hard to find them."

The others looked at each other confused. They remembered Carl and Arthur talking about this historical character but wondered what this had to do with anything currently.

"You're no doubt wondering why this is relevant to what's happening. But here's the thing. They gave some useful information which may be of use to us."

"What kind of information, Arthur?" Bob asked curious, sitting forward.

"Unfortunately, there are no records or physical documents to go by from all those years back. There might have been something, possibly even Seath Mór's diary, but they have since been destroyed or lost over the years. At first, these descendants were *very* reluctant to tell me anything. It took a *lot* of persuading, and some guilt-tripping, not something I'm proud of, but we are desperate … From what they say, some moved away, fearing Canus – The Grey One, would come back, thirsty for revenge one day. Even after all these centuries. Or after already knowing, of Famuli Cani's evil return. They could obviously sense and feel it. Not to mention, the reports about the forest down the years and sightings."

"Hence their name change. Out of fear," Carl added. "Some of the clan, aren't even aware of what happened way back then."

"How's that going to help with anything?" John asked from one of the armchairs, with his arms folded.

"One of the descendants who I spoke to, told me that Seath Mór had a son who went missing one summer. He discovered the cult was behind it and found their secret lair. He took his clan and managed to defeat them, rescuing his son. This is also confirmed by others of the Clan Shaw."

"Really?" David asked. He sat on the sofa next to Carl and Arthur.

"How did he *stop* this demon?" asked John, his arms still crossed.

Arthur looked at Carl.

"The information is a tad sketchy. Apparently, Seath Mór 'killed' Canus with a special dagger." Carl pulled out a folded piece of paper from his jacket pocket with a photocopy of the Clan Shaw's crest. They'd seen it before from the meeting. "It's believed that this represents the dagger on their clan's crest."

The crest had a hand holding up a dagger, surrounded by a belt and FIDE ET FORTITUDINE on it.

"The Latin that you see, means 'by fidelity and fortitude,'" Arthur said.

John sneered. "He killed a demon with *just* a dagger, eh?"

"It's unlikely that you can 'kill' a demon in a traditional, human sense. But you *can* stop it and send it back to where it came from, at least. True evil can never be destroyed completely," claimed Arthur.

"How did he manage to stop this thing with just a dagger?" Gavin asked. He stood next to Bob.

"It was a special kind of dagger. The descendants didn't know where or how he came to have it. To kill or stop a demon, you have to wait until it is in its physical form. Once the cult was defeated, Canus would have lost some of its power. Furthermore, after it was defeated itself ... They are linked as we told you, just as they are today," Arthur explained.

"Am I missing something? So, we just need to get ourselves an army like this *Seath Mór* did, get his special dagger – which could be anywhere – and kill the cult. Great! Simple!"

"John! Please, come on," Bob said. "I'm sorry about that."

"It's okay." Arthur smiled. "We understand your worries and frustrations. If only it *was* that simple ..."

"Where is this dagger, now?" Bob asked.

"We're not entirely sure," Carl answered.

"There's a surprise," John muttered under his breath.

"None of the descendants know for certain. It could be lost or hidden somewhere ... They had one theory that it was buried with Seath Mór," Carl said.

"His grave is situated in the ruins of the old Rothiemurchus Church," Arthur said.

"Even if the dagger was buried there, how on earth would we get it?" David asked.

"Yeah. It's not like we can just *dig* it up," John added.

Both Carl and Arthur looked at one another.

"Oh, Jeez!" John smirked, shaking his head.

"It's … it's a possibility, yes. But how we'd do that, well, we don't know." Arthur bowed his head.

Betty returned with a couple of teacups and biscuits on the saucers. "Here you men are." She grinned. "I thought you'd like a couple of biscuits, too."

"That's very kind of you." Arthur looked up and smiled.

"You're welcome," Betty replied, retaking her seat in one of the armchairs.

"There's no way a dagger's going to work." John shook his head.

"Dagger? What dagger's that?" Betty asked confused.

Bob smiled. "Don't worry. I'll explain later."

"This just feels so helpless. We have nothing. Look at us. We're not fighters, we're not an army. We're just *normal* people. What are we supposed to do, honestly?" David felt the hopelessness of the situation.

"We need to remain positive. Have faith. I believe something will aid us." Arthur took a bite from his biscuit, dropping a few crumbs onto the saucer.

John shook his head again. He felt like saying something but stopped himself.

"These descendants; they said nothing more?" asked Gavin.

"Not much. Other than we shouldn't get involved but move away as quickly as possible," Arthur replied. "I'm afraid I was terribly ill after my call with them."

"Sounds familiar," David said.

Arthur nodded.

"Maybe Samuel and Ralf know more? Particularly Samuel." David looked down at the carpet.

"The two old men from the pub?" Carl asked.

"Uh-huh. Although Samuel didn't seem quite the full ticket," John answered.

"It's possible." Carl ate a biscuit.

"Maybe Emily and Annabel can help? The two girls we know." David considered.

"Yeah … David got to know one of them *really* well the other night!" John smirked, teasing his friend. "Didn't you, Dave?"

The others looked over at David. He felt uncomfortable with all eyes on him.

"Leave the boy alone." Betty frowned.

"It's hard to trust anyone … I'm not sure that's a good idea," Arthur said.

"I'm sure Samuel knows more, but Ralf kept blocking him."

"David's right about that Ralf bastard," John added.

David and John queried their nightmares again. John asked why they didn't have them all the time. Arthur believed that because David and John were good people at heart, their positivity, kindness and good energy naturally repelled such evil, but couldn't stop everything all the time. He stated again that although Famuli Cani had occult powers, it still required great effort and energy to process dark magic, which wasn't always constant, therefore. He even believed that the salt crystals would be having a positive effect too. Worryingly though, the more sacrifices that were performed, the more dark energy the cult and Canus acquired, being able to produce stronger black magic.

Arthur wanted to have a look around the farm. Bob again, told him about the 'frosted blast' incident. On the front lawn, Arthur stood examining the dead hydrangea. "Yes. This is a sign of being touched by evil and negative energy." He took a dried flower head in his hand, crumbling it. "Not good."

Arthur checked the line of salt crystals around the house. "It is possible that you prevented Canus from entering your home the other night, if it indeed had that intention. But the salt stopped it, I feel. Never underestimate the power of what salt can do to evil spirits and entities."

"*Hmpfh*. Yeah, righto," John said quietly and sarcastically to David, following behind.

"We thought we'd stick some salt crystals around here too, even though the animals were to be moved," Bob stated.

"It's good that you did, Robert. I am so sorry about your animals. Not just the ones that were killed, but the ones you had to move. I'm sure they're safe now. It was no doubt a tough decision but indeed, the right one." Arthur walked with his hands behind his back as he looked at the empty animal pens. "I can definitely sense an evil presence has been here … I've sometimes had a sixth sense since a young age, but it's strengthened in the past few months."

"Th-this is where the two-headed calf and its mother were mutilated and killed." Bob showed Arthur and Carl the area. He could feel his eyes starting to fill with tears.

Arthur shook his head. "I'm so, so, sorry. I truly am."

"What do you think about that two-headed calf?" David asked Arthur. "How can they impregnate something like that?"

"Their dark arts." Arthur rubbed his white beard.

"Scary ... If they can do that to an animal, could they do it to a woman?" John quizzed.

"This cult possesses powerful abilities but still has its limitations. They can't just do anything. If they could, we really would be in trouble! However, the more powerful they and their demon, Canus, become, who knows ... I don't have all the answers, but I believe animals are more vulnerable to dark magic. Just like certain humans. Everyone is different."

"Why would they impregnate a cow just to mutilate it and the calf, later?" David asked.

"To hurt you emotionally. No doubt for their own personal reasons, too ... the sacrifice was planned."

"They've certainly achieved that," Bob said.

"Exactly," Arthur replied, looking over his shoulder to Bob.

They walked up to the twin grain silos and to where David had found the ring.

"This is where I found the ring," David said.

Arthur crouched down at the spot, with his huge cross dangling down. "Perhaps, you were meant to find it. A sign, maybe." Arthur then smiled.

"I guess it does seem a little strange that Benji started digging there," David replied.

"Animals are very smart beings." Arthur then rose and frowned. He looked around. "I remember in Carl's office, you told us the farm wasn't as expensive as you expected?"

"That's right. I thought the farm was undervalued. It hadn't been active for many years. The previous family never ran it as a farm."

"Perhaps it was cheap because its history was known, because there was something dark about the area, even before Famuli Cani returned." Arthur stroked and pulled lightly on his long beard. "I would like to talk with you in private, Robert."

"Oh?"

"Come." Arthur led Bob away from the others.

"What's that all about?" David asked.

"I'm sure we'll find out," Carl replied.

"He's a bit of a strange one, ain't he?" John said to Carl.

"Different, I guess. Harmless enough, though. It's only natural for people to doubt demonology. But remember, he's here to help you. All of us."

They watched as Arthur spoke to Bob.

"You think she's in danger, specifically?" Bob asked.

"When I shook your wife's hand to greet her, I felt something. Something cold. Like she was under a dark influence. I'm sorry."

"It's okay, you've only got our best interests at heart. What can I do about it, if she is under the influence of a darker power?"

"Remember that dream your nephew had? The one where she killed you. I'm not saying it was a premonition, but it's all related. Didn't he hear things in your room and experience this coldness, and hear whispers from inside your room?"

"He did, yes."

"She could have been touched by the dark presence of Canus. I'm not necessarily talking sexually. Rather it interacted with her somehow." Arthur put a hand on Bob's shoulder. "It could be targeting her more, because of her vulnerability."

"She was acting strange, but that was down to her not taking her medication, according to the hospital."

"It may have been down to that, or something much darker. Or both."

"Well, what can I do?"

"For now, just keep a close eye on her ... I might just be picking up on the negative energy she's suffered from everything."

"What if you're right? It fits with everything David heard."

"The salt crystals should already be having a positive effect. If she is under their influence, the salt should be keeping things at bay. The good news, as you said yourself, is that you think she seems to be getting back to normal. Her positive energy alone, is no doubt fighting any potential threat, on a subconscious level."

Bob looked down at the ground.

"I may have some things with me where I'm staying that would help. I'll see. But in the meantime, take this ..." Arthur pulled out a shiny red crystal from his pocket and handed it to Bob. "Place this somewhere in the room where you sleep. It can help ward off evil spirits and things."

Bob didn't say anything. He took the crystal from Arthur's hand. It felt warm to touch.

The others watched and waited.

"I wonder what they're talking about?" John asked. "What's he just given him?"

The two made their way back over.

"Everything okay?" David asked.

"I'll tell you later." Bob smiled at his nephew.

David asked if Arthur wanted to see where the strange tree was in the forest.

"I would, but not right now. I need to get back as I have some things I need to do today."

"What are we supposed to do?" John asked.

"Be strong and careful. Stick together. We'll be in touch very soon," Arthur answered.

"I'm sure Emily told me that Samuel and Ralf go on Tuesdays to the pub. Perhaps, we can go this afternoon?"

"It's not advisable, David. Wait for me and Carl to contact you all. I know we lack options."

They set off back to the farmhouse just as the wind picked up.

"I see you took my advice about wearing the ring." Arthur smiled at David.

"What's that? Oh, yeah. It's a perfect fit, actually," David replied, looking at his finger.

"It may help."

"Chance would be a fine thing," John muttered.

"You question my means, John. I get that, I really do. I take no offence from it."

"I don't mean any offence," John replied. "Well, maybe a bit."

Arthur smiled. "Ask yourself this … you question whether the salt crystals work. Maybe you're right? It sounds stupid, impractical, maybe even unrealistic to you. But before all of this started happening, if someone had told you about such experiences, would you have believed them?"

John frowned, staring out into the forest and looked up at Arthur. "Probably not, if I'm honest. I'd say it was horseshit."

"Exactly." Arthur smiled. "So, why would my theories and ways be rubbish, if all that is happening isn't? It's all relative."

John nodded. "I suppose I get what you're saying. I'd like to believe salt could help us, but I'm not counting on it."

Outside the house, Gavin was chatting to a man in his thirties. They had just loaded up three bales of barley into the back of a small yellow van. The man had opted for a third bale.

"Top of the morning to you, Robert! How's things with you?" the man greeted Bob in a mild Scottish accent.

"Morning, Guy. I'm doing okay, thanks. How are you?"

"Good, thanks. Just collecting hay for the rabbits and for the guinea pigs that my little one has got now."

"Just the three bales for now?" Bob smiled, noticing the bales in the back of the van.

"Aye! Probably be back for more, before the summer's out. Those animals get through a lot of this stuff in no time at all!" Guy laughed. He frowned again like he had when he saw the salt crystals outside, as Arthur's silver cross caught his attention. "Anyway, I best be off. Got plenty to do." He got into his van and waved as he left.

"We'd best be going too, Robert," Arthur said, holding out his hand.

"Thanks for coming." Bob shook Arthur's hand.

"I must get off. I've still got some divorce papers to sort out," Carl half-joked.

Bob shook Carl's hand too. "You be safe."

"What we were talking about; try not to worry. I'll be in contact," Arthur said to Bob.

Arthur and Carl nodded to the others as they got into Carl's car.

"What was all that about, with you and Arthur? What did he want?" David asked curiously.

"I'll tell you in a sec," replied Bob.

"What do you think?" Carl asked Arthur, driving off.,

Arthur was rubbing his huge cross. "I feel there's something about that farm. There's certainly a darkness there. We're all in grave danger."

# Chapter Fifty-Nine

## 24th July, 2018

Despite going against Arthur and his uncle's wishes, after lunch, David and John set off to The Auld Drongair Bàrd, hoping to see Samuel and Ralf. Gavin mentioned about going with the two, but they adamantly declined.

"God, I hate driving through this forest. Even during the day." John looked at the surrounding forest. Thankfully, they were almost out of it.

"Interesting that Arthur picked up on Betty not seeming quite right. I kept feeling there was something."

"But does it mean Arthur's right? He's pretty odd, himself."

"It's just the way he is, I suppose. Betty not taking her meds no doubt made things worse. Although maybe this 'Canus' stopped her from taking them? I feel uncomfortable being on the farm and leaving Bob there after my nightmare. Maybe I shouldn't have left Benji there."

"Don't worry about that, mate. Benji will be fine with your uncle. Gavin's there, too. There's the salt as well, don't forget!" John smirked.

"Yeah."

"I wonder how Annabel is?"

"You heard from her earlier, didn't you?"

"Yeah. She said she still wasn't well. She had a relapse or something; she didn't go in to work again today."

"It happens."

When they got to the pub, John noticed Annabel outside, collecting some empty glasses and lunch plates. "That lying cow! She *is* working today. Probably made out she was ill, in case I wanted to meet her later."

"All right. Calm down … maybe she's feeling better and decided to come in after all?"

John shook his head and drove into the car park.

Entering the pub, Annabel came out of the kitchen. Samuel and Ralf were indeed there, sat in the same place near the fireplace, playing dominoes.

"John! David! Lovely to see you two," Annabel said, smiling at them.

"I thought you were still ill?" John asked.

"Not a hundred percent yet, but decided I'd better come in. Not really poorly enough to miss work. Hold on, I'll serve you in a sec …" Annabel went to serve customers who were already waiting. The pub was fairly busy.

"See, I told you she was probably feeling better," David said quietly.

"Whatever." John looked over at Samuel and Ralf.

"Right! What can I get you, both?" Annabel asked. "If you're looking for Em, David, she's gone for lunch." She smiled again.

"That's all right. I'll have a large Coke, please."

"Lemon and ice?"

"Sure."

"I'll have a pint of that, cheers," John said, pointing to one of the cold pumps. "How long have those two been in here?" John used his thumb to gesture over to the two old men.

"Oh, not too long. About half an hour, I think. Why? You're not going to annoy them again, are you?" Annabel winked.

"Me? Nooo," John joked back.

"How long do they usually stay for?" David asked.

"It varies, really. It's usually a good two to three hours at least, I'd say." Annabel poured the drinks and then attended to her other duties.

"We've got a couple of hours at least to work out what we're going to do … Maybe, we can knock Ralf over the head with Samuel's cane and then kidnap old Sammy," John jested.

David smiled. "We need to get Samuel alone. Even then, he might not open up to us."

John gulped his pint. His eyes lit up in thought. "Think I've got it!"

"Got what?"

"An idea."

"What?"

"What if we wait until they've finished and then follow them? If they don't live together, we can find out where Samuel lives!"

"I guess we could. Sounds a bit like stalking, though."

"What choice do we have? Besides, it's more like detective work, really." John turned to look at Samuel and Ralf again.

Samuel had his back to them. They still hadn't noticed John and David standing at the bar. They were too busy focusing on their game.

"It's worth a shot. We'll have to keep an eye on them," David said.

"So, Annabel," John said, "When would you like to take me out next?" He smiled cheekily.

Annabel laughed. "What makes you think that I *want* to?"

"Oh, I *know* you do!"

"It's a shame you missed out on quad trekking. Maybe one evening, later this week? Once I've recovered fully from this stomach bug. I wouldn't want to risk you catching it."

"Ah, I think it would be worth it." John winked.

Annabel shook her head, laughing.

*****

David and John sat at the bar, occasionally chatting to Annabel when she was free. Eventually, Samuel and Ralf noticed them both. Ralf grumpily mumbled something as he went to the gents. John waved sarcastically in response. Samuel turned briefly to see who Ralf had been mumbling to.

"Still a miserable bastard, I see," John said.

"David! What a lovely surprise," came a sweet voice.

"Hey!" David got up and gave Emily a hug.

"Why didn't you let me know you were here when you texted?"

"Thought I'd surprise you!" David smiled.

"Well, you've certainly done that." Emily beamed back. "You okay?"

John looked on, feeling a little envious.

"Fine. You?" David felt a little guilty that the purpose of his visit was not to see Emily.

"Yes. I'm great, now I've seen you." Emily felt uncomfortable knowing John and Annabel were watching them.

"Aw." David gave her another longer hug.

"Argh. Enough of that, in here!" came Jock's loud voice as he exited the kitchen.

"Sorry," Emily replied sheepishly.

Jock laughed. "Don't be silly lass, I was only joking. How are ye both?" he asked David and John.

"Not bad, mate. Yourself?" John asked.

"Good, good. Ticking over." Jock smiled broadly.

When the pub grew quieter, Emily sat in the corner to chat with David, at Jock's suggestion.

"They make a lovely couple, don't they?" Annabel said to John, looking over at them. She was wiping a table close to the bar.

"They do. You know, we could have that," John said in a more serious voice than he usually used.

Annabel laughed. "You think?"

"Never know," John replied cheekily.

Annabel laughed again.

John watched Ralf and Samuel. They hadn't shown any signs of leaving yet. They were still fixated on their game. Neither had approached the bar to order drinks. They rarely even spoke to each other as they played dominoes sitting across from each other.

Annabel noticed John's interest in the two old men. "You fancy a game with them?" She smiled.

"What's that?" John asked, turning his head to Annabel. "Oh." He laughed. "Yeah! It looks so riveting. Not to mention the conversation they're having! They've hardly said a word to one another."

"They're usually like that, aye. Engrossed in their game. Bless 'em."

John sipped his pint, just as he heard a chair scrape to his left. Ralf was going to the gents again. He looked coldly over at John who stared back.

"Miserable shit," John muttered.

*****

Samuel and Ralf's game lasted over two hours. It sounded as if Ralf had won. He got up from the table and rudely demanded Jock order him and Samuel a taxi.

John caught David's eye. He raised his eyebrows and nodded with his head at the two elderly men. He then mouthed that they were leaving.

David had been so busy chatting to Emily, he had almost forgotten why they were there. He sat holding her hand over the table, when he caught John's eye. "We better get back to the farm." He smiled.

"Aw. Yeah. I'd better get back to work as well. I don't want to neglect my duties; Jock's always too kind." She giggled. "I'm sorry again, about what happened on your farm. I'm sure the animals are safer, now." She gripped David's hand tighter.

"Yeah," David replied. He had shared with Emily that his uncle had moved the animals but very little else.

They kissed each other on the lips and hugged.

"I'll see you tonight, then?"

"Of course." David smiled.

"Great!" Emily beamed back.

David kissed her a final time on her cheek and rejoined John.

"Have a nice chat, did we?" John teased.

"I almost forgot about those two." David looked over at Samuel and Ralf's table. They had now cleared away their dominoes and Ralf was holding the pouch of tiles.

"Jock got them a taxi. He said it would be about twenty minutes."

"We're definitely going to follow them, then?" David felt nervous but also excited. It felt as though they were on a stakeout.

"Yep. We have to find out what Samuel knows."

"What if they don't go home? Suppose they go elsewhere first."

"Nah. I heard Ralf tell Jock they were going home."

"Okay," David replied, watching Emily carrying dirty plates into the kitchen.

"I think it's best if we go now. It will look obvious if we leave at the same time. We can pull over down the road and wait to follow the taxi," John suggested.

"Yep, good idea."

They said their goodbyes to Jock and Emily.

"Thanks for coming again, laddies! Ye have a good day and take care," Jock called out to them jovially.

"I'll see you tonight." Emily smiled over again at David.

"Will do!" David gave her a twinkle back.

Annabel was coming down the step as the two were leaving.

"Hopefully, I'll see *you* soon!" John grinned cheekily.

"I'll be in touch, I promise." Annabel smiled.

"Chance would be a fine thing," John muttered to himself, checking out her curves as she walked behind the bar.

*****

"You're seeing Emily again, tonight?" John asked, after parking at the side of the road, a short distance from the pub. It had begun to rain.

"Yep." David sighed. "I want to, obviously. But I think it's time I came clean and told her everything. It's not like I'm lying to her, but it feels like I am, you know? I'm thinking of calling things off."

"I know, mate. Must be tough. I saw you both. It's plain to see that you really like one another. It's love," John teased.

"Dick." David grinned.

"She cooking you dinner, again?"

"Nah, not this time."

"Shit! That must be the taxi," John said anxiously.

A silver taxi pulled up outside the pub.

The two friends waited for a moment. Samuel and Ralf slowly walked out, Samuel with his cane, and Ralf moving more steadily but with an irritable face as usual. Samuel struggled as he made his way to the taxi. Ralf seemed to be nagging his friend to hurry up.

"He really is a miserable shit, isn't he?" John said, shaking his head. "He's not even helping him to the car."

As Samuel reached the vehicle, the chubby lady driver jumped out and opened the door for him, helping him into the back. Ralf sat in the front.

"I wonder who's going to get dropped off first?" David mused.

"I guess we'll find out." John started the ignition.

They watched as the taxi turned around to return the way it had come.

John waited a few seconds before following. "It feels exciting, doesn't it?" John said, tailing the taxi, keeping a reasonable distance. "Like we're a couple of private detectives!" He chuckled to himself.

"It does a bit."

John slowed down as another car turned in between his own and the taxi, which made John feel more comfortable as they were better hidden from the taxi.

*****

After a few miles, they followed the silver taxi through a small village called Kincraig.

"At least we're seeing the sights, I suppose."

"It's a lovely area." David looked out of the window.

It had stopped raining and the sun was trying to come out. They could see the mountains clearly and green fields where sheep were grazing. It was very bucolic. It all felt serene passing through the village. The taxi began to slow down and then indicated left.

The taxi came to a stop outside a small, stone cottage bungalow, isolated some distance from the other houses in the village.

"One of them must live here," David said, feeling a little nervous.

"You think?" John said sarcastically, looking over at David.

They sat and waited to see who got out. It was a few moments before the back door opened. Samuel struggled to clamber out of the taxi, almost stumbling as he did so. The driver again jumped out to help Samuel to his front door. Ralf remained sat in the front passenger seat.

"Ralf is supposed to be his friend, the bastard. You'd think he'd help him," John said annoyed.

"I know. He obviously doesn't care."

"Prick," John added.

The driver returned to the car and reversed round carefully.

John and David scooched down in their seats to avoid being seen by Ralf as the taxi drove past them both, making its way back through the village.

"I don't think they saw us," John said, sitting back up. He then parked outside Samuel's home. "You're sure he lives by himself?"

"Emily said he lives alone but has a carer who pops in two or three times a day," David replied, unfastening his seatbelt. "Let's hope the carer doesn't come while we're here."

"Looks a nice enough place."

"What if he gets angry or calls the police?" David asked concerned.

"Not chickening out, are you?"

"No, just saying."

"I'm sure he'll be more relaxed without that moron, Ralf. He's in his own home as well."

"I suppose so."

"Come on!" John said encouragingly, opening his door.

"Shit," David uttered quietly, following him.

They stood nervously at the small white door to Samuel's charming home, with its stonework and slate details. A darker slate to the right of the door read *Taigh an Dàraich Mhóir*.

Anyone tall, would have to stoop their head to avoid bashing it at the top of the front door frame. Two diamond shaped windows looked out from either side of the doorway.

"That's certainly a large tree," John said, looking at an oak tree to the left of the house.

David looked over. "Sure is … who's going to knock?"

"I thought you were?"

"What made you think that?"

"Just presumed, I guess?" John said, scratching his elbow.

"Fine, I'll do it." David hesitated, his knuckles hovering over the door. There was no doorbell or knocker. He gave three firm knocks on the door and felt his anxiety rise.

John swallowed, beginning to have doubts himself now. "Maybe this wasn't such a good idea of yours, after all?"

"Mine? It was *your* idea!" David said.

"Oh shit, yeah. It actually was!" John replied, trying not to laugh.

"Shhh. I think he's coming."

They could hear the thudding sound of Samuel's cane on the floor as he approached the door.

"Shit, here we go …" John said, his own anxiety increasing.

The silver chrome handle shook. Samuel seemed to be struggling to open the door. When the door opened, Samuel, still wearing his deerstalker cap, peered at John and David without expression on his yellowing face.

"Erm, Samuel! Do you remember us, from the pub?" John asked.

Samuel looked blankly at John and then blinking, turned his attention to David.

"I hope you don't mind us turning up like this, and that we're not intruding, Samuel?" David asked.

Samuel still didn't say anything. His face remained blank. It seemed to David and John as though he didn't recognise them at all. Samuel continued to stare at them both. He blinked again. And again.

"I think we're wasting our time, mate," John said.

"Please, Samuel. We *really* need your help."

Samuel stood, crouched over, still saying nothing.

"Come on, David. Let's leave him." As John pulled on David's arm to leave, they heard Samuel mutter something.

"What was that?" David said, quickly turning back.

"I … I remember, yes." Samuel's voice was slow, faint and breathless.

"Do you remember our conversation at the pub that night? About the cult?" John asked.

"Yes, I remember."

"I know it's difficult for you, but could you tell us more, please?" David pleaded.

Samuel looked down at the ground, gripping his cane for support.

"Please, it's important. We wouldn't be here if it wasn't. We need your help, mate," John stated.

"I … I can try," Samuel replied, his head still bowed.

"Would it be okay if we came in?" John asked softly.

Samuel hesitated at first, but eventually agreed. "Okay." He slowly turned around and started the journey down his short hallway.

John and David looked at one another.

"After you …" John said to David.

Ducking their heads slightly, David followed Samuel and John closed the door after them, clicking it shut.

"It's a, erm, nice place you have here," David said, looking around.

Samuel didn't say anything. He continued down the hall with the help of his cane.

David noticed numerous circular marks on the old wooden floor, where Samuel's cane had hammered in.

Samuel was leading them into a small living room at the back, where fresh flowers in a vase scented the room.

"Sit …" Samuel slowly sat himself in one of his striped grey and white armchairs.

Next to Samuel's armchair was a large green and grey oxygen tank and mask.

John and David sat down on the matching sofa.

An old analogue TV stood on a stand in the corner of the room. Samuel clearly wasn't with the digital times. An old VHS recorder sat connected underneath. Next to the TV in the middle, was a vintage, slate fireplace. Above, hung a painting of a pirate ship. On the opposite wall, an old wooden cuckoo clock was stuck at ten-to-two.

"Thanks for inviting us in, Samuel," David said sincerely. "Could you tell us what you know about this cult, please?" he asked calmly. "It's really affecting our lives, so if you could help us in any way, we'd be really grateful."

Samuel sat there blankly, looking straight at John and David. It made them feel uncomfortable. "It … it wasn't long before my wife died, Edwina …" Samuel's head lowered and he paused.

"I'm so sorry about your wife," David replied.

"Me too, Samuel. I know what it's like to lose a loved one," John added.

"I miss her so much, even now, after all these years."

John and David felt for the old man. Jock had told them that he had been through a lot down the years. A heck of a lot. The years hadn't been kind to him.

"I'm sorry," David repeated.

"Oh shit, wait!" John suddenly said.

David frowned, looking at John. Samuel raised his head.

"Sorry, Samuel, but would you mind if we recorded our conversation so we can play it to someone else who is helping us?" John placed his phone on a blue pouffe between the sofa and Samuel.

David felt John was being rather disrespectful to Samuel but didn't say anything. It seemed like a good idea for Arthur and Carl to later hear what Samuel had to say.

Samuel didn't appear to mind.

"Sorry, Samuel, please, continue," John said.

"It was the summer solstice of 1998."

"What was?" John asked. "What happened? What did you see?"

"Quiet, John. Let him speak," David snapped.

John held his hands up, apologetically.

"Ralf wanted us to go camping for a fishing trip in Rothiemurchus Forest that summer. We used to fish a lot when we were younger. We would light a fire, cooked the fish and had a couple of beers each. They were happier times back then … But we did it less after I got married. Ralf and I didn't see as much of each other after. Edwina and he never really saw eye to eye."

"That's no surprise. We've seen what Ralf's like," John said.

David frowned at him again.

"Sorry! Carry on, Samuel."

"I've known Ralf most of my life. He's often been irritable and temperamental. He's become worse with age, I should add." Samuel looked over at John and David as he spoke. "It was a beautiful day as I recall. My memory isn't as good as it used to be, the same as my health in general. But, I'll never, ever forget, what we encountered that night. It's like it was yesterday, still fresh in my mind …" Samuel had to stop to get some air from his tank.

John and David watched as Samuel breathed in the fresh oxygen. His mask steamed up from his breath.

"We set up camp close to the River Spey in the middle of the forest. The rules are a bit stricter now. I think you need permits … There were certain rules even then about catching fish, not that it really stopped Ralf, though! He was never one to abide by rules and hates being told what to do. He's certainly caused a fair few arguments down the years." Samuel began to laugh, causing him to cough. He needed more oxygen. "As I was saying, it was a fine and beautiful day, at least most of it was. Not a cloud or other person was in sight. To begin with, it felt very serene and peaceful. But it all began to change later on that afternoon …"

There was a longer pause this time as Samuel drew more oxygen from his heavy tank. He spluttered a few more times before continuing.

"Later that day, whilst Ralf was still fishing, I went to fetch some kindling for a fire so we could cook the fish we caught. As I went back into the forest, I felt a strange sensation, like I was being watched from all directions. It's hard to explain … Then I heard this whispering come from all around me. I remember suddenly feeling sick and vomiting."

Samuel stopped again for more oxygen, closing his eyes as he inhaled deeply.

David began to worry that Samuel would stop breathing any minute. Telling them his account was straining Samuel's breathing. David was tempted to stop quizzing him.

Samuel continued regardless. "I collected some wood for the fire, nevertheless. When I returned to the embankment, Ralf was chatting to a strange man. He claimed he was a forest ranger, but the funny thing was, he had no uniform. Ralf told me later that he had appeared from nowhere, startling him."

"Sweet Jesus," John said. "I bet his name was Harold, wasn't it?"

Samuel nodded. "Yes. It was. He looked awfully gaunt, balding and spoke slowly. Worse than me." Samuel laughed a little to himself. "He was telling us we needed a permit, and how we shouldn't be there, and needed permission to start a fire. Something along those lines … Ralf told him where to go and this man took exception to that." A little laugh came from Samuel, followed by a cough.

"Maybe Ralf's not so bad after all, if he told that Harold to fuck off," John commented.

"What happened after that, Samuel?" David asked. "Thank you for telling us this."

"He told us that a storm was coming … me and Ralf thought he was mad. There was no sign of rain, let alone a storm. The sky was clear and the forecast was fine." Samuel coughed before continuing. "About ten minutes after he left, some clouds appeared. Before we knew it, the sky was dark with menacing clouds and it poured down … There was a violent storm that lasted well into the night. Even a nearby tree got struck by lightning close to our tent."

"My God! That's what happened with me and Emily on our walk. It was fine one minute and then clouds came over the mountains and a thunderstorm came out of nowhere." David frowned in thought as John looked over.

Samuel continued not even acknowledging what David had said. "But that night, was when the worst of it happened." Samuel's voice held a raw sadness.

He looked down again at the maroon carpeted floor.

"What did you see?" John asked, sitting forward now, on the edge of the sofa.

"We managed to get shelter from the storm. Luckily, we'd pitched our tent under some large trees, not too far from the river ..."

"It's okay, Samuel," David said, positioning himself forward next to John.

"The storm had died down by the time we went to bed, but I woke sometime after midnight. I'd only been asleep for a couple of hours. I was shivering and I could hear chanting nearby ... Ralf was still asleep, snoring, so I left the tent. I remember the moon overhead. It was so bright. I never saw it so large. The chanting became faster and louder and I could see this strange mist on the river ... the way it moved; it didn't appear natural."

"We've seen this strange mist too, Samuel," David said.

"I didn't know where the chanting was coming from, but it seemed as though it was coming from deeper in the forest from the north-east. I ... I felt drawn to it ... I had to investigate. I ... I wish that I hadn't ..." Samuel's voice was getting louder. "The chanting was so loud, so mesmerising ..." Samuel put his hands over his ears. "I can hear it now. Make it *stop*!" Samuel called out, cowering and shaking as he had at the pub when they met him previously. *"Please!"*

"Oh-oh. Here we go. *Shit*! What are we going to do?" John said, standing up in a panic.

David stepped over to Samuel and placed a hand on his right shoulder. "It's okay, Samuel. You're safe. There's no chanting here."

*"I can still hear it!"*

"Just relax. Deep breaths, Samuel. Here, have some more oxygen ..." David handed the plastic mask to Samuel. David looked over at John, worried.

Samuel took some deep breaths and managed to calm himself. He then looked up at David with his watery, yellowy eyes. "Th ... thank you."

David smiled. "It's okay."

Gradually, Samuel regained his composure. "I'm sorry. Everything that happened that night has scarred me. It will haunt me for ever."

"It's all right, mate. We're here with you." John felt saddened.

"As I went further into the forest, I saw a clearing ... There was this ugly looking tree in the centre of it, not big, but it didn't look right and in front of the tree, was this huge fire ... In front of that, there was a log set up as an altar. Around the edge of the clearing were people dressed in hooded robes, kneeling. It seemed so light with the moon and the fire. I, I can see them now …" A tear ran down Samuel's left cheek and disappeared into his white beard. He shook his weary head.

"How many people were there, Samuel?" David asked.

"I … I don't know. Twenty, thirty, maybe? I'm not sure … I got as close to the clearing as I could, without being seen. I got close enough that I could feel the heat on my face. I sort of welcomed it, because I was still shaking from the inexplicable cold. It didn't feel normal.

"The people chanting were rocking their bodies and heads, like they were in a violent trance … The mist from the river started circulating throughout the forest and there was a sort of static electricity in the air." Samuel stared in front of him as he recalled the events of that night. "I became even colder. I … I started to shake so hard. The mist, the way it moved, it wasn't normal as it flowed around me. It was like it was trying to touch and reach out to me. Grab me. It never went inside the clearing, though …"

"Jesus," David said. "Are you okay to go on?"

"And then. Then the chanting just halted. The people around the clearing stopped convulsing and stood. There was silence for a short while. And then …" Samuel paused, shaking his head again. He began to weep and sniffed a couple of times.

David put his hand on Samuel's shoulder again and sat on the arm of his chair. "It's okay, Samuel."

"Th … there was this bright white, yellow flash from the tree. I … I thought it was going to blind me. I instinctively turned my head away from it … When I looked back after the flash had gone, there was this tall, cloaked figure, just hovering above the ground in front of the fire, near the altar. Its head was covered and it had no visible arms nor legs."

"Fucking hell," John said, his mouth open.

"The rest of the group took off their hoods. Some were wearing masks, masks made from human faces."

David and John remembered Samuel briefly mentioning masks before.

"T-two people entered the middle of the clearing, a man and a woman. They took off their dark robes and stood naked … They began to have intercourse on the dirty ground, whilst the others watched and the chanting started again."

John intuitively wanted to break the tension by joking crudely, but he thought better of it.

"The man then picked the woman up and placed her on the altar … He began sodomising her from behind. The other hovering figure – I still couldn't see its face – was watching, enjoying what it saw. I could *sense* it. That was when Ralf appeared … The mist began to fade and I saw Ralf a few feet away from me behind another tree. He didn't notice me at first. When he did, he came over carefully trying to be silent. He'd woken and heard the chanting and finding me gone, he'd come to search for me."

A sound from the letter box in the hallway startled John and David. David went out to check and could see the afternoon post. There were a few envelopes lying on the black mat.

"It's the mail. It often comes later, nowadays," Samuel stated.

"I'll get it for you," David offered. He picked up the post and returned, placing it next to John's phone on the pouffe. "There you go."

"Would you like a cup of tea?" Samuel asked randomly.

"Erm, no. We're fine, thanks," John replied, looking over at David.

"What happened after Ralf joined you at the clearing, Samuel?" David didn't want the interruption of the post to delay them discovering more.

Samuel started to shake. "Wh … whilst the man was sodomising this woman, another man wearing a mask with horns on came from the side of the clearing. I … I hadn't noticed him before. He seemed like a leader. He, he handed a long sharp knife to the naked man … Sh-she was moaning." Samuel's voice was broken now. He shook his head as tears streamed down his face.

Behind his tears and breathless voice, it was becoming more difficult to hear his words. David and John listened wide-eyed, shocked, their pulses soaring.

"This man. He flipped the woman over onto her back, still penetrating her. He … he held the knife aloft with both hands, chanting something. And then … he plunged it again and *again* into this naked woman's chest. Over and over and *over*. So much blood. Her screams and gargling. He … he … held up her heart. The rest of them cheered. The figure hovering seemed to sense that we were watching. I could hear it laughing and mocking inside my head." Samuel put his hands to the side of his head again. *"Noooo!"* His hands and body shook and tears flowed.

David tried to calm him. "Have some more oxygen."

Samuel swiped the plastic mask away from his face. *"Get away from me!"* he cried. He became more agitated, slapping and thumping at his armchair, almost knocking over his oxygen tank. *"Get out of my head! Get away from me!"* He was hitting the sides of his head, making them sore and red. "GET OUT! GET OUT! GET OUT!"

"What are we going to do?" David asked frantically, looking at John for help. "We can't just leave him!"

John got up. "*Shit*! I don't know! Maybe we can?"

"Maybe we should phone an ambulance?"

"And how would we explain who we are?" John started pacing around the room. "*Fuck*! I knew something like this would happen!"

Samuel continued to rock his body and hit his head against the chair back.

"What the *hell* is wrong with him?"

"Clearly, his experience affected him," David replied, concerned for Samuel. He tried to calm down and think.

After a few moments, Samuel appeared to calm.

"Samuel? You okay, buddy?" John asked, keeping his distance.

Samuel stopped his thumping and rocking and focused his attention on the two young men. His yellow eyes were swollen and red. "I'm … I'm okay."

John let out a sigh of relief. "You had us worried there for a while, Samuel!"

"Would you like a cup of tea?" Samuel asked again, randomly.

"What the …"

"I think it's best if we leave him be, John. He may know more, but it's clearly all too much for him," David advised. "We can't risk another episode like that. It's not fair."

"He may know more, though? We *need* answers. We could be running out of time. We're in danger."

David didn't say anything. He didn't know what to think. John was right but he was worried for Samuel. Before he could speak, Samuel continued with his story. He seemed to have returned to normal. He even replaced his hat, which had come off.

"I remember seeing her naked and lifeless body there. The man … he rubbed her blood all over himself. It seemed to arouse him further."

"What kind of sick fucks are these people?" John uttered in disgust.

"That's when … when they saw us."

"They saw you?" David frowned.

Samuel gave a slight nod of his head. "This thing … it hovered slowly towards us. Me and Ralf. We … we couldn't believe our eyes. It stopped at the edge of the clearing. It raised its cloak and a hand appeared, not a human hand, it had large claws. It pointed at us. I'll never forget the staring cold eyes of those people, fixated on us through their masks. My … my blood froze." Samuel seemed to have composed himself, although his eyes still looked fearful.

"What did you and Ralf do?" David asked. He felt uneasy listening to Samuel's story.

"Our first instinct was to run, naturally. Back then, I could! We were scared beyond belief. We sprinted as fast as we could back towards our tent ... We didn't know where else to go. We were in the middle of the forest at night. Even with the moonlight, we panicked and lost our bearings."

"Man, I would have bricked it. I thought what we'd been through was bad, but that has to beat it, for sure!" John shook his head.

"Ralf and I got separated. I remember looking back and he was gone. He'd tripped apparently and was too scared to call out. He hid under a log until daylight, petrified. I ran into a large branch. At dawn, I woke in the forest. I'd knocked myself clean out."

"What happened in the morning, Samuel?" David asked.

"When I woke up, I thought perhaps the previous night had been a nightmare, until the brutal reality sunk in ... My head hurt badly and there was dry blood from where I'd knocked myself out. I still have the scar." Samuel lifted his deerstalker cap and showed them a pink scar an inch long on top of his forehead. "I could just about walk so I made my way back to the tent. I wasn't too far away from it as it turned out. Ralf was already there, worried about me."

"I'm glad you made it, Samuel, and that you're alive to tell the tale," David said.

"I wish I hadn't survived after the repercussions."

"What repercussions?" asked John.

"When I got back to where we'd pitched the tent, Ralf was reading a note written in blood on the side of our tent, warning us not to tell anyone what we'd seen. Ralf burnt the tent before we left. I don't know why."

John swallowed. "Why didn't they just kill you? I don't get it."

Samuel took some oxygen from his tank and began to laugh ironically. "They wanted me to suffer. To cause us fear and paranoia, too."

"How do you mean?" David asked.

"My Edwina ... She asked how I'd banged my head. I couldn't bring myself to tell her what had happened. She, she could tell something was up. I said I tripped and fell. She wanted me to go to the hospital to get it checked. I insisted I was fine, but she made me go ... Call me paranoid, but I knew I was being *watched* at the hospital. The way they looked at me."

"It must have been so horrific for you. We're so sorry. But what of these repercussions you spoke of?" David asked.

"I, I made the mistake of going to the police a few days later. What I saw that night was eating me up inside. That poor woman who was killed … Ralf seemed to cope better than me. He never spoke of it but I could tell he was affected by it all as well … He blew his lid when I told him I'd been to the police. He raged at me how stupid I was when we'd been warned not to."

"What did the police say, Samuel?" John asked calmly as he ran a finger round his chin.

"Not much. I never mentioned I was with Ralf. I said that I was camping alone. I told them about what I saw, including the floating figure … Perhaps, I shouldn't have, as it just sounded silly. They laughed … They tried to find the clearing but there was nothing there. No blood, no tree, nothing … They said it might have been druggies or a re-enactment, or roleplaying!" Samuel laughed triggering his cough again.

"Roleplaying?" John screwed his face up. "What the fuck?"

Samuel's laughing soon stopped. "Edwina. Sh … she's dead because of me. A day after going to the police, I received a note through my door, again written in blood, with a couple of strange symbols … Edwina didn't see it." Samuel got up from his chair and slowly walked out into the hallway and to his bedroom, his cane banging on the floor as he went.

John and David looked at each other.

Samuel returned soon after, holding something in his left hand. "This was the note they left that morning. And this, this is my Edwina …" Samuel handed David a photo and the note before sitting back down. "It was the last photo taken of us. Of her."

"She's a good-looking lady," David said as he and John looked at the photo.

Samuel and his wife looked happy. They had their arms around each other in a garden, with a smoking barbecue in the background. Samuel looked healthy and much younger.

"Sh-she was," Samuel replied glumly.

David and John then looked at the note, which appeared a little wrinkled and had slightly yellowed over the years. The writing and symbols had faded:

YOU WERE WARNED, NOW YOU MUST PAY!

"This looks like the same handwriting as on our notes," David said. "Certainly similar."

"Yeah, it does," John replied. "Could we keep this note, Samuel?"

"It's of no use to me," Samuel replied.

David handed back the photo. "Thank you."

"Why do you feel responsible for your wife's death? Did they do something to her?" John asked, glancing again at the old note.

"Edwina was diagnosed with cancer a short time before that night … She was diagnosed early and the doctors insisted that she was fine as long as she had treatment … It wasn't life threatening and not too much to worry about … Four days after I'd received that note, I found her lying in bed one morning. She was dead … The post-mortem reported the cancer had become so aggressive, she didn't stand a chance. But she had been fine. Then she was dead." Samuel began to cry again.

"My mum died from cancer. It's a bastard of an illness, Samuel. It can happen like that. It's not your fault. There's nothing you could have done." John tried to console Samuel.

*"They did it!"* Samuel hissed, his eyes full of tears. "I'm to blame for going to the police. Their *black magic* did it."

"It could just have been a coincidence, Samuel?" David considered.

"No. A week after her funeral, I had a phone call. There was static on the line. I could hardly hear, but I heard somebody laugh and then ask how my dead wife was … They said she was waiting in Hell for me and that I shouldn't open my mouth, again."

"Fucking sick shits!" John was both angry and sad.

"They did something to her, to make her cancer worse. I know it! Killing me would have been nothing compared to the suffering they've given me … They want me to suffer and feel this guilt and sorrow every day. I can still hear the chanting whenever I try to sleep … That's why Ralf keeps quiet. He has a grown-up daughter to protect. After Edwina's death, he said we would never talk about any of this again, and we haven't. Until you two showed up."

"I understand, Samuel. It's so good of you to talk to us," David said.

"I don't care anymore what happens to me. I'm ready to die, now. I want to be with my Edwina again … I never even told her about that night, nor did she see the note. I, I miss her so much … *Oh, God, my Edwina*!" His tears spilled uncontrollably.

"Come on, mate. You can't think things like that." John tried to sound upbeat.

Samuel cried for a couple more minutes before being able to speak again. "There isn't anything they can do to cause me any more pain and suffering now."

"Did you ever hear about other disappearances? There was a little boy, Charlie Begsbie?" David queried.

"A few, yes. Charlie? Maybe, I don't remember … Would you like some tea, I can brew the kettle for you boys?"

"Erm, no. We're fine," David replied, looking at John.

Samuel got up and made his way to the kitchen and put the kettle on.

"What is it with him, and making us tea?" John asked.

"I don't know. It's probably dementia."

"I think we've pumped this well dry. He's told us everything he knows. Not that it really helps us, though. Poor bastard," John said.

"I know. He hasn't even asked us questions, like how are we involved and how we knew where he lived."

"Yeah. His story seems similar to what happened with Charlie, when the family went camping."

They heard Samuel rummaging about in the kitchen and then someone putting a key in the front door.

"*Shit*! Who the fuck's that?" John asked.

A middle-aged woman wearing a dark blue tunic with black trousers, made her way into the living room, where David and John were standing. "Oh. Hello?" She smiled. She sounded polite but curious in her light Scottish accent. She looked confused to see them standing there.

"You all right?" John tried to smile.

"I'm sorry, I don't mean to be rude. But you are?"

John and David both looked at one another.

"I'm John and this is David. We know Samuel from the pub. We erm, we live nearby and sometimes when we can, we pop in and see how he's doing." John tried to sound confident. "And you are?"

"I see. Well, that's kind of you. I saw a car outside and I did wonder. Samuel rarely gets guests apart from Ralf. I'm Harriette. I'm the carer who checks in on Samuel, daily. Surprising, he's never mentioned you." Harriette pulled out her ID for them to see.

"Shame on him. Shame on you, Sammy! Not mentioning us to this lovely lady!" John called into the kitchen. "You know what his mind is like? I don't think he's even mentioned you to us either, before. Mind you, we've only known him for barely a month, to be honest," John lied.

Harriette smiled. "Oh, I know! He has good and bad days. Sometimes he even forgets who I am, and it takes a while for it to register with him. Bless him, aye?"

"That's old Samuel for you!" John laughed.

"Are you okay, Samuel? These two nice young men looking after you?"

"He keeps asking if we want some tea. We kept declining, but now he's making it," David explained.

"He's the same with me." Harriette smiled fondly at Samuel.

"We were about to leave, actually," John said. "We've been here a fair while."

"We don't want to stay too long and confuse him, further," David added.

"Of course," Harriette replied.

Samuel started to cough from the kitchen.

"Come, Samuel. Leave that for now." Harriette led Samuel back into the living room and sat him down.

John picked his phone up.

"I see he showed you the photo of his wife?" Harriette smiled, noticing the photo on the arm of the chair.

"Yeah. It's a shame what happened to Edwina," David replied.

"Yes, it really is," Harriette said.

Samuel started coughing, spluttering everywhere. Mucus flew from his mouth, sticking to his white beard. Harriette handed him the oxygen mask to aid him.

"Bronchitis." Harriette tutted, shaking her head.

"He's going to be all right?" John asked, screwing his face up a little.

"He should be, in a bit ... His TV doesn't work, but I'll put on a VHS tape of some trains and railways. He likes that. Helps him settle. Isn't that right, Samuel?"

When the coughing fit died down, Harriette asked if one of them could get a glass of water for Samuel. John obliged.

"We best be off. You take care, Samuel. We'll see you soon. Thanks for the chat." John raised his hand.

David patted Samuel on the shoulder and nodded to Harriette.

Harriette smiled. "Well, it was nice meeting you both."

"Would you like a cup of tea?" Samuel asked a final time.

# Chapter Sixty

## 24th July, 2018

"I understand why you did it, David. But it was still a risk to follow that Samuel back home and then visit like that," David's uncle repeated.

They were sat in the living room, Betty included, where they had just listened to the conversation John had recorded on his phone. Samuel's breathless voice was harder to understand when recorded. David had also shown them Samuel's twenty-year-old note.

"That poor, poor man," Betty said. "And we thought we had it bad. You think he really did see all that, that night, and it isn't just his dementia?"

"One hundred percent, Auntie," David replied. "We've encountered similar things. Look at that note for example. We believe it's the same handwriting as our notes, although it's from two decades ago."

"Despite his dementia, he could recall that night perfectly. I suppose it's easier when something so awful has carved its way inside your mind, scarring you," John added.

"Yeah. I guess it's hard *not* to remember something so sinister and tragic as that." David bent down and stroked Benji.

"It's like Carl and Arthur said, they get pleasure in seeing people suffer, as opposed to 'just' killing them straight away. They could have silenced Samuel and Ralf, long before. Perhaps they knew Samuel would blab? And this was *worse* than death." John scratched his cheek.

"It was heart-breaking. We could feel his pain. Despite all that, we haven't really got any more answers." David sighed.

"Yeah, it was gut-wrenching. It was a good job that carer woman didn't come in earlier, when he was flipping out."

"Totally. John tried to convince her we knew Samuel from the pub, gift of the gab, and all that." David looked over at his friend.

John smiled back, raising his thumb. "I try."

"It certainly goes to show what happens when you try to alert the authorities," Gavin said. "Again, just as Carl and Arthur warned us."

"I think we need to tell those two about this, so they can listen for themselves," Bob replied.

"That's why I recorded it." John winked. "For what good it will do."

*****

David was feeling anxious again; listening to Samuel's story hadn't helped. He hoped that Samuel was all right after they had left him. At least the carer had been with him. He was also thinking more about confessing all to Emily. After he'd showered, David joined Bob in the garden with a beer for each of them.

"You're going to tell this girl about everything, then?" Bob asked. "You sure it's a good idea?"

David clicked his tongue, thinking. "Honestly? I'm not sure. It feels like I'm keeping things from her, almost lying, although I'm not as such. Like I told John — I really like her. More than that. But I can't risk her getting involved. Maybe, I already have? *Damn*!" David stamped the ground with his foot. "If only the circumstances were normal? Either way, I have to cool things between us. I should have done it already. It's just so hard when I really like her, Uncle … How do you even *start* to explain something like this?"

Bob smiled, and placed a firm hand on his nephew's shoulder, giving it a shake. "I know, boy. I know how you feel. I get you."

"I'll see what happens. Believing me is one thing, but I don't want to scare her, either, especially as she's by herself at the moment. I think her mum isn't back until the weekend. I doubt she even noticed that figure in the photo … What would you do?"

"Just go by your gut instinct, David. Do what you feel is right. Me? Personally, maybe I wouldn't tell her. Not everything. It's a heck of a lot to tell someone. Or I would just say something like now isn't the best time to start anything serious, seeing as the distance will be a factor as well."

"I know, Uncle. I'm considering that as well. But I *hate* not being honest with her."

Bob sunk down the remains of his beer. "Ah. Nice beer this." He looked down at the empty bottle in his hand. His hands were rough from having laboured on the farm over the years.

"I guess we'll see. Thanks, Uncle."

"Thanks? What for?" Uncle Bob smiled.

"Just for listening. I really appreciate it."

"Likewise, David. I appreciate you being here." Bob gave an affectionate slap on David's left thigh.

The nephew and his uncle smiled at one another and sat chatting for a few more minutes.

"You ready to go?" John asked, coming out to the garden. "The taxi will be here soon."

The two friends had decided on getting a taxi as it was potentially safer. John wouldn't have to drive back by himself through the forest.

"Sure … I still don't like the idea of you coming back by yourself in a taxi, even if it's still light." David got up from his seat.

"It's fine. I'm not overly keen if I'm honest. But it's what mates are for," John replied. "Besides, I want to try out this chippy not far from Emily's, which I saw online. I guess I'll just be a brave boy." John grinned.

David smiled. "I'm really not happy about it. Not with what happened to us that night after our dates."

"I could always take you instead, David? Or come with you two, so that John's not on his own coming back?" Bob suggested. "It would save you money, too."

"You don't have to do that. Besides, it's best you stay here with Betty, Uncle. I think it's best if we get a taxi. Gavin already offered again, too. You best stay on the farm. I'll leave Benji with you this time."

"I'll be fine, guys," John said strongly, but he still felt a little uncomfortable.

"It might be the last time anyway, if I break things off with Emily. I still haven't decided what I'm going to do." David planned on staying over at Emily's again but if he revealed all and cooled things between them, he wasn't so sure what would happen.

*****

It was after seven, when they reached Emily's home again.

"Have a good night," John said through the back window of the taxi.

"Thanks," a nervous David replied. "You make sure you take care getting back … Enjoy your fish and chips!" David gave a smile.

The middle-aged taxi driver frowned at the 'take care getting back' comment.

"Count on it!" John winked back.

As the taxi drove off, Emily opened the front door and stepped out. "Hey!

I thought I heard a car pull up. How are you? I've missed you." She chuckled and walked over to David and hugged him as they kissed.

"I'm good." David smiled, hugging her back. "Better now, that I'm with my little Irish flower."

"Aw. That's so cute." Emily embraced him tighter.

"How was work?" David asked.

"Good. It quietened down a little after you guys left. Jock even let me and Anna finish a bit earlier, which was nice of him. He still paid us for it, too." Emily giggled.

"That's all right, then." David smiled back as they walked inside.

*****

John sat quietly alone on a bench he found in Aviemore, eating a large portion of fish and chips. He had asked the taxi driver to pick him up in around half an hour. As he munched away, Grant rang. "Granty! How are you, mate?" John chewed away.

"John! I'm okay, mate. I decided to go back to my flat last night and stayed the night."

"That's great, bud. Did you have some chick you needed to bang?" John joked.

Grant laughed. "Chance would be a fine thing. Nah … things have been fine since you guys left, but I'd have to come back at some point, you know? Plus, my folks are annoying." Grant laughed again.

"I'm proud of you, Grant."

"What are you up to? Any developments?"

John didn't know what to say. "I'm just in a small town here, eating some fish and chips by my lonesome. David's at that girl's again."

"Oh, right. Yeah. David told me about her. It's serious, then?"

"I think so. David's unsure about things though, with everything that's been happening."

Grant paused over the phone. "Everything that's been happening? I thought things weren't that bad?"

"I didn't want to worry you, mate. I've held back on a lot of things. It's … it's worse than we thought. We're in deep shit up here, actually. I don't know where to begin."

"I … I see. What's been going on? Please, tell me."

John told him everything he could. John assumed Grant was safe as he'd said nothing had happened to him since they left, but he wondered whether he was doing the right thing telling him. "… That's the shit we're dealing with," John finally closed on his account of everything. "You still there, Grant?"

"Y-yeah. I am. Sorry. I just, I don't know what to say … Maybe I should go back to my folks."

"It might be best, my friend. If you do, make sure you don't say anything to them, though. I can't stress that enough," John warned.

"I, I hear you. You think that old man you mentioned, who saw them in the forest, *really* saw what he did? It wasn't just his dementia?"

"Completely certain. It relates perfectly to what we've encountered too, mate. I'm sorry; I wanted to be honest with you." John felt guilty for worrying Grant now. He lost his appetite for what was left of his fish and chips.

"It's okay … I appreciate you being open with me. I'd rather you were honest."

"I know how you feel, buddy. But how do you think we feel? At least you should be safe down there." John gave a slight laugh.

"I feel bad for not coming up with you guys."

"Don't! You're safer back there." John empathised.

"What … what if I don't see you two again?" Grant said sadly.

"C'mon, Grant. Don't talk like that. Try and take your mind off things. Go see some of your other friends, yes?"

"I don't know. I've got to go, anyway. I've got to fix someone's computer."

"No worries, big boy. Keep positive and we'll speak soon. Look after yourself, okay? *Love ya*!" John ended the call and finished his cod, but there were still a fair few chips left.

Giving up on what was left of the chips, John placed the greasy box in a nearby bin. Making his way to where the taxi would pick him up, he was about to cross the road, when an elderly couple holding hands from across the street further down, waved and smiled at him. He checked behind him, to see if they were waving at somebody else but they clearly weren't. Perhaps they had mistaken him for someone else.

He waved back half-heartedly just to be polite and tried to smile. "Who the hell are you?" he said to himself. "Silly old duffers."

The couple carried on smiling and waving. John thought they were a couple of nutcases. No one else was about.

What happened next, made John's blood freeze.

The couple stopped waving and smiling at him. Instead, their eyes became wide and their faces serious. Both in unison pointed towards John, lifted their chins up and used their forefingers to gesture slitting their throats. The gesture was clearly intended for John.

He stood in shock for a moment as the couple then continued to stare ice-coldly at him. He swallowed. He felt sick. He couldn't turn away from their stare. He remembered how Samuel had described the cult members looking at him through their masks in the forest that night.

A car to John's right, beeped its horn making him jump. The noise snapped John into action. The male driver held their hands up to query what John was doing just standing there. He then drove off. The incident had more than unnerved John. He wanted to get back to the farm as *quickly* as possible.

John sat quietly in the taxi. He never said a word to the driver. At least it was still light and there were a few other cars around. As they drove further into the forest, with the sun behind them, they saw a police car and an ambulance up ahead. There was also another car pulled over, a blue estate. Someone had clearly been in an accident.

John could see a blue and white police cordon go up as he got nearer. He and the taxi driver were both curious; the driver slowed the taxi down, passing the vehicles. They saw a young woman, who looked quite distressed, talking to a police officer. She was possibly an eyewitness. She wore a white cycling helmet and there was a mountain bike on the ground near her. John then caught a glimpse of a dead body on the ground, just as two paramedics zipped up the black body bag.

"Poor bastard," John said to himself, wondering what had happened.

The taxi drove on as John suddenly realised who the dead man was, with his ginger hair and beard. It was *Angus*. "Woah! Stop the car!"

The taxi driver slammed on the breaks. "What is it?" He turned to John, alarmed.

"Go back. I think I know who that dead guy was back there."

The taxi driver turned the car around and drove back to the scene. He pulled up a few feet away and John got out, leaving the car door open. He could hear the woman talking to one of the police officers.

"Like I said, I, I saw his car parked up as I cycled past and I just saw him hanging there, on that tree in there. The p-poor man. To do that, to take your own life, he must have been suffering awfully ..."

John could hear that the young lady was emotional.

Another of the police officers caught sight of John walking over. "I'm sorry, sir. But there's nothing to see here. I'm going to have to ask you to return to your car and leave." He was wearing a police hat and held his hand out, to prevent John from getting any closer. "Please, move along!"

"Can I ask what happened? I think I know this man," John replied, not sure what to do.

The paramedics carried the body into the back of the ambulance.

"You're a friend? How did you know he was here?" The police officer interviewing the young woman now approached John, serious faced. He was holding a small note pad with a pen pushed through the wire rings at the top.

"I just saw the body now, as we drove past, before he was covered up. I recognised his car as well. His name is Angus. He runs a farm somewhere around here," John answered. He noticed two suitcases in the back of Angus' estate as they stood by the car. He remembered Bob telling them that Angus had planned on going away after what had happened on his farm.

"I see. He had ID on him, so we have his details. So, you're a friend; you know him well?" the officer asked.

"Not exactly, no. He's a friend of my friend's uncle. He came to his farm like a couple of weeks back. That's how I recognised him … Can I ask what happened?" John didn't mention what Angus had been through.

"There isn't much to say, really. Other than that we believe it to be a suicide. Nothing suspicious. There was no note left. This lady here, saw him hanging up over there." The officer gestured his head to the left in the forest.

It didn't make any sense to John. Why would Angus pack his bags to go away somewhere, only to pull over at the side of the road and hang himself? He could surely have done that closer to his farm too. He wasn't even sure if these policemen could be trusted. "That's awful," John replied.

"Well, shit happens." The police officer smiled. He temporarily removed his police flat cap to scratch his head.

John frowned. "Gee. Don't sound too compassionate," he said sarcastically.

The officer sniffed as the other one smiled.

While the police were talking to the paramedics, John used the opportunity to talk to the young lady. She had been crying and looked to be in her late twenties. "You okay?"

"I suppose," the woman replied. "I've … I've just never seen a dead body before. Certainly not a suicide victim."

"You didn't see anything suspicious, then?"

"Nothing. Well, maybe something. It's silly really. Never mind."

"What? You can tell me. I'm open-minded," John replied, trying to be persuasive. He wanted to know if the woman saw anything else before the police intervened. He needed to be quick before they returned. They seemed to be having a joke with one of the paramedics.

"It was nothing. It's just that I thought I heard a child laughing, when I walked over to the body, from inside the forest. It was probably just the wind that picked up. It was very brief. The police officers didn't really pay much attention to it, when I told them … I still can't get his face out of my head, his tongue hanging out and his eyes." The woman wiped her eyes and nose with a tissue. "His cold and staring eyes, looking up. So lifeless. I hope he's at peace, now. It's a shame that people think it is the only way out."

"I guess. I'm sorry," John replied. He was now thinking what the others, especially Bob, would say when he told them.

"Please, don't talk to the witness, sir," one of the police officers interrupted.

A third police officer, a female, suddenly came out of the forest. "Crikey … I really needed that piss!" she joked to her colleagues.

John looked on; something didn't sit right about any of this. It all felt odd.

*****

David and Emily spent most of the evening snuggled up on the sofa watching telly, kissing and cuddling.

David was still trying to find the right time to tell Emily about everything. But the more Emily spent time in his arms, the more he felt his feelings growing for her. He wondered too, if telling Emily everything was more likely to put her in danger. Not just her, but even her mother. David was in limbo and hated it.

"I'm going to get some more wine." Emily smiled and kissed David as she got up.

"Okay." David smiled back.

Emily soon returned with a fresh bottle. "Back. Did you miss me?" she joked.

"Of course. I was almost getting withdrawal symptoms," David joked back.

"Aw. My poor baby." Emily cuddled back up to David, repeatedly kissing his neck. She wrapped her left leg over his.

"You working tomorrow, then?" David asked.

"Yep. Not until late morning. It gives us time for a lie-in." She glinted.

*"Us?"* David smiled. "And what makes you think I *want* to stay over?" he teased.

Emily gave him a gentle slap on his chest. "Meanie." She giggled.

*****

Emily yawned and stretched as she switched off the television with the remote. They had been watching an old comedy film that they had both seen before; *The 'Burbs*. It was one of their favourite films since childhood. They had then watched the last part of a Gerard Butler action movie; *Olympus Has Fallen*. Emily had giggled and said how her mum fancied the actor.

David had become a little quiet, thinking through what to do. When asked by Emily what was up, he said he was tired. He decided he would tell her everything in the morning. He yawned himself, making his eyes water.

"You coming to bed then, sleepy head?" Emily smiled.

"I guess." David squinted, his arm still around Emily.

"I hope you're not *too* tired?" Emily winked. She had that sparkle in her green eyes again.

As David sat up, the cordless phone that rested on the sofa arm rang.

"It's a bit late for a call. I wonder who it is?" Emily climbed over David and reached for the phone. "Hello …? Hello …?"

There was no answer and the line went dead.

"No one there?" David asked, frowning.

"I didn't hear anything. The line just went dead. I thought it might have been my mum, but she wouldn't normally call this late. It's probably just someone playing silly buggers." Emily chuckled.

David wasn't so sure.

Emily held her hand out to him. "Come."

David took it in his and she led him upstairs to her bedroom.

*****

Back on the farm, Bob was still trying to get his head around what had happened to Angus. It wasn't that he didn't believe John, but he needed to know for sure and had phoned the police. He was still in a state of shock.

Bob was close to tears again as he walked up and down the living room. "I still can't believe he's dead. I'm sorry for keep saying it. I know Angus has had difficulties down the years with his wife and of late, like we have. But I don't believe he would ever have killed himself. He was stronger than that. Or so I assumed. I guess … I guess he was suffering more than I thought." Bob poured himself a very large glass of brandy and drank most of it in one go.

Gavin and John were sat down watching him. Betty had already retired to bed before John got back. Again, complaining of a headache.

"I still can't believe he's gone. I always liked him. It just goes to show that people can be hurting more than you think," Gavin said, shaking his head.

"Perhaps the pain of losing his wife resurfaced with everything that's happened? It's only been, what, two years since she passed?"

Bob nodded.

"Like Samuel's wife all those years back," John said.

Bob looked at John, thinking. He was hoping a pattern wasn't emerging with husbands losing their wives.

"It's certainly terrible news … I need a drink, myself." Gavin got up and poured himself a large Tomatin Scotch.

Bob couldn't get his mind around any of it. "I only spoke to him this morning. It's so strange. He seemed calm. He said he was going away to Nottingham for a while to where his wife, Wendy, grew up."

"What will happen to his farm, now?" John asked.

"Someone he knew was going to check on his farm and the house every now and then, whilst he was gone. Obviously, there were no animals to look after anymore." Bob knocked back the rest of his drink and poured a new one. "He has no children, so I don't know what will happen to his farm, or his relocated animals. He had a younger brother, who's still alive. They live up in Scotland somewhere. I don't know where, or if he even still talked to him."

"What about his workers?" John wondered.

"He never really spoke about his workers. A lot of the time, he preferred to work on his own. Especially the past couple of years since his wife died. A bit like a 'one-man band.' I guess it occupied him more. Usually, when he had workers, they'd be temporary or agency employees … Poor Angus." A few tears ran down Bob's dishevelled face.

"I still don't think he killed himself, Bob," John repeated. "Sure, he could have changed his mind about going away, but why go to the effort of packing your stuff and driving through the forest, just to pull over and hang yourself? I'm not buying it. It doesn't make sense. He could have done that on his farm. Someone would have found him. Either someone, or something, influenced him to do it, or someone did it to him, literally made it look like a suicide … What about the laughter the girl heard?"

"John makes some valid points, boss. It does seem suspicious."

"I know, Gavin. But there's no way of proving it," Bob said dejectedly.

"I didn't like the way the police behaved either, Bob. They were joking. All right, they didn't know Angus, but surely they should show some sympathy? Even one of the paramedics was joking."

"I'm hearing you, John. It does sound like it's linked to this cult, but there isn't anything we can do about it, regardless. But we'll call Arthur and Carl, tomorrow."

After the others had gone to bed, Bob sat alone with his thoughts of Angus. A few more tears rolled down his face. He couldn't believe Angus was gone and had taken his own life. Or perhaps worse, that someone else was responsible. Either way, the official verdict was suicide.

# Chapter Sixty-One

## 25th July, 2018

After another night of passionate love-making, David shot upright in Emily's bed that Wednesday morning, his naked body, covered in sweat.

He was breathing heavily. Almost panting. He had dreamt again. It was almost the same dream he had had before, in the clearing and with the tree and the large moon turning red above him. However, it was slightly different. Instead of being sucked into the tree this time, he remained as he was, in just a pair of jeans, in the centre of the clearing. Again, there was a bloody inverted pentagram on his chest. This time, at the edge of the clearing, he could see the cult members in their robes and 'skinned' masks, their haunting eyes staring at him, chanting. It terrified him. He remembered what Samuel had said.

They then began taunting and laughing at him, in languages he couldn't understand. He believed some of it sounded Latin. The other language, he didn't know. He could feel a sharp coldness from behind him, freezing his body. Something was behind him. He closed his eyes in fear. Despite being too scared to look around at first, he then did so.

He turned to see the huge, hooded figure towering above him, holding its arms out. David could see the long grey hairs on the warped hands and jagged fingers of the entity. Dangerously black, large talons grew from its fingers. The inside of the cloak, including the hood, were black.

The demon pulled its arms back further to almost behind its back and then suddenly, they flew forward almost like a catapult, to smash David's head, at which point, David woke.

"Hey! You okay, babe? What is it?" Emily asked. "My God, you're caped in sweat." Emily put her hand on David's sweaty back.

David tried to calm himself and slow his breathing. He could see his torso twitch from his high pulse rate. "I just. I just had a bad dream. That's all." David placed his hand on his forehead.

"Aw. It must have been a bad one. You're okay, now. I'm here … What did you dream of?" Emily kissed David's upper back.

"Huh? Oh, just something silly."

"Come here!" Emily pulled David towards her. She kissed his hair and then his forehead. "I can make us breakfast, if you like? After I've showered, that is. We've got some time yet, before I have to go to work." Emily smiled.

"What time is it?" David asked, his throat was dry.

Emily looked at her alarm clock on the small dressing table next to the bed. "Twenty past eight. Still early."

"Yeah," David yawned.

"I'm going to hop in the shower. You're free to join me." Emily winked, leaving the option open as she got out of bed with her petite and perfectly formed, naked body.

David took her up on the offer. A shower might do him good after his latest nightmare.

*****

Following their shower together, David still had no real appetite so they decided on cereals instead of a cooked breakfast.

David decided now was the time to tell Emily *everything*. "Emily?"

"Yes, handsome?" Emily smiled. She was washing the bowls in the sink.

David sighed. "I really need to talk to you. To say it's important, would be an understatement."

"You're, you're seeing someone back home, aren't you?"

"What? *No*, no. Nothing like that. It's probably worse than that. Please, sit down, Emily," David tried to joke, but it didn't work.

As Emily was about to sit down, the phone rang. "Let me get that, first," Emily said, grabbing the cordless phone from the worktop.

Like last night, there was no answer, but she could hear some interference and then the line went dead.

"No one there again?"

"No. There was just some interference," Emily replied, sitting back down at the kitchen table.

*"Shit!"* David's face looked shocked. His eyes became large.

"What is it, David? You're starting to worry me, now."

David swallowed. "I wanted to tell you this before. I tried over the weekend, but we got distracted with you having to go into work. It's … it's about my uncle and his farm, and the reason I'm up here."

"I know, David. You told me why. Someone was killing your uncle's animals, and you're here to try and help support him." Emily held David's hand, rubbing it with her thumb.

"Yes. But …" David breathed in and then out. "It's much more serious than that."

"I don't understand?" Emily frowned.

"What I'm about to tell you, it's going to sound so messed up, but please try and believe me. Let me explain *everything* first." David squeezed Emily's hand, looking straight at her.

"Okay, I'm listening …"

*****

That morning on the farm, Bob, who was slumped in the armchair, slowly opened his dry eyes. His head hurt a little from too many brandies. He heard Gavin's voice in the hallway chatting to Brian, the postman. Slowly getting himself up, Bob made his way out of the living room.

"Morning, boss. You sleep okay? I heard you snoring earlier, so I left you be." Gavin smiled and was holding the mail.

Bob approached the open front door. The sun hurt his head more as he squinted and sneezed.

"Bless you," Gavin said. "You all right?"

"I'm fine," Bob replied, shielding his eyes from the sun. His throat felt dry and his voice was croakier than usual. "Just a bit headachy after a few drinks last night, after the news … Morning, Brian."

"Morning, Bob. Terrible news about Angus. I'm so sorry. I know you two were friends. Sorry to hear about your animals as well."

"Thanks, Brian," Bob replied, adjusting to the sunlight.

"I can't say I knew him too well, other than delivering mail out to his farm. But I'm still shocked at the news. Especially, after the way it happened. I've not long come from there. I had no idea until Gavin just told me. There's certainly some strange things happening of late … and with that Jones girl."

"Yes, it's a shock … Jones girl?" Bob's brow lowered again.

"The daughter from one of the houses on my round's gone missing, since Sunday; she's heavily pregnant, too," Brian stated.

"Really? Not heard anything about it ourselves," Bob said.

"Aye. It is odd. Hopefully she'll turn up safe and sound. I best be going, anyway. Mail to deliver and all that. Good day!"

"Sounds a bit worrying with everything we know about this cult," Bob said as Brian drove off in his red van.

"I'm thinking the same thing," Gavin replied, shutting the front door.

"We need to speak to Arthur and Carl about the latest developments," Bob said, walking into his study.

*****

Emily was in tears sat at the kitchen table. She tried to grasp what David had just told her. He got everything he possibly could out, with all the sickening details. That included showing her the photos on his phone. He had even shown her the ring that he was wearing.

Emily was incredulous at first, but as all the details unfolded, she became shocked. She was particularly upset, when David talked about them not seeing one another until everything was 'sorted.' Almost angry at one point, she asked if this was just an excuse to part ways after he had slept with her. It had then been David's turn to become annoyed; he argued that he would *never* lie to use someone for sex like that. Emily then felt guilty for thinking badly of him. She knew he was better than that and apologised. It was their first argument. David also showed her the photo of the man in the blue raincoat from their Sunday afternoon walk. After what had been a passionate and uplifting night, the morning became a dark and depressing affair.

"I didn't know how to tell you before, Emily. I wanted to. I really did. I should have fought my feelings for you, and not allowed us to get close with everything going on. *Christ,* I tried. But every moment I've spent with you, I felt myself falling deeper and deeper for you. I've *never* felt like this towards *anyone,* before … I'm so sorry. I didn't mean to get you involved in this," David said sincerely.

Emily looked up at David with those emerald eyes of hers. Tears still ran down her soft face. She gave David a sad smile. "I feel the exact same way. I'm glad, you didn't fight your feelings … Every minute I spend with you, I feel my love growing stronger. I love you, David." Emily squeezed his hand.

David felt a tad better for getting everything off his chest. "I'm worried that I've got you involved too, now. Those phone calls last night and this morning — it may have been *them.*"

"Perhaps it was a legitimate call, a wrong number? I believe you, but at the same time, I can't help but think you're wrong about the supernatural side of things." Emily held David's hand tighter. She wiped some of her tears away with the other hand.

"I was the same, Emily. I've never believed in things like that before. But believe me, this is all real. Different but the same accounts of things prove that. We can't all be wrong. Like with poor old Samuel. You saw the photos, too."

"Th-that poor man … that certainly explains why he's like he is, and why you asked those questions about him. I wondered why you were so often deep in thought."

David wiped a few more tears from Emily's face with his thumb.

"I never noticed that person when we were walking." Emily shuddered. "What if I *am* involved, too?" Emily wept again.

"Shh, it's okay. You have me. And the others … *Shit*, I could have spared you from all this." David got up.

"Then, we wouldn't be together," Emily replied softly, looking up at David.

"I've put you in danger, you and your mum. I even thought you may have been involved with these sick bastards at one point, but I couldn't believe that, not of you." David turned his back and looked out of the back door.

Emily got up and held David from behind. "I don't blame you for thinking that, David. This has all obviously messed with your mind. You've been through *so* much. *All* of you. It's terrible." She rested her head on his left shoulder.

"I can't leave you alone here," David said, just as the phone rang.

David turned around and they stared at each other.

"Sh-shall I answer it?" Emily said nervously.

"I'll answer it."

An Irish woman's voice said, "Hello? Who's this?"

"I'm, erm, David, a friend of Emily's," David replied awkwardly.

"Oh, is she there? It's her mother."

"She's just here," David said, passing the phone to Emily, while mouthing it was her mum.

"Hi, Mum." Emily tried to sound her normal self. She wiped the tears from her cheeks. "I'm fine. Just a little tired. Yes, that's David." Emily looked over at David and smiled slightly.

David smiled back and gently rubbed her arm.

Emily chatted for a few minutes and then ended the conversation. "I love you, too. Bye, Mum." She frowned.

"What is it?" David asked.

"My mum. She's going to be away for at least another week. They're still short-staffed." Emily paused. "I don't know what to do. I can't stay here by myself. I think Mum sensed something was up. She always knows when something is bothering me." She sniffed.

"Come here." David consoled her, kissing the top of her head. "What if you stayed with us on the farm? But then, I don't know ... maybe that's more dangerous for you. *Shit*!"

"Wouldn't your aunt and uncle mind?" Emily looked at David. Her eyes were puffy from the tears.

"It wouldn't be a problem. I'm not having you here by yourself. It's just not safe alone."

"I could stay at the pub, maybe? Jock has room and would let me. It would certainly be more convenient, but I'd have to tell him why."

"*No*! You can't tell anyone, Emily. Not even Annabel. Even your mum. It isn't just about risking ourselves, but you may be putting others in danger. It's hard to trust anyone anymore."

"I would feel safer with you and the others on the farm. I don't want to be alone, David."

The couple embraced.

"It's going to be all right," David said into Emily's ear. He didn't know if he was trying to convince himself, or Emily. Either way, he found it hard to believe the words.

*****

Emily was reluctant to go into work, but David thought it would help to be occupied. He made her promise not to mention anything to anyone and particularly Jock or Annabel. David promised to meet her from work later and help her pack up some things. David had taken a taxi back to the farm and arrived a little after midday. He was shocked to hear about Angus and the elderly couple's throat slitting gesture aimed at John. Bob was unsure whether Emily would be safer at the farm but agreed that David could bring her. Betty was also informed of Angus' death. She didn't appear too fussed or upset.

Arthur and Carl came in the afternoon and had listened to the recording of Samuel on John's phone.

"Once again, I'm so, so sorry for your friend," Arthur said. "From what you have told me, I do not believe it was a suicide; it doesn't make much sense."

"I've had the local radio station on all day and Angus' death hasn't been mentioned," Bob said.

"As we've mentioned, things linked to Famuli Cani are often covered up. I don't think you'll see anything in the local newspaper either," Arthur replied.

"That poor Samuel. The way he's still affected and suffering. That's what this cult is about. Not just sacrificing, but for ever torment," Carl said.

"Interesting that he mentioned the tree. He said it wasn't overly large? It's no doubt grown over the years, due to the evil and sacrifices," Arthur added.

"If they can make his wife's cancer worse, or whatever they did, what else can they do? Well, we've clearly seen what they can do. We're *way* over our heads, here. Well out of our depth," John said.

"They are capable of doing terrible things. Supernatural things. That much is clearly evident. But even their powers have limitations," Arthur said, trying to reassure the group.

"What of the dream I had last night?" David asked. "So much for being naturally strong."

"I think they're trying to break you, slowly. They enjoy toying with people, making them suffer. Perhaps, testing your resolve? To see what you do. You said you stayed at that young lady's house, last night?" Arthur asked.

"Yeah. Why?"

"I believe that the salt crystals may have been helping with the nightmares. Without them last night, you were more prone to their attacks and dark powers."

"Not that salt again," John said sarcastically.

"I still don't get why it's me and John. Why haven't either of you, *especially* you, Arthur, had these dreams? You've known about this cult for years."

Arthur smiled. "There's obviously something about you two that these people and the demon have targeted. A strong possibility is that with you going against their warnings, perhaps they admire you both. For the moment though, we need to remain focused on our objective."

"Our *objective*? What the hell is that?" John asked.

"Our objective is to try and get to the bottom of things and stop these people. I know we're going over old ground here, but we may have a lead," Carl said, trying to sound positive.

"A lead?" Gavin asked.

Arthur leant forward; his large silver cross was almost flush on the kitchen table. "If you recall, we mentioned the burial place of Seath Mór in the grounds of what's left of the old church in Rothiemurchus, known as St Tuchaldus Church. Well, I spoke to another of the descendants. They've insisted I don't contact them again, though."

"And?" John asked.

"They too, believe the dagger is buried with him, possibly together with information on where their Satanic lair is … their unholy sanctuary. The same place as it was many centuries ago."

"What's so special about this lair? Why would they even have a lair, if they do their rituals in the forest?" John asked.

"That's a good question. They enjoy their activities in the forest because it is a place of power for them. Their sacrifices enhance the power … Remember as well that they like leaving little hints for people, to remind that they are about, without giving too much away. As for their lair, they use it for their more evil and potent rituals … They can also hold their captives there until the required sacrificial date," Arthur explained.

John scoffed. "They save their more 'evil' work for their lair? So, what's been happening on the farm and what Samuel saw in the forest, weren't evil enough for the lair? Unbelievable!"

"We, erm, we'll need to dig the grave up to access the information," Carl added.

John scoffed again. "You guys are kidding, right? How can you get away with digging up someone's grave? And what we want, might not even be there!"

"What choice do we have?" Carl replied. "We're out of options. We feel as if we're running out of time, too. This cult and its deity are getting stronger with each sacrifice. They are on the verge of reaching their peak. This is why you are hearing more whispers, too … We are *all* at risk!"

"I sense things are now coming to a head. Next week, is *Lammas Day*," Arthur added, looking round at the others. "It's the first of August and another powerful day and night for Satanists. It's a festival to celebrate the wheat harvest and the Satanists have sequestrated it to perform the wickedest of their sacrifices and rituals. They still stick to the dates on the Satanic calendar which are powerful for them, but have also created their own dates … We have a *very* bad feeling for next week's Lammas Day. We *have* to try and stop them." Arthur's eyes showed sheer fear and willingness.

"By digging up an old grave that's centuries old?" John asked.

"It's a start," Carl said.

"What if you got caught?" Gavin asked.

"Well, we're going to do it at night," Carl answered.

"When are you planning on doing this?" Bob asked.

Carl and Arthur both looked at each other.

"That would be tonight," Arthur said. "We know it sounds absurd, but we have little else to go on. I believe we *will* find something that can aid us in our fight."

"But then what? If we find the location of this cult and the dagger, what are we going to do next?"

"One step at a time, David," Arthur said.

"It's just going to be you two?" asked Bob.

"Yes. There's no reason for more of us to take the risk. We both have a little experience in unearthing things, albeit, not graves," Arthur replied.

"What if someone catches you?" John asked. "How on earth would you talk your way out of something like that?"

"It's a risk we're willing to take. Or rather, we *have* to," replied Carl.

"Maybe it's best if one of us at least goes with you? You might need someone to keep an eye out. I can come and help," John suggested.

"I don't think it will be necessary. But thank you," Arthur declined.

"You know, Arthur, it wouldn't be a bad idea to have someone watch out? John's right."

Arthur sighed. "I don't know, Carl. Maybe."

"Maybe I should come as well?" David said.

"No. One of you, yes, maybe. But we can't have any more," Arthur said firmly.

"It's okay, mate. I'll be fine. Besides, you'll have Emily tonight. She'll need you."

"That's true," David replied, just as Betty came into the kitchen. She had been out doing some watering.

*****

Arthur and Carl stayed a little longer, so Arthur could watch Betty's behaviour a little more. She seemed fine most of the time, but there were moments when she appeared a little strange.

Before leaving, Arthur wanted to speak to Bob alone. "I've been monitoring your wife since I got here. I still feel she's under some kind of influence. This should help her." Arthur pulled out an oval-shaped stone on a silver chain and placed it into Bob's hand.

"What is it?" Bob frowned, looking at the light blue-purple stone.

"It's agate. It helps protect from evil spirits and dark magic. Even demons. It's similar to the salt crystals that you have around your farm. I take it you already placed the other item in your bedroom? This will give your wife added protection and strength. Get her to wear it. As you can feel, it's very light."

"What shall I tell her? Is she aware she's under this influence? Is she possessed?"

"I don't believe she's possessed, no. She'd be a lot worse if she was. I just feel a dark presence has a grip on her. I feel she's naturally fighting against it. Her soul is warm and good in nature, which will help block the dark forces. But this pendant should aid her further, along with the other things."

"So she does know?"

"Maybe at times she is aware. But it's soon forgotten. It's perhaps more on a subconscious level she is fighting against it."

"What if she refuses to wear it, or whatever is affecting her doesn't allow her to?"

"She'll wear it. Just say it's for her protection. She is still wearing her silver crucifix."

"What influence is she under?"

"It's most likely to be this entity, and maybe the cult has put a spell on her as well."

"But why her? What has she done?"

"Evil sometimes has reasons, sometimes it doesn't. Sometimes, it just picks on someone randomly. Just keep an eye on her. I know it's a silly thing to say but try to remain positive. Be strong. Negative and dark energy prey on one's fears and negativity." Arthur smiled and placed a hand briefly on Bob's shoulder.

"I will try."

After Carl and Arthur had left, Bob gave the necklace to Betty. She put it on straight away, without questions. Bob said it was for added protection to make her feel better.

# Chapter Sixty-Two

## 25th July, 2018

"You don't think I should have told Grant everything, then?"

The two were sat outside The Auld Drongair Bàrd, waiting for Emily. They were chatting about Grant again.

David sighed. "I don't know." He scratched the side of his head. "I guess I would have held off, seeing as he had just moved back to his flat and was feeling a little better."

"Shit, yeah. I shouldn't have done, I suppose."

"It's done now, mate. Don't worry about it. The chances are he's safe. I'll call him later. You're definitely going tonight?"

"Yep. It seems a bit sick digging up somebody's grave."

"It certainly seems an extreme measure. But I guess we're in *extreme* circumstances." David saw the front door of the pub open and an elderly gentleman came out.

"Tell me about it. Still, it's not like there will be a body in there. Even the bones would have long gone by now."

David was looking at the swaying sign that hung from the pub. "True."

A short while later, Emily walked over to John's car holding her forehead.

David got out of his seat to greet her. "Hey. You okay?" he asked, placing a hand on her shoulder.

"I've just had a nasty headache all day. It got worse this afternoon. I'm sorry I'm a bit late. I got talking to a couple of customers."

"That's okay. Have you taken anything for your headache? You should have finished early, if you're feeling poorly." David was worried. He remembered the headache he'd had when he received the note through his door.

"Yes. I did earlier. It hasn't done much good, though. Jock wanted me to go home, but we were kind of busy. Plus, I didn't really want to go home unwell and be, you know, alone."

"Aw. Come here." David hugged Emily gently.

"I might leave my car here for now. It should be fine out the back, there. I told Jock you guys were coming to meet me."

"Annabel and Jock didn't suspect anything was up?" John asked, looking back at Emily now she'd climbed into the back seat.

"No. They could tell I was pretty quiet but I suppose having a headache explained that."

"That's true," John replied.

"I still find it hard to believe all this. This beautiful area and its surroundings. It's almost *impossible* to fathom that there's something so dark and evil happening. And in the lovely forest, too." Emily screwed her face up from the pain in her head. "I don't feel so good; ignore me if I'm rambling. I've been here a fair few years and never heard anything about this. Nor has my mum."

"I know. You okay?" David asked. He sat next to her in the back, with his arm around her shoulder.

Emily didn't look well at all. "I, I think I'm going to be sick."

"We better pull over, John," David suggested.

John pulled the car over. "It could be a migraine. I get them."

Emily quickly got out and threw up behind a tree.

David rushed over and placed a supportive hand on Emily's back. "It's okay, Emily," David said softly.

After she retched a few times, she slowly stood upright. Her eyes were all watery. "I think I feel better now. The pain doesn't seem as intense."

David smiled at her and helped her back to the car.

*****

Back at Emily's, David patiently helped her pack some things into a suitcase in her bedroom.

"How are you feeling now?" John asked, standing in the doorway of Emily's bedroom. "I've just put the kettle on."

"Better, thank you, John." Emily looked up and smiled. "There's still a slight pain there, but I can feel it going now, thankfully. I don't recall the last time I had a nasty headache like this. Let alone be sick from one."

"That's good. I just went out into your back garden. Lovely field at the back. It's a really nice place you have here."

"It is … which makes it harder to believe what's going on around these parts."

"I've been thinking about tonight. My stomach's starting to get some butterflies," John said. "It's going to be my first grave, you know," he joked.

The other two smiled.

Emily had recently learned about tonight's 'grave-digging event.' "Well, just don't make a habit of it, hey?" Emily joked back.

"Ha! I'll try not to." John laughed.

As Emily placed a final item of clothing into her suitcase and zipped it up, they could hear the phone ring out on the landing.

"You want me to go fetch that for you?" John asked.

"No, it's okay. If it's important, they can leave a message or ring back," Emily replied. She was nervous to answer it, after last time.

"Is that everything?" David asked.

"I think so. If I need more items, I can always come back. It's not *too* far away … Are you sure your aunt and uncle won't mind me staying with you?"

"They're fine with it. They think it's probably for the best as well. Safer perhaps. I'll carry this down for you."

"Okay." Emily smiled. "It might be a bit heavy. Be careful."

"Nonsense. It's fine." David winked. "Mine was a lot worse."

"I can make us something to eat before we leave, if you like?" Emily offered as they went downstairs.

"I'm okay, thanks. I had something to eat before we came," John answered.

"Since when has that stopped you?" David joked.

"True." John grinned.

"I'm good as well, Em." David placed Emily's suitcase near to the front door.

"It wouldn't be any bother. I'm starting to get my appetite back. I've not eaten since lunch. And that wasn't much. I might just make a sandwich before we leave."

"It's fine. There's no rush. As long as we get back to the farm before nightfall. I don't fancy going through the forest at night. It's bad enough during the day," David said.

"What time are you going to the old church ruins?" Emily asked.

"Grave robbing? Arthur and Carl are going to let me know. They said sometime after midnight. That's if they decide to take me with them. They weren't sure."

Emily made herself a peanut butter sandwich and put the jar back in one of the kitchen cupboards. As she did so, the phone rang again.

"Do you want me to get it?" David asked.

"No, it's okay," Emily replied and picked up the phone. "Hello?"

There was a pause and some interference, then a dull, slow voice. "Hello … Emily."

"Wh-who is this …? Do I know you?"

John and David moved closer to Emily and listened to the call.

"Not yet … but … you will," said the voice.

"S-sorry, who are you?"

David snatched the phone from Emily. "Who is this?"

"Hello … David."

*"Harold?"*

Harold laughed. "How … was your … walk that … Sunday?"

*"What the fuck!"*

"You will … all … be seeing … us soon. *Very* soon!"

A sharp burst of electricity from the phone jolted up David's right arm, causing him to drop it. *"Argh, fuck!"* David held his arm.

"David, what is it? Who was that?" Emily asked frantically.

"I got another electric shock." David reached down to pick up the phone. "It feels cold."

Emily and John both touched it.

"It was Harold, the supposed forest ranger we encountered in the forest when we first arrived up here," David explained. "He asked how our walk went."

"Wh-what does he want with me? How does he know my number?" Emily's voice was trembling.

"They just *seem* to know everything," John replied.

"How did he know about the walk we went on?" Emily questioned again.

"He must have been the person in the blue raincoat, with the electricity coming from his fingers … it makes more sense, now," David said.

"Not to me," John replied.

"I'm, I'm so scared." Emily started crying.

*****

David sat in the back of John's car to keep Emily company. He kept his arm wrapped around her the whole journey back. Annoyingly, John pointed out where Angus' body had been found. David didn't want Emily any more upset than she already was.

"It's amazing how big the forest is," Emily said. "I didn't realise. I guess it's no wonder people go missing and that these people get away with what they do."

"People? More like monsters," John said.

"It's certainly darker and creepier, the further you go in."

"That was why I didn't want you picking me up from the farm. I didn't like the thought of you driving out here on your own. I couldn't have lived with myself, if something had happened to you."

"Aw," replied Emily, kissing David on the lips. "I can feel the temperature dropping."

"Yep. We often feel that, too. Though, it isn't always the case. We also get the sense of being watched," John added.

"Yes, I know what you mean." Emily shuddered.

David rubbed her upper arm. "My uncle's farm's not too far now."

"Maybe it's just me, but it just looks so dark."

"Again, another thing we've all noticed," John confirmed.

*****

"Well, this is it," David said, glad they'd finally got Emily to the farm. "Obviously minus the animals now, sadly."

The three got out of John's car.

"It's a beautiful house and front garden."

"You okay?" David asked, concerned that she was having second thoughts about staying at the farm.

Emily half-smiled and nodded as David took her case. She noticed the salt crystals around the house.

"You must be Emily." Bob smiled warmly and held out his hand to her as he came out of the front door. He squeezed her hand gently. "You're in every way as beautiful as David described you ... I do recognise you. We've not been for a while, but me and my wife, Betty, have been to the pub numerous times."

"Thank you." Emily smiled awkwardly. "You look familiar, too. It's a lovely place that you have here. I hope it's no bother, you having me here?"

"Don't be silly, sweetheart. It's hopefully safer for you here, whilst your mum is away. Safety in numbers and all that." Bob smiled further. He wasn't convinced himself that Emily would be safer on the farm. "It's no trouble you being here. Come, I'll pop the kettle on." Bob ushered the three of them inside. "Benji's snoozing in the kitchen."

"I'll leave your case here for now," David said. "Gavin and Betty upstairs?"

"They are. They should be down in a minute," Bob replied.

Benji scampered over, wagging his tail, jumping up at David.

"Here he is, my boy!" David said, bending down and showing some affection towards his furry friend.

"Aw." Emily grinned.

Benji went in turn to Emily and John, greeting and licking them.

"He's so adorable," Emily said.

"Apart from when he's farting. Ain't that a fact, eh, Benj?" John said, ruffling Benji's face up.

As Bob put the kettle on, he sensed something was amiss. "You okay, David?"

"Something happened back at Emily's; there was a phone call. It was that Harold."

"What did he say?"

"He said they would be seeing us all *very* soon. He asked how our walk had been on that Sunday when we got caught in that thunderstorm. I then got an electric shock again from the phone."

"H-he also knew my name," Emily said.

Bob looked at Emily. The poor girl looked terrified.

David put an arm around Emily and held her.

"We should let Carl and Arthur know. As long as we have each other, we're safe," Bob said, trying to exude a confidence he didn't feel.

Gavin joined them, quietly whistling to himself. "Now, there's a sight for sore eyes," he said, smiling at Emily.

Emily couldn't help but raise a slight smile.

"And this towering figure of a man, is my number *two* in command of the farm." Bob tried to make Emily feel better.

Emily looked up at the tall, bearded figure and held out her hand. "Hello, I'm Emily."

"I'm Gavin. Nice to meet you, darling." Gavin softly shook her hand with his large one. He looked at David and winked. She was certainly a stunner and a sweet little thing. He recognised her from the pub.

Emily could sense the warmth and bond between them all. It made her feel a little more secure.

"Is Betty coming down?" Bob asked Gavin.

"Soon I think, boss. She's just doing some dusting upstairs."

David told Gavin what had happened at Emily's and Betty soon joined them, turning her attention to the now seated Emily.

"Why *hello*, Emily, dear." She beamed.

"Hello," Emily replied, feeling a little awkward again. David's aunt sounded polite enough but seemed a little intense.

"This is Betty," Bob introduced his wife. "You probably guessed!"

Emily gave a half-hearted smile. "Yeah."

"Arthur and Carl haven't contacted me yet," John suddenly said. "I wouldn't mind giving it a miss, tonight."

*****

"How do you think John's getting on?" Emily asked David as the two of them lay in bed cuddling.

Arthur and Carl had collected John from the farm, some time after eleven. They had introduced themselves to Emily and were concerned to hear about Emily's phone call, and that she now appeared to be targeted, also. They recommended that Emily wasn't left alone. They had then made their way to the old church ruins and the resting place of Seath Mór.

"Hopefully okay," David replied. "I wonder if they're there, yet. I'd text him, but my signal keeps dying. It might be why I haven't heard anything." David looked at his phone.

"Yeah. Mine does, too."

David noticed Emily's phone as she held it. She had the photo of the two of them from their walk as her background picture. "Aw. You've made that your background picture?" He smiled.

"Yeah. I cropped it a little, though. I wanted to cut out that man in the background with the blue coat on." She looked up at David and smiled.

"Aw." David kissed her. "Yeah, I can see that."

"Is your aunt okay, now?"

"I'm really not sure. I still sense something is not quite right with her. Arthur thinks she is under a dark influence. He gave my uncle a gemstone for her to wear and some other crystal to place in their room, to help her. Like the salt crystals around the farm you saw, it's supposed to repel dark and evil energy. Things like that. Supposedly."

"She seemed polite enough … just, well a little creepy. Maybe, it's just me."

"It's definitely not you, Em. Trust me." David squeezed her.

Laying there, they heard a rasping sound at the side of the bed.

Emily couldn't help but laugh, in spite of everything. "Was that Benji?"

David chuckled. "Yep. That was Benji farting, all right."

# Chapter Sixty-Three

## 26th July, 2018

"I still can't believe we're going to do this," John said.

The three of them had arrived at the old Rothiemurchus Parish Church and burial ground. Carl was carrying a light grey bag with a couple of shovels sticking halfway out, and a cordless metal cutting saw.

"Mind where you walk. It's still used for burials nowadays, though rarely," Arthur warned.

"And how long do you think it's going to take?" asked John.

"Hopefully, not too long," Carl replied, shining a bright torch in front of them.

A few old tombs and headstones loomed up in the light, casting dark shadows behind them.

"Be careful of the smaller headstones sticking up from the ground, too," Carl advised.

John could see what was left of the old church and its derelict brickwork in the torchlight as they walked past it. The ruins smelt fusty. "I guess that was the old church, then?"

"Indeed it is, or was," Arthur replied quietly. "The site itself is ancient."

"Where's the grave?" John asked lowering his voice.

"Over this way," Arthur whispered, leading the way. He also had a torch pointing ahead now.

John started to feel anxious as Arthur stopped at a worn headstone. A large, iron mortsafe with some rust covered the grave. The trees rustled nearby.

"This is the grave of Seath Mór," Arthur said.

Carl placed the bag down on the long grass and shone his torch over the resting place.

Grass was jutting up through the mortsafe.

"What's with the metal grate?" John asked.

"It's known as a mortsafe. Used to prevent graves from disturbances and robbers," Arthur answered quietly. "And in this case, to prevent the removal of the stones."

"Seems a little ironic, seeing as we're about to *do* just that," John said sarcastically. "Why would anyone want to remove these heavy looking things, anyway?"

Carl looked at Arthur in the torchlight. "You want to tell him, about the supposed myth?"

"What myth?" John frowned.

"You see those five cylinder-shaped stones on the grave slab?" Arthur said as he and Carl again shone their torches downwards. "It's said that anyone who tampers with them will suffer a horrible fate at the hands of an elf, or goblin-like guardian spirit, called *Bodach an Duin* ... A couple of centuries ago, it's believed that a young man threw the centre stone into the River Spey. Come morning, the stone was back in its place and the man was found dead, floating in the river."

"Interesting. But someone did that and died, so who told the tale?" John replied. "And thanks for telling me. Now we'll have some other entity after us!" he added sarcastically. "As if we don't have enough problems."

"Who knows." Arthur smiled. "Regardless of whether or not the myth is true; we will be fine. We are worthy of touching these stones and grave ... It's best we get started, anyway. I already feel as though someone is watching."

"If you say so." John watched Carl take out a couple of lithium powered lanterns from the grey bag and place them diagonally to each other across the grave. "You need to saw to cut the grate? Won't someone hear?"

"Hopefully, we won't need the saw," Arthur said.

"No?" John scratched his chin.

"We've examined the grave more than once. Some of these mortsafes connect to concrete underneath the ground. We don't believe this to be the case with this one." Arthur gave the iron mortsafe a slight but firm kick with his right boot. "Although, it seems pretty damn solid."

"How do you know it isn't connected to concrete?"

"The mortsafe has been here many, many, years. An old groundskeeper I got chatting to once told me about it. He was here when it was fitted into the ground. There was a small ceremony."

"I see," John replied.

"The saw is just in case," Carl said, looking around.

"How are we going to do this, then?" John asked.

"We'll start digging each side to see how deep the grate goes," Arthur said.

“What do you guys need me to do?” John asked. “Just keep watch, yeah?”

“That would be good, for now. You can perhaps take over from one of us, if we get tired. We can see how we go. We’ll get it started.” Carl bent down to retrieve the two shovels from the bag; they appeared shiny and new.

“Fine by me, mate.” John would have preferred to be doing some digging to occupy his mind. “What if someone catches us? I don’t necessarily mean by *them*, but anyone? Like isn’t there a groundskeeper watching the site?”

“There is a young groundskeeper, but he only comes once a week to cut the grass. If anyone else comes, we’ll just have to make a run for it,” Arthur said.

John couldn’t help but find the whole idea comical. Three of them, an old man, a middle-aged man and himself might get caught grave-digging and needing to make a run for it in the middle of the night. But then he heard rustling in the bushes again and an owl hooted. He stared around in the dark, whilst the other two got to work.

*****

Almost an hour had passed. John offered to take over from the other pair, but they insisted they were fine. John didn’t want to venture too far, but he approached the other nearby headstones. He noticed a newer grave and some fresh flowers. He rested up against one of the headstones, watching them dig. They had made considerable progress. Mounds of dirt had piled up as they dug. John texted David but there was no signal. He watched Arthur pause again for a brief respite, stretch his back, and return to work. Some moths were attracted to the LED lanterns. The feeling of being watched intensified; he felt goosebumps on his arms and the hairs on his neck rose. Arthur and Carl continued to dig. There was an eery silence, apart from the sound of the shovels at work and John wished he hadn’t come. It had also started to rain and the temperature had dropped. John also wished he’d brought a jacket like the others.

“Shit,” muttered John to himself.

Carl looked around and saw John standing behind him. “There’s an old jacket you can wear in that bag.”

“Cool, thanks!” John replied. He walked over and pulled out an old green jacket. It was a little big for him, but he didn’t mind. It would stop him from getting as wet. “It’s getting colder out here.”

“Yes,” Arthur replied out of breath. His limbs ached.

“You want me to take over? At least you’re getting there.” John tried to encourage the pair.

"Yes, please. I think it would be best. My arthritis is playing up. The cold isn't helping."

"The ground is quite soft the deeper we dig," Carl said. Younger and fitter than Arthur, Carl had dug deeper.

John took over and eventually finished what Arthur had started. The iron mortsafe went a few feet underneath the ground. Thankfully, it was not connected to any concrete or anything else. It remained strong and fixed into the ground by its own weight and the surrounding earth.

The rain was now coming down fairly steadily and softened the ground more. Arthur was having a drink of water from a bottle from the bag.

John swiped some moths away from his face. "Damn moths!"

They freed the heavy mortsafe that was covering the grave slab. Between them, they then removed the five cylindrical stones from the grave slab and placed them near to the grave, next to the mortsafe. John remarked that if the story was true about a man throwing the middle stone in the river, he must have been very strong to carry it.

John also asked about some coins that were placed on top of some of the stones. Arthur explained that coins were placed there out of respect and also to pay the ferryman, *Charon*, who would bring the recently deceased souls across the River Styx that separated the land of the living and the afterlife.

John joked about taking the money for themselves but Arthur was adamant it would be disrespectful and he was even superstitious that something bad could happen if they did. John found that ironic, seeing as they were technically robbing a grave and legend had it that anyone removing the stones they just had displaced would likely have something bad happen to them anyway. Arthur, however, didn't answer.

The next task was to remove the heavy stone slab and get down to the bottom of the grave itself.

*****

David got up to fetch two glasses of water. He nor Emily felt like sleeping, despite both feeling tired. As he walked downstairs, he heard his uncle cough in the living room. "You okay, Uncle?"

"I thought I heard someone coming down the stairs. I'm fine, I guess. Just having a hard time sleeping. You?" His uncle was holding a glass of brandy and sitting in one of the armchairs.

"Yeah. Em's the same. I just came down to grab us both a glass of water. I'm worried about John and the others as well."

"Me too, David. Have you heard from John?"

"I had a couple of texts, yeah. He said he didn't have much signal, that it was creepy, and that it felt like the three of them were being watched. Nothing new there." David yawned. "The signal keeps dying."

"I can imagine. Digging up a grave in the middle of the night." Bob sipped his brandy and then stared into the glass.

"Yep. Even if they do find this dagger, I'm not sure how it can help."

"We'll just have to see, David. Take each day as it comes and just watch out for ourselves and each other. Aren't your mum and dad due back tomorrow? These two weeks have gone quickly."

David had to think for a second. It was now the early hours of Thursday morning, so his uncle was right. "Yeah, they've flown by. And yes, they should be back tomorrow. They know nothing yet. I'm not sure if I should tell them. It might be too dangerous for them."

"I understand, David. My brother is open-minded, but even he would have trouble believing all this. You and Emily should try and get some sleep. I'm going to try myself, soon. Once I've finished this." Bob raised his near empty glass.

"Okay, Uncle. Night."

"Night, David."

David fetched the water and returned to Emily.

*****

The grave was roughly six feet down. They were all drenched with their wet hair. They had removed the heavy stone slab covering the grave with difficulty as it was much heavier than they had anticipated.

Carl sighed. He had finished the digging and stood below in the opening. Arthur had told him to stop, as he believed this was the bottom.

*"Empty?"* John said confused. He was standing over the open grave with Arthur in the rain, shining their torches down. "We've wasted our fucking time for nothing?" John exclaimed angrily. "Fuck's sake!"

"Lower your voice," Arthur chided, staring into the grave. His white beard and hair were knotty with debris and dirt. His limbs hurt and his back ached more. The digging and heavy lifting had aggravated his arthritis further.

"Don't tell me we've done all this for nothing?" Carl said softly. He shook his head. "You think we need to keep digging, Arthur?"

Arthur slowly climbed down to stand at the bottom of the hollowed out resting place too. "No ... I believe this is exactly where Seath Mór's body was placed."

"What a waste of fucking time, eh?" John said from above. "No dagger, no *nothing*!"

Arthur remained silent with a blank expression on his face as he repeatedly swung the torch about. There was nothing but dirt and soil.

Carl and John watched as Arthur then knelt to examine the soil.

John laughed. "I think it's clear, there's nothing in there, Arthur," he mocked.

"There's something here. I can sense it." Arthur pulled out his glasses to examine something in one of the corners of the grave focusing his torch there. He traced his fingers over something. Pulling away a fair amount of soil and dirt, he uncovered a small metal plaque.

"What is it?" Carl asked, also crouching down.

*"Hiort,"* Arthur said.

"Hiort?" Carl said confused. "What does that mean?"

"Look." Arthur pointed. In small writing, there was an inscription that read *Hiort*.

It would have been so easy to overlook and almost impossible for anyone else to have identified. There were a few scratches and marks on the metal plate.

John carefully jumped down, almost slipping. He wanted to see for himself. "How did you know that was even there?"

*"St Kilda."* Arthur sounded serious.

"St what?" John almost banged his head on Carl's as he bent down.

"Hiort. It is the Scottish Gaelic name for *Hirta*. The largest island of the St Kilda archipelago."

"Archi, what?" asked John.

"Archipelago. It's an island group, or a chain of islands. I'm not too familiar with St Kilda. But I have heard of it. It's west of the other Outer Hebrides islands, if my memory serves me correctly," Carl answered.

"Your memory does serve you correct," Arthur replied, still scrutinising the small carved word.

"Well, what about this island? What has it got to do with *anything*? Why is it scratched into this piece of metal and hidden like that?" John was confused, tired and agitated. As well as wet. He just wanted to get back to the farm and sleep, now.

"It's quite possible that whatever was here, like the dagger, has been removed to St Kilda. This is a clue." Arthur still examined the plaque.

"Jesus," John replied. "Who would do that and why? And more

importantly, how the hell can we find the dagger with no real idea of where it is, even if it is on this island?" John felt his eyes grow heavy.

Arthur checked all around the grave a few times, making sure they hadn't missed any other clues.

"It's a valid point, Arthur. John's right. Let's say you are correct about this dagger and other information being on St Kilda. It would be like looking for a needle in a haystack."

"I believe that whoever removed items from this grave did so to prevent Famuli Cani from finding them. They obviously believed that this resting place wasn't safe anymore. Perhaps, the inscription was done when the mortsafe was installed? The engraving certainly isn't centuries old like the grave … But if someone moved the dagger, they wanted to leave a subtle hint of its possible new location for someone worthy enough to find it."

"I understand that. But why St Kilda?"

"I don't know why they chose St Kilda, Carl. I can't answer you that. At least, not for now. I don't believe Famuli Cani have been down here and taken it … I sense that this dagger *was* here, but I don't believe *they* have removed it. Don't ask me how. I, I just know."

"Well, it still feels like we're being watched out here. I don't like it one bit. They may also now know that the dagger's definitely not here, so the secret is out," John warned.

"That's possible. If they didn't know already. Perhaps they knew it had been removed from here, just not where to … but at least they don't know where in St Kilda it now lies. I sense this, also. Of course, the only downside is, we don't know either. For now, we need to refill this grave and get it back to how it was. We can't leave it like this." Arthur picked up the small plaque and placed it in his pocket. His back was stiff, which made him grimace as he stood up and took his glasses off.

"Oh, fuck! Of course, we've got to fill it all back up again. *Shit*!"

"It won't take as long as digging it up. Don't worry," Carl said. "Let's do this and get the hell out of here."

*****

Dawn wasn't far off, by the time John finally arrived back at the farm. His limbs and body were aching, but his clothes had mostly dried out. They had at least survived the night without anything bad happening or getting caught, but now his bed was crying out for him. He was too drained to even think about what they should do next regarding St Kilda.

Arthur had suggested not mentioning anything about St Kilda in front of Betty for now.

Getting out of the car, Arthur and Carl thanked John for his help and told him to get some rest. They were just as tired and aching, particularly Arthur. They reassured John that they would come up with something, or the 'next step,' as Arthur put it.

"Yeah, okay. Whatever, guys. Drive back safely." John closed the car door after him, made his way quietly to the front of the farmhouse and let himself in with a spare key Bob had given him. He could see part of Bob, slumped in one of the armchairs, snoring away.

When John got to his room, he texted David to tell him everything went smoothly and he'd tell more once he was awake. He was 'cream-crackered' and would appreciate not being woken.

# Chapter Sixty-Four

## 26th July, 2018

John was sat upright in the bed, sobbing uncontrollably into his dirty hands from last night. Mucus covered his palms. He had slept for several hours. But he had also dreamt again. This latest nightmare had felt more personal and rawer. He was standing in a clearing, somewhere in the forest. It was daytime but overcast. A faint sound of chanting flowed around the trees, as though recorded on a loop. He was wearing the same clothes as last night including the green jacket that Carl had given him. As the chanting gradually stopped, whispers and zephyr began flowing through the leaves of the trees. Then, a faint voice grew clear and loud.

*"Joooohhhhnnnn ... Joooohhhhnnnn ... Joooohhhhnnnn ..."* the female voice echoed all around dragging the sound of his name out into a long call.

John recognised the voice. "M-Mum?" He looked around, confused and anxious.

The calling continued.

He continued searching around and looked back to the centre of the clearing. There was a hospital bed, in which a woman lay. He rushed over and stood by the dying woman. *"M-Mum?"* Tears rolled down John's cheeks, smudging the dirt on his face from last night.

His mum was wearing an oxygen mask that steamed up where she struggled to breath. She slowly took it away from her face, smiling up at her son.

John could see what little life his mother had left in her weary eyes. Her lifeforce was ebbing away. "Mum? It's okay. I'm here now." He held her left hand in both of his. She felt extremely cold to touch.

"You weren't here when I was dying, John. Why did you forget about me?" Her breathing was laboured.

"Th-that's not true. I love you, Mum! You, you died before we could get there to say our final goodbyes." John started to cry harder, looking down at his mother.

She faded slightly. She snatched her cold hand away from his, turning her head away from him in disgust. "*Bastard*! I loved you so much, John. And that was how you repaid me in my hour of need. You left me to die alone."

"No. Mum, *please*. That isn't true. We saw you every day. We were always there for you," John pleaded. He tried holding her hand again, but she snatched hers away.

"I will *never* forgive you, John. Even when we are together in *Hell*!"

John became hysterical, overcome with such emotion. He had not deserted his mother when she was dying. Nor, did his father. It just wasn't true. He felt so confused.

A mocking laughter came from around the edge of the clearing, making fun of him.

"I *hate* you, John!"

"No, Mum. *Please*! I love you. I *didn't* leave you to die alone."

The mocking laughter intensified and her body faded further, becoming transparent. The hospital bed with her fading body on it then lifted up from the ground, stood upright and began spinning round in a spiral.

John watched, confused as the laughter continued.

The ground in the forest clearing gave way to a black nothingness, swallowing the rest of the trees and bushes. Still, the laughter continued as John stood watching in blackness.

His mother and the bed then fell flat and spiralled quickly, over and over, round and round, disappearing down into the dark, black abyss.

*"John!"* his mother called again as though she were begging for help now, before disappearing with the bed completely into the black nothingness.

John felt a helplessness, his cries drawn out: *"Mum … No … No!"*

All the time, the laughter mocked him.

David had left his friend to sleep as instructed, but on coming up the stairs to fetch Emily her phone from the bedroom, he could hear his friend sobbing. He opened John's door. "John? What's the matter? What's happened?"

John removed his hands from his face. "She … she hates me …" he sobbed.

"*Who* hates you?" David stared at John, shocked to see him in this state. He rested his arm around his friend as he sat on the bed next to him.

Benji, who followed David up the stairs, jumped up on the bed also and cuddled up to John as he explained his nightmare.

"*Listen* to me, John. Your mum *doesn't* hate you. She slipped away peacefully, before you got there. You *know* that. She wasn't even conscious. She knew how much you adored her. She loved you *both*, so fucking much. *Don't* let them do this to you …" David got up to close the bedroom door in case Emily came upstairs. He knew John wouldn't want anyone to see him like this.

It took a while for John to calm down. David consoled him further and gave him their well proven 'best friend hug.' It was something they had come up with when they were little for standing united in difficult situations.

"I guess those salt crystals didn't help much?" John tried to joke.

*****

"It was pretty much a waste of time," John explained to the whole group later when they were sat together downstairs. "All that for nothing. It was exhausting filling the grave in as well, afterwards."

John had made sure Betty wasn't about — as Arthur had requested. She was outside tending to the fruit and vegetable patches. Bob had previously explained to her about the idea of digging up a grave to gain information about the cult and a dagger, but he hadn't said whose grave or where.

"At least you're okay, John. That's the main thing," Bob replied, getting up from the armchair.

"For now," John said. He wasn't over his latest ordeal of the nightmare, but he was feeling a fair amount better, thanks to David and seeing the others.

"Have you heard of St Kilda, yourself?" John asked Gavin and Bob.

"It rings a bell, but I don't know anything about the place," Bob answered.

"It's new to me," Gavin said.

"I wonder what happens next?" David said.

"Only what I told you, mate. No idea what they're going to do, or how they can find this so-called dagger." John scratched his thigh.

Emily sat quietly, listening to the others talk. She had yet to say anything.

David sighed. "We really aren't getting anywhere, are we? Nothing but dead ends, it seems. It's depressing. It makes things worse."

Emily looked at her watch. "I really should leave for work soon and my car's still at the pub."

Gavin had already offered to drive Emily to work, seeing as John had been up all night. He also wanted to do some shopping for Bob and Betty. "Whenever you're ready, lass." Smiled Gavin.

"I'll come, too," David said.

"Okay." Emily half-smiled, squeezing David's hand.

*****

It was dull and drizzly when they left after noon.

"You okay?" David asked.

"As well as I'm going to be, I guess. Hopefully, work might take my mind of things for a while." Emily opened the door. "Thank you, for bringing me, Gavin."

"Anytime, darling. I'll see you later." He gave her a smile and a nod.

"I'll walk you to the pub." David got out too.

Gavin waited as David chatted and kissed Emily goodbye.

David was taking a phone call as he got back in the car. "Okay, Mum … He's fine, too … Yep, okay. Send my love to Dad. Have a great time … Love you, too. Bye. Bye." David slipped the phone into his pocket.

"Everything okay?" asked Gavin.

"Yeah. Mum and Dad are going to stay on a little longer in Spain. It sounds like they're enjoying themselves. At least they're safe out there and not involved in all this."

"It must be tough, keeping something like this from your folks, but good they're out there, and not over here."

They looked over to the beer garden where Emily had begun her shift. She was collecting empty glasses and waved to them before going back inside.

"She's certainly a beauty, that one. Incredibly sweet as well. If only I was twenty years younger," Gavin teased.

David smiled. "I know. I've never known anyone like her. In fact, I've never felt this way about anyone before. It isn't just her looks; it's everything about her. She's such a warm-natured, sweet person. So caring as well. She's a natural beauty, in every sense of the word. It's just a shame that we've met under these awful circumstances and that's she involved now."

"As long as we all have each other, at least we have a chance. Maybe." Gavin gave David an affectionate punch on his shoulder. "I'll look after you."

"I sense that something worse is coming. How on earth, are we going to stop all of this?"

"One day at a time. We'll all just play it by ear. Let's get some shopping done, anyway. I want to stop by my house on the way back, too. Check everything is okay there."

*****

John caught sight of Bob coming out of his study, looking rather glum. "I'm just taking Benji for a walk whilst David's out. You all right, Bob?"

"I'm okay, John, thanks. I phoned around the local funeral directors to find out which is dealing with Angus' funeral. There was no one else I could contact for details. I want to pay my respects and Betty does as well."

"That's understandable, mate. I'd have wanted to do the same. What did they say?"

"They told me his brother is dealing with it. Angus' body is being transported to Stirling for a small service and cremation. I was hoping it would be closer. But then, I guess it makes sense, seeing as his brother lives there."

"Ah. That sucks, mate. It would have been nice to have said your goodbyes. It's a real bastard, what happened to him."

Bob nodded in agreement.

"Those fuckers have a lot to answer for. Have you heard anything from Derek and Jack, too?"

"I spoke to Derek earlier whilst you were still asleep. He's fine, but he still feels guilty about getting paid for not working." Bob smiled. "As for Jack, I left a message on his voicemail. I'm sure he's fine. I also spoke to Eric as well. He seems better and might have another job lined up soon."

"Nothing from Carl or Arthur?"

"Nothing as yet. I guess they're busy figuring out what to do next."

"Yeah. Whatever that's going to be. Anyway, I'll see you in a bit."

"Okay, John. Watch yourself out there."

"Will do."

Bob joined Betty in the kitchen, where she was doing some washing up. "I said I'd do that," Bob said, walking over to his wife and giving her a warm hug.

Betty didn't say anything, but then started to hum quietly to herself.

Bob told Betty about Angus' funeral but she continued to stare out into the garden, humming. "I wonder what will happen to Angus' farm, now? And his animals. I suppose his brother will deal with all that side of things. Such a terrible shame. I know we didn't always see too much of him, but I will miss him." Bob let out a sigh and shook his head. A feeling of sadness washed over him. "Those bastards," he muttered under his breath.

Bob looked at Betty and thought something didn't seem quite right about her. She stood humming with her bare hands in the washing up bowl and her head now bent down. "Betty? You okay?" He gave a her a firm shake of the shoulders. She continued to hum with her head lowered. He looked down at her hands. They were scorched red from the hot water. "Christ, Betty!" He quickly pulled her hands out but she remained oblivious. "What's wrong with you?" Without thinking, he turned the cold tap on full blast and held both her arms under the cool water, splashing both of their clothes.

Still, Betty remained unresponsive apart from her humming.

"You're lucky you didn't scald yourself," Bob said, making sure the water poured all over the redness. "What were you thinking?"

Betty stopped her unnerving humming and slowly began to raise her head.

Bob saw in shock that her eyes were completely white. Her mouth opened, letting out a dull, monotone sound. Her head then tilted back, her mouth widening.

*"Betty?"* Bob shook Betty's shoulders, trying to make her come round. He was shouting by now but still she remained unresponsive. He started to panic.

Finally, her eyes rolled down and stared blankly at him.

"Betty?" Bob tried to stay calm.

"B-Bob ... Bob?" Betty stuttered. "What happened?"

Bob fetched some ice from the freezer and wrapped some in each of two towels. He sat her down in the living room to watch television, telling her to keep the towels compressed over her hands and arms. The cats darted out of the room for some reason. He considered taking Betty to the hospital, but her skin didn't seem scalded. Bob stood for a moment in the doorway, watching her, before he walked outside and dialled Arthur. There was no answer, so he rung Carl.

"Bob, I was going to call you. How's it going?"

"Not great, Carl. How about you?"

Carl laughed a little. "Still a little tired and aching from last night. I couldn't really sleep once I got in. Is John okay?"

"Yes, he's fine, now. He had another nightmare earlier about his mum. She passed away several years ago."

"Another nightmare? Jeez. Poor boy."

Bob told Carl about Betty.

"Bob, I don't know what to say. Just keep an eye on her. I don't know what to do next, either. We need to talk to Arthur, but I think he's probably still sleeping. He's the man with the plan. Just try and remain hopeful. Arthur will work out what to do next. I'm going to call him in a bit."

A few static crackles hindered their hearing on the line.

"Damn. Looks like it's started again," Bob said.

"We'd better go. Listen, Bob. I'll be in touch soon. Just make sure you're all together, especially at night. Take care!"

The phone went dead. "Shit," Bob said to himself. He put his phone away and saw John return with Benji.

*****

That night, although the group sat downstairs with the television on, nobody was paying much attention to it.

Emily was considering having an early night, as once again, she had a headache, although not as bad as the previous one. Gavin and David had met her from work. She insisted she was fine to drive back and David had joined her in her car. Gavin followed, never too far away from them at the rear.

There had been no further word from Carl or Arthur.

Bob had repeatedly applied some soothing cream, so that Betty's arms were well cooled now, although they were still pinkish. She sat wearing her reading glasses in one of the armchairs doing a few crossword puzzles in a book. After a while, she headed up to bed for an early night.

"You okay, Em?" David asked.

"Not too bad. I think the painkillers are working, now. I'm glad it isn't as bad as the last headache."

"Do you often get them, Emily?" Gavin asked.

"Hardly ever. Rarely, actually."

A sudden, sharp gust of wind outside startled them. It made the house groan and creak. A few twigs lashed against the window. Benji, who had been lying on the carpet, looked up quickly, wide-eyed.

"Damn wind," Bob said, although he wondered if it was the wind.

The telephone then rang in Bob's study. Bob got up, not saying anything and went to answer it.

"Bob? It's Carl. Everything okay? I know it's a little late. I tried calling your mobile a few times, but it seemed turned off? I've been trying all afternoon and this evening. The same with your landline but it wouldn't connect. I texted, too. I was worried. I even tried John's phone as well."

Bob pulled out his phone and saw that it was still turned on from earlier and that he had a signal, but no missed calls or texts. "It's definitely turned on. We've had no phone calls on the home line either and John would have said if he had received any calls."

"That's strange. Or maybe not, considering. Anyway, I managed to speak briefly to Arthur. I have some news."

"What's that?" Bob asked intrigued.

"I don't like discussing things over the phone, but it probably doesn't matter now. Arthur seemed a little anxious. He wasn't making too much sense, but he said he'd speak more once he got back from St Kilda."

"St Kilda?"

"He's gone to look for the dagger. He had a dream or vision, from no other than *Seath Mór*, himself!"

"What?"

"I don't know what the old coot is up to, but he believes he knows where the dagger may be buried. He was very vague. He flew out, sometime this afternoon."

"Flew out?"

"That's right. There's a place not too far from Aviemore, which organises flying lessons. Things like that. Arthur knows someone who owns a Cessna, who was willing to take him there as a private hire."

"Oh, I see." Bob wasn't sure what to say.

"How's Betty?"

"She's fine, thank you, Carl. She decided on an early night but the rest of us are together downstairs."

"That's good. And great, that you're all together."

"Is it safe for Arthur to have gone alone like that?"

Carl sighed as the crackling started again. "All we can do is wait. He insisted on going alone. He seemed in a rush, but I think he'll be fine. There it is again, the static interference. I think it's best we end this call. Listen, I'll call soon with an update, okay?"

"Okay, Carl. You take care!"

"You too, Bob. Be safe!"

Bob walked across the hallway and the lights dimmed; he felt a shiver of coldness that lasted only a second, go right through him.

The others looked at him with an eager anticipation on their faces.

"The lights and television just went funny, Uncle. Was that Carl?"

"Maybe the wind? Yes, it was Carl."

"What did he say?" John asked, getting up.

"Arthur has gone to St Kilda, to find the dagger. He's had a vision from the spirit of that Seath Mór."

*"What?"* John asked. "A vision from some guy who's been dead for centuries? He's madder than I thought."

"He's gone by himself?"

"Apparently so, David. Well, he was having somebody fly him out there, someone who he knows. Carl offered to go with him, but he declined."

Another strong gust of wind hit the house. The television pixelated and cut out for a moment before regaining signal. The lights dimmed for a while longer this time and the group started to feel uneasy.

David put his arm around Emily, when he saw how worried she looked.

"I really hope that *is* the wind," Gavin said.

The others didn't reply.

"Well, what do we do in the meantime? Just hope that Arthur finds the dagger and go from there? What if something happens to him?" David asked.

"It's not like he's been that much of a help, anyway," muttered John.

"Apparently, Carl's been trying to ring the landline, my mobile and John's phone," Bob said.

John took out his phone. "I have signal, but no missed calls."

Emily yawned and held her forehead. "I think I might have a lie-down and an early night. I've come over really tired."

"Your head okay?" Gavin asked.

"Still the same, really. I think I just need to sleep."

"We should go up, then. I could do with an early night," David said. "You coming, Benji?"

"I'm going to pour myself a drink. You want one, boss?" Gavin asked.

"I'll have a brandy, please," Bob replied.

"We'll see you all in the morning," David said as he put his arm around Emily and they headed upstairs, with Benji following behind.

**27th July, 2018**

David awoke suddenly that night. He was lying on his back, looking up at the ceiling. For some reason, he could never sleep on his back. He must have turned in his sleep.

Several quick flashes of bright, white lightning in succession lit up the room and made him jump. He squinted against the brightness and sat up, rubbing his eyes. He wondered what time it was. Looking over to the window, he saw Emily standing there with her back to him. The lightning lit her up showing her underwear under a long, white sleep shirt. "Em?" David asked confused as he climbed out of bed. "What are you doing?" His mouth was dry.

Benji was snoring near the doorway.

David's voice startled her; she turned around. "I … I couldn't sleep. I kept waking up. I thought I heard something, so I got up to look out of the window. It was like chanting but the window is closed. There was moaning and groaning. I could hear it clearly, but it seems to have gone now. At least my head's better. It's cold tonight though, isn't it?"

David was in just his boxers. He also felt the cold. The room had dropped temperature considerably since they came to bed. David went over and gave Emily a hug.

"I'm really scared, David."

"I know, sweetheart. But as long as I'm here, I won't let anything happen to you."

Emily rested her head on David's right shoulder. She felt safer in his arms. She smiled a little, but her eyes welled up.

They were suddenly startled by a huge flash of forked lightning, which illuminated the forest in the distance like a stage. They held each other tighter.

"Did you only hear the chanting for a bit?"

"Yes. I kept waking up but managed to drift off until about ten minutes ago, when I heard it. It stopped when I reached the window."

Another lightning flash hurt David's eyes followed by rumbles of thunder. "We should get back to bed. What time is it?"

"It's nearly three." Emily checked the glow-in-the-dark watch she sometimes wore; a gift from one of her Irish friends.

"The Devil's Hour," muttered David.

"What's that?" Emily asked, frowning.

"Nothing." David felt uneasy.

Slowly getting back into bed, Emily said, "*There*. Do, do you hear it? It's the chanting again."

"I can."

"David, I'm scared." Emily held onto David in bed, her head buried into his chest as the room lit up with bright flashes.

"It's okay." David was also scared but he wanted to be strong for Emily's sake.

Emily tightened her grip onto David's body as a loud crack of thunder assaulted their eardrums. The chanting grew louder.

"It sounds so *close*. How can we hear it so loud?"

David could feel her tremble. "I don't know. It's not as close as it seems. It just seems that way." At least that's what he hoped.

They continued to lie there in the dark, watching the flashes of lightning as they lit up the room, listening to the thunder and chanting, until it eventually began to fade. Not too long after, they both managed to drift off to sleep in one another's arms.

Everyone had heard the chanting that night and the storm. A worried Gavin and Bob, had taken it in turns to sleep downstairs, in case something happened. Gavin had also had a strange dream, which featured one of his grandmothers, who had passed away almost twenty years ago. Nothing sinister had happened in the dream, so he didn't discuss it too much. It had just made him feel sad when he woke up.

# Chapter Sixty-Five

## 29th July, 2018

Friday and the Saturday passed with no word from Arthur or Carl. Annabel had asked John if he would like to go for a picnic, but he declined as he wasn't feeling too well; the strain of everything was beginning to take its toll on him. She apologised for not having been in touch much; she had been doing errands for her godparents and was tired from working, but she would really like to see him. She suggested they do something together the following week, but John said he'd let her know. She promised that the next time they got together, they would have a *great* time. John sensed she felt bad for having not contacted him much. He joked a little saying he would hold her to her promise.

*****

In the dark, David opened his eyes sharply. It was becoming a habit. He thought he heard a whisper. He was lying on his side with Emily up against him, fast asleep; her left arm draped across him.

He then heard what he thought were footsteps outside the bedroom door and some slight giggling. Becoming unnerved, he carefully removed Emily's arm away so that he didn't wake her and slowly got out of bed, hesitantly.

Stepping out into the hallway, he could once again feel the coldness, colder than before. The soles of his feet began to hurt from the cold as it increased. The light from downstairs was on, but dimmed.

David became startled. A small silhouette of a person was stood outside his aunt and uncle's room. Due to the lack of light, he had to squint, trying to adjust his eyes. He felt the coldness sweep around him as he stood in his boxers. He walked a little further down. "Au-Aunt Betty, is that you?" David swallowed, becoming nervous. He assumed it was his aunt, as he could just about make out the outline of the figure and the hair, with their back to him.

As his eyes adjusted to the low light, he could see it was definitely his aunt.

An unusual groan then came from Betty as the bedroom door slowly opened by itself. Walking into the bedroom, the door closed again by itself behind her.

David's pulse grew faster along with his nerves. He swallowed again. He slowly made his way towards the bedroom. Like before, he placed his ear up against the door. *Cold again.* So much so, it burnt his ear. As an almost repeat episode from over a fortnight ago, he could hear the sound of some footsteps from behind the closed door. Just like before. *Betty's?* He couldn't hear any whispering this time, but he could still hear some murmurs and groans coming from Betty, so he believed. Gavin's door was shut to the right. David wasn't sure whether his uncle was inside the bedroom or downstairs asleep.

Without warning, David felt nauseous. He quickly but cautiously dashed on his tiptoes to the bathroom and pulled on the light cord just in time to throw up into the toilet bowl. He spat out the remaining bile and stood up over the toilet, shocked to have felt so ill so quickly.

He walked over to the basin and looked into the mirror at his tired, weary and watery eyes. He splashed his face with some cold water. He then washed his mouth out to get rid of the acidic taste. David then heard footsteps out in the hallway. They came from the direction of Betty and Bob's bedroom; they sounded heavy and slow, making a stomping, dull thudding sound. The floor creaked from the pressure of them.

David wondered if it might be Benji as there was also a loud tapping sound, like claws touching and scratching a wooden floor, but the footsteps were way too heavy for a dog. The bathroom light let David see a little out into the wooden hallway. He felt so cold and too scared to move. The cold basin touched his lower back.

The bathroom light began to flicker as the footsteps went past the bathroom, briefly stopping. There didn't appear to be anyone or anything out there. David heard the creak of that one particular stair, the one that made more noise than any of the others. The creak was louder than usual, due to the force of whoever or whatever was making it. The rest of the stairs also creaked and jarred as whatever it was went down them.

David finally mustered the courage to walk over to the bathroom door. He looked out onto the stairs. There was no one there, but he felt static in the air. He heard the footsteps approach the front door downstairs and saw and heard the door open by an unseen force. The light in the hallway downstairs flickered and dimmed further. When the front door closed, the lights returned to normal. Whatever it was, was gone, along with the static and cold; just like that. At least, for now.

Standing and staring, David then reluctantly made his own way down the old staircase. He then froze in fright at the bottom, where he saw the front door opening again.

His uncle came in, surprising him. "David?" Bob looked surprised too. He was holding his shotgun. "What are you doing up?"

David just stared for a moment at his uncle, breathing heavily.

"David, calm down," Bob said again, putting both of his hands on David's bare shoulders. Bob could feel his nephew shaking as they stood in the living room.

David tried explaining what had just happened …

Bob stood, looking concerned.

David swallowed. "It wasn't a person … I literally couldn't see anyone or anything. Betty was just standing there in the dark, outside your room. She made a strange noise and the door opened and closed by itself. Then there were sounds coming from inside."

Bob listened seriously.

"I mean, *it* just walked straight down the stairs and then straight out of the front door, just like that. The door opened and shut by itself …! What were you doing outside?"

"I stayed down here and woke up, feeling strange. I then heard what I thought was children laughing outside. I unlocked the door, and went to take a look. I left the front door ajar. Perhaps, this thing snuck in whilst I had my back turned — we need to check on Betty!"

The two of them hurried up the stairs.

Bob opened the bedroom door and switched on the light. "Betty … you okay, love?"

Betty was fast asleep and snoring. Bob walked over to her and gently shook her left shoulder to wake her up. "Betty …"

"Urgh … Bob? What is it? What time is it?" Betty groaned, still sleepy. She flipped up her sleep mask and saw Bob, leaning over her. Then she noticed David standing in the hallway; he leaned his head into the room and had a quick look around.

David was soon joined by the large figure of Gavin who had been awoken. "What happened?"

"What is it? Is something wrong?" Betty's voice sounded dry and croaky. She shifted to an upright position and let out a wide yawn. "Well, what is it, dear?"

"David was worried about you; he heard you making noises in here. He said he saw you just standing outside our room, too."

"What?" She smiled. "I don't recall. Unless, I was sleep walking." Betty gave a funny laugh. "I do remember having a dream; it was about *Daisy.* I don't remember what it was about, though. Only she was outside near the forest. Just sitting there and watching me. But honestly, I'm fine."

Bob smiled back at her. He didn't mention what else David had just witnessed.

"Honestly, I'm fine!" she said again with added conviction. She smiled as she looked over at David and Gavin.

"Okay. Try and get back to sleep, okay? I'm sorry for waking you." Bob smiled. He saw his alarm clock read 03:13.

After explaining to Gavin what had just happened, the three checked the rest of the house; all was clear.

"I know what I heard and saw, Gavin. I hope you believe me?" David and the other two stood in the kitchen.

"Trust me, I do." Gavin put a large hand on David's back. "We'll discuss it more later on. Go back to bed and try and get some more sleep, okay?" Gavin smiled. "Me and your uncle will stay up and make sure nothing else happens. Right, boss?"

"Right." Bob smiled back.

"I don't know if I can, now."

"At least try," Bob said.

They heard someone cough out in the hallway. John walked into the kitchen wearing black boxers and a white vest. "What's going on?" he yawned widely. "I needed a drink."

"I'll tell you tomorrow, mate," David replied, walking past his friend and back upstairs.

Benji and Emily were still asleep.

"What happened?" John asked Bob and Gavin seriously, frowning.

Despite what had happened in the early hours, David somehow managed to get back to sleep.

*****

"I think it's safe to say that these salt crystals haven't worked. Eh?" John said.

John, Emily and David were sat in the living room. They had recently been joined by Derek; they were surprised to see him. He hadn't turned up so much to help with anything, he just wanted to check on Bob and everyone and see how things were. Bob told him he shouldn't have risked coming in but was touched by the concern.

Gavin was outside checking around the farm and Betty was on her bed reading.

"I know, mate. But maybe they *have* been working, and things would be worse without them?" David replied, staring at the carpet.

Emily sat next to David on the sofa. The poor girl was even more frightened.

"Possibly. I slept through fine. At least I haven't had anymore nightmares since, well ..." John looked serious and swallowed.

Derek hadn't said much. "You didn't dream it, David?"

"*What*? Of course I didn't fucking dream it!" David felt offended by Derek's question. "Why are you even here, Derek? My uncle said you didn't need to come in." As soon as David had snapped at Derek, he regretted it instantly. It wasn't like him; everything was just getting too much for him and for everyone.

Derek's face reddened and he bent his head down sheepishly.

"Shit." David got up and walked over to Derek in the armchair. "I'm sorry, mate. I didn't mean to snap at you. It's just all this shit is getting to me." David semi-smiled and placed a hand on Derek's left shoulder to add weight to the apology. "Honestly though, Derek. It's nice you came in to check on us. But it's way too risky to be here."

Derek looked up at David. He gave a slight smile. "It's okay. I know how tough it is for you all."

"I need a leak." David went to use the downstairs toilet. He looked to his left up the stairs to see Benji on the landing. Benji had been asleep in the bedroom. "Benji? What are you doing up there, boy?"

Benji appeared to have been staring down at something. He started to growl before David got to the top.

"What is it, boy?"

Benji's growl deepened. David crouched down to see what Benji was growling at. On the grey rectangular mat at the top of the stairs, was a large indentation of the same inhuman, unnatural footprint that they had come across in the mud on the dirt track, the first day when they had arrived on the farm almost three long weeks ago.

David swallowed slowly. He walked halfway back down the stairs and called out, *"John!"* trying to keep his voice down.

John quickly joined him. "What is it?"

*"Look!"*

Benji was still growling as John dashed up the creaking stairs behind David. Derek and Emily followed.

"Oh my God …" John said, kneeling down.

The mat was fairly thick, which enabled whatever it was that made the mark to press down onto the fibres, printing an outline. There were of course, other faint human prints on the mat, but nothing so well-defined.

Bob emerged from his shower in a towel, rubbing his hair dry with a hand towel. "What is it?"

"You need to see this, mate," John replied.

Bob looked down in shock.

"This must have been last night, when I heard something go down the stairs and out of the front door."

"Unless it happened after?" John suggested.

"Maybe it's still here …" Bob said, looking around. "I can't believe this thing has been in our house. Our *home*!"

"I'm certain it was from earlier," David said. "Benji was growling over it."

"I'll check on Betty," said Bob anxiously. Making his way to their bedroom, he suddenly stopped and frowned.

"What is it?" David asked. He and the others went to look.

On the floor along with other older marks, were some fresh scratches in the wood. Small pieces of frayed wood splinters stuck up from the floor.

"What is this?" John asked bemused.

Bob didn't answer.

"I know what caused this …" David said worryingly. "They're this *thing's* claw marks, from its talons."

Bob bent down, dripping small droplets of water onto the hard floor. He ran his finger along some of the rough scratches. The pattern the suspected talons made appeared in a row of five next to one another; the marks only appeared briefly. Instead of running all along the wooden hallway to the stairs, they just seemed to stop.

Bob looked towards his bedroom door where the marks seemed to come from. Moving quickly, he burst in, throwing the door open. Betty was sat up in bed eating one of the biscuits he had previously brought up to her.

"Darling … what are you doing barging in like that?" Betty asked as she brushed off a few crumbs from the mauve and white duvet cover. "Darn … I've made a mess." She reached over to the small bedside table to pick up the cup of tea. She took a small sip. A closed book lay next to her on the bed with a red book mark in.

"I … I'm sorry. I just wanted to check you were okay?" Bob answered, feeling a little awkward as he looked around the room for anything suspicious.

"I'm fine, Robert. Nothing like a nice cuppa and a good read." Betty smiled.

Bob looked at her with a little dismay. He couldn't recall the last time she had called him by his first full name. And usually when she had, it was either in a joking or sarcastic way. But this time, she sounded serious. "Okay, love. You enjoy your read." Bob tried to smile and closed the door.

"What is it, Uncle?" David asked, seeing how confused his uncle looked.

Bob walked away from the door before he answered, "It's nothing. It's just that Betty hardly ever calls me Robert … but I'd better get dressed and check the house again."

Bob showed Gavin the mat with the large print on. He then rolled it up and stored it in his study. He didn't want to risk Betty seeing it, at least not for now. If she asked, he'd just say it got marked and dirty. The two cats also seemed reluctant at first to go downstairs.

*****

Late that Sunday afternoon, Bob received a call from Carl. "Carl! We were all getting worried. I've been trying to phone you all day. Again, our phones kept going down."

"I'm sorry, Bob. The same with us. Some strange things have been happening. I know I'm being watched further — it feels stronger now."

"Strange things?"

"Yes. Just phone calls and static and no one there, or laughter, things like that. Weird sensations. Oh, and a note delivered to my office last Friday morning saying 'Very Soon!' But listen, enough about that … it's about Arthur. He's back from St Kilda. After we failed to contact you earlier, we decided to visit you on your farm again. But since Arthur has returned from St Kilda, he's been feeling really unwell. We had to turn back as driving through the forest made him feel even worse."

"What? Is he going to be okay?"

"He claimed he will be, after a little rest and meditation. But he still wants to avoid the forest and farm for a little while. But there's something else …"

"What else?"

"He's found it. He's *found* the dagger!" Carl sounded excited.

Bob told Carl about the latest incident in the early hours. Carl felt even more concerned on hearing this news. They then arranged another meeting.

They agreed to gather at a cricket pavilion this time, rather than at Carl's office. It was a little more neutral, especially after the note Carl had received. But the main factor was that Arthur had been feeling really unwell since he returned from the Outer Hebrides. Although Arthur didn't want to put the group at risk driving to a meeting, he 'sensed' they would be fine. On Arthur's behalf, Carl insisted the group all came, including Betty.

As it happened, however, Gavin stayed back on the farm to keep an eye on Betty who said she wasn't feeling too great. All she wanted to do was stay in bed. Derek also remained.

*****

At the cricket ground just outside Aviemore, a small, gravelly parking lot sat at the bottom of a grass embankment with some flowers, which lead up to a neatly cut cricket pitch with the sweet smell of freshly cut grass.

"Why here?" John asked Carl who was standing alone next to his car.

"It was Arthur's idea. He knows the groundsman. He said he'd wait for us inside the pavilion."

Theirs were the only cars there. They walked up the stone steps on the embankment. Benji pottered between the steps and embankment, lapping up all the exciting new scents. When they reached the top of the steps, they could see Arthur standing with his back to them in the middle of the cricket pitch with his hands clasped behind his back, distinctive with his long white ponytail tied back as usual. The wooden pavilion was small and lay to the right with a dark green door. The window frames had the same dark green iron bars to protect the glass from cricket balls and break-ins.

Carl had to call out to Arthur a couple of times before he finally turned around and walked towards them.

"Does he always wear those same damn clothes?" John asked quietly.

Neither said anything, but Carl turned his head and smiled.

"I'm sorry. Were you there long?" Arthur asked. "I was just enjoying the warm breeze." He smiled at them.

"You okay?" Carl asked his friend, placing a sympathetic hand on Arthur's shoulder.

"I am. It's good to see you all again."

"Gavin stayed to keep an eye on Betty," Bob replied. "She wasn't feeling too well. Gavin insisted I should come."

"I see. But you should all be together now. Though perhaps it's better Betty isn't here. Carl told me about what happened in your house during the night. Things are getting more and more dangerous. I feel Famuli Cani's powers are growing *much* stronger." Arthur walked past them and smiled at Emily, making his way to the pavilion.

"Shall we?" Carl gave a flick of his eyebrows, gesturing with his hand.

John queried with Carl under his breath whether Arthur was a little 'off' today. Carl claimed it was the stress of everything.

Entering the small building, Carl closed the door behind them. They entered what appeared to have been the canteen and sat round a table there.

Arthur had arrived back from St Kilda the same day he left, Thursday. Upon returning to the county of Inverness, he started to feel unwell. In spite of that, he decided to leave the area for a day or two to collect his thoughts and think things over. He had actually felt better, until he came back.

Across the oval-shaped table, the others pondered on how jaded he looked close up. His eyes were puffy and tired. He had a fresh scratch at the side of his forehead. His long white hair and beard appeared more yellowy than usual. However, he didn't beat around the bush.

"After I returned from digging up Seath Mór's grave with you two, I was exhausted. I slept deeply and had a dream — a vision from Seath Mór, himself." Arthur's eyes grew wide as he stared at the others.

John didn't say anything; he was beginning to wonder if Arthur *did* sense certain things. How else would Arthur have found the plaque in the grave in the first place and then the dagger, unless Arthur was somehow playing them. John's scepticism soon returned. He decided to keep quiet and let Arthur continue.

"My vision was very clear."

"Did he speak to you?" asked David, frowning. He held Emily's hand under the table.

"Not exactly. I can't explain it. He communicated through thought alone, without speaking. He showed me flashbacks of things through his eyes, as though I was him: his clan, his life, family, and … and the atrocities that Famuli Cani committed all those centuries ago."

"Wow." David swallowed.

"I was hoping that he would show me more. When I was standing over his grave in the old churchyard, I could sense that he was with me, but I couldn't see him. I think he helped me find what we needed." Arthur breathed out. "I need a glass of water. Would you be so kind, Carl?"

"Sure thing, Arthur." Carl made his way to the back of the canteen and through a side door to the kitchen area. The metal shutters were closed.

They heard the tap run, before Carl returned with a glass of cold water.

Arthur took a couple of large swigs.

"What happened in your vision?" John asked.

"We were back standing over his grave. It was snowing. I could feel the coldness of the snow as it swirled around us. The next thing I knew, I was gliding across the ocean from above and it was warm, and the sea was calm and glistening in the sunlight." Arthur stopped, to drink some more water. He wiped his mouth and beard with his hand. "After a short while, I was above St Kilda. The island of Hirta, green expanses, with cliffs and deserted huts."

"Deserted? Doesn't anyone live there anymore?" John asked.

Arthur shook his head. "No, not now. It has long since been abandoned. Apart from a military base there, and an old inn that's no longer open. The remaining population were evacuated long before the Second World War, supposedly at their own request, due to life becoming too hard and difficult there for them to live and survive there, especially, during the winter. So, they moved to the mainland."

"Ah, I see," replied John.

"The next thing, I was on the ground. But I felt at peace. Tranquil. Especially, after what I'd seen Famuli Cani do."

"What sort of things?" Bob asked.

"I'd rather not go into that. Let's just say, the most awful things you could imagine."

"You mean, like sacrifices and stuff?" asked David.

Arthur didn't answer. He gave a slight nod and closed his eyes, steadily exhaling from his nostrils. "I could feel Seath Mór pulling me towards the edge of a cliff to something; something he wanted to show me. I stood near the edge of the cliff and looked down. I had to get down there, somehow." Arthur drank some more. "I don't know why, but he suddenly disappeared. I could no longer feel his presence, but I had to get out there as *soon* as possible."

"Wait, that was it? What if it had been a trick, from those sick fuckers?" John asked.

"I can't explain it, John. But I knew it was a genuine vision. I could feel it. It was benevolent. I knew it was him. Time was of the essence, so I arranged a chartered flight with a friend who owns a Cessna, an ex-military pilot."

"Did you tell him why you were going?" David asked.

"Not exactly. I've known him for a number of years and he knows what I do, but I don't want to involve anyone more than needed."

"So how did you find the dagger?" John asked.

"I felt like Seath Mór was trying to guide me. The dagger wasn't far from where we landed."

"I think I need a glass of $H_2O$, myself," Carl interrupted as he made his way to the kitchen area.

Arthur waited for Carl to return before going on. "I wasn't sure how long I'd be, but Francis, the pilot, said he'd wait. I wondered how on earth I would get down to the bottom of the cliff … but by putting thought out to Seath Mór, he guided me along the top of the cliff towards some shrubs and overgrowth. Then he told me to look down. Hidden in the grass and dirt was a small, wooden hatch with a rusted bolt holding the rotted hatch closed. Fortunately, it wasn't rusted shut. There was an old rope ladder attached to the top of the entrance, so I climbed down. I only had a torch and some crystals with me, but I was glad of them.

"The rope ladder stretched down to around a hundred feet into darkness. At the bottom, was a single narrow pathway in the cliff. After walking for a few minutes, I could see a golden light ahead. I finally reached a small ledge with another short rope ladder going down, finishing in a domed open cavern with a closed stone tomb in the centre. It was the tomb that was radiating the light. I could feel the warmth from it. I'd switched off my torch by now, but when I reached within touching distance of the tomb, everything went dark, so I had to switch it back on. I felt a benevolent presence though, so I slid the lid off the tomb and shone my torch inside."

"Did you see the body of Seath Mór?" John asked.

"Not quite!" Arthur smiled. "Not after several hundreds of years."

"Shit. Oh yeah." John remembered.

Arthur closed his eyes and gave a slight nod of the head and continued. "Inside the tomb lay a dark yellow and blue léine croich under a white mortcloth. A brown cloth with the dagger wrapped inside lay next to them. I could hear Seath Mór urging me to take it, so I did … a centuries-old dagger that can kill or stop a demon." Arthur took a few breaths as though he didn't want to remember the next part of his story.

"There was an envelope there, too. I was about to pick it up when Seath Mór warned me to leave. He shouted inside my head to leave quickly and the cavern began to shake violently. Everywhere was crumbling down around me. I stuffed the envelope and dagger inside my pockets and scrambled up the first ladder, along the tunnel and back up the second ladder to the top. It was terrifying. Just as I reached the top, everything caved inwards. But that wasn't the worst part … I could now sense pure evil all around me. Something was angry that I'd found what I was looking for. I needed to get back to the plane, pronto. We had a really rough flight back because a storm came in, so we were both glad to eventually land."

"Fucking hell," John said. "You almost died."

"I know … God and Seath Mór were looking out for me. *Us*, as we made our way back … Escaping, I cut my forehead on a thorn bush." Arthur smiled slightly and pointed to his forehead.

John shook his head. "Why didn't this Seath Mór just show you this vision from the off? Why let us go through the effort of digging up his grave in the first place?"

"I understand your annoyance, John. Your question makes sense. But I cannot answer that. Perhaps, we had to show our 'worth' to him first? Or he wasn't able to do so."

"So, this demon, this evil presence, was responsible for the cavern falling in? That means they know that we have the dagger now?"

"Yes, David. We were never able to keep this a secret. Not for long, anyway. They watch us. They know a lot of things," Arthur replied. "That's why both Carl and I never like talking over the phone. The interference isn't just from the souls of the lost ones, but to do with the dark magic."

"And because Betty's under their influence, you don't want her knowing what we're up to?" Bob asked.

Arthur nodded. "Though it matters not, now."

"What about the envelope? And do you have the dagger with you?" Bob asked.

"The dagger is in a safe place."

"And the envelope? Was there anything in it? Who would have put it there?" David quizzed.

Arthur suddenly frowned, looking serious. "Now, is not the time. They are here. We have to leave, *now*."

"Who? You mean the cult?" John asked. "They followed us?"

"I don't know. But I can sense they are close. It isn't safe here."

"Where *is* safe, now?" David asked concerned.

Arthur got up from his chair and gave a knowing nod to Carl.

"Come on, let's get out of here," Carl agreed quickly.

The air turned cold as they exited the pavilion, they could see that the sky had clouded over.

Arthur locked the building up as the others waited. Pushing firmly on the door to make sure that it was locked properly, he pulled down the dark green shutter for added security.

"Fuck me, it's got cold. Or is it just me?" John shook.

"It isn't just you," Carl said. He gazed ahead of them. Something had caught his attention.

Turning to follow his unblinking stare, their spirits were chilled as they saw a dozen or so figures holding hands, up past the boundary line across the neatly cut lawn of the cricket pitch.

"What the ..." John murmured.

"It's them. Well, some of them," Carl responded, still staring.

"Famuli Cani," Arthur whispered.

Benji started to growl before whimpering to silence as Emily held David tightly.

In the middle of the chain of people, John and David noticed a tall and slender figure.

"That's Harold, the supposed forest ranger we met when we first came up here."

"Oh my God. It is him. And he's *still* wearing the same uniform as well," John confirmed.

"Why are they just standing there like that, staring at us?" asked David.

"We shouldn't stand about and find out. We need to leave. Come on!" Carl said, finally breaking his gaze and quickly moving along.

John burst out at them, *"Hey! What the fuck are you looking at, you freaks? What do you want?"*

"John!" David said, frightened his friend would provoke trouble.

*"No! Fuck them! I'm sick of this!"* John shouted again, his adrenaline rising.

They didn't respond or acknowledge John's outburst. Everyone sensed the chain of people were laughing at them with their piercing eyes.

"Come, let's go!" Arthur ushered them away from the pavilion and towards the stone steps.

None of them took their eyes off the line of figures holding hands, until they were out of sight at the bottom of the embankment, where their parked cars were.

"Let's not hang about. We need to all be together now. Me and Carl will come to the farm as soon as we can. But I have to do some things first and prepare myself," Arthur said adamantly.

The others became more frightened.

"That's fine," Bob replied unnerved.

"We can go over things, then." Arthur made his way to the passenger side of Carl's Audi.

"Why were they just standing there, looking at us like that? Why not run after us and get us?" John asked. "So much for us meeting at a more neutral location!"

"I don't know," replied Arthur. "We'll get together soon. But now, let's *go* ..."

*****

Travelling back, the group's nerves were a wreck.

"Jesus ... that creepy Harold. That's the first time we've seen him, since the incident in the forest. Why were they just standing there like that? *Ugh*." John shuddered and screwed up his face.

"I don't know, John. But it was certainly one of the creepiest things that I have ever seen," Bob said.

"And why were they holding hands like that?" David asked.

Nobody answered as Bob pulled up outside the farmhouse on the small pebbles.

As they got out of the car, Gavin came rushing out. "I've been trying to call you, boss!"

"Gavin? What is it? Is Betty all right?" Bob replied alarmed, locking his car.

"I've been trying to call you. Why didn't you answer? The phones kept going dead as well ... I couldn't get anyone on the landline or mobile."

"You've been ringing? I didn't hear any calls. Let me check. No signal. Is everything okay? Is it Betty?"

"I'm not sure. She was acting strange. But you'd better come inside!"

On one of the armchairs, was a young woman wearing only a light green towel. Her face and limbs were covered in mud. Her dark hair was tangled in clumps and she was heavily pregnant. Her huge bump was protruding through the towel, her belly button clearly visible.

"I found her outside," Gavin said quickly, before the others had a chance to ask anything.

"Who are you?" Bob asked, walking towards the girl.

"She hasn't said much. She seems very confused and disoriented."

"Why is she in just a towel?" asked John.

"I sent Derek home an hour before ... I just saw her there, out of the kitchen window. She was just standing there, staring at me, completely starkers. Almost gave me a bloody heart attack, I can tell you!"

John thought of saying something funny, but bit his tongue when he saw the state of the girl. After what had happened at the pavilion, he wasn't feeling his usual jovial self.

"Has she said her name?" Bob asked.

"Florence. Or Florrie, to her friends. I managed to get that out of her." Gavin put his hands on his hips as they all stared at her. "When the phones started working for a bit, I considered calling the police, but I wasn't sure, after everything ... I wanted to wait until you came back."

The young woman looked wide-eyed at the floor at nothing in particular, rocking her body back and forth slightly.

"I wonder if this is the woman Brian told us about? The Jones' daughter, was it? Their pregnant daughter was missing ... Are you Florence Jones?" Bob asked calmly, crouching down in front of this young woman.

She didn't answer or look up at Bob.

"She said she came out of the forest. She said she managed to get away and was led to the farm."

"Led? By whom?" Bob asked, frowning.

"She wouldn't say. I wrapped her up and sat her down in here. I've hardly managed to get anything out of her. Oh, and something about her baby being in danger. I did offer her something to eat and drink. She just asked for water. Sorry, my head's all over the place, boss. I tried calling. Thank God, you're back."

"No worries, Gavin." Bob smiled, understanding. "Why hasn't Betty come to help?"

"I can't get through to her. She just kept wandering around the house humming before going upstairs to read. She was creeping me and Derek out. The place has gone mad!"

They left the young woman who must have been around twenty, sitting in the living room and gathered in the kitchen. But not before Bob went to check upstairs on Betty, who was now asleep.

"The plot just keeps getting thicker and more fucked up, doesn't it?" John said.

"Where did she escape from? And how did she get here? Who led her here and why? She must be due any day now. She's in no condition to be walking around deep in a forest like this, and naked at that! And *why* was she naked?" David asked.

"It's surely no coincidence," Bob said, before shaking his head and exhaling. "Arthur and Carl will be coming over soon, hopefully. We can see what they suggest."

"You think we should phone the police or take her to the police station?" Gavin asked. "We can't take her home, if she doesn't tell us where she lives."

"I know. In normal circumstances, of course, it would be the right thing to do. But as you say, Gavin, after everything Carl and Arthur have told us, I think it's best we hold off for now. The police can't be trusted. We can try asking her more in a little while. See if she responds. The poor girl is clearly in shock."

"What happened at the meeting? Is Arthur all right?" Gavin asked.

"You *really* don't wanna know!" John answered, before they filled Gavin in.

Bob and the group were undecided on whether to phone Arthur and Carl in advance about the naked, pregnant woman who had randomly turned up. They decided against it. They didn't want to risk anyone listening in on the call and knowing Florence was at the farm, especially if she had escaped from the cult. The chances were high, however, that they already knew, particularly with the way Betty was behaving. They had to be on extra guard.

The poor young woman still didn't say much. All she would mutter every now and then, was about her baby being in danger. They didn't know what else to do. They couldn't even get her to tell them where she lived or confirm her surname. She just sat there in her towel.

Bob asked Florence if she wanted to have a lie-down. She gave a nod of her head and Bob helped her up the stairs to the spare bedroom across from Gavin's.

He then went in to check on Betty again. She was still fully clothed asleep on the bed. All she seemed to do lately was sleep. Bob couldn't believe that she wasn't interested in helping the young woman. This wasn't his wife, somehow.

*****

Carl and Arthur arrived well into the evening. Arthur apologised for being later than he expected. With no signal yet again, they hadn't been able to ring earlier. The others were also concerned. Although not a hundred percent, Arthur was feeling considerably better after spending more time meditating. He was able to arrive at the farm without any difficulties. He brought his brown satchel that hung over his right shoulder.

Arthur and Carl were informed about Florence and about Betty's continued strange behaviour. Bob also showed them the imprint on the mat and the marks upstairs in the hallway. Bob checked in on Florence, who was sound asleep under the covers. Arthur wanted to question her, naturally, but rather than wake her, he considered it would be better when she had slept and might be more responsive.

"It was almost like she was catatonic," Bob said quietly. "Though, she managed to put on a pair of Betty's pyjamas. You sure you don't want to wake her? We should return her to her parents."

"I still believe she needs to rest. Not just her body but her mind. I feel it could make things worse or even dangerous if we disturb her now. Although we need to get her home to her parents, she could also have answers to what we need to know … It would have made sense to contact the police, but I believe you did the right thing not doing so and also not phoning me about it when you had a signal. This young lady might have been brought here for a reason," Arthur suggested.

"What?" Gavin asked.

"We will get to that," Arthur replied. "We can perhaps wake her after we have discussed further about the dagger and the envelope I recovered from St Kilda. Let us gather downstairs."

"Do you want me to wake Betty?"

"We can leave her be too for now, Bob." Arthur smiled.

Inside Bob and Betty's bedroom, Betty's eyes opened wide and staring.

Downstairs, Arthur sat in one of the armchairs and pulled out the envelope from his satchel, his 'man-bag' as John joked quietly to David.

Inside the envelope, was a letter and a note:

*To whomever finds this letter, it can surely mean only one thing. Famuli Cani, with all its evil have returned.*

*The dagger is the only thing that can stop Canus. The dagger was relocated somewhere away from the initial burial at Rothiemurchus Church. It was too risky to leave it there. At the time of writing this letter, there is a stronger growing fear and impending doom that this cult will return.*

*And if you are reading this, then you have successfully found the clue that has led you here, to Hirta, St Kilda, a special place. Safe from Famuli Cani.*

*I can only assume that you have found this tomb through a vision from my great ancestor, Seath Mór, who vowed before he died to guide anyone, who was chosen and worthy enough to stop this cult, if it returned.*

*I wish, for whomever finds this letter, the strength and courage to destroy Famuli Cani and Canus, once and for all!*

*May God, be with us all,*

*Alban Shaw, 18th March, 1993*

*P.S. Unfortunately, other details, information and documents have long since been destroyed, or lost, but I can include a small note from one of my earlier ancestors.*

Arthur handed the letter to the others after he had read it out aloud.

"And that's it?" David asked.

"Who is supposed to destroy this thing and these awful people?" Emily added. She was snuggled up to David on the sofa.

"Famuli Cani are no doubt concerned that we now have the dagger, and it's clear they know we are in possession of it from what we experienced at the cricket pavilion," Arthur said.

"I don't mean to sound negative, but why would they be worried that we have the dagger? It's not like we're in a position to take all these guys out. We are nobodies. Who are *we* to worry them?" John said agitated raising his voice. "We don't even know where they are, or *who* they are! And why is it down to *us*, to stop them?"

"We *must* have faith," Arthur said. "And I can't really answer that question, John. Obviously, things were different back then with fighting warriors. But I believe it is down to us. For whatever reason, we have been chosen."

"But we aren't *warriors*!" John shook his head. "How can we compete against them and their powers?"

"I know that it's terrible. *Awful*. But we need to remain strong. The other note I have here is many, many years older. It confirms that Seath Mór infiltrated the lair of Famuli Cani all those centuries ago. He took some of his men with him one night and defeated them. Canus had been summoned during a sacrificial ritual involving his twelve-year-old son. Seath Mór is believed to have stabbed this demon in its blackened heart. Their lair or hideout was somewhere underneath the Cairngorms mountain range. That could still be the case, but where, I do not know. Yet." Arthur pulled the note from the envelope and handed it to the group, who each read it in turn and passed it around. It had become yellow and wrinkled with age, more so than the letter.

"That poor child must have been petrified. Thank God, he was saved," Emily said tearfully.

"Just like that, eh? He stormed the fortress and killed everyone and the demon? Simple enough, I guess," John said sarcastically. "We don't even know where their place is. And even if we did, are we just supposed to waltz in there and kill them all? Not to mention, that this *Seath Mór* was a soldier and had an army."

"Please, John," Arthur said calmly.

The others were all thinking the same, however.

"As discussed before, it is believed that true evil cannot be destroyed completely. I don't believe that's always the case. But Canus could have been sent back to where it was initially summoned from, like to Ben Macdui; it most likely became weaker and more dormant, only being able to manifest itself on a number of occasions, like when Norman Collie encountered it, and others in the forest. And then it was resummoned by the returned Famuli Cani. It is contradictory, I know. You'd think a demon would either fail to exist after being killed, or at least, be sent and banished straight back to Hell."

"It's possible that Seath Mór was somehow mistaken into thinking that he killed Canus for good, at the time. Unfortunately, we are still lacking details," Carl added.

"So basically, even if we did the impossible and killed this demon, it could all be a waste of time, as someone might summon it again, anyway?" John argued.

"In theory, yes. It's possible. But still *very* unlikely. There aren't many who have the capabilities and know-how of Famuli Cani. Even stopping them alone could be enough to weaken the demon, rendering it no longer a dangerous threat," Arthur explained.

"Well, at least we have the dagger. That should be enough to take them all out. Maybe, we can just hurl some salt crystals at them as well, seeing as they've been a great help, so far. Especially with stopping the dreams," John spat out.

Arthur bowed his head without saying anything. He didn't blame John for being facetious.

"Who was this Alban Shaw, who wrote the letter?" Bob asked.

"I am not too familiar with him," Arthur said, looking up. "I've heard of him in my research, though. But there isn't much about him, other than that he died in 1994. He no doubt wanted to keep a low profile. For obvious reasons. He did live around these parts. So, I guess he felt something more sinister than his other family members who had immigrated."

"Not too long after he wrote this letter, then?" Gavin added.

Arthur nodded. "We can assume that it was him who moved what was left of the grave and placed the remains in that underground cavern in Hirta. No doubt with some help. He was obviously right about the cult returning. And it not just being paranoia."

"How did he die?" David asked.

"Through heart failure. But that isn't completely confirmed," Arthur answered.

"I still don't understand why this demon wears a cloak, though?" Emily suddenly asked.

Arthur smiled at her. "None of us are too sure, my dear. We believe it doesn't always wear a cloak. Reports from people in the forest and climbers near Ben Macdui claim to have seen a huge grey figure, although not close up or fully."

"I take it you have the dagger with you, in that satchel?" David asked, pointing.

Arthur reached inside the satchel that lay next to him and pulled out the old brown cloth. He unwrapped the shiny dagger. The group were eager to see it.

"That's it?" John said. "It doesn't look anything special!"

The blade was roughly six inches in length. It looked incredibly sharp, narrowing off at the end to a dangerous looking point. The dagger had a plain wooden handle with a silver rounded head at the bottom. It looked very ordinary.

Arthur smiled. "I thought exactly the same thing. But believe me, it's *far* from ordinary. The blade is specially made. Even after hundreds of years, it still remains like brand new."

The silver blade reflected the late evening sunlight that shone through the living room window. Again, like the letter and note, it was passed around the group. They all noticed how light it was and could feel a warm, tingly sensation as they held it.

"Is it silver?" David wondered.

"It is," Arthur replied as Bob handed the dagger back to him. "Solid silver and mercury."

"Mercury?" Gavin asked. "Isn't that poisonous?"

"Yes. But this is completely safe." Arthur smiled. "Mercury, or Azogue, which is another name used for it, has been used for many years to ward off evil and for protection in rituals as well. Silver, as you probably know, is a very powerful element when it comes to stopping evil. Here ..." Another smaller note was inside the cloth with the dagger. The same handwriting as the old note. "It mentions about how powerful this dagger is and a little about it," Arthur pointed out.

"Like silver bullets?" John said.

"Correct." Arthur swept a few strands of his long white hair from his eyes. "It was also blessed with salted holy water by a priest, according to the note, and had spells cast upon it. Benevolent ones. *White* magic."

"It's hard to believe we are holding a dagger that looks brand new but is actually centuries old. I mean, this has been inside a demon's chest!" David remarked. "I wonder how Seath Mór managed to do it? I don't think I could do it."

"What's next?" Bob asked.

"I do believe we will be shown a way. Things happen for a reason. An opportunity will present itself. This young girl who is pregnant ... it's possible this was *meant* to happen. She was sent to us for a reason. Perhaps she has some of the answers we are looking for," Arthur suggested.

"It's definitely related, then? Her showing up like that?" Gavin asked.

"Oh, most certainly, my friend. Most certainly." Arthur looked at Gavin.

*****

The group continued to chat further into the evening about things and Bob decided to make a hot drink for them all. Carl gave him a hand bringing in the hot cups of tea, along with a plate of biscuits. As they sat back down, they were startled by someone screaming upstairs.

"It's the girl!" Gavin said, jumping up.

"Maybe she's in labour?" John suggested.

"We *must* go to her," Arthur said, standing up.

Bob rushed upstairs and the others followed. Betty was outside the woman's room and said she had been about to go in when she heard the terrible screams. Bob told her to stay in the hallway. He and Arthur entered the room while the others stood in the doorway looking in.

The young woman, wearing a pair of Betty's white flowery pyjamas, was soaked through. She had stopped screaming, but was sitting up in bed with the duvet pushed aside. She was clutching her huge bump, sobbing and shaking. *"My baby, my baby. Please don't let them take my baby!"* she sobbed.

"Shhhh … it's okay. No one is going to take your baby," Arthur said softly as he sat on the edge of the bed. He put a gentle arm around her wet shoulders. "You're okay."

The others watched as Florence slowly raised her head and looked at them with her red eyes. She turned to see the face of Arthur, with his long white hair and beard. She sniffed a couple of times, but sensed they were good people.

"You're okay," Arthur said again, then smiled.

A few moments past, before she spoke again. "I, I have seen you all before. These dreams I have been getting. These people …" Florence's accent was English.

The others looked at each other. Concerned.

"What people?" asked Arthur. "Bob, could you fetch her some tissues?"

Florence was a little calmer now. "Worshippers. You know who I mean. They, they have been talking about you." She wiped her nose. "They make people have bad dreams. Nightmares. Oh, the *worst* nightmares. They are so *real*." Florence almost started to cry again, but she refrained. She felt awkward, being in some stranger's house, wearing someone else's pyjamas, sobbing, and being stared at.

"Maybe it's best if you all give Florence some breathing space?" Arthur suggested, looking at the others. "That's your name, isn't it?" Arthur looked back and smiled.

Florence nodded. "Florence Jones."

"No. No way," John replied. "This concerns *all* of us. We need to know *right* now, what she knows." He looked straight at Florence. He felt awkward for her, but he needed to know. Nobody had challenged him, so he assumed they agreed. She was actually quite attractive. Tears, bump and all.

"If you don't feel like speaking right now, then that's fine. Just say so. We don't want to push you," Arthur said calmly.

"It's okay." Florence sniffed again. "You, you need to know. You are all in *great* danger."

"I'm Bob. This is my farm. How did you end up here?"

"I, I know you're Bob … they've been watching you. All of you." Florence looked at them all.

Arthur asked her to start from the beginning.

She inhaled strongly, before breathing out. Then she began to talk. It had started a little under a year ago. She had met a young guy, named Jacob Johnson, or *JJ* to his pals. He was slightly younger than she was; she was twenty and he was nineteen when they met. He liked to smoke weed.

John thought 'JJ' sounded like his kind of guy.

Jacob had been a sincere and really sweet guy to start with, when they first started dating. Cheeky too. But after a few weeks in, things had started to change. It was little things at first. Mood swings, ignoring her when she chatted to him, staring at her awkwardly for no reason.

He wasn't on social media like most people. She didn't think that was too strange. But the more they dated, the more secretive and closed off he became. He was also vague about what he did for work. She worked part-time in a small clothes shop in Aviemore. When asked what he did for work, he would usually just say "This and that," or that he was helping a friend paint someone's house that had taken for ever, because it was so big. She never really paid too much attention and it wasn't a concern. But what *was* a concern happened around eight weeks after they had first begun dating.

"He had a small run down flat in Aviemore, just a few minutes' walk from where I used to work. He used to sometimes stay with his mum, but he liked his own flat and freedom. But one evening after I had finished work, I stopped by to see a friend who was also nearby, and then went on to see Jacob at his flat. He had his window open. I could smell the weed. I never smoked the stuff myself and don't really like the smell.

"But he often made me do it and would get aggressive if I declined. I went to ring the buzzer, but noticed the main door was already ajar. So, I walked up the steps to the door of his flat inside. I knocked a couple of times and he finally answered for me to come in, as it was open." Her eyes began to fill again. "Oh, those *poor* little mice."

"Mice? What mice, dear?" Arthur asked. His arm never left her shoulders.

"I could hear him chuckling to himself from in the living room. I called out to him, but he didn't respond. I walked in and saw him sitting there, naked. He was sitting inside what looked like an inverted pentagram, made out of entrails and bodily organs. He had some of them on his naked body. He looked up at me grinning, holding a small penknife. He had pinned down one of his pet mice by its neck. The … the other two were already mutilated. He said he was just doing his 'homework.'"

*"The sick fuck!"* John hissed.

"H-he had three pet mice. Two of them had their heads cut off, and their bodies cut open and torn apart. It was *awful.*" Florence started to cry again. Arthur pulled her head into his chest.

"Who does that to innocent animals?" Emily started to well up herself.

"These sick bastards," David replied. "That's who. It's what they do."

"I, I then watched in horror, as he cut into Louis' neck, severing his head from his body. The squeaks and squeals. I'll never forget it. I asked him what he was doing. I was in shock. I didn't know what else to say or do. He just started laughing. I started to walk out backwards and then managed to run out of there."

Florence was so shook up by the incident, she hadn't told anyone for several days. Even her own parents. She felt ashamed too, that her boyfriend had done something like that. Then, a few days later, she mentioned it to one of her friends, who was more than shocked and told her to go to the police. She thought about it, but she wasn't sure what the police would do. It would only have been three mice to them. She also felt scared.

"What happened after that?" Gavin asked.

"I, I realised I was pregnant a week after. I cried *so* hard. I wasn't ready to be a mother. But worse still, I knew *Jacob* was the father. After what I had seen him do, how could I give birth to his child? How could I have been *so* careless and stupid?"

"Hush. It isn't your fault," Arthur said.

"But it *is*. I should have been stronger. I think I conceived one night after we went out for a few drinks. I wasn't in the mood to ... you know? But Jacob, was adamant he *wanted* it. He was quite forceful and said the 'timing' was just right. So, I, I allowed him." Florence bent her head in shame. "It's all my fault. I should have broken things off sooner but I was scared. Now, look at me." A few tears dropped down onto her covered bump. "I considered an abortion, but I got a letter through my door telling me that if I did that, not only would I suffer, but my parents would, too ... that we would suffer and die. It was handwritten in blood ... and I assumed it was from Jacob. Who else could it have been from?"

"Did you go to the police?" asked Carl.

Florence shook her head, which was still bowed down. "I couldn't. I was too frightened. Part of me wanted to keep the baby, too. But if it wasn't for the threat, I would have gone through with the abortion."

"And how did your folks react to the pregnancy?" Carl asked further.

"I, I never told them about what Jacob did, nor about the note. I just couldn't. They have always been so supportive of me. I could tell that they were disappointed I got pregnant so quickly into the relationship, especially, when I didn't see Jacob again after that incident in his flat. I had texted him saying I didn't want to be with him anymore. I never told him about the pregnancy, either … I just told my parents that we'd split up. But they insisted they were there for me. Always."

"What about Jacob? Have you seen him since?" Arthur asked, refusing to let go of Florence's shoulders. She appreciated his warmth.

"I didn't see Jacob, nor hear from him again apart from that note, until three weeks ago." Florence raised her head and breathed in deeply. "I was coming back from the supermarket. I was about to turn into my road, when I heard someone whistling from across the other side of the street … I could smell weed and knew it was Jacob. He, he said he would soon be taking what was *his*. He stamped out his joint and walked away down the street, whistling."

"Are you okay to go on?" Arthur asked.

"I have to." Florence looked up at Arthur.

"Take your time," Arthur said.

"A few months into my pregnancy, I started to get these strange dreams. They were mild, compared to what they are now. But this one night, after I saw Jacob again, I had the worst *ever* nightmare … I had woken up in my nightmare, but it was like I was paralysed. I was lying naked on some kind of blackened altar in the middle of a forest. A tall-masked figure stood over me, splashing blood onto my stomach and making symbols on me. I was pleading, begging for him to stop. I tried to scream, but I couldn't. And then Jacob appeared, standing over me, with that *grin* of his.

"I could hear chanting and see other people around me in a circle. A fire burnt brightly near to me. I could feel the heat from it. It was so real, so lucid. And then, then this masked figure pulled out a huge knife, and plunged it into my stomach. That's when I usually wake up. Since I last saw Jacob, I've been getting these same nightmares almost every night. Until now, but this time it was different … I've also seen your faces and this farm in a couple of different and nicer dreams." Florence tried to smile.

"Different this time, how?" Arthur asked.

"I could see my baby … ripped from my, my womb. The baby was alive but crying. This masked figure was holding up my baby whilst Jacob stood next to him, grinning. I could *feel* the pain." Florence looked down at her bump and cradled her unborn child. "*Please*, don't let them take my baby."

"How did you end up on my uncle's farm?" David asked.

"Perhaps we should give her some rest?" Arthur suggested.

"No, it's fine … you have to know. Time is of the essence."

The others looked at each other. They had since moved a little into the room, apart from Betty.

"A fair amount of it is all a blur … I lost time. I honestly don't know how much. I remember waking up one night in the early hours to the sound of a baby crying. I hadn't dreamt that night. I thought perhaps I was dreaming again. I could hear the baby's cries coming from our back garden … I put on my dressing gown and slowly made my way downstairs to the garden. I felt very cold.

"I didn't want to wake my parents. I opened the back door and the ground was covered in a white mist. I could still hear a baby's cry. It seemed to be coming from the other end of the garden. My feet burnt on the frozen ground. As I got closer to the cries, I could hear a whisper. I began to get anxious, and I felt like calling out. My belly started to ache, too … but before I knew it, I could feel myself begin to faint, and then everything went black."

Arthur insisted Florence took a break before she continued. Bob fetched her a glass of water. Betty continued to stand in the hallway without saying anything. John and David played with Benji for a few moments on the landing to break the tension, until she continued.

"I woke up every now and then and felt drowsy and disoriented. I could feel that my hands and feet were bound. I had no idea where I was or what was happening. I was alone and naked and kept falling in and out of consciousness … sometimes, I was wrapped in a black gown but my eyesight was blurry so it was never that clear. I had no idea what was happening."

Arthur insisted she drank some more water.

"One time, I could barely open my eyes at all. But I could hear a conversation briefly, about all of you … they were saying that those on the farm would soon perish. I don't remember it all."

"It's okay." Arthur had his arm around Florence again. She welcomed it.

"But … there was one night I woke up to an awful scream and chanting. I managed to stay awake a little and I'm sure I wasn't dreaming. I was in a cage, suspended several feet off the ground by a chain. I could see below me, some form of a black altar, and a lifeless, bloodied body draped over it. I assumed that it was the poor woman, who had screamed. The masked figure from my nightmares was standing over her, holding up a knife and cheering, with both arms aloft in the air. I'm fairly sure that there was another body on the ground at the other side of the altar; I could see a pair of legs.

"My eyesight was still blurry and I was dazed. I'm sorry … but there was also another huge, hooded figure near the altar. I don't know why, but it seemed and felt different to the rest of them … the room was lit by torches. I saw flames to my right. A red carpet? Groups of hooded figures stood in rows … I think there were others near to the altar in darker red robes. I passed out then, although I remember hearing some form of water dripping from above me. It felt like I was drugged."

"Interesting," Arthur said. "I'm so sorry, my dear, about what you've been through."

"What else happened? How did you manage to escape?" asked Bob.

"I … only have two recollections of what happened after that. I woke up once when the cage was on the ground. I saw this horrible gaunt face, looking at me, smiling horribly through the rusty bars of the cage. He had a lazy eye and a visible scar on his forehead. He was wearing a hat too, and some form of uniform."

John and David looked at one another and said simultaneously, *"Harold!"*

Florence looked at them confused but didn't say anything. She was exhausted mentally and physically.

"Yep. That sounds like the guy we encountered in the forest, all right," Gavin said.

Florence's throat was beginning to dry from all the talking, so she finished her glass of water. "The last thing I recall, was waking up again. I had no clothes. My eyes weren't fully returned to normal, but the cage door was open and there was a small child wearing some worn clothing. His expression was blank and he just ran off before I could say anything. That was it. The next I knew, I was outside. I soon recognised where I was. I was at Loch an Eilein, the small island and castle in the middle of the loch. I only knew it, because me and Jacob went for a picnic there when we first met, back when, when things were nice and, and normal." Florence bowed her head again.

"Interesting," Arthur said for the second time. He was in thought.

"Where is Loch an Eilein?" asked David.

"It's basically a castle ruin on a small island in the middle of a loch. It's very beautiful," Carl answered.

"Indeed, it is. Me and Betty have been there a few times ourselves over the years. A lovely place," Bob added.

"I could feel my baby kick. I was so relieved we were both still alive. But I had these markings and symbols over my belly and on my breasts. It looked like blood stains, so I washed them off in the loch."

"How did you end up here?" John asked, clearing his throat.

"This will sound silly, I know … but I heard a voice in my head. It was telling me to leave, and I could see an image of a farmhouse and all of you, so

I started walking. It didn't even feel as if it was me doing it. Sometimes, there was a golden figure in front of me, pointing the way. I sound crazy, right? It was all like a blur, still."

"*Seath Mór*. He was showing her the way. Guiding her," Arthur said.

"Well, he could have at least found her some clothes," John joked.

With the tension released a little, everyone laughed, including Florence.

"Seath who?" Florence asked confused.

"We'll explain another time, my love." Arthur smiled.

"The next thing I remember, I was sitting in your living room, with just a towel around me." Florence blushed.

"We should try to contact your family for you. And get you home before it gets too dark," Bob said. "Where do you live, sweetheart?"

Florence looked over at the bedroom window and had a worried look over her still dirty face. "I want to go home. B-but it will be dark soon. It's already clouded over. I don't want to drive through the forest when it's dark or not as light … it's bad enough during the day. What if I put my parents in danger?"

Arthur sighed. "I'm afraid Florence is right. It will get dark earlier tonight. If it was earlier in the day, perhaps, by all means. It may be too risky to even phone her parents."

"We could all go? Safety in numbers and all that. Take the shotguns, yeah?" John suggested.

Arthur sighed again. "In theory, it would make sense, John. But even though we are in the middle of the forest out here, I still believe we have the security of our surroundings. It would be safer here, tonight. We can get her back first thing tomorrow. We just need to be on alert in case anything happens."

"I guess you're the boss," John said a little sarcastically.

Arthur suggested Florence should rest up some more and try to sleep, even though she was frightened about having another nightmare. He had taken off his large silver cross, lifting it over his head and putting it around Florence's own neck. He told her it would help her. They then closed the door and made their way back downstairs.

Betty had remained in the hallway. Bob had to gently pull on her arm to lead her away. She ended up downstairs, sitting and staring blankly at the television.

"What do you think, Arthur?" Carl said, scratching the back of his head.

The rest gathered in the kitchen.

"I don't know. I believe that Seath Mór brought her to us. It's quite possible that the lair is near Loch an Eilein, or below it," Arthur answered, "and no longer underneath the mountains."

"Why would Seath Mór bring her to us? And do you mean underneath the water?" David asked.

"Seath Mór perhaps believes we are key to stopping all this and protecting Florence. As for the lair, Florence could hear dripping water, so perhaps, it's likely."

"How far is it from here? It seems strange nobody saw her on the way."

"It's a good few miles, David," Bob said. "Coming through all the trees in just bare feet would take a while. It's surprising she has no cuts or anything."

"Seath Mór was looking out for her, I am *certain* of that." Arthur gave his beard a stroke.

"What about this girl's parents?" a nervous Emily asked.

"They certainly need to know that their daughter has been found and is safe. Well, at least for now. But can *they* even be trusted? We don't know how deep this all goes. Who's involved and who isn't."

"Carl is right," replied Arthur.

"Well, what do we do?" Gavin asked.

"It's too late, now. But in the morning, I can take her home and try to explain things to her parents. I'm not sure about going to the police, but she needs to get away from here. It's too dangerous for her to be here," Carl said.

"We can sleep on it. The most important thing right now is that we stay together," Arthur said.

"Safety in numbers, eh?" John said again only half-serious. He wouldn't have felt safe had there been fifty more of them.

"Something like that," said Arthur.

"What about this young child that she saw?" Emily asked.

Arthur let out another sigh. "Famuli Cani's chances of having children are no doubt very slim, or they can no longer have children, period. This is due to their practice of the dark arts and black energy that flows through their veins. They perhaps bring children they already have, or take them from elsewhere, bringing them slowly into their sect. Though, they would have to be chosen specifically."

"These arseholes get sicker and more twisted, the more you hear about them." John looked with disgust and shook his head.

"It is possible that this young child opened up the cage and let her out. How she really got out of the lair, only she would know." Arthur considered.

They were alerted by a text from John's phone. He pulled it out of his pocket. "*Ha*! How's that for timing."

"Why, what's that?" David frowned.

"It's Annabel. She asked if I am free to meet up tomorrow. Typical. She wants to meet with all this shit going on and getting worse."

"Yeah. She has the day off tomorrow," Emily confirmed.

"I don't think that's for the best right now, John," Arthur said. "Plus, we can't risk getting anyone else involved."

"Oh, I know. I'll just tell her I'm busy on the farm. I'm not up for anything right now. Even though, we might all be dead soon."

# Chapter Sixty-Six

## 30th July, 2018

Everyone had slept upstairs but Gavin, Arthur and Carl each took shifts downstairs. Nothing happened throughout the night except that Carl had a strange dream. He could see himself, standing next to his car in the middle of the road in the forest. Some school children had walked across a zebra crossing, with a tall and slim lollipop man holding a yellow and red stop sign, with his back to Carl. A large truck was on the other side of the road opposite. He was then lying on a beach somewhere, enjoying the sun as it beat down on him. He laughed when telling the others as it seemed so random.

When everyone was up, Betty, who seemed her usual self for a change, had offered to cook breakfast. She was still wearing her agate necklace along with her crucifix. "Here you go, sweetheart," Betty said to Florence as she served up a second round of fry-up. "Get that down you. You need to eat plenty for your baby as well!"

"Thank you," Florence replied, still feeling awkward in a stranger's house, although they didn't really feel like strangers. It all felt very surreal. At least she hadn't had any nightmares last night. She had also showered and Emily had kindly lent her some of her looser clothes to wear.

"We need to get you back to your folks, Florence. They must be so worried," Carl said.

"Maybe we should *all* get out of here? Go somewhere else?" John suggested.

"I believe the rest of us need to see this through and put an end to it. But we can't risk Florence and the baby. They are a priority. We are a part of this now. I don't believe we can run away. It's fate," Arthur replied. "We have been chosen."

"Why is it fate? I mean, we aren't special. How can *we* stop a demon?" David countered.

"Some things are just meant to be. People are chosen whether they like it or not. It's their destiny. You chose to come up here and help your aunt and uncle, your family. If it wasn't already, it became your destiny. You too, John. You came to help your friend," Arthur tried to explain. He looked over at Betty who was attending to a frying pan.

Florence stopped eating and looked up from her plate, startled. "*Demon*? Wait ... I think I remember another victim. A huge, cloaked figure was swerving around these robed people. All I could see, was its cloak. There was a naked body stretched out on that altar. It was a man. He was begging for help. Crying out. He, he said he had two daughters." Florence could feel her eyes tear up. "That poor man ... that could be me. That's all I can remember."

Arthur, who was seated next to her, held her hand. She sensed he had a warm soul, that he was a genuine, good-hearted man. They were all good people. She felt it; their love and bond for each other.

"That's terrible," Emily said, who had hardly touched her breakfast.

"There might be something else, too."

"What is it, Florence?" Arthur asked.

"I remember some people near to me discussing something about *The Big One* coming."

"The Big One?" Bob asked.

"Yes. Oh, wait ... it's coming to me now. One of them spoke about having sacrifices to look forward to and how it was *arousing* him. He said he could barely contain his excitement for it. Another agreed and said the word 'Lammas,' I think?"

"Lammas Day," Arthur said dejectedly. "Possibly the worst day of the Satanic calendar. It's tomorrow night, 1st of August."

"I think one of them was called Anthony, although I doubt that helps." Florence looked down at her near empty plate.

"We've met him ... I bet that was the same guy who weirdly lied about going to a wedding, the one whose wife, Melissa, freaked Em out at the disco that night," David said.

"I remember," Emily added, clearly remembering Melissa. It seemed so long ago now. She'd been so happy to meet David.

*"Sick bastard,"* John hissed, throwing a small piece of toast back onto his plate.

*****

The group chatted amongst themselves, whilst Carl and Arthur spoke outside in the back garden in the warm and welcoming sunshine.

John started to take a liking to Florence. In spite of everything that had happened, he still managed to make her laugh. She seemed to like him too, or he hoped so. She let them feel her baby kick. She must be close to giving birth any day now. You could see its tiny feet pushing up against Florence's stomach which made them all laugh and smile.

"Okay," Carl said as he and Arthur returned. "I'm going to take Florence home to her folks and to explain things to them."

"Is that a good idea, though?" Florence asked. "I don't want to endanger my parents' lives. But I guess I'm putting your lives at risk further, being here."

"We believe it's the only sensible option," Arthur said. "They want you and your baby for Lammas Day." Arthur tried to play it down; he didn't want to use the term 'sacrifice' to Florence.

"M-maybe I should disappear by myself, so they don't find me or my baby."

"You may be safer once you've had your baby," Arthur said, although he wasn't sure if that was true.

"No. You must *not* be alone," Carl said. "That is *not* an option. It would probably be best if you and your folks left together."

"I do know a place not too far away that might be safe, but I believe it would be safer the further away you are," Arthur added.

"When do we leave?" Florence wasn't sure in her heart that leaving them was the right thing to do. She felt a connection with them.

"The sooner the better." Carl smiled.

"I'll stay here. I need to do a few things and it's best I stay with the rest of you," said Arthur.

"But you said that it was best if we all stayed together?" John pointed out. "We could all go together, in separate cars, if need be?"

"Carl will be fine. It's daylight, and hopefully others will be about," Arthur said, trying to reason.

"But at least one of us should go with them … I'll go," John said emphatically.

"I'll be fine, John." Carl smiled. "They won't harm Florence or the baby until Lammas Day. She still has a chance until then."

"It's still too dangerous for you both to go alone. How do you know something won't happen?" John said worriedly.

Carl looked at Arthur, then back again. "I didn't mention it before. I wanted to tell Arthur first. But apart from my dream last night, before waking, I heard a voice claiming to be Seath Mór. He advised me that we would be safe, and that we had to take Florence this morning."

"What?" John frowned. "But what about the rest of us? What if they track Florence and her parents down?"

"If we can find a way to defeat them, then that won't be a possibility," Arthur said strongly. "But she needs to get as far as possible away until this is all over."

"But we still don't even know where their lair is?" John replied.

Florence looked at them. "I am here, guys." She tried to smile.

"Sorry, Florence," Carl said. "We didn't mean to speak like you weren't here."

"Carl is right, though. I don't want to put you guys at risk any more than I already have. We should get going … I guess this is it. Thank you for looking after me. You are all such good people. And thank you, Emily, for lending me your clothes. I'll be sure to give them back to you, after … I mean, if I see you again."

"Aw, come here," Emily said, offering her hands. "You can keep them."

"Thank you," Florence replied, holding Emily's hands.

They embraced and the others put their hands on their shoulders. They certainly felt a strength together.

Arthur and Carl then hugged and Arthur gave Carl an orange crystal. He said it would help 'protect' them further.

John wondered what the deal was with Arthur and these crystals.

"Oh," said Arthur. "Please, take this!" He removed the large silver cross Florence had returned back to him this morning.

"Are you sure? But it's yours."

"It's fine. It will help you." Arthur smiled.

Florence, teary eyed, took the heavy cross from Arthur. "Thank you."

Arthur cupped it firmly in her hands and wished her well.

As Florence opened the passenger side to Carl's door and was about to get in, she had another memory and then froze.

"What is it?" Carl asked her.

"I, I, just remembered something else." She walked back over to Arthur.

"What is it?" Arthur's brows lowered.

"There was someone else. A young man, who arrived not long after I escaped. I didn't see his face. He was curled up in another suspended cage. He was whimpering. I wish I could have done something to help him."

The others looked at one another. The poor guy. They wondered who it could have been.

"It's not your fault. There is nothing you could have done," Arthur said, reassuring her. "You got out. That's all that matters right now."

Florence got in the car and waved as they drove off. Carl gave a beep on the horn as the rest of them waved them off.

*****

"We still should have gone with them," John said. "At least *one* of us."

"Possibly," David replied.

They were standing near the empty pens giving Benji some exercise.

Carl and Florence had been gone for well over two hours. They would be with her parents by now. They wondered how Carl would explain it all to them.

"I wonder who the other poor guy was in the cage?" John said.

David shook his head. "Who knows? The chances are we'll never find out. They're possibly dead by now ... Arthur's adamant that we're the ones to bring down this sect, but how?"

"I know. Scares the shit out of me," John said.

"Me too."

"What do you think he's up to?" John thumbed behind his shoulder, to where Arthur was now standing, about a hundred feet away.

David turned his head. "No idea."

Arthur walked all the way up to the forest line. He was trying to reach out to Seath Mór, *demanding* he help them. Seath Mór had helped him get the dagger from St Kilda and brought the vulnerable Florence to them. Now, he needed to know where this secret and unholy sanctuary of Famuli Cani was. He too, also wondered who the other poor soul was, who was still encaged where Florence had been held. There might be others as well.

Arthur pulled out a small polythene bag that held some strange looking pink and white powder. He sprinkled it onto the dried ground and used his finger to make four small, single symbols in front of him. Resting on his aching knees, he pulled out the dagger and sprinkled what was left of the mysterious powder onto it. He muttered a few unclear words as he placed the dagger to his forehead closing his eyes. Then, he placed the dagger to the ground over the symbols. With his eyes still closed, he started muttering some more, deeply focused. He started to meditate, looking for answers.

David and John had walked up after him, keeping their distance.

"What *is* he doing?" John asked. "He certainly does some strange things."

"I have no idea," David replied. He scratched his left cheek.

Benji sat looking up at David, waiting for him to throw a stick for him to fetch.

"Strange man. Very strange man," said John.

"That's a bit harsh, mate. I'm sure he's doing his best to help us."

"Oh, don't get me wrong," John replied. "I genuinely like the old boy. I really do. It's just hard to understand his methods."

"I know what you mean."

David dropped a stick for Benji to chew on instead, whilst they continued to watch Arthur.

Arthur still had his eyes closed. A strong breeze had come up, rustling the trees a few feet away from him. It blew away most of the powdered dust, dispersing it into thin air. Still on his knees, he felt a warm presence blow against his face. He smiled faintly, his hair blowing. He remained that way for another few minutes and then slowly opened his eyes. The breeze came to an instant halt. Still breathing slowly and relaxed, he got to his feet and exhaled. He had all he needed to know.

David and John were still watching, when Arthur got to his feet and turned around, placing the now warm dagger back into his jacket pocket. For once, he was wearing a different jacket for a change, although it was the same style, but brown in colour. He noticed them and casually walked towards them, brushing a few strands of hair back with his hand.

"Erm. Everything okay?" asked David.

"We need to go inside and talk." Arthur placed a hand on David's shoulder and walked past them, back down to the farmhouse.

Arthur still felt uncomfortable when Betty was with them, so he asked her if she wouldn't mind leaving them alone for a little while. Arthur explained how he had contacted the spirit of Seath Mór, using the dagger as a conduit.

"What did you see?" Gavin asked.

"Similar things as before. Awful things. But this time, I could see Seath Mór himself, stab Canus all those centuries ago. I could feel its pain, as the dagger plunged right through its evil heart. I could also see the top of Ben Macdui, where the acolytes first summoned it all those centuries ago, and the second time round."

"Was that it?"

"No, Bob. I know where their lair is."

The others could feel a chill run through them.

"Where is it?" David asked.

"As I suspected from what Florence told us. It's underneath Loch an Eilein."

"How do you get to somewhere underneath the water?" John asked.

"There's a secret passageway, not too far from the loch. It's inside a tree."

"What?" John grimaced. "In a *tree*?"

"Yeah, how does that work?" David queried.

"There's an opening that leads down below, going underneath the loch," Arthur explained. "It's a different place from all those centuries ago, where Famuli Cani were first defeated."

"So, do we just go there and kill them? Like shall we go now?" John said sarcastically.

Arthur smiled. "Not quite. I believe we will be shown the way, when the time comes. We will have to wait for Carl to return. I thought he would have called by now, but perhaps there's a problem with the phones still. However, there is one other thing."

"Which is?" asked Gavin.

"I now know for sure how Canus returned, The Grey One. The dagger indeed, wasn't enough to kill Canus fully. It was sent back to the top of Ben Macdui, where it became weakened and dormant throughout the centuries, fading in and out of existence, and like an apparition at times. This explains the appearances down the years. Then *they* summoned it again."

"Why wasn't the dagger enough? Will it work this time around?" Bob questioned.

"To kill and destroy Canus for *good*, it needs to be stabbed through the heart. The same as before. Only *now*, the dagger is much more powerful."

"More powerful, how?" Emily asked softly.

"More positive energy and magic is bound to it. Seath Mór still wasn't sure if Canus was destroyed for good, after the first battle towards the end of the 14$^{th}$ Century."

"So, they made sure that the dagger was more powerful, just in case? Why didn't they make it more powerful to start with? Who made it? John asked.

"Before Seath Mór died, he had a vision. He saw the return of Famuli Cani and Canus, which confirmed his initial doubts about whether it was fully destroyed. Even though it has been centuries, it explains why his own spirit has never been fully rested."

"And he then made sure that the dagger was more powerful?" David asked.

"That is correct. They obviously believed that it was enough, initially. But they made certain after Seath Mór's death, which is why the dagger was buried, and then moved to St Kilda all those centuries later, as a more secure measure. As for who made this dagger and gave it its powers? I don't know. A special swordsmith, most likely. Then, it would be blessed by a priest, and given to a spellcaster, no doubt. It's quite possible too, that the plaque we found, also had mercury put into it. To make it more hidden."

"You can perform spells too, then?" Emily asked intrigued.

Arthur smiled. "Yes, and I studied crystals and gemstones — gemmology and crystallography. It's vital in my line of work."

"I guess that explains a lot," John replied.

"Whoever gave the dagger its magical powers, no doubt gave Seath Mór other tools to help him defeat Canus. Possibly, something to turn the demon into its physical form, in order to try to kill it. Even back then, I could see it wearing a cloak."

"At least if we do 'kill it,' it might be for good, then?" David asked.

Arthur gave a slight nod, stroking his beard.

"Think you're jumping the gun a bit there, mate. That's assuming we get a chance, or even *close* enough," John replied.

"I believe we will in time. We *will* get a chance. Seath Mór and God will guide us," Arthur affirmed. "I'm going to phone Carl, if you'll excuse me."

"He might even be on his way back now," David said. "Christ knows what Florrie's folks thought. Speaking of which, I'll try ringing mine later to see how they're getting on."

"Yeah," John said. "I'm going to phone my old man as well. It's been almost a week. It might be the last time I get to speak to him."

Gavin got up and arched his back. It was the first time in a while that he wasn't wearing his flat cap. "I'll go make us all a brew."

*****

The time was approaching six in the evening. There was still no word from Carl, although the phones were working and static free. The group started to feel more than anxious and worried.

Although Arthur couldn't reach Carl, David had reached his parents without any issue. David half-joked to the others about it being 'all right for some,' after chatting to his parents, who were having such a great time on holiday. John called his dad too and Bob even made some calls. But no one could reach Carl. The calls went through to Carl's voicemail greeting. The phones were now fine, it seemed.

"I'll try again in a bit," Arthur said. "Just as long as he's back before nightfall."

A brief topic of discussion followed about cows; Bob and Betty, along with

Gavin, didn't believe in artificial insemination. They referred to it as the *rape rack*. They then spoke about the animals down in Carlisle.

When Arthur was about to phone Carl again, his phone rang. "It's Carl!" Arthur sounded cheerful. "*Carl*! We've all been worried. Where are you? Are you on your way back?"

There was a pause and a crackle over the phone call. Arthur spoke again. Still nothing.

But then, a voice spoke. "Hello, *Arthur*." The voice was cold and sharp and emphasised his name in a way that shook Arthur.

"Who is this? Where's Carl?"

Everyone could hear this evil, twisted laugh over the phone. There was then a scraping like sound on the wall. They watched as the wooden crucifix began to shake. Before turning upside down.

"Th-that cross!" Emily said frightened.

"Turn on the news," the voice said.

Laughing again, the phone call came to an abrupt end, but not before giving Arthur an electric shock up his arm to his shoulder. He dropped the phone on the carpet and cried out in pain.

"Who was that?" Emily held David tighter.

"They ... they want us to turn the news on." Arthur winced and held his arm as he picked up his phone. It was cold to the touch.

Without hesitation, Bob rushed over to the television and switched on the news. A female presenter was reading the headlines.

"... and a man has been killed in a collision earlier today in Rothiemurchus Forest, when his car veered over to the wrong side of the road and hit an oncoming truck. The car driver was killed instantly."

No one said anything. They stared at the television, which briefly showed the smashed up red Audi and a covered-up body with a black sheet over it.

John and David both looked across at Arthur who was standing there blank-faced. Nobody could find any words.

Finally, Arthur spoke. "P-please. No one say anything. Let me listen."

They waited to hear more details on the crash. The driver hadn't been identified and the details were sketchy. The truck driver, naturally distraught, was interviewed.

It had happened sometime this morning; the red car just came racing down the other side of the road and suddenly steered into the truck driver. There was nothing he could do. The front of the truck was shown and it had a fair amount of damage to it, but not as bad as the car, which was a complete write-off. The truck driver said he would never forget the man's face, who looked, "terrified beyond belief," just moments before they crashed head on.

Arthur didn't say anything. He walked over and switched off the television. He then slowly sat down, his arm still aching.

"Is … is he really *dead*?" Emily asked. She hadn't really known Carl, but was devastated. They all were. None of them noticed Betty sitting with a grin on her face.

"Perhaps, they're mistaken," Bob said sounding subdued. "Maybe it *wasn't* his car. Or maybe, he's still alive?" First Angus and now Carl. Bob was holding out with as much hope as possible.

"He's … he's gone." Arthur swallowed and bowed his head. He had come quite close to Carl during all of this. He had lost a friend. "I … I can feel it. It was his car. That's why that voice told us to turn on the news."

*"What about Florrie?"* John suddenly shouted.

"Famuli Cani have her now. They caused this. It was on the way there, not on the way back. Carl wouldn't have made it out of the forest to Florence's parents.'" Arthur clenched both his fists in a silent anger. "They must have tricked Carl before he woke up. Making out that it was Seath Mór saying it was safe for them … I, I should have known."

David held Emily as she started to tear up.

"Such terrible news. Oh well, I'll go and make us another nice brew," Betty said in an uncannily cheery way, considering the dreadful circumstances.

"What the …" John commented.

Everyone watched her eery movements as she got up and left the room.

"I'm sorry, but I need to be by myself for a little while. May I take your car, Bob? I'll be back shortly."

Bob frowned. "Erm. I guess. Here." Bob took out the keys to his Land Rover.

Arthur unclenched his fists and took the keys. Picking up his satchel, he then left by the front door. This news had hit him like a brick wall.

"*Wait*? What about Florrie? What happened to her? Why wasn't she in the car? What about us all staying together — safety in numbers and all that?" John called out.

Arthur, didn't answer.

*****

By the time Arthur had been gone for three hours, the others also became concerned that John had been right and they should all have stayed together.

Not only were they worried about Arthur, but they were unsure what they would do next, if Arthur wasn't there to guide them. He hadn't answered his phone since he walked out on the group.

"I still can't believe Carl's gone," said David as they all waited in the living room for Arthur to return.

Betty had yet again mentioned of another headache and went up to bed early.

"I *knew* we should have gone together," John barked.

"But maybe we'd all be dead by now if we had?" Bob said.

"Well, we probably will be, soon," John replied.

"Don't say that, John," Emily said softly.

"I wonder where Arthur's got to?" David shook his head.

"Probably out casting some *shitty* spells or laying more of those salt crystals. They didn't help Carl and Florrie," John said angrily.

"Poor Florrie. I hope she escaped," Emily said.

"Maybe they're trying to trick us?" Bob suggested.

"No, I don't think so, boss. Carl's gone. I need a drink." Gavin got up and poured a Tomatin whisky. It seemed such a long time since Bob had brought it home. Everyone accepted his offer of a drink, even Emily, who usually hated the taste of whisky.

"Maybe we should keep drinking and get completely and utterly wasted," John said, necking his drink and burning his throat.

"I know you're angry, John, but we need to keep our heads clear," Bob replied, sipping his whisky.

"My uncle's right, mate. We mustn't get drunk. We can't help anyone then."

# Chapter Sixty-Seven

## 30th July, 2018

Arthur still hadn't returned by nightfall and there was a steady downpour now, so it was strange that he hadn't returned. Everyone had gone to their bedrooms, except Bob and Gavin, but they were unlikely to sleep. Carl was gone and there was a sense of helplessness and melancholy in the house.

David and Emily were on their bed together and John and Benji were lying on the floor.

"I liked Carl," John said. "He was a good guy."

"We all did, mate," David said, running his fingers through Emily's hair.

"Maybe we should just fuck off? Go abroad and never come back. We could all just *go*. And what is it with your aunt? She's been like this for weeks, now. She seriously scares the shit out of me, mate." John's head hurt as he sat up.

"She's not right, that's for sure. Even if we left, they may find us wherever we go. I think it's too late. We need to see this through, now. It's like I *can't* leave. Or *we* can't. It's like we are supposed to be here. Don't you feel it?"

"You're not buying into this being our destiny and fate crap too, are you? I think Arthur's done a runner. Typical, leaving us all here to get killed."

"No, no. I don't believe he would do that. Don't you feel the same — that we *should* be here?"

"Maybe. I don't know. *Jesus*. At least Granty isn't up here, anyway."

"That's true."

"I can't help thinking of Florrie as well. She's such a sweet girl," Emily said, moving closer to David.

They then heard a car pull up outside and a raised voice from downstairs.

"That sounds like Arthur!" David said.

They rushed downstairs just as Gavin came out of the bathroom.

*"They're coming!"* Arthur blurted out again, pointing outside.

*"Who?"* Bob asked nervously. "Where did you go? We've been *worried* for hours!" Bob clutched his shotgun, which he'd kept close to him all night.

"I needed some time. I'm sorry. It won't happen again but listen to me. They're coming. *Famuli Cani*!"

*"What?"* David said, his pulse starting to race.

Was this it? Were they all about to die?

*"Come and see!"* Arthur raced up into David's room, almost tripping over Benji.

They looked out through the rain-smudged window. They could see a glow of several fire-lit torches making their way through the edge of the forest, heading in their direction.

John opened the window and they could hear chanting getting nearer and nearer.

*"Oh my God. David!"* Emily started to cry as she clutched David, almost winding him.

"Why are they coming, Arthur? What are we going to do?" David tried his best to remain calm.

"Bob, go wake Betty! We need to get out of here, *now*. While we still can," Gavin said frantically. "I'll grab my shotgun from downstairs."

"Yes, we need to go!" Arthur tried to remain calm, but he was petrified as well.

As they hurried out of the room past the top of the stairs to fetch Betty, they heard a whistle from downstairs. They stopped abruptly and looked down the stairwell.

Jack was standing in the hallway near the open front door. The smell of the joint he was smoking reached them at the top of the staircase.

"*J-Jack*! Wh … what are you doing here?" Bob asked, frowning. His heart was beating through his chest. "You need to get out of here. They're *coming*!"

Jack didn't say anything but continued to watch them with a disturbing gaze. His hair was drenched as were his jeans and black T-shirt. He took in a few last puffs of his joint, before dropping the butt on the wooden floor and stamping it out, lowering his head.

Bob knew something wasn't right. "*Jack*? What are you doing here?" he asked again.

*"He's fucking one of them!"* John shouted.

"What?" Bob looked at John in dismay and then back down to Jack.

Jack started to laugh.

*"David!"* Emily grasped David. "What's happening?"

Slowly raising his head, Jack started to applaud, slowly, mockingly. "Good call, *John-Boy*!" Jack no longer had a Scottish accent in his voice. He sounded strange and different.

"Wh-who are you?" Bob asked, his mouth becoming dry. He started to sweat. "Your, your *voice*!"

Jack started to laugh again, but then switched to become deadly serious. "I can speak like this, if ye want?" he mocked to Bob.

"Boss, we need to *go*!" Gavin said.

"I don't think so," Jack said. *"I fucking hated speaking in that Scottish accent!"* he spat.

The chanting was loud now. *They* were much closer.

*"Fucking shoot him, Bob!"* John cried out.

"*What*? Are you mad?" Bob replied.

"Just you *fucking* try it," Jack said. His eyes became more sinister and piercing.

"What do you want?" David asked.

"It's not just what I want. But rather, *we*, and what *it* wants."

"He's referring to Canus," Arthur said.

Jack clapped again at Arthur's comment. "I'd like for you all to come outside," he said almost politely. "Please, come."

The chanting sounded as though they had reached the farmhouse now.

Jack quickly pulled out a revolver from the back of his jeans and aimed it up at the group. "I *won't* ask a second time." Jack's tone had turned dark again and there was pure evil behind the young man's eyes. This wasn't the Jack they had enjoyed being with on the farm.

"J-Jack. Where did you get that gun from?" Bob said saddened.

The group slowly made their way downstairs. Bob had his shotgun hung over his shoulder. He didn't even think of removing it. He was in total shock. Jack, still aiming the gun, waited for them to walk out of the front door before following them into the rain. Jack asked them to stand in the middle of the lawn and he did the same, all the time keeping the gun raised. The rain drenched them as the chanting grew louder and closer. They could see the glow of torches from the side of the house approaching, close to where Arthur had parked the Land Rover.

Bob started to remove the shotgun from his shoulder.

Jack noticed and aimed the gun more at Bob. "Ah-ah, Bobby … don't be stupid. Actually, toss the gun over there. Like you'd have the *guts* to use it, anyway." Jack laughed.

Bob slowly removed the gun from his shoulder and threw it a few feet away.

The chanting came to an abrupt, eery halt. The figures were wearing black, hooded robes, with their faces only slightly visible from the light of their torches. There were six of them. Seven, if you included Jack. Despite the rain, the torches continued to burn, occasionally flickering and dimming. Jack tilted his head back, letting the rain hit his already soaked face and hair as the bare-foot figures spread out and encircled them on the sodden lawn. Jack then put the revolver back behind his jeans.

"What are you going to do to us?" Bob asked, his stomach churning.

Jack could hear Bob's stomach. "Don't shit yourself now, Bobby. Angus already did that." He started to laugh and the hooded figures echoed his laughter.

"Y-*you* killed Angus?" Gavin asked shocked.

"I like to think, that I played a part," Jack replied sarcastically. He seemed proud of himself. "I actually helped string the old bastard up. Old *Ginge*, begged for his life as we dragged him from his crappy car." Jack chuckled. "The bloke smelt like he shat himself when he was dangling there, begging and gasping for breath."

"But why*?* What did Angus ever do to you?" Bob felt a few tears stream down his face.

"*Aww*. Don't cry, Bob," Jack mocked.

"How could you do that? He was a *good* man," Gavin said, his anger rising.

"Well, they usually are." Jack laughed. "That's the *fun* of it!"

*"Why?"* Bob wiped tears from his cheek with his cuff.

*"Because the bastard blabbed. That's why. He went to the police. He could have jeopardised our plans!"* Jack hissed, eyes wide. "Good job they're on our side." Jack grinned. "Mainly, I knew you were friends with him, so we took pleasure in knowing you'd suffer if he died."

"You didn't have to kill him … What kind of *sick* bastards, are you?" John asked, rage building up in him.

Jack approached John. "*Ha*! I think you know, by now." Jack winked.

"But … I gave you a job. We were *good* to you."

"Well, Bobby … we all still work and need the money." Jack laughed again. "I was even the one who found your farm up here. And before you ask, yes. I *did* help slaughter your animals. But I can't take all the credit for that. And Daisy, was it? Yes, yes that was me who killed your *shitty*, little cat and hung it on your washing line. The way she screeched out in pain, as I skinned her. *Beautiful.* I had considered letting it live but she bit me one day, so I thought, nah, fuck it. My Master, was proud of me."

*"You sick little bastard!"* Bob cried.

David hated seeing his uncle like this. He wanted to lunge at Jack but it was too risky. The other figures might be armed.

"Whatcha going to do? *Shoot* me? I *dare* you! Pick up that gun," goaded Jack. "*Ha*! I didn't think so. And yes, I also helped sacrifice your cow and the two-headed calf." Jack seemed proud of his actions, smugly boasting of them. "My mum's fall was an act. Once Dippy Derek had passed out and big Gav ran off in the direction of those screams, we all got to work. Not that that idiot Derek would have done anything to stop us. But we wanted it to be a surprise for you all. And we knew Derek would feel guilty and how upset he'd be." Jack laughed again. He wasn't normal.

"What about Florrie? Where is she? And that other sick bastard, Jacob?" John asked. "Wait a minute … *you're* Jacob, aren't you?" John suddenly pieced it together; the weed smoking and how Jack had always played down things that happened to them on the farm.

Jack clapped. "Right again, *John-Boy*." He laughed. "You're the smart one, all right. Though, not *that* smart to have not figured things out sooner. I was going to come for my girl and child, but you played straight into our hands, when you let Florrie go with that *dumbass*, Carl."

*"Don't call him that!"* Arthur yelled.

"Or *what*, old man? Get a haircut!" Jack was enjoying this. It was so beautifully satisfying to him. He had been waiting for this moment. "Florrie, is back where she belongs. *And* my child. We have great plans for her tomorrow night. And for all of you. Well, after midnight. Plus, there's a surprise in it for you two, especially." Jack flicked his eyebrows up and down, looking at John and David in the low light. "Florrie should never have escaped. Christ knows how she made it way out here to you. She'll be punished further for opening her mouth to you. As for the little *shit* that opened her cage up, let's just say, they got what they deserved."

"What did you do to Carl?" Arthur asked, tightening his fists again.

"Maybe Carl isn't dead," Jack teased.

"What?" Arthur asked, hoping. His fine white hair fell in rats' tails down his face in the persistent rain.

Jack whistled and a robed figure came forward to join him in the centre.

Jack temporarily took the torch from the figure who slowly pulled back his hood and revealed his face. "Here he is!" Jack grinned wickedly.

Arthur looked at the person he thought was his friend and then keeled over and threw up. The unhooded face was indeed Carl's but it wasn't him. His face had been sliced off and used as a mask, still fresh and bloody.

John lunged at Jack. *"You sick FUCKS!"*

But the figure wearing Carl's face swung a right arm at John, catching him perfectly in his stomach, winding him to the ground. John gasped for air as David went to help him up.

Jack laughed. "If I could, I'd *fucking* kill you all now. I'd rip your hearts out. I would have done it a *long* time ago. Even before you pair of idiots came up here. It was pretty damn funny, watching Carl speed off down the road without any control. Oh, and I think you've met Anthony?"

The masked figure tore off Carl's face and tossed it to the ground like a piece of garbage.

"You, you *bastard*!" John struggled to say, still bent over trying to get air back into his lungs.

"Hello again, gentleman!" Anthony said, smiling. Carl's blood still stained his face.

"How did the wedding go, you lying piece of shit," John struggled to say.

"It went great! Thanks for asking," Anthony replied sarcastically and began to laugh along with Jack.

David pulled John back a step, hoping to calm him down. He respected John for lunging at Jack, but knew they were in a weak position to attack. "But why, why *us*? What did we do to you? We did *nothing* to you."

"I think I'm almost done talking. But I'll answer your question to that, Dave-O." Jack cleared his throat. "You didn't heed the warnings. Even our *Master* didn't stop you. We only managed to stop that other weakling friend of yours, who pissed himself." Jack laughed and Anthony smiled.

"That thing you call a Master had already been in my flat before I knew anything about all of this. Why not just kill us then and there?" David asked.

"Oh, David … we didn't want you up here, getting involved in our business and affairs. But our Master, Canus, *The Great Grey One*, admired your courage. You should be honoured that Canus chose you like that. It was like a test to your resolve. Canus liked something about you. Your bond, your friendship, your love for each other. Your goodness. It was like a challenge to us, although it angered us. You were hard to break. No matter what we did, you insisted on coming up here and refused to leave. But for that, the punishment will be even *greater*. And sweeter. Your courage will ultimately be your downfall and your sacrifices will be more powerful and stronger to us."

"I'm aroused even thinking about it," Anthony added and then laughed.

"As it turns out, we're glad that you did come, as contradictory as it may sound. After that failed fishing trip, we let you live. We wanted to see how things would play out. Let things develop. Proving your worth. The more courage and resilience you showed, the better for *us*. Oh, and not to mention you brought poor little Emily into it all. *Tut-tut*, David. How careless of you." Jack laughed some more. "Either way, we've saved you for the special occasion. *All* of you! The rewards will be *huge*."

"Oh, yes," Anthony said, still smiling.

"Killing, is the easy part. We could have done that, *anytime*. We *enjoyed* watching you suffer. We like to *savour* the moment, fully. Your aunt and uncle were already on our list to fall at Lammas Day. I have to hand it to you. You are brave. Unlike that other wimp friend of yours, back home." Jack folded his arms.

"You really are a bunch of sick individuals," David said.

"Thank you." Jack bowed sarcastically to him.

"And what of our dreams?" David wanted to know.

"We wanted you to suffer even more. You subconsciously blocked many of them out without even knowing. You're strong, David. And of course, that old bastard put down salt crystals and started using his spells." Jack gestured towards Arthur.

John looked at Arthur. He felt guilty for having doubted him. Arthur looked very old and sad now that Carl was dead and they all seemed defeated. John wished he hadn't been so hard on him.

"And what about my wife, Jack? What did you people *do* to her? She hasn't been herself for weeks, now," Bob demanded.

"She is under the influence of Canus, who wanted her to suffer more after the slaughter of your animals. We also used your bitch of a wife to spy on you, but the old bat seems to have lost her mind due to it. Those damn salt crystals and other methods used weakened our Master's control. But we are gaining *more* power. Rest assured; she *will* get her comeuppance!"

*"You leave my wife alone. You hear me!"*

"Ooooh, such anger, Robert." Jack beamed and teased. "I *like* that …" His eyes grew large.

David had to hold his uncle back.

"And speak of the bitch, here she is." Jack pointed to the front door.

"Do we have guests?" Betty said, standing at the door in her nightie.

Jack laughed. "What a stupid old cow!"

"J-just go back in doors, love," Bob called over.

Betty didn't answer.

"Derek … he isn't part of all this, then?" David asked.

"Who would want that thick shit to join them?" Jack answered.

"What's the story with that *freak*, Harold?" John asked, his stomach better.

"I think we're done. Enough talk. Oh, and I believe this is yours." Jack pulled out a bent silver cross from the back of his jeans and tossed it at Arthur's feet.

Arthur bent down to pick it up. "M-my cross."

"It didn't help Florrie. And it *sure* as hell won't help you," Jack sniped. He slapped his forehead. "How could I forget. Another thing. I'm going to need that dagger that you recovered from St Kilda, Arthur. We've been searching for it for years. It's great, that you managed to find it for us. Another reason we let things play out … As if you could ever have stopped us and Canus. But I admire your ignorance. Pathetic."

"I, I don't have it," Arthur replied anxiously.

"I don't have time for this, you old fool. Tell me where it is!" Jack's eyes glared at Arthur in the rain. He waited only a moment and continued. "Fine. We'll do it your way." Jack gestured towards Anthony.

Anthony stepped forward and yanked Emily away, throwing her to the ground at Jack's feet.

*"Emily!"* David reached for her.

Jack had pulled a red penknife from his pocket and held it to Emily's throat. "I will ask you *one* more time. *Where* is the dagger? I'm allowed to take one life tonight, if need be, so it really doesn't bother me."

Emily began to sob. *"Please … "* She was trembling in fear.

Jack pulled at Emily's hair so that her head twisted to the side, facing upwards, exposing her neck more.

"*Please*, Jack. Not her," David begged. "Arthur, *tell* him where the dagger is! *Please*!" David's eyes filled.

At that moment, Bob leapt for his shotgun on the wet grass. He grabbed it in time just before a robed figure did, by pulling on the strap. He aimed at them as they retreated and then took aim towards Jack.

Jack laughed at Bob. "If you shoot me, you'll also kill Emily … Even if you do kill me, you are outnumbered. You only have one round in that gun. I also have my revolver." Jack pushed the penknife into Emily's throat firmly. He wanted to hurt her, to hurt David.

*"Tell him, Arthur! Where is the dagger?"* David shouted desperately.

"I hid it. Further down the dirt track. I ... I panicked, when I saw you coming through the forest." Arthur dropped his head.

Jack laughed. "Careless fool. I did see you in the Land Rover ... Anthony, take another with you. Get him to show you where he hid it. I'll stay here with the others." Jack kept the knife at Emily's throat. "Just in case the old bastard tries anything, take my gun. And if anything happens to me or the others, feel free to use the revolver. Don't kill. Just maim them." Jack grinned.

Anthony nodded and took the small revolver out of Jack's jeans.

The others watched as Arthur lead Anthony and another hooded figure off down the hard dirt track.

The heavy rained continued but the group weren't concerned anymore about the cold and wet. They were frightened for Emily's life.

"You aren't going to shoot at us, Bob. But I'll let you have the satisfaction of aiming that shotgun at me, until they arrive back with the dagger. Then you *will* drop it again ... and you better hope they bring that dagger back, or I'm going to seriously enjoy slitting open her *pretty* little throat."

"Well, we're all going to die anyway tomorrow, aren't we, Jack? Or after midnight," John replied, fully recovered from his blow.

Jack smiled. "Well, that's true. But at least you'll have some more time with each other before the *big* night."

David looked at poor Emily's face. She was soaked through. He mouthed the words *I love you,* to her. She didn't say it back as Jack's other slippery hand was now pushing her chin up. She just tried to smile lovingly back, praying to God inside.

Anthony walked behind Arthur with the revolver pointing towards his back. The other hooded figure was in front. None of the three said a word.

"It's just up here." Arthur pointed to a small soft mound of dirt at the edge of the forest. The mud was soft and wet. He was praying to himself. "It's here." Arthur looked down.

*"Get it!"* a sharp and disturbing voice from the other hooded figure commanded.

Arthur's pulse increased as he knelt down and started scooping the mud up with his hands, trying to ignore the pain in his old knees. He could just about see from the torch light as he felt for what he had buried earlier; an old wooden box.

"Give it to me," Anthony snapped as Arthur removed the box from the ground.

Arthur handed over the box and hoped that Anthony would open it.

"You ... you just push the buttons on the sides there and it opens." Arthur stepped back.

*"Silence!"* Anthony ordered. He pushed the buttons and his colleague stepped forwards to see the box.

As the box clicked opened, a green and purple puff of smoke sprayed up into their faces, leaving them gasping for breath and clutching at their throats.

Anthony dropped the gun. *"You ... you bastard!"* Anthony collapsed to the floor unconscious and his acolyte friend soon followed.

*Fools.* Arthur bent down and picked up the revolver. On his way back after disappearing earlier, he could sense some of Famuli Cani were coming even before hearing and seeing them. He knew that if they came, they would no doubt ask him for the dagger. That was when he pulled over and set his trap, in case the situation needed it. He tapped on his jacket pocket to reassure himself the dagger was where he'd kept it all along. He then heard some shouting and a gunshot. He headed back to the others as fast as he could.

*****

Once Arthur had left with the others, David soon heard barking from inside the house. He'd hoped Benji would stay asleep upstairs. It was the safest place for him. He closed his eyes in despair.

The bark caught Jack's attention. He smiled. "Of course. You've got your mutt with you. Benji, isn't it?" He grinned, looking over to the house. "*Mmmm* ... this could be fun. Go get him. Bring him out here. He should be part of the fun." Jack motioned to another robed figure to go into the house. "Stupid dog. He didn't even suspect me, but I guess we *do* have our ways." Jack grinned at David.

David had to do something. He must inspire the others. After all, they had a gun right now. He needed a window of opportunity. Thanks to his furry friend, the opportunity soon arose. As the hooded figure walked past a bewildered Betty, Benji came bolting out of the front door like lightning. He leapt up at the hooded figure, knocking him backwards. The figure fell to the ground, dropping his torch and his hood fell away, revealing the young man's face.

*"That fucking dog!"* Jack shouted.

Benji darted towards Jack and Emily and took a gigantic leap at them. Jack fell backwards with the impact of the dog and lost his footing on the wet grass. He swiped his penknife at Benji, narrowly missing him.

David instinctively shouted, *"Now!"* to the others, hoping they would spring into action.

For just a split second, they remained frozen but then sprang into life.

Jack screamed as Benji bit into his arm. He struggled but managed to reach for his dropped penknife and thrust it twice into Benji's side, causing him to yelp in pain as blood shot out. Benji let go of Jack's arm just as David approached but Jack kicked David backwards in the stomach. Emily was shocked and too scared to move. David got back up but Jack sent him rolling and they wrestled on the ground, with Jack once again dropping his penknife.

The four remaining hooded figures had also hesitated. But soon ran towards the others, dropping their torches.

*"Use your gun, boss!"* Gavin shouted.

Bob aimed his gun at one of the onrushing figures. Closing his eyes, he pulled the trigger. The shotgun jolted back, hurting his shoulder. The blast knocked the figure clean off the ground and killed them instantly with a blow to the chest. That was one down.

Gavin used his strength to dive at another one, knocking him to the ground and repeatedly punching him.

John did the same, but he was nowhere near as strong as Gavin. He seemed to just bounce off them. He could hear the one he was attacking laughing in a deep feminine tone as she lunged at John, who was now on the floor. He hadn't been in a scrap since Year 8, when he'd helped David with a school bully.

Bob had soon been jumped upon by the robed man who Benji had knocked to the ground. Bob managed to fight off his assailant by hitting them across the head with the butt of his shotgun. He then saw John struggling. He had a few more shells inside his pocket, but he rushed towards John instead, as it was too dangerous to shoot. Doing so, the robed man instantly recovered from the blow to his head and hit Bob with a garden rock from under the hydrangea, which rendered him semi-conscious. The figure then jumped on the back of Gavin, who had knocked the other one out. Gavin threw the figure off, launching him into the air.

*"You fucking arsehole!"* David shouted as he pushed his thumbs into Jack's eyes. Adrenaline flowed through David's veins.

Jack screamed in pain.

Jack managed to get David in a chokehold, leaving him gasping for air. Emily started pulling at Jack frantically, trying to get him off David.

*"Get off me, you Irish bitch!"* Jack shook Emily off, without too much trouble and reached again for his penknife on the grass.

David wriggled free from Jack's grip just as Jack stabbed him in his right thigh. David yelled out and retaliated by throwing his elbow to Jack's cheek.

Jack ran away a little, sensing defeat, for he saw Arthur return, holding his revolver. Jack slipped on Carl's face in doing so and very oddly, picked it up.

Arthur could see John being choked on the ground. Arthur pulled the figure off John with a kick to the ribs. The figure fell onto Arthur and rolled over, now trying to choke him. Their heavy weight pinned Arthur's frail body down. Arthur tried using the revolver but it was knocked from his hand and slid along the lawn. The robed figure quickly went after it.

Gavin, after knocking out his second robed figure, picked up the garden rock used on Bob and smashed it with force over the head of the hooded figure from behind, causing the figure to hit the deck like a sack of potatoes. To Gavin's surprise, the hood fell away to reveal a dark-haired woman with shortish hair. She was surprisingly strong for a female.

Emily had run to embrace David, who staggered to get up.

*"Benji!"* David called. Emily helped him to limp over to him. David's heart was pounding and he started to sob.

Benji was bleeding out onto the grass, whimpering.

They turned to look at Jack who was running towards the forest.

"You're going to pay for this," Jack said panting. He held his penknife up in one hand and Carl's face in the other. "All of you. For *all* of this. Tomorrow, you'll be *ours* ..." Jack coughed and started to laugh again.

Gavin picked up the revolver and considered aiming it, but Jack quickly disappeared out of sight into the dark forest.

The group seemed safe. For now. Two were dead and four unconscious.

Betty had watched the whole episode unfold, expressionless.

"He saved us." David wept, holding Benji. "He's ... he's dying."

*****

David had picked Benji up and carried him into the kitchen. He lay him on some kitchen towels on the table. Benji was clinging on to life but he had lost a lot of blood. Arthur was stemming the blood flow with a couple of bathroom towels. He said it wasn't looking good, but he might still stand a chance. He had asked John to fetch his satchel from the Land Rover.

Bob had since come to. He was fine, although a little dazed with a bump at the back of his head that hurt, unlike the female acolyte who had fallen victim to Gavin. Bob had reloaded his shotgun and put a few more shells in his pockets. Gavin had fetched his own shotgun from the living room and had the revolver in his possession.

Both of the hooded figures Arthur had overcome had disappeared. Two of the others on the lawn were clearly dead. Two others were tied up outside with some rope and were still out for the count.

Arthur was examining Benji on the table. "I don't think there's any major organ damage." Arthur briefly took off his glasses and rubbed his eyes.

"Is he going to be okay?" David asked softly.

Emily was holding David as they all stood around the table. "He's such a brave boy."

"I didn't think he had it in him," David said, stroking Benji gently.

"Sometimes, it doesn't matter how soft or gentle an animal is. When it comes to true evil, they'll do anything to protect their owner and loved ones," Arthur said as he put his glasses back on. "At least, the bleeding is slowing."

"Poor baby," Emily said tearfully.

Arthur took out a white sachet from his satchel and tore it open with his teeth. "This will hopefully stop the bleeding."

"What is it?" David asked, holding one of Benji's paws.

"It's a haemostatic powder that prevents bleeding. It can also help seal wounds. You could do with some of it on your leg."

"I'm fine. Just concentrate on Benji, please. My bleeding has stopped. It just hurts."

Arthur used another product from his satchel that helped numb Benji's wounds and cleanse them, but not before making him yelp.

Arthur asked Bob to fetch him a needle and thread. He sterilised the needle with alcohol and stitched up Benji's wounds. He then used a green powder on the stitches and muttered some words over Benji's body, moving his hands over him, with his eyes closed.

The others watched on. Arthur certainly knew his stuff.

After he was done, he was confident Benji would be fine, but they wouldn't know for sure for a few hours. In the meantime, Benji needed rest.

"Thank you, Arthur," David said warmly and sincerely.

"You're most welcome." Arthur smiled back.

# Chapter Sixty-Eight

## 31st July, 2018

They had been up all night, scared that Famuli Cani would send more members for them during the night. The two dead bodies were still out on the lawn, covered now with a couple of blankets. John was surprised to find that they were naked underneath their robes when they had searched them. The hoods had been removed to reveal the faces of the two tied-up men; one had a ponytail and one David and John had recognised.

Arthur had also explained that last night, on his way back to the farm, a truck was parked further down the old dirt track. It was no doubt to be used to transport them all had they been captured.

"I say we just kill the fuckers," John said.

"John, please remain calm," Arthur said. "We're not murderers."

"We should have known that this *fucker* here, was one of them," John said, gesturing.

One of the tied-up men was Marcus, who had been working at the church when David and John looked into Anthony and Melissa's wedding story.

The two tied up hadn't said a word. They sat stone-faced on a couple of plastic chairs out front with their beaten and bruised faces.

"I want to thank you, Arthur, for saving me from that *butch* cow over there on the lawn."

"You're welcome, John."

"I still can't believe I got my arse handed to me by a *woman*."

Arthur smiled. "It happens. She was strong."

"I'm, erm … also sorry, for doubting you about those crystals and your methods." John bit his lip.

Arthur placed his hand on John's shoulder. "It's fine, John. No need to apologise."

David was checking on Benji who was asleep on the sofa, along with the two cats. He seemed to be recovering well.

Emily sat next to them. “I love you, David.”

“I love you too, Em.” David gave her a warm embrace. “When Jack had that knife up against your neck, I thought I was going to lose you.”

“I know. B-but they’re still coming for us. What are we going to do?”

David took in a deep breath. “I honestly don’t know. I should *never* have got you involved in this. I’ll never forgive myself.”

“D-don’t say that. I’m glad you did … I’m glad I met you. We’ve had some great fun in the short while we’ve been together.” She kissed him passionately.

Betty had gone upstairs to change the bed that Florence had slept in. Arthur took the moment to speak to everyone else.

“I still can’t believe that Jack was one of them all along. He seemed such a nice boy,” Bob said.

“Some people are just naturally bad apples, or they are easily influenced,” Arthur responded. “Perhaps, he hasn’t been part of them for too long. He told Florence he was doing his ‘homework’ with the mice. It may have been part of his initiation. He was a neophyte. Like virtually all of them at one point. It explains how he managed to get Florence pregnant. He hadn’t lost the ability to reproduce children. It was before the dark magic flowed too strongly in him.”

“It’s just as well they can’t keep reproducing. Otherwise, they’d be sacrificing babies all the time!” John said.

“There surely has to be an endgame, now?” David asked. “They obviously want us for tonight. They will be coming for us.”

“I know. May God be with us all. But by fighting them off, it gives us time. I don’t think it matters if we run or not, now. They *will* find us. Even if they miss the deadline of after midnight. We need to save Florence and the other guy she mentioned. There may even be others.” Arthur had shaved his beard off and ran his hand over the unfamiliar feel of his face.

“What do you suggest?” asked Gavin, holding his shotgun over his shoulder.

“We need to take Betty and Emily somewhere safe. Your dog and the cats, too. We need to get the women safe. We can’t take any chances.”

“Take them where? Who can we trust? Jack all but admitted that the police were in their pocket. I can’t leave Emily, Arthur. Maybe we should all get the hell out of here?”

“Here, here! I’m with David. Maybe we should just call in the army?” John semi-joked. "*Or* take a chance with the Old Bill?"

"It's too much of a risk ... but we need to act fast. They could already be on their way, or out there now, closing in on us. You know we can't run. We can't let them sacrifice Florence and her baby."

"That's true, Arthur. She must be terrified. Especially when she'd already escaped them once. Now she's back where she started." John sighed and shook his head.

"The clock is ticking. What are we going to do, Arthur?" Bob said worried.

"I know of a place. But I don't wish to say where, yet. Not here. Not with them outside and Betty upstairs. You can take anything you feel that you need or want."

"What about the two out there?" David asked.

Arthur sighed. "I haven't decided," he said, unsure.

"We can't let them live. Not after everything they've done!" John raised his voice.

"I still don't believe we should kill them. Not in cold blood ... Perhaps, we should keep them tied up and in the boot. Drop them somewhere."

"*What*? Are you kidding, after what they did to Carl and all the others?"

"I have to agree with Arthur, John. It was bad enough in self-defence. I don't believe I could do it any other way," Bob replied.

Gavin looked in thought. But before anyone else said anything, Betty walked in with a pair of scissors, humming and smiling.

"Oh no ..." Bob said.

They dashed outside to see that the two tied-up men had gone. Even more surprising, was that the two dead bodies had also disappeared. All that was left, were the two blankets and some blood stains leftover on the still wet grass.

"I guess we don't have to worry about what to do with them, now," David said.

"Until tonight," John added quietly.

*****

The group took two separate cars that morning, with Bob's Land Rover leading the way and Gavin following close behind in his own car. They still hadn't any clue where they were heading off to. Like yesterday, Emily had phoned Jock saying she wouldn't be in today as she had another headache; she hated lying. Jock knew she wasn't well of late and told her to have the week off. It was fine. She had earnt it and hadn't had any days off sick for as long as he could remember. Nor had she taken any holiday for a while.

John and Emily left their cars at the farm. They wondered if they'd ever see them again. Small things like that went through all their minds. Things they normally took for granted.

Emily and David sat at the back of Bob's Land Rover with the two cats, Sammy and Josie, in their cat carriers. A fast-recovering Benji sat in the front passenger seat. John sat in Gavin's passenger seat and Arthur sat in the back keeping watch on Betty. He had managed to do a 'blessing' over her not long before they had left. He used his index finger to paint an invisible symbol on her forehead and gave her another necklace to wear with a white crystal on it. He hoped this would help block any information about where they were going, nullifying any evil influence. They all prayed and had a group hug before they left, with Arthur muttering words that didn't make sense to any of them.

Sat in the car, Arthur's thoughts returned to the sadness he felt at losing Carl. He wished Carl was still there with them.

They were hoping to get out of the forest as quickly as possible. They couldn't wait to get out. It was raining again and there were few cars about. They all wondered how Carl had lost control and whether the same would happen to them. John, David and Emily in particular, couldn't stop fidgeting. They were also anxious to know where Arthur was taking them.

Bob suddenly raised his voice and slammed on the breaks as a couple of rabbits ran straight out in front of him, marginally missing the front tyres. Gavin then had to brake rapidly to avoid smashing into the back of the Land Rover.

Eventually and to their relief, they exited the forest roads.

*****

They stopped off at Gavin's to pick up some more shells for his shotgun.

"I'll come with you, buddy," John offered. "Just in case. I need a leak, too."

"No worries. We won't be long." Gavin took off his seat belt and looked behind to Arthur and Betty. He opened his door and put one of his long legs out onto the ground below.

Betty had not spoken on the journey, even when Arthur had tried talking to her. She had simply stared out of the window.

Emily got a text from Annabel, asking how she was feeling. She said she would see her soon.

Gavin returned after a few minutes with a bag of ammo and a black ammo belt. He had got his ammo belts as part of a deal when he first purchased his shotgun. He never in a million years thought he'd use them. It still hadn't sunk in that he had killed someone. A woman, at that. But unlike Bob, he didn't feel one bit of remorse.

*****

Gavin's car took the lead as they arrived in Newtonmore, a small and pretty village, with a population of less than a thousand. Gavin and Bob had both been there a few times, but not for a couple of years at least. The two cars pulled up at the back of a church near to a house, where there was less chance of them being seen from the road.

"Cute church," David said, admiring it. Scotland certainly had some nice little attractions as well as some big ones. "But why here?"

The church was fairly small with its pretty beige and grey brick work. A pointy bell tower sat on top.

Arthur hadn't phoned in advanced, hoping to avoid being tracked. "You guys wait here. I shan't be long. I'll explain everything when I get back." He smiled.

"Where's he going?" John asked, frowning.

The group watched as Arthur trotted up to the small bungalow, whilst the others waited inside the two cars.

After a few minutes, Arthur came back out and explained why they were here. The rest got out their cars, apart from Betty. Being on holy ground, the chances were higher that Famuli Cani couldn't detect where they were.

"Why here, Arthur? Who lives here?" asked Gavin.

"I know someone here and it is sometimes where I have been staying. He knows what I do."

"Who's 'he?'" Bob asked.

"Father Joseph Adan. He's semi-retired. I've assisted him in performing a couple of exorcisms down the years. I've known him, going back to the early '80s. I believe the women will be safe here. And ourselves, whilst we discuss our plan of action."

"Would that be around the early 1880s?" John couldn't resist having a little dig, regarding Arthur's age.

The others smiled, including Arthur.

"You honestly think they'll be safe here? David asked. "Can this priest be trusted?"

"Safer than anywhere, David. He's a *very* holy man. The holiest I've ever come across. It will be harder for them and Canus to find us here. I did consider moving us here sooner and discussing it at the cricket pavilion. But of course, *they* turned up. I even considered Florence being brought here …"

"Why didn't you?" John asked.

Arthur sighed. "It was maybe too much of a risk. Because she was pregnant and more linked to them, I wanted her as far away as possible until Famuli Cani were defeated. I didn't have the required time to work my magic on her, along with my other methods. Time was too short. I've had more time with you all, to try and help protect you."

"But why this church?" Emily asked.

"I still don't see how we can stop them," John added.

"Father Adan has a special place underneath the church, like a holy shrine. It's very hard to get down there. Of course, it's still a risk. They have the power to know things. But we've already weakened their powers like with Betty with the crystals we've used and subconsciously, she's fighting against it. Along with other things." Arthur looked at the group. "Although we will be walking into the lion's den, we have the spirit of *Seath Mór* with us. We *can* stop this."

"What's the plan if we manage to get into this lair? Just start shooting?" Gavin asked.

"We can discuss that more inside," Arthur replied.

"Well, it certainly looks a pretty little church," Emily said, looking up at the bell tower. She shielded her eyes with her hand from the sun that had now reappeared.

The others all agreed.

*****

The living room of the small bungalow smelt of jasmine due to the flowers that sat in a pot on the windowsill. Above the television hung a rather large-framed painting of Jesus, with a bright halo above his head. Father Adan had gone to make some tea for his guests.

"You think Jesus posed for that painting?" John joked to Emily who was sat between him and David on the soft grey sofa.

Emily couldn't help but giggle. "Maybe?" she joked back.

Betty occupied one armchair and Arthur the other. Gavin and Bob stood. Benji and the two cats in their carriers were on the burgundy-coloured carpeted floor in front of the television.

"How much did you tell him?" David asked.

"He's aware of a certain cult and presence around these parts. He knows I've been looking into it. He's always been a brave man and willing to put his neck on the line to stop evil."

They could hear the rattle of teacups as Father Adan walked back in carrying the drinks on a small metal tray. "Here you all go. Robertson's Herbal Tea. The *best* in Scotland." Father Adan smiled, placing the tray on the small coffee table. His accent was soft, his voice calm and warm.

Father Joseph Aldan Adan was sixty-eight years old. His virtually grey hair had receded almost all the way to his crown. His chubby face had a caring smile and he wore glasses. He wore a casual pair of blue trousers and a tanned coloured cardigan, along with some red slippers. He wasn't exactly the sort who look liked they fought evil.

"Thank you," they all said, not quite in sync.

"Arthur here, tells me you're in quite a bit of a pickle?" Father Adan grinned.

*"Pickle?"* John whispered across to David.

David shook his head slightly. "Don't." He raised a finger discreetly to stop John's jesting.

"You should be safe, here. It's very difficult for evil entities to see in a House of God or in buildings on holy soil." Father Adan sounded and felt confident. Fighting and shining light against darkness was part and parcel of being a priest. No matter how dangerous it was, he believed he was doing God's work. He believed that someone had to do it. Like Arthur, he had seen his fair share of things over the years, especially, when he had worked in Africa many years ago.

*****

Arthur had discussed things in more detail. "I just think it is for the best, that the women stay here with you."

"Oh, yes, Arthur. I completely agree. Downstairs, should be particularly safe, until you get back."

"What exactly is downstairs?" Emily asked intrigued.

"Finish your tea, sweetheart. And I'll show you all." Father Adan smiled.

There was something warm and genuine about this man that Emily liked. She guessed that most priests were like this.

Father Adan soon led them to the back of his house to a large wooden door with dark metal embellishments. He punched a six-digit code into a mechanical door lock and pulled down on the rather large handle after it clicked open. It seemed that the door was usually covered by a red curtain that was drawn open to the end of the rail.

"Come, follow me." Father Adan smiled further.

They followed him down some white, hard surface stairs. Emily held onto the red railings. At the bottom, they moved along a straight corridor with a hard white laminate flooring, lit from the ceiling. They could see another room up ahead.

"What is this place?" David asked.

"You'll see." Arthur gave a knowing grin.

The well-lit room was like a shrine or 'underground holy sanctuary,' as Father Adan put it. They admired the room which was directly underneath the church. At one end of the room, on the right as you went in, were four neatly made beds; two on each side of the room facing one another. Each had a red duvet and a large white, plumped-up, single pillow. They looked comfy. Religious paintings of The Last Supper, Jesus, and the Sermon on the Mount broke up the white walls. Along with a few pieces of furniture, a huge gold cross was fixed on the far side wall. On the denim-coloured decking, in the centre of the room, was a fairly large, circular red and white rug, with a stitched gold cross in the centre. Steps at one end led up to a second dark brown platform, where an altar stood, covered in purple and gold draping. To the right, was a smaller set of steps that led down to a small bathroom.

"It's a bit like a holy nuclear bunker, then?" John said.

Father Adan chuckled. "Yes. You could say that, my son."

"What makes this room so special?" asked David, looking around.

"I always bless this room once, sometimes twice a day," Father Adan replied. "But the walls are made of certain materials. They have special symbols painted behind them to help ward off evil spirits and other dark energies."

"I guess we should just stay down here for ever, then," John said. "Have you ever had to use it before, for things similar to what we're going through?"

Father Adan hesitated. "No, not quite. But certain other things, yes."

"What other things?" Emily asked.

"Let's not discuss that right now. Why don't do you all take a seat?" Father Adan smiled again and gestured towards the line of white pews with red cushions.

*****

Father Adan had performed some kind of mass and prayer that took around twenty minutes. He had even got changed for it, donning a white vestment with a gold cross pattern down the front. He had also said a prayer for Carl, which was nice. He had never met him, but knew of him from Arthur.

Once he had blessed them all, he again did the sign of the cross at the altar and then draped a dark red blanket over Betty. He explained that it would further help protect her from negative influences. He then stood to the left near the wall.

"Well, I guess this is it." Arthur cleared his throat. He was standing in front of the seated others. "Tonight, we will hopefully put a *stop* to Famuli Cani, once and for all." He tried to sound strong and confident as though he were rallying his troops before going into battle. Inside though, he had started to have doubts. But the others were looking to him for guidance.

In spite of everything, John couldn't resist the urge to smirk. Seeing Arthur standing there, trying to galvanise them all seemed comical. It seemed so silly. How the hell, were they supposed to take out a whole cult and some kind of supernatural being? They had no idea how many of them there were. His smirk didn't last long though. Reality soon kicked back in.

"I've been thinking about our plan of execution and there are a few ways we can go about it."

"I think we're all keen to know, Arthur," Bob replied. He could feel butterflies start to form in his stomach.

"I think we should go into the forest early evening before it's too dark."

"That's pretty obvious, Arthur," John quipped raising his voice slightly and making the others laugh a little.

Arthur smiled. "What I mean is, we need to get to their hideout before they arrive. We can then keep our distance and see how many there are. Or, we could even sneak in before they arrive. I don't believe they will arrive until sundown. At least the majority."

"Why not go in now and rescue Florrie and whoever else, before they all turn up?" John suggested.

"I don't believe Canus will be summoned until after midnight. If we stop Famuli Cani, it *could* be enough for Canus to become weakened and dormant again. But we need to stop it for *good*. We could attempt to rescue them sooner as there may not be many, if any, of them there."

"So why don't we?" David asked. "Maybe we can go back later to confront them all? We can rescue Florrie first, and anyone else."

Arthur breathed in and exhaled. "Going into their lair without knowing in advance how many there already are in there is too risky. We also don't know the full layout … I don't believe Florence is currently being held below

Loch an Eilein as we speak."

"How on earth can you know that?" John questioned.

"When I disappeared yesterday evening after … Carl had gone, I meditated in the forest. I saw that tree you three came across, after you first arrived up here. It was still there, along with the bones of the dead animals, shaped in an inverted pentagram. *Arbor Animarum.*"

"Arbor what?" Gavin asked.

"Arbor Animarum. It's Latin, for *Tree of Souls*," Father Adan said, then bowing his head slightly.

Arthur nodded his head in agreement. "The poor souls that have perished under Famuli Cani are trapped in a kind of purgatory in that tree." Arthur quickly thought of Carl and wondered if his soul was now trapped too.

"How, though?" David asked further. "All of them?"

"Maybe not all, no. Some have perhaps been lucky enough to go to the light and get to the other side. Regardless, only destroying Canus and most likely its acolytes too, can set them all free. That includes the souls of the poor animals."

"There's a lot of things resting on tonight, then?" David said.

"Yeah, no pressure!" John was slouched forward on the pew, but sat upright, flexing his neck somewhat.

"What is the tree used for? Didn't you say something about teleporting?"

"Yes, Bob. The demon can appear anywhere it wants within Rothiemurchus Forest without the need for this tree, and the tree allows it to travel further afield, outside the boundaries of Rothiemurchus. The tree grew larger as more lives were sacrificed." Arthur looked at the faces in front of him. He could tell they were frightened. "Take for example, when Canus appeared in your flats miles away, back home."

David caught a glimpse of Father Adan bowing his head down again. He seemed to be mouthing silently, praying perhaps for the lost and trapped souls.

"Anyway, I meditated in front of the tree. I could feel the pain of the tortured souls, reaching out for help. I could also feel the evil that came from it as well. I could see Florence chained to a bed somewhere, some cabin."

"Why doesn't Seath Mór help more? Why can't he show us more?" John became annoyed. "It would save a heck of a lot of time."

"There's only so much spirits and magic can do. Especially, when these acolytes are so strong. There's definitely another captured person being held at Loch an Eilein, as Florence mentioned. I could see them terrified in a cage, curled up."

"Shit. Poor bastard," David muttered. "One thing I have sometimes wondered, Arthur: why the need to summon this Canus? Like tonight; why will it not already be there, when the cult arrives? Surely it can appear anytime, anywhere it wants?"

"It's a good question to ask, David. It's part of their rituals. It isn't like they are summoning it back into existence, in that sense. For they already have done. It may even be an ego thing from Canus itself. It can still see and feel the sacrifices even if not currently present. But Canus wants its followers to continue to pay homage to it, and make themselves worthy of being graced by its presence."

They were distracted by a doorbell sound. It came from a small speaker to the left of the entrance. Benji and the cats pricked their ears up.

"You'll have to excuse me, sorry," Father Adan said. "I'm expecting a delivery."

"Okay." Arthur smiled and gave a nod of acknowledgement.

Arthur and his friends discussed their plan in more detail. They planned to reach the lair by eight at the latest, whilst it was still daylight. Arthur suspected the acolytes were expecting them anyway. This would be one of the biggest, if not the biggest events of the Satanic calendar, when everything dark and supernatural would potentially be at the highest peak of its powers. Arthur insisted that the group stay inside, either up in the house or down below and rest up before six in the evening.

*****

It was time for the group to head out and leave the two women behind. The hours had dragged and were emotional to say the least. They had mainly stayed and chatted below the house. They tried to eat but could barely touch anything.

"How do I look?" Gavin tried making light of it all. He was wearing the camouflaged shotgun belt that held twenty-five red shells and was fastened tightly around his broad waist. A machete was fitted inside a leather sheath on his right side. Attached to his normal leather belt hung the ammo bag that held several more shotgun shells. The revolver they had recovered was tucked into his jeans at the back below the waistline. Gavin made sure a couple of times, that the safety was definitely on. He wore no flat cap.

John and David both remembered joking and making a slight mockery of Gavin, along with Bob, when he had kitted up to investigate the fire, which ultimately led them to the tree and animal bones and Harold. It wasn't really a laughing matter back then but now, it certainly wasn't. This time, it was real. And this time, it really did look and feel like he was ready for war.

"Looking good," John replied.

Bob had his almost identical shotgun and wore the spare black ammo belt of Gavin's. It carried twenty red shells. Both were praying that they wouldn't have to use their shotguns.

Arthur wore his favourite black jacket again. The sacred dagger was inside his inner pocket. He had swapped his usual satchel with a slightly larger one that hung over his right shoulder. He was also wearing another silver cross around his neck. "Have you still got some of the things I left here before?" Arthur asked Father Adan.

"But of course. They're still in the trunk over there." Father Adan smiled and gestured.

The crew wondered what things Arthur had left. They watched him walk over to the trunk and pull out a few vials of holy water that he placed in his satchel, some other vials that contained some form of coloured liquid and finally a small black crossbow.

"I never did like guns, much." Arthur looked over at the others and smiled. He then picked up a pack of crossbow bolts with silver tips and placed them into his satchel. He closed the trunk.

"I'll bless those vials again for you, Arthur. They've been in there a while."

Arthur took out the vials and Father Adan blessed them individually, before Arthur returned them to his satchel.

And then, it was time for the dreaded goodbyes.

"I … I love you so much, David." Emily sobbed. She was a wreck as the others watched.

"Back at yer. My little Irish flower," David said, holding Emily tightly. "Always and for ever." He could feel his cheek wet from her tears as she held him tightly.

"*Please, please,* come back to me."

David placed his forehead to hers. He was close to tears too. He gently held her face with his hands. "I promise." He smiled. He never made promises he couldn't keep, but this was one he may have to break. He didn't know what else to say. He kissed her passionately.

"Shit," John muttered.

"And you, you big *hero*!" David walked over to Benji.

Benji whimpered; he perhaps knew that something was up.

"I love you, boy. Thank you." David knelt down and cuddled his dog and Benji licked his face. "Be good. Look after them for us."

Betty still seemed fairly oblivious to what was happening, but Bob hugged her goodbye and stroked the cats. Arthur and Father Adan believed that if Canus was destroyed along with its followers, she would regain her free spirit.

There was a few more hugs with Emily wishing them all good luck and to be careful. Father Adan promised to look after the pair, until their return.

"Group hug?" John said, beaming. He held his arms aloft. "Even you, Betty. And come in here, Father."

Everyone laughed but came together, even a confused Betty still wrapped in her blanket. The priest joined them too and they all held each other for a good minute or so. Father Adan then said a prayer and blessed them all. He told them to have, and always remember their *faith*.

The men left the bungalow in the Land Rover and Gavin drove. Emily and Father Adan stood in the doorway waving them off. As the Land Rover drove off tooting its horn, Father Adan comforted Emily with his left arm, signing the cross with his other.

After several weeks of terror, confusion, fear, and even death, the brave five set off for Loch an Eilein to do battle against the dark forces of evil. They were in God's hands now.

# Chapter Sixty-Nine

## 31st July, 2018

Arthur was proud of them all. He could sense their fear, yes. But also, more importantly, this unique and special bond they all had with one another. It was a light in the darkness. This would prove powerful against the evil sources that lay in wait. He started to feel more confident about their goal.

It may have been paranoia, but John and David could have sworn that a few passers-by gave them strange looks as they were stuck in the traffic on the way. One in particular, gave them what John referred to as *The Daggers*. Arthur had thought the same thing. But they weren't too far now, to where Arthur believed the best spot to park up was.

*****

"I think this will do," Arthur said, pointing to the side of the road. "Just up here, on the left will be fine. We can walk from here. It's pretty open, until we go further in."

"Sure thing, Arthur," Gavin replied, slowing down the Land Rover and pulling into a space at the side of the forest.

Arthur told him to drive a bit further into the overgrowth to try to conceal the car. The Land Rover became covered with leaves and branches.

"I guess this is it, then?" David had been texting Emily until the signal began to fade.

"I hope you've got your wills written out, boys?" John joked, taking off his seat belt.

"Can't say I have much to leave, or to many, anyway," Gavin replied, adjusting the machete at his side. "Other than a brother I rarely see, and my parents. But I'm not sure they'd need my money, at their old age."

"Hopefully, it won't come to that." Arthur smiled. He made sure his hair was tied back securely.

"At least it's still dry and clear," David noted.

"For now," Bob said. The forecast had said it would stay clear, but with possible rain and thunderstorms in some places.

"Which way do we go and how long will it take us to get there?" John asked.

"I would say around an hour and twenty. We need to head in this direction." Arthur pointed up ahead.

"Don't forget the torches," John reminded Bob.

"I know, I know." Bob walked around and opened the boot.

David took one, John another and then Arthur. They turned them on and off a few times to check they worked and put them in their pockets.

Bob locked the car and gave Gavin a spare set of keys, in case something happened to one of them.

"I guess we should set off, then?" Arthur said.

"No point hanging about," Gavin replied.

"There's certainly a nip in the air, now," David said.

"Yep. Walking will soon warm us up, though," Bob replied.

"*Penitus in nemus*, we must go," Arthur said to himself.

David frowned. "What was that?"

"Deep into the forest, we must go," Arthur replied this time in English, leading the way.

It was still pretty light as they started walking through the forest. At first, the foliage was sparse. Arthur pondered whether Canus knew that they were on their way. Canus was a denizen of Rothiemurchus Forest, but Arthur had crystals and other things in his satchel that could potentially block Canus and its acolytes from detecting them. He had instructed to the group to try not to mention the name of Canus.

Arthur had also been muttering things under his breath as they walked. The others assumed he was saying spells or praying in Latin as they couldn't understand what he said.

There was no signal in the forest, which they'd all expected.

About half an hour or so in, they came across a fairly large open space. The soft ground was awash with violets, a sea of purple. They could smell them before they had reached the opening.

"Wow," said David as they stopped for a short breather. His thigh had started to ache from the wound inflicted by Jack. "Beautiful."

The others admired the view and Arthur took out a couple of large water bottles from his satchel and passed them round.

"It certainly is, David," Bob said. "You can't always smell violets, but these ones are very strong." The back of Bob's head had started to throb. He decided to take some aspirin.

"Further up, you can see we will start to go much deeper in. It's going to get darker, so make sure we all stick close together. And be careful of any dangerous overgrowth," Arthur warned.

"Along with anything else," John added.

They started making their away across the violets, which were surprisingly tall.

Across the other side, the violets continued under the trees for a while, but as they walked further, there were fewer and fewer and the gloomier it became.

"I can't hear any birds, now," David said, looking up at the towering trees.

"I don't think it's a coincidence," replied Gavin who switched his shotgun over to his left hand.

"Yes ... we are heading further into Famuli Cani territory, now," Arthur said. He bent down to tie up one of his brown boot laces.

The others shivered at the words *Famuli Cani territory*. It started to become darker in the forest, with clouds forming overhead. Maybe it was just paranoia but it seemed as if the sun was setting faster than usual, despite it still being early. The further in they walked, the more unsettled they felt. Arthur stayed in front of the others but the towering mass of trees and overgrowth still stifled them. They passed a small swamp, which smelt foul. Three dead ducks floated on the green-brown surface.

"Do you think Seath Mór will help us, Arthur?" David suddenly asked.

Arthur stepped over a fallen log and advised the others to be careful. "Yes, I do. I'm not sure how exactly. But I have faith he will aid us. Particularly when the times comes."

"Before we came up here, David and I, and our other friend, Grant, looked up this place. I remember we read something about Seath Mór."

"I remember that," David said. "Carl showed us it, too."

"Was it something along the lines of him being a formidable warrior, having a wicked smile and striking fear into even his own people?" Arthur turned and smiled. A large twig snapped and broke under the weight of his boot.

"Yes, something like that," John replied.

"Yeah," David agreed.

"It's not entirely accurate," Arthur replied.

"How do you mean?" David asked. He almost slipped on some wet muddy leaves.

"Seath Mór was indeed a formidable warrior. That much is plainly evident. But that description of him having a wicked or sinister smile, is clearly not true. It kind of depicts him as evil himself, when he was anything but that. He was very well liked and respected, particularly after he had defeated Famuli Cani."

The others listened intently.

"As for his spirit wandering the forest, looking for a challenge and killing people who show fear, but releasing them if brave, *that* is completely false." Arthur laughed slightly to himself.

"Yeah. That all rings a bell, now," David said.

"It's likely that Seath Mór's spirit is trapped here. Not quite like the others. But bound here. Either due to *it* or because he can't fully move on until they are defeated for good. Like we discussed before." Arthur noticed something up ahead.

"Is that a tent and a fire?" David noticed it a couple of seconds after Arthur.

Slightly ahead of them, they could see a blue tent, along with a campfire.

"You don't think it's them, do you?" John asked, swallowing.

"I'm not sure they'd be out here camping?" replied David.

Bob and Gavin looked at one another and nodded. They held their shotguns in both hands, pointing ahead. They felt as if they were in a war movie, aware of the enemy, but unfortunately it was real life.

"Steady," Arthur said, raising his left hand. "Let's approach slowly."

Walking carefully, John winced as he trod on a stick, making it snap.

As they got nearer, they felt the air grow colder. They had foreseen that the forest could get unnaturally chilly and they had dressed warmly although it was summer. Their clothing was also protecting their arms from any thorn bushes too.

The camp site appeared empty. The tent was unzipped open. They searched inside. There was nothing but a pair of identical brown sleeping bags. An unused, portable barbecue stood between the tent and the dwindling fire.

"Strange," Gavin said.

"You think so?" John said, touching the grill. It was cold and unused.

"Well, I guess not, considering. I thought there might have been a couple of rucksacks. Something like that?" Gavin replied, looking around the now deserted camp site.

"Perhaps they left in a hurry?" Bob suggested, scratching his neck, where he'd been bitten.

"Or worse," David said. "Maybe, they were taken. What do you think, Arthur?"

Arthur walked around the perimeter thinking. "It might not have been too long ago, seeing as the fire is just about still burning."

A strong breeze rustled the trees around them. They began to feel they were being watched.

"Well, there certainly isn't anybody here, guys," John said. "No trace of anyone. Or anything."

"We still have a fair bit to go. We should pick up the pace," Arthur said, adjusting his satchel. "Let's move, guys."

They left the camp, just as a strong gust flowed through the forest, blowing out the fire.

*****

"You think he's lost? Or that we are, rather?" John asked the others, while Arthur was further ahead.

Arthur stood still and appeared to be thinking. He ran a hand through his ponytail with his back to them.

"Let's hope not," David replied. "Then again, that might not be a bad thing, considering where we are going."

"I'm sure he knows which way we need to go, boys," Bob replied. Although the bump remained on the back of his head, the aspirin seemed to have taken his pain away. Even the bite on his neck had stopped itching.

It was already much darker. The trees were fast blocking the majority of the sunlight and the cold chill remained in the air. It was eerily quiet. There was no sound, apart from the occasional wind in the trees, the crack of a branch as someone stepped on it, or the sound of something falling from a tree, and of course, the sound of their own voices every now and then. Arthur insisted, however, that they kept the chit-chat to a minimum.

They could smell pines and other scents of blossom and flowers that had been growing in the forest. Arthur had told them that certain parts of the forest no longer had flowers or other things growing at all, most likely due to the evil that dwelt within. For whatever reason, some parts remained unaffected, however.

"We need to go this way." Arthur pointed to his right and turned to face the others. "It shouldn't be much further now. Maybe another twenty minutes."

"How does he know where to go, anyway?" John asked.

"I guess he just 'knows.' Maybe he senses it, like all the other things he's sensed," Gavin replied.

Suddenly, they could hear whispering and laughter all around them, like a child's giggle. Something dashed past them on the right and through a row of shrubs and bushes, disturbing the foliage.

"What the fuck?" John grew concerned.

They moved forward closer to Arthur who smiled.

"Why are you smiling?" David asked, remembering when all the apples had fallen back on the farm.

"It's a child's spirit. A benevolent one. Nothing to be frightened of."

"How do you know that?" John asked.

"Trust me. I know. It means us no harm. Even though the souls are trapped here and in that tree, some of the children's souls are more naïve. They perhaps don't know that they are trapped. They can still act mischievously."

"Right," John replied, frowning.

"This entity sometimes mocks the trapped souls by whispering itself. It can be hard to determine between them. But that one was definitely a young child."

They continued in silence and soon they could see Loch an Eilein, about a hundred metres away, through the trees. Unless they were to walk all the way around, they had to slice and hack their way through rows of sharp and deadly rose bushes. Gavin used his machete. Most of the roses had died or were close to it, dried and shrivelled up. After making their way through, they were thirsty and so drank. It was well past eight, although it seemed much longer since they had left Father Adan's. The journey had taken around an hour and forty minutes of trekking through the forest and they had arrived before nightfall as planned.

"Well, this is Loch an Eilein," Arthur said. "A beautiful place if you ignore what lies beneath it."

The others admired the view. Gavin remembered it now; he had never been here himself before but he used to see it in magazines and in the paper. The ruined castle sat on its own little island in the middle of the loch, surrounded by trees and overgrowth. The water was calm, reflecting what was left of the blue sky as it began to turn yellow and as the day slowly came to an end.

"Is the loch deep?" David asked.

"Not really," answered Arthur. "It's around eight metres or so, I think. Ten max, at its deepest."

"Where is the entrance to their lair?" asked John.

"Judging by what I saw in my vision, it's somewhere to the right down there. There should be a large rock nearby. We can perhaps use that as our vantage point."

They started to make their way along the loch. It was eerily quiet. You wouldn't have thought it was a popular tourist attraction. Any normal person who came here with their family for a picnic, or a paddle in the loch, would be oblivious to what was underneath them.

"It's hard to believe how something so striking and beautiful hides such evil, isn't it?" Arthur said.

"If people come to fish and have picnics and things, doesn't this cult run the risk of being seen, even though their activities may be late at night? People obviously camp and things?" David asked. "And why here, specifically? How did they build this place?"

"It's believed that people who do see something are not to be seen again. They also have their ways of not being seen, unless, they *want* you to see them. As for why this place, I don't know other than that it may be a place of power and energy, with ley lines perhaps, or tectonic energy. I can feel some form of energy, positive and bad. Mystical," Arthur replied. "As for how they built this lair? Your guess is as good as mine."

"Yeah. Dark energy coming straight up from Hell itself," John said, making David and Gavin look at him.

They walked past a couple of strange looking trees but Arthur said neither were the one he was looking for. Bob however, noticed a few strange markings and symbols on one of them. He queried what they were.

"Marking their territory," Arthur replied. "I'm not familiar with a couple, though. Possibly, they're magical symbols."

They then found the large rock.

"This is the rock," said Arthur. "The tree should be very nearby. Let me think ..." Arthur composed his thoughts, recalling the vision that he had had. "It's over here."

Following Arthur, they walked past the rock, and about another fifty yards on, to a large tree. It was surrounded by other slightly shorter and smaller trees and the ground was covered in overgrowth.

"You sure this is it?" asked Gavin. "It doesn't look anything special."

"Oh, it is. I can feel its negative energy. This is it. What better way of hiding a certain passageway, than in plain sight?" Arthur ran his hand over the bark. "But at the same time, you wouldn't even know that it was here."

"How does it open?" asked David, looking around their surroundings, nervously.

"I'm not too sure. But we will find out soon. We can see fine from behind that rock."

"It might be too dark for us to see how they get in," David said.

"We will see them fine. Trust me." Arthur smiled. He then led them back to the rock, where they waited patiently, glad of the rest.

*****

They had admired the setting sun, a fantastic orange and pink sky reflected onto the surface of the loch. John had mentioned whether it would be the last time they would see a sunset. By ten, it was completely dark.

John had also joked about the need for night-vision goggles, but soon they realised that Arthur was right about being able to see. The torches that were carried were put away in Arthur's satchel too.

"I don't think I've ever seen a moon so big and bright, before," John said quietly.

"I have. In one of my dreams," David recalled.

John then looked to the northern sky. "Wow. I don't think I've seen a group of stars as bright as that before, neither. Why does one of them look reddish?"

The others followed his gaze.

"That's the Perseus constellation. That's the star Algol ... although I have never seen it appear red like that before. It's also known as the *Demon Star.*

David swallowed. "Appropriate," he said worryingly.

It was twenty minutes past ten, when the first group of acolytes arrived.

John was about to say something else.

*"Shhh ..."* Arthur intimated, peering out from the rock. "It looks like they've started to arrive." He gripped his newly worn cross.

Heart beats rose. There was no turning back. It was their fate. Their destiny. It felt so surreal. Half of them had only met each other in the past few weeks. And here they now were, plotting to take down a group of Satanists and save the day.

An orange glow emerged through the trees from the torches they carried. They were walking slowly in their honorary robes, towards the tree entrance, once again, bare foot. There were around fifty of them, approaching in pairs and holding hands. As they got closer to the tree, they began slow, unnerving chants.

"What are they saying?" whispered John.

"It's Latin," whispered Arthur. "Canus is great and wonderful. Our thanks to Satan and Canus."

An owl hooted somewhere nearby. It was the only animal they had heard in the forest. They peered out, watching the robed, bare footed figures as they stood for a short while lined up in front of the tree, still chanting. Then the chanting stopped. One of them at the front muttered something but it was too far away to hear. A rumbling sound came from the tree and an uneven arched passageway opened up in front of them.

"What the ..." David whispered.

The torch carriers then disappeared into the tree one by one, with the passageway closing shortly after the last one had entered.

Shortly after, a second group of a similar size did exactly the same. Arthur counted that there were approximately a hundred cultists. These must be the *core* of Famuli Cani.

It was colder now. They had started to shake a little, crouching behind the rock, through a mixture of cold and fear.

"How are we supposed to take down so many?" David asked.

"I-" Before Arthur could answer, he noticed something.

In the bright moonlight, slowly coming down the loch, he could see a small boat. A lantern hung on a pole at the bow.

As the boat came nearer, they could discern four hooded figures. One sat alone rowing and the other three sat opposite.

"What the hell?" Gavin said.

They shifted their position slightly to make sure they couldn't be seen. A cloud moved over the moon, plunging the loch into darkness for a few moments.

"Why are they using a boat?" Bob asked.

No one answered as they watched the small boat stop at the edge of the loch, less than twenty metres from the rock. The one rowing was the first to get out.

*"You two. Bring her,"* said the rower in a gravelly voice.

The two bent down and picked up someone who had been lying in the boat. The body seemed lifeless and was also wearing a hooded robe. The moon came out fully again as the four hooded figures made their way to the tree, two of them carrying the lifeless body by the arms and legs at the rear.

They also murmured something at the tree and disappeared into it via the strange passageway.

"Who do you think that was?" asked David.

"I don't know," Arthur replied.

They waited a few minutes, but Arthur was sure that these last four were the last of Famuli Cani to arrive. He told the others they needed to hurry and get down there themselves.

At the far end of the loch, from where the boat had come, a strange white and grey mist appeared. It was steadily making its way over the water, spreading out and surrounding the forest as it did so. It seemed alive.

"Shit," Bob muttered.

"Come on, we need to get in that tree." Arthur jogged over, slightly hunched.

The others followed him to the hidden entrance.

"How are we going to get in?" John asked, looking behind them at the loch.

The mist was already half away across and seemed to be moving faster.

"I think I know what to do." Arthur reached into his satchel and aided by the moonlight, took out one of the small, coloured vials. He quickly pulled out its rubber bung and sprinkled the whole of it over the bark in the shape of the passageway.

"What is that stuff?" John asked.

"There isn't time to explain. It detects and opens magical doorways. But you need more than just this," Arthur answered quickly.

"Huh?" David said.

Arthur muttered something and started moving his hands over and over the bark of the tree … *"Arbor aperiatur,"* he finally said strongly and sharply, but in a low tone.

A slight rumble and vibration were followed by the passageway opening.

"Come on," Arthur said, looking behind them at the eery mist, which had now moved up the bank and past the rock where they had hidden.

The five of them went quickly through the passageway. The passageway shut after them, just as the mist reached the tree and descended on the rest of the forest. They were in.

# Chapter Seventy

## July 31st, 2018

Arthur looked at his wristwatch; 22:44 — less than an hour and twenty until midnight and a new day: *Lammas Day.*

They stood near the now shut passageway on a wooden platform that led down a spiral flight of stairs.

"I guess this really is it," David said, swallowing hard.

"Before we go on, I just want to say how proud I am of you all. You are all so brave." Arthur tried to smile. "Whatever happens. We *must* have faith and believe. Believe in God, believe in Seath Mór. And perhaps even more importantly, believe in yourselves, ourselves. We have been brought here together for a reason. God, loves you all." Arthur then pulled out a vial of holy water and splashed it over them and himself. He then took a swig of it and told the others to do the same. "Now, let's go!"

The inside of the tree had been carved hollow, with a central beam down the middle around which the staircase wrapped.

A torch had been fixed to inside of the tree near the top of the stairs, which seemed to wind down endlessly. More torches along the way provided light as they descended. The five of them welcomed the warmth of the torches, but as they went down further, it grew colder. Eventually they started to hear chanting again.

"There it is again," John said. His legs were shaking from the steps and his fear.

"You can expect a lot of that tonight," replied Arthur.

Once they had finally made it to the bottom, they stood facing a stone passageway that sloped down, which again had several lit torches on one side, lighting the way.

Behind them, was a small stone room with two bloodstained body trolleys in the corner. A bloodied whip and braided cat-o'-nine-tails hung on the wall, with a pair of rusted iron handcuffs and some chains.

They made their way slowly on the uneven surface of the passageway. The flames from the torches flickered and the chanting grew louder, echoing.

"I'm shitting it," John said.

"Me too, mate," David replied. "Love yer."

"Right back at yer, pretty boy."

"I think we all are bricking it," Gavin said, firmly gripping his shotgun.

The air was musky and damp. They were well under the loch by now. They could hear water trickling around them. It seeped through the walls and ceiling and they felt splashes every now and then. Occasionally when the water splashed a flame, they heard sizzles.

"This might all cave in on us," David said, looking around them.

"It'll be okay," Arthur said, looking back at David.

Eventually the pathway levelled out and was stoned off straight ahead, so they could only turn to the left. The chanting was loud now. They continued round the path.

John heard a crunch on the ground, where his right boot stepped on something. He looked down and picked something up to examine it in the light of one of the flamed torches.

"What is it?" Bob asked.

They all stopped and waited for John to answer.

John had frozen. He was staring at a pair of broken glasses.

*"John, what is it?"* David repeated in a harsh whisper.

"Th-these glasses ... *they're Grants ...*" John couldn't help but raise his voice slightly in his shock; his tone echoed along the stoned walls.

*"What?"* David went over and checked the black-framed glasses.

"G-Grant wears these glasses and they have a crack in the middle of the frame, here. He fixed them with a blue plaster, *look*!"

The others looked as John showed David the plaster. He tore it off and showed him the crack.

"How can that be? It's just a coincidence."

"Don't be so fickle, mate. *Look*! These are *his*. I'm telling you! He's *fucking* down here!" John struggled to keep his voice down and shoved the glasses under David's nose.

"When did you last speak with him?" David asked. "I texted him Friday morning and he answered."

Before John could answer, they were distracted by a woman's loud scream.

"That's Florence," Arthur said. "We need to hurry. If this is your friend, then we can still help him."

John put the glasses in his back pocket and they continued.

As they progressed, they smelt something. It smelt of death.

*"Ugh,"* said Bob. "What is that?"

John and David pulled their tops up to cover their mouths and noses.

"It's like rotted flesh," Arthur said, coughing.

The smell was filling the passageway. To the left, they saw an opening and the smell was getting stronger.

"It's coming from in there," Arthur said, coughing but trying to remain quiet. He walked slowly to the opening, gesturing for the others to wait. The room had four lit torches.

"What is it?" Gavin whispered.

Arthur stood in the opening, staring in. "My God," he said eventually, slowly walking in, covering his nose and mouth with his hand.

The others joined him. David had to turn his head away and John almost threw up.

Stretched out and nailed up against the back wall was the skin of a grown man. He had been flayed.

The room was only small. To the left, was some kind of bloodied workbench with a steel metal bucket that had body parts in it. A heart and some intestines were mashed up in the bucket, along with an arm and a leg. Next to the bucket, were a couple of tools; a bloodied saw and knife with a slight curve to it. On the hard cold floor, drawn with the victim's blood was an inverted pentagram. A few sigils had been drawn on the circle itself. In one of the corners were a pile of maggots, wet and glistening in the torch light, wriggling.

*"Jesus fucking Christ!"* John said, "Just when you thought these *fucks* couldn't get any worse. That poor bastard." He could feel his eyes sting.

Bob walked closer to the flayed skin. The stench was unbearable. "Oh, no. No, no, no," he muttered. His eyes were beginning to well up, his face one of sadness and pain.

"Uncle, what is it?"

Bob recognised the man. "It's … it's Eric."

Eric's heavily beaten face was still recognisable.

"Eric?" John asked.

"Oh, my sweet Lord," Gavin said, walking closer to the nailed-up skin. "It … it is him … Eric quit before you guys came. He saw that cloaked figure and was too scared to carry on working for us." Gavin's eyes flooded.

The skin was bloodied and heavily beaten. It appeared yellowy and pink. A couple of tattoos Eric had made him even more identifiable. On his left inside forearm, he had a few Chinese symbols. On his slightly hairy chest, was a small tattoo of a dove just above his right nipple. They were still visible.

"Oh, Eric. I'm so sorry." Bob tried to hold himself together. His emotions were a mix of fear, rage and anger. "I *promise* you, Angus and Charlie ... I *will* make these people pay for what they have done." Bob breathed heavily, nostrils flaring.

David hadn't seen his uncle like this before and it scared him. "I'm sorry, Uncle." He put his hand on Bob's shoulder.

Bob patted David's hand with his own. "The pain he must have endured. *Bastards*!"

"I'm sorry for your loss, Bob ... but we must move on," Arthur said with sympathy.

Bob turned one last time to pay his respects to Eric.

Continuing, the chanting suddenly halted. After a couple of minutes, it started up again.

Arthur told them to only speak if necessary and in whispers if possible, as they really were close now. They were on the final stretch of the passageway. The stench had been replaced by the dank and musky smell again. There was another opening just ahead. Again, on the left. They stepped carefully and peered in.

The room had an old and rotted drawless wooden desk and a chair with a blue raincoat hanging over the back of it. On the desk, was an old leather grimoire that was closed shut with a faded brass inverted pentagram on its cover. There were several photographs on the desk by the grimoire.

"That's us," David said as they examined the table. "I recognise this raincoat, too."

There were photographs of them all, mostly on the farm. There was even one of John and David leaving The Auld Drongair Bàrd. Another was of David, Emily and Benji on their walk before the storm. There were a couple of Arthur and Carl together. Most of the photos had symbols drawn on them in blood.

"They have certainly been watching us," Arthur said. "This explains the dreams you've been having. Amongst other things, they've been casting their black magic over you. This book is full of spells." Arthur opened the grimoire and skimmed through a few pages. He hadn't the will nor the time to look through it properly.

Before they left the room, they noticed a portrait on the wall next to the entrance. It was a dusty, framed portrait of Harold. The painting looked incredibly life-like. It was just an expressionless face with a forest background. The ill and gaunt-looking man stared straight out of the frame as though he was watching them.

It felt creepy to all of them, especially in the low light with the chanting in the background. The date scribbled on the top left of the portrait was 1972.

"Look at the date. He looks the same age in that picture as three weeks back. How is that possible?" David asked.

"That's the power of black magic," Arthur replied.

"Who *is* he, though?"

"I don't know, David. It could be more a case of *what* is he. But let's go. Our destiny awaits."

Walking on and further up ahead, they could see where the passageway came to an end with an orange and red glow. The chanting grew louder. They checked one final opening on the right. Apart from the torches that lit the room from the walls, just like the other two, the room was empty, except for three stone tables that had metal chains and shackles attached to them. The three tables were all stained in blood.

Once they had finally exited the dank passageway, they were at last at the centre of Famuli Cani's secret sanctuary: the most *unholy* chamber. The acolytes were still preparing for their big ritual. Or perhaps, rituals. A stone gantry curved both to the left and right halfway around, overlooking a large rectangular-shaped room. Torches lit the space. Red draped banners hung over the sides of the gantry each with an occult symbol stitched in black on them.

Stone steps stretched down from the middle of the exited passageway to the shiny black floor of the chamber, which had red occult symbols marked onto it. A large red strip of carpet led straight to an elevated platform where a large, old and black altar rose up from a plinth. Four tall black candles flickered at each corner of the altar. The chamber was also lined with torches mounted at varying heights from the floor. At the back of the room beyond the altar, burning flames rose from grooves in the ground in an inverted pentagram but did nothing to abate the cold. In the middle of it, was a black platform. To either side of the inverted pentagram were two burning upside-down crosses. A pile of burnt-out torches had been ditched in a neat pile in one corner of the chamber.

Hanging in the air, just past the altar and before the flames were two rusty metal cages raised through winches on the walls either side. The one on the left was manned by a half-naked man facing the front of the chamber. He was curled up into a ball. The ceiling was adorned with sharp stalactites of varying sizes.

Famuli Cani were grouped together facing the altar on either side of the red strip of carpet. They bowed their hooded heads.

The five of them had quietly moved round to the left of the gantry and peered through several gaps that were carved out in some symbols in the parapet. The low light gave them more protection and cover.

"What do we do now, Arthur?" Gavin whispered.

"Let's just be patient and see what happens," replied Arthur, fixing his gaze on what lay ahead of them.

"I can't tell if that's Grant in that cage," David said worriedly, looking at the suspended caged man.

They remained crouched down watching below and ahead of them. The chanting still continued as if it were on a loop.

"What the hell are we going to do, Arthur?" John asked.

Before Arthur said anything, they could hear a woman cry out, coming from below them.

*"Florrie?"* John said. "We have to save her, Arthur!"

Arthur didn't say anything for a few seconds. "We're going to have to go down there," he then said, still looking at Famuli Cani.

"What if they see us or hear us?" Gavin said, gripping his shotgun.

"We will have to be quiet and step carefully. We need to hurry. Gavin, you come with me. The rest of you stay here."

With Famuli Cani's backs facing them, Arthur and Gavin slowly and very carefully, made their way down the stone steps — hearts in mouths. The group were praying that the acolytes wouldn't turn around. At the bottom, there were two other arched passageways either side of the stone steps. They could hear some chatter and laughter down the passageway to their left. The two carefully walked down some smaller steps down the passageway on the right.

They could hear sniffing and crying ahead. There was a room on the right at the end. Arthur held his hand up to Gavin, peered in and saw Florence on a raised stone table.

Florence was completely naked. Her hands were bound by iron chains and shackles either side of the table and her ankles also. Arthur rushed over to her, followed swiftly by Gavin. She had markings in blood all over her body, face and forehead. Her huge bump stuck up in the air. Arthur thought she could give birth any minute.

"Florence, it's Arthur. We're here to rescue you." Arthur stood over her, head bent. He repeated himself, but this time, he gently slapped her face to help her focus.

"Arth ... Arthur?" she said, looking up with her bloodshot eyes. "My baby ... *My baby.*" Florrie bolted upright, almost hitting Arthur's chin.

Arthur quickly put his hand over Florence's mouth to prevent her from shouting. *"Shhhhh ... "*

Florence wrestled a little, but soon calmed down, when she managed to focus on Arthur's eyes and face, so he removed his hand.

"Keep your voice down. There are others nearby," Arthur whispered.

"Wh-what are you doing here? How did you find me?" She then looked at Gavin. She had forgotten that she was naked but despite the embarrassment, she was so glad they were there.

"That doesn't matter right now," Arthur answered. "We need to get you out of here."

Arthur saw an old key hanging on the wall next to a couple of black robes. Freeing Florence and getting her to put on one of the robes, they carefully made their way back into the cold chamber.

"*Fuck* ... here they come," John said.

The others up in the gantry watched with incredible tension as the other three made their way back up the stone steps. Arthur signalled with his finger to follow.

They gathered in the empty room with the other three stone tables.

"I ... I can't believe you are here and found me ... They stopped us in the forest, not long after we left the farm. One of them was lying in the road near a parked car. Another waved us down, pleading for help. Carl got out, and that's when they jumped him. They were too much for him ... then Jacob came out of the forest and dragged me from the car. We sped off in the other as Carl got up and followed in his car ... Wh-where is Carl? Is he okay?"

"He's ... he's dead, Florence," Arthur replied.

*"What?"*

"There's no time to explain. Try to be strong. We have to get you out of here before the ritual starts." Arthur started to think.

"What are we going to do with her, Arthur?" John asked.

Arthur paced a little around the half-lit room. He had no idea what to do and little time to think. *They* would most likely be coming back for her soon.

"What if we get her out and came back for them another time?" John suggested. "No, we can't. We *must* find Grant ... *Shit, shit, shit*!" He paced about too.

"Who's Grant?" Florence looked confused.

"He's a friend we believe they've also taken. He might be the guy in the cage. We found what we think are his glasses," David explained.

"Try and remain calm," Bob said.

"*Calm*, Bob? You just saw what they did to Eric. I'm worried I am going to end up like that. *All of us*!" John said.

*"Enough!"* Arthur raised his old voice slightly. "Here's what we're going to do ... one of us can take Florence back up to the surface."

"Wh-who's Eric?" Florence was even more confused.

"We'll explain later," Arthur replied. Usually a calm head on old shoulders, he was now beginning to lose focus. "We can leave Florence here, with one or two of us, whilst the others go and deal with *them*, or one of us can try and get her out."

"But what if whoever does that gets caught?" David asked.

"Then you'd just end up back down here. But if we could at least get her out, it gives her and her baby a chance," Arthur suggested.

"What about that mist up there? That might be just as dangerous?" John pointed out.

"I don't think that's so much of a threat. We need to decide *fast*. How many others are being held captive? Do you know, Florence?" Arthur tried to sound calm.

"I ... I don't know. Apart from the guy in the cage, I think I heard another girl scream. I can't be sure."

"It's okay." Smiled Arthur. "Who's going to take Florence back up?"

They were quick to agree who should go. Arthur needed to lead the party and Gavin and Bob were his gunmen. David refused to leave his uncle, so that left John.

"I'll do it ... How am I supposed to get us out of the tree, if we make it that far?"

"Take this," Arthur said, pulling out a purple vial from his satchel. "Pour this where the door was and if it still doesn't open, say *arbor aperiatur*."

"Arbor aperiatur," John repeated. "What if it still doesn't open?"

"It should, John. But if it doesn't, stay up near the passageway. Do *not* leave Florence, okay?"

"Okay. But what shall we do when we're up there? We can't just run through the forest."

"Get to that rock and hide behind it," Arthur answered. He was completely lost for ideas.

"And that's it?"

"If we don't succeed, then try and wait until dawn."

"And then what? Arthur, we'll be stuck in the middle of the forest. I can't remember the way we came. What if you all fail?" John sounded frantic.

"Then you take Florence and get as far away from here as possible. Just try and remember the way that we came. Try and put thoughts out to *Seath Mór* for guidance."

"Maybe I should go?" Gavin said.

"No, I'll do it," John said adamantly.

"Take this as well." Arthur pulled out an orange crystal with white speckles over it. "This will help prevent them from finding you. And this ..." Arthur pulled out his small crossbow and bolts and offered them to John.

Gavin told John to take the revolver instead because it would be easier for him to use. John took the revolver and handed back the crossbow and bolts to Arthur. John had never held a real gun, so Gavin quickly showed him the safety catch and how to switch it on and off, and how to point, aim and fire.

An emotional John gave David a firm hug, prayed that they succeeded and wished them all luck. With the soon to give birth Florence, John returned the way they had come. Florence had her arm over John's shoulders for support. The chanting seemed to be intensifying as they left.

The hopes of the others began to dwindle, after John and Florence had left. They then carefully made their way back to the gantry and resumed their crouched positions.

*****

After a little while, the chanting changed in tone and volume, slowed and then stopped completely.

"Look, something is happening ..." Bob said.

Famuli Cani were now lined up evenly in rows — five rows of ten on either side of the red carpet, heads still bowed and facing the front. Arthur counted a hundred worshippers.

All was quiet.

A few seconds later, another robed figure walked out from underneath the gantry to the right of the steps, dressed in black like the others, but with a black mask and horns, their mouth and chin visible. Just behind them, were twelve others dressed in dark red hooded robes. The masked figure led them in pairs up the carpet between the rows of worshippers.

"Who are they? Why are they dressed in different colours than the rest? And that one, with the horned mask?" asked Gavin quietly. He could feel his pulse pounding in his neck and ears as he gripped his shotgun in both hands.

"The ones in red are *The Elders*," Arthur answered.

"The Elders?" David asked.

"Yes. They are the eldest and most wise of the sect. Most likely responsible for bringing back the cult and Canus, after all these centuries. The one wearing the mask is the High Priest, who does their evil sermons and the sacrificing." Arthur swallowed.

The four watched as the High Priest stood behind the altar. The Elders stood a little behind him and to his side in sixes, their heads now also bowed and their faces undetectable.

The Satanic priest started speaking in Latin, addressing the others, who after a short while, raised their covered heads. The priest's voice was deep and dark as it echoed around the stone walls.

"He's basically saying again, how grateful they are to Satan ..." Arthur translated for them. "And for giving them Canus ..." Arthur then looked at his watch. It had gone half eleven. The watch then stopped ticking and he tapped the soft glass a few times. "... And how they will soon be blessed again to be in the presence of Canus."

"Tonight, shall be our finest and greatest Lammas Day, yet," said the High Priest, speaking in English now. "An extremely powerful one. A great night. The blood we will shed and sacrifices we shall make for Canus will make us more powerful and closer to immortality. Tonight, we honour ourselves, as well as our God, Canus, *The Great Grey One*!" The High Priest's voice boomed.

*"Ave Canus! Ave Canus! Ave Canus! Ave Canus!"* all the robed figures and twelve Elders shouted back excitedly. Their voices too, boomed around the walls.

It reminded David of his dreams. "God help us," he said quietly.

*****

Meanwhile, John and Florence were halfway up the stairs back up to the hidden passageway. John had made sure Florence didn't see into the room where Eric was.

"I'm too tired." Florence had to keep stopping for breath and because she ached all over and her stomach was hurting. "It's too much strain with the baby."

"I know, Florrie. But we have to get out of here *fast*, before they find you've gone." John was aching too and out of breath. He was helping her with one arm and holding the revolver in the other.

Florence tried not to look down. She could feel her baby kicking. "I think the baby's coming soon." She looked up at John, slouched over, her gown half open, her face and body sweating although she felt so cold.

"What? *Shit*! Don't say that!" John felt panic. This was the last thing he had wanted to hear. He too began sweating.

"Okay, I'm ready to go again," Florence said, standing back upright.

John was relieved that she was being so stoic. They finally reached the top.

"Okay, we're here," John said panting. They stood on the platform and he pulled out the vial Arthur had given him. He tried to remember the word he needed. "Are you okay, Florrie?"

"I think so." Florence tried to catch her breath. Her back ached the most. She looked up at him and smiled. Her hair was tangled with sweat and her face was grubby. "Thank you for coming with me, John."

"Don't thank me, yet," John replied. "We still have to get out of here."

"I'm sorry that you had to leave your friends," Florence said softly.

"It's okay. They're a strong bunch. I felt I should stay but I felt I should help you, too. You know what I mean?"

"I do." Florence smiled again. She was soaked in sweat.

John got his breath back and ran his hand through his hair. Florence looked so scared and vulnerable. He looked down at the sweat showing through his grey top. "It's a good job I used deodorant today, or my BO might have killed you before you reached the top!" he joked, trying to break the tension.

Florence laughed. "You are silly," she said.

Even in the darkest of hours, John's sense of humour shone through. It was, however, the last joke that he would make that night.

John composed himself and poured the contents of the vial over the bark as Arthur had done and repeated the phrase ten times. He began to panic. "Why isn't it working?"

"It ... it doesn't matter, John. Even if we get out, we still won't be safe," Florence said downbeat. She rubbed her belly with her right hand.

"We have to try, Florrie. For your sake *and* your baby's."

Florence admired John's selflessness. "Just keep trying."

John closed his eyes and took in a deep breath and breathed out. He said the word more slowly and calmly this time. "Ar-bor aperi-atur ..." Just as he was about to curse again, there was a rumble. The old tree shook and the passageway opened. "It worked!" John said almost in a state of shock. "Come on!"

John took Florence's arm and pulled her gently out of the hidden passageway and into the forest where the thick mist swirled around their knees. They could feel the cold energy and static from it as they made their way to behind the rock. Behind them, the passageway shut. There was no way back in now, not without another vial. John wondered if he would ever see David or the others again.

"I f-feel so c-cold, John." Florence was shaking uncontrollably.

"Some great plan, Arthur," John said, although he knew he was being unfair. Arthur had got them this far. He held Florence as they both shook from fear and cold. The strange mist danced around them, as though it was trying to reach out and grab them. Florence's bare feet began to freeze. John put his socks on her feet and then put his boots back on.

"I d-don't feel gr-eat," Florence said, closing her heavy eyes.

"Me, n-neither ... Florrie? F-Florrie ..."

*****

"What are we going to do?" David asked.

They were all fixated on Famuli Cani, watching as they chanted and worshipped Canus. They were paying homage to their *God* and preparing for whatever they were going to do.

Arthur knew it was almost midnight. "I have a feeling they won't come for Florence and her baby until later. Perhaps, as their final sacrifice. That's the biggest one. I do not believe they yet know that John has taken her. Nor do they know that we are here."

The four of them were crouched down biding their time to act, their backs and legs aching from the crouching and cold. Especially Arthur's.

"That guy in the cage still needs saving," David reminded Arthur. "I still can't tell if it is Grant. There still maybe others down here, too."

"I know, David. I'm trying to think."

Yes, they were armed, but with single barrel shotguns, which were also difficult to reload when nervous. There were only four of them against over a hundred cult members; they were badly outnumbered. Arthur also knew that they needed to do the job in full, destroy *all* of them at the same time, so they needed to wait until Canus arrived.

David didn't want to think about what might happen. At least John, Florence and her unborn child might have made it safely out of the lair.

Several minutes later, things started to develop further.

# Chapter Seventy-One

## 1st August, 2018 - Lammas Day

At just after midnight, the chanting had lowered significantly in volume. One hooded member of Famuli Cani, walked over to the old rusty winch on the left wall. The winch creaked as it turned, slowly lowering the cage from above them. The chain in the ceiling screeched and groaned as it came down. As the cage landed on the ground, the acolyte dragged out the half-naked sobbing man.

*"It is Grant, Arthur! John was right. Oh God!"*

Perhaps, this was the 'surprise' Jack had referred to.

"*Shhhh*, David. Keep your voice down," Arthur said. He could feel David's pain.

"But we have to help him. *We need to do something.*" David felt hopeless. "We can't just let him be sacrificed."

Grant, who had his hands and ankles tied, was wearing a black loincloth around his waist. He shuffled as he was pushed over to the carpet and then up to the High Priest, who stood behind the altar.

"Look at the *bastard* pushing him." David began to breath heavily.

*"P-please. D-don't kill me."* Grant sobbed. *"I haven't done anything."* Without his glasses and along with his tears, his vision was blurred, but he could see enough to know what was likely to happen to him.

Although he couldn't hear anything, David could sense Famuli Cani were laughing at Grant. "Grant," he said quietly to himself. David's eyes pricked with tears.

Grant still sobbing, was trying to wrestle free from the clutches of the acolyte who was trying to position him on the cold altar. He started screaming and shouting, crying out and begging for help. Famuli Cani were then heard laughing and mocking him, as he urinated over himself.

Another robed figure helped to lie Grant on the cold altar, forcing him flat. Grant kicked out at them as they untied his feet and arms. They captured his arms and ankles in metal shackles to each side of the altar, so that he could barely move. Grant was completely helpless. Finally, they fixed a metal throat brace.

The four from the gantry still looked on.

*"Please. I'm begging you! Let me go … Mum! Mum!"*

David closed his tear-filled eyes. "Please, God."

Famuli Cani began to chant louder, more passionately and excitedly. Seeing Grant placed upon the altar had increased their thirst for blood and sacrifice. Their chanting blanked out the hopeless cries of Grant … Then the chanting stopped. The only remaining sound was Grant still sobbing. Something else was about to happen.

"You! Go bring the other one, the girl," ordered the masked High Priest, pointing to one of the figures on his right, second row.

The figure obeyed, bowed their head and headed for the entrance the High Priest and The Elders had entered by. Less than a minute later, he returned. He walked out pulling a young dark-haired woman by a worn leather leash around her throat. She was sobbing as she was led up the red carpet. Her hands were tied together behind her back. She was also wearing a black robe but unhooded.

"My God," Gavin said. "They have another one. It must be the body we saw them carry from the boat."

It took a while for David to realise, perhaps because of the low lighting or because the woman's hair had fallen over her face. When he did realise, it hit him like *nothing* before in his entire life. "*Emily*! … But how?"

*****

While Betty rested downstairs after the men had left, Emily offered to help Father Adan unpack his delivery upstairs.

"They go up there, my dear," said Father Adan, pointing.

The Catholic priest had ordered some fine cutlery and plates online to treat himself. He loved proper crockery.

"Okay." Emily reached up to place a plate carefully in one of the small open cupboards in the kitchen.

Father Adan knew that it was impossible for Emily to take her mind off things, but he needed to try at least. Benji had also joined them and was sitting watching. The priest had given him some leftover chicken; the two cats were asleep in the small conservatory.

"Have you known Arthur, long?" Emily asked, turning to the opened box on the kitchen table. She extracted another plate from the excessive bubble wrap and cardboard packaging.

"You could say that." Father Adan smiled again. "He's a good man, Arthur. The best. He knows his stuff. God knows how to choose the right people." The priest put away a couple of knives and forks in one of the drawers and closed it. "Well, that's the cutlery put away, anyway." He clapped his hands rubbing them together.

As Emily finished putting away a couple more plates, there was a knock at the front door. She was a little startled.

Father Adan noticed her concern. "It's okay," he said, placing a hand on her shoulder, walking towards the front door. "Go into the living room."

Emily did as told and took Benji with her.

Father Adan looked through the small spyhole in the door and could see a man with short dark hair with his hands in his jacket pockets.

"D-don't open it," Emily said. She was a bundle of nerves.

"It'll be all right," Father Adan replied, although he hesitated before opening the door.

"Hey … I'm sorry to bother you, but my car has broken down. I was wondering if I could use your phone, please?" The man was polite and had a friendly tone.

"Well, erm, of course," replied the priest. "Do you not have one on you?"

"I do, but the bloody battery died." The man grinned.

Father Adan wasn't entirely convinced. He still took precautions. He stepped outside, pulling the door to. "I think it would be best if I get my mobile for you to use. Now isn't really a good time to come in."

"Oh, that's fine. I completely understand. I don't mean to be a nuisance or intrude," the man politely replied.

"Hold on one second …" Father Adan fetched his mobile and returned, standing a little further outside this time.

The man could then see Emily through the crack of the door. She had moved back near the kitchen, concerned and curious.

"Here you go," Father Adan said, handing the phone to the short-haired man.

"Thank you." The guy smiled, turned and walked a little way from the house. "Oh, I'm sorry," he said. "I don't think your phone is working."

"Really? It should be." Father Adan walked over to check the phone for himself.

Before Emily had the chance to warn him, another man approached and smashed him across the back of the head with what looked like a large plank of wood. The force knocked the priest's glasses off his face and he fell to the floor with a thud. The man with the short hair laughed and dropped the phone at his feet. Then he stared at Emily just inside the doorway. Both men darted towards the door before Emily could close it.

"I don't think so," the short-haired man said, sticking his black boot in the gap to prevent the door from shutting.

Emily screamed and ran through the open door down to the basement, frantically. She didn't have time to close the door behind her. They were just too quick.

Benji leapt at the shorter guy who had attacked Father Adan, who caught Benji in mid-air and threw him like a ragdoll at the wall, just missing the Jesus portrait. Benji hit his head and all along his side, where he'd been stabbed. He dropped to the floor, winded and whimpering.

The other guy dived at Emily's legs, pulling her to the ground.

*"Get off of me!"* Emily cried, kicking her short legs at him.

He laughed as she wriggled her legs free.

*"Betty, Betty … they're here … they've found us!"* Emily cried out as she exited the corridor.

Betty sat up in bed but didn't say anything. The two men were both on top of Emily now. One pinned her down on her back whilst she struggled and the other tied her hands and feet together using cable ties. Emily let out one final scream, before she was gagged with a dirty white cloth that cut into the corners of her mouth as it was pulled tight.

"What you want to do about this one?" the shorter guy asked, pointing at Betty on the bed, who just sat there looking blank.

Emily lay on the floor trying to scream, looking up at Betty for help.

The short-haired man had his right knee pushed into Emily's lower back. "Anthony said not to worry about this daft old bat. She's not worth the hassle. She will be under our Master's influence for good after tonight. That will be her punishment until the day she dies. And after tonight, she'll hopefully have no one."

"Hello. Would you like something to eat?" Betty asked.

"Ha! Good. Stupid old cow. Look at her," the shorter one said and they both laughed.

"Let's get you out of here anyway, beautiful … we've got *big* plans for you." The short-haired one, picked up Emily and threw her over his shoulder, whilst the other guy followed them, still laughing.

"It's a shame what's going to happen to her, tonight. She's a cute little thing, ain't she?" the short and stocky guy said, seeing Emily's tears streaking down her pretty face.

"She sure is. But a shame? As if ..."

The shorter guy laughed. "Nah. It isn't really. I can't *wait* for tonight."

Walking past Benji, who was still winded, the shorter one stopped and asked about the dog, but it seemed their orders were only for the girl.

"And what about this pathetic, old sack of shit out here?" the shorter one asked again.

Father Adan was either dead or out cold. He hadn't moved and was bleeding from the back of his head.

"Fuck him. We can save him for another night if need be. Anthony's orders were only for the girl. We can take her to the cabin in the forest before the main event tonight. Besides, the priest can live with the guilt of not having kept the girl safe and knowing how she suffered and died. He failed."

They both laughed further as a black car reversed up the driveway. The driver stepped out and greeted Emily as he opened his boot. "Hello again, Emily," he said with a smug smile.

Emily recognised Anthony. She tried to scream and struggle, but it was in vain, as they dumped her in the boot and closed it.

*****

*"How did they find her, Arthur? You said she would be safe?"* David said hysterically in a whisper. One of his best friends was about to be slaughtered and now his beloved Emily.

Arthur couldn't find the words. "I don't know. It should have been safe there for them."

David wondered if Betty, Father Adan and Benji were already dead. He had no idea if John and Florence had made it out safely, either.

"Arthur? What about Betty? What have they done to her? The cats, Benji and the priest? Are they also here?" Bob asked frantically.

"I don't know," Arthur repeated.

"We need to *do* something. We can't just sit here and watch this happen. We need to at least try to do something," Bob said.

"*Fuck this*! If we're going to die, we may as well die fighting." Acting on impulse, David yanked the shotgun from his uncle's hands and suddenly got up. He had never fired a gun before in his life. He then made his way down the steps, his bad leg hurting.

*"David, no!"* Arthur hissed after him.

David's heart pumped ferociously through his chest as he slowly walked onto the red carpet at the bottom of the steps. Rage and adrenaline drove him. Famuli Cani hadn't noticed him as they had begun chanting quietly with their heads bowed. Emily was to the left of the altar, next to six of The Elders in their red robes. David could hear her sobbing, with the leash tight around her neck and Grant's cries.

"*Arthur*. We need to do something," Gavin said in panic.

Without thinking, David shouted, pointing the gun at no one in particular as he got closer to the rows of acolytes. *"Hey!"*

The robed figures stopped chanting and turned to face him. The High Priest and Elders also lifted their heads, looking straight at David.

*"Let them fucking go!"*

"D-David? Is that you?" Grant asked in disbelief. He managed to twist his head to catch sight of his friend holding the shotgun.

"It's okay, Granty. I'm going to get you out of here." To David, his words sounded stupid. As if the cult would just let David waltz in here and rescue two of his friends.

*"David!"* Emily yelled, but the robed figure yanked on her leash, causing her to choke.

There was silence for a few seconds. Then all the robed figures including the masked High Priest started clapping their hands, first slowly and then picking up the pace.

"Well, if it isn't the handsome hero, here to save the day. We were hoping that you would come," said the High Priest. "You are either very brave, or very stupid. But I think I speak for us all, when I say you are a *very* brave young man. We knew you would come."

*"Let my friends go!"*

The High Priest laughed. "I don't think so. But now, you can witness your friends' sacrifices firsthand. And then, your own. You have saved us the trouble of sending pieces of them to you …" The High Priest laughed further. "I take it the others are here, with you?"

"I came alone. The others were too scared," David lied.

The High Priest was having none of it. "Don't think you can fool me. Do not lie! It was your disobedience and ignorance that caused this. If you hadn't come here, you and your friends wouldn't be in this situation. Particularly green eyes, here. But we are glad that you did. This makes it all the sweeter and more powerful. Plus, you found the dagger."

"You shouldn't have messed with *my* family. My uncle's farm. Angus, that little boy, Charlie, all those years ago. Your *God* already started on us before we came up here. My flat, scaring Grant. Did you just expect me not to do anything?"

The High Priest laughed again, walked round the altar and jumped off the platform. "Your courage and failure to stay away has been your downfall. *Canus* admired you. All of you. It's what gives us power. *Will* give us power, when we take your lives and souls … And yes, that little boy all those years back — I remember him. The screams he made that night and when we took his life. I was still learning my trade back then. I was merely an initiate and worked my way up." He moved closer to David.

Bob clenched his fists as he heard the High Priest talk about Charlie.

*"You're bastards, all of you!"* David spat. "And where is this great *God* of yours?"

The High Priest laughed and grinned. "You will meet Canus, soon enough. *Properly*, this time. It will be the last great thing that you will see before you fall and die at its feet."

David aimed the gun at the High Priest.

"*Pull* the trigger, David. See what happens," the High Priest goaded in his dark voice.

David pulled the trigger three times. It just wouldn't fire.

The High Priest laughed harder and the others joined in.

Arthur, Gavin and Bob looked down at David. They knew he hadn't switched the safety catch off.

"Jack … why don't you bring David to me," the High Priest asked, before turning his back and making his way up to behind the altar.

"My pleasure, my lord," came a voice from a robed figure. Jack then stepped out onto the carpet. He walked towards David, took off his hood and smiled. "Hello, David." He grinned. "Why don't you give me the gun, now?"

"Fuck you, Jack … Jacob."

As Jack went to grab the gun, David tried striking him across the head with it. Jack ducked just in time and sucker-punched David hard in the ribs and face, knocking him to the ground. Emily screamed.

Jack quickly scooped up the shotgun, beating David to it. "Looks like round two, doesn't it?" Jack laughed, now pointing the gun at David. "Only this time, you won't escape us. I underestimated you and I received my punishment for that …" Jack opened up his robe. He was naked underneath and showed his back to David, who still lay on the cold black floor. Jack's back was full of deep lacerations, red and sore, still bloody, where he had been whipped. "But you can never hide from us. We are far too powerful."

David slowly rose to his feet. He winced and clutched his left ribcage. His lip was bleeding and his wounded leg was throbbing again.

"We knew you would come, and Emily confessed, confirming you were on your way to us. Let's just say, she wasn't exactly willing to blab at first. We had to get it out of her." The High Priest laughed, his mouth clearly visible through the bottom of the horned mask. "We would have got all of you regardless, if not tonight, at some point. We had a feeling that old bastard, Arthur, would find a way down here. But I am surprised we didn't detect or sense you down here. We believed that we would."

"What is wrong with all you people?" David tried to fight back his tears.

The High Priest chuckled. "We wondered where you went, after we went back to the farm. You know, we only found out you were at Newtonmore by chance, when one of our newer members who lives there saw you leave that church."

"Lammas Day is a powerful one for us." Jack beamed. "Bringing your other weakling friend up here, dragging him from his sleep and bed, was most satisfying."

"I think that's enough talking, Jack," the High Priest said in a strong authoritative tone. "You four, bring David up here so he can experience close up the wonderful and excruciating pain of watching those closest to him suffer and die." The High Priest smiled broadly and pointed to other members of the cult to assist Jack.

As Jack and the others went to grab David, he fought back but was knocked to the ground again and repeatedly punched and kicked by the bare feet of the acolytes. Jack used the butt of the shotgun to hit David's body. David tried protecting his face with his hands and put up a good fight but was soon overpowered.

*"Stop! Leave him alone! Please!"* Emily pleaded, her voice breaking with emotion.

David hoped the others would step in and do something. His nose and mouth were bleeding. He was carried up to near the altar where Grant lay.

"We've certainly got some *events* lined up for tonight," Jack said, grinning. "We hope you enjoy the show." Jack fell back into line, replaced his hood and placed the shotgun on the floor next to his bare feet. The other three stood with David, gripping him tightly.

"You have courage, David. Unlike the others. I do not believe you came alone. I suspect that they are up there somewhere, watching on, including that coward, Arthur." The High Priest looked up towards the gantry. "Let them watch you die. And the others. They won't do anything against our number down here. We'll get them when it is their turn to fall."

"*Arthur*! That's my nephew down there, and his friend and girlfriend. We can't just stay here and do nothing," Bob whispered anxiously. "They know we are up here. We're sitting ducks."

"I know. I might have a plan. But we need to be patient and wait for our moment to strike."

"We have to do something, *fast*," Gavin said. He was tempted to go down those steps himself. But he had to be sensible.

Arthur explained that he had potions which would render people unconscious, but not enough to wipe out all of them. Canus was yet to be summoned and they might never get a better chance than tonight to defeat the cult. They had to be patient and bide their time for a window of opportunity.

"What about his friend on the altar?" Gavin asked.

"I'm … sorry, but there's nothing we can do for him. If we attack now, we will be overpowered by them in no time at all. Yes, we would be able to take some of them out, but it won't be enough, and it will be all in vain. We are heavily outnumbered. We have to wait for our moment. It will come — trust me."

*****

John woke up lying on the freezing cold ground with the mist still swirling around. *"Florrie?"*

Florence was lying next to him, in only his socks and her half-open gown.

John fastened the gown around her. *"Florrie. Hey."*

Florence slowly opened up her eyes. "John. Wh-what happened? I'm so cold."

John holding Florence, rubbed her hands to try to warm them up for her.

"Oh, *no*!" she cried out. "My waters broke. The baby's coming!"

*"What?"* John replied, his eyes widening. "It can't be. Not now, not here!"

"My baby, my baby …" Florence's voice faded; she seemed to be drifting back into unconsciousness.

*"Florrie!"* John shouted. He then saw something out across the loch. A bright yellow ball of light floated across the water, causing the mist to part and casting a reflection as it did so. John had to rub his eyes to make sure he wasn't imagining it. It looked warm, whatever it was. "What is that?"

The light stopped a metre away from the pair. John swallowed, nervously, wondering if it was something to do with Famuli Cani. John then heard a voice in his head.

"Do not be afraid," it said. "I will protect and look after her. Go to your friends. They will need you."

"Who are you?" John asked, already trusting the light. There was something about it. Something warm and trustworthy. It seemed to dissipate the coldness from around them.

"Seath Mór. Chief of the Clan Shaw."

"Seath Mór? The one who killed them, centuries ago?" John thought he was hallucinating from the cold.

"Yes. But you must hurry. *Go*!"

John, who was usually sceptical, knew that this was the spirit of Seath Mór. He believed Seath Mór would protect Florence; he had already protected her from the cold. His friends down below surely needed him. He looked at Florence again, where she lay resting. He knew she would be safe. He heard a rumble coming from the tree and the secret passageway opened up again.

*"Go now!"* said the voice.

John felt the ground through the mist for the small revolver that had slipped from his hand and made his way to the passageway. Looking back, he could see the ball of light envelope and expand behind the rock, where the unconscious and soon to give birth Florence, lay. John headed back down the stairs, hoping his friends were still alive.

*****

The three still crouched behind the stone gantry, watching in fear as the torches around the chamber began to flicker and dim. The High Priest removed the sodden black loincloth from around Grant's waist, tossing it to the floor. He then pulled out a small grey vessel from inside his robe and shook blood from it, all over the naked body of Grant who winced and tried shaking his face away, as it spluttered over him.

David's hands were now tied behind his back and his ankles were tied together. They had pushed him down to sit on his knees and watch his friend. The High Priest began chanting and The Elders and worshippers joined in. Grant's heart could be seen beating through his chest. He was begging David to help him but there was nothing David could do. He had to take his eyes off Grant; he could bear it no longer. Famuli Cani chanted louder and swayed as one, their chant ringing throughout the stone chamber.

John stumbled on his way back down the tree staircase and dropped the revolver. The gun fell into a black hole at the base of the staircase. He reached in, but there was nothing but thin air. He continued and once he reached the passageway, he started running. He tripped on a rogue stone and grazed his right hand. He could hear the chanting echoing throughout the passageway as he got nearer to where he had left the others. He had to hold his side, where he had a painful stitch, but eventually he slowed down as he approached the end. He crouched down to walk out and hid behind the gantry, seeing Famuli Cani down below. Their heads were held high looking up and the High Priest was standing behind the black altar, arms aloft, head facing up too. The naked body of Grant was stretched out on the cold altar. But John had yet to realise it was him.

John couldn't make out Emily's face but he saw David's straight away. He froze and stared. His heart sank, seeing his best friend kneeling there. He then focused on the naked man screaming out and recognised Grant. The two people who meant the absolute world to him were down there about to be sacrificed. Before he started to panic further, wondering where the others were, he heard Gavin.

*"John. Over here."*

John quickly made his way over. *"Why are you just sitting here?"* John hissed.

"Where's Florence?" Arthur asked.

John anxiously explained what had happened back up on the surface, and the others explained briefly what had happened back down below, and that Emily was also down on the altar platform.

Arthur handed John the small crossbow.

*"We have to fucking going down there, Arthur!"*

"If you go down there now, John, you'll end up the same," Arthur said.

John peered through the gantry gap, watching. He looked back at Arthur. He was right. *"Shit!"* he whispered to himself. He formed tears of frustration and fear for his friends below. He sat on his knees, scratching and digging his nails into his thighs.

The masked High Priest chanted alone now, holding out his hands and looking down at Grant on the altar:

*"O Satan, Princeps Tenebrarum,*
*Magne qui de caelo lapsus es,*
*Expulse,*
*Deus Vere, Domine Sabaoth.*
*Nobis enim famulum tuum, illum Canum tulisti.*
*Accipe hoc oblatum, hoc sacrificium."*

In unison, all of them chanted, *"Ave Satan! Ave Satan! Ave Cane! Ave Cane!"*

The chanting in unison carried on and the High Priest then took out a large sacrificial knife from inside his robe and held it high aloft, behind his horn-masked head.

Amongst all the turmoil and noise, David couldn't help notice that it was the same slightly curved knife from in his nightmare of Betty killing his uncle. "Please, God … Grant. I'm so, so sorry," he whispered to himself. Tears ran down his bruised and bloodied face.

"You will love this part," came the voice from a robed figure standing over David.

David tried to turn away, but the robed acolyte held his face in place, so he couldn't avert his eyes. When David closed his eyes, the figure forced them open with his dirty fingertips.

*"Tibi hoc sacrificium offerimus … "* the High Priest said.

*"Ave Satan! Ave Satan! Ave Cane! Ave Cane!"* the rest still chanted as it got faster and reached a crescendo.

*"We offer you, this sacrifice …!"* The High Priest threw down the knife with incredible force, plunging it deep into Grant's chest.

The chanting stopped immediately.

The tearing of Grant's flesh and the cracking of his rib cage could be heard from the gantry. Blood splashed onto the black candles snuffing one of them out. The sound of the masked High Priest cutting Grant's bones as he pursued his task was unbearable. His eyes were wide with evil and excitement and his gritted teeth smiled in *ecstasy*. Dribble came from his mouth.

Grant let out the most horrific scream and his restricted body and head convulsed from the pain … *"D-Da-David … "* came his dying last words as he tilted his head round sorrowfully to David. His eyes flickered and then there was a lifeless stare. Blood trickled from the corner of his mouth. He was dead. His right leg spasmed involuntarily for a few seconds.

The High Priest, with his now bloodied mask and mouth, dug his hand into the gaping wound in Grant's chest cavity and yanked out his heart. He held it up to show the rest. They cheered euphorically. Grant's blood rolled down the sides of his body and dripped from the altar onto the floor.

*"No, no, no, no … "* John muffled a scream in Gavin's chest, thumping it as he did so. Gavin held him tight to stop John's cries reaching below.

Emily fainted when the knife went into Grant's chest. She was half-held up by her leash.

One of The Elders pulled out an old wooden skull bowl from inside their robe. The masked High Priest squeezed the heart into it. Taking their time, they then passed it around, each drinking the blood from it …

David too was forced to drink the warm blood of his friend. The masked High Priest grinned and thrust it into David's mouth. David, looking into the dark eyes through the holes of the mask, spat the blood back at the mask and threw himself at the High Priest with a fair amount of force, using his right shoulder. It knocked the High Priest back into the altar sending his mask flying. The dropped skull bowl toppled over, spilling its contents and another robed figure grabbed David.

The now unmasked High Priest turned to face David, laughing. "You really are quite a feisty one, aren't you?"

David recognised the dark, black-haired man. He had first seen him coming off the motorway and then driving the taxi for Emily, Annabel and Nigel the night of the disco. Emily had mentioned his name but David couldn't recall it. It seemed like a lifetime ago, back when Grant was alive.

Emily came round. She looked at the flaccid dead body of Grant, still bleeding out. She then saw the High Priest as he bent down to pick up his bloody mask. *"Z-Zac?"*

Zac, held the mask in his right hand. "Hi," he said sarcastically. "Well, that's one of you down, anyway." He then laughed. "I can already feel the *power* flowing through me. All of us … who is going to be next? But we don't want to go there just yet. Something to look forward to later on. I think it's time for a break. Time for a *different* kind of entertainment, don't you think?"

# Chapter Seventy-Two

## 1st August, 2018 - Lammas Day

Zac motioned for two people to come forward to the raised platform. Jack took off his hood, and the other was a woman, judging by the shape of her large breasts through the robe. She stood for a few moments and then pulled back her hood. She turned to David and smiled.

*"Annabel,"* David said incredulously.

*"That bitch!"* John whispered sharply up in the gantry.

"A-Annabel," Emily said sadly and shocked. *"Why?"*

"Hello." Annabel smiled again. "Well, isn't this a night for surprises?"

"But how? Why?"

"Because, Em. I *want* to … You've met my godmother, haven't you? And my godfather? Ilene and Gerald."

Two of the dark red dressed Elders on the left near to Emily removed their hoods. The old woman, well into her eighties, approached and stood in front of her.

"Hello, my dear." The Elder grinned, exposing her yellow stained teeth and fusty breath."

David recognised them too. *Ilene* and *Gerald* were the elderly couple he and John had met near the farm, who Benji didn't like.

"They introduced me to all of this, when they took me in after my parents left," Annabel explained. "They and the others brought Famuli Cani and Our Great Grey One, back — Canus."

"But, you're a good person, Annabel. Y-you're my friend." Emily began to sob. "How could you do this to us?"

"It proves how little you know me, Emily." Annabel started to laugh. "Aw, don't cry, Emmy," she teased, squeezing Emily's cheeks together with her hand. "If it wasn't for your boyfriend here, and his band of merry men, you wouldn't be in this predicament. Too bad!"

"Anna ..." Emily continued sobbing.

"I said, don't cry!" Annabel slapped Emily's face so hard that it left a red mark and strained her neck against the leash.

David looked on. A mixture of pure sadness and raw rage.

The Elder, Ilene, stepped nearer Emily. "I may be very old, dearie, but with each sacrifice, my youth gradually returns. Soon the effects will last for ever. Our patience will bear more fruit. We *will* be rewarded thanks to Our Great Grey One. Or Canus, if you prefer." Ilene chuckled showing her yellow teeth.

Emily tried to turn her face away from the stale breath of Ilene, whose old grey eyes looked straight into Emily's green youthful ones.

"Drinking the blood, the sacrifices of the innocent, in particular, children and animals makes us stronger. Our afflictions will soon disappear for good. Thanks to Canus, we will regain our youthful looks and gain immortality. Tonight, takes us a great deal further towards our goal. The sacrifices and the blood: it's our elixir of life." Ilene laughed and the rest of her cult joined with her.

"And don't forget to tell her, dearest," Gerald called out, "we enjoy doing it!"

The laughter intensified.

"How ... how could you do all of this?" Emily continued to weep.

Annabel smiled as Ilene's face turned serious. She pushed her wrinkly old face to within touching distance of Emily's, staring right into her. Emily couldn't help but gaze back as she watched Ilene's face start to change. It transpired into a younger Ilene right there in front of them. Emily's jaw dropped in shock.

"You see, pretty? *This* is why." Ilene pulled her younger looking face away returning to her older version.

Emily swallowed. "It's no excuse for killing innocent animals and children, and people."

"I guess that's a matter of opinion, *brèagha*!" Ilene laughed. "My ancestors remained my age many years, until Seath Mór and his clan stopped us. *Bastards*!" Ilene hissed spittle over Emily's face.

Emily winced, turning her neck and throat awkwardly to the side in the leash.

Ilene spat on the floor as a mark of disgust towards Seath Mór. "But we have long since returned and are more *powerful* than ever. Thankfully, there were still some of us left all those centuries ago, and we discovered our lineage."

Emily started to shiver. She was scared and her feet were cold on the black floor.

"You'll have to excuse me anyway, Emily. I've got some *fucking* to do." Annabel smirked.

Putting his mask back on, Zac, the High Priest, explained that it was Annabel's turn to choose who she wanted to have sex with after the latest sacrifice. He unshackled Grant from the altar.

Annabel chose Jack. She undid her robe and let it drop to the floor, revealing her huge breasts and naked body.

Jack did the same as he approached her, already aroused. "I've been looking forward to this." He looked to David and winked.

"Enjoy yourself, my dear." Ilene grinned.

Annabel shoved the limp body of Grant from the altar in a disrespectful manner, and then climbed up and laid back. Jack started to mount her and the others watched on with pleasure. Ilene grinned, gently nodding her head up and down. The pair grew more excited as they became covered in Grant's blood.

*****

Jack finished by sodomising Annabel from behind, with her huge breasts hanging down; she moaned in ecstasy.

*"Sick bastards. They will pay!"* John hissed from above.

Zac stepped forwards. "We are now approaching the big event, or should I say *events*, of the night. I suspect the others are up there somewhere, watching. Well, apart from Carl," Zac cruelly mocked. "I hope they enjoyed the show, seeing as they were too *gutless* to come down like your good self, David."

Arthur knew he had to come up with something. Grant had already lost his life, and unless they did something, David and Emily would too. As would all of them. He had prayed to God for guidance, and also to Seath Mór. He had been focused on that whilst Annabel and Jack were having intercourse on the sacrificial altar.

"*Harold*, take David," Zac instructed. "He needs to be prepared sufficiently for his own sacrifice, whilst we prepare for the summoning. Let him keep his jeans for now. We can remove them when the time comes." Zac laughed. "You two, go with him. Take the shotgun, just in case the others try anything. We'll get them soon enough. They can't stay hidden for ever."

The tall and thin, hooded figure of Harold walked out from his row, to in front of David. He looked down at him, his lazy eye drooping and watery and his horrible gaunt face smiling. He and another robed figure carried David to the back, whilst a third followed behind carrying the shotgun. They disappeared into the opening where Zac and The Elders had come from and Emily, the other passageway next to the stone steps.

Arthur saw this as his window of opportunity.

"Arthur? We need to do something!" Bob said.

"This could be our chance to act. We need to get down there and rescue David," Arthur replied, peering through the gap in the gantry on his haunches, his thin old legs, aching.

Zac and the others began to chant again. Zac's arms were held upwards, looking to the ceiling. They were preparing for the next step in their ceremony. Emily was alone on the platform, shaking. Famuli Cani were already facing the front. But now Zac the High Priest and the twelve Elders turned around and faced the flaming inverted pentagram and upside-down crosses.

*"Arthur!"* Gavin said.

"Let's move to where they took David. Quickly, whilst they're chanting and have their backs to us." Arthur made a move, his knees cracked as he rose.

The others followed him slowly, hoping that they wouldn't be detected. Carefully, they walked down the stone steps and then down the other small passageway.

With some small steps leading down, it was an identical stone passageway like the other where Florence was. A few torches lined the walls. They could hear voices at the end and there was light in a small room to the left. As they came closer, John and Gavin recognised Harold's slow drawl as he spoke to David. He was telling David how brave he was and how this would make his sacrifice to Canus more perfect and powerful.

Peeking into the partially lit room, they could see David was now gagged and had been strapped to an old wooden table at the back of the room.

Harold, tore open David's dark blue top, exposing his chest and torso. The other two figures stood back and watched Harold fetch items from a drawer. He brought a bowl, which contained a small brush and some brown powder, a brass ornamental jug and a small decorative blade to the table. He then cut his inner right arm with the blade, and filled the jug with his own blood, squeezing on his arm to speed the flow.

David was watching and struggling to get free; still bound. He was trying to shout through the filthy gag.

Harold then poured the jug into the bowl with the powder, and started to mix them together with the brush, grinning to himself. He then started to speak in Latin, holding the bowl over his head, after which he brushed some markings and symbols delicately over David's body. "This … is one of … my favourite parts … I'm making sure … that you will feel … the most pain." Harold grinned wickedly, drooling, looking over David. The sweat from Harold's face began to drip onto David.

David turned his head away, cursing Harold.

Arthur reached into his satchel and pulled out a small breakable vial. This was one of his 'bombs' and the only way he could take out the two robed figures silently. Arthur tapped on Gavin's shoulder, and pointed towards Harold and gestured 'throwing' his elbow. Gavin nodded, knowing what he meant.

The hooded figures had their backs to Arthur. He closed his eyes for a moment and then stepped a little closer to them. Opening his eyes, he tossed the bomb down with force. A purple powder shot up from the ground in a puff, into the faces of the two figures.

Gavin held his breath dashing past the figures as they clutched at their throats gasping for air. They soon dropped to the floor, including the shotgun. Gavin smashed into Harold, who was in some kind of trance, crashing him into the wall behind David. He crumpled to the floor in a heap.

Bob picked up his shotgun and they freed David.

"Wh-what took you?" David asked. *"They killed Grant … Ripped out his fucking heart!"*

"We know, David. We saw everything. I'm sorry but we couldn't do anything. There aren't enough of us to overcome them just like that." Arthur put a hand on David's shoulder. "I'm so sorry. This could be *our* opportunity now, though."

"John!" David saw his friend in the open doorway. "Where's Florrie?"

"She's safe. Seath Mór is looking after her," John answered.

*"What?"* David asked confused.

"We can explain later, if we get out of here," Arthur said.

"What about my wife, Arthur? Is Betty down here, too, somewhere? Is she even alive?"

"Shit. *Benji*!" David quickly remembered.

"I do not believe they are down here. I am not completely sure, but I still feel they are alive. But we can worry about them after." Arthur searched the drawers and found some rope and rags to gag and tie the hooded figures. He also found a set of four heavy keys, attached to a ring.

"I can't believe that Annabel is one of them, too!" John looked angry and sad.

"I know, mate!" David replied.

Arthur planned to disguise themselves in the robes and return with David. Arthur would try to pass off as Harold as they both had slim builds. Bob and John would disguise as the other two acolytes. Luckily, they were both roughly the same height as them.

They took off their tops, shoes and socks to look the part but kept their jeans on. John put his robe on and pushed the crossbow down the back of his jeans with the bolts. Gavin would stay out of sight until needed. Arthur slid into Harold's sweaty gown.

"Ugh," John said, looking down at the tied-up naked body of Harold. "Why does he look so ill and fragile?"

"I don't know, John," Arthur replied. He took what he could fit in his pockets from his satchel. The dagger was slipped down the front of his jeans. He took off his crucifix and stuffed that in one of his back pockets. "I'm not sure that he's even completely human."

Harold's yellow and pale body looked starved; his skeleton clearly visible through his skin. A large blue bruise had formed on his side, where Gavin had slammed him into the wall.

"Why didn't they just come up to the gantry and get us, seeing as they knew we were most likely up there?" John asked.

"They didn't believe we were a threat against their numbers and they enjoyed us watching on helplessly … Their pride and ignorance may be their downfall," Arthur answered.

"What about the bodies, Arthur?" David asked.

Before Arthur could answer, they heard a bump from underneath the stone floor.

*"What was that?"* John asked. "Is that someone underneath us?"

They heard the noise again. Arthur sensed something. "There are people underneath us."

"What?" Gavin said.

Arthur walked to the far corner of the stone room and knelt down. There was a trapdoor built into the floor, bolted shut with a metal ring latch. Arthur opened it. A small ladder went down and they could hear muffled sobbing. Arthur climbed down. There were four cages at the bottom in a row on the left side and three lit torches on the opposite wall.

A young Chinese couple were huddled, tied up together in one cage, sobbing and gagged. In the second cage, lay a short balding man, who was also gagged and tied. The third cage was empty. In the fourth, were six young children, who stared blankly at Arthur. One young boy of eight or nine had a black eye and other bruises on his face and neck. There was another boy around six or seven, two girls the same age, and a boy and girl who looked older.

Fifty to sixty human face masks hung in pairs on the wall, their flesh looking grey and old.

"I'm not going to hurt you," Arthur said, holding his hands up, aware he was now robed like the others so they would assume he was an acolyte. "I'm *not* one of them."

The others wondered who he was talking to. Arthur told them to come down. But to hurry. There was one more surprise in store for them all.

*"Derek!"* Bob exclaimed, when he saw him in the cage.

Derek and the young Chinese couple were dazed, confused and frightened, but other than that, they were physically fine. Arthur warned the others that the children may have been primed for sect membership. He decided to keep them where they were for now. They sat silently, watching.

Gavin suggested lowering Harold and the other two acolytes' naked bodies down to place them in one of the cages. They also hid the rest of their own clothes and belongings and Arthur's satchel. They then shut and bolted the trapdoor and Gavin put the keys in his pocket.

Arthur decided to send the Chinese couple, who turned out to be the missing campers, back up to the surface, so he gave them another vial and told them the 'magic' word they needed to open the entrance. He instructed them to make their way to the rock, where Florence was hiding, hopefully protected by the spirit of Seath Mór. Famuli Cani were still facing the front; using that to their advantage, the Chinese couple hastily made their way up into the chamber and up the steps. Derek was also advised to leave with them, but he wanted to remain with his friends.

Arthur found another leather leash and tied it loosely around David's neck. His hands were also loosely tied, so he could easily undo the knots to free himself. In this way they were imitating how Emily had been taken out.

The three in disguise pulled their hoods in to cover their faces more. Pulses began to soar.

"Are you ready?" Arthur asked them all.

David struggled to swallow. "Let's do this."

John and Bob both took in a deep breath and exhaled sharply.

"I can't believe we're about to attempt this," John said. Like them all, he was scared beyond belief.

Arthur, posing as Harold, slowly walked back out of the opening from the steps and onto the red carpet. They had no idea what would happen once David and Arthur reached the altar. Famuli Cani were still chanting. Arthur led David up the carpet between the Satanists and closer to the platform and altar. Grant's body lay as before. David closed his eyes. Bob was to the left behind David and Arthur, holding the shotgun and John was to his right.

John took his position back with the acolytes — surrounded by evil. Annabel was two rows to the right in front of him. Bob did the same, carefully resting the shotgun on the ground near his bare feet.

The chanting slowly came to a halt, less than a minute after David and Arthur reached the altar close to Zac.

"Ah ... here is our *special* one," Zac, the High Priest said, turning and looking at David.

The Elders also turned around.

Emily still had her head lowered. She glanced up at David and saw the blood stains on his body and had to turn away. Seeing the symbols and markings on his body was too frightening.

"Nice work on the symbols, Harold. Perhaps, your best work yet," Zac praised, though with a little sarcasm.

Arthur gave a brief nod to acknowledge the compliment, his head already bowed. He was hoping that he didn't have to say anything.

Zac instructed 'Harold' to stay where he was. "Go bring us Florence," Zac then ordered two different acolytes. "I'm sure she is about to *pop* soon." He grinned.

David and the rest of his group wondered what the hell would happen when they realised Florence was gone.

*"She's gone!"* one of the robed figures shouted in a rasping voice upon his return. The other figure went up the steps to search the gantry.

The rest of the cult turned to face him, then back to the front. John and Bob could sense the anger and rage amongst them.

*"She's what?"* Jack shouted.

"*Calm* yourself, Jack. They won't have got far. They couldn't have escaped, unless ... unless I have underestimated you." Zac turned and frowned at David. He was certain they had been hiding up in the gantry.

One of The Elders joined him.

*"We need her!"* Jack raised his voice. "We should have fetched her when David came down!"

"Silence, Jack! She's still here … You will tell me *everything* that I wish to know, David," Zac demanded, grabbing at David's throat tightly, digging the leather leash into his neck.

"Shall we go and search for them?" the rasp-voiced figure asked as his fellow acolyte returned from the gantry.

"No, not yet. How many of you are there, David? *Tell me now*!"

"Th-three," David lied, with his throat gripped.

"Who's with you?" Zac released his hand from David's throat.

"Me, John and Arthur. That's it." David included Arthur's name to sound more believable.

"Where are they? How did you get in through the passageway?"

David tried to swallow and hesitated.

*"Speak!"*

"Arthur did it. He used something on the tree, which opened up the passageway down here. We freed Florrie and watched from the gantry. That's who we came for. We saw the vast numbers of you all and realised we could never defeat you. We were about to leave. That was, until I saw Grant and Emily. The others told me to leave them as there was nothing I could do. But I couldn't walk away from them without trying." David sounded convincing.

"That bastard demonologist certainly does have his ways. He no doubt *blocked* us from seeing you all here. I have to hand it to him. But it will all be in vain … Why didn't the others come with you? You all left that priest's house together."

"My uncle and Gavin got too scared in the forest. They left us and headed back. They tried to convince me to do the same but I carried on."

"Admirable of you," Zac replied. He then muttered and then began to laugh. "So, your chickenshit of an uncle and his sidekick did a runner, eh, and the others left you down here by yourself?"

*"He's lying!"* Jack shouted. "Let me go look for them. You said they couldn't get out, so they should be stuck at the top."

"I believe he's telling the truth, Jack. I can see it in his pretty blue eyes. Either way, it matters not. Even if that old fool, Arthur, and his weak magic got them out, they won't get far in the mist. We *will* find them and Florence. We still have David and his other half for Canus, and the other three. Our Master will not be too disappointed. We have more than enough."

*"But I want Florrie and my baby!"* Jack was enraged.

"Remember your place, Jack!" said The Elder standing by Zac, in an old Scottish accent. "We won't accept insubordination. It was your mistake last night that caused this. If you had brought them to us then, as you should have done, we *wouldn't* be in this situation."

"Forgive me, My Elder. You know how much this means to me. The chances of us having our own children to sacrifice are so remote. I *want* their sacrifices."

"And you shall," replied The Elder. "Even if not tonight."

"We should still check if he is telling the truth. They may still be here," said the raspy voice.

Zac ordered the same two acolytes and a third to search while they began summoning Canus. He instructed them to take the shotgun.

One of them approached Bob and bent down at his feet to pick up the shotgun. Bob's heart pounded as he closed his eyes, praying that he wouldn't be detected.

Arthur and the others, started to get more afraid and anxious. They wondered if the Chinese couple had managed to escape.

Gavin tried to remain out of sight at the foot of the small steps. He knew that he had to act quickly, so he took Derek and himself back down through the trapdoor in the corner. The children stared at Derek. Harold and the other two were still unconscious. Gavin nervously aimed his shotgun at the trapdoor, in case it opened. He started to sweat as they heard the footsteps thud above them, checking the room. Strangely, the children remained silent. Then the sounds faded and disappeared.

Gavin turned around and saw Harold slowly open his eyes. His tied-up skinny, naked body wriggled towards him like a worm, his cold, staring eyes looking straight at Gavin.

"You ... won't ... defeat us," Harold muffled through his mouth gag that had loosened. Thick saliva dripped from his mouth. "*Never* ... You will ... pay. Death ... awaits you." Harold then laughed and raised his tied-up wrists to the bars and clung onto them with two fingers of his thin, veiny, right hand. *"Die ... die ... die ... like Eric."* Harold's laughter began to choke him.

*"Never."* Gavin smashed the butt of his shotgun over Harold's fingers, breaking them instantly.

Harold cried in pain and cursed Gavin and Derek. He started to laugh again.

Gavin then opened up the cage door to fasten the mouth gag back and instinctively smashed the butt of the gun down onto Harold's struggling, laughing face. After several hits, Harold went quiet with half his head caved in. Derek looked away in shock, but the children watched on without a word.

Gavin tied the mouth gag back over Harold's wet and open mouth. He could hear a crunch, where using his boot against the back of Harold's head, he pulled the mouth gag as tight as he could, splitting his mouth. For good measure, he booted the bruised side of Harold, breaking his ribs. As he locked the cage up, he told Derek that Harold deserved it and much more. "Trust me," he said. No remorse. Gavin was on the warpath now for vengeance for his friends.

*****

Zac and The Elders again faced the flaming inverted pentagram and upside-down crosses, with their arms aloft, chanting. The rest of Famuli Cani, were chanting and holding hands:

*"Ad nos veni! Ad nos veni! Ad nos veni!"* they were all chanting in unison.

John and Bob joined hands with their enemies, who all gripped hands strongly. The two tried to chant to play their roles. These Satanic worshippers appeared to go into a trance. The chanting came quicker and quicker, becoming hypnotic. Arthur and David still stood near the altar. Arthur reluctantly played his part a little too. Emily started to feel sick and dizzy from the chanting in her ears from the robed figure who still held the leash.

David looked over at Emily. She seemed to be falling unconscious. The whole of the chamber was echoing, through every stone and crack.

David had thought he had done enough last night to save Emily. He started getting emotional — thinking of the things he loved and any possible regrets that he had in his life, what was left of it. As well as Emily, he thought of Benji, his parents, Gino, his flat back home and the last time he was in his flat with Grant and John, laughing, having fun — pizza, beer ... he couldn't help but smile a little through his fear and profound sadness as tears rolled down his bruised and beaten face. Feeling dizzy too, he closed his eyes. He knew the chances of seeing those things again were so very remote. *No chance.* Grant was gone for ever, whatever happened from here on in. And one of the worst things of all, was that his parents in Spain had literally no idea what he and the others had been through. And their only son, was *here*, in an underground Satanic lair, trying to destroy an evil that no one could possibly believe or comprehend.

"Be *strong*, my boy," Arthur whispered in David's left ear. "Believe in yourself. This is what we came for. Be brave in the face of evil. Show no fear in the face of Canus when it comes. We *will* get a chance to defeat them. God and Seath Mór will grant us that. Be patient. Remember the pain and *use* it. Avenge Grant and Carl. *Avenge all of them*!"

Arthur's words seemed to inspire David.

Famuli Cani then sank to their knees, pulling Bob and John down with them, still holding hands. They were violently rocking their heads, their eyes raised upwards, fluttering and flickering like a warped camera shutter on automatic, with their bodies twisting and contorting. Bob and John were finding it increasingly difficult to mimic their actions.

The robed figure holding Emily's leash sank to their knees, forcing Emily to hers. Arthur did the same, telling David to get down with him. Famuli Cani were now in such a trance that they seemed oblivious to their surroundings. The chanting became so quick and fast, yet so clear, repeating itself over and over. The air grew colder and alive with static electricity. David started to shiver and grew colder. Goosebumps covered his naked upper body.

*"Hail Satan! Hail Satan!*
*Hail The Grey One! Hail The Grey One!*
*Oh, Grey One, come to us, come to us!*
*Come! Come! Come!*
*The Grey One! The Grey One! The Grey One!*
*Ad nos veni!*
*Ad nos veni!*
*Ad nos veni!"*

Famuli Cani were in such a trance they mixed their words with Latin and English.

The black circular platform in the middle of the inverted pentagram, began to smoke. The smoke rose higher and higher, white-blue to begin with, then growing black and thicker with a smell of sulphur. All the flames from the torches dimmed and flickered making a disturbing, hypnotic light show — frighteningly fast. A dark outline, a silhouette, started to form on the platform.

*"Ave Satan! Ave Satan!*
*Ave Cane! Ave Cane!*
*Ave Satan! Ave Satan!*
*Ave Cane! Ave Cane!*
*We are Yours! Your Disciples!*
*For we are The Acolytes of The Grey One!*
*We are FAMULI CANI . . . !"*

As the chanting stopped abruptly, an enormous, inhuman roar exploded around the stone chamber like an earthquake and the walls, ceiling and floor violently shook. It was deafening. David looked up, wincing at the ceiling, wondering if the sharp stalactites would fall onto them. Their eardrums rang with the impact.

And then there, on the platform in the middle of the flaming inverted pentagram, a huge, cloaked figure hovered — it was *Canus.*

Everything was suddenly quiet. The room had returned to normal. Everyone in the whole chamber was still on their knees, heads bowed. Bob, John and Arthur, daren't look at the huge, cloaked figure for more than a second; they still had to play the part. David couldn't help but stare up at it.

Slowly, starting with The Elders and the High Priest, Zac, they all rose to their feet and started applauding.

One of The Elders spoke. "Master Cane. Our Great Grey One. We are honoured with your presence, once again. We hope that you are satisfied with your sacrifice."

At first, the cloaked figure didn't react. It hovered there unnervingly. It then glided slowly past The Elders and High Priest and went over towards the altar, where it hovered over Grant's dead and naked body.

Arthur, only a few feet away, could sense the pure evil aura from Canus. He had never, ever felt anything like this before. He prayed it wouldn't detect their presence. For a second, his hand went towards the dagger he had under the robe. But fools rush in. This wasn't the right time.

Canus laughed with its evil, dark and twisted laugh.

David recognised the sound.

A different Elder spoke this time. "Unfortunately, the girl who was pregnant with Jack's child has escaped … You are already probably aware, Master."

David discerned a slight tremor in The Elder's voice.

"Jack failed us last night but rest assured, he has been punished. He will *not* make the same mistake twice."

A growl could be heard from Canus, which grew louder. It was angered.

"We have sent some of ours to look for her in case she is still here. But we still have this young girl and others being held. These can still provide a strong sacrifice to make us even more powerful on this Lammas Day, including you, *O Great One* … And David, the courageous one you admire so much, is already prepared for you, here."

*"Yes,"* Canus replied hissing the word out. Emily and David being presented to this entity had pleased and abated its anger.

Jack, however, had become enraged again as he stood there, and also afraid. Arthur was responsible for ruining all their plans. He wanted Arthur's blood.

The man had to die, more than anyone.

"We can start with the girl here, first. Let her innocent blood flow for you, Master Cane." A different Elder again, now spoke.

Emily was yanked to her feet via the leash, making her choke.

David became driven by anger. His beautiful and soft Emily was going to be slaughtered.

Ilene, The Elder, stepped over to Emily and placed her veiny hand on her left cheek. "It's your turn now, my dearie." She smiled with her yellow-toothed grin.

Emily screamed and kicked out. *"No, please, please. No!"*

"Shhh, don't fight it," Ilene whispered.

They removed her robe to reveal cuts and bruises on her petite body and lacerations on her back where she had been whipped.

*"David, please! Don't let them kill me. I love you!"*

"Aw, isn't that sweet," Ilene said mocking them. "Aren't you going to do anything, David, dear?"

Her provoking grin fuelled David's wrath further, especially after seeing Emily's wounds.

Canus started to laugh together with all its worshippers. Emily's naked body was lifted onto the old black altar and laid on Grant's blood. She fainted, which seemed to provoke more laughter.

David noticed that they seemed distracted by her fainting and hadn't shackled her down. Then he heard a whisper in his ear from Arthur.

"Patience, David. I know it hurts but keep calm. *Wait* for it. Be ready." Arthur sensed their cover would soon be blown.

David had no clue as to what Arthur intended to do. But he had to act fast.

Zac once more opened the lid of his vessel and poured blood onto Emily's unconscious body, chanting as he did so. The others chanted with him. Canus began hovering around its acolytes, giving off static.

"Arthur ..." David whispered quietly.

"Get ready. Untie your hands," Arthur said, reaching into his black jeans through his robe. He waited until Canus moved further away from him. His pulse was racing in anticipation and fear.

Adrenaline soured through David's body, making him shake. He was struggling to grip the end of the rope and undo the already lose knot. Canus was turning back round, just as Zac took the sacrificial knife and held it high above his head. The chanting grew louder and louder and David still struggled, panicking further.

He decided to use his teeth to grip the end of the rope. It worked. He loosened it with his right hand and was completely free, dropping the rope to the ground. He took off the leash around his neck.

Famuli Cani had their heads bowed, apart from Zac who looked up to the ceiling.

Canus was now only a few feet away, gliding closer to Arthur and David, and as it did so, it saw that David was no longer bound. A couple of Elders had also noticed. But it was too late …

Arthur held three breakable vials in his shaking right hand. Two held holy water with salt, and the third, a pale white liquid that would temporarily turn Canus into its physical form. He prayed that they would work as he had planned. When Canus was a foot away, Arthur *smashed* the vials through the spectre of Canus. The vials instantly dispersed.

Canus let out a huge howl.

Arthur felt wispy cold static as he smashed the potions, and burning on his hand and lower arm. A force thrust him off the raised platform down onto the hard floor.

Canus threw back its invisible hooded head, howling and made its way back to near the black platform in the middle of the inverted pentagram, twisting and writhing in pain.

Famuli Cani seemed to feel their deity's pain as though they were all linked as one. The chanting was replaced with screams and shouts and their bodies were shaking violently. Zac, the High Priest was still holding the knife up but was now shouting in pain and wriggling as though he had been electrocuted.

Emily came to just in time to see David charge at Zac. She had never seen him so angry.

*"You fucking bastard!"* David repeatedly punched Zac in the face, breaking the mask in two and revealing Zac's face again. The ring he had found that he was still wearing, helped with his punches. *"You took my friend! You tortured Emily!"*

Blood splattered onto the black floor from Zac's broken nose and mouth. Still screaming, he tried to fight David off. The sacrificial knife fell to the floor.

John and Bob watched the commotion around them and were unsure what to do. Gavin and Derek, hearing all the noise entered the chamber. Two of the figures who had gone to search for Florence returned down the steps, stopping at the end of the carpet. They were obviously starting to feel the effects, the same as the others. They met Gavin's wrath.

*"Hey!"* Gavin half-shouted, getting their attention.

One of them came running towards Gavin. Gavin aimed his shotgun without hesitation and fired straight into the chest of the robed figure, before he could even take the shotgun he was carrying off his shoulder. The figure fell back sharply to the ground, arms flailing. Gavin discarded the fired shell and reloaded quickly.

*"You!"* shouted the rasp-voiced figure and pointed. He ran at Gavin, past his now dead comrade. It was the last words he ever said.

Gavin blasted into his upper chest and reloaded again. Turning, he took out the third one before he even reached the bottom of the steps.

The second of Gavin's shots galvanised Bob into action. He ran out of the crowd to join him and Derek, pulling down his hood and revealing his face. It mattered not now. He reclaimed his shotgun from the dead acolyte. He took the ammo belt from Derek who seemed to be in shock and attached it to his waist. "You stay back, Derek. We need to finish this *now*, whilst they're weakened." Bob's gruff voice sounded fast and full of adrenaline. Seeing Gavin take down the three had encouraged Bob. He then called out to Emily who was in shock herself, sitting upright and naked on the black altar. *"Emily … over here!"*

Emily quickly got up and pulled her robe on. She hesitated not knowing whether to help David, who was still on top of Zac, or run towards Bob and Gavin. *"B-but David?"* she called out.

*"We'll get him!"* Bob shouted back, flicking the safety off from his shotgun.

"Go over there with Derek. Stay back. Let us handle this," Gavin said over the screams and shouts.

"Derek?" Emily queried.

"Yes, he was captured too. Now, *go*!" Gavin was looking for his next victim.

Emily ran back to Derek, while Gavin and Bob moved closer to the screaming and flailing acolytes.

They saw John try to run out from his row to assist David. But he got knocked out by a flailing elbow to the chin.

Bob and Gavin knew what they had to do. Never in their lives, had they thought they'd take lives.

"You ready for this, boss?" Gavin asked breathing heavily.

"Y-yes. Let's do this. *Payback* for Eric, Angus, Charlie, Grant and *all* the others!"

Some of the pained, robed acolytes, started to come at the armed pair. In spite of their obvious intense suffering, they tried to run and attack, struggling as they did so. Gavin and Bob took aim and opened fire at them. *No mercy.* Firing. Reloading. Numerous smoking empty shells hit the floor. The robed figures dropped like flies, their screaming halting as they hit the hard deck.

Some of Famuli Cani had been shot, others were rolling around on the floor, screeching and screaming. Some were pushed and kicked back before being shot, as they tried grabbing Bob and Gavin. Through the crowd of acolytes, it was hard to reach John who was still unconscious. But he was safe in disguise. For now.

Zac had found his power again to David's surprise. "You won't … beat us. You see? The power of sacrifices … gives us strength. The blood of the innocent. Like your dead friend, there." Zac grabbed his sacrificial knife. Still laughing, he managed to kick David off him and rise to his feet. "Time to meet your maker … David. Say *hello* to Grant for me." Zac tried to laugh. *"For Canus!"*

The blast of a shotgun went straight through Zac, just as he was about to thrust the knife into David. David looked to his left, open-mouthed, to see his uncle standing there with the smoking shotgun. All in a glance, he could see Emily and Derek at the back of the chamber, and Gavin still shooting at the acolytes.

David stood and checked that Zac was dead. Zac lay dead-eyed with blood oozing from his nose and mouth, and with a bloodied gaping wound in his chest. "Not going to be immortal now, are you?" David said over him. "The blood of the sacrifices couldn't save you. *Burn in Hell, Zac*!"

Arthur had been winded and dazed as he crashed to the floor from the shockwave from Canus. All his energy had been zapped from his body. As he struggled to focus, he knew now was their last opportunity to defeat the cult.

He rose to his feet and focused. Bob and Gavin were firing at the robed figures, with some still coming at them. David was standing over Zac's body. John was still out. Then Arthur saw Canus within the inverted pentagram. He threw himself towards it and took out the dagger and his final vials of holy water.

Canus was changing into its physical form, flickering into solid matter. But the effects of the holy water were starting to wear off. It could see Arthur approaching and raised its huge hairy hand. It was using its returning power to halt Arthur, lifting its left arm up higher through its cloak. Arthur became suspended in the air, clutching at the vials in one hand and the dagger in the other.

David saw Arthur suspended in the invisible grip of Canus. He heard Arthur trying to call out, but he was being held by his throat. David ran past some Elders, who were still suffering from the initial attack on Canus, to try to help Arthur. *"Arthur!"*

"Canus ... is getting ... its strength back ..." Arthur struggled to speak.

As David approached, he too was lifted up into the air by the throat. He felt the cold of frost as Canus lifted its right arm directing its powers at David.

David could see some of the physical body of this demon now with its huge hairy grey feet.

*"Shit!"* Gavin shouted. *"My shotgun is jammed!"*

Bob looked over to him: he was running low on ammo from his belt. *"What?"*

"It won't fire!" Gavin struck an acolyte in the face with the butt of his shotgun, then kicked away another firmly in the stomach with one of his strong, long legs.

Bob was then jumped on by a couple of Famuli Cani. There were still a lot of them left. They seemed to be recovering with an anger. Bob managed to fire and kill one, but the other was a tougher opponent.

Before Gavin had a chance to help Bob, he too was jumped on by two robed figures.

Emily and Derek feared the worst. They seemed to have been winning the fight but now the tables had potentially turned again. *"We have to do something!"* Emily shrieked at Derek.

"Stay here," Derek ordered and then rushed to Bob's aid, pulling the robed figure from him to the floor.

The robed acolyte stood back up, but Bob shot at them, hitting them in the stomach. The scream of a female assailed their ears as she flew back, with a fatal wound.

Gavin was strong, and he was doing well against perpetual attacks, trying to shove them off with his fists and shotgun, taking blows to his face as he did so. Bob couldn't shoot in case he hit Gavin, but he and Derek went to help him.

*****

Arthur and David were choking to death, with the grip on their throats tightening.

*"Mere mortals."* Canus laughed. *"I was defeated once, but not this time. I am stronger,"* it bellowed, its voice, evil, deep and rough.

Arthur closed his eyes and prayed. He prayed for strength and help and reached his thoughts out for Seath Mór and God.

Canus could read his thoughts and mocked him but Arthur resisted. He raised his right hand and threw the last two vials of holy salt water straight into the physical body of Canus. The sound was more horrific than the first time. David dropped to the ground and winced in pain. Arthur was slung against the wall, dropping the dagger.

Bob, Derek and Gavin were now under attack from more of Famuli Cani, whose strength had returned. Bodies pinned them down. But when the holy water reached Canus, the acolytes were weakened again. Bob and the others used this to their advantage, struggling to break free.

Canus howled agonisingly on its platform.

*"David!"* Arthur called across, struggling for breath. "The dagger, my boy. Fulfil your destiny. It is your fate. *Destroy* Famuli Cani and Canus once and for all!" Arthur's shaking hand covered the dagger next to him. He slid it along the smooth black floor towards David. It stopped a couple of feet away from him, spinning around and around on the floor.

As David caught his breath back, he went to grab it. A bare foot slammed down hard on it. David looked up to see Jack smiling above him.

"I don't fucking think so, David. This … is how I … redeem myself." Jack's body and head shook in agony. *"Give me the strength, Master!"* Jack shouted to Canus.

Jack suddenly seemed to find strength from Canus from what it had left. He kicked David in the face and picked up the dagger. David quickly rose to his feet and punched Jack back in the face, knocking him to the ground. Jack retaliated by getting back up and swiping the sharp dagger across David's bare stomach, cutting it. David let out a shout in pain.

*"Come on, David!"* Jack taunted. He was energised through Canus. He held the dagger in his right hand, and with his left, he gestured David to come at him. "After I'm done with you, I'm going to *cut* Emily's pretty little face off and *fuck* it."

"Bring it …" David said, finding a new courage.

Jack laughed through the pain and took another swipe at David, but David jumped back this time, anticipating the attack.

Canus looked on. Having diverted its energies to Jack its powers were depleted, but the platform was replenishing that.

Jack shouted in pain as he made another lunge at David with the dagger. David dodged and then swept Jack's right leg from underneath him with his foot using an old karate move he'd learnt in school. He then jumped on Jack and began punching him in the face. He then hit Jack's hand repeatedly onto the hard floor, causing him to drop the dagger. But Jack fought back and tried to get David in a choke hold.

"Just like last night, eh?" Jack said. "Only this time, you won't survive."

"Be strong, David!" Arthur's weak and broken voice filled David's mind.

Jack laughed.

*****

John came to. Lifting his still robed head up from the floor and giving it a shake, he heard the screams and shouting still. Dead bodies lay around him. Then he saw Jack holding David in a chokehold. He ran towards them.

Emily managed to free herself after she too, had been attacked and jumped upon. She saw the hooded figure running towards David and ran to jump on him from behind. She thumped on his chest and hit his head, so that his hood fell off, revealing his face.

"Emily. It's me, John!" He shook her off and turned to face her.

*"John? You're one of them?"* Her face turned to despair.

*"No, silly! I was disguised. We need to save David!"*

David struggled to wrestle free while he and Jack competed to reach for the dagger.

Jack loosened his grip as David elbowed him in the chest and grabbed for the dagger. David stabbed Jack in his right foot. Jack bellowed in pain.

Arthur told David he had to hurry.

Jack tried to grab David's foot as he attempted to reach Canus, but David managed to kick himself free.

The flames from the inverted pentagram shot higher as Canus began to restore its power, but it was too late. David took an almighty leap through the flames — the highest he would ever jump, feeling an invisible force from under him. Arthur smiled to himself.

David plunged the sacred dagger *deep* into the thick chest and black heart of Canus.

*"Die!"* David shrieked. The ring that he wore glowed a bright yellow.

*"No!"* cried Jack.

Bob, Gavin and Derek had freed themselves just in time to watch this defining act. The defeated Canus threw its head back and screamed. The acolytes' pain was now tenfold.

David threw himself away from this now solid entity, by pushing off its body with his feet, landing on the stone floor, over the flames. He then looked up at the true evil image of Canus as the hooded black cloak was thrust away from its body.

This huge grey entity was over seven feet tall with curved black horns rising from its head, bald apart from a few sparse grey hairs. Its grey face twisted and flickered in agony with its black eyes and piercing yellow irises. Its mouth was full of jagged fangs. Its large hairy body had greyish-white hairs and its arms and legs were muscular and its feet and hands huge, all with dangerously sharp, black talons. It had no genitalia.

*"Die, you dickless fuck!"* John shouted as he looked on with Emily.

Canus, with the dagger still rooted deep inside it, oozed black blood from its body. It knew it was dying. Rays of yellow and white light burst through numerous holes in its body, making it cry out.

Jack was in full tears now, seeing his Master suffering. His pain also grew, as did that of all of Famuli Cani. The screams from them all were deafening. The good amongst them had to cover their ears.

The chamber began to shake and crumble.

*"We need to get out!"* John shouted.

David got to his feet and ran to Arthur to help him up. Arthur put his arms around David and John's shoulders for support. Debris began to rain down on them. The Famuli Cani still alive were screaming on the ground in agony, oblivious to the group as they hurried through them.

"We need to go down those steps," Arthur tried to shout. "We need to get the children out."

*"What children?"* Emily shouted back.

Bob, Gavin and Derek rushed over to the others.

They made it down the steps just as the ceiling in the chamber fell and Canus exploded into a huge ball of blinding white light. Stalactites came crashing down onto the black granite floor, smashing the altar and main steps. Famuli Cani everywhere were screaming, some crushed and some stabbed with the stalactites. Then all went quiet.

*****

"Are they dead?" Emily asked. "Is it over, now?"

"Not until we get out of here," John replied, his pulse still high.

The three naked bodies in the cell were dead. Their bodies were lifeless, their cold eyes staring.

"You knew, didn't you?" David asked Arthur. "You knew that killing it would hurt the others?"

Arthur gave a slight nod, holding his side, screwing his face up. "Yes. I've always believed and sensed that hurting and killing Canus would inflict pain onto its acolytes. I saw a similar thing in my vision, from when Seath Mór killed them the first time around. Despite them being linked as one, I wasn't sure that killing Canus alone, would be enough to kill the rest of them. But I knew something would happen, that would lead to their demise."

"Why didn't you tell us?" asked John, rubbing his chin, where he'd been knocked unconscious.

Arthur sighed. "Although I've always believed and had faith, I still wasn't completely sure it would work, being down here in their territory … I am so *proud* of you all. You showed so much bravery and courage. You have all fulfilled your destiny." Arthur smiled through his pain.

"Why is his body melting like that?" Emily asked Arthur, watching Harold's body as it continued oozing out on the floor and onto the other two dead naked acolytes.

"This Harold is, or was, some kind of *ghoul*, perhaps … not completely human. An abomination. His oozing body is what killed the other two next to him."

"But where did he come from?"

"That is probably a question that we will never have an answer to, David … it matters not, now. But it is likely that he was possibly brought back from the dead. Maybe something went wrong along the way? Ghouls are also known to eat human flesh. Judging by the date of that portrait we saw, he may already have been resurrected prior to the rebirth of Famuli Cani, by someone else. Or *they* brought him back from the dead themselves, years later. The process of evocation. It could even have been a different and other malevolent spirit, entering into a different body … Come, we will take the children with us. I know a place where my friends can bring them back towards the light. There is still much hope for them."

The children still stared at them unblinking.

The group returned to the chamber where the ground was covered with debris, with the odd arm or hand stuck out from the wreckage.

John removed the hoods of two semi-exposed bodies to reveal their faces and check for himself that they were dead; their eyes were completely devoid of life. One of them just happened to be Anthony.

They then heard some crying and moaning.

"Someone's still alive," Gavin said, gripping his shotgun although it was still jammed.

"Careful," Bob said, holding his own shotgun in front of him.

They made their way across the uneven rubble. The noise was coming from Ilene, one of the dying Elders. She was bleeding from her mouth and nose. Only her neck, head and a hand were visible above the mass that had crushed her. Next to her, holding her hand, was Annabel, her body also mostly trapped.

They turned to look at David and the group, looking down on them.

*"Bastards!"* Annabel screamed.

"Where is your *God*, now?" John mocked.

Annabel started to laugh. "You're still trapped down here … you've achieved nothing. Famuli Cani, will return."

"If that's true, we'll be ready. And anyway, it won't return with *you*," John said calmly with defiance. Revenge was sweet.

"Oh, Anna …" Emily said sadly. She had a mix of contradicting emotions; anger, satisfaction, such raw sadness and pity. She had regarded Annabel as her friend and for a brief moment, she thought she perhaps saw regret in Annabel's hazel eyes.

Annabel sobbed as she saw Ilene take her last breath.

"So much for all those sacrifices and killing people," John sniped.

Annabel said nothing.

"Even The Elders couldn't survive," David added.

Arthur noticed something shining on the platform where Canus had been defeated. They left Annabel and made their way up. Jack's body lay there lifeless, eyes wide, staring. A huge and single stalactite had fallen straight into his sternum.

"Fuck you, Jack," John said.

The light Arthur had seen was the dagger. It was spinning around by the point of the blade. He knelt down to pick it up. It felt warm in his hand. "Best I take this with us."

While they all looked on at the shining blade, a noise drew John's attention. He turned to see Annabel lunging towards them. She started to scream. Without thinking, he pulled out his crossbow and fired a bolt. He stared in shock as the bolt pierced through Annabel's left eyeball. She fell forward onto her face so that the bolt pushed through her brain and killed her.

*"Shit!"* John said in a whisper, his mouth and eyes wide open.

*****

"How are we going to get out?" Emily asked again.

The group searched the wrecked chamber for any secret entrances they might have missed. There were none. They were trapped and sat to contemplate what they could do next.

Arthur wasn't concerned though. He had a 'feeling,' the same way he now knew that the others back at Father Adan's would be just fine.

After a few minutes, a strange humming sound started to fill the room as though another earthquake would demolish the chamber, but Arthur smiled and told everyone to remain calm.

A yellow ball of light appeared at the end of the passageway at the top of the chamber. It slowly moved down towards them and stopped about ten metres away. It was radiant and warmed them. It then expanded into an oval shape.

"There, there's our way out." Arthur beamed.

"It's the same light I saw with Florrie!" John said excitedly.

*"The spirit of Seath Mór,"* Arthur said.

First to walk through it were John and Derek — to show a nervous Emily it was okay. Emily and David held hands and went next, followed by Bob and Gavin, and finally, the children with Arthur behind them.

It was a strange but pleasant sensation entering the light. Extremely bright. They stepped out surprisingly through the *Tree of Souls*. It was now daylight, early morning. The warm sun shone through the trees. The forest appeared much lighter. They could see the blue sky above them with the birds singing. Numerous scented and pleasant looking flowers had now started to grow in the glade that was previously dark and grassless, covered in old animal bones. Everything felt so normal and calm. So tranquil.

"Have we died?" Emily asked. "Is it a trick?"

Arthur laughed affectionately and was quick to reassure her that this was all real. The pain from his side was diminishing.

Then they heard another humming sound and the ground started to shake. There was a blinding flash of white light from the still sinister looking tree, and the feeling of pure, raw energy in the air as it flowed past them. Their hair stood on end and they could hear the mixed sounds of animals, people and children chatting and laughing, and the words "Thank you" could be heard. The flash then grew and disappeared, as did the tree.

"What was that and where did the tree go?" David asked.

Tears ran down Arthur's old face. His head and neck were arched back, his face looking up into the summer sky through the tops of the trees. "They are free … free of pain. No more, will their souls suffer. They are *free*," he said again.

*"Look!"* John said, pointing to where the tree had been. "Granty … Carl …"

Grant was wearing his favourite white trainers and a green T-shirt and jeans, and his glasses. Carl wore a grey suit and navy tie. They each raised an arm to wave goodbye.

Watching the spirits of the fallen pair smiling at them brought tears to all of them, even the young children. The images of the spirits soon began to fade until they were gone, gone for ever, at peace. John sank to his knees crying uncontrollably, his face in his hands. David did the same and went to comfort him and they held each other. Emily wrapped her arms around them both, also in tears.

They were all soon distracted by the distinctive crying of a new-born baby, along with the soft singing of a woman. Making their way through the now well-lit forest, they could see Florence still in her robe, sitting on a tree log. The Chinese couple were with her, smiling and holding hands. Florence was gently serenading her baby, with the sun shining on them. She could hear the others coming and looked over at them, happy.

# Epilogue

Some wounds can never fully heal or the scars always remain. After everything they had all been through together, all of their lives had changed for ever, but they still had each other and new friends: Wang and Chen.

David stayed in Scotland and he proposed on Christmas Day. He and Emily were married by Father Adan in Newtonmore, in July 2019. John was naturally the best man. Benji brought the wedding ring up the church aisle as Emily giggled. Reggie held a disco at their wedding reception, which was held at Hamish Farm in a couple of large marquees. Jock and Gino catered for them. There was much laughter and fun involved. David passed his driving test in the New Year a few months before and started to work on his uncle's farm. Emily continued working at the pub.

John fell in love with Florence and was the perfect father figure for her baby girl, Anita. Arthur stated there was nothing to fear in regards to the baby. The couple rented a small house near Aviemore and John found work delivering pizzas. It wasn't the best job, but it was money, and he enjoyed the free food.

Betty had returned to normal almost instantly when Canus was destroyed. She had woken up confused in Father Adan's holy basement. She hardly remembered anything about what had happened during her ordeal. Bob and Betty were thrilled to have David and Emily living with them. Gavin also still worked on the farm and started dating an older woman by ten years, who he brought to David and Emily's wedding. Derek was still single, but John and David convinced him to try online dating, which he was enjoying. Even Samuel's health improved once Famuli Cani was eradicated.

Arthur was looking into something over in Australia for a few months. He said it would be his last job, and he planned to retire in Scotland and put his feet up, for however long he had left in his old life upon his return. The children were now somewhere safe and were doing great. During the first few weeks after their adventure, Arthur was often asked if Canus and Famuli Cani would ever return. Arthur didn't completely dismiss it as impossible, but said it was *highly* unlikely. Arthur said the real core and deep evil of them had been wiped out. Still, Arthur had hidden the dagger somewhere safe, just in case.

Regardless, their job was done. Famuli Cani and Canus – The Grey One – were defeated and gone. Their reign of terror was finally over. The race was won. *Team Arthur* had come through and was victorious.

**October, 2019**

Emily, David, John and Florence went on a double date night. They had booked a table for dinner at a fancy new restaurant in town and had a great night, full of laughs and happy memories of the wedding. They all felt more normal with each day that passed.

Emily had refused any alcoholic drinks, even though she was tempted. She didn't want to risk it. Not even one.

The others fully understood, especially Florence. "Aw. I can see your little bump slowly growing, now," she said smiling as she gently touched Emily's belly.

Emily giggled.

David and Emily had already decided on a name if they had a boy … *Grant.*

# AUTHOR'S NOTE

Many thanks for reading/purchasing my first novel. I sincerely hope that you enjoyed reading it as much as I enjoyed writing it. It was always my aim to create something any potential reader would enjoy. I hope I've achieved that. Creating fiction that people enjoy reading would give me a great deal of satisfaction.

For several years, I considered writing a horror novel based on a Satanic cult inside a forest, with a 'nephew visiting his uncle somewhere up north.' However, it wasn't until spring 2015 that I finally began.

I always liked the idea of creating a novel that mixed fact and fiction and included a real place, with a mix of folklore and myth attached to it. After researching online, I discovered Rothiemurchus Forest up in Scotland, which was the perfect setting for my story. Seath Mór did indeed exist but the part played by him in this novel is purely fictitious.

When writing a novel, I believe that it is important to be as original and unique as you can. Nowadays, it is becoming more and more difficult to come up with complete and original ideas, but I feel with *Famuli Cani*, I have managed to achieve that. At least to a certain extent.

One major concern with my novel was perhaps the size of it. It was originally much longer, but thanks to great editing, it has been cut down significantly from over 400k words to around 271k. Due to the nature of the story, I believe it justifies the length; a story is as big as it needs to be told. Like a lot of things, this is all subjective and people's opinions may vary. But personally, I believe cutting certain things out would have meant the story losing substance and potential character or relationship development. There had to be a build-up in the story and a build-up to the finale (which was my favourite part), and an ending after a long read mustn't let the reader down. Also, when writing a novel this long, the character development becomes even more important.

Regarding the characters, I really enjoyed creating them and I hope you enjoyed them too. It was one of the most enjoyable parts of working on my novel, particularly the friendship between John and David. Character development is always very important, I feel, in any novel. When things happen — good or bad, I wanted the reader to be able to bond with the characters, feeling their pain and joy and the bond of love between characters. I wanted to make the characters appear real and for them to be remembered after the story has been read.

As for the Latin parts, I wanted the novel to have some authenticity with the Satanists speaking in Latin. Latin can be a complicated language, which is why you see different variations of the name 'Canus.' How it is spelt depends on in which context the name is used. For example, it is spelt as 'Cane' when addressing him/it. 'Famuli Cani' literally means *Acolytes of The Grey One.*

Thank you again for taking the time to read my first novel. If you enjoyed this book, please recommend it to others by leaving a review.

Alan :)

# ACKNOWLEDGEMENTS

Many thanks to the authors Roddy Martine, Stefan Vucak, Matt Knight, and also to Jon Watkins from www.exposingsatanism.org and William G.A. Shaw of Easter Lair for their help and advice. Big thanks to Sherwin Little, Aleksandr Sol'ka and in particular Gregory Klyve, who were kind enough to spare me time to give advice and suggestions with the Latin translations. For the Scottish Gaelic parts, thanks to Àdhamh Ó Broin and Kenneth McManus. Thanks also to tutors Geoffrey Sammons and Jason Bond for their explanations and suggestions with the language. Big thanks to Ken Dawson from www.ccovers.co.uk for his very friendly service, help, designs and perseverance regarding my ideas and fussiness! Thanks too to Eleanor Pigg from Nielsen Book Services. An even *bigger* thanks to my editor, Kirstie Edwards (www.kirstieedwards.org.uk), for her *very* hard work, dedication and patience. And of course, thanks to Google and Wikipedia for much needed research! :)

# ABOUT THE AUTHOR

Alan Golbourn was born in Essex, England. He enjoyed writing stories at school where he was known for his writing abilities. Amongst several interests and hobbies including football and computer games, he holds a love and compassion for animals. *Famuli Cani* is his first novel, with hopefully more on the way.

Printed in Great Britain
by Amazon